the bear comes home

the bear

comes home

rafi zabor

w. w. norton & company

new york london

Printed in the United States of America

Part One originally appeared in *Musician* magazine in somewhat different form.

The text of this book is composed in Janson
with the display set in Rabbit Ears
Desktop composition by Gina Webster
Manufacturing by the Haddon Craftsmen, Inc.
Book design by Chris Welch
Title page and part opening illustrations by Jane Winsor

Library of Congress Cataloging-in-Publication Data
Zabor, Rafi.
The bear comes home / by Rafi Zabor.
p. cm.
ISBN 0-393-04037-2
1. Bears—New York (State)—Fiction. 2. Jazz musicians—New York (State)—Fiction.
3. Saxophonists—New York (State)—Fiction. I. Title.
PS3576.A157B4 1997
813'.54—dc21 96-48184
CIP

W. W. Norton & Company, Inc., 500 Fifth Avenue, New York, N.Y. 10110
http://www.wwnorton.com

W. W. Norton & Company Ltd., 10 Coptic Street, London WC1A 1PU

2 3 4 5 6 7 8 9 0

To: the Musicians, all of them

In memoriam
Steve McCall
Julius Hemphill

“How can you make fun of Me, you whose hopes abide in Me?”

“My trace is Yours and my quality is Yours. . . . My inexistence implies Your existence, my avarice Your generosity, my muteness Your word, my whisperings Your discourse. . . . Everything in accord with Your gift is made into Your praise.”
—Ibn ‘Arabi

part one

I didn't come here and I'm not leaving.

—Willie Nelson

1

It was a hot day and the Bear worked hard for his money, dancing to Jones' harmonica, a disco cassette, a couple of Austrian marches and some belly-dance music. He guzzled a bottle of beer and shambled around groaning and pawing at the air. He let Jones wrestle him to the ground and plant his foot on his deep barrel chest to let out a victory cry. He let himself be led around in a circle by a chain through the ring in his nose so that the shoppers could laugh at him and applaud. He rolled in the gutter twice without looking up. They made about forty dollars.

The Bear was a good act. He was a muzzy medium-brown bear who looked small enough to be safe when on all fours but absolutely huge when he reared up and stretched out his arms to get the oohs and aahs, that moment of awe without which no artistic production, even one that rolls itself in the gutter twice daily, can completely succeed. It was a small transfiguration, but it was sufficient unto the day, and it was probably what the people on the corner, after they had stopped laughing and wiping their mouths, took home with them when they left. Otherwise, the Bear knew his cues, never gave Jones any trouble on the job, and didn't pee in the street. When Jones led him home toward evening, the Bear's walk rolled him shoulder to shoulder, his head swayed genial and empty, his face was vacant and his eyes were glazed. Passersby were interested of course but seldom afraid. They may even have wondered more about Jones, a lean, almost spiffy man with lank brown hair and well-drawn if subsequently smudged features, apparently attached by a chain to a dancing bear. The Bear knew how to behave in company. He had the social number down.

When they got home and upstairs—a narrow three-flight walkup with bare bulbs in the hall, cracked tile floors, old red paint and roaches—Jones undid the locks on the door and went in. The Bear came in after him, unsnapped the chain from the ring in his nose and dropped into the old green armchair beside the door. Fine dust whorled up from the upholstery in response.

"Another day," said Jones.

"Another dollar," completed the Bear.

"Want a beer?"

"Whatever's right." The Bear started drumming his claws on the threadbare arm of the chair.

Jones opened a couple of cold Anchor Steams and sat down on the worn old trunk across from the Bear. "How you feeling," Jones asked him.

"If I have to do another day of this shit," said the Bear, "I'm gonna go out of my mind."

"What's the alternative? You think people are gonna accept you as you are?" Jones was getting shrill more quickly than usual. Maybe it was the heat. "They'll put you in a fucking freakshow, a museum. They'll stick your head so full of electrodes you'll think you're Goldilocks." He took some beer. "Stick with the act. The act's good, anyhow it's the best we can do."

"It's undignified," pronounced the Bear.

"Don't I do it? Don't I do it too? All the same shit you do?"

"Tomorrow," the Bear told him, "I step on your belly and yell like Tarzan and you take the roll in the gutter."

Jones composed an elaborate frown, then let it slide.

The Bear continued regardless. "You get to wear the chain in your nose but I still drink the beer. . . . By the way," he said more seriously, "I want to work another beer or two into the act. And I'd like them cold."

Jones said nothing, with unusual clarity.

"Whatsamatter," said the Bear.

"I worry," said Jones.

"About?" the Bear prompted.

"About you."

"About li'l ol' *me*?" the Bear said with a servile grin and a little bow in his seat. "You think I'll be an unruly beary-poo? Sexually or otherwise assault the clientele? Crap in the gutter? Go public and break into *King Lear*? Why ursine, wherefore base? Blow ye winds, crack your cheeks, and break the molds that make ungrateful man? Y'all worried about *me*?"

"Sometimes," said Jones, "you can be a real pain in the ass."

"Whereas the rest of the time I'm just your bread and butter."

"Bear . . ." Jones pleaded.

"One more lousy beer is all I ask," said the Bear, "when I can drink you under the table four or five times over."

"Bodyweight," said Jones.

"Character," said the Bear. "One more beer, Jones. I don't think that's so dangerous or temperamental. You see me playing the prima donna here? I don't think so. Get real."

"Drinking on the job," said Jones, shaking his head and taking another swig of Steam.

"That's the kind of job it is."

"Exactly," said Jones, and burped. "Which is why an extra bottle of suds or two is dangerous. I wouldn't want to see you getting dependent on beer to get through the day. Remember, you had a problem once."

"I was a comic little cub back then. I fell down a couple times."

"Bad precedent, man."

"I ain't," said the Bear, "a man."

A silence ensued. They drank their beers and allowed themselves to relapse back into friendship, as they generally did after the ritual tiff about work. Sometimes they wondered if they had been together too long, but where else in the world could the Bear go and what, exactly, would Jones do in it without him?

The Bear riffled through the fur of his chest and Jones wiped sweat from the pale skin of his brow and brushed a lock of his brown hair back.

It was getting twilight out, and the world was making twilight sounds: the calls and cries of a few kids in the street, cars prowling for a parking spot, Brokaw or whoever doing the news on TV, someone kicking a bucket around in the gutter, someone else whanging away at a streetlamp with a stick. The smell of frying chicken wafted in.

"What's for dinner?" asked the Bear.

"Can you deal with spaghetti again?"

"I can deal with spaghetti."

"I'll get a can of salmon and some berries for you tomorrow."

"Aarh," said the Bear, "salmon's only good fresh, and we probably don't have enough cash for a couple of pounds."

"Not after I pay the overdue electric bill we don't," Jones confirmed.

"You got maybe some chopmeat?" asked the Bear.

"I got."

"Then make me a nice steak tartare appetizer."

"I was saving it for the sauce."

"You make a very nice meatless sauce and I need more protein than you. Make me an appetizer."

Jones made a pass with his hands. "You're an appetizer," he said.

"Aarghr," said the Bear.

"You walked into it," said Jones. "Fair is fair. You set me up. You said it twice: make me an appetizer."

"Right," said the Bear, swiping idly at the air. "You're an appetizer too."

"What kind?" Jones perked up. "Beluga?"

"You're chopmeat, Jones," said the Bear. "At the very best a can of salmon and a couple of very small berries."

Jones and the Bear laughed at the old jokes and opened two more bottles of Anchor. Jones lit a cigarette and they sat across from each other as the summer evening came on outside, bringing the first cool breeze of the day in through the open window.

"Ah," said Jones.

"*Come with me*," sang the Bear, "*if you want to go to Kansas City*." A pause followed, to accommodate the piano break.

"*I'm feeling so sad and blue, and my heart's full of sorrow*," sang Jones, who did not sing well and came in three beats early.

"*Don't know just what to do*."

"*Where will I be tomorrow?*"

"*Got to go there*."

"*Really got to go. Really want to go there*."

"*Really got to go there, sorry-but-I-can't-take-you*," completed the Bear. There had been some omissions and mistakes.

"Heh heh heh," said Jones. "And heh."

"Heh. Make dinner."

Jones got up. "All through thick and thin," he said.

"*Parker's been your friend*," sang the Bear. "*Man!*" he shouted, slamming his paw on the threadbare arm of the chair. "Charlie Parker!" The Bear beamed, a rippling wave worked its way through his fur, and there was a suggestion of a subtle glow about him from from top to toeclaw. "*Bird!*"

Jones busied himself with the steak tartare, grumbling at the inadequacy of the beef, and the Bear laid his case flat across his knees and unpacked his alto. He checked the reed, worked the keys and blew a couple of phrases. Satisfied that both he and the saxophone were in working order he began to play "Parker's Mood," adding his own comments and emendations as the solo advanced. After five choruses, his eyes closed with pleasure, he leaned back in the armchair. "You know," he said, "I don't even have to play a bunch of weird outside shit to be happy. There's so much wisdom in bebop it's enough for a lifetime, really. All the things you have to know just to make one chorus work right. You have to know life pretty good. Not to mention the horn."

"You play all right."

"I know I play all right. Not the very first rank maybe, not world-class, but good enough to make a living in New York."

"You phrase nice."

"Of course I phrase nice. Bears are soulful and inventive people. We're friendly, we're creative, and we're cool. But the world," he told Jones, "knows us not."

"I know you."

"You. Yeah. You know me." The Bear put the saxophone to his mouth and arpeggiated his way through a typically murderous late-fifties Coltrane turnaround—C major 7, E-flat 7, A-flat major to B 7, E major to G 7, and finished on a resonant C, which he flatted slightly for emphasis. "*You* try that with paws, mutha. *You* develop an embouchure for a snout. Yeah, *you* know me. Sure. Could *you* do that?"

"Steak tartare," said Jones, presenting him with a plate of raw chopmeat topped with a dusting of paprika and mixed with fresh green spices. "You're in a lousy mood."

"I'm sorry," said the Bear. "I just get so frustrated. You want a hand with the spaghetti?"

"Naw. Thanks."

"I could give you a hand with the spaghetti."

"That's all right." Jones cleared his throat and put a hand to his collarbone. "I like to cook."

The Bear played whole-tone scales while Jones chopped onions, garlic, dry red peppers and flatleaf parsley. Jones heated olive oil and put the spices in to sauté, reserving the garlic. The Bear switched to some legato phrasing in the Dorian mode and Jones eased ten fresh plum tomatoes into a pot of boiling water. "You want to go up to Woodstock this weekend and jam with Julius? Julius is cool. I could call Julius."

"Yeah, Julius is cool," said the Bear, lowering the horn, "but when a guest comes over I have to go out in the yard and act like an animule."

"We could go."

"And I think Julius is in Europe this month."

"Good for Julius," said Jones, easing the garlic into the pan and beginning to peel the tomatoes he had spooned from the water.

"Yeah. Good for Julius. We got any decent wine in the house?"

"I think an okay Italian red."

"Let's hear it for an okay Italian red," the Bear said dully.

"Bored?" Jones asked him.

"To death," said the Bear, and downed the mound of steak tartare in two large mouthfuls. "I mean, dance is all right, even street dance. It's the poetry of the body, flesh aspiring to grace or inviting the spirit in to visit. But music." He shook his big head side to side. "That's different. That's one level more subtle. I mean, if the universe is vibration, and after Einstein who's gonna deny it, energy sifts down matter and before it gets there it manifests as sound. So playing music—playing music *well*," he corrected himself, "it's like taking an active part in the future. . . . Jones? You with me here? Do I detect a glazed look about the eyes?"

"It's a little obscurant for me," Jones admitted amid rising veils of steam. "You been reading the wrong magazines."

"Bears have a good head for metaphysics, Jones, but our feet never leave the ground. I know what I'm talking about."

"Well that makes one of us."

"You understand me all right." The Bear licked his muzzle clear of flecks of beef and reattached the saxophone to his neckstrap. "You're just afraid I'm gonna wig out and get unmanageable."

"I just don't want you getting any funny ideas."

"Too late," said the Bear. "I got a headful." He got up and started walking around the living room, the saxophone steadied by a touch of his paw. "Man I'm restless."

"I could give Mirelle a call," Jones offered.

"I'm sick of hookers," said the Bear, "and they don't dig me. The ones that do dig it, I think they're sick. They wig out so much on doing it with a bear I'm not even there, me. Later for Mirelle. Maybe we should go upstate and I could nose around in the woods."

"That's the spirit," said Jones. "A she-bear from Big Indian."

"A nice country bear," the Bear chimed in. "No mind for ideas. A regulation roots-and-berries type. A hippie. But what'll we have to talk about after? Never read Proust or Victoria's Secret, acts territorial after you're done. . . . This world gets dull, Jones. It's a bad fit. I'm not from around here."

"You know what your problem is?" Jones asked him, tasting a bit of sauce he had blown cool on an end of a wooden spoon. "You're too good."

The Bear nodded vehemently. "Nail on the head. Too good. So often thought but ne'er so well expressed."

Jones and the Bear had another little laugh on that one.

"Remember the days I used to jam up in Harlem with those guys out of Lionel Hampton's band?" asked the Bear.

"Who could forget."

"They didn't know what to make of me, did they . . . Uh, where you, uh, *from* . . ." The Bear trailed off into laughter. "Wasn't for Julius the whole thing would've been untenable. But I could play, couldn't I? And I kept your ass safe in Harlem. 140th Street mind you, not just One Two Five."

"The whole thing," said Jones, "was a calculated risk."

"I even made that record date."

Jones, easing the stalks of spaghetti into boiling water, laughed softly, then mimicked the nasal voice of the union man. "Uh, who is that artist with the ring in his nose? He uh plays uh alto? Alto saxophone? I don't seem to see his name here on the list."

"Julius walked up to the guy," and here the Bear did Julius' voice and towered down on the union guy to speak: "'Excuse me but have you ever wondered how the Dogon knew without the aid of a telescope how Po Tolo does its dance around Sirius and perturbs its orbit? You might inquire of the ahhhhh gentleman wearing fur and as you observed a ring in his nose. He may be willing to share some facts with you. You never know.' The union man about died."

"'The wearing of fur,'" Jones continued in his own rendering of Julius' deep slow voice, "'signifies the putting on of primal power—'"

"Speaking of put-ons," said the Bear.

"'—an assumption of the ritual cloak of wilderness and night. Have you really never worn the mask of God? Or do you only operate the external human form.'"

"God that man was stupid," said the Bear.

"But persistent. All good things," Jones said, "must come to an end."

"Sometimes they got to begin again, don't they? Lord knows I got the itch to go out there again."

"Just 'cause you're round and brown," said Jones, "don't mean everyone's gonna take you for Arthur Blythe."

"There anything on TV tonight?"

"It's Friday. We could pick up a rerun of *The Rockford Files*."

"All right!" said the Bear. "Save my life. Let's hear it for Big Jim Garner!"

"Dinner's almost ready. You want to eat in front of the television?"

"Does a bear shit in the woods?" asked the Bear. "Present company excepted."

"I liked the show better before they wrote Bev out of the script," said the Bear, cleaning sauce from his plate with a crust of bread, "but even in reruns it's still about the best thing on the box."

"Bev? Who's Bev?"

"Rockford's lawyer, dummy. A good actress, a nice presence."

"Her name was Beverly. Or Bess."

"Yeah," the Bear said derisively, "Bess Myerson."

"Myerson?" said Jones. "Myerson? You sure? Myerson?"

"You sure get stupid come evening," said the Bear.

"I get tired. I'm getting middle-aged." Listlessly he shook his empty wineglass. "I get tired. Leave me alone."

The Bear regarded Jones' hairless white chest, on which his shirt had fallen open. "That was nice spaghetti," said the Bear, thinking, Poor Jones.

"Thanks. I like Angel," Jones said.

"I like Dennis," said the Bear. "Rockford's friend Dennis Becker, the cop.

"He looks like a bear," said Jones. "That's why you like him."

"The hell he does," said the Bear, "and the hell I do."

"Nya nya," said Jones. "I'm tired. I like Rockford's dad. Lea' me 'lone."

Poor Jones, thought the Bear. Poor weak Jones. Such slim resources. Life was down. Time was up. The Bear had to get out of there. He packed his alto—nothing out of the ordinary in that—then went to the closet, put on baggy khaki pants, a long flappy raincoat and a hat.

"What are you doing?" said Jones, sitting up, rousing himself, trying to be equal to the situation.

"*Sorry but I can't take you*," sang the Bear. "Don't worry. I'll be back around two, three the latest. We can work tomorrow, but tonight I got to get some air."

"Where you going?"

"Tin Palace maybe and jam. Maybe I'll just do like Sonny Rollins, go up on the bridge and play. Stand there suspended between heaven and the deep and wait for something to happen."

"Wait up, I'll go with you, run interference."

"Not tonight," said the Bear, showing teeth. "What I do I must do alone. Go quickly. Robert Jordan felt his heart beating on the pine floor of the forest. Gary Cooper. Ingrid Bergman. The End."

"Don't talk crazy. I'll come with you. Wait up."

"Look, if I go up on the bridge and play we might get a writeup. Which bridge was it?"

"Brooklyn. Williamsburg. I forget."

"Rainbow. The spectrum. See ya."

The Bear was already out the door and trundling down the stairway when Jones started buttoning his shirt and looking around for his socks. Shit, he thought, I knew this was gonna happen one of these nights. He's going out there looking for trouble. *Looking* for it. Thank God he can handle himself in a fight but New York's changed a lot since the last time he was out alone. Too many people out there carrying heat.

Jones found the other shoe and slipped it on. I've got to get a move on if I'm gonna catch him at all. He ran slapdash for the door and made sure he had the keys.

But the Bear was already standing outside the glass doors of the tenement, adjusting the brim of his hat. I may be wearing a hat and a raincoat, thought the Bear, but no one's gonna mistake me for Paddington. I have always rejected the cutesy-poo. And I am, objectively speaking, one heavy bear.

He came down the seven steps to the sidewalk and turned right, toward the Avenue. From behind he looked like an enormous, burly man in a coat, his body thick with power. The weight of the alto case did not affect his walk in the least. He didn't roll, didn't lean or sway, but went straight in a line along the pavement.

Maybe, it occurred to the Bear, someone seeing me from behind might think: he's carrying a gun in that case, or a bomb, or the secret of my life that I myself have lacked the courage to live completely, or the secret of this great and terrible city, or perhaps instead—something strange was happening—an oblong, self-illumined emerald three feet by one by one and a half that glows neither like the moon (silver), the sun (gold), nor the stars (diamonds) but like some inner, unsuspected, spiritual globe or light, of which man has hardly begun to learn the existence, the qualities, the name: an all-suffusing green gem with unprecedented powers: the key and catalyst to new emotions, attributes, lives and unifications, the secret of secrets, center of centers: the microcosm, the mandala for real, the obverse of the manifest and the key to all possible liberations. Perhaps, thought the Bear, someone behind him might have thought this, and perhaps for a moment, flickering wholly in and then wholly out, the saxophone case might actually have contained the sole and abiding principle, the locus of revelation—who knows?—but at the moment the only person behind the Bear was Jones, coming scattered and dishevelled down the seven steps to the street. His first impulse was to run after the Bear and bring him back, but then he thought better of it, dropped back and followed at a distance.

In the meantime, the Bear had attained the Avenue, where blinding, brilliant traffic travelled like a line of light from north to south, as if between worlds. But it was Jacob who saw the ladder, wrestled with the angel, and obtained a birthright under false pretenses. The Bear had done none of these things. He pulled the hatbrim farther down on his face and walked south beneath the vault of darkness, above him like guardians or heralds the electric signs of bars and stores—white, orange, yellow, gold, red, brilliant blue and green, occasional imperial purple—as if they were angels that had descended to earth only to hire themselves out as lures for business, possibly for reasons of pity. The Bear walked beneath them like a resolute and powerful man, the saxophone case at his side swinging like a cache of fate, love, gold or vengeance. When he realized that he could have his pick of them—that all options, attributes and possibilities actually were open to him, that he was, at the moment, exalted, liberated, free—he stopped walking for a moment, put down the saxophone case, looked gradually around him at the Avenue, raised his snout and smiled broadly, and there on the pavement stretched out and aloft his great and inevitable arms. Aah. The night entered him like honey, and he began, so heartily and with such a depth of pleasure that it might have been for the first time in his life, to laugh out loud.

2

despite the fact that the Bear weighed about four hundred pounds, carried a saxophone case and wore baggy pants, a raincoat and a hat, only a few people noticed him in the dozen blocks from his apartment to the Tin Palace. He was trailed by Jones and a remnant of grace. Jones bit his nails and wondered when to make his move. Grace kept the police cars on other streets and serious troublemakers out of the Bear's path. Some people saw him coming from a block or so away, but even at that distance they were sufficiently impressed by his size and shape to cross the street and feel their hearts hammering against their ribs until he was gone. They did not get to see him for what he really was. One young man came out of a tenement doorway and saw the Bear up close, but he had just come back from a year with the dervishes in Turkey and took the Bear for a curveball God had decided to throw him that night, either that or an elemental nature spirit off his turf. A second individual was merely confirmed in his opinion of what life in New York was coming to these days, and only an hour and a half later in the middle of a movie uptown did it dawn on him that he had seen a large and literal *bear*; he gripped the arms of his chair and let out a little scream. The third human the Bear encountered was the inevitable wino two blocks north of the Palace who, the time-honored gag to one side, did not swear to give up drinking on the spot but offered the Bear half his pint of Night Train. The Bear took it. "I haven't seen you since lemme see," the wino said.

"Only you can prevent forest fires," the Bear advised him.

The Bear came through the doors of the Tin Palace like a force of nature. The band, he noticed, was between sets and the house half empty: a deep room sided by a brick wall on the right, a long bar with a mirror behind it opposite, cheap wooden tables, a worn slat floor, and a diminutive piano and bandstand tacked on as an afterthought halfway back. He headed for the tables at the rear of the club behind the bandstand past the end of the bar. Most of the people in the club failed to notice him in significant detail. The few that did were too wary of being uncool to say anything. A jazz critic sitting at a front table decided that since Lester Bowie was in the house the guy in the bear suit was Joseph Jarman stopping by to say hello. The bartender, a large man with Hemingway hair and beard, had taken the Bear in for what he was and checked his supply of ice.

It turned out that the band was sitting at the tables at which the Bear had aimed himself. Without nodding hello, he swivelled his enormous body into a seat against the wall and did his best to exude the air of being where he belonged. The first person to speak to him was the girl who worked the door, pale, dark-haired, dressed top to toe in black. She had been on the phone when he came in and had hurried to the table to ask him for three dollars admission. She looked at him just before speaking. "Gack," she said.

"Gack," said the Bear, and politely raised his hat.

Steve McCall, the drummer for the night and, it must be admitted, a large and bearlike man, was in the seat next to the Bear on the right. He had a large oval face, the bottom half of it covered by a beard, and wore round-lensed steel-frame spectacles. "It's okay," he told the waitress. "The gentleman is with us."

The woman backed uncertainly away. She felt overwhelmingly sleepy, and wondered if coffee would help. Coffee would not help, but she would settle down in about an hour.

Lester Bowie, who was not on the bill for the evening but had dropped by to sit in for a couple of sets, had meanwhile come out of the men's room and was staring at the Bear with a wild, delighted grin on his face. His goatee was waxed to two fine points, he wore an immaculate white surgeon's coat and a stethoscope hung from his neck. "Holy shit," he said finally. "Ho-lee shit." Bowie had recently come in from the street, where he had been smoking an unusual cigarette that rendered him peculiarly susceptible to hilarity and awe. "Hey," he concluded. "I think I'm gonna like this."

"Doctor doctor I got this terrible pain," said the Bear. "Every time I walk into a room people make a fuss and I feel just awful."

Bowie's grin became, if possible, even wider.

"Want a beer?" asked McCall.

"Sure," said the Bear.

McCall raised a glass and waved to the bartender, who nodded back.

"I even love it," said Bowie, and jolted himself into a seat across the table from the Bear. "And I know I'm gonna love it one hundred fucking times more when I find out what it is."

"It's a bear," said the Bear.

"One . . . hundred . . . fucking . . . times . . . more," repeated Bowie, with the kind of rhythmic variation for which he has been noted.

Jones had gotten hung up at the front door trying to pull three dollars out of his pants while watching with mounting panic the tables at the rear—it's all over, it's all over, he was thinking, it's only a matter of minutes before someone calls the cops—but he had worked himself clear and now he lunged into the seat next to Bowie, and ran a hand through his sweat-soaked thinning hair, his mind in tatters. "Now this is not what it looks like at all," he said in a hurried voice. "My friend here is my friend here he's okay and there is absolutely no need for for for panic. Right? Nobody move."

McCall raised two fingers to the bartender, who already had one beer in his hand and nodded again.

"Who's this guy," McCall asked the Bear.

"My manager. My best friend."

"How you doing," McCall said to Jones.

"I'm a little edgy," Jones told him.

"I see that," said McCall. "Try to relax."

"Look," said Jones, "if he's seen here, if anybody sees him, and the cops come in, or the scientists, it's all over, I mean his freedom goes out the window, you know? It'll all be over. It's very dangerous for him here."

"He's right," said the Bear. "He's absolutely right."

"Wait a minute," Bowie said authoritatively. "If anybody tries to fuck with the Bear they're gonna have to deal with us, with me, with Steve, with the management and with ev-ry fucking musician in this place, you understand? So you just take it easy, ain't nothing gonna happen to him and ain't nobody, no *body*, gonna fuck with a friend of mine while I'm around. Okay?"

The bartender brought the beers himself, put them on the table and nodded a discreet hello to the Bear. "Anybody tries to leave in too big a hurry," he said in a low voice, "or has to make a sudden call on the phone, is gonna run into delays. Make yourself at home."

The Bear nodded and took a first sip of his beer. "Aah," he said. "Well, I want to thank you all for your, um, hospitality, and while I'd really love to sit around and talk," he went on, "what I really came in here for is to play.

Would it be all right if I sat in." Noticing the general look of incomprehension that greeted this speech, he picked up the alto case by its top-handle and set it on the table.

"Can you sit in," said Bowie.

"Goes without saying," said McCall.

"Where's Fred and Hilton?" asked Bowie.

"Outside," said McCall. "What do you say we all have another beer for a minute. And what do you want to play?"

"Say we start with a blues?" the Bear suggested.

At length and a few beers later, the band reassembled and regained the bandstand, although the Bear had chosen to remain in his seat, hat pulled low, until it was time for him to play. The blues the band had decided on was "C. C. Rider," mid-tempo in B-flat, no customary shuffle this time out but loose-limbed, *au courant*, at its ease, a groove. The main thing that the Bear had failed to realize about the band was that it was Arthur Blythe's date, and as the band finished the repeat of the head and the human altoist stepped forward to the mike for his choruses, the Bear marvelled at the fluency of his playing. It was a pleasure, as he remembered having read somewhere, to hear the alto saxophone played so well. I could never play like that, he thought, and took his own axe out of the case and assembled it, turning toward the club's rear wall and warming up inaudibly. Working the mouthpiece down, he tuned it before returning his attention to the bandstand and Blythe.

He saw the short, round, brown man in profile, the golden saxophone held delicately out in front of him toward the microphone, each note coming out of it perfectly shaped and finished, as if turned on a lathe. The saxophone, as Blythe held and played it, began to seem less and less like a musical instrument and more like some part of a jeweler's apparatus, something that might be used to cut and facet a precious stone. The Bear enjoyed Blythe's approach, but it was far more polished and deliberate than what he felt drawn to personally, and although he knew he could not in some respects match Blythe technically—listen to those two-octave leaps, those cleanly articulated sixteenth-note runs over chord substitutions, the way he milks the reed for inflection—he felt a competitive edge rising in his chest, felt, for the first time as a musician in fact, his very bearness rising in him to assert itself against what he had always thought of as the merely human world. He felt a great mammalian warmth begin to fill his deep barrel chest.

"You sure you want to do this," he heard Jones' thin voice ask him.

"Abyssolutely," said the Bear, feeling his great fur-covered body sitting like an original form of Power in its seat. Soon, this Power would act. Only I can prevent forest fires, he told himself. Only I can shape, harmonize and render generous and benign this rising conflagration.

Blythe was finishing up his solo with a series of fast runs that ripped repeatedly into the lowest octave of his horn and came up shining, then, no, he was returning to the poised, perfectly positioned blues figurines with which he had begun. The Bear, realizing that his moment had come, rumbled up from his seat and made his way to the stage, finding himself thinking with unusual rapidity as he did so. He was led instantaneously to consider, now that he was onstand with the demonstrably bearlike McCall and the smaller but equally ursine Blythe, whether there was some deep, even fundamental connection between his own species and that of the jazz musician in general. Bird had taken on some bearish qualities when he put on weight and years. Mingus was a grizzly. Jaki Byard. Jack the Bear. But Ellington was a tiger, everybody knew that, elegant too, to the tips of his claws and his velvet voice.

Finding himself completely onstage now, with Blythe stepping discreetly backward, the Bear dismissed his thinking as frivolous and prepared himself to play. Lord what a rhythm section, he found himself thinking as he raised his saxophone to his snout and heard McCall's unfashionably simple cymbal beat opening up a free infinity of time and space, Hopkins' bass sinking deep shafts of darkness into the beat and Ruiz's chords, even from that scandalous piano, feeding him strength and ideas from bar one.

The Bear proceeded to attempt a few things he had never really done before, partly in reaction to Blythe's lapidary style but far more for reasons that overwhelmed him and which he could not all identify. He began his solo with violent, almost inchoate downward smears of sound—hadn't Ornette Coleman's early recorded solos always reminded him of broad smears of red paint?—which bled down over bar lines and the beat but stayed somehow within the statutory framework of a B-flat twelve-bar blues. He heard someone in the audience call out "Yeah!" and this, surprisingly (since he had always thought such exclamations tasteless and out of place), spurred him on. He continued squeezing sound out of himself like paint out of a tube until it was gone and then, having established this crude, expressionist impasto for a few choruses, he began to raise up out of it fast runs that blurred past him like fireworks, like the streak of ambulances at night. From this he passed to something nearer the conventional blues with which he had begun, as if he were riding the storm of what had gone before, but not entirely: the conventions, like the notes and phrases themselves, had been bent, bled and burned away: they were collapsing houses and flaming cities of themselves, they were flying doorways and bursting lives, they were pretty damn good. This is all right, the Bear told himself as he played, this is really all right.

Hilton Ruiz played a last block chord on the piano and laid out, and in response McCall and Hopkins bonded their sense of time still more indissolubly together and gave the beat such urgency the Bear thought for a moment that they had sped up. But they were solid, on the money and sailing clear.

The Bear had never played with musicians like this. He reared his head back to take a larger breath, and had he been aware of the audience he would have realized that the sudden sight of his opened jaws—great white tearing teeth, livid purple gums and broad, slavering tongue—had made it collectively gasp and jump back a foot, where space allowed.

The critic had leapt from his front-row seat and made his rapid way to the pay phone at the far end of the bar. He had already dialled the first four numbers of his photographer's exchange when the bartender reached over, dashed the receiver's brains out against the wall and told him, "I'm sorry, but this telephone is temporarily disconnected."

The musicians in the house—and David Murray, who lived upstairs, was among them, his lidded savvy eyes already calculating what use he might make of what the Bear was putting down—all found themselves most impressed by what the Bear took most for granted in his work: his unmatchable capacity for breath, the incredible volume he could get from the instrument without breaking up his tone. As for what he was playing, yeah, it was all right. Maybe there was a new musician in town, maybe not. One solo does not an artist make.

The Bear found himself doing a few more unexpected things, although there was precedent for one of them in Dolphy: he began incorporating ideas that had no proper place in the solo, stray thoughts, overheard sounds, freaks of inspiration, arguments played out rapid-fire in the dark theater of the mind. He inserted them when he felt like it or when they obtruded sufficiently—he liked the idea, why shouldn't the solo pick up on what's going on outside it, why shouldn't it interrupt itself to say something irrelevant and inspired?—but then just as suddenly he got sick of the tactic and began playing as many notes as he possibly could, as if to blot them out and obliterate the divided mind in which an argument could take place, even an inspired one, and substitute for it the more whole and harmonious instrument that had been given him from above in the street on his way to the club. He became aware that the illumination he had received, fragmentary and unsatisfying to him now but wholly adequate to the needs of the music, was beginning to inform what he was playing, and his solo had begun to even out, to reflect, in the middle of what was still a tumult, a kind of peace. Yes, he thought, there is my true, eternal self and native song. How did I even begin to get interested in this other shit? He attuned himself to what was most complete and timeless in him and tried to let its music through.

Something came through for a couple of choruses and floated above the demands of the time and turned slowly on its axis, but then, even before the Bear was aware of it, he had lowered his saxophone and begun to walk offstage. His solo, apparently, was over. Trouble was, he wanted to go on. He raised his saxophone to his snout again but found himself apprehended by the Law of what he had already done. *Ich habe genug*, his spirit told him, and with uncharacteristic docility he nodded okay and left the stand. Lester Bowie came up past him and began a sputtering and electric trumpet solo. About halfway back to the table he felt the material New York world return to his consciousness with a crash. A sweat of terror broke out under his fur. Holy shit, he told himself, we got to get out of here. "Jones?" he said weakly.

"I'm with you," said the man who was his friend.

"We gotta split," said the Bear.

He made his way back across the nightclub through the blur of his mixed emotions and the unanimous recoil of the audience. He did not remember having packed up his instrument, although he had, and swabbed it roughly clean too. When he and Jones left the club through the two sets of doors and turned right, the Bear found himself facing the Avenue: it was a wilderness of human darkness and unnatural light. The Bear began to shake. "I can't deal with it," he told Jones. "I'll never make it home. I can't do it, I'm caving in."

"There's only one way," said Jones, and although the Bear saw little or nothing, he recognized in all the tumult of the street the sound of Jones unsnaking his length of chain.

"Right," the Bear agreed, and began to strip. When he had gotten all his clothes off, Jones compressed them into a bundle he secured with the trench-coat strap. The Bear attached the chain to the ring in his nose and got down on all fours. "Ready," he said, and they started uptown.

The Bear applied all his attention to getting his brainless, rolling, after-work walk down, and was terrified of not being able to get it right. He found himself surprisingly near the verge of tears. Was it the emotion left over from his solo? A sorrow was welling up from deep in his body that had the shape of his whole life to it, the captivity and loss, the quirks and pitfalls of character and fate, everything that had shaped him and he didn't want to know about just now. Oh Lord, he thought, here it comes, the Big Sad, not portioned out but all in one gulp. I am about to disappear. "Be cool," he heard Jones hiss at him severely.

"What?" the Bear asked hopelessly, and began to sink to the pavement on his belly, as if ready to vanish into the earth.

"That's it, play dumb," he heard Jones say. "It's the police."

The Bear was just able to stop himself from saying, The what? He was aware of a red light—ha, the lower worlds, he told himself, whirling in their profitless and eternal cycle on the roof of a car—and then of an officer shining a bright white light into his eyes, which began to water in response.

He heard an unkind voice asking Jones a question: *"Have you got a license for that animal?"* No, he's not evil, the Bear reminded himself, only unfortunate, only bereft of his sustaining principle. How can people live like that? How did they manage to get that way? It's such an illusion.

"Of course, officer," he heard Jones say, and then the unrustling of a piece of paper. The Bear felt his earlier sorrow change its shape, and sensed himself filling with something like compassion—he was having a busy night—and it came to him that he should stand up and heal the police officer's spirit just by standing up and speaking the truth to him. You must, he told himself, live the unconditioned life. You must adhere to the Real or consent to die piece by piece. If this night has taught you anything it must be that a life lived halfway is the deadliest thing on earth. You must be fully born.

"You know you're not supposed to be out with him at night," he heard the cop's voice say. "And what's in the suitcase?"

"His things," said Jones. "I had to take him to the vet in a hurry. Just look at him how sick he is, there wasn't a cab that would pick us up on the way back, it's night out, so we started walking."

"What was wrong with him?"

"Distemper."

"Hey, my dog had that."

"Bear's just a big dog," said Jones.

"Whaddaya say, Jack?" said the policeman.

"I dunno," said a similar voice nearby. The Bear heard a car door open and shut, then shoesteps on concrete. "I dowanna take him in, the animal shelter, the paperwork, it's a drag. Man's got a sick bear. It's not my job, sick bears."

"We can't just leave 'em out on the street, Jack," the first officer reminded him.

"You're right about that," the second officer said.

"We're a working team," he heard Jones tell the policemen in a pleading tone. "A street act. Taxpayers. We just got written up in *New York* magazine," he lied.

"Really?"

"A revival of a great old tradition, it said."

"Oh. Hey. Hum."

"Listen," said Jones, sounding exactly as if he'd had a sudden inspiration. "How about if you guys gave us a lift home. It's only a coupla blocks and we don't wanna scare any people on the street. He's cool in cars, won't crap on the seat or anything."

There was a moment of silence, for the sake of deliberation or its imposture, and the scales of justice were raised aloft to balance the possibilities of the moment. The night hung suspended. A cloud covered the moon. A bottle crashed to pavement half a block away and a voice cheered its destruction. "Okay, get him inna car."

As the Bear shambled obediently into the backseat of the police car he was preparing himself to speak. Because it was time. All the world's compassion, sorrow and love had gathered in his chest—well, maybe—not to tie itself into the usual complicated knot but finally to do its proper work. It was time, thought the Bear, for all that truth and feeling to flow out of him unaltered and change men's lives. It was time to blow the quotidian categories, not out of egocentric glee but because the human world had trudged the circle too many times and it was getting hard for anyone in its ambit to wake up in the morning, sleep lay so heavily on one's eyes.

He had played his little solo and now it was time for him to have his little say. No big thing. Just another incremental set of recognitions, the straitjacket worked a little looser under the arms. It may be time to do it, nudge the epoch two or three degrees sideways into the light. Now's the time, said Bird. The Bear would pick it up. Why have I been such a coward for so long? He counted off the tempo and got ready for his entrance.

When the Bear raised his head to speak, his eyes encountered the strong steel mesh that separated the backseat from the front, and he remembered, or foresaw, some more decisive encounter with everything that was wrong with the world, and his spirit contracted, dampened, chilled, and resolved into a mire. Thus conscience, he thought. Doth make. Why? Why does this always happen? He had no answer. His big night out was done.

"Howja get the bear?" he heard a voice ask Jones from an unbridgeable distance. No, check it out: from the front seat. We're back. The clock is ticking.

"Won him in a poker game," he heard Jones' voice say, correctly.

"Wadja have in ya hand?"

"Full house actually."

"Houseful of bearshit's more like it."

"Hey that's a good one," said Jones, and laughter was general in the car. The Bear joined in and Jones shot him a quick elbow in the ribs, but the cops seemed not to have noticed.

And then, the Bear observed, the cops forgot about him completely. They punched the siren a burst before pulling into traffic, then hooked the car through a wide U-turn and pointed it uptown.

The ride took five minutes, the farewell warning another two.

"Yes," said Jones, easing out of the car when the driver popped the back-door locks by remote. "Yes sir."

With a farewell blip of siren, the police car pulled away.

On all fours at the end of his chain, a subdued Bear followed Jones up the stoop of their building, then up the stairs to the apartment. "*When you see me coming raise your window high*," he sang on the second-floor landing, "Parker's Mood" again.

"*When you see me going hang your head and cry*," Jones returned.

In the third-floor hall Jones looked in his pocket for the keys. He opened the locks, they went in. The television was still on but they both sat down and looked at the floor.

3

the Bear woke up an hour before his usual time to find that he had clawed the corner of his mattress to shreds again, another night of bad dreams. They had begun to plague his sleep since the jam session at the Tin Palace, peculiarly vivid, with all the weight and authority of waking experience. The remains of last night's feature clung to him now but he didn't want to look. He unwound himself from the ropes and tangles of his sheets and walked hazily into the bathroom, where he turned on the shower and stared at his reflection in the mirror while the water heated up. He seemed lusterless and oppressed. His eyes were sparkless. Is there anything, he asked himself, in this undignified hulk of a body that is capable of being raised up to Beauty? Or was that just another dream. While he was wondering about it, the glass fogged over and his image vanished into mist.

He pulled open the pink plastic curtains, stepped into the tub and under the hot spray of water. Purify me, he asked it. I am the oblation and the sacrifice. I am the offering and the flame to which it is offered. I am the clarified butter. I am the yak out back behind the lamasery. I am the blue-green thing in the far corner of the fridge behind the bulging month-old milk carton. I am that I am and that's all what I am. I'm Popeye the Sailor Man. *Ich narr*.

The Bear shuddered. Cheer up, it'll all be over soon.

Speaking of dreams, what had last night's been? Recently he had been assassinated—shot between the shoulderblades in his white-gold robe and miter trying to conduct High Mass before a mixed animal and human crowd in an old wooden barn. The night before that, he'd been hunted by the Mafia—seemed he'd pocketed the wrong money or informed on someone—to a dingy 1950s hotel room in Cincinnati, soiled soup-green carpet, rumpled bed, the sound of a streetcar clanging past outside in slanted sunlight while two men in coats looked up at him from the sidewalk as he parted the curtain. Some fitful half-waking part of himself kept asking, Wait a minute, wait a minute now: this doesn't make sense, how did I get *here*? But the dream's sense of detail had done him in, and he had plummeted heavily into belief and imminent doom. The night before, as the captain of his submarine, he'd been trying to save the world from a bunch of hideous green ghoulish creatures, but they found a hidden entrance down below and came up at him through a maze of ladders and hatches that he recognized as untended regions of himself; they enveloped him in their unspeakably loathsome presence and calmly, methodically ate him alive.

Last night's feature, he now remembered, had been less routinely nightmarish but somehow more depressing. He had been walking down a vaguely outlined city street toward evening when, as if a force were driving his head downward, he found himself looking at the backs of his paws: they were changing into pink, worm-fingered human hands, and he felt deeply nauseated and afraid. Then, too quickly, the dream had changed: he began to fly headfirst across the pavement at tremendous speed, and the street was no longer vaguely sketched: despite the fact that his eyes were fixed in shock on his half-paws half-hands, every stone, every speck, every fleck of light on every pane of glass and every filament of floating city soot was brought home to him in riveting, unnatural detail. He did not recognize the street but it came to him, as he flew through its preternaturally detailed gridwork of matter, light and shade, that he would see it one day when he was awake, possibly at the same speed. This reflection made no sense to him and he woke briefly in the dark room, where ladders of carlight coming through the blinds swept across the ceiling in a noiseless clash of optics. He lapsed back into vague dreams and partial sleep. He followed a pale, half-familiar woman through a maze of alleyways till dawn.

The shower hadn't helped much, and the night still had its hands on him. He turned off the water, got down on all fours in the tub and shook himself dry. After he pulled the curtain open and climbed out he took a last look at himself in the mirror. What can ail thee, wretched wight? he asked himself. The sedge is withered from the lake and no birds sing? Is that what's troubling you, bucky?

In the kitchen he made eggs and toast and coffee, sat at the table to eat them, and found the phone company's Final Warning concealed among the napkins, where Jones must have inserted it the day before. Soon, the Bear smelled the day's first cigarette, and in a little while Jones himself appeared in his bedroom doorway, yawning and rubbing at his eyes. "Gumorning, Bear," he said, and scratched randomly at his underwear.

"Morning, Jones," said the Bear. "Coffee's up."

"I need a shower. Keep it hot."

Ten minutes later they were seated across the table from each other, Jones eating the Breakfast of Champions while his eggs got cold, the Bear having another coffee, black no sugar, in his widemouthed cup.

"You left the bathtub full of fur again," said Jones. "I wish you'd um . . ." He waved his hand vaguely in the air.

"I thought I wiped it."

"You forgot."

"Sorry," said the Bear, and held up the message from Ma Bell.

"I was hoping you wouldn't find that. Don't worry. I'll pay."

The Bear took a puff from Jones' cigarette and replaced it in the ashtray. "How can you smoke these things?"

"Jesus, look how you lipped it. Look at that thing. You expect me to smoke that?" Savagely Jones mashed it out in the ashtray.

"Consider me your therapist," said the Bear. "I'm trying to get you to quit. You know my methods, Watson."

"Up yours," Jones observed, and lit another Lucky.

"We have the money for the phone bill?"

Jones shrugged. "I'll pay it. All the calls are mine."

"I use the phone too." The Bear had acquired the habit of conducting lengthy late-night conversations with long-distance operators in Denver, Idaho City, Des Moines and K.C. He told them he was a businessman, a writer, a son in search of his father, a father in search of his son. After five minutes they'd be swapping stories about their lives, and he'd tell them lies in return, fitting out a human life, working his way into whatever character happened to be emerging that night. They were good people, the operators. He enjoyed talking with them. If you could believe what you heard on the phone, America was full of blameless, generous folks.

"Doesn't cost you," said Jones. "I was thinking of finding a job in a restaurant."

"What about the act?" the Bear asked him. "If we're out of cash I'm ready to go back to work."

"Aah," said Jones, "take a break. I can wait tables a couple of weeks, it won't kill me."

"What do I do, sit around the apartment all day? Terrific."

"Watch TV," Jones suggested. "Read a book."

"Get sluggish," the Bear counterposed. "Die of boredom."

"What the hell else am I supposed to do? I can't just drop you upstate anymore. The forestry commission's tightened up its act. You're the wrong breed and you're not banded. They'll fly your ass to Manitoba."

"The wild's not what it used to be," the Bear allowed.

Jones stretched his arms above his head and cracked his knuckles back. "Things will have their revenge," he said, "but right now I'm gonna go out for a paper and look at the want ads. Anything l can get you?"

The Bear washed the cigarette taste out of his mouth at the sink, then unpacked his alto and ran through a few rudiments among the breakfast litter. Seeing Blythe up close had made him want to extend his usable range and speed up his fingering. He had been putting in an hour a day on exercises alone. The same genetic crapshoot that had enlarged and detailed his brain had laid a set of opposable thumbs on him, which was cool, but his paws did not have the degree of articulation those nightmare wormy hands would have taken for granted. Was that the point? Was it a saxophone dream? It didn't feel like a saxophone dream. The Bear often played saxophones in his dreams. On occasion he had made love to saxophones in his dreams—tell it like it is: he had *fucked* them, with a ruthlessness he'd never have directed at another living being, and then would wake amid sheets of sound or cotton gone sticky thinking, How perverse. He was getting off the subject, and in his distraction the rudiments he was supposed to be working on were losing their contours and turning almost into music. Which at the moment was not the point. He reapplied himself to the anatomical machinery and allotted it the necessary focus.

Practice was a cheerless task but you couldn't deny that it worked: his paws gradually accustomed themselves to working faster, and, tonguing his way through some maniacally intricate turns of phrase, he began to gain a better grasp of the reed, and saw new ways, some time off, of bending this grasp to the purposes of living play. The seed of music needed this husk of persistence and repetition, but it seemed a shame that the whole thing couldn't be done on just the sweet, searing fire of God, music winging down and sweeping you up in some sweet chariot.

Ecce the Last Romantic, he thought, put down the horn, and looked at the breakfast mess on the table. Jones had put a cigarette out in the hardened yellow of an egg, and the Bear had spilled the dregs of his own last coffee. This is supposed to inspire me? This is supposed to provide a basis for Art? The fire, the inspiration, the whatever-it-was that had filled him just a few nights before at the Tin Palace lay dormant or damaged somewhere in the workings of his chest. He tried to play "Giant Steps," but although he could make the changes in tempo it sounded listless, empty, not even nearly right. Funny how it works and then the next minute doesn't. He put his alto down, went to the sink and washed the dishes clean.

When Jones came back, banging the door almost off its hinges, he seemed excited, red in the face and nearly out of breath.

"What's up, doc?" the Bear asked him, and halted in the middle of a chorus of "Brilliant Corners." "I know you ain't been jogging. You land a job at Lutèce?"

"Not exactly." Jones held an opened newspaper in front of him. "You made the *Voice*."

The Bear squinted his eyes and just made out the headline. "*Ecological-Jazz Fusion*?" he read.

"Oh yeah."

"Oh no."

Jones brandished the paper and began to read aloud. "'Amid the drastic imbalances inflicted upon the natural world by human avarice and stupidity the great enveloping silence of the natural kingdom has begun to unfold itself into sound,'" he said.

"No shit?"

"No shit. 'No single alto solo at this point can raise a voice sufficient to the wounds of the butchered planet—'"

"No?" asked the Bear.

"Apparently not," said Jones. "And what do you think it means that you made 'analogical reference to Albert Ayler, Lee Konitz, Albert Schweitzer and Chu Berry'?"

"Beats the shit out of me," said the Bear.

"Here, take the paper." Jones handed it to him.

Smoothing it down on the breakfast table, the Bear wrinkled up the top of his head and scratched himself midway between the ears. "Did you catch this?"

"Which."

"About how if the human race has any hope left it will enter through the portal of the extrahuman?"

"It's looked like that for a few years now."

"'By extrahuman,'" the Bear quoted, indexing the air with an upraised claw, "'I mean to include not only bear-solo and whale-song but the less articulate utterance of the mineral world, vegetation's language on the stave of the seasons, pools of water aiming their hearts at the moon.' Did I play that? I forget."

"What I said before," said Jones. "Things will have their revenge,"

"I ain't," said the Bear, "a thing."

"Sure you are," said Jones. "We all are. It's a thingy world. The sun shines down equally on the good and the bad, the just and the unjust."

"Also," the Bear read on, "I seem to be 'the first enunciation of a new age of possibilities not only animal but human, the unlocking of a bizarre and singular door in the mansion of the future, and possibly the best altoist to show up in New York since Zoot Finster.' How's that grab you?"

"Sounds like our man drinks a lot of coffee. Does he say anything in there about me?"

The Bear retired to a far corner of the living room with the newspaper, and after awhile his laughter grew softer and more contented. "I mean it's got nothing to do with me," he announced finally, "but it's made my day. Glory be."

"You still want to work the street today?" Jones asked him.

"Can it wait till tomorrow?"

"We got two days to pay the phone bill before they shut us off and I can get some credit at the grocer's."

"Do I seem like a first enunciation to you?"

"First time I saw you I said to myself . . . there's a bizarre and singular . . . uh . . ."

"Door." the Bear prompted.

"Exactly," Jones concluded. "So what should I get for dinner."

"Hinges," said the Bear.

The next day they were out on a midtown streetcorner at lunchtime. Their police permit was posted, a decent crowd of workers and wanderers had gathered and the Bear was flat on his back, moaning and crooning and waving inarticulate paws at the sky. He wasn't sure he'd be able to complete the routine. Time and the city were pounding him to a powder, and something weaker was fighting for life in his heart. Faces looked down at him in a ring and laughed, showing teeth and tongues. There's so little of me left, thought the Bear, why not take it all? The Bear felt himself beginning to slip away. "Harooo," he said, and waved blurry paws. "Haroooo."

Jones knew that Harooo was not in the script, and when it was time for him to walk over, look triumphant and plant his foot on the Bear's panting chest, he looked down to see if everything was all right. "Haroo?" the Bear asked him, and looked with unforgettable clarity into his eyes. Jones felt his entire life rise up to accuse him, and he stepped away from the Bear in confusion.

They cleared nineteen-fifty on the first show. Picking himself up and dusting off his jacket, the Bear wondered idly if anyone in the audience had read the piece about him in the *Voice*.

Looking out at the Bear, who stood waiting on the pavement in the middle of a ring of shoppers, Jones felt like tearing himself to pieces rather than go on. He should never have let the Bear talk him into taking the act out on the street again. It was torture for them both. For Chrissakes the Bear was a *musician*, and if he was afraid of standing there in the human world as what he really was, it was Jones' job to help him, give him strength. I'm the only one who knows him, Jones told himself. I raised him from a cub, I gave him records and an education. When he turned out to be special I protected him, but I should have been able to give him more than that. If I'd been a better human being . . . If I'd been man enough to stop the money I had from running through my fingers, we wouldn't have to do this. We'd be living in the Bahamas, plucking our food off the trees and making it with beautiful women of all races. . . . On big occasions the Bear would slap a fish out of the waves for dinner. If I were a better man I could have given him a life. If I'd been able to hang on to the family cash I could have given him a hideaway, but good Lord look at us now.

A three-deep crowd had gathered in a ring around the Bear, and it was time to begin. Well, thought Jones, making a living is a bitch even in the best conditions. You get eaten alive, a little at a time. He tipped back his straw boater, cued up his harmonica and began to play "Columbia the Gem of the Ocean" in C major. The Bear saluted in sprightly fashion, then began tap-dancing in a circle, a desperate, toothy grin on his face as he passed before the faces of the crowd. He pulled a small American flag from the breast of his plaid jacket and waved it aloft. There was a small, merely ritual ripple of applause.

And there they were: Jones with the beginnings of tears in his eyes, inhaling and exhaling into a small chromium harmonica as if the device had been surgically attached to his face, the Bear dancing in a circle with a terrible grin on his face and the crowd just beginning to loosen up and enjoy itself, just starting to clap its hands to the music. Above the tops of the slab-and-crystal buildings the sky was a clear and brilliant blue. It was another working day in the fallen world.

Jones put down his Hohner and switched on the Sony. The Bear did an effectively funny belly dance, followed by an adept disco parody (paws pedaling the air), and then, while Jones put on a Shore Patrol armband and got out the white sailor hat, the Bear did his strutting, avuncular Viennese bit to waltzes by Johann Strauss. When Jones tossed him the sailor hat and the tape segued to "Anchors Aweigh," they looked at each other across the pavement for a moment as if across a chasm, an identical pain piercing their hearts, before going on. The Bear was the drunken sailor, Jones the SP barraging him with questions as to his unit, ship and status. The Bear's groaning, monosyllabic answers were perfectly timed, his impersonation of human drunkenness uncannily exact for a beast. The crowd loved it, the men and women laughing and wiping at their mouths, and the bit was beginning to find its rhythm, but when Jones popped the Bear over the head with the foam-rubber billy and the Bear groaned and took his second roll in the gutter the show went suddenly slack and the hilarity ceased. It was Jones. The billy dropped to his side and his shoulders slumped. "C'mon, Bear," he said, "let's go home."

Lying there on the pavement looking up, the Bear blinked twice and let his mouth fall open, surprised. "Suits me," he said finally. "I feel like homemade shit."

"We can't do this anymore," said Jones. He pulled off his armband and walked away.

At first the crowd thought this was a brilliant new wrinkle in the performance, some combination of signals, ventriloquism and pathos, and although they were uneasy they applauded. But when the Bear started helping Jones pack up, switching off the cassette machine with weary casualness and putting it with his sailor hat in the valise, uncertainty set in, as if the crowd were seeing a piece of modern theater no one had written an essay about yet.

"You go get the cab," said the Bear, "and I'll collect the money. *Alms for oblivion*," he announced to the crowd. As he went around the circle, hat in hand, collecting dollars, matchbooks and a smattering of fear, the Bear could feel the skin of his life tearing almost audibly open, a membrane that had kept him from what? It was either new life or fatal illness from here on out. Anyhow that bit of prophylaxis was gone. "Only fifty cents?" he said to an olive-skinned lady with hollow cheeks and tweezed, Dietrich eyebrows. "For a first enunciation, a bizarre and singular door?" He saw her mouth drop open, her eyes register pain. "Sorry," he mumbled, and moved on down the line. "Sorry. I didn't mean . . ."

"Cab's here," he heard Jones call him.

"Hope it's a Checker," said the Bear. He looked back and it was. Nice roomy backseat.

The Bear pocketed the money and made his way to the big old satisfying taxi. Jones was already inside. As people parted like the awestruck waters of antiquity left and right, the Bear realized that it was time for his last public gesture as a street entertainer, but the necessary poetry wouldn't come. What could he say? O you people, change your lives? Somehow it lacked the necessary punch.

He reached the taxi door and turned. They were still there: good. But as he waited for the buildup of rhetoric that would enable him to call down the fire of heaven on a nation of vacated grinning fools, he recalled the woman he had just wounded with a passing remark and realized that like her all of them were innocent, whatever he had suffered under their eyes. The crowd was no target, merely human, merely a little uneasy due to a momentary, Bearish breaching of the laws of nature, and the only thing he wanted was to restore to them their fragile, baseless sense of peace. I'm just not ruthless enough, he told himself. It'll be the end of me yet.

"Our revels now are ended," he told his public gently, "and our little life is rounded with a sleep." He bowed deeply, hand on heart. "You're all in deep shit," he muttered under his breath. "Good luck."

The applause began as he straightened, and continued as he backed into the taxi. "That's New York for you," he remarked to Jones as he pulled the door closed. "If they think it's art they clap their hands, and if they think it might be real they turn pale and hope it goes away. You realize we cleared fifty bucks plus?" He smiled and waved to the crowd as the cab pulled away.

"What came over us?" Jones asked him.

"Gee I dunno," said the Bear. "You wanna try it again and find out?"

"Nope."

"What it was," the Bear said sagely, "was the law that says, Whatever the reality of a situation is, that's what has to come out in the end. There's no going back. I mean, that was a genuine change of state."

"Shucks," said Jones. "You don't have to explain absolutely everything to me. I can keep up with the basic stuff okay."

"Hey, where downtown?" asked the cabbie.

"Stay on Second," Jones told him, "and I'll tell you when we get there."

"Great costume you got there," the cabbie said, looking back.

"Thanks," said the Bear. "I'm beginning to develop a fondness for it myself." He reached forward to pull the Plexiglas partition shut. "So that's it," he said to Jones. "When we get back to the apartment I'm gonna call Lester Bowie and tell him that the guest shot with the Art Ensemble is on, if it's still okay with them, but I don't know what happens after that, how we make a living or what."

"You know," Jones said, settling back in the seat, "with that article in the *Voice* behind us we could probably manage to book you a little tour."

"A tour?" said the Bear.

"You said yourself there was no going back. Why not go straight ahead?"

The Bear ran a paw across his face as if to wash it. "Jones, I dunno. My family has a long tradition of silence. Twenty generations of talking bear and I'm the first to so much as open my mouth to a human being."

"That's because I'm such a sweet guy," Jones told him.

"I'm not sure I can go any farther than that," said the Bear.

"You've done that already. You want to cross the next line," Jones cleared his throat, "I'll be with you."

"I know," said the Bear. "But a tour . . ."

"Think about it. You've got the time."

The Bear looked out at New York City rocking past the taxi window. A stone jail with humans bunched at the major intersections. Ten million dazed and mortal beings hypnotized by love, work, hate, family and the past. What were the odds—the Bear asked himself, trying to be realistic—in all that multiplicity, on gaining sufficient purchase on real freedom? Looking out at this sampling of the millions is just the thing to convince me that I have no meaning and no chance. What could it possibly matter if one more or less creature toots on a horn?

They were passing Fourteenth Street, where drugged-out husks shambled past the storefronts like ghosts in coats. Living in the world means becoming part of *that*.

On the other paw, he thought, the right, the brave thing is to grasp your personal grain of truth and take your stand no matter what. God help me, he thought, I'm the genuine article, I'm a sap. He turned to Jones. "Guest shots?" he said. "A tour? I'm ready if you are."

The Bear looked down at his paws. Oh no, he thought, realizing what he had to do. I was never good at dramatic gestures. "Do I have to do this?" he asked aloud.

"What," said Jones.

"The ring."

"Maybe you should wait till we get to the apartment."

"I think it's time for it to go."

"Just remember it was never my idea, okay?"

"I know. You wanted to stay with the collar," said the Bear. "It was my sardonic bullshit take on things when I was a kid. It should have gone some time ago. It's going now."

"I think you'll want some towels," warned Jones.

But the Bear had already inserted his index claws and begun to pull the ring in his nose apart.

"Steady, steady," Jones advised him, but the first bright droplets of arterial blood began to spatter the Bear's chest.

"Get my jacket off," the Bear managed to say.

"Wait a minute . . ."

"Bunch it, bunch it, pull it off."

"Shit, you've done it now," said Jones when he saw how much blood the Bear was losing.

"What the *fuck*!" the cab driver said, taking notice, and then a squeal of tires and blare of horns as he swerved his taxi to the curbside.

Jones got the Bear's plaid jacket into position beneath the Bear's bleeding nose and thrust a chunk of the day's fat take at the cabbie. "Two blocks south, then take a left. I got the nosebleed covered here, and this money is for you."

The driver blew out air. Which about summed it up, thought Jones, looking forward to the fall of eventide, when all this would be over and something unforeseen would begin at last.

4

two weeks later, they were halfway across the Brooklyn Bridge and the Bear was tired of hiding in the back of the van Jones had rented for the day. He clambered forward into the shotgun seat and rolled his window down.

"Bear," said Jones, while changing lanes, "please don't make a spectacle of yourself."

"Me?" the Bear asked him, then stuck his head out the window into the breeze and did his St. Bernard impression for two fair-haired kids down there in a passing Oldsmobile. "Woof," he said. "Woof woof woof," then let his tongue loll out the side of his mouth full length and drooled into the wind.

The kids waved and pointed at him and pounded at their parents, but the folks weren't having any.

"Spectacle, shmectacle," said the Bear, and pulled his head inside. "Nobody gives a shit. But what a day. Ain't it a brilliant day in the harbor? Sun with thy shiny rays! Water with thy gleamy gleams! Harp of steel stretched above the deep! O Sonny! O Rollins!"

"Oh shut up."

"We really ought to get out more often. You never take me anywhere."

"We're getting out now."

They made their landfall in Brooklyn, passing between the Eagle Warehouse and the Watchtower—Read God's Word the Holy Bible Daily.

"Jones," said the Bear, "what do you know about this band really?"

"They're the best we can do under the circumstances."

"Circumstances," said the Bear, "will be the end of me yet."

"Look," Jones told him. "It's summer. Everyone who can is touring Europe and Japan. Even aside from all the security considerations and the kind of money we can afford to pay, there's this general sense of Huh, a bear? And it's partly your fault, for being so careful to point out to everyone that there's a danger of you getting busted and the whole band with you. I wish you'd let me handle the phone calls."

It was true there could be troubles on the tour. In their early days together they were discreet about the Bear's real nature, and had confined the news to a small circle of friends. Even so, inquiries came, polite and academic at first, mild solicitous souls in ill-fitting clothes and fashionless spectacles: a couple of days at the lab, such a privilege, if you'd be so kind. And it might have ended there if the Bear hadn't been so adamantine in his refusals. Subsequent bids had been more forceful, eventually even threatening: of course we could take matters into our own hands, sir, but we won't if you volunteer, and a week is all we want of your animal I promise. Nuts to you had been Jones' reply. The research theme reached it ripest development with two men in narrow-cut suits, short hair and steel-frame shades who offered Jones a "book contract"—two books would appear under his name and royalty checks would be paid him on a regular basis—for the "use" of the Bear: in our facilities we can look after him better than you can, and he'll have a good and, nudge-nudge, *full* life with us. Even after Jones and the Bear changed addresses twice there had been doorway figures in the street at night, new neighbors in the next apartment, an irritating echo on the telephone and a suspicious fire in the building. After years of extreme discretion, in which they had narrowed their social life to a virtual circle of two, Jones and the Bear had achieved anonymity again, they hoped. In any event no strange nose had poked through the curtains in awhile, but now that they were stirring the waters who could tell?

"I don't want to get anyone into trouble they don't know about," said the Bear.

"That's big of you, but maybe then you shouldn't tour. Some tour. A couple of unadvertised gigs in New York and a quick ramble up to Boston. We're lucky to get anyone at all. But," Jones recited, "Julius talked to Tim Berne and Marty Ehrlich, and although they couldn't spare their own bands they did know these other guys . . ."

"The Bear and These Other Guys. Terrific billing. I had hopes, I really had hopes, that between Julius and McCall and the guys in the Art Ensemble we could manage to find some real cats willing to come out with us."

"You sat in with McCall and Lester and it's spoiled you. You haven't earned guys like that for a working band."

"So I got nowhere to go but down. Traffic jam." The Bear pointed at the cars bunching up at the light.

"I can handle it," said Jones, braking, lurching. "Fucking suspension."

"Fucking suspense," said the Bear. "Please don't crash." But he wasn't really worried about a traffic accident: how good would These Other Guys be, and if they actually did the tour would he survive it?

The one-night stint with the Art Ensemble had come off well, but that was down to Lester Bowie, who had done everything to ease the Bear's way and make sure the joint was secure: the loading doors at the back of the Bottom Line swinging open just as Jones and the Bear pulled up in the van, Bowie hustling them inside and introducing the Bear to the rest of the Art Ensemble in the backstage dressing room.

"We're overdoing the costume shit tonight. You'll be lucky if anyone even notices you," Bowie said, and he might have been right: bassist Malachi Favors had painted his face white and wore tribal-style robes of silver lamé; Joseph Jarman had topped off his cloaks and warpaint with a pair of fluffy pink bunny ears; drummer Don Moyé was wearing approximately Dogon regalia; Roscoe Mitchell, in streetclothes and black cotton watchcap, merely nodded hi. The Bear wore what seemed to be his regulation music costume of raincoat, baggy pants and widebrim hat.

"And dig this," Bowie said, showing him the gun, a small black automatic lying on the palm of his hand. "The piece of resistance. Ought to scare off intruders, right? Sometimes I like to shoot it off at the end of a trumpet solo, blanks of course, but it also takes flare cartridges and tear gas. Brought them along in case of trouble. When I bought the thing I wanted to see what the flares were like and I damn near set fire to the house."

Malachi Favors finished applying bright red lipstick and smiled out of the mirror at the Bear. "I'm interested to hear how you play," he said. "I'm sure, from what Lester tells me, that I will be delighted."

Roscoe Mitchell nodded again and again said, "Hi."

In the event, the music had been interesting.

After standing with the band in silence facing east—a nice moment actually, an effective tune-up—things had begun in a rumor of gongs and birdcalls, and the Bear had stayed out of it, a few stray notes excepted. Standing at his bass, Malachi Favors began muttering into a bullhorn, Lester was breathing hoarsely in and out of his horn, and something in these gathering strands of music caught on his fur and before he knew it he was involved in a converse of whispers with Roscoe Mitchell on the other alto while Joseph Jarman roamed the gong-world behind him, occasionally punctuating the groundswell with a bicycle horn. Now, the Bear had never considered himself a flat-out free atonal player—he hoped he sounded like himself, though it was pretty obvious he came out of Bird, Ornette and Jackie McLean—but as he and Roscoe tangled further and drums and bass came up under them like some thickening storm and Jarman raised a rattle of bells and chimes before the rising wind, in a matter of minutes the Bear was involved in successive tumults of freeblow with Roscoe's pretty much atonal alto, and the band's whole sound rose up in a wave. When the crescendo subsided, the rest of the night was blown clear of obstruction, and the Bear went into it happily and without much worry. The audience, which applauded pretty much on schedule after each of the music's episodes, didn't bother him either.

There was a long sort-of blues, the rhythm section solid, Malachi Favors' bass huge and warm without, the Bear noticed in some surprise, the benefit of amplification. The Bear had some fun with Bowie, trading choruses, then drifting into some less marked-out call and response. There was a long percussion jam in which he crossed the stage, grabbed a mallet and whomped away at a big bass drum, and then someone called Jarman's impossibly uptempo Coltrane tribute, "Ohnedaruth," and all the horn players blew their brains out in succession. Bowie played last, pulled out his pistol at the end of his outing and emptied his clip of blanks into the lights.

So far so good, thought the Bear as he squeezed tight on the reed and blew out a skirl of multiphonics, but then Bowie, looking as if he'd gone mad, for all the scientific sobriety of his labcoat, reached into his pocket, loaded another clip into the automatic and fired another brace of blanks into the avid, crowded tables of the nightclub yelling, "Bang bang bang motherfuckers," and a busload of tourists at a row of tables near the front—some tour director must have sent them to see the Art Ensemble by mistake or for laughs—who had been only mildly alarmed at the first shots and the presence of what seemed to be an actual bear onstage now went into blind panic, flinging chairs aside and bolting through the tightly packed crowd for the exit. Their panic spread through the club, no one sure what had happened or what had not, and it pretty much cleared the house. The band retired backstage laughing, Jarman threatening to kill Lester Bowie twice, and the Bear stood there onstage looking through pistol smoke.

He heard Jones calling from the club's front door, but he also saw a lone figure seated at a table, and the Bear's jaw dropped in deference: it was Ornette Coleman: the master: he made me.

The Bear stepped down from the stage through the remaining gunsmoke and walked to Ornette's table. Ornette was wearing a black silk suit and he seemed untroubled by the gunshots and the emptying of the club. He smiled up at the Bear. "That was interesting," Ornette said in a faraway, gentle voice, "but what I wonder, even though you play a thousand times better than I ever could, was how come you play so much like a human person. What I would like to know is do you transpose from bear to human and if so why you do it, because if I played with you what I'd like is for you to play bear without transposing and I could play like me even if I don't know if that says man and then we could see what the total added up to if no one did the adding. You know?"

Even though he felt the hemispheres of his brain crossing, the Bear was sure Ornette was right. Why *did* he transpose? Why was he so weak as to want to assimilate? "You're right," he told Ornette redundantly.

"You see," Ornette told him, "I think you play quadripedally, so what would a quadripedal tone be if you didn't transpose it to two-footed music. That would be the really interesting thing. By the way," he said, "I wouldn't worry about the audience leaving. They used to walk out on me all the time."

"Bear," he heard Jones calling, "there's a mob out on the street and I think I hear a siren."

"Let's play sometime," Ornette suggested.

"Maybe we could leave together," said the Bear.

"No that's all right," Ornette told him. "I'd like to hear the rest of the set." He gestured up at the empty stage.

Jones came up, grabbed the Bear by the arm, and they made it to the back door and the van just as a noise of entrance began swelling through the front.

It had taken the Bear a couple of days to get his alto case back, but the Bear considered his evening with the Art Ensemble a qualified success, not least because there came an unexpected check from Lester Bowie in the mail, and for no minuscule amount either. He would have played the gig for nothing. Of course you would, Bowie told the Bear when he phoned to say thank you, but we couldn't let that happen, could we.

The check had paid for today's rent-a-van, and some of it remained to finance the makings of a tour.

Which would be like what, exactly?

The van negotiated a tangle of intersections between the municipal court buildings, then found its way along a commercial slot of street and pulled up to a parking meter in front of Tim Berne's place—the Bear knew Tim from when they were both studying with Julius. They trundled through the door and up the stairs past a hair salon one flight up, then through the open door into Tim's apartment, said their hellos and entered the music room, where a rhythm section was waiting.

Piano, bass and drums, and when the Bear came in, the three guys behind the instruments exchanged quick looks with each other and smirked out loud.

The Bear turned to Jones. "I don't think I like the look of this," he said.

By the time the actual tour got under way the worst of the summer heat was gone, and that first night autumn blew in on a black wind down Fifth Avenue, where the Bear and his band unpacked their gear from a dark green van, menaced by flying newspaper and bits of wind-driven ash. Eager to be off the street as quickly as possible, the Bear picked up both halves of the Fender Rhodes piano like two valises and hurried them into Beefsteak Charlie's, dropped them onstage, then disappeared into a dark, highbacked booth while Jones and the rhythm section rigged up a curtain to cover the show window at the front of the club. The Bear felt ready to deal with an audience but he did not want to be observed from the street. Everyone was telling him to relax, but he was still worried about the police.

Finished with the curtain, Jones joined him in the booth while the rhythm section set up their axes. A waitress came by and Jones ordered two cognacs.

"Naw," said the Bear to the waitress, "make mine a draft beer. You have Guinness on tap? Even better. I'll have a pint of that."

"Sure," said the waitress, smiling at him and trying to get a better look under his hat.

Making an effort to be sociable, the Bear took it off, ruffled the fur on top of his head and smiled up at her. "Hi," he said. "You've heard about me all week and you wanted to see if it was true, right?"

"Right," she said.

"It's true," he said, "and I've changed my mind, I'll take the cognac alongside the stout. But I need a very big snifter." Making another effort, he patted his snout and smiled again. "Cold nose, warm heart," he added, looking her up and down.

"Jesus, Jones," said the Bear when she had gone, "how many people am I gonna have to deal with tonight? I'm not used to this."

"That's what I like about you," Jones told him, "you're not too tough to be sensitive, even sometimes a little shy."

The Bear curled a black-and-purple lip at him, disclosing sharp canines and incisors. "And where did they get all this turn-of-the-century crap?" he complained, gesturing at the ornamental woodwork, fake studded leather cushions, wrought-iron frosted-glass imitation gaslamps and dim period paintings on the walls. "What am I supposed to do, play cakewalks to match? Did we come to the right place?"

"Restaurant consciousness is heavily into reproductions these days, I can't help that," said Jones. "I'm glad you're in such a good mood." He craned his head momentarily out of the booth. "Cummins just came in."

"Thank God for that," the Bear said.

Bob Cummins slid into the booth alongside Jones. "Hi fellas," he said.

"Hiya Bob," said the Bear. He liked Cummins, and much to his surprise had trusted the man immediately upon meeting him the week before. Cummins was a gentle-featured man around forty, face framed in curly brown hair going grey and a ditto beard. He owned India Navigation, for which small, almost infinitesimal record company the Bear was supposed to record toward the end of the tour.

"How's it going?" Cummins asked.

"Oh great," said the Bear. "I feel like bolting out of my seat and ditching my axe in a sewer but otherwise everything's just peachy. Cummins," he said more seriously, "are you sure that's the best rhythm section we could get? I mean, I'm glad for your help, but they've been busting my ass in rehearsal, they hardly talked to me on the way over here, plus they don't really play that good. What's going on here?"

"They're young and nervous," Cummins lied.

"And I'm big and hairy. So?"

Cummins considered for a moment, then went on, "First of all the Musicians Union's heard about you and they don't like it. They've yelled at a few people, asked a lot of questions and filed suit against Circus Performers International, who haven't got the slightest idea what they're talking about."

"And," the Bear prompted, sensing Cummins' unwillingness to go on.

"And there's some flack around town among musicians about you being a novelty act and a ripoff. There are a few people I called that don't want to work with you."

"Oh," said the Bear. "That's swell. That's great. Makes me feel really good to be here. I enjoy feeling guilty. What would I do all day without guilt, I don't like what they have on TV. So I'm taking bread out of people's mouths, is that it?"

"You've got to understand," Cummins explained, "that, aside from not knowing you or having heard you play, most of these musicians lead a very marginal kind of existence and make a very marginal living."

"I *know* about marginal living, Bob," said the Bear in a surly voice. "What about our friends?"

"They're all on tour with their regular bands and we can't afford Dave Holland and Jack DeJohnette."

"Are you still my buddy?" the Bear wondered. "Do you still want to record me?"

"I'll be happy to have you in the catalogue, Bear. I like your work and you might just sell enough records to get me out of my law practice and into the record business full-time."

"Us novelty acts tries real hard," the Bear assured him.

"And we might be able to improve the band as the tour gathers steam."

"Steam?" the Bear wondered. "Why steam? What has steam got to do with it?"

"You know, somebody from Warner Brothers called me the other day and wanted to know if you were for real. If you wanted to make some money you could probably work something out with them. If you're interested, I could return the call and represent you as your lawyer."

The Bear looked across the table at Cummins. "I want to be a musician, not some famous freak of nature. That's why I'm dealing with you. Besides, this is about as much world as I can deal with just now."

"I didn't mean to offend," Cummins said.

The waitress brought the drinks, and the Bear raised his big dark glass of stout. "On the other hand, Bugs Bunny's always been a hero of mine and do you think they'd let me record with Yosemite Sam?"

The first set, as the Bear would later maintain, was an irremediable disaster, however much Cummins and Jones would assure him that he had turned it around. It had begun with the Bear standing in front of the quarter-full house (votive candles in colored glass columns meshed with plastic fishnet on every table), stomping off "Straight No Chaser" and the band coming in behind him at a markedly slower tempo. They were out to test his mettle, ran the charitable interpretation; more likely they just wanted to fuck him up. Then, because he had no experience of playing lounges, he ran into the acoustic double bind of all stageless rooms: he could hear either the rhythm section or himself, but never both at once. To top it off, once the tempo got settled—he giving way to theirs—his employees were acting up on him again. The drummer, a hotshot kid with Turkish cymbals hung so high he could hardly reach them, started cracking out loud, irrelevant breaks behind the Bear, interrupting his line virtually every time he tried to get something more than just another phrase off the ground, and punctuating the choruses as if they were eight bars long instead of twelve. The pianist kicked in a little later with some intrusive and inappropriate chording and opened three consecutive choruses with fake modulations that made it look as if the Bear had landed himself in the wrong key. The bassist behaved, but there wasn't that much damage you could do from the bass, although he did break up his walk whenever the Bear began to swing despite the odds and opposition. The Bear looked back and snarled over his shoulder at the three of them; the drummer paled and dropped a couple of beats, the pianist laid out and looked away, and the bassist had his eyes closed. Thanks a lot, thought the Bear. I need you guys like I need another fur coat.

What galled him most was that, bear or not, novelty act or bizarre and singular door, he played so much better than they did. It wasn't as if they were razzing an incompetent. Looking out at the unimpressed house and remembering the Kansas City story about a contemptuous Jo Jones throwing his cymbal at the feet of the teenage Charlie Parker, the Bear decided almost wearily to do what he had done in rehearsal once or twice and try to turn the show around. Here we go, gentlemen. This way forward. Let's take it a little out.

First thing he did was start dismantling the tune. He played a series of violent lower-register honks, then some angry, disordered runs that violated the cadence at the end of the chorus. And there went the tempo: the rhythm section was forced to break ranks and stutter to make it look as if they might be playing free. As the Bear applied more pressure, the time splintered like boxwood beneath the weight of his phrasing and the home key collided smartly with two or three others, motivic fragments flying off at the edges like electrons from a critical mass about to go fission.

Divide and conquer? On the contrary; say Allah and leave them to their confusion.

Either way, with the rhythm section cut out from under him, he started slow, played a mid-tune, out-of-tempo cadenza that reduced the drummer to cymbal filigree, then began a long, deliberately constructed accelerando they all had to pick up on or look foolish, and took it up to a tempo so fast they could not really manage it in style. He played a few furious straight blues choruses with more fire than they could muster, then turned his back to the audience and played a vile twelve-bars blues in no particular key hideously out of tune straight into the three faces of the band. He lowered his sax, showed his teeth in all their rending horror and stomped his way offstand, setting the microphone stands awobble. The audience applauded as if it had been wonderful, wonderful, and the rhythm section, once restored to trivial competence for the duration of their own solo outings, granted him a wary and uninspired professionalism for the remainder of the set: "Skylark," "Afro Blue," "Oleo" and out.

"I don't understand," he complained to Cummins and Jones afterward in the booth. "I've tried to talk with them, be a buddy and like that, but it's always the same. Bob, you gotta help me out, you've got to find me some other people to play with. Razzing the novice may be the oldest ritual in the book, but I've had it with these guys, it's enough."

"I'll see what I can do," Cummins promised.

"I mean, how many of these tours do you think I'm gonna do?" the Bear continued, then noticed that there was a woman standing beside the booth, waiting on the brink for a break in the conversation. "Excuse me?" he asked her.

"*Sybil,*" Cummins greeted her, half rising. "Join us. Sit down."

Cummins and Jones were sitting opposite the Bear. The only empty seat was the one next to the Bear, and Sybil looked uncertain.

"You're perfectly safe," he assured her. "It was beauty killed the Beast."

After a moment's pause, she sat alongside him and gave him, within a general context of shaky eye contact, a remarkably clear-eyed look. "You look pretty impregnable to me," Sybil said.

"What you see is nothing," he said. "I have a feeling heart and severe self-division."

Sybil laughed, and raised her right hand to cover her mouth.

"No," he told her. "Go ahead, laugh. It's why I live. Nice to meet you."

"Nice to be met." She took his paw with a polite if unconvincing show of fearlessness and shook it hello. "Sybil Bailey."

"The Bear. Bear to you."

"I'm Bob's law partner."

"Yes," said the Bear. "I've heard of you."

Sybil, the Bear decided, had a graceful, softened beauty to her rather than the imperious, heart-conquering kind—Jones looked like he might see things differently—but there was fire in her despite any trepidation she might have felt in the presence of so much living fur. She had tumbling light brown hair, a clear unworried forehead and greenish eyes. He liked her implicit warmth, even if for the moment it was veiled by whatever else. And had she just moved marginally closer to him on the banquette?

Jones was doing a nervous cough routine and chewing on his plastic cocktail straw. The Bear decided to give him a break and turned away from Sybil in his seat.

Sybil looked across the table and said, "Hi Ray."

Ray? Who's Ray? the Bear almost asked aloud, but finally remembered that it was Jones' first name. It had been so long.

Jones and Sybil touched hands across the table and the Bear felt a stab of his own loneliness. Jones had been telling him about Sybil, how happy he was to have met her, how maybe they were going to get something going. . . . The Bear was brushed, then saturated by the memory of a small slim woman with a radiant, beautifully detailed face, large bright eyes into which, it seemed, he was always falling, and red hair tumbling about her small square shoulders. Iris had been a biochemist friend of Jones' left him from his college days, and after the bear he had won in a card game began talking a blue streak and developing a musical gift of surprising proportions, Jones had called her in to test the animal's capacities. Astonishment loves company even more than misery, and craves lots of reassurance.

Jones still had some of the family money then, and they lived in a fairly spacious apartment. Iris came over, listened to the Bear's family lore, and over the weeks ran what tests she could on him without taking him down to the lab—portable EKG, cell samples, blood, urine, semen (the Bear had refused to masturbate but he did allow the leavings of a wet dream to be placed upon a slide). Soon Iris was hanging out at the apartment, staying for dinner and sitting up talking with the Bear late into the night, the radio on, the ashtray filling, and Jones trying to sleep in the next room, bothered by the sound of their laughter, their equable, affectionate conversation. What had emerged from the genetic inquiry was not a pat quotidian answer to explain the Bear away but an intimacy that surprised the Bear and Iris both, and as it deepened, as the correspondences between them multiplied and wove them closer, they found that the obvious next step was one they were too shocked or surprised to take. Iris in particular was pained and confused—while she was not in any obscene or kinky fashion attracted to the transgression of doing it with the Bear, thank God, she had fallen in something resembling love with him and didn't know what to do about it—and the Bear, with a delicacy of feeling left him from cubhood of which his hookups with hookers had not entirely deprived him, would have done anything, or been anyone, to relieve her of any pain and disarray he might have caused to trouble her spirit. He began by suggesting that she stay away from him, go away more or less forever.

She asked why she should be deprived of the pleasure of seeing him.

The Bear said, Um, I thought, whatever.

Iris and the Bear were allowed their season of indecision and then, without knowing exactly how or why, they were separated from each other, like swimmers in opposing and indifferent currents, and were swept into separate, self-coherent streams. Although since then the Bear had slept with three she-bears (two in the woods and one rented from the circus for a night) and too many human prostitutes, and although between him and Iris there had been everything but, finally, physical union, she remained the only woman he had truly, in the complete and soul-transpiercing sense of the term, ever loved. Oh, he had been able to rationalize it away, and apply the balm of irony to the wound, but that was the last stone laid on his heart and the sharp final edge whetted on the grudge he held against the world: he had never been able to complete the circuit of his love. By now, unused and suppressed for so long, that capacity for love was not what it had been—weaker certainly, grown morbid like as not, turned bitter . . . the works. Iris was receding from him, not only into the past but into a world of sensibility he could hardly even visit anymore. Life had coarsened him. All he had left was the insufficient substitute of art. The last he had heard of Iris, she had gotten married, had two kids and moved to Kansas City.

Someone had spoken to him. "What?" said the Bear, and collected himself back from memory and regret to find himself still at the table and still the only bear in the house. He tried to feel happy for Jones' possible good fortune with this Sybil, but when he trundled back onstand for the next set all he wanted to play were ballads, and his beloved saxophone seemed to him the cruel and sinister instrument of his own undoing. Instead of the cross, the albatross. *Vita brevis*, he thought, *ars nada, nada, nada.*

A few days later the Bear came into some good fortune of his own. Billy Hart, who had recently left his longtime stay in Stan Getz' band, was picking up every available gig and record date he could get his hands on in order to keep his family afloat now that he was off a steady wage. He had agreed, Cummins told the Bear on the phone, to do the bulk of the Bear's clubdates and be on hand for the recording session at the end. In addition, he would bring the rest of a rhythm section with him—Scott Lee on bass and Armen Donelian on piano—and although a hefty chunk of the Bear's tour bread would go to pay for them he was ready to part with it by then. The first night he played with them he felt sure the expenditure was way past worth it. Ideas surprised him coming out of his horn; he began to touch again on the deeper pleasures of playing, the joys of an evolving line happy in its element, and felt the intermittent stirring of fresh creativity, the uncoiling of new energy in his belly, chest and limbs.

The Bear effectively dismissed the self-suggestion that this new mastery of the materials of his chosen music would enable him to rule the world, and found himself developing a particularly tight accord with Billy, a mellow brown cat in his forties with his hair gone white and a sweet habitual smile more or less ever-present on his features, even when he was pounding drums and cymbals to bits and threatening to roll thunder all across the night. There was a smile in Billy's drumming too, a smoothness that suffused it, for all the transgressed barlines and all the smash and scatteration. Something friendly, something warm. The Bear was learning to run with it, and sometimes even fly.

He got along with Scott Lee pretty well without ever getting to know him much. Armen Donelian opened up when the Bear told him that his ancestors had always been grateful for the kindness of Armenian keepers on the Turkish circus circuit.

They did a round of unadvertised gigs in the city, letting enough word of mouth leak out to half fill the nightclubs. The Bear thought himself an inconsistent player, but the rest of the section and particularly Billy Hart kept assuring him that he was doing fine. "You mean you don't know about the three kinds of chops?" Billy asked the Bear one night when he was accusing himself of greater inconsistency than usual on the horn.

"Something to do with Goldilocks?" the Bear asked him. "There's a bear in that story too."

Billy's face broke into a wider grin. "You're a trip, Bear. Look, there are three kinds of chops and they have less to do with each other than you think: the kind of chops you have when you're practicing alone, the kind when you play with other people, and then there's the kind of chops when you play with other people in front of an audience. They're three different things. The way I understand it, you've been sittin' home for a long time. Of course you're gonna have some off nights. There's no possible way you can expect yourself to know how to road."

"No?"

"How could you know how to road? The tension you're feeling? That's one of the things that puts cats on booze and drugs just to take the edge off. You've got to lay back, you've got to let yourself develop. Otherwise how are you gonna get ahead? I got to tell you, you're doing better than I expected the first time I heard you. I think you've got the talent to take it as far as you want to."

"So I just need more chops, type three?"

"There you go." Billy had such a winning smile and so positive a spirit that the Bear lost track of whether he thought the guy was conning him or not. "Lay back, Bear, take your time, learn how to road and you'll be fine."

But the Bear, an expert in giving himself a hard time, felt sure there was more to it than that. Even accepting what Billy said, because until now he hadn't been out there performing night after night there were large areas in his music that were blurred, insufficiently realized in conception and execution both. It might be that when he practiced he had gravitated to his strengths and left the rest unconfronted. Now that he was out there palpably exposed, and especially since Billy was raising the level of play, it showed, it showed. He heard the absences and unworked areas, the dead transitions, the insufficiently attended lifeless notes and the wholesale acres of unfinished business—heard it every set, every night, heard it without shelter or mercy, and felt that whatever guilty rush of practice he attempted now was too little, too late.

He said some of this to Billy Hart.

Billy told him it was always like that. "The *music's* like that, B. Whatever level you get to, there's always something further to reach for, something you haven't seen and didn't know was there. Once you stop feeling that, you're finished, basically."

"Really?" asked the Bear.

"Yeah. Once that happens it might look like you can play, but the light's gone out. The thing is dead. It may feel uncomfortable now, but that's because you're alive and kickin'. Trust me on this," Billy said. "Trust me on this one. It's true."

The Bear nodded yes and tried to believe it but something in the pit of his belly said no and tightened its grip on his innards. Some stupid self-will demanding doom. Or a case of nerves most likely.

The band took a weekend trip in two rented vans to play New Haven and Boston. The Bear enjoyed the Boston gig more than any other he had played so far. It was at a place called Michael's, near the conservatories and Symphony Hall, and he found the bandstand ringed by bright and eager faces turned up toward him, smiling and nodding yes while he played. Music students: Berklee, the Boston Conservatory. They had come in fair numbers to hear the advertised rhythm section, but after the first set they must have phoned their friends: by eleven-thirty the place was full; there were even some people sitting cross-legged on the dusty wooden floor around the bandstand.

Between sets he was besieged by questions—up until now he had hidden himself in the backs of clubs, in booths and dark corners, but in a student-heavy joint like Michael's there was no room. They asked him not what was a bear doing playing alto but where did he pick this or that lick up, did he do deep-breathing exercises and if so what were they, what kind of reed did he use, what did he think of Anthony Braxton and had he done anything special to adapt his mouthpiece to his, um, you know. The Bear was unused to coping with so much acceptance and felt desperately awkward and out of place. He tried to be friendly, but seldom had he been so aware of his physical size and obvious potential for violence—no way to sheathe those claws—and his fugitive impulse to run for the door made him realize that acting it out would injure a couple dozen friendlies and break some chairs.

On the late ride back to New York, he sat in the front seat of the utility van—the rhythm section making its own way back to the Apple—occasionally woofing out the window at passing cars. Jones, who had accepted gift reefer at Michael's by the handful, giggled to himself and drove more unpredictably than usual: a certain tendency to drift from lane to lane. "Who would have believed it, man," he said finally, at about four a.m., when the highway traffic had diminished. "A few months ago, that it would come to this."

"Uh huh," said the Bear dully. The gig at Michael's had been tonic, but as so often after pleasure his useless crapstrewn unconscious nature was kicking clods of misery at him, and they were beginning to soil his regalia.

"You having trouble coping?" Jones asked.

"I don't feel with it all the time. It's getting better but sometimes I feel out of phase."

"Jesus, Bear. You ought to get stoned more."

"I don't like smoke," the Bear told him firmly.

Jones waved his arms for a moment before resuming his grip on the wheel. "This is the stuff of legend we're doing here, Bear, riding out of the night in vans and playing music at unannounced gigs in dark and midnight America. We used to dream about this. You ought to be participating, Bear. This is what you wanted."

"You're right," the Bear admitted. "I'm just slow to adjust. It's been a big change very fast. Parts of me aren't catching up."

"I wonder if the Indians in these parts had a myth about Participating Bear, the van-riding saxophonist of the American dream. . . . The audience is just starting to latch onto you, you know. I sense a groundswell. I intuit recognitions. . . . Jazz people, they're such outsiders you're the kind of mythology they can relate to. You're a dream figure, you're their hip little secret. I think they're beginning to catch on."

"Being everybody's dream figure's not exactly what I had in mind," said the Bear. "All I wanted was to play some music and go home. . . . Maybe I'm really best as a contemplative, you know? Sitting back from it all and, um, dreaming about it on my own."

"We're all contemplatives," Jones assured him, "only we found out we couldn't pay the rent. So you want to go back to the apartment and frustration and the street act? You amaze me, you really do. Look at us, B. We're rolling."

"I know," said the Bear. "I'm a crank and a complainer. I get everything I've wanted handed to me on a platter and all I do is criticize the silver plating. I'm a schmuck."

"You're doing fine." said Jones. "Considering."

"That's what everybody tells me," said the Bear, "but I dunno. I mean, is this what I wanted? I don't recognize it at all."

"Cummins wants to record as soon as possible. He wants to try live two nights at the Tin Palace next week and if it doesn't work out he's got a studio on tap. I already know you're too good for this world, Bear. What is it now, you're too good for art?"

"How come," the Bear asked Jones, "it used to be that whatever was wrong with my life was the world's fault and now apparently it's mine?"

"Parallax," said Jones. "You're growing up. You're becoming a star."

The Bear leaned into the van's front window and looked up, squinting, at the sky. "The Great Bear," he said.

"Can you see it?" Jones asked him.

"Dim the dashboard lights."

"How about this. . . ." Jones switched off the headlights. The highway appeared before them, pearled by the waning quarter moon, and then, when their eyes had adjusted, the massive, patient night emerged, high and filled with stars.

"Wow," said the Bear.

"There without you all the time, world without end." Jones switched the headlights back on.

The Bear settled back into his seat and closed his eyes, trying to feel, in the rushing forward motion of his life, the stars that framed his bones, and in his own large body his true geometry of light, the larger peace he knew he lived in but could not entirely find. Why did it have to be such a guessing game? he asked himself, when the truth is right there, when we're made of it? He failed, for the moment, to understand why ignorance should exist at all, why there should not be only complete realization, perfect peace. He recalled the taste of his timeless self from his handful of meetings with it and savored its repose on the other side of strife. O freedom, he thought. O freedom over me. Before I'll be a slave I'll be buried in my grave, and go home to my Lord and be free. Is that the only way? The grave? I don't buy that. "I've been thinking about archetypes," he confessed to Jones, by way of opening up a conversation.

"Great," Jones replied. "Have a ball but don't get spacey. While you were checking out Ursa Major I saw Orion's Belt. Big fucking hunter, man. Keep one eye on your archetype and the other on your ass."

The Bear pondered a moment. "Point taken," he said, and then, "You mind if I put on the overhead light? You got some paper? A pencil? Pen?"

"What am I, God the provider?"

"You're not?"

When the Bear got the illumination and his writing materials sorted out, he roughed out a motif or two on paper, saw the way ahead and wrote down the first four bars, then sketched the likely changes in a subscript.

Interesting, he thought, taking a step back from it. Not my usual thing at all. An obvious Mingus tip to it, and someone else in there . . . Strayhorn? But what intrigued him was the uncharacteristic harmonic density, as if he were investing some new portion of himself in a study of understructure, girderwork, taproots running down into the dark, when usually he went for a flow of melody and an open chordal field for it to spread in; and even an untrained ear would pick out the tune's emotional ambiguity: it seemed obvious the tune was the beginning of a creative response to aspects of his new experience.

On the other paw, maybe he'd better finish writing it before all he was left with was speculation. After a moment's quiet, he pencilled another four bars down:

Which made it to the end of the A section. Obviously the tune needed a bridge. He had no idea, not a whisper, not a wisp, of what it might be, and he thought, if that's all I've got we could play it anyway.

Jones leaned over. "You have a name for it?"

"How about," said the Bear, and then wrote across the top of the sheet, "Billy Heart." Hardly enough to repay the debt I owe him, but he'll like it.

The Bear switched off the pinlight and looked out again. Thumbprint moon descending the western sky, first grey reef of dawn rising into sight on the horizon east.

"Still a hundred miles to go," said Jones.

"It figures," said the Bear.

Whatever Jones' conceptual handle on the Way of Heaven and Orion's size, the Bear decided that the man was right about the way the tour was working out and that his optimism wasn't idiotic. Two nights later at Sweet Basil—the curtain pressed back into service for the front windows of this converted drugstore, an unadvertised Monday night before a three-day break, then two nights of live recording at the Tin Palace—he looked out at the audience over the top of an original blues he might put on the record and noticed fewer sensation-seekers in the house and maybe more real listeners than usual. There were even a couple of people, journalists most likely, taking notes while he played, although he was obscurely bothered by the plainness of their shoes. It was a shame he felt so unready to record. Not that he was playing badly or that the music wasn't working out, but he wasn't quite ripe yet, and what he and the rhythm section had going was still an incompletely glorified version of a pickup band. They were just beginning to move into something more fully their own, perhaps, and he would rather make a record of that, if it showed, than this incompletely shaped swarm of hope and things he'd practiced.

The Bear had begun to suspect that he had a shot at being an original—something he hadn't really anticipated—but if it was done on schedule the recording would be made a notch too soon. Ornette's comment at the Bottom Line rankled him. He wasn't there yet. He had always held the naive but understandable assumption that once he really got started in music he would have things exactly the way he wanted, but he was learning something new about that virtually every day. The world was not holding still so he could take its conceptual snapshot, and there seemed to be no place within the music's ambit immune to the flux of life around it, no privileged spot on which to stand unmoved and stable, and this was what the Bear, in his exile from it, had always conceived a musical life to be.

Odd, wasn't it, how life turned out to be when you got there. Sweet Basil and bitter herbs together.

The Bear played a bittersweet little run reminiscent of Jackie McLean, pressuring the notes slightly flat to underline the point, and realized, as his eyes swept the darkened nightclub and its vague attentive forms again, that there was one spot in the room he had instinctively been avoiding: toward the rear, almost into the windowporch, at a table partly obscured by a hanging plant, where a small graceful figure sat holding a cigarette, smoke rising in an unbroken blue thread above it like a line of thought. It was a woman, and she looked familiar in the dimness, but every time he began to make her out something distracted his eyes and mind and he looked away.

Suddenly and still without seeing her, he knew that it was Iris. His time faltered, he played an egregiously wrong note and earned an admonitory rimshot from Billy Hart, shook his head, squinted across the room, couldn't identify her, tried to play again, it didn't take, he rubbed at his face and waited for Donelian to play a transition to cover him. The Bear wanted it to be her, the Bear didn't want it to be her, he did he didn't he did. The Bear would go to the insufficient backstage space and forget about it, he would not go to her table, he would he wouldn't he would. The Bear felt himself being bound back onto the gain and loss of the earthly wheel and despite his unfinished love it was not what he wanted. I'm just trying to play some music. Why bother me with larger stuff? He shook his head to clear the insufficient brain within. Ludicrous that anyone, whether actually present or not, should have such power over his heart.

Apparently he had walked across the room to her table. She stood up, smiled, and took his paw as if she had rejoined him after a five-minute absence at a cocktail party. "I knew it was you when I saw the article in the paper," she told him.

"Iris," he said, always a hotshot with the right word at the right time. Her impact on his heart was immediate and overwhelming; he was still bound to her however much life and time had changed him. In other words, when you got down to it he was still the original unmodified idiot. "Good God it's you."

"I would have come to see you sooner," she said, with her usual delicacy and poise, in a polite and sociable tone, "but you don't advertise your appearances."

"I'm like that," said the Bear, and wondered what to say next. "Always was."

"I know," Iris said.

5

actually, as the Bear would reflect later, when he had plenty of time for contemplation, his life had had a refreshing solidity to it that night after meeting Iris at Sweet Basil's. As he looked through the club at the people enjoying his music and, near the back, at a small table beneath a hanging plant, at the smallish figure of a woman he loved and who possibly loved him, it had seemed to him that the terrible rift that had been driven between him and the rest of the world might finally have been healed, that perhaps he had at last been granted, as if by courier from the king, the imprimatur of reality. He looked at the assortment of friends and lovers in the candlelight and for the first time in his life felt approximately equal to them. Before this, he had always felt either immensely better or immensely worse. Provisionally at least, the burden of comparison had been lifted.

Although something bothered him still. All this instant fulfillment, didn't it make too simple a creature of him? What possible dignity did he have if all it took was for Iris to walk back into his life for him to feel Completed? And wasn't there more than a faintly proprietary air in his attitude towards her, some cheap, possessive, anticipatory lie? And—hey Bear, how come you forgot to ask her? is she still married? Try that one on for size. He watched her from the stage, once he had regained it to finish the set, and tried to remind himself, for all his years of wanting her, that she had her own existence and was probably as subtle and elusive as ever. By the time the band had packed up and Jones and Sybil had driven him to Iris' apartment in the van—she had gone ahead to straighten the place up—the Bear knew she wasn't married anymore, but wasn't sure he really wanted to see her. Oh, of course he wanted to see her, but he didn't know that he wanted his boat rocked this hard just now.

Jones pulled the van up outside Stuyvesant Town on East Twentieth. "You know the apartment number?" he asked.

"Yup," said the Bear.

"And she told you she's divorced."

The Bear nodded. "You want to go ahead and ring me in?"

"It's four in the morning. There won't be anyone around. Go 'head."

"C'mon Jones," the Bear said. "At least check out the street for me."

Jones yawned without covering his mouth. "A bear's gotta do what a bear's gotta do. Me, I'm not getting out of this van until I'm home."

The Bear pulled up his coatcollar and lurched uncomfortably out of the van, feeling abandoned by his friend and betrayed into the anonymity of the night. The street was empty, but he had the unpleasant feeling that he was being watched. He walked across the black lawn and into the entrance hall, where—a Skinner box, he thought—once he got the buttons figured out and Iris rang him inside, the elevator came up from the basement, and when the aluminum doors rolled open a short sourfaced woman with dyed red hair and a cigarette stuck in her face stood inside holding a blue plastic basket of laundry. The Bear walked in, pushed four and tried to look inconspicuous. He took a quick glance sideways as the doors shut. The woman was looking directly at him. The cigarette smoke rose into her eyes, but she did not blink. "Just what are you supposed to be," she asked him.

"Delivery boy," said the Bear. "How'd your wash come out? You get those whiter whites?"

"What are you, some kinda joke?"

"That's it," said the Bear. "I'm some kinda joke."

"Well you don't fool me." She narrowed her eyes to demonstrate how difficult she was to fool, slapped at the bank of buttons behind her, and the elevator stopped at the next floor. She got out and turned to face him. "I know exactly what you're thinking," she said.

"These days that's more than I manage," the Bear told her, and tipped his hat good night. You know, he thought as the doors rolled shut and the elevator resumed its upward journey, if I have that effect on all the ladies I'm gonna be fresh out of luck tonight.

Iris was waiting when the doors opened on four. She smiled up at him, her face small, bright, and about as perfect as it always had been. "Didn't Jones come up with you?" she asked.

"He thinks I should learn to take care of myself."

"That's not the point," said Iris. She took him by the paw. "This way."

"There was a woman in the elevator on the way up," the Bear explained as Iris led him down the hallway. "With laundry."

"And red hair? Did she squint at you and tell you she could read your mind?"

"She do that to everybody?" asked the Bear.

Iris nodded yes and laughed into her free hand. "I think coo-coo is the technical term. You thought it was you but you were wrong this time."

"Paranoia," the Bear admitted.

"Vanity," Iris said. "Here we are. I'm afraid the place is a bit of a mess." She let him go in first.

"It's beautiful," said the Bear, spinning around the living room in a kind of domestic ecstasy. "So spacious, so big and bright."

"It used to belong to my father. I came back to town and took it over when he moved to Florida. It's bigger than I need, but the rent is low."

"You should see the hole Jones and I are living in. This is gorgeous."

"You two used to live pretty well," Iris remembered. "Big stereo, fresh salmon, good champagne . . ."

"That was a long time ago," said the Bear, "and a lot of water under the bridge." He refocussed his eyes on Iris. "Your hair used to be red."

"You just noticed that?"

"Iris, the fact is I'm too dazzled to take in much detail just yet."

"You are not," said Iris. "You just don't remember me very well."

"I've thought of you, you don't know, I've—"

Iris put out her small hand firmly, like a traffic cop. "Don't. Just don't."

This produced a pause in which it would have been difficult for the Bear to feel more awkward. Meeting Iris again was like walking into a wall of subtlety, a dazzle of gentleness, an immaterial aura he had lost the refinement to see; but it acted on him anyhow. He wanted to live in it but he was not ready. He was insufficiently transformed. So what? He loved her. Wasn't that enough?

"As to my hair," Iris resumed when she judged that sufficient time had passed. "After I left my husband I lived in an unheatable cottage in winter. I contracted scarlet fever, nearly died of it, and when it was over my hair had gone this dishwater brown, dark blond, whatever it is."

"You're still so lovely," said the Bear.

"I am not. Please don't lie to me."

"I have never lied to you," the Bear said firmly enough, it appeared, to finish with the subject for the moment. He had stopped beside a coffee table, looking down. "*Winnie the Pooh*?" he asked, picking up the book. "You leave this out for me?"

Iris blushed and her eyes shone. Her features are so mobile, the Bear remembered, but that's not it. Something subtler comes through her skin, her eyes. A kind of light. "Oh I uh, I was reading it tonight before going down to the club. When I came back I didn't know whether or not to put it away, I put it away twice and finally left it out."

The Bear sat down on the couch and propped his feet on the table. His feet looked enormous. He wiggled his claws. "And do I remind you of Winnie the Pooh?" he asked.

There was still some red in her face, but it was fading. "Of course not," she said. "Don't tease me. Would you like something to drink?"

"A beer if you have one."

"I see your tastes haven't changed. I prepared." Iris went around a corner into the kitchen, and the Bear looked around her living room at the tasteful but worn furniture, the old stereo and TV, and at her paintings on the walls. He had always liked the way she painted, the general shape of the pictures, her use of color, the emotion that came through.

"You can stay the night," came her voice from the kitchen along with the sound of bottles and glasses, "if it's a hassle going home. I made up the extra bedroom."

"Um," said the Bear, and toyed with a heavy glass ashtray on the table. "I don't think so," he added, but too softly for her to hear.

She came back carrying two large glasses of beer. The Bear watched her body moving under her dark green dress."That copy of *Winnie the Pooh*," Iris was telling him, "was one of the few things I took with me when I left my husband." She handed him one of the beers and sat a certain distance from him down the sofa, letting her shoes fall to the floor and curling her legs beneath her. "I used to read it to the kids." She put her glass on the coffee table and appeared to forget about it completely.

The Bear took a first sip of beer and collected a moustache of froth on the front of his snout. "How come your husband got custody of your children? Don't women usually . . . you know."

"Herb is a well-known psychotherapist and a nearly pathological liar. He diddled the court. He can do anything."

"He convinced a judge you're crazy? That's not possible."

But Iris nodded. "I'm unstable. I'm an unfit mother." Her eyes were very bright, and she had composed her hands in her lap to conceal a slight but irrepressible trembling. "He had colleagues come in and tell lies about me. It was horrible."

"Why did you leave him?"

"I didn't like him anymore," she said, as though it were a simple thing to marry someone, have two kids with him, then not like him anymore. The Bear, who had never married but believed in lasting relationships, was so unable to come to terms with the casualness of her statement that he failed to recognize it as a way of closing the subject. Iris placed her fingertips lightly on her forehead, as if to steady her mind, but when she resumed speaking her voice retained its usual poise. "When I read the stories to my daughters I told them Pooh was an old friend of mine from New York. Then they only wanted to hear stories about Pooh and me, and never mind the book." She laughed down into her lap. "I started telling them about you, growing up crazy, playing the sax, beating Jones at chess, your family in the old country and here. You became their favorite character, and then, funny thing, they must have picked up on it, they asked me if Pooh was in love with me."

"Pooh was in love with you," the Bear told one of her paintings.

"And they wanted to know why I didn't go away with him."

"You know anyplace we could have gone?"

Iris cleared her throat. "I used to tell them, 'So I could have you guys.' Anyhow, when I left Herb I rented an apartment, packed up everything I would need the day before and put myself and the kids into a cab after he left for the office the next morning. At the last minute I grabbed the book and took it with me."

"He shouldn't have been able to get custody," said the Bear.

"I was messed up, Bear. Some bad things happened. I was panicky. I couldn't handle myself well. I had a few bad years. He had the career and had married himself a wonderful, loving and accomplished woman. It wasn't hard for him to get Tracy and Amy away from me." She paused. Iris was speaking of deep uncertainty and pain, but she looked happy and her voice remained pleasant. Her eyes were bright. "Bear," she said, "I'm not what I used to be. I don't have the strength. I've been damaged. I am very easily hurt, and I can't fight back."

"You seem together."

"Oh, I'm good enough at seeming. I practice all the time. And you were always taken in by appearances. But I can't do very much. I can handle the lab job. Beyond that I manage to cook for myself, get the phone bill paid and have apparently social conversations, but in here," she pounded her chest with a small vehement fist, "it's broken up, it doesn't fit together anymore, I don't have the energy, I'm not anyone at all."

"Oh baby," the Bear said. He couldn't help it, but to him the fact that someone as exquisite as Iris could have gotten damaged was an indictment of the world in general. He felt something in himself, part protectiveness and part desire, move in her direction across the couch.

She may have sensed something of this, because she got up quickly and walked across the room to needlessly check the blinds. "You must be pretty happy now that you're in the open playing music," she said, attempting a change of subject.

"Oh I don't know," said the Bear, resisting a moment before giving in. "I don't know. Maybe it was better the other way. I don't know."

Iris sat down again and it was the Bear's turn to walk around the room. "What do you mean you don't know?" Iris asked him, and he could hear the relief in her voice now that she was talking about him. "You know. Tell me about it."

"I don't want to complain," the Bear protested, waving his arms a little.

"You *love* to complain," Iris told him. "You're a terrific complainer. Fate has singled me out, et cetera. You're one of the best."

The Bear cocked an unsporting eye at her.

"Did I step on a sensitive toe? I'm sorry. Go on."

Gradually, the Bear removed his eye from her and resumed. "I don't know. I mean, it's all new to me. I don't like being *seen*. I don't like people thinking they know who I am. Utter strangers, you know? Do they think they know my insides because they've heard me play a couple of choruses on a horn? Where do they come off, where do they think they get the right? I feel violated. Sometimes I get actual spasms, I flinch, I double up, I can't do anything about it. I can feel their eyes working on me. It hurts. I know it's terribly immature of me or something, but there it is and I can't help it. A subconscious is a terrible thing to have."

"But Bear," said Iris, "you always used to talk about how you wanted to get your music heard. There were all these things you wanted to express, to get across, to give."

"Express?" said the Bear. "Give? That must have been a long time ago. I was a kid back when you knew me."

"You were a sweet, romantic bear," Iris said.

"I'm still a sweet, romantic bear," the Bear growled back at her. "I'm the sweetest, most romantic bear in the whole wide world, but life was a lot easier when what I did had nothing to do with who I am."

"You don't really believe that."

"Everybody's at me all the time. Everybody knows what's good for me, everybody's an authority on me but me, everyone's got a piece of advice. Like I'm some dink without a brain." Encountering Iris' subtlety and finesse, he felt the root stupidity and coarseness of his responses. It had been so long since he had seen her, or been with anyone remotely like her. There was a blunt, undetailed quality to him, but he could not change it now. Given time perhaps. Or more of her influence. In her absence he had grown crude. He had forgotten so much.

"You're not some dink without a brain," Iris told him.

"I'm getting close, though. And I see you've got your piece of advice for me too. Very therapeutic I'm sure, but . . . Iris, I'm," it was very hard for the Bear to say the word, "hurt. Something's getting to me and I can't fix it in the middle of the tour and everything. There isn't a pause." He pounded lightly at his chest to indicate the location of the problem. "The one thing I need is privacy, not people peeking in. Now that I can talk to someone about it I see how bad I feel. And I'm supposed to make a record in this condition. This is nuts."

"But if that's how it really is," Iris said sensibly, "why shouldn't a record be made of it?"

"Uh-uh. No way." The Bear shuddered a little. "The race belongs not to the addled but the swift."

"Forgive me for saying so, Bear, but you sound petulant."

"I *know*," he said, and worried his chestfur with a paw. "This way madness lies. I can't live like this."

"Bear, I hate to tell you this, but this is what life is like. You go along for awhile until you've had more than you can deal with and then you go the rest of the way in pieces. It's not the worst thing in the world, and you're not the Lone Ranger, either."

"That's *not* the way it is," the Bear insisted, standing over Iris and gesturing with his arms. "That's the crap that gets in the way. Perfection *exists*. Don't be hustled into partial solutions. This is accident, garbage, delusion."

"I don't think you realize," Iris told him, "how much of life is made up of failure."

"Human life maybe, but not me. What pisses me off is that I should be able to handle it, just knock it flat the way I used to do."

"If that's how it's been for you, then you've been very strong or very lucky."

"Yeah. I'm all over luck . . . I should be able to do this though. I'm not like you. You human people, you have emotional lives your bodies can't support, you lack the strength to keep things from getting to you, so naturally you crap out and get exhausted halfway through. . . ." The Bear stopped himself. Iris' head seemed to have raised and stiffened atop her graceful neck. "Aw, Christ I'm sorry. . . ."

"Bear? Is that you in there? I've heard you angry before, but I've never heard you speak like this. You have changed."

"I haven't said any of this to anyone, Irish." One of his old nicknames for her. "A little, maybe, but not like this. Is there any room here for how I really am?"

Iris raised her arm and held out her hand to him.

He came around the coffee table and sat down beside her. She let him draw her to him and they held each other, comfortably for a moment, but then they stiffened awkwardly, Iris first, the Bear responding after. All the same, it felt so good to the Bear. It was as if he had not touched another living creature in an eternity, as if he were slowly being welcomed back into the warm community of flesh. As if there were a place for tenderness in the world yet.

"Do you remember," Iris asked him, "way back when, before I met you for the first time, I had dreams about a talking bear for a week and then Jones called me up?"

"Do you remember when we started hearing each other think?"

"The first time I heard your voice out loud in my head," said Iris, "I nearly jumped across the room."

"We belong with each other," said the Bear. "Isn't it obvious?"

Iris pulled away from him so she could have a look at him. "Listen, I know you've got a big drama built up and I'm the next act," she said. "But I'm not that, I'm not the answer to that, I'm not a function of that. At least, don't jump to any conclusions. A lot of time has passed and in some ways you're a stranger to me. There may be a connection between us, but we've both changed. It may be that we've changed a lot."

"Funny," said the Bear. "I feel as if no time has passed and nothing has changed."

"You're wrong on both counts." She was straightening herself up and smoothing down the hem of her dress so that its edge just covered her knees.

"Nothing essential has changed," the Bear said.

"No? I've heard you talk tonight."

Good Lord, the Bear realized, it was a mistake to have said anything.

"There's something I want to show you." Iris got up from the sofa without looking at him, and as she walked across the living room she kept her face averted. She rummaged in a pile of magazines on top of a bureau and came away with a copy of *Rolling Stone*.

"Oh no," said the Bear, and put a pair of troubled paws to his head. "Did I get written up in the *Stone* too? I can't stand it. I feel like I'm being opened up, being destroyed, like my insides are being pulled out."

"Funny you should say that," said Iris, who had found her page. "And no, you didn't get written up in the *Stone*. It's a quote from a book review. 'If you bring forth what is within you, what you bring forth will save you. If you do not bring forth what is within you, what you do not bring forth will destroy you.' "

"Heavy," said the Bear. "What's it from?"

"*The Gnostic Gospels*."

"So you got God on your side, huh?"

"Doesn't everyone?" Iris asked.

"Aw, you're probably right, kid. I've just become a crumb, that's all. I used to love you so pure and true, now I spend half my time thinking how much time it might take to seduce you."

"That seems natural enough," said Iris, looking him in the eye without blinking.

"It does?" asked the Bear. "God, I'm such a stranger in this world."

"Well, good luck," she said.

He walked home alone under the pylons and girders of the FDR Drive, smelling the fetid night and watching the colored lights shimmer on the black surface of the river. Waiting for Godzilla, like the rest of the city. The Bear had already begun to successfully argue Iris down in his mind. There was too big a pileup in his life. Worse, he had been living with a dumb, unregal automatism, his nose glued to the iron rail of events, stupefied by sequence, rapt, somnambulous, unalert. He had been stupid enough to hope for something from people and events. The gigs, the music, Iris—he had stood in front of them like a man at a cafeteria counter, expecting to be fed. It didn't work that way. You didn't walk through the world with your hand out, begging your meaning from whatever happened along. A truck rolled past him under the highway, braying on its horn, and he pulled up on his coatcollar and down on his hat. The only way to live was to be free of what happened to you, and he had lost that. He was stuck. He had lost everything! The Bear heard the unreal melodramatic note in his voice but continued nonetheless. The recording session in two days meant nothing. And Iris. More bondage. Vulnerability! Give and take! The whole crock of shit! Letting her tell him that all this garbage was good for him when he knew he was being destroyed!

The Bear scanned the river before heading inland to the apartment. Godzilla might not be coming up to chomp the city down to size, but some monstrous ambiguity or other was rising through other waters. It was threatening all the hip ironic accommodations he'd made with the world to keep his fear of it at bay and a coherent self alive. Godzilla in the river, and who knows what in me. I should never have come out of the cave. I should have stayed with the shadow play. The world is unremitting. On your own, you can keep things cozy.

This is what I wanted.

He had a sneaky feeling that, somewhere unattended, he was dreaming up a catastrophe to wreck the set so he wouldn't have to go on evolving. If that's what he was doing.

As they carried me away, I was overheard to say: but I was cool.

He got home without incident before first light, went upstairs and despite his agitation fell asleep almost at once. He had a dream that purported to part the veil and reveal to him the secret perfection of his life. Not only were the events of his life, some of them fine, others correspondingly awful, rendered perfect by the beauty of the overall design, but each individual event itself was perfect. He was handed a large flower on whose petals his life's individual events, past present and future, were displayed in a beautiful arrangement and harmonious form: there was not one wrong note in the composition. In the middle of the dream, the woman with the dyed red hair and the laundry basket walked up to him and kissed him full on the mouth.

When he woke up on the day of the recording session it was midafternoon and Jones had gone out for lunch with Sybil, leaving a note behind. The Bear grumbled around the apartment practicing and wondering whether or not to be nervous about the date. Cummins phoned around sundown to ask how things were going. The Bear told him they were going dynamite.

Night came too quickly, and too quickly after it Jones showed up with a vapid, eager expression on his face and the van downstairs. "This is it, eh Bear? The night of nights. You ready for posterity?"

"No," said the Bear. "And I ain't dressed yet either."

"Don't know which pair of baggy pants to put on? Whether to button the raincoat or belt it? Stage fright? Is that what's troubling you, bucky?"

"Jones," the Bear told him, dusting off the raincoat and wishing he had a black one instead, "try not to be such a pain in the ass."

They went down the stairs with the Bear in the lead, Jones behind him trying out an Edward G. Robinson impression to the tune of I made you and I can break you so don't doublecross me tonight or you'll be sorry, see? The ride down to the Tin Palace passed too quickly, and when the Bear entered the club he knew without possibility of error that nothing was going to work out. Maybe he would lay out a lot and the rhythm section could put out a trio record. They'd been playing well, so why not?

Some people were drifting into the club, but what for? Ordering dinner. That's rational. That makes sense. My being here does not.

A little while before the first set he phoned Iris.

"Are you sure you don't want me to come down and watch?" she asked.

"You'd only make me nervous. Or I'd forget about everyone else and only play for you."

Her voice softened. "That's sweet," she said.

"No it's not, it's stupid and it'll fuck the music up. Look, I'd love to see you. If a couple of sets go well maybe I'll call you and you can come down later."

She made a goodbye kiss into the phone, and he hung up the receiver.

The rhythm section showed and the Bear yakked and laughed with them and felt completely alone in the world, without an answering echo. This of course was an illusion, but that's how tight and apprehensive he was.

Cummins set up the tape machine and the microphones, the Bear worked his way distractedly through a conversation with the bartender about his first visit to the establishment a few months earlier, and gradually more people came in and assembled themselves over drinks from the bar and dinner from the kitchen in the rear. Too quickly it was time for the first set. He told Cummins not to run the tape machines, and Cummins only pretended to obey him—he could see the tops of the reels turning. The Bear played feeling only half present, beginning with "Au Privave" and a couple of standards and playing short, perfunctory versions of two originals he wanted to record later. The rhythm section sounded okay, but they were trying to goose him, and they got a little twitchy in the face of his nonresponse. After the set everyone told him he was doing fine, but he could tell they were lying and his inquietude deepened. By the time he went up for the second set he was ready to call it a night. The club had filled rather suddenly, but he hardly noticed it. Where was he going to get the music from?

He looked out at the people in the club, but he wasn't noticing detail. There was something unreal about the night. Something provisional. Something, it occurred to him, not yet made clear.

Then, after playing a furious blues he hoped would open him up but didn't—all he heard in the noise of his playing was the rage of discontent—the Bear had a new experience. It came to him, so that he was not able to doubt it, that whatever battle he had been trying to fight in his life, it was over and he had lost it. Everything he had tried to accomplish was gone, and his efforts were shot. Whatever it was he had been trying to store up inside himself was, if not gone, a dead issue. A sense of his true and undeniable desolation entered him and he waved the band away from the Monk tune he had meant to call and began playing alone. Some distance ahead he would meet up with the nettlesome ballad he had written for Billy in the van coming down from Boston, but for now he wanted to play by himself.

What an empty life I've always had. I tried to fill it up with passions and objects and other stray bits of stuff but I never really succeeded. Because I could not. Because the thing could not be done. He could see it clearly and it was empty for good now. Something had given way and left things bare of striving and illusions, and the music came out of him ordered and dispassionate, according to an unfamiliar principle and feeling less like a language of emotion than one of fact. So this is how I'm going to be for awhile, he thought. I'm not sure I like it but it's not going to go away. It has too much gravity. He sensed himself as a large dark space in which everything had calmed down and settled into position. He didn't know if it was good or bad and he didn't think it was the end or the goal of all perception, but after he had played alone for five minutes or so and then taken the band through the body of the tune he felt that he had gotten some unsuspected portion of himself into music for the first time and that it would have to stand. It wasn't particularly pleasant but it was true.

The Bear heard a new heaviness in his tone come forward to meet the density of the changes and curl at their base like waves around a rock at the sea's edge, and he modified his mouth's grip on the reed to emphasize the intentness of his attack and detail the implications of the encounter: adaptive music meets world of obdurate fact: question: will the water ever wear the rock away? In one lifetime, for example his? At the moment it seemed unlikely, but you never know: there are other waters, other shores.

He heard the rhythm section part behind him and make way, opening a space before framing a response. Thank you, guys. It's a gesture of respect and I'm grateful. Donelian played a chord stacked with fourths and sixths not normally in his repertoire; Scott Lee rumbled through the lower storeys of his instrument and threw open a few dark rooms, disused till then; Billy muttered amid his tomtoms to imply a shaking of foundations, a shifting of low stones. The Bear raised up a cry and let it fall dissonant and unresolved, certainly unsatisfied, perhaps forlorn. He didn't want to live in this house but he was certainly there for the moment. He extended his solo into another chorus and entered every room. His life was going to change.

What's more, he thought, looking through the strangeness of the nightclub at Cummins behind the recording console, that was twelve, maybe fifteen minutes long and a keeper no matter how weird it was. So they were getting something done.

He played a fast impromptu blues straight out of the cadenza to blow some of his steam off, and although he played fluently and bitterly enough he knew he would do better by the end of the night, and probably better than that tomorrow. By then there would be enough for a record. Okay, he thought, and allowed himself the smallest and most sardonic of smiles. Okay. It's not what I planned but it will have to do. He walked up to the microphone to say a few words of nonsense and announce the next tune.

They had been told to wait for the end of the set, but the youngest man on the squad must have gotten edgy. "NEW YORK CITY POLICE!" he called out, and jumped to his feet with a strange-looking gun held stiffly out in front of him in both hands. "FREEZE!"

The Bear was aware of screams, falling tables and breaking glass as he threw the mikestand and took off for the kitchen doors. He heard an oddly muffled-sounding gunshot, and when he looked back over his shoulder he almost laughed: they were getting it all wrong: the cop had fired into the air all right, but it was a tranquilizer gun, and a brightly feathered tranquilizer dart was quivering anomalously on the ceiling. To top off this bit of farce, someone shouted, "*Stop in the name of the law.*"

Good Lord, the Bear asked himself as he raced through the kitchen and splintered the back door open with his shoulder, did somebody actually say that? He upended the patrolman who had been waiting for him in the alley, vaulted a low cinderblock wall, landed on all fours and took off at forty miles an hour down a parallel alley. Now that the long-feared bust had finally come down on him he felt oddly liberated. No more half measures. No more obscurities. Let's have it out. Let it come down. He climbed a section of cyclone fence, came out on the sidewalk and sprinted through the dark for Second Avenue, listening for the sound of pursuit and hearing only his claws on cement. But they'd be coming.

A portrait of the artist as a hunted animal: he paused at the edge of the Avenue's brightness to consider his possible strategies. He could look for some indoor place to hole up in or brazen it out among the populace. The latter alternative appealed to his sense of humor, besides which he was only five minutes' walk from his apartment and maybe ten from Iris' place—it was twice the distance but no one would look for him there.

Pulling down on his hat and up on the collar of his coat, the Bear raised himself onto his hindlegs and prepared to face the music of the Avenue. Almost immediately he could tell he wasn't going to make it. He'd succeeded in passing through crowds before, but tonight he was out of phase. He reeked anomaly. As soon as he turned the corner, people started backing away and making noises. A skinny girl in black leather and a head of rooster hair let out a scream. A number of dark mouths dropped open. "It's all right," he told them. "Let me through, I'm a doctor." A young couple in down jackets staggered backward away from him into traffic. A taxi swerved to avoid them and a chorus of horns went up; everywhere the Bear detected faces spinning in his direction. Here it is, he told himself, you've defied the laws of gravity long enough.

With a sweat breaking out under his fur and the distinct sensation that he was acting something out that had happened long ago, he dropped again to all fours, aimed himself uptown and took off along the storefronts, running through banded light, a shock of purple and green, then white, as the thin legs of the people skittered and scattered. He was aware of a gathering tumult some distance behind him and took the first available left into relative dark. Passing alongside a high brick wall down which rivulets of water ran, he found a rusted metal door, broke it in with his shoulder and headed down through a wilderness of stairs, aware at the same time that he was passing through some landscape implicit in himself. He collided with a number of heavy objects and came at last to a halt. He stood in darkness and listened. A siren dopplered off outside and his nostrils filled with the smell of rusted iron. Someplace nearby, water dripped regularly onto stone.

In a few minutes his perspiration dried and his heart quieted closer to normal. He groped his way forward and then slowly up the first iron stairway that presented itself, followed it through a series of precarious and irregular turnings, and then had to clamber up onto some kind of shelf. He had the sensation, as he stood, of having come out into a large open space. When his eyes adjusted themselves he made out, very high above him, a bit of broken ceiling through which faint light filtered slantwise down. He was on a kind of platform, overlooking a landscape of broken timbers and upthrust flooring. In fact he was on the stage of an abandoned theater, and as he retraced his run up the Avenue he understood that he had broken through the side door of the old Fillmore East, descended to its basement and then come slowly upstairs. Fifty years before, Carnovsky had done his famous Yiddish Lear here, and more recently the psychedelic age had blown east to this platform on a sea of purple billows. Now it was his turn, the one and only Bear.

"World," he said.

There was a noise from the pit and three powerful flashlights clicked on and shined in his face. "Hello," he told them, doing the voice. "I'm Mr. Ed." A fourth policeman standing behind the first three raised a kind of lantern and the Bear was able to see them all. It may have been the irregularity of the lighting, but they appeared to be wearing red or blue rubber noses. And why not. Wasn't he a bear in a raincoat and a hat? The Bear felt terribly sleepy. His eyes closed; he wanted to lie down.

This is what I get for rising to the bait, he thought. What a sap I've been. Music, a career, even love. Can you believe it, ladies and gentlemen? I wanted to live.

"We can shoot you with a dart full of PCP where you stand," a big white-haired man in an overcoat told him in a conversational tone of voice, "so it would be better if you don't try to run."

One of the uniformed cops, stepping uncertainly through the rubble on the floor, then pausing, had a question for his superior: "How do we get the bear off the stage?"

"You can't," the Bear told him. "It's in his blood."

"*What was that?*" the detective asked him sharply.

They shot him full of animal tranquilizer before leading him out of the theater into the street. He was semipleasantly dazed, but recognized the true iron cold of winter on his fur when they reached open air. A heavy black truck—CORRECTIONS, he read on its side—had pulled up to the curb, and rings of people were watching him. He felt so ashamed. This was something he himself had produced. It told on him, accused him of lapsed taste, bad imaginative form. Paranoia is the last refuge of the unimaginative. And you call yourself an artist. This is very crudely done.

There was a movie poster peeling on a wall: The Ultimate in Alien Terror. There was a van from an exterminating company: We Are the Pest Doctors! All Our Patients Die!

There was a dark green tanker truck: Mystic Transport: By Serving We Grow . . . no, there was no such truck. He'd seen it somewhere else, some other time. The overabundance of signifiers was a trick of the increasing blur of drug and spin of mind. It was his doing.

As he stumbled forward a cry rose from the crowd. Obedient to the occasion, he covered his face with his hat, then tried to laugh at the gag but could not.

They threw him semiconscious into the back of the Corrections truck. He was sped dazed and blinded through half-familiar streets. Later, his body would retain the memory of painful blows from blunt instruments. Bassoons? Miscellany ensued. His last clear memory was of being thrown heavily into a cell. "That oughta hold you for awhile," a voice told him. His saxophone was thrown in after him. Someone must have retrieved it from the club. It hit him in the face, and before he spun downward into a brown and uncomforting darkness he became aware of eyes watching him. Was the world shrinking to a dot or expanding beyond recognition? Possibly the eyes were his own. No, too intent, too steady.

Iris? Jones?

They were not there.

Was he?

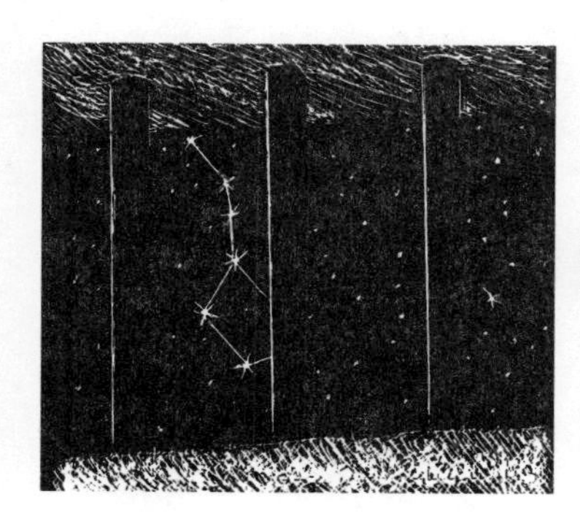

part two

Listen to this reed forlorn,
Breathing ever since 'twas torn
From its rushy bed: a strain
Of impassioned love and pain:

"The secret of my song, though near,
None can see and none can hear.
O for a friend to know the sign
And mingle all his soul with mine.

'Tis the flame of love that fired me,
The wine of love inspired me.
Would you learn how lovers bleed?
Then listen, listen to the reed."

—Rumi

1

jones opened one eye and the entire physical universe reappeared, in all its smug ubiquity. Considering it, Jones closed the offending eye and succeeded in going back to sleep for another half an hour. But that was all he could manage and eventually he had to wake up.

When he opened his eyes again, the waking world discovered him lying on his back, arms flung melodramatically cruciform, a corner of cotton top-sheet covering his privates. Looking up, he saw what might have been the first fly of spring doing its geometry lesson in the air above him, inscribing a series of severely cut, highly regular angles against the veined white background of the bedroom ceiling. Jones couldn't decide if the bug was building triangles or squares or some phantom revolving unresolvellogram—the angles seemed exact and absolute but the overall form of the figure kept shifting by inscrutable increments and he couldn't make out what it really was. Maybe it was weaving the shape of his fate, if he still had one, which he doubted. In any case, Jones told himself, this was quite a fly. It also occurred to Jones that the Five Platonic Solids would make a good name for a doo-wop outfit. He also liked the Peptides, and was partial to the Thousand Natural Shocks, but thought the name unwieldy.

Another thing he didn't understand about the fly, about all the flies of spring for that matter—did they grow out of this exacting schoolwork into the larger roving, eating, mating model, or were there two entirely different kinds of fly in the world, one of them interested only in food and fornication and the other inexplicably obsessed with the demands of ideal form? Was such a thing possible? If so, it implied a pretty severe division of labor in the kingdom of the flies, and a host of tedious things about the world in general.

"I'm not quite carrion yet," he told the fly in any case. Jones was the kind of guy who talked to animals.

"Little fly, who made thee?" he asked it after awhile. "Dost thou know who made thee?" He lit a cigarette, inhaled its dose of poison and blew the smoke off to one side of the fly's workspace. Who set you so exact a lesson? How inscribed it in your genes or tiny mind? Did He smile His work to see? Did He who made the Bear make thee?

This last consideration landed heavily in his heart and prodded the beast of his guilt back into being. Jones lurched up from his mattress insufficiently armed into the accusative light of day and stumbled out of the bedroom pursued by a Bear. Whom he had failed. Whom he had abandoned into imprisonment or annihilation or worse for how many months now? Get out of this bedroom. Jones blinked into the long daylit rectangle of the living room and found a moment's sweet unconsciousness standing there naked in the doorframe until his moral clock ticked again, audible and relentless, and the beast resumed its motion. He dragged his rambling sense of catastrophe toward the bathroom at the rear of the apartment but stopped en route to browse for a paperback to read while on the toilet. Bookshelves lined the right-hand living room wall floor to ceiling and front to back. Jones himself was a scattershot reader, but the Bear was a hardy omnivore who consumed virtually everything in his path. Fiction. History. The mystics. Time was, start him going on Meister Eckhart or Ibn 'Arabi and you could close down the store for the day. Jones himself had not had much mystical experience—unless his liaison with the Bear counted, and he wasn't sure—and so could only follow the Bear's line of thought with insufficient rational analogues. When the Bear got on a long mystical jag, it seemed to Jones, he could be tedious to listen to after the first twenty minutes or so.

Jones pulled down a copy of the Penguin *Charterhouse of Parma*—the Bear's favorite novel, although Jones had never understood why—and lapsed with it heavily onto the sagging green sofa, which as he landed exhaled along with galactic whorls of dust an unforeseen intensity of Bear-smell. For a dizzy moment Jones reeled at the richness of that remembered life. Although his time with the Bear had been no picnic, it had been incomparably meaningful to live through, had been a life worthy of the name which had allotted him, for a time, a special fate, someone to be in the world and a niche in which to be it: a role he understood, something stable and resonant and sure. Now it was not the Bear but the Void that snuffled around the apartment and took up all the available space, the Void that nipped at his heels in the street and ate away at him morning, noon and night. It was his fault the Bear was gone, or dead, or whatever, wherever, he was. Everything had been his fault, always. *Selah*.

When younger, Jones had been a man of obvious potential, smart, funny, not too bad-looking, with an engaging manner and a certain flair: a typical strolling boho with artistic tastes and predilections, if no art, and the habit of ready money; but in the conversion of his potential to actuality, the *solvae* and *coagulae* had fallen short of alchemy and left something leaden behind in the alembic. Too hip for corporate life, too funny a take on things for academia, he had waited tables, hacked a little journalism, done a couple of character roles off-off-Broadway—had a small hit as Dr. Van Helsing in an avant-garde *Dracula* but never realized his dream of playing anyone, absolutely anyone, in Chekhov—hung out around petty crooks and carny characters, in short had done a lot and not much really. Which was cool as long as the years didn't add up and the talk and food were still good. But by the time he started hanging out with Russian emigrés on the circus circuit, money was running short, the outlook was grimming out, and he was starting to feel that he had pretty fundamentally fucked up the practical project of his life.

One of the bright moments, he'd thought at the time, but certainly not one of ultimate consequence, had been drawing three cards into a full house, kings up jacks, that night against the Great Vichinsky. Vichinsky had been drinking too much vodka and grinding on as usual about the popularity in Ameriky of those focking *kets*, and the lack of feeling for his old, once-respected specialty—they were, Jone, the soul of all real circus, all the filling and pothos of real circus, and me with only the one cub left I been able to defect with in great democratic city of Cincinnati and what good? Who recognized? My cousin physicist still driving keb. And why? Jealousy is why. No understanding of life is why. Ameriky is why. Nice shiny surface, *nichevo* underneath. I see you and raise you feefty. I know I don't have. You win you take bearcub, okay? I all finished with life already anyhow.

Looking back through the flawed optics of retrospection, Jones had to admit that by the time he beat Vichinsky at poker he had reached the same dead end a few times over and had begun to daydream idly about the gaspipe. Which was how Vichinsky had tried to end it a couple of weeks after the card game. Jones had offered him the bearcub back and Vichinsky had refused, with the usual melodramatic trappings, no matter how much Jones insisted. Where was Vichinsky these days? Jones hoped he was doing all right.

He read the same sentence ten or so times over—something about that idiot Fabrizio del Dongo buying a couple of barrels of Nebbiolo for someone or other—without gleaning any sense from it, until his cigarette was done and then, still drenched in the unexpected scent of Bear and before the waking world could tug him into further motion, he remembered the earliest days in the apartment with the bearcub he'd only kept as a goof on how low-comic a thing his life had gotten to be—going by the name Jones when his real name meant Garden-on-the-Mountain in another language was another one-man in-joke on what a nonentity he'd become. The dumbhead furry fucker blundered into the furniture and scratched up the woodwork but also seemed at times to understand his subtlest inner workings: would sometimes mimic his moods, it seemed to him, with a finely honed parodic edge—he'd be sitting in an armchair, say, feeling sorry for himself, and on the floor at his feet the cub might put its head in its hands in a classic woe-is-me pose and start moaning and rocking. Then to amplify the point it would get up and walk nose first into the wall right next to an open doorway, as if to say . . . Then there were the things that really didn't tally: you'd come into a room and find the cub with a book open on its lap—it'd look up, clock your entrance and start licking the pages or put on a glazed expression and pee on the carpet. Then, of course, there was the intent if more explicable way—since bears were known to respond to the stuff—the cub listened to music.

Yup. There was that, all right.

And even before the vocal denouement, there was the fact that the bearcub had already begun to evoke from him the one good quality he would still admit to, call it by its proper name: devotion.

Jones got up and walked away from the memory.

In the shower, he prayed for cool clear water to come down and rinse those nagging stains from his soul, but when he turned the shower off the world was still breathing slow and steady on the back of his neck in its usual overbearing show of constancy and presence and weight. Oh give me a break, Jones asked it. I outran you for awhile, for a few years even. Give me another couple of minutes now.

Whom the gods would destroy they first deprive of his magic bear.

In fact, what time was it? Soon he would have to begin the trudge to work.

Jones towelled himself down but fresh sweat beaded on his brow: it would drip down and blind him later, he knew. What point was there to any effort, any motion, any feeble twitch of will? Jones felt the complex geometry of his depression advancing upon him, the invisible cage that kept him patrolling his bit of air under what hidden orders? He blinked at himself in the mirror and his face looked back at him, unimpressive and not very healthy-looking in the glass. One face too many in the world, he thought. One face he'd just as soon not see. Did He who made the fly make thee?

He had to get going or he'd be late for work at the bar and Johnny Coyle would give him one of his all-day special hard times. He had to get a move on.

But came to himself again slouched on the sofa so redolent of Bear today, the same unread book open on his lap. And Jones remembered his way-back bearcub sitting on the living-room floor while a record was playing, his shoulders rounded with what almost seemed human concentration as if, Jones had thought at the time, the thing was shaping itself to music. Even before he'd had any real inkling what intelligence was resident there, Jones could almost feel the cub drawing music into itself, the rounded furball form immobile or rocking intently in front of the speakers, its eyes out of focus or fixed on some random spot on the floor while Coltrane burned his way to God on a minor blues or Ornette raised his saxophone and centuries of cognitive imprisonment fell to the dust without especial drama. Jones used to test his new animule's tastes with different records. It seemed to like Bach and Bird a lot—there'd be that oddball stillness in him, he'd get that funny elsewhere look in his eyes—but put some Mantovani on the box and the thing would bumble off to the bedroom on all fours. Switch back to Mozart or Sonny Rollins he'd be back on the carpet in front of the stereo, looking at the backs of his paws in a spill of sunlight from the windows as he listened, or would swat placidly at the golden dustmotes and watch them spin in the day's declining beam.

Cuter than a dog and maybe even a little smarter, Jones had thought at the time, and isn't it odd how exactly he seems to understand what I say to him? Although sometimes, true, and usually perversely, he does not. But what am I gonna do with him when he gets bigger? You can't keep a full-grown bear in a New York apartment. I'll have to have him put down with a needle at the vet's or contribute him to the zoo. Jones hated to admit it: in the isolation of his life at the time, the bearcub had become his closest friend. He talked to it, he confided, he told it everything. Some absurdity of symbiosis had evolved between them; it felt all right but thought all wrong. At night, noting the particular stupidity of this descent, Jones would have long, one-sided conversations with the cub, and sometimes it would seem to nod yes to some salient point, or tacitly express some nuance of sympathy with a comprehending paw atop his knee.

I know I'm a fuckup, Jones would tell it, but is there anything good left in me? The cub would pat him consolingly. This was idiotic. Then, if he'd say, Come on, you understand me really, the thing would drool out the side of its mouth and start gnawing on the toe of his slipper.

He used to put the cub on a leash and take him out on walks around the neighborhood, and he'd met a lot of good-looking women that way. Is that what I think it is? You're kidding me! Really? They'd come up to the apartment for coffee or a beer, but all it had ever led to was them playing with the

Bear for hours and hours, hugging him to their supernatural slender waists or those taut-nippled East Village bosoms poking T-shirts and tube tops, letting the cute li'l thing paw them wherever it wanted, enjoying its big sloppy random-looking kisses and even getting a laugh out of its shocking-pink erections.

If they'd only known.

For fuck's sake, if *he* had only known.

Finally there came the day. A man if anything overstocked with halfway talents, Jones had always noodled on an instrument or two, and one week he unpacked his old metal clarinet and played it persistently for an afternoon or two at the growing bear. He played some Sousa, a sort-of blues, almost-klezmer, an impression of belly-dance music, all the little bits of this-and-that he knew. Maybe I can get you to dance, he told it. I'm playing pretty well, ain't I? even with the occasional squeaks and squawks? The reed's a bitch to control sometimes. Maybe that's what we can do with ourselves when we grow up. I'll play, you'll dance, we'll make some bread and retire upstate like a pair of merchant princes. What do you say to that? I know it sounds like a joke, but how would it be as a real-life prospect? Think I can get you to play along? Because, man, I'm sick of waiting tables. I tell you, bear, I'm an artist at heart. Always was. Jones played another snatch of tune on the clarinet and ended the phrasing on an interrogatory upnote. What do you think? What do you think really?

The bearcub rose onto its hind legs, waddled up to Jones, snatched the instrument out of his hands and said, "I think that if I have to hear you torture this poor thing another five minutes I'll go out of my fucking mind."

Jones had gasped and nearly fallen down. "Ack," he said.

"You mean you never guessed?" the Bear asked him, coolly examining the reed of the clarinet.

"There were clues," Jones just managed to say through a constricted throat. It was the strangest conversation he had ever had, and he didn't know what tone to adopt. Civilized outrage clearly wasn't working. He shuffled his deck of roles and voices and found no card he could play. "Clues," he repeated in a voice he barely recognized as his own.

"Yeah," said the Bear. "I laid a few out for you but you seemed kind of, uh, slow on the uptake."

"Kind of *what*?" said Jones, aghast at the insult, the offense, the affront to his—

"I know it's a big conceptual leap and all but I thought you were a little, how should I put it, thick, and I was going to let you pass. I mean, maybe you weren't up to it."

"Oh thank you very much."

"But the clarinet was the last straw," the Bear told him. "You had to be stopped. And here we jolly well are," he paraphrased one of Jones' Lord Buckley records, doing the voice, "*ahn't we*."

"W-what are you?" Jones had protested absurdly, his hands fluttering at the end of his ridiculous arms. "Some kind of expert on the clarinet?"

"Expert might be too strong a word," said the Bear. He moistened the end of his snout, then played the opening bars of the clarinet part of the K.581 Mozart quintet through the first arpeggio, with the rhythm nicely pointed up and his breath well controlled but some inconsistencies in tone production across the range of the instrument: Mozart was not as simple as he seemed. From the arpeggio's end he segued into Charlie Parker's "Au Privave" and improvised two not-bad choruses before lowering the clarinet from his distended black-and-purple lips. "When you go out to wait tables I only pull the couch apart and rip the carpet for realistic effect. Most of the time I read books or practice horn. I'd rather have a sax, you know. Probably an alto would suit me best, but without trying one it's hard to say."

"You've been practicing while I was out," Jones managed to say coherently and in his own voice.

"What did I just tell you."

"I think I need a drink," Jones said.

"Sit down and I'll make you one. There's just enough Scotch left for a stiff one. The usual half an ice cube and a soda back? The whiskey's already watered. I take some now and then and make up the difference from the tap. You never seem to notice. Not much of a palate, apparently. You sure you want a drink? You don't have a very strong constitution and the stuff's not good for you."

Not much more than a pup, Jones had thought to say but kept silent, and already so fucking uppity.

"Look," said the Bear when he came back with the drink, exactly as if he'd read Jones' mind, "if I didn't like you I wouldn't be talking to you in the first place. I'm nervous about it myself. Overcompensating. I'm not as assured as I seem. It's a big jump for me too. A break with family tradition. I mean, it's obvious you're a fucking mess in the practical sense, but you've got a good heart, and that's what I respond to."

"You *like* me?"

"What's not to like? You're one of the human race's few true gentlemen."

"I am?"

"Trust me. For generations back my folks have known every kind of human cruelty. You're not one of Them. You're a good man. You wouldn't hurt a fly."

"I'm a good man," Jones repeated in a sort of wonder.

"Drink up and get used to it. You are now The Man Who Owns a Talking Bear."

"Own? How could I own you?"

"Proves my point," the Bear told him, "but your life's defined anyway. So tell me, what do we do next?"

Jones awoke years later on the sofa, looking at the unread words in his lap. What book is this? Why do I smell you so powerfully today? I've sat on this sofa before. Are you still out there somewhere? Is it possible you're still alive? Is it possible you're trying to tell me something?

Jesus McChristmas, he realized, I'm late for work.

Jones murdered another clam, added it to the paper plate that held the five he had already opened and handed the half-dozen littlenecks through the sidewalk window to the big brownskinned man outside, traffic bright and noisy behind him, blue exhaust smoke rising and a game of hoop starting up in the court on the other side of the Avenue.

"You got another little cup of hot sauce for me?" the customer asked him.

"Here you go." Jones passed it out into the daylight and took the man's money. Then he wiped his hands dry on his apron, ate another few cold shrimp with cocktail sauce he had mixed up heavy on the horseradish and took a swig of beer from a paper cup. Sometimes it amazed him that he could stand there all day and down a simply unbelievable amount of seafood: shrimp, clams, oysters, the occasional filet of sole more or less *meuniere*: it all went down the hatch without even beginning to overstuff him. How did he manage to eat so much? Just because he didn't follow it with a carbohydrate chaser? He wasn't about to eat the fries here, not with that month-old tub of oil in the fryer. The management didn't seem to mind how much fish he ate, but that was mostly Coyle's good nature. It wasn't the worst job he'd ever had. Not by a long shot, no.

"Ah, excuse me, Jonesy," Johnny Coyle's voice said from just behind his right ear, "but if you're not too busy eating shrimp and jerking off could you possibly go down to the basement and bring me up another couple cases of Miller's?"

Coyle was a retired longshoreman with a habitual I'm-just-another-dumb-fucking-Irishman riff going most of the time, mid-forties, curly hair and moustache going grey but still in fighting trim. He made the job livable and got between Jones and the mafioso who owned the joint whenever that short squat reeking heap of psychotic violence put in an appearance, usually fresh from beating some poor son of a bitch half to death with a tire iron. Coyle was supposed to be the only guy alive who could keep this heavy, sweating, widespread monster at bay, used to ride with him on the bad months to make sure he didn't kill someone out of season. With Jones, Johnny Coyle was sociable and easy, and quite a sensitive guy, in his way. "Sure," said Jones. "I think I can get you a couple of cases cheap."

"Since you seem to be drinking it all," Coyle persisted.

"It's the Champagne of Bottled Beers," Jones informed him.

"If you'd be so fucking kind. When you have the time. If you'll forgive me for asking."

"All right all right all right."

Jones checked out his short-order emplacement—the tubs of clams on ice, the spread of cooked cocktail shrimp on a pizza tray, and on his right the deep fryer and the grill—to see that everything was in order. The Bear had long ago told him that there was no facet of your essential self that the world will not find out and one day travesty. No. Check that. There is no travesty of your essential nature to which life will not eventually subject you, was how the Bear had put it, and from this vantage point it seemed that the Bear, although of course his experience of life had prejudiced him in this regard, in fact was right. Jones' job at Filet of Soul on Sixth Avenue in the Village had put stigmata on his hands and placed a crown of paper on his head that read Soup Burg in blue-and-red letters across his brow. The stigmata were easy to explain: when he opened clams all day, the heels of the shells wore a hole in the palm of the hand that held the clams against the pressure of the knife. Later this hole callused over, but a small red eye remained in its center. Jones was ambidextrous and had grown a callus on each hand from which a livid eye looked back at him, like everything else, accusatively. To complete the sketch, the runoff from the tubs of clams and ice had soaked through his white canvas deck shoes to leave a mottling of rash on the tops of his feet. Not quite a spikemark, but under the circumstances it would do. The Soup Burg hat was a leftover from another restaurant that the owner wanted him to wear at all times. Better, perhaps, if less truthful, than Filet of Soul, but after a full day's work Soup Burg was about what he felt like he had left for brains.

But the imagery had not come entirely without compensations: on Jones' second day, the runoff from the clam tubs had made its way through the basement and whatever stonework intervened beneath to interfere with a portion of the city's basic power grid, and the whole string of subway lines that ran beneath the boards of Filet of Soul blew out at the rim of the evening rush and crammed the streets with stranded civilians for a couple of hours. Jones had punched New York City's lights out! He felt that he had struck a blow for freedom and in some sense made contact with the Bear.

Jones usually worked the nightshift, serving up clams and shrimp for the street trade and working the grill for people in the high-backed booths in Filet of Soul's dark interior—he had to wait the tables too, and work a full-scale kitchen in back if anyone ordered steak or mussels—but today he was doing the daylight stretch, lunchtime through evening, get off after he'd buddied his relief pitcher, the Dominican guy, whatsisname, Esposito, Vergíl, through the worst of the dinner rush. Most nights, by the time Jones closed down the grill and finished mopping out the bar, there'd be first light in the sky and nothing out there but yesterday's papers navigating the updrafts and a few last vampires scuttling home along the gutters through the early blue.

Tonight, though, there'd be some time to live through after work. And Sybil Bailey had called to say she'd be dropping by around seven or eight or so. They were no longer seeing each other—in fact it had been awhile since he'd literally seen her at all—but she had the final layout of the album's cover art and she wanted him to see it. He had almost forgotten about the album. With the Bear gone, what really was the point of putting it out?

"Jonesy," came Johnny Coyle's voice again. "That beer. Anytime you're ready. And say hello to Spooker for me if he doesn't bite your balls off first."

"You mind if I bring him down some hamburger? I mean, you never know."

"Sure. Take him one for me."

He was all right, was Johnny Coyle.

Jones took two flat round patties from the cooler and lifted the basement key from its hook, and even though he knew he had his apron on he patted himself to check for sure. If you walked down the basement stairs without an apron on, the dog would tear your throat out before you knew what had hit you—there's no training like Mafia training like no training I know. The hamburgers were insurance, just to be sure.

"Spooker, sweetie," Jones sang out from the top of the steps when he had shut the basement door behind him. The lights were always on down there, a few bare bulbs hanging from the ceiling, unplaned plank walls nailed up rough, a freezer vault, and he could see a few hardened dog turds on the cement floor at the bottom of the stairs, but the Doberman hadn't made his entrance yet. "Yo, *Spooker*." A quick tapping of uncut toenails on the concrete and there he was, a reddish-brown overstuffed chunk of walking meat, mouth open, looking up and wagging his stump of a tail for all he was worth. The animal was obviously half demented with its life down there. The boss didn't want him socializing with anyone, though Johnny Coyle was able to sneak him out for a walk on the end of a heavy leash a couple of times a month. On rainy days usually or late at night, when there weren't too many people out there.

"Look what I got for you, baby," Jones announced, then tossed Spooker down half a burger. The dog scarfed up the meat in an instant and looked up at Jones with renewed enthusiasm and an expansive doggy smile, tongue lolling out the side of it. Brain of a puppy and an overpacked body programmed for attack. Hiya, Spooks.

Jones nerved himself up for the descent.

For all he knew, every restaurant in Manhattan packed a brainwashed chump like Spooker in its basement. For all he knew the whole city was underwritten by a layer of buried animals living under lightbulbs and crapping on poured concrete floors. It was part of a hierarchical, metaphysical scheme of things Jones had been working out for himself over the last couple of months, a sort of outsized mental fresco: the dreaming public walked the upstairs maze in daylight while like the image of their own buried, denied or damaged selves a layer of animals lived trapped and incommunicate beneath. One level lower, just above the sewage, ran the subway full of worker drones and stupefied consumers, and in the co-opped heights above it all the rich reclined in golden condos against a sky of Fra Angelico blue. But watchit, ladies and gennamen: when the Big Day dawns, the first might get to be last, the last might just jockey into first position, you never know, and in any case everything's gonna get jumbled in all kinds of unpredictable ways and the animals will be set free and they will render justice.

But probably not today. No, probably not today.

At the bottom of the stairs, Jones hunkered down and offered another piece of hamburger, which Spooker gulped down quick as worlds vanishing into the maw of Kali. Then the dog thrust his strong insistent head into Jones' hands for a little human contact, a quick fix of love, and Jones rubbed him behind the ears. Jones had to admit to the absent Bear that the travesty level was running pretty high this year.

"How you doing, dumbbell," he asked Spooker, working his hands behind the animal's ears, the dog pushing against his fingers to say harder, harder, more. Jones kneaded his way down the Doberman's spine. "Just another poor working stiff with the wrong instructions," he said. "Ain't you."

Spooker looked up at him with crazed adoration and nodded yes.

"Come down here without my apron on I sometimes wonder, would you go for the throat or take the low road and rip my balls off?"

Spooker wanted more friction behind his right ear and down his neck.

"Of course one day your programming is gonna snap and you'll go for me anyway. The apron might protect the family jewels, though. Which I might as well have hocked with the silver for all the use I'm getting out of them these days."

Spooker was getting very very happy. He'd found a buddy. Look at that stump of tail go. Jones worked the other side of his neck.

"So have another burger on me."

Spooker looked up at him with sudden serious focus.

Oh shit, thought Jones. "Uh, how about I give it to you in the freezer?"

Jones stood up and survived the transition. Brandishing his last half of hamburger, he walked to the freezer vault, turned on the light switch, pulled open the heavy door and tossed the piece of meat inside. Spooker ran into the freezer, pivoted on the concrete, looked happily at his old good buddy Jones without even bending to the meat and stood his ears at their ultimate degree of attention. Jones slammed the freezer shut on him, and while counting to twenty examined the double-X oak girderwork of the vault-strong door. In the middle of my life, dark wood. Look at how that thing is made. And they say craftsmanship is dead. Bet you the door they slammed shut on the Bear wasn't this well put together. Eighteen, nineteen.

When Jones yanked the freezer open, Spooker still hadn't eaten the burger, and looked at Jones with his eyes wide and the skin pulled tight atop his skull, from which Jones could almost see waves of manic energy radiating outward. Jones didn't know which Spooker liked best, the cold in the freezer room or the thrill of imprisonment and release. Spooker's untrimmed feet did a quick little up-and-down tap dance on the concrete. Spooker's neural circuits were overloading and he had hit the wheel of bliss: bright sparks scattered with the friction, and the dog was on the verge of seeing its God.

This is dreadful, he thought. Wonder if they've made something like this out of the Bear's brain by now.

"You cool?" asked Jones. He slammed the door shut again, went to the wall for his two cases of Miller's and stacked them at the foot of the stairs.

When he opened the freezer room again he beheld what appeared to be a dog in bliss. If Spooker could have turned his body inside out to express his gratitude he would have done so in a flash. "Out," Jones told him, and noted that the meat had been eaten. "Much as I enjoy dicking around in the underworld with you, it's time for us both to go back to work."

Jones gave the Doberman a few farewell thumps on the ribcage and asked it again not to kill him next time he came down. As he hefted the cases of beer up the steps one at at time, he wondered how many hours it would be until Sybil showed up and did he really want to see her.

Jones had long known that he lacked the knack for avoiding romantic disaster, but it came as a shock to him how fatally he was still in love with Sybil Bailey. It didn't take long to make the rediscovery. The day's last light behind her obscured the details of her beauty as she came out of Sixth Avenue into the relative gloom of Filet of Soul, but once she had settled the warm generosity of her form on one of the tall uncomfortable barstools, Jones, canted on the edge of the one beside her toward the rear of the bar, felt his cresting soul plummet into the depths like the sinker tied to his whole life's sum of hook and line. Sybil removed her dun possibly Armani jacket and laid it across the bar and he was lost completely.

Could he believe the warmth of smile she turned upon him? Believe the "Jones, it's so good to see you again" that accompanied it? And what about the deliberate beat during which she held his upper arm, and the half-moment during which she pressed her lips, first softly and then with a last ironic push, to his own in greeting? The tenderness of her lips' first pressure devastated him, he had experienced none for so long. Could he trust the sense the gesture seemed to make? Truth was, he was such a fool for love it hardly mattered.

"Good to see you too," he managed to say. Peripherally he noticed Coyle's goggling appreciation of Sybil from the business side of the bar and watched his social stock soaring here at the close of the trading day. "Is it still cognac?" Jones asked Sybil with, he thought, a certain degree of smoothness and cool, and followed with, "I'm afraid Rémy Martin's the best the joint can offer."

Johnny Coyle poured her an ample measure and waited to be introduced. The obligatory speeches gave Jones a moment in which to collect the remnants of himself. Was it possible that Sybil was willing to give him another tumble? In the early days of their, call it that, love, there had been so little trouble and so much hmmmm. It had been remarkable.

Had what he felt for Sybil been only a heartfelt tribute to her body's warm amplitude or the depth of welcome it had once accorded him, Jones could have called his feelings by a simpler name. It had been a long time, actually it had been forever, since a woman of such beauty and intelligence had directed her tenderness and passion upon him. It was the woman suggested behind the clear grey eyes into which Jones had fallen so deeply, for Jones at least, that had made the kind of lovemaking they had done possible. Sexually they had sometimes reached unprecedented heights together, if speech could be trusted on the subject. Certainly it had been fine. What had puzzled him, even amid the interglow of their mixed auroras, had been the inexplicably high regard in which she seemed to hold him, as if there were some substantial trace left behind in him of the man he might have been.

It had taken awhile for normal life and its routine denials to intervene, and her eyes to clear of the last veils of romantic haze. *Do* something, *be* something, she then entreated him, with what had seemed an uncharacteristic hysteria of emphasis, a command flung against the annihilating weight of experience as he had known it theretofore. Make something of yourself in the world and I'll stay with you, she had said, expressing an inexplicable commitment to him but also an explicit intolerance of nonentity and failure, Jones' longtime traditional domain. In this culture a man expresses his masculinity by hunting and gathering *money*. Only do it, Jones, and I could be yours for a long time, who knows, maybe for life, think about it. . . . Don't you know *anything* about adaptation? Oh why are men such fixbrained idiots all of you?

Beats me, Jones had told her. Beats me every time.

Sybil's proposal had inspired him, of course, but he had not known what to do about it. In this worldly regard Jones had never quite known what to do. To such entreaties Jones could only respond as he had to the material demands of the world in general all his life, that is, like a man who had just been thwocked between the eyes by a tennis ball, served hard. The ball was in his court, apparently, but it was not a game Jones knew how to play. Standing there on the asphalt, he had all the practical smarts of a jacklighted deer. That stare. Oh look. The pretty lights. Whammo.

"What could you possibly want with me? What do you see in me?" Jones had asked her honestly.

"Don't be an idiot," she had replied with a throatiness he had not thought her voice possessed, and then she had gathered him to her. He loved the feel of her body, less skeletal than those currently in fashion; womanly, rounded, and blushed by a softness that was a sign of mercy in this world. He remembered their first kiss, which, like their current inconsequential conversation, had taken place in a transit between barstools. She had come off her stool and walked into him with her mouth open, and Oh Jesus he had said around his tongue at the energy vibrating with fine intensity between their lips, even as she sucked his tongue almost off its root.

Not long after the Bear's disappearance and Jones' obvious inability to return the volley or dodge the Buick, Sybil was gone. Jones had not been entirely surprised, although in the immediate afterquakes of the Bear's arrest Sybil's departure had registered with nearly negligible intensity on the Jonesian Richter, a bit of routine dustfall amid the larger shaking of the foundations of his life. In the interim, however, his doubled loneliness had beaten against him with a fury whose edge was sharpened by the removal of everything Sybil's contentious love had seemed to promise. Who did he miss more? On an essential level the Bear, but that was at least partly in response to all the time invested and experience involved, while Sybil was the image of every fulfillment he had ever felt his life deny him. The accusation of her absence was definitive in your basic, garden-variety *mene mene tekel upharsin* kind of way.

"Well actually," Jones told Sybil now, "not a hell of a lot. You?"

"I've been busy," Sybil said.

"I bet you have."

"Work. Paperwork. Office hours." Sybil sighed routinely. "Another failed love affair."

"You fall in love with another Cary Grant?"

"Please don't be merciless," she asked him, as if that were a possibility, and the grey irises of her large eyes seemed momentarily to kaleidoscope and retract.

"You didn't."

"I did." Her eyes recomposed themselves into their original clarity and she rearranged her weight on the barstool as if to readjust her center of gravity.

"And he was a shit," Jones pressed on, "like all the last times."

Sybil nodded a slightly melodramatic yes.

"You know," Jones mused aloud, "it's funny. I mean, to me you're the very image of someone who's got normal life worked out."

"I mostly am."

"But there are some unresolved areas in there behind those intelligent eyes, huh."

"A few," Sybil allowed, and took refuge in a sip of brandy. "Look, Jones, it's pretty cold out there, and a feeling heart is hard to find."

"Well, there's me."

"There's you." She extended an arm as straight as a girder and laid the hand at the end of it atop Jones' shoulder.

The Bear was right, Jones decided. People were funny. "And you'd like a taste of refuge," Jones suggested.

"You know," she said, "that wouldn't be such a bad idea."

This was pretty good, thought Jones, but he remained on his guard. There was an odd clumsiness to Sybil, and sometimes, just when intimacy seemed to have been achieved, she could say the most unguarded, wounding things and not even notice. "Okay," he said. "But I love you a lot and I'm very vulnerable to you. So try to go easy on me."

She nodded yes, then they both breathed out.

"You want a little something to eat?" he asked.

"I wouldn't say no to an oyster."

"They're highly aphrodisiac. Want to split a couple dozen?" He felt his face break open in an easy grin.

"Absolutely," Sybil said.

I'm in, he told himself, amazed. Politely, medectophobically, he crossed his legs. "*Holá* Vergíl," he called out. The short dark Dominican, installed up front between the griddle, the clam tubs and the street window, raised his head in reply. *Domini canes*: the hounds of God. Spooker. Very funny. "A string of pearls if you please," Jones announced. "Twelve of them."

"*Sí señor*," Vergíl called back, and bent about his business.

"The *señor* must be in your honor," Jones told Sybil. "Usually he just calls me *maricón*."

"How charming."

"He calls everyone *maricón*."

"Does he call Johnny Coyle *maricón*?" She nodded her chin at the bartender, who was pouring a short row of boilermakers for three dockworker types who had just come in.

"He does not."

"Well."

Vergíl showed up with the fresh dozen, which he had thoughtfully arrayed on a white porcelain plate rather than the statutory paper item. He had come up on the customer side of the bar, and as he laid down the pair of napkins and oyster forks, placed the bottle of hot sauce and withdrew, his glance slid over Sybil with insulting directness and an accompanying grin.

Jones and Sybil made faces at each other in acknowledgment of this vulgarity, then squeezed lemon wedges and each gulped down an oyster. Jones found himself looking at the butt of his cigarette pack on the bar. LSMFT. Lucky Strike Means Fine Tobacco. Loose Sweaters Mean Flabby Tits. Not her.

"Not bad," Sybil said.

"The place don't look like much on the outside," said Jones, uncomfortably aware that he was putting in a subliminal plea for himself, "but the shellfish here is cherce."

Sybil ingested a second one. "Did you notice the ring Vergíl was wearing?"

"The which?" asked Jones, adding a single drop of hot sauce to his next intended.

"The ring."

"I don't notice such things. Too bad the champagne here's so bad. A glass of decent fizz would go down nicely just now."

"It's the one I gave you," Sybil persisted. "The silver one with the blood opal set in it."

"*What*?" gasped Jones around an inefficient swallow.

"Vergíl is wearing the ring I gave you. Are you two guys going steady or something?"

"I *knew* I misplaced it here," Jones exclaimed, his volume drawing a quick sideglance from Coyle, who was accepting a shot of bar Scotch from the dockworker types. "I knew I took it off down in the basement, put it aside when I had to carry a bunch of cases up, then lost track of it. I asked Vergíl if he'd seen it and he said no."

"I think he might have been lying to you. Take a look."

"I will."

Once off the stool, Jones hiked up his jeans with what might have been a movie-cowboy reflex and moseyed up to the grill emplacement and the square of diminishing twilight beyond it, where colored lights were coming on all over the avenue.

"Nice oysters," he told Vergíl. "Plump ones. This month has an R in it and the moon's just past the full. Are you all set for the night? I'm about ready to leave, but if there's anything you need . . . *Hey*, look at that ring," he said innocently, and reached out to grasp Vergíl's wrist. "I had one just like it."

What Sybil saw down the length of the bar lifted her from her stool: Jones lashing out to seize the little Latino guy's hand, the Latino pulling violently back, Jones tightening his grip and hanging on, then the knife coming up.

It was the big ten-inch chef's knife, and when Jones saw Vergíl pass it twice across his belly, quickly but as if weaving a spell, he let go of the Dominican's wrist and arched his body away from the blade, banging into the side wall of the short-order box. Then something odd happened to Jones' perception. Things slowed down. He stared at the knife like a sparrow caught in a cobra's eye: the thing had hypnotized him. The knife *meant* something but it was like looking at anything basic in your life. In the end you couldn't read it, you couldn't tell what it was saying.

Jones tried edging out of the emplacement in order to find a bit of open floor but the knife followed him, and before he knew what he had done he had grabbed Vergíl's knife hand and was pushing the smaller man back onto the grill. Vergíl's eyes and mouth went wide when he felt the heat behind him, and his knife hand grew more lethal and insistent. Jones understood that if he let go now he was going to find out what it was like to be gutted by a ten-inch chef's knife. The stillness receded, the racket of time resumed, and fear hit him again. Holy shit! How did I get into this?

It was at about this time that he heard Johnny Coyle's voice say, "Hold it. Nobody fucking move."

Jones was relieved to see that both he and Vergíl had obeyed Coyle for the instant, but their bodies remained tensed, their eyes alert, jockeying for an opening, the Dominican's knife hand probing for a weakness in Jones' center of gravity or his stance.

"Two things," Coyle told them. "I got one hand on the thirty-eight revolver here, and the other one's under the bar on the button for the basement door. I don't know which one of you the fucking dog is gonna go for first when I buzz it open, but I do know, Vergíl, that even if you stab me in the fucking belly I'm gonna shoot you in the leg and stick your head in the French fryer until it's fucking done. You understand me? Put the knife down. You've got five and I do it."

Jones could see all the moment's wonderful potential: the knife stuck in his gut or Coyle's, Vergíl's head bubbling in the fryer's ancient oil while a bleeding Coyle held it down with his last strength, and Spooker, whose image filmically interflicked with the Bear's in Jones' very busy mind, rushing upstairs to tear his balls off—look Spooks, no apron!—or rip the tonsils out of one of those three dockworker types who had stepped away from the bar in a frieze of shock or savvy. Maybe, the moment was so wonderfully pregnant with possibility, the dog would go for Sybil—where was she? Jones could feel her presence in the room but she escaped his sight. This was when the Bear ought to stroll in the front door saying casually Hi, how you been, man? Lord knows the Bear had bailed Jones out of even more perforated boats than this one. But of course the Bear wasn't there. Though wait a minute, this was the real thing: suddenly he knew for a certainty that this knife business has something to do with, was directly connected to, the Bear. Huh! Trouble was, he didn't exactly have the time in which to piece out how and why.

Vergíl was still pushing the knife at him. The little bastard wasn't letting up.

Johnny Coyle banged the butt of the snubnose revolver on the bartop. "*Comprende*?" Coyle's voice insisted with climactic severity. "*Comprende*, motherfucker?"

"What a nice job you have," Sybil said once they were strolling on the avenue arm in arm.

"Hey, I got the ring back, didn't I?" Jones raised the ring in a handy access of streetlight and noted that in its absence from his hand the stone had acquired here and there another mottled droplet of red. His hands had stopped shaking about five minutes ago.

"Yes, and you did it with such aplomb. You could have a record company job, you know. The pay is better and it's a bit safer."

It was true. In the simultaneous days of their first involvement and the

Bear's repeated debuts, Jones had proved himself organized and adept at publicity and general tactics. He had handled business negotiations with the allegedly real world and had composed himself into an interface with the Bear's at least slightly paranoid sense of it to find his abilities already in place, his engines gassed up and throbbing—as long as he was doing it for the Bear. He had impressed a few significant people, but try to parlay the situation into something for himself apart and the usual hams were strung and crucial tendons severed. In the aftermath of the Bear's arrest his inability to cope with the wilderness of grotesque formalities—composed in equal parts of police, court attendants, prison-system bureaucrats, music journalists and a widespread blanket of denial that anything had happened to anyone at all—had been nearly complete. Jones had been something like the sole surviving votary of a vanished sect, bereft of everything occult and bearshaped that had been of use and sense to him. He knew that it was this spherical ineptitude that eventually had sent Sybil packing. She had needed to see some progress, and circumstances had found him fresh out of the stuff. Could he do something with himself now? Sybil was obviously dangling the sex-scented lure, and he had a whole host of good reasons for going for it, wide-mouthed with beating gills. Why not make something of his life now that he was on his own? It was a good question, but he could feel all his old internal complications swarming up a way for the answer to come out No. Fact was, he still felt linked to the Bear by chains he could not see but which had absorbed all his sense of faith and service. What a contraption, this self he'd wound up having to live with. It was his own construction, of course. He wished he knew the way out, but no one had thought to mark the exits. Fire, he thought. It was not a very crowded theater.

They dined at a chi-chi but not too pricey pasta place. Jones ordered clams stigmata and the moose-and-squirrel combination plate but Sybil didn't get the joke.

When the leavings of their meal had been cleared away and they lingered over coffee, Sybil laid out the proofs of the cover art. It was not bad—a blue-filtered photo of the Bear, his face compressed with the intensity of playing and the saxophone gleaming bluely; a slanted, artful insertion of white block letters above his head for the title—but Jones didn't know if it would look like much when reduced to CD size. "It'll do," he told Sybil. "I only wish the album didn't end the way it does."

At the end of the long ballad, during which the Bear's saxophone tone had grown now explicably more bitter, came a short blues, then the interruption of toppling tables, the cop's announcement, breaking glass. They had decided to fade it after the pistol shot.

"I think it sounds pretty dramatic as is." Sybil shrugged, and took a sip.

"That wasn't what I meant."

"Would you like another coffee or do you want to take a stroll over to my place, come up for a sip of something," her eyes dipped, "especially nice I know you like."

"You're pretty frank," said Jones.

"You're pretty too, Dean," Sybil parried.

So that he found himself, a short walk after this truncated cadence of espresso, sitting with Sybil in her living room as she smoked a joint to loosen up. Jones only took the odd toke. It was nice to know they were going to make it, but it hurt him that Sybil needed loosening. By the time she stopped dodging his caresses she had something of a doper's laugh going, and Jones had always been a fairly serious lover. When, finally, he was sprawled hungrily over Sybil's rounded and welcoming naked form in bed, O Sybil, he thought, looking down at her in the dusky light: the warm ship that sails beneath me in the night.

Her eyes brimmed with happy light and her ripe breasts were raised to him. This did not seem like a strategy or a ploy, did not seem some sneaky way of getting him to play along with the big economic plan, record company job and then maybe a couple kids, though of course it was not a bad idea. It seemed like she really dug him. It seemed to be for real. He remembered how it had been between them before. It had been just fine for them both. It wasn't bad right now.

He sucked at the big sweet buds of her breasts until he was sated and she seemed sufficiently lost in preliminary bliss, then lowered his mouth to the joint between her legs, already running with sap, and licked along the length of her opening. She had always been a sweet-tasting woman. Jones anticipated her returning the favor and then the final sweet conjunction, the Big Hello, the two-backed animule feeling good and wagging its tails for the sheer pleasure of the activity. He swallowed down some of her loxy, viscous flow and before applying himself seriously to the nub of the matter let out a low spontaneous growl, louder than he had thought to make it and surprisingly deep. Deep enough to almost sound like—

He heard a low stifled laugh burst from above him in response. Not the tone he had been anticipating, if there was to be a laugh, at this juncture. Damn grass. Doper's laugh. He paused a moment until she stopped, but as his tongue entered her more deeply the laugh came again and convulsed her unwilling belly and finally she twisted her hips away from him and lay laughing on her side.

"What," he said.

"Your brother," she managed to say before disappearing into fresh gasps of laughter and tucking her legs up to her stomach, showing him only her hind parts.

Even though he knew that women would always remain a mystery to him, Jones was a patient man. He waited for her to subside before asking, "What about my brother." Brother? He felt a hot flush pass with angry anticipation over him from top to toe.

Sybil fought for control of herself and lost. "Your brother," she said.

"What."

"Your brother is an hairy man. And you are an smooth man." Having concluded, she lost herself to laughter completely.

Jones knew this particular riff, the Bible via a hip old comedy record from the sixties he and Sybil had listened to once. He deflated, subsiding sideways onto an elbow and a crook of arm to support his learning head until she was ready for conversation. He looked her in the eye, and with all the subtlety of the pie-in-the-face of farce she rolled, still laughing, off the side of the bed and landed heavily on the floor. Jones watched her curved back and rounded ass disappear with a too-savvy sense of loss. He waited until what rose from the unseen floor beside the bed was the relative silence of recuperating breath. In the meantime he scanned the tasteful shaded lithographs on her bedroom wall, admired the rich reds and blues of a kilim flung with calculated carelessness across the back of a chair. Sybil had such good taste.

"Sweetie," he inquired finally, "what exactly do you mean."

The unseen Sybil conquered her gusts of breath, and there was a factual blankness in her voice when at length she replied, "I mean, you always knew, didn't you."

"What did I always know," Jones asked her, already clocking in depressing detail the previously unsuspected answer. What a sap I am not to have seen it.

"Can I come back up there?" Sybil asked.

"Make yourself at home," he suggested.

When Sybil climbed back onto the plateau of her bed she had compressed herself into a semblance of her business self. When she noticed him goggling at her breasts, so warm and globey, as if at paradise lost, she extracted a hissing white sheet from her heavier bedding and gathered it to her body. For punctuation she cleared her throat.

Here we go, thought Jones.

"You knew it was always him," she said.

"No, but I should have figured."

"The first time I sat down in the booth with him—remember?—I went weak in the legs. Dear Jesus I just about spilled my cup. But the actual prospect, good Lord, of *doing* it with him—are you kidding?—was too terrifying to contemplate seriously."

"So you transferred the feeling over to me. The proxy. Did you ever imagine him when you were doing it with me? You did, didn't you. Aw shit, you did."

"Jones," she said, her lovely grey eyes going marginally wider—he noticed that, a lawyer, she had mastered the movie-actor trick of not blinking as she made an important speech—"it may have started that way, but as things developed, as I got to know you, to see who you really are . . ."

"That's a movie line," he told her. "Spy stuff. Drop it." There were conflicting waves of heat and energy passing through his body, and, trying its best not to acknowledge the violence of this riptide, his mind was managing not to peer too deeply into the waters. But impact, thank you very much, had been achieved. Yet there was one more thing he wanted to know. "You were imagining him this time too," he asked Sybil, "weren't you. And that was why . . ."

The beautifully mottled grey irises of her eyes were large and startled but she did not blink.

"I think I have to get out of here," he said.

"Jones," came her voice—in which despite his turmoil he could detect a note or two of sincere music—from a deepening distance, and there was a lovely arm reaching out toward him somewhere in the picture, but Jones was pulling his pants on and checking the pockets, Jones was looking for his socks and thinking about his shirt, his shoes, and about making the transit to the door of her apartment without suffering a second, possibly lethal, wound. He was getting his shirt on without awkwardness or a hitch and keeping his eyes on the carpet and the intricate figures that composed it. In short, thank you very much, his exit was going reasonably well under the circumstances.

He got out of the bedroom without looking her in the eye and across her living room without incident, sweeping up his old suede jacket from where he'd left it on the back of the sofa, but as he fumbled with what were certainly too many knobs and levers and chains festooning her entrance door he was aware of a rustling sound pursuing him from across the apartment and looked up to see grey-eyed Sybil Bailey, wrapped in a white sheet like Athena, advancing upon him with a face full of intelligence and concern.

"I'm not walking out on you forever," he told her, thinking coward, coward, *worm*, "it's just that I really didn't see this coming, silly as that may sound, and I have to walk away from it for awhile. Okay? I'll be in touch."

"Jones?" That arm reached out to him again. "Don't go out there. Sit down on the sofa. I'll make you a drink. I won't bother you. Sit down with it for as long as you want and then we can talk."

"I can't. I really can't. You talk too well and you know how lousy I am in an argument. Maybe I'll be back in half an hour. Keep the home front burning. I need a breath of air. I'll come back in half an hour or phone to say I can't. Okay? How the fuck do you open this lock?"

She had to do it for him.

Going down the squared-off helix of her stairway he felt the weight coming down on him and shrugged it off, wanting to do about ten minutes of nightwalk and get some streetscenes in his eyes before he had to deal with it in detail. At that hour, West Houston Street was ideal, three lanes of asphalt bare in both directions except for windblown bits of scrap, Walk and Dont Walk blinking at him, a car alarm getting all worked up about a block and a half off. Over toward Sixth warning lights blinked around a Con Ed excavation—Dig We Must—from whose pit rose a banded-orange-and-white smokestack pouring steam into the air: another boatload of souls Charoning off to the boroughs of Lethe.

Jones turned to walk north along MacDougal, and after a silent townhouse block with the sober facades of the funeral place, the Mafia restaurant and Dylan's old house came the trashy block of falafel trinket shops and beyond them the Empire State Building rising phallic against a scud of moonlit cumuli. But it was a sidebar joke and the wrong signifier. Because what was hitting Jones now was not the mirage of some sexual insufficiency but hollow illusion at the core of every self he had ever tried or imagined himself to be: there was not a person there, there was lack of being, an ache, there was nothing, or nothing much. He would never add up to a self on his own in this world, would never become a sum sufficient to spell out Man. Though three letters ought to be easy enough. The Bear's sidekick at his very best, therefore no one really, and in the end of course he had failed the Bear at that.

Good Lord, did rejection from a woman really mean all that? It hardly seemed possible.

He had progressed another block and the prospect had altered.

Hey, look at New York City. Big dark brick walls, ranks of high blank windows, dully silvered clouds passing sideways across the black; up there the lit and looming thrust of Empire, and down here an infinity of self-loathing, no end of opportunity for failed promise and thwarted desire.

What was the worth of any human life: that was the question.

From this perspective the prospects did not look good.

Jones had reached Washington Square Park, whose trees were waving bare and pleading in the wind. What the hell, if it looks cool let's cut through the park. As he scanned the park's segmented expanses for troublemakers, found none, and walked up the path between the trees, on whose branches early black buds had begun to form, he noted the new contents of his emotive self.

How could I have been such a doormat all my life! How could I have been such a schmuck! It was the *Bear* that robbed me of my life, he heard himself thinking with unexpected speed and vehemence. The *Bear* took over and there was nothing left for me. He stole my birthright. Jones thought of Sybil spread beneath him in her bed, then pivoting away. Usurper. Even though his heart began to burn more bitterly than he would have believed possible, he was able to hear a voice in him protesting: Help, I don't want to think this. But hatred for the Bear flooded him, and it was as if all the rooms they had lived in together over the years were turning themselves inside out and reversing their meanings. I might have *been* somebody, Jones told himself, but the Bear took over as if it was the most natural thing in the world and I became nothing but a sidekick and all I might have been just dried up and blew away like leaves, like rind, like that scrap of newsprint on that patch of stunted city grass. *He* was a special case. *I* of course was nothing. I let myself be robbed! When you come right down to it, I hate him, I hate Sybil, I hate every brick of which this city that has denied me over the years is built, and I am walking beneath the dark and stars of a useless fucking sky.

What about *me*!

Stop this, he tried to tell himself. It's the worst. I have never felt so soiled by thoughts. This is the nadir, the lowest of the low. Help.

How to be human, how to be human, I don't know how it's done.

What is a man anyway?

This is bad. Maybe I better get out of the park.

He had emerged from between the trees and reached the center: the plaza, the wide parched fountain in its middle, and at the top the triumphal arch that stood lit against the receding wallscape of Fifth Avenue like a monumental pair of pants. Jones decided to leave the park beneath the arch and cut east toward home on Eighth Street. He lit a quick cigarette against the wind, listening to his lighterflame in his cupped hands, and blew out smoke before he heard the voice behind him and saw three forms detach themselves from the wrought-iron tracery of a bench backed up to a length of rail.

"Got some smoke for me?" one of these forms asked him from beneath a shock of white-blond hair. Jones looked at the pale raw face and thought, Here we go.

"Sure," he said, and started walking. "Have a Lucky. They're toasted."

"Toasted?"

"Says so on the pack. Take it. Read. Improve yourself." He tossed them the pack of Luckies, hunched his shoulders to buffer himself and increased his pace toward the arch and safety, but they got in front of him. Ah youth, he thought, and the legs it walks on.

The three were lean and angular and what he could see of their faces seemed ravaged, raw. "Hey we need a light for these," one of them said, tossing the pack casually up and down in one hand.

"Right," Jones said, realized that giving them the pack had been too legible a sign of weakness, and dug for his trusty Zippo in his jeans. The amazing thing was that he had lived in New York for so long without getting mugged. And here he was, going through a change of life at this late date. His heart knocked hard and fast on the moment's breastbone door. Listen to it. Thump thump thump. What exaggeration.

"Hey thanks," and one of them closed his fist around the lighter and took it from him. "Got any cash?"

"Ah yes, I was wondering when you—"

"I said *money*," and this time the voice was hard: a typical hunter-gatherer, perhaps. He saw their three heads pivot through three circuits, clocking the park for possible cops. Jones didn't see any either.

"A few bucks," he allowed. "T-twenty, twenty five." A stammer. How pat.

"Let's see 'em," and for the second time that evening, as if someone was trying to tell him something, a knife appeared before him. This one was a stiletto, the blade six inches long and chromed. This one didn't mean anything to him beyond the perfectly obvious, but he was staring at it anyway.

"Hey, you got the ticket right there," he told the kids, and pointing his jaw at the knife he managed a little laugh. "Just let me get your wallet out. My wallet I mean."

They snickered at him. "Yours, mine, what the fuck's the diff you schmuck, let's have it."

Jones took the wallet out and held it in his hand.

It would never be clear to Jones if the kid had stabbed him outright or if he himself had walked onto the blade, but he knew it when the knife went in above his navel for its full length. He felt a powerful sledgehammer impact that expanded spherically within him like a bruise in a nightmare, the sharpness of the blade concealed in the depths of its blur. Jones, his mouth gawped open in shock, registered some preparatory tension in the knifer's arm and begged, "Please don't rip me."

The kid's arm tension clutched. Jones saw the hatchet face, knew for a certainty the kid had meant to cut a circle through his guts to kill him but that now he was thinking twice about it.

"What the fuck," said the kid, shoved the knife in deeper, hard, then pushed again to urge Jones off the blade. Jones obediently fell back onto the pavingstones on his ass, holding his middle, tipping sideways, his head coming down, finally hitting cool city pavement, there.

After he heard their footsteps recede, Jones, thinking it either unwise or improbable to rise, began to crawl. If he didn't reach the perimeter of the park, where someone might find him, he knew with unpanicked clarity that he was going to die. Which in many respects didn't seem an entirely bad idea, but this night came at a moment in which a number of chords hung unresolved in unspecifiable keys and in the end it didn't seem like an ideal time in which to close up shop. His left hand clutched to his punctured gut and reaching forward with his right he advanced, on the second pull noticing a sharpened edge of damage at his core, no help for it, and kept his eyes fixed on the bits of glitter worked into the concrete across which he too slowly and painfully progressed. He noticed that his concentration on the visual texture of the pavement was heightened, his mindfulness unnaturally refined. Above him, he knew, the branches of the trees reaching up to the insufficient moon also felt a curve of mortal sympathy for him. Love of life, look at it working, look at it crawling for all it's worth despite pain and loss of love, he meant loss of blood, no, probably he meant love—we're familiar with it, we don't have a conflict with it here. Thank you. No applause please. It's not a very crowded theater. A tide of blackness was rising and if it took his head it would knock him out and that would be the end.

I don't think I'm gonna make it, thought Jones. Too far to go, and not enough me.

But just then the pain ceased to affect him seriously and he began to experience an entirely unexpected kind of relief.

The odd thing was how the bits of glitter impregnated in the floorstones mirrored the glints up there in the sky, stars they called them. These stars were getting closer. The really odd thing—that hurts!—was how more clearly legible the signs were from here. The Walk, the Dont Walk, the Fifth, the Lion, the Archer, finally of course the Scales, in which he was getting lighter and lighter all the time. The sympathetic arms of the trees moved him, and the friendly grid of the buildings composed an affectionate formal tribute to what had always been the elevated and compassionate disposition of his heart. From up here, where he did not even need to climb, in the ease of his ascent, the lit ladder of Manhattan between its rivers, the text was so clear to read it amazed him how he had missed the point of it walking the maze down there so many years. Then of course there were the constellations, among which he was quickly drawn into the orbit of the Twins—Jaycub and Heehaw, Lucky and Stricken, Castoff and Pollinator, Omelet and Baloneyus, but no, he said to that: no no no. He was tired of dyads and of dya . . . dyadl . . . say it again . . .

dadl . . . one more time . . . dyadaladaladality—there!—for the simple reason that he was looking for his *friend.* Thank you thank you but what I'm looking for is an Ursa, is an Ursa something, is an Eartha something, a Birtha someone, is an Eartha Kiss, no no no, sorry, my mistake, it's not any of that.

"Sybil?" he gasped aloud, his breath to the pavement. "Bear?"

And protesting the dualistic insufficiencies presented him amid the varied lights, he passed upward—mortal life beneath him now a slip of the tongue, a wisp of the will, a mere declension of the celestial noon, no, nume, no, noun, so *this* was the stuff the Bear always usedta go on about—through the heaven of the fixed stars, where he found sketched out in lights before him the astrological signs he had always most admired: the Saxophone, the Beerbottle, the Shabby Apartment, the Eviction Notice, the Deposit, and yes the Return, and finally—Jones knew the way by the big geometric tracery of light the Bear had always told him was the mnemonic of his eternal self outside the cramps and keeps of time—it seemed to him in some strange way that he had found his friend.

There you are! Hey dig it, Bear! We're together again, dead or alive on this side or that of the Great Divide! Can't tell you how much I missed you, man. Never mind all that silly shit I said down there. Hey baby we're *home.* It don't bother me a bit. We finally made it! Look where we are! This is the big time! Look at that beautiful swarm of light coming to gather us home! Look at the size, look at the inconceivable beauty of the thing! Look at the love that's coming to meet me. I'm bursting with it. I'm ready, I'm ripe. Oh look at that wonderful, look at that beautiful extended arm!

Jones began to weep at the beauty of it and at the welcome it accorded him.

He beheld, above the smoldering LSMFT of the lower worlds and the ROYGBIV of the visible spectrum, the floodlit archway of PRNDL signifying the available range of suprasensible illumination—as every initiate understood, the letters stood for Purple, Rurple, Nurple, Durple, Lurple, Flurple and Twurple—but why, amid so much that was radiantly unific, why be so damned enumerative, eh? Eh? Can you tell me that? He saw the light change to green, he wanted to put the petal to the medal and go go Go. The Bearmobile rides again! So why was the Bear holding him back? Jones had always been the slow one, and he was flying free. So what was the problem now? This was the last straw and it was breaking the back of his pack of Camels. You want one? What do you mean you need a light? In the middle of this? Man, you've got to be kidding.

No, Bear, I don't want to go down there to that nightclub. I don't care who the fuck is playing.

What I want to do is flee, I mean fly, I mean look at how much sky we got to play in and I don't have to cramp back into that uncomfortable contorted identity no more. He who made the Bear made me! And, what's more amazing, He smiled His work to see! You're no better or bigger than I am, so don't bother me, what I am right now is home. The doorstep anyhow.

As the stars threw down their spears, Jones saw himself sketched out in a tracery of lights against the dome of after midnight blue. He saw the face he'd had before he was born, and tears poured down it in relief.

Jones was first surprised, then reassured to find himself where he had always been—if he had ever been away, it had been for the blinking of an eye—a soul in a green wood where others like him, for the moment unseen, meditated the resolved puzzle of their being in the dappled light, aided by the trickle of a stream that ran through the middle of the garden. Mottlings of shade provided cognitive assistance, just a hint of shading and divagation. Reclaimed by the garden. Which I have never left. So this is the obverse face of time's coin, and all eternity to spend it in. Yes. He said yes to it.

The light entered him like honey, and if he had had arms he would have raised them and said Aah.

Look at the size of what's coming to gather me home and help me make my last landfall on the shores of light. What a party. For me? No, let me say it, you're too, too kind.

But what I really want, thank you very much, is to lay my head down on this comforting stone. And they say the son of man has no place to rest his head. What an idea. What a thought. All is provided. Soup Burg.

What I'd like is just a little bit, it feels so sweet, of sleep.

Give me five minutes. Give me a break. I'll get right back to you. And hey there, stop that pulling on my arm.

Jones laid down his head and began to die.

A young Japanese couple found him a few minutes after he had reached the floodlit cobblestones underneath the arch. Tourists. He stood over the body while she went running for the phone. They both had cameras, thank you very much, but neither of them thought to take a picture.

Of the body pulled fetal. Of the kidney-shaped puddle of blood almost black as it spread across the stone, tilted a piece of cellophane, bore up bits of dust and city soot.

Of that gaunt and strained and expressive face lying on its side, biting at the air.

2

the Bear's gums had begun to bleed again. "Tim," he said. "Come on, man, you got to get me another fish. I can't live on hot dogs, powdered potatoes, chipped beef on toast, side of succotash and canned string beans so limp they couldn't fuck a bowl of oatmeal. Look at this." The Bear hooked a claw under his upper lip and lifted. "Look."

"You're bleeding a little. What a drag." Tim, a heavyset guy in a rumpled blue uniform but a scrupulously trimmed beard, nodded his slow yes and peered between the bars at the Bear. Baggy face, friendly eyes, maybe forty years old but no grey yet, didn't really look like a jailer. Tired shoulders and a flop of gut. Talked in hipster argot like a musician or even Jones, but his words were tugged down by a sad sagging cadence, a weariness, a familiarity with loss. Said he was Greek but looked and sounded American to the Bear. Badge and shoulderpatch said Department of Corrections, which the Bear found pretty funny under the circumstances. Correct me if I'm wrong. Oh we will, we will.

"Tim, I'm gonna lose a tooth. You want an amulet for your wife, is that it? Shopping around for a totem?"

"Not at that price, Bear."

"So?"

"Tomorrow."

"Tomorrow what."

"Tomorrow a fish."

"If possible a whole fish, not a filet."

"Sure thing, Pierre," said Tim in his slow big lazy voice.

"Not because it's larger but because I have to eat it raw and the whole fish has a better chance of being fresh and free of parasites."

"Hey, the world is full of parasites, man."

"I am not," the Bear said wearily, "a man. Bring me a bag of apples in case I can't eat the fish. Apples are cheap. I'll pay you back someday if you let me out of here." He attempted a smile.

"Like to letcha go but I can't," shrugged Tim. "Way of the world. How it is."

"No, Tim, it's you and your lack of guts mostly."

"People like me make the world go round."

"I know it."

"You probly think I don't know about all that cool, creative, souly-soul sensitive shit, but you're wrong. It's just that I understand the working-stiff model of reality too. We all got our parts to play. No one out there to maintain the form you'll get all the pretty lights but before you know it the whole thing loses track of its orbit and what generally ensues is chaos and disaster."

"All I do is play a horn, Tim. Toot toot toot. Dangerous shit. Suppress the dormouse. I agree with you entirely. I couldn't agree with you more than I already do. I agree with you in such a way that I couldn't agree with you any more entirely than I already entirely do. I hope I make myself clear."

"Yeah, musicians make such good legislators. Your average working stiff is tied into the big picture a lot better than you imagine. Trust to the day-to-day. Render unto Caesar. Miracle will take care of itself. That's how I know you're gonna be okay, see? Miracle will take care of itself."

The Bear regarded Tim's attempt at a beatific grin and lapsed heavily backward onto the iron cot. The already overstressed springs and bands screeked in protest, then sank another increment lower toward agony and collapse. The Bear closed his eyes. "Tim," he said. "When you're right you're right. What can I tell you. You're a luminous being."

"Tell you a story," said Tim.

"Goody," said the Bear.

"When I started working for the city I was with Health before I came over to Corrections. What I did basically was they had me drive the wagon for the Brooklyn morgue. I was only doing pickups, man, no ambulance facilities in the truck, couple of stretcher racks, a supply of body bags and just the one assistant. So one day after I'd been on the job a couple years I got a call to pick up one deceased indigent female in a clapboard tenement district down near the waterfront, and when I got there all kinds of shit was going on, there was a crowd on hand, and the attending physician, this young inexperienced guy, came out all embarrassed. It seemed the woman'd been dead for about an hour, then come back to life. I went in there past the doctor and there on the bed was this little old lady with young-looking skin and nice white hair and she was lying on her back talking nonstop about food, man, about different kinds of food in this faraway singsong voice: I'm gonna buy some cantaloupes and some watermelons, some cantaloupes and apples and plums, some cantaloupes and peaches and plums and some sweet sweet melons and some tunafish and some cool clear water . . . and What the fuck is this? I asked the doctor. I could have you up on disciplinary charges I told him, calling me out here and you don't know the difference between a living woman and a dead one, and we fought about it some and he swore up and down she'd been solid dead for at least an hour and he asked if maybe I could break for lunch—he would buy, okay?—so we did, and when my assistant and

I finished our roast beef sandwiches and orange sodas we came back and the lady was dead, and we took her body away in the truck and put it on ice back at the morgue and we were done."

The Bear looked up at Tim from where he lay, expecting to hear more, but it seemed that Tim had finished. "Tim, I'll have to work at this," said the Bear. "Let me guess. This is your story about how miracle takes care of itself?"

"Yeah," said Tim, as if that should have been a lot more obvious than the Bear was making out.

"What an inspiring story," said the Bear. "I've been underestimating you all this time. You're not just any run-of-the-mill luminous being. You light the world. You light up my life. In fact I'm burning up in here because your light is too much for my poor capacity for witness. Your knowledge is not my knowledge. Your ways are not my ways."

"Aw, gimme a break."

"The scales are in your hand. The eye with which you see God is the eye with which God sees you. It makes wonderful sense to me now." The Bear shut his eyes.

"Bear?" he heard Tim's voice ask him. "You okay?"

"I'm plum apple fucking candy peachy, what you think? Just bring me a fish tomorrow and spare me all the impotent concern." No doubt about it, the Bear was getting mean. Testy at the very least. Why, in the old days he would bend over backward—no easy trick for someone of his anatomy and nothing, to his knowledge, that any of his circus ancestors had been tormented into doing in the spotlight—to avoid bruising the delicate sensibilities of another, who knows, holy subjectivity; but captivity, although it had its compensations, like privacy and time to think, had coarsened him more than somewhat, in this regard. "Tim?"

"Still here."

"Sorry."

"Noted."

"Thanks. Tomorrow a fish and half a loaf?"

"Do what you can with it."

"Who could ask for anything more? Rhythm I always had."

"Look, I gotta go," Tim told him with some wist clinging to his voice. "Sorry but I gotta go."

"See you tomorrow. In fact I'm incredibly grateful for whatever measure of kindness you can manage. You're an angel. I'm just very, very tired." Which was one way of putting it.

"Okay. Bye."

"Arrrh," said Tim, and retreated down the corridor tearing obscurely at the front of his uniform jacket, chest high.

"Hmph," the Bear snorted after him, "some hipster you turned out to be." The Bear was happy to have sent him packing in at least some degree of moral anguish.

When Tim had gone, the Bear thoughtfully sucked salt pungent blood from his gums and swallowed it down, trying to assess its current mineral content. He pushed his heavy tongue against each of his major teeth in turn. Right incisor, he decided, was the loosest, but the root runs deep so I'm probly safe awhile. With a shudder, he remembered meeting this friend of Jones' who'd been jailed on a manic jag one time; he had destroyed most of his teeth chewing on the bars of his cell. Awful to think how I'd look without mine. I'd be a sad piece of work all toothless, a target for every specious form of pathetic regard, gumming down porridge, scratching absently at my unemployed testicular dependents. There he is, the one and only Bear. Don't worry folks, those mind-forged manacles are made of mind-forged carbon steel.

He looked at the books stacked on the table in the next cell. He had not been reading much of the good doctor's one-volume complete Shakespeare. What he had gotten into instead was a good cheap prose translation of the *Iliad*, and he hadn't even read much of that.

The Bear's cell sat at the end of a side corridor of some forsaken city lockup: a precinct house perhaps, or some outlying cousin of the Tombs or the Raymond Street Jail. The Bear didn't even know what borough he was in. The facilities seemed to belong to an earlier epoch, the fifties maybe, which argued Brooklyn? Queens? the Bronx? He couldn't tell, though it seemed too quiet out there to be Manhattan. Some backwater of brick and steel. The cell's iron bars were lacquered white but flaking here and there to show earlier yellowed coats and, beneath that, stray small pits of black. Inside his cell the Bear had off-white-painted breezeblock gone yellow, and old chain mounts still hooked inquiringly at him from the rear wall—hang yourself today, sir?—but the hinged flatbed and its chains had been removed and a narrow iron-frame camp cot shoved in, followed a day or two later by a flattened bluetick mattress that was mercifully free of lice. After trying it in a couple of other spots, he stuck the bed against the bars dividing his cell from the one next door. The sheets were mostly lost to sweat and claw by now, and the mattress ticking had begun to give way and the innards to unstuff themselves, but the two brown army blankets were still pretty much intact. They lay indiscriminately rumpled beneath him now.

Bars separated him from the adjacent cell but breezeblock ended the view after that. If he angled himself forward against his left-hand wall and didn't lose his balance to the lidless toilet, he could see a distance down the hall to his right, but there wasn't much to see. Tall barred windows high up the opposite, institutional-green wall revealed only slants of sky through the reinforced glass across from a line of what the Bear estimated to be twelve cells in six walled pairs—assuming consistency from his own premises, a universal subjective constant but always a chancy prospect. The windows—their height suggested a second storey of similar cells, but he had never heard a sound up there—let some blessed daylight in, but little of it ever contacted him directly. As the season advanced, who knew? Anything was possible, within reason.

The concrete details were well enough made, but in his clearer moments the Bear knew it all for the cheapjack flummery he'd had to live with ever since he'd wawled his way into the farce of matter. Lord was he ever weary of it. As far as he was concerned, any actual imprisonment was pure redundancy, unsubtle explicitation, was getting stuck in the rear with a point that had already been made clear some time ago. It was an error of taste for him to be here.

At the hall's unseeable end there was an audibly heavy door that opened and shut to admit or occlude Tim and the Bear's other less sympathetic keepers, and the wandering Doc Friedmann when he was of a mind to set a spell; beyond that door, it seemed to the Bear, was another zone devoted to absence and amnesia, the better for him to be forgotten, and beyond that, perhaps, the full vitality of bureaucratic life went on, thickly populated and on regulation march to the suppositious music played on this part of the planet. Life without syncopation and solos, but there were water coolers out there and people chatting beside them. Typewriters. Coffee machines. Life in all its forms, no matter how thinly made or how hard it got for him personally, he would always love it. Was that his big mistake?

Yes, truth was, he felt a little isolated here.

The Kabbalists were right: where essence is restricted, form becomes explicit and pronounced, all bar and slab, barrier and plane: no curves, no life ticking over but lots of form. As in the subways, so here: Qlipoth: the land of shells, and he was in it.

Almost wistfully he turned his head to the right on his pillow to scan Doc Friedmann's belongings in their modest homey array in the next cell. Friedmann was not a fellow prisoner, nor was he a keeper, anymore. He was, given the joint's restrictive conditions, something like a friend. The management had let Friedmann bring in a small wooden table and a chair. On the table sat an alarm clock that needed winding, an ashtray, a yellow packet of pipecleaners beside which a couple of rudimentary tar-browned pipecleaner animals attempted to stroll and graze despite their deficiencies of form.

The good Herr Friedmann had also left behind a bunch of curling clippings from the *New York Times* and a crooked stack of books. Bible, too much Thomas Mann for the Bear's taste—if it's German make mine Kafka, though this was not really the place in which one wanted to read him—tiny green volumes of Chekhov stories as stilted by Garnett, and various scatterings mostly from the last century, fiction and memoirs, no straight histories as such. The Doc, of course, lent freely, and would bring in things for the Bear on request. When the Bear asked for Shakespeare, though, Friedmann had actually asked if he wanted the Schlegel edition or "the English version." To his credit, Friedmann had quickly slapped himself on the forehead after this *faux pas* and said "Akh" in the approved comic manner. The Bear turned his head left and rolled his eyes back to look at his alto leaning in the corner like a tout. More dead weight. Leaky pads and Rico reed forlorn. Full moon and empty arms. Should I play a little?

Nah. Nap is what's called for. Still the tail end of winter, by what I can tell from the advancing windowlight, and sleep should be my natural talent, though I was never much of a hibernator. Nap and then let's see. Confirmation. Now's the Time. Constellation. Good Night Irene.

The beginning of the Bear's imprisonment had conformed to the melodramatic expectations he had had of it. In the Bud Powell Wing of whatever bunghole they had sent him to, the Bear got hosed down with ammoniated water and zapped with electric prods when he charged the bars of his cell screaming about how they couldn't cage the light—a memorable phrase that had come from some drugged correspondence between his own sense of himself as a cosmic tree reaching up toward fundamental sun and the memory of the lightbulbs he'd seen in the subways of his cubhood when Jones had taken him down into the stations and the tunnels: the yellow bulbs grinding out their sallow light were caged in black bulb-shaped matrices of iron. When he was still small enough to ride the trains without freaking out the populace, Jones used to hold him up, not without difficulty, to the front window of the lead car so that he could see the brown square frames of the tunnel coming at him, the inset lightbulbs, the little keynote points of blue. The best ride was the A train between Fifty-ninth and 125th Street of course, longest stretch in the system, a subterranean jet ride, a vision of time's excitement, a taste of things to come. At the end of certain stations there had been green-lit control rooms with men and women in dun-colored uniforms working boards of intricate red and green lights with silver levers; in his youth and innocence it had seemed to the Bear that they were regulating the movements of all the people up there in the daylit maze of the streets.

Later on, it had been a dream of theirs to work the act on the trains for memory's sake, but not only was it illegal, they had already learned that people could assimilate the Bear outdoors but would go into shock in enclosed spaces. In his maturity, the Bear only took the Coltrane, and sometimes the East St. Louis Toodle-oo.

For a while, though, there had been the Bearmobile, one of the ultimate late-fifties tailfin cars, a three-tone Chrysler New Yorker St. Regis—charcoal-grey roof, cream at midlevel, and beneath the chrome streak a slant of deep Bordeaux—that had a push-button transmission, PRNDL, and went a couple hundred yards to the gallon. But didn't the thing purr! It purred like a dinosaur mated to a boiler factory. And weren't they going to have fun in it! That was in the days of the Bear's relative adolescence, when the two of them, Jones and the Bear, were going to go out there and really fuck the world's head up. Let us go down there and confound their language! Babble babble babble, y'all! Behold, the Unconditioned is upon you! There had also been some talk about buying a motorcycle and a sidecar and riding around the city at night in comic-book costumes, shouting out surrealist slogans and heaving the occasional red balloon full of ink at a major building. Oh yeah, they were gonna knock a few kinks in the local version of reality. They were gonna build a whole new wing on the brick shithouse of the quotidian. Deal with it, Horatio! In any case they had certainly laughed a lot in those days. They had rolled around the floor of the apartment, shrieking and holding on to their ribs—Jones had actually dislocated his rib cage once, but the Bear had been able to perform the adjustment—hilarious with the sense that they held the whole world's liberating and intoxicant secret in the antic cup of their lives.

Well, the Bear had always thought it a sign of small character to cringe at the fooling and excesses of your youth. Let it go, let it be what it was and God bless its pointed little head.

What had happened, mostly, was that the last of Jones' family money ran out and they found out they had to make a living. And they got on with the show, like no business I know. The Bearmobile? After some terminal black cough from beneath its enormous hood, they had taken the plates off and left it abandoned on a sidestreet.

In the early days of his imprisonment there had been bright lights and drugs and electrodes, the loss of all sense of time, and a paranoid's paradise of faces drifting before him in a cloud, leaning individually in at him out of the unclarity, fading, going, gone, then roaring back with indecipherable demands. There had been a terrible period in which some combination of the things they were doing to him scored a direct hit on his capacity for language and thought, and he felt those faculties in him bob and weave, then fall to their knees in the middle of the ring, and his heavy tongue struggling for liberty and speech.

Wwwwwwwwwwwww, he remembered saying repeatedly.

Remembered trying to locate a memory in the appropriate room in the house of himself and finding the room explicitly, exactly gone. And not just memory either. It went the same for specific components of his sense of self and its contents: words, music, love, ideas, friendly faces, identity, the whole medulla, he meant megillah. Sometimes he clung to the sight of Iris as if to a prayer, but most of the time he couldn't even manage that.

Wwwwwwwwwwwww.

So much for the secret and intricate effort of generations that had carried him to this degree of individuation and speech. They were taking him all the way down. He could identify tracts of his root nature going blank. He had a few bracing out-of-body intermezzos—stars and lights and colors, and a little extratemporal relaxation in the lesser garden—but the general sense was that of the slow intent progress of calm and comprehensive horror. As he lost more and more cognitive ability, the rubric of Stalin's face in some way became the mnemonic of what was happening to him. He saw the pitted cheeks, the yellow eyes, the big moustache. In any case one picture, whatever its weight in words, was all he had left to put a name to what was happening to him.

Wwwwwwwwwwwww.

He had managed a decent wisecrack or two on occasion. Table, chair, electrode, labcoat, nice tie you got there, Hermès? See? I can name things fast as Adam, I got opposable thumbs, a good eye for silk—*of course* you're scared shitless! C'n you loosen my neck restraint? As above, so below. Adam's apple. Nylon. Brogan. Knee. Nice break in those trousers there. I'm telling you, God's had it with you guys and he's sending in replacements. Oh shit, here we go again. Wwwwwwwww.

What's your name? had been one of the major questions.

I'm just trying to make my report to the members of the Academy.

What's your name?

Just the Bear, he'd finally said.

Not enough. What is it really?

Kukla.

They rejected it.

Would you believe King Pleasure, he said, and they didn't even zap him for it.

Sackerson, he said once, and saw one old lined face on the perimeter do a take in response, as if it had caught the reference, the famous bear who had been baited outside the walls of the Globe Theater in Shakespeare's day. Sackerson, fierce and bleeding, had held off many packs of dogs before going down for the count. Once, that name had been passed like a talisman among the members of the Bear's worldflung family. Now, for the Bear, this last mention of Sackerson had been no more than a farewell triumph of in-joke wit. It was not a very crowded theater.

Because mostly all he could manage was Wwwwwwwwwwwww.

He didn't know at which point he became aware of disputation in the phantasmal ranks of his attendants, but it must have been going on awhile in his virtual absence. In one of the first modica of clarity he recognized a face from among the earlier apparitions, an old man's face about as gnarled and wrought and lined and carved as an old man's face could be, an ugly face that when first he had seen it he had thought looked like a devil's but which now, as it leaned down to him out of the fog, had come to seem rather pleasantly ugly. "I sink I haf gotten zem to relent awhile," this face had said to him in a remarkably deep voice and a thick German accent. "Vee vill see vat vee can do."

Ich habe genug, the Bear had wanted to say, in preference to Vee haf vays of making you talk, but it came out some variation of Wwwwwwwwww.

"I know." The ugly man patted him on the shoulder and checked the straps on his wrists for signs of chafing. "There is help."

Friedmann.

As the machines receded and the drugs mostly went away, Friedmann came into focus and was a friend, but wouldn't phone Jones for him. Couldn't, he said—too dangerous still—but the man had a cot and a table and a chair dragged into the adjoining cell and would go into it and converse with the Bear from behind the bars. It wasn't long before Friedmann's German accent began to seem less thick to the Bear, and his heavy ugly face a map of the most pleasant country he could afford to live in just now. Being old, the doctor would lie down on his back after a stretch of talk or a lunchtime sandwich, fold his hands across his paunch, and take stertorous afternoon naps, from which the Bear was careful not to disturb him. Then, after awhile, Friedmann spent a night or two sleeping in the next-door cell.

Be careful, the Bear told him, they don't lock the door on you one day.

I know the story, grunted the good doctor, scratching at his skull through stray white wires of hair.

They had both read the story, and fell into long conversations about Chekhov, whom of course they both loved. But one must be careful of loving him sentimentally, they agreed. Although it would not surprise the dead author, he would not like it if you did.

Yes yes, thought the Bear, how civilized this is. But the conversation was almost infinitely fatiguing to him all the same.

Friedmann was mostly retired and wholly a widower. He had outlasted his wife by more years than he wanted to know about, and his two major heart attacks had not succeeded in reuniting them. He commanded a medley of medical disciplines but had specialized professionally as a neurologist and a counselor; he preferred the word to "analyst," certainly preferred it to the invidious "shrink."

It had taken the Bear awhile to shuck off the suspicion that Friedmann had moved in next door as a management shill and that his name was bait, a fake.

"I like to talk vith you. I like you personally and you bring back many childhood dreams und memories."

"Of course," said the Bear.

"The animals. I always vanted to befriend them."

"Sure."

"Zey were—excuse me I still have such trouble with ze dipdthssong—zey were my bruzzers."

"Yes. On the other hand," said the Bear, "and subjective sentimentality apart, the aboriginal population of Hokkaido, having observed that bears hibernate for the winter, decided it would be cool to drag a bear out of his cave and sacrifice it so that Spring would come again that year. They would bind its limbs and cut its throat open with a sharpened stone."

"You vish to express somesing about missology?"

The Bear smiled at the good if unintended pun but let it go. "I wish to suggest that if you do anything the least bit unusual or interesting in this world, people will figure out a way to catch and kill you for it."

"Ah," said Friedmann, and took the indicated pause. "It's a kindness for you to let me stay here," he resumed. "I have so little else to do. Most of my friends und colleagues, *todt*, dead, all of them. *Meine frau ist gestorben*. It is impossible to have an intelligent conversation with my neighbors. Look at my face. How will I die?"

The Bear examined Friedmann's face, its harsh-cut lines, the redness, the weight. "Heart attack," he said. "Maybe a stroke."

"It vill be the heart. I have no especial wish to die soon, but vhen the next one comes I vant one big punch and that I go out like a light."

They paused, paying respect to death and its presence in them both.

"Speaking of being dead," the Bear asked, "what's my situation here now exactly?"

"Vhat I hope has happent is you have fallen down an administrative hole. Lost papers, a forgetful computer. I may have helped vith this a little. The *idyots* didn't know vhat they vanted to do with you ectually. Maybe somevon elsewhere is dichesting data. But I think, and let us hope, that for the most part you haf been forgotten. It is best so. This is best of possible vorlds for the moment."

"Yeah but do monads have windows?"

"Interesting question. Shall ve discuss?"

"No," said the Bear.

As it happened, Friedmann and the Bear had the experience of music between them, although this didn't come out in conversation right away.

"You know, when I first saw you I thought you looked like the devil," said the Bear after some time had passed, unknowingly providing the prompt.

"I know vot my face is," said the doctor.

"By now I like your face," the Bear assured him.

"It is qvite a map, and the face of the devil, absolutely. When I was young it was quite striking however."

"So you were a handsome devil then," the Bear suggested.

"Never handsome, but as it happens a success vith ladies, alzo in fact I debuted in a starring role at the opera playing the devil himself. At the Vienna Staatsoper. *Not* Volksoper mind you. *Staats*."

"I'm impressed."

"In the title role of Boïto's *Mefistofele*. I had a chest problem finished with the month before—pleurisy, a small valking pneumonia—but my physician has assured me I was vell enough and could sing. So: I strode onto stage in a long machestic robe, in a starring bass role at last, and began the first aria, you know the *Ave Signor, Perdone se il me gergo si lascia un po' da tergo*?"

"No."

"Vhen I got to the *Il dio piccin della piccina terra*," his deep voice boomed the notes, "*ogar tragligna ed derra e, al pardi guido saltellante, a casa spange fa gli asti al naso*, the little God of the little world, you understand—he expresses his contempt for Man—sticks his nose in the stars and flowers. At this point I suffered a massive arterial hemorrhage and blood poured from my mouse exactly as if from a hydrant. On stage! Some debut! Unprecedented I believe and possibly not eqvalled since! From that time on I sang only in the chorus. I vas already a medical student and that decided the choice of career." He shrugged. "Possibly it was better so. *Poi con tenere fatuita superba fa il su trillo nell 'erba*," he sang. "*Botioso pulve! Tracotato atóma!*"

"Maybe you shouldn't have debuted as the devil."

"Perhaps not."

"Because it was not your nature."

"Really who knows my nature? You?"

Whether doctor or devil in Vienna, Friedmann had seen the storm coming—"Jewish both sides of family, but assimilated, totally assimilated, so foolish we were"—assembled parents, wife, son, daughter and as much of the silver and memorabilia as could be carried, sewed jewels into coat linings and had crossed the ocean to America well before the downpour of Hitler and the war. Haphazard professional circumstance on this side of the water, and many people to support, accounted for the sometimes miscellaneous nature of his practice. "I am two, three specialists. Really I am interested, alzo I am too old to assimilate organically the new disciplines and technology, in molecular neurology, brain chemistry, especially as regards aspects of evolution. Somesing of a reputation but too late now to accomplish something vundamental in the field."

"Aha," said the Bear, enlightened as to the source of Friedmann's presence there, initially and now.

"Yes," the doctor said, and leaned intently towards him: "*So?* You are special. Do you have special information?"

"What exactly do you want to know?"

"What you know."

"I'm not a medical bear."

"Then tell me anysing, so long as is honest. You have opposable sumbs, elongated toe und finger structures in forepaws."

"Also an altered palate."

"To say nothing of your brain."

"The less said about my brain at this point the better. Look where it has got me. Also, if nothing happens to me here I should live much longer than your usual run of bear."

"A human lifespan?" Friedmann wondered. "So much?"

"Some of my ancestors," said the Bear, holding the information back, "lived a good deal longer than you might think."

This seemed to move Friedmann in some odd way. "Are you prophetic? Do you know somesing of the future?"

Oh Lord, thought the Bear. The difficulty of converse between disciplines. "Are *you* hip to all the secrets of *your* construction?" he asked.

"No," Friedmann admitted.

"Can I play you some music?"

"I don't like yatz. In music I vant streams, mountains, blue skies, not more of city life. I have too much of this already."

"I can understand that. But can I play a little and then talk to you? As if I were a little drunk. As if I still felt something. Let a little something happen, could be."

Friedmann sighed heavily.

"Maybe you could ask me another kind of question," the Bear suggested.

Friedmann's face deepened and his eyes got suddenly intent. "Is there anuzzer life? After, I mean." The question was not scientific but personal.

"Before, after, during: yes."

"You know this."

"Yes."

Friedmann took off his glasses and wiped his eyes with a clean white handkerchief. "You know this personally, from experience."

"What I find strange," the Bear told him, deciding to be a lot less guarded on the subject than usual, "is not the fact that there is an overarching transcendent realm, but that in the breadth and generosity of the universe as it really is, there is room for such narrowness and constriction as this." He gestured around him at the walls and bars and paint in the limited light. "And the fact that I've generated enough anguish to wind up stuck inside it, when it's illusion top to bottom—what can I tell you, I'm ashamed. It's such a failure of taste."

Friedmann sighed heavily, shrugged, then let his shoulders slump. "Ja, things are tough all over," he said.

The Bear had known that music was a dead or at least differently animated thing in him at the Tin Palace before his bust, while playing the long ballad—an odd, doubled moment in which his creativity seemed to have been enlarged and eliminated simultaneously; so much so that the bust had seemed an afterthought, the gross materialization of a prior event and no more. Now, in his all too material cell, with his proper brain and motor functions more or less restored to him after the episode of pure monstrosity, he didn't know what music was to him anymore. Once the fogs and cobwebs were sufficiently cleared from his working consciousness, although an ambient fog of drugs still interposed itself, a veil—they were still dosing his insufficient supply of food—he worked the keys of his horn and bent to the instrument, sitting on the edge of his iron-frame bed. Scales, a few preparatory maneuvers and some fretting over the short supply of reeds and minor damage to the instrument, then, out of some sense of the wryly appropriate, the head of Bird's "Relaxin' at Camarillo," Bud's "Un Poco Loco," and although he didn't remember all of its fractures, Mingus' frantic "Lock 'em Up," also known as "Hellview of Bellevue." Truth was he didn't much feel like playing. Truth was he felt like an intruder on this terrain or someone impersonating himself, making the moves and noises he might have made if he were still alive and in love with his locus of manifestation and the music that might be found there, latent.

Other repertoire: Lady Sings the Blues. Nutty. Justice. Evidence. Criss Cross. Moanin'. Fables of Faubus. Alabama. A Question of Sanity. I Thought I Heard Buddy Bolden Say. Hellhound on My Trail. How Much Is That Doggie in the Window. Que Sera Sera. Kryptonite. Doxy. Lush Life. Glass Enclosure. So What.

It would have been hard to play even if he felt like it. It was damp in here, his one reed was about shot, its fraying edge felt horrible on his tongue, he didn't have a swab to clean his horn out with, a few pads were working loose, the springs were probably rusting, and one of the rods had gotten bent when they tossed the horn after him into the Black Maria.

As he went further into it through the days he didn't bother to count, in a time during which it partway occurred to him that Friedmann and the slowly emergent friendly keeper Tim might be more destructive than any outright tormentor—since being savaged by a dead sheep, or by two of them, robs one of all the dignity of righteous outraged response—and as he began to find the thing in him that long ago had seized on music and learned to work it into an instrument of his secret self, it sometimes seemed that what was monstrous about him in this world or any other was not his sizable bearform and his impolitic gift of speech but this apparent talent for music, this powerful equipage that he had always prized above all his other contents: that fine instrumentality that played itself into intelligible shapes of sound and knew what lay ahead uncharted in the seas of time, and could fashion forms that lived their way into the obscurities of that future and thereby lit them: it seemed hideous to him now. Monstrous, to use the proper word. Following the force behind this perception led him logically to agree that he belonged in some sort of prison after all.

The Bear was turning inward, dropping like a stone down the well of himself in the dark: not a sound: hadn't reached water yet. Neither was he caroming back and forth between the walls. Straight down, then, into what he hoped was the mothering dark, stars reflected on the face of the water. All his previous solitudes had been masks that this deeper one had worn. Either this was some scary but authentic repenetration of himself, from which renewal eventually might come, or it was the most banal and pointless solo game that external circumstance and interior error could wring from him. It was impossible to tell, but he was making the descent will-he nill-he nonetheless.

If this is only more emotion, thought the Bear, the hell with it. Depression gets you nowhere. What I want is extinction, effacement, death.

As he went down the shaft his own smell came back to him and he did not like it, he found it ugly and unfamiliar. Plummet, then, and don't censor what you make out in the dimness. The music thing: he didn't like the blank intent look in its eyes and he could feel the greed churning out delusion and ambition at its heart. It had closed his eyes to the love of everything that did not serve it—Jones, Iris, whatever and whoever in the breathing piping world, without exception, that did not feed its maw. The music beast fed, it seemed to him, on a rich stew of denial and whatever local greenery could be torn from its roots and chomped down whole. It pitched its tent on one small field and saw the rest of the wide world's landscape as pointless waste. From the rough look of the canvas, the armaments stacked around the perimeter and the forms standing guard around the fire, it had pitched this tent for war. So: his beautiful talent was an ugly thing at heart, and if it came across authentic beauty in its march, it soiled whatever trace was resident there with its own smudge, trod the music into the mud and marched on hungry and destructive as before.

The Bear's self-disgust, at this turn of his contemplation, was so strong that he had to remind himself not to kill the musician, only peel him, if that was still possible, and refine him as far back to the holy as could be managed under the circumstances and sufficient unto the day. Find something in him, if possible, that would not coat itself in the travesty of a self you could put a name to.

Too much fucking fur, he told himself.

I got lost in it. It's me.

Imprismed.

Exit, pursued by a bear.

If he didn't feel like playing, he didn't much feel like listening to music either. Certainly not to jazz, certainly not to anything he had spoiled with his touch. Mozart maybe. Start with angel Mozart and after awhile of that see what still seemed alive and uncorrupt.

Friedmann of course loved Mozart. "I could bring you a Valkman," he said, "and cassettes."

"Headphones have to be pretty much destroyed to fit my head and most of them hurt my inner ear, probably do some damage in there. Do you have a radio?"

"This I will bring."

It was a black plastic thing, it stayed in Friedmann's cell because of regulations, and for the most part the Bear used it only to listen to the news: to details of the world he had never paid much mind to because he'd thought that by knowing it in general he had known it well enough. Not true.

When he did begin to feel like noodling at the horn it was to explore the architecture of certain chord changes—checking out the cornices and capitals of the structure, as it were—and this surprised him too. "Chelsea Bridge" showed him how much work there was to do. Although he knew his way around the halls of modern harmony, the Bear had always been an essentially melodic player who liked his harmonic materials simple enough to get out of his way when he wanted them to: he liked the option of an unobstructed field. He'd always seen himself pitched somewhere between Jackie McLean and Ornette Coleman, his tough-talking tone close to Jackie—although the Bear had never tugged his intonation Jackie's trademark bittersweet increment flat—his sense of abandon and free choice nearer to Ornette. Then too, sometimes, a fury with everything that was not the Absolute filled him and his music screamed its quest with a love that must have been something like Coltrane's but which he understood, finally, was the only thing he had that really was his own; and the Bear followed this long-phrased love or rage through the lifts and volutions of its laws, each note he played laying the next stone of the road ahead toward a series of theophanies, forms rising up like prayerful approximations which the Absolute graciously if only provisionally consented to inhabit, then falling away as burning husks before successive revelations and final, epistemological fire.

All that felt pretty far from him now. He was in no condition to shake the world or its pillars, or even light the most mundane book of its matches, much less seek out, beyond the life and death of ephemeral forms, some ultimate fundamental flame. So he was picking his way through old chord sequences now, as if through bones to see what edible scraps remained. "Stablemates." "Lotus Blossom." "Blood Count." Was there anything Billy Strayhorn hadn't said? "All the Things You Ain't." "Reincarnation of a Lovebird" he'd save till later. And it half seemed to him, in the half light of his contemplation, that the regular rotation of any given tune's harmonic cycle—which had always seemed a weary round to tread when the free road was there for the taking and the key to the highway always in his hand—represented the spirit's chance to make accommodation with worldly circumstance and learn from it. A humbling thing to be sure but maybe necessary if the whole job of living down here was to be done in full. Anyhow he could hardly be said to have avoided this world and its circumstances now.

This was a jail, he felt, that he had built brick by brick during the long anxiety of his emergence into public music—oh yeah, and before that too—in short by a couple hundred errors of perception and judgment and taste: all those misgivings, all that quailing: this is a prison of your own construction, bodied forth in the hidden workshops of your fear. Did I really pull this down from the available pictures? What's the alternative? Put on the red rubber nose and funny hat? The Bear cast a weary eye around the walls and corners of his cell.

What he had always liked least about himself was the anxiety at the back of his being. No doubt it was by nothing else that he had been betrayed into the materiality of the slammer. So where was the chrismal drop that might save him?

It was at about this time in his downward progress, the Bear felt, that he began to make some good, monastic, *via negativa* use of the cell to which circumstance had confined him, and to turn this shut-in shutdown of a winter into something at least potentially restorative. But to think that he was succeeding at something, think that he was getting anywhere at all, was to kill the process dead, if process there was. To even hope for progress raised before him the monstrous egoic form of himself that it now seemed more than ever necessary to slip away from or outright slay, if he was to find sufficient freedom.

The Bear had never gone in for hibernation, had dismissed it as ancestral old-hat pre-bop, but at the moment something like it, only vastly more internal and dangerous, promised him his only possible scrap of refuge, and since choices were limited, he went further in, or down, whatever.

Another thing he disliked about this descent was the fact that the light of Iris had been shone upon him immediately before it, as if that were the signifier and love the thing that the world—himself wearing a mask, of course—most denied him; that in his present cell it was the cathedral of love that loomed over his depth of exile. Let love get real and the jailhouse shadows gather, find their form, and here I am, caught in an absence I have myself provoked.

Is that how it is?

The Bear didn't know, but he hated the way it looked.

And music, once his whole grip on life, dead as a doornail and visibly rusting on the concrete floor of his cell.

Then one day it happened, or maybe happened: what he'd been waiting for, or maybe what he'd been waiting for—it was hard to tell in the dark. In any case something within him gave way and he began to die. That is, the being he had always felt himself to be within his body, that energy, that identity, began to fall away in him for good. He could reach into his body to it, but couldn't haul it back into daylight or even shake it by its shoulders. It was going, it was seeping out of him into the earth. Or maybe into the earth, he didn't know where it was going really. It was going somewhere gone.

So he sat there on the edge of his bunk feeling the life run out of him, but was in no pain. It was unnerving, though. It had happened to him twice before, when he was a sweetsouled visionary cub with a more accepting nature, and it had been unnerving even then. Now, in this cell, without external consolation or support, it was worse, this passing away of what the human world was pleased to call the animal soul. You never knew how much you were losing, or what if anything you might gain in return. This time it took three days and while it was happening he didn't feel like doing or saying much. Good thing Friedmann wasn't around. If the Doc had been around, the Bear would have had to talk with him. The process would have gone on regardless, but it was better not to have to talk.

When the Bear's inward dying played its last fadeaway cadence on the afternoon of the third day and he knew that it was over, he listened, he sent out every subtle emissary of sense to see what new light might befall. When earlier versions of this little death had finished with him, capacities in him had been unleashed and given freedom. Set loose from prior constriction and unknowing, they had been empowered and enlarged. Those gifts and their attendant celebrations, in the end, had been everything he possessed: they'd animated his music, and done the same for him. Without that, zip. Which was what he seemed to be left with now.

The Bear listened. The Bear sensed his way as far out into the breathing world as he could manage, and no new resonance came back to him; he scented no fresh air, sensed no newly minted light. And peering down into himself, the place was dark and empty still.

The Bear sat on the edge of his bed and thought, Hm. Inner death and no resurrection. The world was void, the joint deserted.

Evening fell.

Hm, he thought, still sitting there, not having moved except to scratch his nose or nuts.

And that's the world tonight.

Over, if not quite out.

The Bear lay down on his bed and thought of music. No help.

There was one way out. The Bear, no dope, he took it. Slept.

"I think possibly you are too hard on yourself," said Friedmann, to whom he had confided only his misgivings about music, a few days later. The deeper metaphysics were of course unspeakable, and the name Iris would not pass his lips in this place, although he wondered if he thought of her so little in order not to go mad or because he was so self-absorbed by now that even she didn't count for much. "This has the suspect flavor of introjected cruelty."

"You think so?" asked the Bear, leaning back against the bars and listening to the doctor's uselessly deep voice, whose accent the Bear hardly noticed now.

"It is natural in artists for there to be a certain tyrannism of the ego. Even Chekhov vouldn't let his sister marry. Vanted her to look after him in tuberculosis. Tyrants, monsters all, zerefore normal and to be forgiven."

"You only say that because you played the devil and lost."

"Irrelevant," said Friedmann. "You suffer from unreasonable perfectionism and haf begun to consider yourself a monster for reasons completely normal."

"Look at me, old man. What's normal here? What kind of story are you making up? What kind of hackney are you trying to hitch me to? I'm getting sick of our interesting little talks."

"Normal resistance," said Friedmann, knocking his pipe clean against the edge of the table and groping for his pouch, entirely the analyst now. It diminished him, thought the Bear.

"Either help get me out of here or go away."

"At the moment," Friedmann told him, "you are an administrative error, a thing forgotten and I think best so. Do you know what they had planned for you? If you died, an unmarked grave, like Mozart's. If you damaged and they decide not to kill you, then lobotomy and a cage at the zoo. All this is still possible. You are living the best option."

"Lucky me."

"Sink about it."

"I've sunk enough."

Had he, though? Perhaps he hadn't touched bottom yet. Who's to say? Odd, in any case, to speak up now. Fallen so far into inability and silence, making it his home. Wwww. Did he still recognize the authority of what had sent him here, or was it possible that he was done?

Not yet, an inner voice told him.

What do you know about it, he told it back.

Silence, then more dark. He went to sleep in it.

"How about a codpiece, man?"

What ho, it was Tim in the morning, carrying a couple of plastic shopping bags smelling of fish that was not entirely fresh.

The Bear was waking slowly. Dream of Jones last night. Jones, *dio piccin della piccina terra*, had been wearing feathers and flapping his arms. There had been flashes of light and Jones had begun to sing, and much to the Bear's surprise he had sung in tune. So it was a happy dream. How come the Bear's main feeling had been that Jones needed his help, needed it badly? How come, too, that in the dream's fallaway it had been Iris who stood clear in his mind, calm and self-aware in her own delicate light? Don't think of her. It'll tear your heart to pieces if you do. Too much beauty. Too much hope, and too much of that hope suspect. "Give me a minute," he told Tim.

"Hey here I am," said the big affable guard, "loaded down with fish and fruit and you're all jeez what a grouch."

"They still drug me," the Bear reminded his keeper. "My head's not right. A minute. A sec. Be right with you. Don't go 'way."

"*Vuss?*" Friedmann's voice rumbling up out of a cavernous sleep next door. Apparently he had spent the night again. In any case he was huffing and puffing himself awake, clearing his nose, working an angry finger into one of his ears.

The Bear thought: world too heavy, brain not lift it anymore. He had woken up once around dawn. Had noticed dawnlight in the slant of windows, then gone back to sleep. It was then he'd dreamt of Jones, or had it been earlier, during the night? Bear didn't know. Tim's fish smelled, how did it smell, good? bad? It was getting harder to tell. His eyes registered a subtle freshening in the available daylight. "Is it spring out there?"

"Has been, technically, a coupla weeks already," said Tim, "but it's only now the weather's changing so you can feel it."

"The daylight looks different."

"It's a clear one out there, yeah, and there's a kinda softness in the air, now you mention it."

"Mine head," came Friedmann's voice, still clogged.

The Bear sat up on the edge of his bed and scratched his balls. "I don't know about that fish, Tim, but I could start with an apple. Brought any?"

"Does the Pope shit in the woods?"

The Bear, his eyes squeezed shut as he yawned again, heard a rustling of plastic bags. Then the crisp smell of fruit came to him. Oh man.

"Granny Smiths," said Tim, "and not bad. Had a couple myself." Tim started passing small apples one by one through the bars. They landed on the blankets at the foot of the Bear's bed, plop plop plop. "Have a ball."

"Knock myself out."

"Vhat day of the veek?" asked Friedmann, sitting up, ruffling his stray white wires of hair and groping on the table for his specs.

"Same as usual," said the Bear. He took an apple, turned it in his paw, admiring the blush that must have faced south on the branch, thinking of the breezes that must have cooled it, swayed it, then popped it into his mouth whole. Juices ran and he chomped it up and swallowed it down. "Oh man, these are good." He put two more in his mouth and chewed, letting foam and juice run out the sides of his jaws for the pleasure of it. Abundance. Sweetness. World without end.

"You eat 'em cores and all," Tim was saying, his big head shaking appreciatively left to right.

"Leave nothing out of your experience of life is my motto," the Bear told him. "What else would I be doing in this godforsaken slammer? Do the circuit. Harrow the lower realms. Get harrowed in return. Always say please and thank you. You got any more apples in that bag?"

"What about the fish?"

"Smells a little funny. Not bad, just funny, and these apples—I can feel vitamins pouring into me—has it ever occurred to you, Tim, how gratuitous and beautiful fruit is, nodding on a branch in the air?"

"People work to grow 'em, and usually I buy 'em in the store, where people have to work too, but yeah, sure, I know what you mean."

"So let's have the rest. I have a sudden thirst for fruit. Morning, doc," said the Bear to Friedmann as Tim began letting the remaining apples through the bars. "If apples go over the rainbow," the Bear asked the doctor, "why can't I? Can you tell me that? Only Art Pepper ever did anything with those changes."

"You are being obscure," Friedmann told him.

"My policy always." He took another apple in and quickly made pulp of it, then let it slide down his gullet like a song. "Hey, you two."

"What," they said more or less in unison. Must work on this ensemble shit, get it right.

"What say you get your four balls together and turn the key today? I'll take it from there, deal with the gunners up the hall or be dealt with. Haven't you noticed the change of season? I know I'm acting a little manic, but my blood's up, sap's rising. Whaddayou say?"

"Hey man," said Tim, "we been through this before."

"Hey, sympathetic soul," the Bear replied, "what are you waiting for, the angel Moroni to come down and tell you special?"

Tim reached under his uniform jacket and pulled out a pocket watch on the end of a chain. "I'm waiting for this silver watch to turn gold. I got a wife that probly needs another kidney operation and two daughters drawing a bead on college."

"Gimme the fish you useless motherfucker."

Tim turned a supplicatory face to Friedmann. "Can you explain it to him again? We can't get you out of here even if we are your only friends."

"You're not, actually," said the Bear correctly.

"There is one epple you did not eat," said Friedmann, casting an eye down upon a fold of brown army blanket. "If you don't mind, it vould freshen my breaths."

"By all means," said the Bear, passing him the apple. "By all means cover up the inconvenient smell of internal rot, failed will, suspect sentiment. Tim, the fish. I thought I asked you to get me a whole one."

Tim held up the long white filet of cod. "It was all I could get, okay?"

"Story of your life. Give it."

Tim passed it slickly between the bars, grimacing. "What's got into you today?" Tim asked him.

"I got into me today. And now this fine if questionable-smelling filet of cod will get into me today. Observe the result." He took a chomp from the thick end of the filet, which, he estimated, weighed five or six pounds in all, had not spoiled but wasn't as fresh as he would have liked. Good Christ, he thought, and took another large helping, it had been a no more than normally innocent creature patrolling the deeps earlier that week. He swallowed more of it down. You ate others too. How it is down here.

"How was it?" Tim asked him. "Good?"

"Just watch." The Bear stood up. He thrust his muzzle between the bars, fixed Tim with a look between the eyes, convulsed his stomach and began to vomit.

"Jesus Christ!" Tim jumped back, but did not escape being stained.

"Like a hydrant," said the Bear, feeling his life inverting itself inside him—this was not just the revulsion of his gut against current circumstance or dicey fish but a reversal, like an umbrella turned inside out by wind, of his prior images of himself, idols all, whatever their aesthetics and geometry. He turned toward Friedmann but decided no, swung back and let the rest of it go into the lidless toilet. When he raised his head he saw that Friedmann looked as horrified as if the Bear had let loose on him literally. Intelligent man, thought the Bear, who can read the book of things in the short version. "I believe I have expressed myself correctly," the Bear told him.

Friedmann nodded, and Tim looked understandably appalled, but the Bear could see that one more straw was still needed to break the camelback of his imprisonment. There would be no big news today.

Friedmann's face had gone unhealthily red, and had begun to flicker like a dysfunctional video picture.

"Wait a minute," said the Bear, "don't you cheap me out with your promised fucking heart attack," and the Bear's perception seemed to split in three. In one version, Friedmann clutched his chest and tumbled to his bed under the punch of an attack, and in a rather sentimentally conceived tableau the doctor died holding on to the Bear's paw, panting convulsively and alternating last wishes with childhood reminiscence and words about his wife, with the Bear promising to conduct him through the veils to his best, most appropriate home. In the second, more plausible segment of perceptible event, life went on, after the Bear's eruption, much as it had for months now, Tim ineffectively wiping himself off and saying something about the roach-infested staff washroom and the stinking utility sponge, the doctor making inefficient consoling sounds, and the Bear submitting to the unjust authority of his continued enclosure. In the third version, however, and the Bear was nearly at a loss to determine which of the three was actually taking place, he not only rushed the bars to get a grip on Tim and put a murderous paw to his lying throat, but in the ambiguous daylight coming through the gridded windows the Bear got to see all the consequences of his attempted violence: other guards rushing up the corridor festooned with ordnance, the mortal sting of the tranquilizer dart, the annihilating jab of the cattle prod, and yet another descent into the riotous, wrong kind of dark, and perhaps prosaic death as punishment at last.

In this superabundance of imagery, all that the Bear could find to ask was: given such a wealth of travesty, none of it up to expressing his reality or anyone else's, was it worth waking up dressed in any kind of self, if that was how you had to do it, on a fine spring morning in this world or any other? Was the project worth the weight and labor? And what, if any, was the issue?

3

"**roger.** I told you this before," said Iris to her supervisor, once her colleague. "I can't do the data concordance this afternoon but I'm perfectly willing to stay up late in order to do it at home and bring it in tomorrow."

Roger cleared his throat and sat with an increasingly male proprietary air on the edge of her desk. "Because you have to visit a sick friend."

"That's right," Iris said, "and I can bring the work in tomorrow morning, or, if you like, modem it to the database when I'm done tonight so that it will be there for you to access at home after your morning jog. That's at seven a.m. I believe?"

Roger the Jogger removed his glasses, pinched the bridge of his nose to demonstrate frustrated patience, and inclined toward her over the surface of the desk. In the slight redness of his face and the condescending embers that burned in his eyes, he reminded Iris of her ex-husband Herb. But perhaps she was exaggerating, perhaps confusing two entirely distinct predatory personalities. "Can I trust you to get it done?" Roger asked her, and she decided that, whatever her confusion, she had not been exaggerating one bit.

"I beg your pardon?" Iris gave him what she hoped was a modestly offended look, but she could feel her face reddening despite herself. For the moment, she hated the mobility and expressiveness of her features, which all too often gave her nowhere to hide.

"Fine," said Jolly Rodge, "fine. I just, uh, worry about you sometimes. I sometimes feel, let's say protective."

Iris wanted to tell him not to strain himself so much, and that he was confusing protectiveness with an activity in his pants, but what she managed was, "I'm sure you already have enough people to protect," a veiled reference to his wife and kids; on this veil also flickered a politely misleading short film of the laboratory and the rest of the research department, also more or less under his care. Iris counted on the mildness of her tone, as always, against the chance of outright attack.

"All right," Roger told her, and she saw him begin to recede.

"I can check in after lunch if you like, but after that I do have to go, if I'm to make my visit."

Roger withdrew after an excuse me or two and another bit of marginal thrust and parry. Iris kept her hands in her lap in the shadow of the desk so as not to betray what she felt as only a slight trembling, whether of fear or rage she would not have liked to say. Rage.

After Roger left her glassed-in little office, she gave herself a minute in which to feel offended. The job he wanted her to do was little more than skilled busywork, an interlogging of five streams of research data having to do with computer models of proposed new medical compounds and their possible interface with the known characteristics of some two hundred primary neural receptors in the brain and central nerve stem. It was work in which she might have had a creative hand only a few, let's say four or five years ago, but now . . . now let's not go into it. Too late: the door had opened and a chill wind had entered the glassine cubicle. Within a minute the rage she had felt toward Roger had turned conclusively inward upon her, and, shaken by a sense of her own frailty and by the failure of her mental and spiritual materiel, she decamped to the ladies' room, key in hand, where she hoped to find sufficient peace and quiet in which she might regroup her forces.

She found herself fortunately alone in the wonderful world of soothing blue tiles, splashed her face with cold water from the basin, and found a mask of obvious panic looking back at her from the square of mirror set above it, although perhaps it was the draining quality of the fluorescent light that made her look so skeletal and rigid. She had installed full-spectrum daylight tubes in her own office, but that was too much to expect here. These lights, while leaching nutrients from all who passed beneath them, exaggerated the redness of her flush and greened out the remainder of the general picture. There she was: a stricken doll: water beading on its too livid skin.

Get a grip on yourself, please.

Iris Tremoureux—the name described the unsteady, oddly questing voice that characterized all the male members of her family, but no, she had always had a fine, even lovely speaking voice, and her diction was excellent. The name's signification had devolved, in recent years, to the shameful disorganization of her limbs; but that was not genetic, that was accidental, she hastened to assure herself; that is not essentially me. Iris lived, these days, accompanied by a background music of anxiety in which the breakdown of all coherence was persistently if vaguely suggested and sometimes outright threatened. Hers was a glassine or perhaps crystalline world which, if its coordinates stayed in place most of the time, always seemed too easily susceptible of being shattered.

Oh God you know I used to be capable of more than this.

The delicacy and refinement of her nature that now only defined the geometry of her fear had once extended to her intellectual functions. She had been capable of keeping her world sufficiently well ordered, and, in her professional life, although she had never been ultimately ambitious, let's say, of that speech in Sweden, she had been capable of original and, it would not be too much to say, difficult and concentrated work. After the end of the marriage, which in retrospect was almost nothing, and the loss to that bastard Herb of her two irreplaceable daughters, which in retrospect filled the view from sea to shining sea, her descent through the ranks of her profession had been ticked as if by index markers on the side of a graduated glass tube, constant in its rate of fall. Level by level she had surrendered degrees of intellectual autonomy, degree by degree submitted to the demands of mere system and departed from the clear-lit landscape of independent research.

Her defining mistake may not have been the marriage after all. Perhaps it was traceable, in a sense, to her liaison with the Bear, and to the thrilling but dangerous sense of miracle and possibility it had once suggested. But what point on the continuum of that liaison had been the critical one? Perhaps if she had had the courage to step into a world of monstrosity and wonder by following her heart and becoming his lover everything would have been different? Then there would have been no Herb, no marriage. Also there would have been no Amy, no Trace, and not only her life but she herself was unimaginable without them. Therefore what? Where was she? What, apart from a bit of discarded ash after she'd been burnt up by the Bear and his appetites, might she have become? And what if anything, apart from less and less, might she become now? I'm so afraid that there is no help available from here. There is no way I can be reached in this corner, into which I have so neatly and conclusively painted myself. Just look at the quality of the brushwork. You have to admit that it was very finely done. Nemesis, I endorse your efficiency even as, helpless, I hate your intricate guts.

What shamed her additionally, as she dried her face on two paper towels she withdrew from the dispenser, was that it was her prettiness, which men found beautiful, but which she, at least for the moment, detested as a doll-like caricature of who or what she might really be . . . where was she . . . that it was her prettiness and what could be done with it that had protected her from dismissal and oblivion, in such world as her profession afforded. No, call it by its proper name: not what could be done with it: what she had done with it herself, in the male world, with all manner of obscene protective flirtation, to ensure the continued existence of a niche in which she could live and breathe. Roger and his bulging shorts were wages she had earned with accumulations of petty sin. She had no grounds for complaint. As for a real love life, it had been awhile. Oh, she wanted one all right, now and then, and had once taken to sex easily and well, had regarded it as a natural enough component of a world of normal appetite, but these days once she saw the banal and blinkered hunger her own light, introductory music of desire evoked in the one or two men for whom she had played a few bars, she was repelled, not only by them, but by the whole hot compulsive machinery of the dance, and by the inescapable, demeaning note of puppetry in it all.

Her face was still there in the bathroom mirror, dry now, too articulate and precise, too expressive, there for all to read, a giveaway. Her good French clothes, bought from discount fashion outlets, fit her well. Iris looked at her watch. Yes, she could seem sufficiently busy for the next two hours, then go out for lunch and, if she had to, come back to the lab and appear briefly conscientious before tearing off to her other life downtown. She was still woman enough to manage that.

Crosstown traffic that day was heavy and the city came at her in pieces, the details too diffuse and at the same time too clearly rendered for her to navigate the maze in comfort: a beggar's pained face, a litter of rags and bodies, predatory looks in men's eyes, the odor permeating the backseat of fate's allotted taxi.

But at length she had reached St. Vincent's Hospital, solid on a corner of Seventh Avenue just up the street from the Village Vanguard, where she had once gone to see Miles, Trane, Ornette, Mingus, Sonny, Shepp, just about everyone who counted. For a moment she remembered in a quick shuffle all the musicians who had tried to pick her up, how they had leaned over her table, the variety of their smiles. Goodness, she thought in a mixture of embarrassment and pride, there were more than a few of them, down the years. One drummer, stricken by a single look it seemed, had fallen down half the Vanguard's entrance stairs and landed at her feet, provoking general laughter. Hey, one musician's voice said to a buddy somewhere in the halls of memory, look what I just found here.

—O my America? she remembered asking the guy.

—Huh?

—O my America, O my newfound land. Is that what you've got on your mind?

No question about it, she'd been pretty nervy once upon a time, and she did know how to shed musicians. She'd tried wide-eyed poetry on the Bear too, but he'd grinned back at her and come up with a deliciously obscene pun about a well-wrought urn and a bracelet of bright hair about the bone.

Iris looked up at the slant brick face of St. Vincent's newest wing, overtipped the cabbie, decamped onto the asphalt beneath the building and felt an anticipatory, Bear-connected and therefore threatening movement in her heart.

How long had Jones been out of Intensive Care? Two days? Three? No news yet on any proposed release but it seemed in any case that he would live.

All set to enter the building, though, she retreated in momentary panic and bought herself an intermission at the little patisserie-café tucked into the street that ran behind the Vanguard, where she lit a cigarette—she'd been trying to quit but couldn't, which struck her as odd, since she was usually able to manage a break from the habit without much effort—drank down two mugs of good black coffee—one too many for the health of her nerves, she knew: there was the beginning of a twitch in her right eyelid—and nibbled her way, it was such a literary café, through an order of four madeleines placed beside her coffee on a small white saucer. Her memory did not need the additional stimulation, however; the vessel of Iris was already full, and trembled with sufficient surface tension at the brink. Her mind's eye skimmed two images in the middle depths: the Bear in her old apartment years back, one day when the sex-question that had been hovering between them raised an obvious and alarming head from the Bear's lower regions—she remembered the furious embarrassment in his eyes, and her own confused mixture of panic and not quite desire; then the second, less threatening memory of the Bear in her living room before his arrest that winter: it had been good to see him. And then gone. In place of whatever music had hovered at the brink of audibility between them, there was a palpable lack of resonance, worse than silence, now.

Before going into the hospital, Iris looked up long enough to acknowledge the brightness of the day and wonder if spring had arrived for real. Just when you think it's here, the sky broods itself into one last grey knot of concentration and unleashes upon you a staggering mindstorm of snow. It was a lovely day, though, whatever its duplicity or sequel.

Jones looked, Iris thought, a bit like . . .

"Death warmed over?" Jones suggested from his pillow.

"Microwaved," said Iris, surprising herself with something the Bear might have said. "You do look haggard, Jones, which is not surprising under the circumstances, but you also have a certain cat-that-ate-the-canary air."

"Do I?"

"I'd say."

"Then you're very observant. I did in fact eat a canary. A large one."

"Romance with a nurse?" Iris asked him, arching an orthodox eyebrow.

"Wrong guess," said Jones, smiling, thought Iris, more than a little smugly. "You could just say I'm more than usually glad to be alive. So: ya bring me anything? Chocolates? A fifth, despite my perforated intestines, of VSOP?"

"Afraid not."

Someone coughed weakly on the other side of the white cloth partition that divided the room. Against the daylight, Iris could make out the outline of an uptilted bed and at the top of its slant the silhouette of an aged male head with its mouth fallen open. "*Rose*," it said.

"It's his late wife's name I think," said Jones. "Sleeps most of the time. Very weak."

Iris composed herself before inquiring: "I understand you nearly died."

"Nearly doesn't cover it," Jones told her, laughing weakly. "I was out there, Irish," once upon a time one of the Bear's nicknames for her. Nearly all her ancestors were French, but in fact Iris resembled her Irish grandmother Kathleen.

"Out where?"

"There," Jones not very helpfully said, waving a vague arm. "Among other things," he continued, "I saw the Bear."

Iris felt herself flushing red. "Saw him where?"

"In my mind's eye, Toots. Well, sorta saw him. I don't know if he's dead or alive but we certainly made some kind of contact. You all right, kid?"

"Fine." She was not. "You do look changed."

Jones profiled left, gaunt and a trifle melodramatically on his pillow. "Everything's changed."

"Your eyes seem a little wild," she hazarded.

"Oh yeah, pretty lady," Jones said, and hoisted himself up a notch amid his bedclothes. "I finally saw some of the stuff the Bear used to go on about years back."

"I see," said Iris, feeling the outline of her world beginning to waver, but keeping to her normal voice nonetheless.

Jones looked away again, Iris thought, with a certain gauche sense of specialness. "It was a trip and a half, as we used to say in the good old days."

"Has Sybil been in to see you?" Iris asked, wanting to change the subject, but mused on the fact that in the good old days she had taken a few trips and a half herself. Which was where, she was convinced, her fracturing or shattering had come. In the aftermath of the divorce, when Herb had stripped her of Tracy and Amy, in all the merciless exposure of a court of law, there she had been, stripped and alone in the brutal immensity of America. Without the Bear to reach out to back in New York—she didn't feel, having left him, that she had the right to try—she returned, after a while, to the psychedelics that had meant so much to her back in her schooldays and which, in the sense of expanded possibility they gave her, were linked to the jolt of knowing the Bear. And it had been on one night, when she had certainly dropped too much acid, that she heard, in the middle of a streamfulness whose essence she no longer really could recall, a little click, and in that moment some fundamental connection between her body and her soul had been severed—simple as that: click: for what was after all so insignificant a body, so simple a soul—so that she could put a precise finger to the moment in which her personal shattering had taken place and, later, in its inescapable train, her professional decline begun. This click and its consequences had left her not a little afraid of transcendent experience of any kind—keep to the earth, her uncertainty had advised her, and to your fragile stance upon it, lest worse things overcome you—and recently, when she'd seen the fragmentary newspaper reports of the Bear's presence in the nightclubs of New York, it had taken some ultimate degree of courage for her to taxi down to Sweet Basil and say hello to him again at a small table while wielding a protective cigarette. And here she was in a hospital room with Jones, where his path of glory had led him, and her. It was a small circuit, it seemed to her, perfectly round and without sufficient issue.

"Sybil," Jones replied in the perceptual shards of Iris' present time, and laughed a little. "Sybil is more or less consumed with guilt—now there's a change of roles for you. We, um, had a little lover's tiff and that was why I was out walking late and got knifed, but she's not the responsible party. If you ask me, that's not what it was about at all."

"When do you think they'll let you go home?" There was something, thought Iris, vain and offensive in Jones' tone, and she wanted to keep the conversation fixed on the matters immediately at hand.

"Any day now I think. I nearly bought the farm from loss of blood, but what's keeping me here now has to do with the patchwork job they did on my intestines. The outer incision's still pretty raw too, though they'll leave the stitches in awhile. Need an office visit later to take them out. Wanna see?"

"Not really."

"I only meant on a professional basis."

"That's not the kind of work I do," Iris reminded him.

The figure in the next bed groaned weakly in its sleep. "*Rose*," it said again.

"Hey," said Jones, "wanna go out in the lounge with me for a smoke? You still smoke? Really? One of the few of us left. You got a pack? I'm out. They won't let me light up in here." Jones jerked his chin at the silhouette. "It's okay, I can get up on my own. Just grab ahold of the IV pole so I don't send it flying."

"Oh look what a beautiful rose you brought me," said the sleeper's voice as they left.

The corridor, thought Iris, was a typical hospital hallway, the routine number of efficient-looking nurses with done-up hair shuttling between doorways of disaster and collapse—Iris looked in at bodies strewn on beds, attendant relatives, televisions craning down on articulated iron arms offering diversions or the news—was it that late in the day already?

"Looky there," said Jones, nodding backward at the words NOT AN EXIT printed large on an arch midway down the hall. "I looked up at that from my gurney when they wheeled me down from ICU and I felt kind of reassured. Hello, ladies," he said to the nurses' station. "They're cool," he told Iris.

"That's nice," she said, but with one still half-professional eye read the label on the two IV drip bottles hanging from the aluminum tree that rolled between them and decided that Jones' condition wasn't as wonderfully stable as he seemed to assume, even though, she was glad to see, the nurses weren't telling him Now now, Mr. Jones, and directing him by an ambulant elbow back to the safety of his room.

"But the smokers' allotment is tiny and out of the way," he was telling her. "Soon there won't be anything left for us."

When they found the smokers' nook, after a bend and then another bend, it was a small alcove with a rudimentary loveseat—lacquered pine frame, worn floral-print cushions—two companion armchairs, and a rounded pinetop table on which old *New Yorker*s socialized with stray *Scientific American*s and rootless *Cosmopolitan*s. An overweight sloppy-looking guy was asleep on one end of the loveseat, a cigarette burning down in one corner of his mouth. A premature wallow of gut hung over his beltline, and he seemed to wake halfway up when Jones and Iris lowered themselves into the armchairs.

"Hey man," Jones nodded.

"Hey bear," the man nodded back, and scratched randomly at his beard.

Jones and Iris did a small doubletake between them in answer.

"In-joke," the guy explained, and pretended to straighten himself in his seat.

"I'll say," Iris told him.

"Visiting my wife," the guy said back. "They're looking to see if she needs another kidney operation or not."

"Visiting him." Iris indicated Jones with a suddenly colloquial jerk of her thumb, and pulled her tin of tobacco from her purse. "Do you mind?"

"What I'm here for," said the guy, and took a last pull from his diminished cigarette. "Was I asleep?"

"Looked like," Iris informed him.

"Bad job, bad hours," he said. "A real jail."

"Ain't they all," Jones commiserated.

Jones and Iris nodded at him in polite dismissal, then rejoined each other exclusively.

"You still smoke those rollups?" Jones asked her. "Three Caftles?"

"You do know that the additives are more harmful than the tobacco itself," she reminded him. "Sometimes I smoke American Spirits, available by mail order from Native American tribes and also free of additives, but more often I—"

"All right all right all right, I'll take one, if you can make it for me."

Iris rolled a couple of cigarettes and they lit up, trying to ignore the heavy guy on the sofa so they could talk at ease.

"You heard Cummins is bringing the album out?" Jones asked her.

"Sybil called me," Iris nodded.

"So have you heard any news," said Jones, reverting to a long habit of secrecy in the company of strangers, "of our mutual friend?"

Iris shook her head side to side, resisting the tendency to go tearful on the subject.

"You ask around some more?"

"I've already asked everyone in my profession who might know," she said, offended, "or who might know someone who knows."

"Hm."

Iris unpleasantly felt the attention of the big bearded guy, but when she looked up at him he had lit another cigarette and appeared to be examining the false-marble black-and-white vinyl tiling of the floor. "Is your wife all right?" she asked him politely.

"We're waiting to hear. Tests and more tests. Thanks for asking."

"You're welcome," Iris said, but something bothered her about the man. "I hope it works out."

"Yeah." He nodded with what seemed a weary stoicism, but something about him still tugged at her attention. Was he watching her too closely? Was he a freak? Iris couldn't put her finger on it. If he lost some of that weight he wouldn't look so tired and defeated and creepy. But why should she think he felt tired, defeated, etc.? She hadn't any right, really, but just look at the slump of those big shoulders.

"Your work okay?" Jones had asked her.

"I get by."

"Me, I'm in shtook," Jones said. "When I get outa here I won't be ready to work anywhere yet, and in addition to being about as broke as usual there'll be all these bills. No health insurance, of course. Perish the thought."

"Stiff them awhile. Claim indigence. You'll get some threatening letters but they'll write you off after awhile. What about living on some of the advance money from Cummins?"

"There isn't much but I don't feel like I have any right to it. It's his."

"If, when you get out the hospital," Iris advised him, "you're not able to work, you should take what you need to live on from the advance. I'm sure he'd want you to."

"Of course he would."

"So?"

"I suppose . . . but for some reason I can't do it. Some form of keeping the faith."

"That's silly."

They smoked together quietly for awhile, Jones pulling uncomfortably hard on the handrolled job. "You have to work to keep it lit," he said of the cigarette.

"Not really," Iris assured him, and puffed easily. When she looked up, the heavy guy was staring at her without social disguise.

"Excuse me?" Iris asked him.

"I don't understand this," he answered. "This isn't logical."

"Is it about your wife?" Iris, noticing that his eyes seemed moist, asked with some concern.

"No," the guy said, a tear starting a run down one of his cheeks but no weeping shakes to accompany it. He didn't even blink. "I don't know why I should say this, but I think, you know, I'm very moved by your beauty, I think it's about . . ."

"Hey?" Jones asked him, but the guy waved him away.

"It doesn't make any sense to me," the guy said, "but I think it's about . . ."

"Hey buddy, you okay?" Jones asked him with some insistence, and this time Iris physically backhanded him aside as an irrelevant buzz. That was when Jones started to realize there was something strange going on, the guy sitting there with tears pouring down his face, and some kind of energy, you could feel it, kind of vibrating off of Iris, whose face was flushing red in successive waves and whose hands had begun to tremble.

"I don't get this at all," the guy was saying now, and ran a troubled hand through his thick dark hair, "but I think for some reason . . ."

Here Iris got to her feet, her eyes wide and this energy coming off her. Her arms were stretched rigid now, held down and slightly away from her body, the fingers out straight and vibrating, her eyes going wider. It was almost, thought Jones, a Bride of Frankenstein effect, just before the scream. In fact her voice wasn't loud, but you would have sworn she was shouting it was so intense: "Say it say it say it."

Now the guy stood up too. It was all very weird. Jones tried to get up, but he had to take it easy because of the stitches and the incision, and it was hard for him to get a grip on the IV pole. The thing kept trying to roll away from him, and he fell back into the chair twice.

"Go ahead and say it," Iris said, only this time more quietly, her voice almost normal, her tone not that of a plea anymore but one of confirmation.

Tim was finally able to get it together, but his shoulders slumped in what looked and felt like defeat: "I think it's about a bear."

To Iris and Jones and Tim it seemed, in a mix of fugues and unisons and as if in a dream state they had somehow all three of them begun to share, that Iris' flushing, tremulous energy was expanding to include all of their reactions to it: Iris seized and shaken by something larger than she really wanted to know about; Jones, the last of his sense of accident swept aside, realizing how far he'd had to fall toward death in order to retrieve the Bear and that, regardless of whatever coincidence had aided or intervened in the process, an Intentionality had driven him there and had now completed its circuit; and Tim unwillingly feeling the structure of his savvy, cautious life collapsing like a dynamited tenement to leave him in the middle of some dispulverated fucking ruin, man, and an unnerving cloud of unknowable dust rising on all sides around him to obscure whatever hip weary humorous view he had once had of things. The quite palpable waves radiating from Iris had some odd optical properties toward the edge of their sphere of consequence, odd quivers of green and violet that began to wobble and blur at the horizon, so that, a few days later, when the Bear stood up from his iron cot, wobbling slightly from the effects of a recent increase of medication in his oatmeal and additionally confused by the unexpected multicolor vibrations mysteriously latent in the air, to see Lester Bowie standing at the door of his cell in a labcoat, swinging a mock-casual stethoscope and saying, "*Klaatu barada nikto*, baby," the Bear had to ask the trumpeter to give him a minute, please, in which to work things out. He took in Roscoe Mitchell's bored, perfect impersonation of an ambulance attendant and Malachi Favors' extravagant, even slightly campy male-nurse impression, but thought that Jones looked a little pekid and unwell in his paramedical whites and Iris' small, perfect features seemed a mite preposterous under a nurse's outsized triangular cap. He was also surprised to see Tim, his eyes going every whichway and his forehead sweaty, coming forward with the keyring while Friedmann, leaning heavily on a cane today and his face red with stress or effort, looked nervously back up the corridor. And who was the hard-looking Irish number with the moustache in the rent-a-cop outfit? The optics of the prison flickering again like a video picture and his own uncomfortable sense of being in too many times or places at once dizzied him, and he wanted a minute's peace and quiet to think it through. It seemed to him, in this complicated instant, that his term of imprisonment was best understood if contemplated in the form of an eye. Read from left to right, this eye showed pink underflesh and a tear duct at its beginning, then opened onto a larger plane shared by pure contemplative whiteness and a beautiful blue-grey mottled iris detailing the emphases and nuances of particular cognitions and events; but at its center this articulated whorl emptied into a paradoxically jet-black locus of uncompromised sight into which he had fallen with no sense that he was ever coming out. After this iris-and-pupil combo, the eyeform symmetrically narrowed to its other end, which, the Bear understood, he had finally reached. There was no tear duct on that end. Now he was able to appreciate the eye's shapeliness and beauty of line, the loveliness of its surrounding lashes, its sly, allusive, cognitive gleam. As if in acknowledgment, he saw this eye blink once, then open wide again, and in the clarity of sight it afforded him, the prison did not need to stoop to the coarseness of visible flicker to stand revealed as an immaterial construction. The jangle of lock and key was mere ceremony, with a tag of late-comic fumbling delay for Tim and Lester, and when the Bear stepped out of his cell, forgetting his saxophone—Bowie collected it, shaking his head and wagging a finger—into a semicircle of familiar, welcoming faces, as if at a birthday party, his lapse supine onto the gurney was more ceremony indicating his fundamental incapacity while Roscoe Mitchell, looking deadpan, taped a fake IV patch onto his arm and Iris raised the bottle with trembling hands. At the last blockade, a difficulty in which papers flurried and Iris made an ameliorative, improbable but ultimately efficacious speech in the face of uniforms and the organized farce of force, it seemed to him that they were already outside together in the lemon light of early spring, that a freshening breeze blew upon their faces and that the year's first pale green leaves were putting on a special show for them on a series of slender extended branches. After a time they would ride the Health Department van that Tim had appropriated through old connections at the Brooklyn morgue down preternaturally detailed streets of actual escape and oh-man-I-don't-believe-we-made-it sighs of relief but for now, in this intermission, these first branches just outside the jail knew the dance and all the local airs, and the old brick wall against which the leaves displayed themselves was beautiful, as were all things the light lay itself so mercifully upon, and it seemed to him that he, Jones, Iris and the rest of them were already free to walk anywhere that pleased them, on this day or any other, in what had always been a freely given expanse of world enough and plenty, plenty time.

part three

On man's heaven's influence works not so,
But that it first imprints the air,
So soul into the soul may flow,
Though it to body first repair. . . .

To our bodies turn we then, that so
Weak men on love revealed may look.
Love's mysteries in souls do grow,
But yet the body is his book.

—*Donne*

1

"mmmmmm," said the Bear. Which, it occurred to him, was essentially Wwwww inverted.

"Get out of my kitchen," Iris told him, and raised her spatula. She was sautéeing young flat spinach leaves, *pousses d'épinard* she called them, in a shiny steel skillet, but with her gesture she seemed momentarily to assume the air of a goddess protecting the lovely uncooked side of salmon lying on the countertop beside the stove.

"You're not gonna cook the whole piece, are you? You're leaving some for me raw, right?"

Iris lowered her spatula and affected a patient, long-suffering tone. "I'm broiling the two pieces I cut off the large end. See them? The rest is for you, if you can really eat that much,"

"I'm a big guy."

"You're an expensive proposition."

"You don't know the half of it," said the Bear. He leaned sideways in the doorframe, and without quite realizing it began to hum the opening bars of "What's That Smell Like Fish, Mama."

Iris, always a good listener, caught it and shot him a dark look. "You're impossible."

"Improbable," the Bear told her. "Unlikely, perhaps. Difficult to adjust to in confined spaces. But impossible, no, that's just not me. As Abraham used to say to God at crucial moments, Here I am."

"Can you please wait outside while I'm cooking? Isn't there something you could do for the next few minutes?"

"I like to watch you."

"You can watch me when we eat."

"I've never seen you in an apron before."

"For the moment," said Iris, "please please *please* wait in the living room. There's a bottle of wine breathing on the dinner table."

"Sounds like a monster movie."

"This *is* a monster movie. Go into the living room and have a glass of wine."

"You're trying to civilize me, aincha. I been there before."

"No you haven't. Git. And will Jones be here for dinner or is he coming over after?"

"After, I think. Who knows? Save him a piece of salmon just in case."

"Whenever he comes, please remember to ask him if he thinks it's safe for you to move back into the apartment with him yet."

"Wha?" asked the Bear—sounding, it seemed even to himself, almost perfectly stupid.

"You don't really expect to stay here forever, do you?"

"Actually," said the Bear, and placed an uneasy hand on his stomach. "Actually . . ."

Actually something was happening down there in his innards. Actually an instability had put in a bid for manifestation. Actually a rift was being riven in his fundamentals.

"Actually," said the Bear, "I gotta go." And he hotfooted it out of the kitchen, pushed open the bathroom door, got his pants down, and made it onto the seat before Richter had a chance to play even the smallest arpeggio of his famous scale.

Well, it was to be expected, he thought.

He'd spent the first four or five days since the jailbreak in and out of sleep, leaving Iris' spare bedroom only to use the toilet or eat whatever was easiest to lay his paw on—by the second day, once the tests on the blood she'd drawn from him with a big syringe had come back from the lab, she'd put a pot of sumptuous oxtail stew out for him along with the antibiotics, and small bottle upon bottle of mineral supplements—before drifting back to sleep, or someplace partway there, where waking life and dreams were more inextricably conflated than usual. He had conversations with his jailers, he introduced the Doc to Iris and engaged in long philosophical dialogues with an unusually articulate section of a large stone wall. Iris tended to wander in and out of these dreamstates; he knew that she was looking after him while he slept, and he felt that his weakness in her presence was both embarrassing and delicious, was some strange indulgence she or the world had allowed him for the moment, some secret buried psychic thing that undid and pleased him both. He distrusted this all-permissive feeling but surrendered to it nonetheless, and not just because he was too weak and drugfucked to do otherwise. A certain sort-of-out-of-body voluptuousness drew him in, and he drifted with the waves and currents of its indeterminate wake and sleep, floating where it took him, sometimes going under and drowning down to deeper levels, more primordial flows, or rising to primary light. Occasionally he dreamt of his mother, from whom he had been separated young.

As for Jones, thought the Bear as he sat waiting for Iris to finish making dinner, shifting on this seat that had been made, like most of this world's items, too narrow for his comfort, tonight would be the first time he'd be seeing him since the jailbreak, and that had been a pretty blurry day. They'd hardly had a chance to talk then, the day so full of rush and the fear that it would all come down on them next minute if they didn't get a move on. It would be good to see the man again, although in fact the Bear had a bone or two to pick with his buddy. A bubble of rage rose in his belly at a few things Jones had done or let be done while he was inside. The title of the record, for one thing. How could he have let them do that?

The Bear felt other currents shift within him.We're moving earth. We're moving on.

When he was done, he hitched up the outsized khaki pants Iris had insisted he wear around the place and checked his face in the bathroom mirror before reentering the general population. He wetted his paws and worked a rudimentary part into the middle of his headfur, finished off combing it with bared claws, then swished his snout out with some fairly acrid blue mouthwash that Iris had lying around. I've always believed in creating a good impression. He pulled the bathroom door open and stood on the threshold. "Ho-ney," he called out as melodiously as he could manage. "I'm ho-ome."

"Dinner's ready," came Iris' simpler voice in answer amid a clatter of ovenware.

Should I be wearing a jacket? he wondered. She'd picked up an old brown tweed monstrosity from Jones a couple of days back. The Bear smoothed his chestfur, looked down at his feet and wiggled his toeclaws on the parquet. Tic toc tic. Spacetime continuum. Ursina Commedia.

How presentable was I ever? He decided that dinner tonight would be come-as-you-are, but wished he might have a splash of cologne. Must get Jones to come by with my bottle of Tuscany. Goes so well with my native musk. Oh go in already.

"Hi there," he said as he advanced upon Iris and the dinner table.

"Hi yourself," she said, looking up, and favored him with a smile.

Iris was arranging the scalloped white plates on the oval walnut table beneath the brass-and-parchment lighting fixture, whose three small bulbs she had turned down to medium-dim on the dial. On the table, two candles burned in voluted silver sconces and an open bottle of Bordeaux sat on a woven straw widget to one side of the place settings.

"Star Eyes," said the Bear. He loved the way Bird had played the tune of that name, and it had always been one of his nicknames for Iris and it still fit, her eyes so large and bright. The Bear was sadly aware that for all the failed noble substance inside him, his eyes remained, as they had since the end of adolescence, small, piglike and dull.

Iris turned a brilliant embarrassed smile in his direction, blushed, poor baby, and invited him to sit down. The apron gone, she wore a simple black dress with a wide neckline that tied at each shoulder to just expose her lovely collarbones. To the Bear she looked heartbreakingly easy on the eyes. If those eyes could be trusted, she wore no bra beneath the dress. Even so, he returned his attention to her face. It seemed to him that he could look at her with increasing interest through the years, the decades, let's face it, more or less forever. This is who I am. This is the best of all I know on earth. Is it really all I need to know?

She was not, the Bear understood, in the first blush of her beauty. The rounded cheekbones had begun to assume a new prominence, the eyes had widened slightly and seemed startled by their own light, the brow had gained character and lines—but good Lord if you have any eye for the poignancy of time, she's more expressive than ever, and her music that much more deeply felt.

"Everything's ready," she said.

"You do everything so well."

"We'll see."

"Probably we will."

The Bear sat down.

The Bear had always expected the possessors of beauty to understand the meanings of the treasure whose improbable wealth they manifested and over which they stood guard. He had expected, ever since he had first fallen in love with the human form, beautiful women not to be dumb and bimbotesque, as local legend had it, but on the contrary to be wiser than anyone else in view. This he knew to be an offshoot of his subjective inexperience and therefore mere romance, although in Iris' case he was sure that it was really so: how she looked was the index of the otherwise inexpressible delicacy of her inmore soul, the merest sign of who she was and what, in the wide and ordered amplitude of the universe, she might finally represent. Her lightly aging looks were a window on more enduring felicities and vistas still.

I haven't changed at all, thought the Bear. Prison, spiritual annihilation, almost death: what the fuck, I endure, and my hurdy-gurdy heart grinds out the same old tunes. How come? And what if I'm getting tired of the music? Can you show me something better? Still, why did the charade of identity, even as it was being freshly reinvigorated by new desire, seem so fatiguing to him tonight? Maybe while he ground out the same old song he didn't quite believe in it anymore. Or maybe it was not the tune but the instrument he no longer trusted.

"You look lovely," he said, consenting anyway to the rules of the game.

"A book by its cover," she said. "Let's eat." A deflection.

"Shall I pour the wine?"

"Please."

It was a St. Emilion, soft Merlot to lay against anything acerbic in the fish. Nice choice. Although . . .

. . . Although the most prominent presence at the table, like Christ at Emmaus only more garish, was still the sexual tension between them. The Bear felt as if the table should be moving slightly, or might wobble into the air as if at a spiritualist's séance, lifted by waves of suppressed energy and sensual heat. But all that happened was that Iris raised her goblet of red wine and smiled at him. The Bear raised his own in answer.

"Freedom," said the Bear.

"Health."

"Beauty."

"You."

For all the Bear knew, the sex thing was a one-sided hallucination, and Iris' participation a pigment of his imagination entirely.

"It smells nice," said the Bear of the wine, "but I can't really fit the glass around my snout. Don't you have one of those wider ones?"

"Did I put out the Bordeaux glasses?" Iris asked him in apparent innocence. "Excuse me. I'll get you one of those 'wider ones' right away. They're Burgundy glasses actually."

The Bear sat alone at the table for the duration of her errand, feeling obscurely humiliated. She's so slick. No she's not. Yes she is. I can't read her. I can't tell.

"There."

"Thank you." He made the transfer. He tasted. "Lovely wine."

"Let's eat."

"What a good idea."

The grilled filets of salmon lay on beds of spinach leaves, and were topped by lightly cooked tomato meat and shallot or was it purple onion. The Bear found this simple combination exquisite, and the teacup dome of lightly herbed basmati rice complemented it well. Steamed asparagus spears lay roughly parallel on the plate under a scattering of shaved almonds and a gleam of olive oil; a bowl of salad showed its colors for later, and he knew that Iris had already loaded the espresso pot and set the cognac glasses and the bottle out. Life chez Jones had not been like this. But it had been easier to figure out. Ah sweet mystery of love at last I've found you. Subtlety upon subtlety. Veil upon veil. The feminine. Duh.

"My glass is empty," Iris told him.

"Is that my job?"

A simple nod sufficed.

Before long the Bear had finished his piece of salmon and Iris brought in the uncooked remainder on its oaken cutting board. The Bear, trying to figure out the right decorum, cut it into two-inch slices, abstracted the first and put it into his mouth.

"Save some for Jones in case," Iris reminded him.

"Rf," the Bear agreed.

Iris almost made a face as he took in the second raw slab of fish and chomped down. "Remember to ask him about the apartment," she said.

Repeating this request was such a low blow that it was all the Bear could do not to drop his jaw in classic fashion. "Yes, dear," he said.

Iris ignored the irony. "What time do you expect him to come over?"

"Depends on how many times he thinks he has to change taxis. The man has so many phantoms to dodge."

"I thought that was your job. Does he think anyone's still looking?"

"I'd like to think that's over."

"But you still won't go out."

"What for?" asked the Bear.

"Fresh air."

"In New York?"

"The river's not far."

"Maybe I'll have a look at it late tonight. See if Godzilla's up yet, ask him if he's still into urban renewal or has maybe found another trade."

The rest of dinner went quietly, with the air delicately frosted in branching crystal patterns of silent tension, and Iris holding firm after her second short glass of wine; the Bear polished off the bottle and yawned when he was done, revealing a mouthful of ivory and purple terror from which Iris could not avert her eyes.

Blocked by his snout, the Bear did not observe this widening of her eyes, and if his ears heard her intake of breath his brain did not take note of it.

The better to devour me with, Iris almost said aloud, and shivered.

When the Bear had finished off the last of the salmon, save a segment for the possible Jones, they sat quietly until, responding to the easefulness of the wine, the Bear sucked too loudly at his teeth.

Saved by the bell, or rather the intrusive blaring buzzer: Iris' exchange on the intercom confirmed that it was his old buddy downstairs, wanting in.

He felt he had to touch Jones' gaunt-cut face when he came in. "You putting some meat back on, man? You're still so pale."

Jones tossed his lank hair back and exposed his crooked teeth in a smile, a bit of bright blood running fanshaped down one of his foreteeth. "I'm making it," he told the Bear.

"You're starting to go grey," said the Bear, noticing the new streaks at Jones' temples.

"All this physical trauma shit took it out of me, but it gives me character don't you think." Jones tugged at his white shirt. "Wanna see my scar?"

"Would you like coffee now?" Iris asked them. "Or, Jones, perhaps you'd like some dinner."

"Naw I ate already. Thanks. Coffee'd be great. You think I could rest on your sofa there?"

"Of course. Do you want to leave your briefcase here?"

"Nope. Got some stuff to show the Creature. I take it black no sugar."

"There's cognac too."

"Then 'tis very heaven."

Iris went off to the kitchen and they both watched her go.

"Hey Jones."

"Hey Bear."

A hug.

Jones walked through the dining area into the living room and slouched himself down on the long beige textured sofa. The Bear took an armchair set at an angle near its end. They eyed each other, looking for the right cadence, didn't find it, nodded anyway, laughed.

"Here we jolly well are."

"Ahn't we."

"You all set here?" Jones asked him, raising inquisitive brows.

"Set?" wondered the Bear aloud.

"You know." Jones snuck his eyes sidewise toward the kitchen. "Set."

"You mean set in a nudge-nudge wink-wink kind of way?"

"Well, yeah."

"I'm offended by the question."

"You mean it's no go?" Jones asked, leaning toward him. "No shit. I'm amazed."

"You always amazed easy."

"What's the matter?"

"We're comporting ourselves like human beings. Well, one human being and a talking bear actually. I'm not talking about it with you."

"Suit yourself," said Jones, and stuck out his chin. "I really like the pants. You wear them all the time now?"

"Mph," said the Bear, and thought about all the cutting things he could say about how Jones had been humiliated by women all his life, but didn't come close to giving it voice. Still, look at the way Jones was assuming a certain skeletal arrogance there on the sofa. What was up with him? Jones had changed somehow. The Bear wondered, just noting in the margin that he was already somewhat stupefied by desire, if maybe he should lose all this delicate beauty jazz and turn his attentions to Sybil Bailey, a woman made more to his own measure than the frail exquisite vehicle of Iris, obviously too finely made to complement his massive energies. I'd burn her up. She'd break. I need a woman with a bit more heft. I wonder if Sybil digs me. Am I really thinking this? Censorship ain't what it used to be. Maybe it's the vino. On the other hand maybe it's the veritas.

"I was kind of thinking," said Jones.

"Really," said the Bear.

"Well, wondering really, how well you were set up here." He looked both ways, as if about to cross a particularly tricky street. "Because like if you were, I was thinking of maybe moving in with Sybil and closing up the old apartment."

"You were *what*?"

"Not that Sybil and I have talked it all the way through yet, but I mean it'd be so much safer. The old place is blown, don't you think? It ain't no safe house no more. I could put the books and things into storage."

"Jones. I'm appalled. I feel as if everything's being pulled out from under me."

"Well, get used to it. Seems to be the law of the land in these parts."

"What is going on with you?"

"You mean you really can't nail her?" Jones asked with what the Bear thought was unprecedented vulgarity.

"Jones, what the fuck has gotten into you?"

Jones grinned and reached for his briefcase. "Let me show you what's been happening. There's a lot you don't know."

"Evidently."

"You're gonna like it."

"I'm gonna lap it up and grin."

"C'mon Bear, get with the program. Things're looking up."

Iris entered with steaming espresso cups, brandy glasses, and a Napoleon bottle on a tray. She walked gracefully, as if on hydraulically cushioned joints, and nothing rattled or shook.

Jones gave her a big smile. "Don't she look great, Bear?" he asked.

Iris set the tray down on the coffee table and sat beside Jones on the sofa. "Now, who wants what."

"Everybody wants the perfectly obvious," said the Bear.

"Coffee and cognac all around then," Iris said.

Jones heaved a sheaf of papers out of his briefcase and onto the coffee table. "Okay. Guess."

"They found Judge Crater," said the Bear. "Shit floats, the Pope's Polish, manifestation's a hoax and we're all really one, man."

"That too," said Jones, "but what's more important in the short run, the whole first pressing of the Tin Palace record just about sold out in two days and Megaton International wants to buy it flat, pay you a quick twenty K, put out a hundred thousand copies worldwide for starters and get you into the studio to cut a new one as soon as poss." Jones grinned at him from his privileged seat. "I been working."

Iris, sitting up straight, clapped flat hands together like a child. "Goody," she said.

"What the fuck happened?" said the Bear, whose first uncensored thought was, This is a disaster.

"In a word," said Jones, taking a large theatrical sip of cognac, "the good guys won."

"How'd they do it."

"Basically because you're such a great musician but also because there was a little item in the *Voice* about the gunshots on the end of the album and *Down Beat* picked it up, and people wanted to know whether you're a hoax or not, and Wynton Marsalis piped up to say you were a degrading image of the jazz musician either way—"

"Wynton Marsalis the young trumpet kid with all the chops and brains?"

"A lot happened while you were inside, B. These days he's the law of the land in this part of the forest, gets to say what's jazz and what's not. Anyhow you offend him enough to talk about in print and that helped Cummins' little pressing vanish from stores quick fast in a hurry on both coasts and also Chicago."

"I like what I've heard of Wynton. It'd be nice to play with him. But I'm degrading, huh."

"Say thanks if you see him, 'cause he gave you the best publicity you ever got. Something about the always false image of the Noble Savage."

"Well," said the Bear, "I'm not very savage, and I can't say I find anything noble about me . . ."

"You have a certain . . ." Jones maintained, and waved a hand in the air.

"Naw," said the Bear, "I always thought I was about the soul's exile on earth and some of the other lesser Gnostic heresies. It's a bunch of shit I've been bored with, personally speaking, for a couple of decades already, but it's more germane than any noble savage variations. If you see Wynton, do me a favor and wise him up."

"Nothing noble then?" Jones asked, pretending to take notes.

"Once upon a time," said the Bear, "but that was only inexperience. What's biting Wynton's ass? I can play. I know my music. I'm no semifinished knuckle-dragger. I'm no faker." The Bear wiped his right paw across his eyes. "God, it's hideous to have to talk like this."

"Don't worry," Jones told him. "I'll stop you before you kill again."

The Bear downed his cognac in one burning gulp and Jones polished his off in answer. Iris refilled their snifters, took a small sip from her own and assumed an attentive air.

"I didn't have to do a thing, hardly," Jones continued. "Cummins started getting calls. Columbia, Blue Note, Megaton. I did the callbacks and Megaton's got the best offer. They're the only one who wants to buy the old record out and redistribute, and they want to make a new one on BFD, give it high-art tone and worldwide distribution."

"I'd love to make a Blue Note record," said the Bear. "Too bad Lee Morgan's dead, I'd do it with him."

"Now there's a guy had even worse luck in clubs than you did," said Jones. "The bullet with his name on it didn't miss."

"Sure," said the Bear. "His girlfriend fired it, not some working stiff of a cop." He didn't look at Iris, but he could feel her looking at him. "If you want the job done right," he said, "what you need is love."

"Well," Jones resumed, "Blue Note's only offering ten to Megaton's twenty. With Megaton you get the first record out there in big numbers now. With anyone else it'll be months before anything new comes out. I say let's keep you current. I say let's move. I say let's take the money and run."

"Whoever it is," said the Bear, "as far as the old album's concerned, they'll have to change the title."

"Shouldn't do that," said Jones. "It's already made its bones under one name. Change it and the buyers'll get confused."

"First," said the Bear, "I'm not sure I want that album out at all—"

"What!"

"Maybe if the cops'd let me do another set before they blew the whistle, but as is . . ."

"What!"

"And I don't know how you let them put it out with that title. You know what I wanted to call the record."

"Everyone agreed that *If There's a Bleecker Street Than This One I Don't Know Its Name* wouldn't fit on the cover, and besides no one but you ever thought it was any good. It was such a downer."

"Jones, is it possible you don't realize it was a joke?"

"Not a very good one, B."

"But *Blues in Ursa Minor*, Jones? Have you lost every remnant of sense and taste?"

"What's so wrong with that?"

"Phphrrr."

"Jesus McChristmas, I come over here with all this good news and you're sending out vibes like a cracked reactor. What the hell is going on with you?"

"You fucked me up," said the Bear, getting down to it.

"I worked like a goddamn slave to find you is what I did," Jones insisted. "I got *stabbed* for you. I crawled bleeding across Washington Square Park for you."

"You got stabbed because you don't know where to walk at night when I'm not with you." The Bear heard a sharp intake of breath from Iris' direction, and looked at her, her eyes widening, face going red, sitting rigid on the sofa. No, he thought. I'm right about this. This has to be said.

"I got stabbed because I'd been looking for you for months and this was the only way the world could figure out to turn the trick."

"Oh yeah?"

"You had to be there," said Jones. "And in a sense you were. In fact I was hoping to talk with you about it, but since you're being so unreasonable, like what's the point."

"When was I ever reasonable?" asked the Bear, with some thunder. "I was never reasonable. What I'm being now is monstrous."

"I'd say."

"Even so I find all this 'I was stabbed for you' a little hard to take. You know where *I* was?"

"Bear," said Iris. "If Jones hadn't been in the hospital, and if I hadn't gone to visit him, if I'd been able to quit smoking, and if Tim hadn't been sitting in the smoker's lounge . . ."

"My grandma'd be a trolley," said the Bear, "instead of dead in a circus cage at twenty-seven."

"Stop this," Iris announced. "I want you both to stop this, or both of you can leave. What *is* it about men anyway?"

"I ain't," the Bear began, but left it there.

"Just stop this."

"She's right," Jones told him.

"Of course she's right," said the Bear. He got up and began to pace.

"Watch the carpet," Iris admonished him.

"Let a bear pace, won't you?"

"Do you have to dig your claws in so?" she asked. "Look at what you're doing to the weave."

"I know," said the Bear. "There's a great disturbance in the Force. I walk through the world doing damage. It's my job." He paced more gently, laying his paws down softly heel to toe. "Howzis?"

"I gotta pee," Jones informed Iris. "Where's the?"

Iris indicated the way. "Bear," she said when Jones had gone.

"You're right," the Bear told her. "You're right absolutely. Let me walk it off. It's your house. It's my fault. Agh."

"If you think I'm going to contradict you you're wrong."

"Was I that bad?"

"You were awful. How could you do that to him?"

"He let them change the name of my album. I think that's an area in which I can legitimately expect to exercise a degree of control."

"He took away your toy," said Iris, "so obviously you should kill him."

"Good idea." The Bear paced more vehemently.

"The carpet," Iris reminded him.

"The eggshell," said the Bear.

In the course of his pacing, during which he tried to see the situation straight and also not rip the rug up, the Bear asked himself, What's wrong with you? Don't you realize we're all in the same old leaky boat?

"What?" Iris asked him. "What did you say about a boat?"

"You're hearing me think again. I was just trying to tell myself that we're all in the same old leaky boat."

"Then you're more of an optimist than I am," Iris said.

"What do you mean?"

"You still think there's a boat."

"Of course there's a boat," he said, but avoided her eye. "Of course there is."

"With you behaving like this," said Iris, "I'm just about convinced there isn't. How can you? Do you think he's your dog?"

"You were hoping for something from me," said the Bear.

"I was hoping for a lot."

"You were? Really? Still?"

"Of course I was. What do you think is going on here?"

"Damned if I know," the Bear told her honestly.

Jones came back from the bathroom smoothing down his shirtfront and double-checking his fly.

"We be of one blood, thou and I," the Bear said wearily.

"Okay, peace. Did you listen to the Tin Palace record?"

"I'm afraid to," the Bear confessed.

"Don't be. It's better than you think."

"I thought it was very good," put in Iris.

"Betrayal on all sides. When did you listen to it?" the Bear asked her.

"Headphones," Iris explained. "You ought to hear it. It's good."

"It's lucky we were a working band. Still, we needed another set to get into it, but by the time we did the gig we never started completely cold. And Billy was so good."

"You ought to hear it," Iris said.

"You'd be surprised," Jones added.

"Maybe tomorrow," said the Bear, meaning maybe a week or so, or never.

"So," said Jones, changing the tone, "what about the offer from Megaton and BFD? Say the word and you can be in the studio within the month."

The Bear made an unconscious face-washing motion with his right paw. "I don't think I can do it."

"What? Kee-rist. Here we go again."

"I'm not doing this just to be difficult, you know."

"You mean it's a bonus?"

"Jones, I really can't find the music in me. I've been practicing around the apartment, and it's not there, or at least not where I know how to find it. I ain't no burning bush. I get consumed. I lose touch with the root. I get all burned up."

"You are what you are. We know you can play. At the moment it would be good for you, and you probly need the bread. How you gonna pay Tim back for all the fish?"

"Yeah, how is Tim?"

"Stunned he didn't lose his job or get busted. Says he sits at home in his armchair expecting the ceiling to fall in on him and after awhile when it doesn't he starts to smile. And his wife won't need the operation."

"Happy ever after," said the Bear. "Friedmann says he's okay too."

"So what's with the record, B? You should do it, you know."

"I know, but I feel like I've lost the thread. What's BFD stand for?" asked the Bear. "Big Fucking Deal?"

"I think it's something Danish. This is a good deal, Bear. Krieger says you can use pretty much anyone you want on the date."

"Sigbjørn Krieger? Mr. BFD? You talked with him?"

"The famous Danish control freak himself. And it wasn't a bad meeting."

"I like the way his records sound. What does he mean anyone?"

"He suggested Jack DeJohnette on drums."

"Uh-uh," said the Bear, recoiling. "I'm afraid of that guy. You ever notice how he always sounds better than anyone he plays with? I can't afford that at this stage of my," he gave a plosive little laugh, "career. Besides, I already have this good thing going with Billy. Is Billy available?"

Jones nodded yes. "Piano?"

"Monk's dead," said the Bear, "so I'd have to think about it. Mingus gone too. There goes the bass chair."

"Krieger suggested Charlie Haden."

"You're kidding. I could play with Charlie Haden? I'd do anything to play with Charlie Haden."

"Even make a record?" Jones asked, looking clever, and raised some papers in the air.

"If I have to. Is there anything I have to sign about selling them the old one?"

"Hey, if your writing paw's still shaky a print'll do. The Bear, his mark. We do the blood contract later."

"You know what I do want to do," said the Bear. "I want to do some press. I think that's the only way to go ahead without getting busted again. I've come to feel that in the last analysis the only way I ever really got hurt was by trying to protect myself."

"Didn't I always tell you that? Didn't I tell you that years ago?"

"Did you?" The Bear sort of remembered something of the sort, but it was unclear and compromised by ancillary circumstance, and anyway he thought it was bad form of Jones to bring it up just now.

"Sure I did," Jones persisted. "I always told you you should go open, but noo, you hadda deal with it your way, you had to be secretive about everything because it was more subversive. Whereas I always felt that was exactly the way to create the very dangers you were afraid of."

"What I remember mostly about what you said is how much money we were gonna make if we opened widescreen. I remember that and how the risk was completely mine."

"Aw, foo-foo. You always think everything's completely yours."

"Thank you for sharing that with me. In any case I think it would be wise to go public now. Radical trust and the open road is the way ahead."

Jones tried to look impressed. "Well, that's new," he told the Bear.

"That is new," Iris agreed.

The Bear saw that both of them had raised their eyebrows, making it four raised eyebrows in all.

"Let me get this straight," said the Bear. "Y'all think it's new."

"You really want to do this big," said Jones, "I could probly get you on Letterman in a week."

"Whoa hey wait a minute. Can't we keep this jazz-size, you know, next to invisible, I think the key word here is small?"

"So what you want? *Village Voice*, *Down Beat*? You want to go daylight maybe you should think about the *Times*."

"I could do a couple of interviews," the Bear allowed. He felt himself starting to sweat beneath his fur. It never ends, does it. What a piece of work I am. "The *Times* is possible."

"Well cool, daddy-o. Here's the one you got to sign." Jones proffered a single piece of paper. "Power of attorney, though don't worry, I won't do anything large without you."

"Can we change the album title back?"

"It might be negotiable. They're not gonna like it."

"What's that clause down there at the bottom of the contract?" the Bear asked Jones, trying to make friends.

Jones picked up on it, gave a little smile. "That's in case you go crazy on us. That's the sanity clause."

"You no foola me," said the Bear, and Jones indicated with a nod that he should finish the line on his own. "There ain't no Sanity Clause."

Iris looked at the Bear, then at Jones, then back at the Bear, and muttered something mostly inaudible about "boys."

"When can you let me know about whether you want to make a new record for BFD?" Jones asked. "Keep in mind that without it, they may not do the deal on the old one."

"Would that be so bad?"

Jones shrugged. "If trust is the way ahead . . ."

"Despite the inexistence of the sanity clause," the Bear promised him, "I'll really really think it over. I'll do my level best." If I can figure out where level is, he thought.

"How could you be so awful to him?" Iris asked once Jones had gone.

"I thought we were over that. Is it still Torment-a-Bear week?"

"You were horrible."

"Ursus horribilis. I admit it. Can we let it go?"

"As long as you know how bad you were."

"Okay okay, I confess. Look, you wanna see my impression of a bearskin rug?" The Bear jumped up from his chair and bellied himself down onto the living room carpet. He splayed his limbs out, exhaled and propped his jaws open. "Howzat?" he asked, and let his tongue loll out and his eyes roll back.

Iris tried not to laugh. "And the only reason you're upset with *me*," she said, "is that I won't be a good girl and get into bed with you."

"Wow, it's in the open," he said from his difficult position.

"It always was," Iris said.

"Well, it would be a nice gesture, wouldn't it?" asked the Bear, turning onto his side, leaning his head on his paw and batting his eyes in her general direction.

"It's not happening," Iris said firmly. "And you didn't ask Jones if you could move back to the apartment."

"We got distracted. I forgot."

"Call him tomorrow and ask."

The Bear got up from the floor and brushed his fur down. "You're a princess on top of a steep glass mountain, aren't you?" he said. "I must perform some appropriate heroic task or other. Have I got it right?"

Iris tried not to smile. "You're so inexperienced," she said.

"Try to think of me as an elderly adolescent."

"Well, wise up," she advised him.

"How?" the Bear wanted to know.

"I'm going to bed. Maybe for once you could do the dishes. Use steel wool on the roasting pan and the long-handled brush on the plates and the glasses. If you come into my room I'll shoot you. Good night." She turned on her heel and split.

The Bear stood there in the living room thinking, Wuh? Huh? Didn't that happen kinda fast and how much did I actually lose in the exchange?

Later, though, lying in his narrow bed alone with an unread book sprawled open on his belly, it all seemed different to him. He remembered how easily he had thought of losing the delicate beauty bit and seeing if maybe Sybil was available for fucking, and in retrospect this made him seem completely monstrous to himself. His heart was dark, a portable beating prison.

After awhile his mind wandered, though, and he allowed himself to think of Iris sleeping. She was probably asleep by now. Once or twice after dinner that week she had fallen asleep on her living-room sofa, lying on her back with her head propped on the armrest, and the Bear had sat himself down on the edge of the coffee table to watch her breathe and dream, her eyes moving left to right behind their lids. The Bear had seen a few other humans sleeping—Jones looking like he'd been poleaxed, and a few women he'd had sex with who had tumbled into sleep afterward and left a residue of shipwrecked body behind—but he had never seen anything like Iris. When she slept, all her habitual tension let go of her, her face relaxed and looked more pure and simple, and everything in her, especially her unprotected throat and face, urged the eye upward: it was not hard to see which way her soul had flown: right out of her, and had left behind an expression on her face of sweet release and perfect trust. She was never more purely beautiful than when she slept. No, that's not it either—she's more radiant and complex when awake, but watching her asleep the Bear understood why people in love felt the irresistible urge to say I'll love you forever, I've already loved you forever, even if they partly know themselves unequal to the task in the chaptering, sequential world. One moment of authentic love, screw it up how you may later on, opens a holy window onto something outside of breathing thumping time that you cannot completely deny, ever, no matter what infelicity or farce succeeds it later on. But because, when the true-blue moment comes, you can't recognize it for what it is, you say something in additive language about forever. As if an additive forever had anything to do with it. It's about the perception of eternity, for all the quotidian ticking of your mortal form. In this respect, it seemed to him, nothing is so privileged as love.

In this way, the Bear had sat over her sleep a few times, feeling like a large dark planet revolving around the delicacy of her light, spun through the elliptical orbits of longing and gazing down through the vertiginous gulf between their species. He'd felt just about broken in two by the gap between his clumsy yearning and the elegance of her perfect formal achievement. Even so, whether in thrall or on guard, whether obeying his heart or the laws of some other subtle physics, he had felt large and dedicated and patient and slow.

If this ain't love, it's the best a poor dumb bear can do.

He would look at the complex cablework, as revealed by her head thrown back, that underwrote the classic thrust of her chin and jaw, and would admire the interweave of tendon and breath, see the pulses beating there, and loving this dreaming face and the spirit it had for the moment set free from its confines, he would surrender to the beauty of the construction and what it might imply about the uncreated, the more than merely built. He would stand guard forever, if need be, over that flown and precious soul, and the breathing house it lived in, to make sure that no harsh or harmful thing might intrude and disturb its being. I will protect her, above all if need be, from myself. Maybe he was no more than a random beast on watch, stunned by the higher music her beauty set loose in him. Maybe that was all there was to it. And that might be enough.

She's right: wise up.

I wish I were more fit for this music than I am.

His heavy bearshaped form had never felt so preposterous to him. There was nothing to be done with this situation. Nothing that he could see at all.

Iris lay in her bed feeling a particularly satisfactory warmth spreading from her flat little belly into her extremities. It felt so good to have the Bear here in her apartment sufficiently tamed, so that she could control the pace of things. It felt almost as if she had walked into the ocean—Iris did not swim—and had laid her hand on the mane of a cresting wave and calmed its ocean-rolling potency momentarily into the sway of her command. If he were to come into the room right now, she would almost certainly be unable to resist him. She would surrender herself to every annihilation, offer herself to be burned up by whatever experience came, even if, as was likely, it would also be sordid and inappropriate and they would both have to pay for it later on. But the knowledge that, actually, he would not come into her room tonight made her strong. It was as if she commanded some large portion of the unmeasured force of nature right here in the rectilinear privacy of her home. It was as if she could lay her hand on that wave's foaming mane and muster its power to her own purpose. She let the warmth of this power thicken the too-thin muscles of her limbs. It felt good. It might strengthen her yet. What would happen to her if she went into *his* room?

Absolutely not. Absolutely not tonight.

In this state it was possible to feel lifted into sleep, as if by a wave, when usually she collapsed into it stricken and seeking refuge. Oh yes, she thought, it was a lovely night.

2

it was almost noon and the Bear was looking out of Iris' living-room window, waiting for the van to come. He could see a bit of the housing project's interior roadway from where he sat. A lot of busy squirrels down there, and people walking their dogs. It seemed to him that the dogs had more interested, curious and intelligent expressions on their faces than the people they led around on a leash, but maybe he was prejudiced in this regard.

The Bear belched. He had downed a salad bowl of black coffee and eight bagels for breakfast and his stomach felt kind of acid. Could be a problem later on. Case of the runs coming on in the studio. He hoped not but it was possible.

He had never gotten it straight whether this was Stuyvesant Town or Peter Cooper Village but it came to the same thing: a housing project built for the postwar middle class, set alongside the East River in the East Twenties, tall redbrick buildings angled a fair distance from each other across green triangulating lawns and walkways, strategically augmented by emplacements of trees and shrubs. What were probably the fattest, safest squirrels in the city were making a big fuss about walking around on all that geometric grass, wagging their plumy officious tails and chattering at each other the way they do. A lot of nickery chitter-chatter under the new leaves in the hazy lemon light. Yeah, city. Yeah, your life on earth. The Bear sank beneath the surface of words and mused on nothing, occasionally coming out with a sigh, for about the next ten minutes.

Iris had come home from work last night happy and singing to herself. La la la, tra *la*. After hanging her coat up in the entrance-hall closet she had danced, her arms raised high, right into his arms and then out of them before he'd had a chance to embrace her, then had kept a careful distance from him for the rest of the night. "I don't feel like cooking tonight, honey, so do you mind if I phone out for Hunan Chinese?" She'd casually called him honey, then gone on with all that tra la la, tra *la*. She'd had such a glow on, and so bright a smile that he'd thought she might be laughing at him. Either that or she was getting laid at work. "Aren't I allowed to feel happy for a change?" she'd asked him when he'd looked bothered. "Is that a problem for you, and if so, can a woman ask you why?" He'd felt so bulky and inept, Iris radiant in her living room, vibrating like a compass needle that always pointed true, and him so dark and shuttered and possessive.

What finally roused him from the dull penny of these musings was an irritated chitter-chatter coming at him from somewhere nearby.

He raised and focussed his eyes to find a squirrel sitting up on its hindlegs watching him from a joint of branch and trunk. Hey, you made it this far up, thought the Bear. Let's hear it for your sense of enterprise. The Bear waved hello and the squirrel nickered at him again, shook its angry tail and advanced toward him along the branch, the bark still black from an early morning shower. The squirrel bared his foreteeth at him and raised up on its hindlegs again in a posture of threat. Wow, thought the Bear, the territorial imperative at work. Just look at it go.

The Bear didn't want to humiliate the little guy but he couldn't help it, he had to laugh. "All right, I give up," he told the squirrel finally, raised his paws in mock surrender, got up from his chair and backed away from the window.

The squirrel chittered at him again to make sure, then walked back along the branch gesturing rhythmically with its tail and showing the Bear its button of an asshole, contemptuous.

The Bear had to laugh again. What a way to put a world together.

Rising from the chair, he decided to take a tour of Iris' apartment. He cast a sidewise eye at his saxophone case standing on end beside the armchair. No, his axe was cool, and all the necessary sheet music was tucked inside the case. He was ready. He was ready to go, although in fact the urge to run away from everything was prominent in his mind. Of course the trouble with running away from everything was that everything, by definition, could not successfully be run away from. It wasn't only the pressure of the recording session that was getting to him though. It was the concourse of ongoing events, including his love or desire for Iris, and all the tributary circumstances that were subtly and invidiously conspiring him back into selecting a single life from the world of infinite options. It was the command aspect of the manifest order that troubled him: if you become this, you cannot become that. It was, as usual, having to be here at all, and the sheaf of laws that came with the package. He knew why he was here. He was here for love, but the consequences were a pain.

He began his ramble through the rooms.

Nothing much happening in the kitchen, and the smell of coffee fading on the air. Should he chow down some leftovers? No. In the bathroom, order prevailed and he had done a good job for once, though time would tell, swabbing up the fur after his shower.

Surveying his own small square bedroom and its single bed, he nodded approval at the near neatness he had left behind, the bedspread smoothed, a few signs of life and inquiry in the interlocutory bookmarks sticking out of the stack of books.

He'd been avoiding Iris' room but finally he went in.

Her room was full of the fine clean smell of her, and she'd left the bed unmade, its topsheet and blankets pulled diagonally back. He breathed her in through his quivering nose a few times but did not thrust his muzzle into the bedding. A faint indentation lay on the pillow where her head had been. A couple of small black lacy diaphanous items were strewn on the floor just inside the sliding doors of her walk-in closet but he wasn't tempted.

Oh yeah, then why bring it up?

Back in place at the window, he checked the view for King Squirrel and when he didn't find him sat in the armchair again. In about a minute he saw the van arrive in the small patch of interior roadway available to view—Jones' aim was true. It braked to a halt and the headlights flashed on and off, as in a spy movie. He could just make out Jones in a peacoat and watchcap behind the tree reflections on the windshield. The Bear stood up and waved, and Jones flashed the headlights back to acknowledge. Time to go.

The Bear put on his trenchcoat and pulled up on the collar, then jammed the big brown fedora on his head. It would be his first time outside in daylight since the jailbreak, which he didn't remember very well. He'd been down to the river a couple of times around four a.m. to see if any of his brother monsters were up and felt like talking, but there had been nothing out there besides water, enveloping dark and rippling smears of colored light. It was spring in New York City but the nights were still chilly. Too cold to work the horn comfortably in any case. A little warmer and he might have done a Sonny Rollins and for want of a bridge walk out on the pilings and play for the fishes.

The Bear opened his saxophone case just to be sure his axe was actually inside it. The horn looked fine. Jones had taken it to Maury, who had worked on it for three days, replacing pads and the occasional cracked mother-of-pearl disk, fixing bent valves and rockers, replacing the springs and lubing its old ligaments and limbs. Then Maury had hand-buffed what remained of the horn's original finish, tossed in some packets of the Bear's usual extra-heavy reeds, and given him a couple of new French mouthpieces to try out on spec. The horn looked almost new laid out in its nest of worn red plush. On the phone, Maury had advised him to get a new molded polycarbon case but the Bear wouldn't hear of it: he loved the old black rectangular beat-up luggage. Then Maury, although one might have thought he'd find such work infra dig, had repaired one of the hinges and braced a disintegrating corner with a piece of steel plate. The case was cool. Maury was an artist. The Bear admired the bronze complexity of his axe, quite a piece of plumbing really, checked his reed supply and fluttered through the sheet music, then shut the case and locked it.

No excuses left. It was really time to go.

The last time he'd done a gig he'd been arrested, but he hoped to do better this time. The image of Friedmann gushing arterial blood in mid-aria on a Vienna stage flashed irresistibly through his mind, but the Bear couldn't figure out what Friedmann's face would have looked like in its twenties.

And then, of course, there was Lee Morgan, who'd been shot to death in the middle of a set at Slug's Saloon. Morgan's death had meant the end of Slug's, and the Bear had learned just a few days before, in the middle of a phoner with Lester Bowie, that his own bust had shut the Tin Palace down. The place was gone, Bowie told him, a shuttered box on the Bowery. As far as the world in general knew, the Tin Palace had never been.

Time to get a move on, Bear. Curtain up, light the lights, cut a record. Only question, how to do it when, at the present moment, you couldn't play for shit? He'd practiced enough to know that he was fucked in every essential musical regard. He had worked a few strategies out to cover this little difficulty but he wondered, even doubted if these strategies would work.

Why is life so provisional, can you tell me that? Why are you never properly supplied?

On leaving the apartment, he made sure the door had locked behind him. He turned the knob a few times and it held. So there was no way back.

"One thing," said Jones while they were heading uptown in the van. "When we get to the Power Station, let's not have a repetition of what happened at the rehearsal studio."

"What was so wrong with that?" asked the Bear.

Jones looked sideways at him from the driver's seat before returning his attention to the milling traffic headed north on Sixth—a lot of cabs out there, bright yellow carapaces competing with each other for a good spot in the swarm, accompanied by a major-league blowing of horns. Fifth chords and thirds clashed with each other without, however, producing developmental consequences of much interest, and there was no universal system of tuning. Ives might have done something with it, thought the Bear, but the given day did not.

"What was wrong with the *rehearsal*?" Jones asked him incredulously. "You mean aside from it being just short of World War III and there was no blood on the floor when you left?"

Well, even the Bear had to admit, although of course not audibly, that the rehearsal had been a little strange. Sigbjørn Krieger had booked two consecutive evenings at S.I.R. in the West Forties and the Bear had said cool on condition that Krieger didn't show. Of course Krieger, famous for his ambitions toward total artistic control of the recording process, had shown up, and of course Jones, still angling for a gig with the parent company Megaton International, had lacked the necessary two olives to keep him out of the rehearsal room. The Bear had hardly met the band, had hardly had the chance to say hello to Billy Hart again, a lot of warmth there, and to meet Charlie Haden for the first time—a pink-cheeked Clark Kent–looking guy the Bear regarded as the greatest living bassplayer on the planet. And he'd hardly had a chance to meet the young pianist Billy had angled onto the gig despite Krieger's objections and the Bear's doubts: Rahim Bobby Hatwell, this kid in his twenties Billy said the Bear just had to hear to believe. Well, the Bear felt he owed Billy a lot and he had given in. And Steve Kuhn had turned out to be out of town that week. The Bear would have given a lot to play with Steve Kuhn.

Krieger showed up as the Bear was eyeing Hatwell hello and the small athletic-looking piano-playing cat was wondering if you were supposed to shake hands with a bear or what, and if so how. "Hallo, everybody," Krieger had called from the rehearsal studio's doorway while shucking a massive shearling overcoat into the hands of an attendant, and the Bear had shot an angry sidelong look at Jones, who shrugged in response and muttered something about how the guy owned the damn company, after all.

Back in spacetime present, Jones stomped on the brakes and barely managed not to crush the rear end of a Chevy full of Chasids. The Bear could see their sidelocks wobble. It was heavy traffic. It was daytime in New York. It was the world as given. "Naw," he said, "it wasn't all that bad, not really."

"In the sense that Krieger didn't cancel your deal on the spot I'd have to agree with you," Jones told him. "Otherwise, are you kidding me?"

"I thought it went pretty well," said the Bear, "musically speaking."

"You hardly played."

"It was enough," said the Bear.

"You're out of your mind," was Jones' opinion.

"Nyah nyah," said the Bear.

While they sat in silence for a few heavily trafficked blocks the Bear wondered if he'd done the right thing at the rehearsal after all. His tactics had been based on the intuition that his music was doornail dead and the only way he was going to get a decent record made was to do it so fast he'd hardly have the chance to know he was doing it at all. That, and instead of getting into the intricate harmonic architecture that had absorbed his real attention lately, he would have to imitate himself, make believe, basically, he was the musician he'd been before his imprisonment: more simply impassioned, better possessed by naive and suppositious yearning for freedom and release. He'd have to forget, as experience had taught him, how complex and unsatisfactory even a small degree of freedom could be, once achieved. Have to dodge his nagging sense of the ambiguity of all experience and pretend to burning unicity again. Appetite he might have, but passion, not these days, no, not really. He was still living under the aspect of annihilation, in the spaces between the atoms. The world as given tasted primarily of ash. Iris? That was another story, not yet told.

What he had to do in order to make the date was dodge his ego or throw a whammy on himself so he wouldn't be looking when the music got made, disguise his right paw from his left so one of them wouldn't know what the other was up to.

He had walked into the rehearsal at S.I.R. with all these problems prominently in mind, had said hello to Billy Hart, met Haden for the first time, and had a looksee at the Hatwell kid. He'd passed out four of the five tunes he wanted to do on the date, rushed everyone through the heads, blew a couple of trial choruses, let Hatwell get a few licks in—Billy was right, he was gonna be fine—heard the music starting to build, and then, coolly certain that if he let it build any further there'd be nothing left in him for the recording session, he'd stuck his paw in the air and called it an afternoon. Everyone said Huh? and that's when Sigbjørn Krieger, expecting to watch the music brew and jell and move in the direction of the perfect record he wished to make, objected. The Bear made it known, through Jones, that he didn't want Krieger in the room. Krieger likewise made it known, through his own intermediary, that he was personally involved in every phase of every record he produced, and his sole concession to the Bear's demand for privacy had been arriving at the rehearsal a half hour late.

They might have had a fullblown battle on the spot, but Haden had somehow got between them and had started telling Krieger about how he had to change his hotel room again—something about the damp, or a draft—and how he wanted the producer to talk to the management for him. This enabled the Bear to get into his hat and coat and pack his alto before Victory-Bear Warrior, which was how the Bear roughly translated the producer's name, knew what was going on. When Krieger did figure out that his altoist was leaving he threw an intellectually restrained and cold-blooded tantrum at the Bear and told him to rehearse the date or else.

"You want to cancel?" the Bear had asked him, but cheated the moment, baring his teeth more than he needed to, strictly speaking, and bristled his neckfur in waves. "Fine."

Krieger stared at him and the Bear put a gentle but still bearish paw on the man's shoulder. "Fine?" Krieger asked him, his voice wobbling critically.

"Yeah," the Bear told him. "On an essential level I don't need to make a record, so if you'd like me to leave, I will, no problem." Then he let his voice modulate to something more reasonable: it was like performing an aria. "But I do want to make this particular record, and I'm doing it the only way I know how. Granted I'm a bit unusual. Eccentric even. A bear of mystery, sometimes even to myself. At the moment it's fine with me if the rhythm section wants to loosen up and get to know the material I've written for them, but purely for the sake of my ability to make the record, hello I must be going, dig?"

The Bear thought it was a pretty speech and hoped it had confused Krieger. Anyhow it was all he had. As the Bear swept out of the studio all footstep and trenchcoat and untamed force of nature—anyhow that was the impression he was anxious to create—Jones had stayed behind to wheedle peace at the producer, and Charlie Haden had followed him out into the corridor, a mischievous grin on his boyish middle-aged map.

"Oh man," Haden told him in the tremulous tenor the Bear had read was a result of childhood polio of the throat, "I don't know if there's going to be a recording date this week, but it was worth a million bucks just to see you talk to Sigbjørn, man." Haden doubled over laughing.

"Glad you liked it."

"I *loved* it. Are you sure you're okay for the date, assuming it happens?"

"Charlie, you think I made a mistake?"

"It's possible. You sure you don't want to play some more today?"

"I'm saving it."

"Well, you must know what you need to do."

"That's the general idea," said the Bear.

"But are you sure?" Haden asked him.

"No. Unfortunately I'm not."

"Has it occurred to you," Jones asked the Bear, as he pushed the intercom button of the Power Station a second time and still no one answered, "that you might have loused things up enough with Krieger that he cancelled the date?"

"Someone would have called. You know," said the Bear, "they should never have changed the name of this neighborhood."

Jones pushed the intercom button again. "See?" he said. "Nobody's answering. It's all over. Fuck."

"I mean, Hell's Kitchen was such a cool name," the Bear continued. "But realtors interfered and the city knuckled under." The Bear sniffed the air, in which some tang of the waterfront remained. "I'd rename New York City Hell's Kitchen if I could."

"Still no answer," said Jones, and actually wrung his hands. "When you fuck things up you fuck 'em good."

"Hell's Brick Shithouse," mused the Bear. "Nah, even I think that's a little strong."

"What are we gonna do now?" Jones asked the air.

"Hell's Pay Toilet."

"Bear, puh-leeze." Jones pushed the button again and wiped sweat from his forehead despite the breezy cool of the day.

"Did you know this actually was a power station once?" the Bear persisted. Jones was so easy to annoy. "Some relay in the city's early electrical system. Nice to know it's not just another ego-of-the-music-business name like the Hit Factory. Have a little faith, Jones. Someone's home."

"I don't think so. I really hate you sometimes."

"I know," said the Bear.

"Khoo zzit?" an electric voice rasped through the small square speaker-grid set in the concrete doorframe.

"Animal crackers," said the Bear, leaning into the microphone aperture.

"Well, *someone's* here anyway," said Jones when the buzzer unlatched the door and he pushed it open. "If we're not making a record maybe we can get up a game of poker. Maybe I'll get lucky and lose you to an engineer."

"That's very funny," said the Bear, and laughed. "That's really very funny, Jones."

"He said something nice to me!" Jones announced to a heavyset guy in a black T-shirt, old jeans and a Monster Cable cap who was sitting at a table sorting gold-tipped lengths of insulated wire. "You were a witness. He said something nice!"

"We're the Bear," the Bear told the guy in the cap.

"I guessed. You're in Studio A, through there." He indicated a way down the piney-woods corridor past the equipment cases and the lounge. "Door on the right's the control room, the left's the studio proper."

"Thanks," said the Bear. "Nice cables you got there. Expensive stuff?"

"So you really are a bear," the guy said, looking up, the cables bundled in his hands. "I thought maybe it was a nickname, but no, huh."

"One morning," the Bear started telling him, and put his alto case on the table, the better to converse, "I woke from a night of uneasy dreams to discover that I had been transformed into an enormous—"

"Yo, Gregor!" Jones was calling from the control-room doorway. "We got some musicians here! Looks like we're actually gonna make a record!"

"I knew this was gonna be a shitty day," the Bear told the guy at the desk.

"There's no avoiding it."

"Later."

"Later."

As the Bear shoved his way through the control-room doorway, he took in the scene as if scouting the place for danger. None was visible. A thin, alert-looking guy in a plaid shirt and a neat haircut and beard was working a slider on a control panel that looked like it could pilot the Starship Enterprise, and the sound of Charlie Haden playing his bass came through the enormous speakers set into the wall above the picture window that opened on the playing space. The Bear stooped to look through this window—it was set a couple of steps lower than the control panel—into the studio and saw Charlie Haden's back bent over his instrument—a French bass, the Bear understood, from the late eighteenth century. He saw Billy's drumset in an annex past Haden on the other side of the big piney-woods asymmetrically octagonal room—there was so much rawcut wood the Bear could smell it clearly enough to know it wasn't all pine: he distinguished at least two distinct other saps but could not name them with all that polyurethane in the way, besides which he was a city bear and did not know the names of enough trees. He looked out there for Billy, but the drummer was nowhere to be seen.

"I'm James," said the engineer, looking up from the control board. "I'm getting some levels."

"Hi," said the Bear. "So am I." He felt sufficiently in place now to hear what Haden was doing. The bassist cycled his way down a series of triple stops, the root in perfect tune and the higher notes slid infinitesimally sharp to lend his chording a questing tone. When Haden reached the bottom of the cycle he cut loose one of his core-of-the-earth tones from the bottom of the bass and bent it with some powerful fingerwork so that the note arched up into beauty and pretty much devastated the Bear's by now wholly attentive heart. The Bear couldn't quite believe he was really going to get to play with this guy.

"Hey man," Haden's voice came at him from the speakers. The Bear opened his eyes to see Haden smiling at him from behind the glass. "Killed anyone yet today?"

"It's early," said the Bear.

"What?"

"Hold on, I'll open a mike for you," said James from his emplacement.

"Nah," said the Bear, pulled open the heavy control-room door and ambled into the studio proper. Haden was laying his bass gently down on its side, cushioning it on a rectangle of carpet. The bassist looked up at him and smiled.

The Bear had seen a lot of people walk up to him over the years, but none of them had done it quite like Charlie Haden. Usually, especially on the first few tries, there was something freaked-out about them, whether it was covered by irony or bravado or not, but Haden, as at the rehearsal the other day, walked up to him more simply than any other human ever had, a social smile softening his features and a look of interest in his eyes. Haden put his hand out and the Bear took it firmly in his paw.

"It's really great to see you, man," Haden said in his wavering tenor.

"I ain't . . ." the Bear began to say, his usual riff, but then dropped it. "It's good to be seen. I mean it's good to see you too. Both. Whatever." Haden was one of the few people he had met who had the power to disarm him more or less completely.

The prelims done, Haden allowed a devilish grin to break out and play across his features. "I've played with a lot of animals, man, but this really is a first."

The Bear joined him in the laugh without thinking twice. Our first duet.

Suddenly Haden was a trifle anxious: "I didn't mean that in an offensive way."

"No, it's cool," the Bear told him. "I got it. I knew what you meant."

"I was afraid, hm, of having made what might be thought of as a humanist statement."

The Bear had to chuckle. "That's the first time I've heard the word used in that sense," he said.

"Well it shouldn't the last." Haden nodded yes with a certain meditative seriousness.

"Stick 'em up," said a voice from behind the Bear, and something like a gun barrel poked him in the back.

"Billy," said the Bear, "if I didn't recognize your voice I might've spun around and taken your head off. You got to be careful around me just now. I'm in no mood for another arrest. What's that in my back, the butt end of a drumstick?"

"Yeah," said Billy, coming around front to say hello. "I wasn't thinking. Sorry, Bear. How you feeling today?"

"Some days you eat the bear," the Bear told him, "and some days the bear eats you."

Billy shook his head. "I could think about that all week and not know what you could possibly mean by that."

"I'm a little wired. Where's Bobby Hatwell?"

"Here."

The Bear had to blink at the piano player. First he had not been there, then he was. Where had he come from? "First there is no Hatwell, then there is," he said. "Nice trick. How you feeling?"

"I'm a little wired," the piano player said, like an echo-delay effect. Rahim Bobby Hatwell was a small medium-dark-brown guy in his twenties with a bullet head, small ears tucked tight to his temples, a delicate mouth, an articulated Ethiopian nose with arched nostrils, and dark Persian-almond eyes that looked right at the Bear the way most people's eyes did not. He was well muscled, highly articulated forearms coming out from under the pushed-up sleeves of his charcoal-grey cotton sweater. At the ends of these forearms, just the other side of a pair of delicate wrists, hung two enormous hands, veined and sculpted with extraordinary attention to detail. "You're looking at my hands," Hatwell said.

"Uh, yeah."

"I'd, ah, rather you didn't. I know I'm physically eccentric, but I'd rather you didn't stare."

"I think I can relate. I thought you were a little tense about playing with me because I'm, well, a bear."

Hatwell took a breath before speaking. "Actually I kind of dig the concept, and this isn't the weirdest gig I've ever played, if you want to know. One time I toured America with Tiny Tim, John Carradine, Pinky Lee and Zippy the Chimp. We did, like, Hadawank New Jersey, Fuckaduck P.A., Assawatchie OH, East Potato and St. Bump—the whole circuit. The tour was booked by this mobbed-up guy so of course what we played was a transcontinental series of, you should pardon the expression, Policemen's Balls. Mr. Tim headlined, but John Carradine did these sweeping versions of 'The Raven,' 'Now is the winter of my discotheque,' and 'To be or not to be.' Then, in his biggest hambone voice, he'd introduce the Lovely Karina and Her Young Charge. Karina'd come out to 'Saber Dance' in a spangly red costume swinging Zippy in a circle in the air on the end of a rope the monkey had in his teeth. It was a buffalo show. After Zippy did his shtick we'd get Pinky Lee in his check suit and derby hat singing 'Hi ho, hi hee, my name is Pinky Lee,' and then Mr. Tim would make his entrance, showing all his strange-looking teeth and strumming on his ukelele, which was tuned like to R-sharp minor, telling us, 'In the Key of G, gentlemen.' And it would almost never fail: the wife of some cop or other would come flying across the room to put a flying liplock on Tim and we'd have to keep the cop husband from pulling out his rod and packing up his troubles right there. After that we'd go out to a Chinese restaurant and Zippy'd get up on a table, pull down his pants and moon the house before putting down a whole baked fish and a couple of noodle dishes. At the end of the tour they found the mobbed-up guy who booked it in the trunk of his Buick Riviera with a longnose .22 in the base of his skull. I also did an episode of *The Love Boat* on a ship off Italy in the Mediterranean and dropped my whole paycheck playing cards with, of all people, Polly Bergen. This woman is a lethal weapon when she got a deck of cards in her hands, just in case you ever happen to run into her. Last week I did five gigs in two days and lost money. I'm a working musician, Bear. You can't show me nothing new."

The Bear turned to Billy. "You didn't tell me he did vocals."

"Yeah, well."

"How do you like the piano?" the Bear asked the pianist.

"This Hamburg Steinway Krieger got flown in by albatross, none of your New York shit, you kidding me? Look at that mirror-black finish. Listen to the way it sounds. When we're done with the record I want to be buried in it. One more thing," Hatwell said. "I'd rather you called me Rahim than Bobby, if that's okay with you."

"Rahim," said the Bear. "The Compassionate. Are you a particularly compassionate man?"

"Sometimes you're given a name because you already have the quality," Hatwell told him, "and sometimes because you need it. You speak Arabic?"

"Just a few of the Divine Names is all."

Hatwell looked both ways at Billy Hart and Charlie Haden. "He's unusual," Hatwell said.

"For a bear," Billy Hart allowed.

"So what you guys do after I split the rehearsal the other day?" the Bear asked his rhythm section generally, as a change of pace.

"We talked to Sigbjørn a lot," Charlie Haden said.

"We took his temperature," said Billy. "We tried to cool him down."

"Then the three of us played for a couple of hours," said Hatwell. "We really worked through your shit, you know? got your pieces down. We figure if Krieger comes in and cuts you out we're ready, the three of us, to record an album called *Ha Ha Ha Plays Bear*."

"Ha Ha Ha?" the Bear inquired.

"Haden Hart and Hatwell."

The Bear slapped himself on the head as stoopidly as he could manage. "I didn't realize. Thanks for working the material through."

Another party cleared his throat. It was James, the recording engineer, being polite on the outskirts of their grouping, accompanied by Jones, who, casting furtive eyes at the band, seemed painfully outcast from life's feast. The Bear had to admit it, it was still pretty cool to be a musician.

"Jones," said Charlie Haden. "It's good to see you again, man." Haden turned upon Jones the same interested attention he had directed at the Bear, and Jones responded like a morning glory that had sensed the sun.

"What is it," the Bear asked the engineer.

"I just wanted to show you," the man said. "We have Rahim and Charlie playing on opposite sides of the main room here. We'll close the door on Billy's drums in the booth, and we're putting you in this room over here." He indicated a glassed-in chamber on the other side of the studio.

"I'm playing in a condo?" the Bear asked him. "I'm looking out at the band through a window?"

"Sigbjørn gets his sound by isolating the instruments," said James. "Everyone does it. It's standard."

"We have a problem," said the Bear.

"Then we have a problem," said James. "What's up?"

"James, I don't have a clue how to play in a situation like this. I'm used to being with the band. I've got to be in close personal touch. Isolated like this," he gestured at the walled-in instruments, "how am I supposed to play? I know people do it all the time, but . . . Also, I'd have to use headphones to hear the band. One, they don't fit my head—"

"We could customize a pair for you."

"—and two, they hurt my inner ear intensely."

"You understand I'm not producing the date," James told him, "only engineering the sound. If it was just a matter of not wanting to separate the instruments you wouldn't have a chance, but the headphone problem gives you an in. You're not lying to me, are you?"

"Only a little," the Bear confessed.

"What I suggest is that you take it up with Sigbjørn when he comes in, and when he goes berserk I'll step in and suggest a way of recording the band in the main room. Meanwhile I'll get my gear set up so I can make the switch. Cool?"

"Bless you," said the Bear. "I'm still panicked but it's cool."

Sigbjørn Krieger swept in about fifteen minutes later, followed by his aide-de-camp. Krieger wore a dark overcoat over his shoulders like a cloak and then flung himself, as the Bear observed through the control-room window, into the leather sofa in front of the glass and dropped his face into his hands. When told to expect a Dansker, the Bear had anticipated some sort of blond or at least honey-colored individual, but Victory-Bear Warrior—the Bear's still unconfirmed translation of his name—was dark and sallow and hollow-cheeked and looked more like a suffering artist than any artist the Bear had ever met. He watched Jones bend solicitously over the melancholy Dane, and after awhile Krieger nodded yes, shed the overcoat, and rose, displaying dutiful fatigue. Nice dark turtleneck sweater, observed the Bear, lush corduroy slacks in subdued, almost indeterminate colors. Artist's clothes. The way I'd dress myself if I could manage the effect. Krieger acknowledged the Bear through the window and waved a weary hand hello, then headed for the control-room door, right. The Bear stood his ground, the alto hanging from his neck, and let the producer come to him.

"I understand we have a problem, the Bear," Krieger told him, then looked down at the floor. "Something about headphones?"

"My ears are positioned funny compared to humans'. See? They're up top of my head."

"We can modify the armature on the cans," Krieger said, although he looked pained at the prospect.

"Well yeah," said the Bear, "but they hurt my ears a lot. There's pain in there, damage being done. I can't do a Beethoven scene in my old age. You ever see a deaf bear? Pathetic."

The Bear was sure Krieger was within an ace of cancelling the session. "I don't know if we have time to reorganize the studio for you," he said.

At this point James materialized on cue. "I think I may have a solution," he said.

"How," Krieger asked James.

Then the Bear listened to James lay it out for Krieger: "I can isolate piano, bass and horn with panels in the main room, bring Billy forward, and baffle him left and right. We'll put three ambient mikes high up to pick up the harmonics. Promise you, Sigbjørn, we'll get something you'll like."

Krieger pinched the bridge of his nose and the Bear wondered if he really cared whether the date went on or not. On reflection, it turned out he did.

After Krieger nodded yes and withdrew, it took about twenty-five minutes for James and the guy who had been sorting cables to set the panels up and reconfigure the wilderness of microphones that attended the musicians. Jones walked around the studio through the whole procedure looking obscurely supervisory and generally getting in the way.

The Bear sidled up to him. "How'm I doing in there," he asked, and jerked his snout toward the control room, where Krieger sat brooding on the sofa.

"You're just getting away with it," Jones said. "I may have gathered from a conversation with Krieger's assistant, that the reason you haven't been shit-canned for misbehavior is not your ineffable charisma but because Megaton is pressuring Krieger. BFD records haven't been selling the way they used to, and you're expected to move product and help keep the distribution deal in place."

"You mean I have leverage?"

"Don't push it, B."

Preliminary levels took fifteen minutes, with James back in the control room asking individual members of the quartet to play a few notes for him. Then the band did a few desultory choruses of "Au Privave" and James said through the sound system, "I think we're ready for a take."

Here goes nothing, thought the Bear, not for the first time in his life. "Okay, guys," he said. "I think we should start off with the uptempo blues."

It was called "Vehicle," only he wanted it pronounced Southern-style, Vee-hickle, and now was thinking of changing its name to "Ha Ha Ha." He had liked writing it, felt he had come up with a bright idea. The line was nothing special, a wisp-and-fragment thing the regulation twelve bars long, but the first chorus was in the major, and the second a variation in the related minor. Wayne Shorter had done the same thing on an Art Blakey shuffle once, but "Vehicle" was fast and seemingly casual in its architectonics, and the Bear had some ideas about how it could be played.

"What I'd like to see here," he told the band, "is a sense that the major-minor alternation is there, but it's also kind of optional. I might start off my solo with a chorus of one, a chorus of the other, but then if I feel like playing three minor choruses in a row that's the kind of freedom the tune is written for. You guys have the same freedom, of course. So we'll have to listen to each other to see which way it wants to go. And if we feel like dropping the changes awhile, that's fine too. Charlie, I know you're familiar with this kind of thing. Everybody happy?"

Haden blew into his hands and said, "Uh-*huh*."

Hatwell piped up: "So, what you're saying, we feel like it we could play some free jazz."

"I was thinking pay as you go," said the Bear.

"One more thing," said Hatwell.

"What."

"You can call me Bobby if you want."

"Actually," said the Bear, "we need all the mercy and compassion we can get."

Getting the nod from James, the Bear grunted a countoff at an energetic but not intolerable uptempo and the band came in like the pros they were. What uplift, he thought as he launched into the head. I mean, these guys start off as if they're already in the middle of the thing, no touchy-feely probes into what the tune might be about. Immediate arrival. They start off at a level other guys might never reach after weeks with the material. What sophistication. Hope I'm up to it.

Billy laid some asymmetrical punctuation into the gaps in the tune's head and implied some facets of the architecture the Bear hadn't known he'd written. As the Bear attained the beginning of his solo over the bridge of a cymbal swell from Hart and a chord pileup from Hatwell, he hoped again he was up to it, and remembering that he wasn't, he resorted to a prior strategy. Because he knew he couldn't play in time present and would have to imitate himself, for the first time in his checkered career he had worked something out in advance. He would do his first choruses in fragmentary fashion, playing some piece of thematic variation oddly placed within the barlines, then lay out for little stretches and let the rhythm section fill. This would extend the strategies of the written composition and, who knew, might pass for music among the uninitiated. Then he'd lay in more bits and fragments awhile and try to pull them together with some long lines and runs for the finish so it would look as if he'd really done something with the solo. It was an inauthentic, connect-the-dots way of playing music, but it seemed like something to go out there with for starters. He might just get away with it. It might just sound like something had really happened.

Accordingly, the Bear put his first bit of phrasing out there and laid back to listen. The band called his bluff with snappish responses from three directions at a deeper level of invention than he had proposed. Then they settled, waiting to hear what he had to say next. Oh shit, the Bear told himself, you can't lie to these motherfuckers. But I'll have to keep trying this stuff out till something better comes along.

His first four choruses kept to the regular major-minor alternation indicated on the page. Billy was producing rounded swelling waves of rhythm on the drums and cymbals, ocean surges that overspilled the barlines while still kicking the beat at him—just the kind of drumming the Bear liked best, only he didn't feel exactly equal to contending with it now. Haden was digging methodically into the rhythm while opening up, within an increasingly free harmonic field, worlds of implication in which the major and minor blues as given had begun to interpenetrate each other, almost, in a way, to cancel each other out. To make matters worse, the Hatwell kid was laying in all this large-scaled architectonic chording that kept upping the ante drama-wise on the Bear every time he proposed a new bit of phrasing or line of thought. In essence they had seen his two preconceived bits and raised him more than he had in his wallet. He either had to fold his hand and forget the whole deal or rise to the occasion somehow. Okay, he thought, let's pretend I can play. Let's pretend I'm comfy and at home. If I were, if I could—soul of Jackie Mac, intercede for me—I might do something, uhh, I might do something like this.

The Bear successfully doubletimed his way into the next chorus, not an easy thing at this tempo, and thought: not bad, but there was still a lot of Cannonball in that. He didn't know if his bid had succeeded, but everyone responded as if he was good for the amount, and from that moment on he pretty much lost track of the proceedings. Oh, he knew that Billy was bashing it and that Haden had dropped strict timekeeping to wrench explosively placed double-stops out of the bottom of his instrument, the strings protesting bodily against the fingerboard—and once, Haden did that droning, rising pedal-tone thing, like a choir of basses, against what he was playing on the horn, and the Bear took it as a compliment, since Haden usually only ran that stuff behind Ornette. He loved the way Hatwell was working his shit in—nobody out there was playing piano like that, laying out for awhile then hitting the music's uprush with this strong two-handed harmonically intensified blockwork, then giving him a bit of the usual connective chording before entering a repetition cycle that responded to what the Bear was playing and demanded that he think about it some more—but what he was aware of, mostly, was the feeling that he would have to sink or swim and that he was doing a bit of both. He wished Billy would give him a bit more breathing room—he was bashing those tom-toms pretty hard—and then, despite the fact that he knew he couldn't play like this anymore, at last he began to dig into what the band was giving him, grudgingly at first, because he had no alternative and it was probably better than packing up the horn and going home, and so despite himself he lit into the day's offered music, streaked and ran and just generally behaved as if he could still tear things up. He stole a lick or two from Coltrane's long recorded solo on "Impressions." Ah well. If you have to steal, steal from the best. The music was either dead or alive or a bit of both, he figured, and the whole time, compounded of what remained of his talent and his frustration with its inaccessibility and limits, there was a kind of shuttered tumult in him, as if all this equivocal music were being generated by a drama taking place from behind the closed doors of a room somewhere deeper in the house of his nature than he could bodily reach, light gleamed around the edges of the doorway and occasionally he could hear some word of dramatic argument rise articulate in the air; but all he could do here, amid the covered furniture and general gloom, was use what he knew about music and the horn to make some sense and energy out of such echo of real event as reached him. Occasionally he got into something real, but then it would slide away and leave him with whatever lay ready between breath and tongue and paws. He didn't know how long his solo lasted, though he ticked off the major-minor switches when he felt like it and took note when the blues structure fell away entirely, but when he was finished he knew that a bunch of time had passed, that he was sweat all over, and it seemed he had drifted into an out-of-tempo dialogue with Haden, Hatwell laying out and Billy flicking in some cymbal trills and mini-bashes on the outskirts. The bassist played beautifully, sounded notes in the Bear's nature that the Bear himself would have played if he still resonated that deep. It was a kind of call, and the Bear responded to it in his current piecemeal fashion, partly able, due to Haden's beauty, to forget how deeply incapable of music he was: in fact the issue of self fell aside, only provisionally and for the moment, but sufficiently far so that something living could get through the barbed wire and perimeter defenses at the prison's edge. Why was the place such a battlefield? How had it gotten to be this way? How did I manage to do this to myself? This should be completely fucking simple!

There was a long section in which the Bear's and Haden's lines intertwined in diminishing volume. The Bear liked it while it lasted, and said goodbye to it with a dying fall, a breathy trill, took two steps back from the microphone and tangled his feet in a mess of cables.

That's where Hatwell picked things up, lingered awhile with Haden in the stillness, rumbling around in the piano's lower storeys, then Herbie-noodled his way back into tempo and got the tune racing again. Bass and drums sleeked themselves down and took off after him, low to the ground, running smooth and steady. The Hatwell kid had some ideas, thought the Bear, as he listened to the little bastard outplay him. The pianist built his solo out of long swift lines whose general curve was upward but which curled back into themselves before unloosing their charge of drama. As Hatwell homed in on his eventual destination there were stops and starts, big two-handed chordal pileups that sometimes topped out with a bit of humor—the Bear heard a polytonal demolition of "Stars and Stripes Forever" ride one buildup in the treble, and a bit of "All You Need Is Love" stumbling out of another climax in bits and pieces—and basically Hatwell's solo was riotous and unpredictable and disported itself over the entirety of the instrument as if the keyboard were still an undiscovered country anyone with a sense of freedom and some soul and muscle could romp in ad infinitum. Nobody outside the outright avant-garde attacked the piano with quite this much abandon, and the Bear felt like shaking hands all around, packing up his alto and handing the album over to the pianist with his blessing. The solo ended out of tempo with Haden buzzing a repeated, slightly flatted triple-stop against the wood, and the Bear had enough sense to wave Billy off it: he'd always liked Haden's solos best when they were unaccompanied and he had room to go wherever he wanted, in or out of tempo. Haden's initial questings, once Billy fell aside in cymbal-whispers, gave way to some plummets into his instrument's bottom range. The Bear closed his eyes and listened rocking as a series of would-be lyrical melodies rose, each of their notes nettled by minute variations of pitch and placement, as if they had entered a moral field under siege. Haden's struggle, whatever it was, made the Bear feel less alone. The bassist seemed to turn upon his notes some ultimate degree of attention and to question them as if at any moment they might drop their masks, fess up and tell him the secret of his life. At that level of inquiry Haden's secrets, whatever they were, were identical to the Bear's, to anyone's, own. The whole band leaned in, listening, a palpable hush seized the room just in case appearances fell away and the world of unmeasured Meaning, from which music came and at which it was always pointing back, was of a mind to put in an appearance, against the odds, pull the scrims down and leave the stage bare of illusion, full of truth. It came close. At the end of his solo, Haden had shifted almost imperceptibly back into the tune's fast tempo and Billy was playing quietly and looking at the Bear over the top of his baffle, eyebrows up. Did the Bear want to play again or should Billy take a turn?

The Bear thought a drum solo would be a pretty good idea just then, and to communicate this thought to Billy he put the saxophone to his snout and began to play a sort of prelude for him. One thing led to another, and without meaning to he was beginning a second alto solo. It had taken him unawares. Hatwell was laying out, there was plenty of room, and, since the bassist and drummer were keeping the volume down, there wasn't any pressure on him. As far as the Bear was concerned, he was playing a little intermission between main events and was only paying a sort of half-attention to the proceedings. His mind had a chance to slip the noose and wander awhile. Listen to these guys, he thought, hearing Haden and Billy's accompaniments and insinuations, the flex of beat, the suggested harmonic divagation, the threat or promise of distant thunder, eventual rain. Where else could you find a music like this? Where else encounter such simultaneous discipline and abandon? It was a whole rich multifarious world, and if you went outside its visible parameters you could draw from anything out there and bring it back in without bowing obeisance to any foreign gods. All you had to do was be able to play. All you had to do was know how to put it together. All you had to do was see how it already was together in potential, articulate and complete, and at the same time throw yourself wholly into the maelstrom of unknown process. All you had to know was the little secret that made it swing. It was no big deal. It was life, is all, no more no less.

They were still playing, Billy was laying back, and Haden was starting to get to the Bear—where he might have expected the bass to walk or run alongside him, there was this bup-bup-bup-bup triplet thing going on, pure comedy, and the Bear thought, Like what the hell is this? Hatwell was coming in with some spare, spaced octaves: tonic, dominant, nothing in particular, relative minor and lo, the music was starting to do what it was rumored or fabled to do, i.e., carry him past the rambling catastrophe of himself into greater knowledge and release. He could not, because of his continuing imprisonment, enjoy it in the full amplitude of his essence, but he could sit there at the fountain and regulate the flow as it came to his horn according to laws anyone with half a brain in a similar position ought to be able to acknowledge and a listener enjoy. In fact this is just what he had been looking for, the subtly right ingress or egress, the chance to know and not know what was going on. Right paw, left paw, note after note, who knows, it might add up to music. In any case, for the first time in living memory he was situated smack in the center of something more real than he was, still feeling nothing but awake enough to tick off the necessary moves and meanings and just generally let it flow.

Haden vocalized, letting out one of his well-known Whooos. Yeah, but what does he know? Dead-eyed but with his heart on some slow-burning fire too interior to warm him, the Bear played what he knew from this equivocal position, rolling out his lines, chafing against the law of rhythm before consenting to its authority again, pulling on harmony's ropes and hawsers, getting those sails up, winching a few down and sailing on into the body of the day. If he had wanted, in the interest of greater speed, to heft the full weight of his emotions into the music's swirls and currents, he would have come up against the problem that for all the moment's intensity he had no feelings really. This was still some sort of intermezzo between the weary self he lived with and the world he wanted to get to, so that it was nothing, really, in itself; and at the same time he knew that this was precisely the best he could hope to do with the moment and its pawful of material. Just don't think you're doing something ultimate or important and maybe you can keep it up awhile.

When the Bear was done, Billy took a solo that rummaged around the set and exploded amid the cymbals, and then the whole band played the out head staggered and almost out of tempo due to some mutual unspoken decision they had made. At the end there were a few last thrashes from the hilltop of one instrument to the valley of another and then they were out. After a four-second pause for the reverberations to die away they looked at each other again. Haden was the first to laugh. Then Billy and Hatwell assented. The Bear did not. He was in some other, blank, terse state of mind and felt like maybe he could play for awhile today and that was the business at hand and there was not much of him left over for laughter or chitchat or camaraderie or whatever.

James' voice came through the speaker: "You want to hear that back?"

"No," said the Bear, his voice so loud it surprised him, but then it seemed that you had to hear it back and so the Bear excused himself. While everyone else listened to it in the control room, he wandered out of the studio and up a hall, found himself in a huge recording room they must use for orchestras and heavy metal bands, an indoor football field, a place for a swimming pool, anyhow something cavernous and gymnastic. The Bear wandered through it, looking up at the dark hangings that could be let down for damping the sound. He clapped his paws a few times to check out the reverb. The light was dim, the place deserted. The chrome of microphone stands gleamed under dulled-down service lights. Interesting. Wonder if they're done listening in there. Give it another five minutes. Better safe than sorry. I don't want to hear it at all.

When he got back it seemed that the musicians all liked it a lot but that it was seventeen minutes long—really?—and there was a certain amount of audio overspill that James was tending to between the gantries, baffles and mikes. Krieger wanted to do a second, acceptably shorter take, under improved acoustic conditions.

"No," said the Bear. Nothing mattered to him at the moment, except getting on with it. He was pretty one-pointed about that, but even that did not count, not ultimately, he felt that cold and void.

"And the drummer was singing while he played," Krieger complained.

"Because he was enjoying himself," the Bear told him. "You've heard of enjoyment, right? Good. Now we have to play the next tune." His voice was so level it occurred to him that he sounded hypnotized.

Some argument ensued but it did not touch him, and even though he contributed a few lines to the discussion it took place at a great remove, in some pointless contingent non-time, and when things got real again they were ready to try the next tune. Which one should it be?

"'Book the Hook,'" said the Bear, "and we can keep it short." It was a jump tune built off a repeated riff spelled by a break figure, eight bars of A-flat 7, eight of B 7 +11, an eight bar release in A 7 flat 9 + 5, and then a last eight in B-flat 7 to close. "If it goes on too long, the changes'll start sounding like a trap. Under seven minutes it might be okay. So."

The Bear counted off, slower than "Vehicle" but still up there.

They played it, and not surprisingly Haden found some variations to work on the repeated rhythm figures that underlay the piece and Billy made the piece's foursquare structure tilt and stretch and rock itself silly. The Bear and Hatwell took their choruses, then Charlie and Billy found a way to share two in tandem and they finished in brisk unison.

"Cool," Hatwell said. "That's like half a record already."

"Charlie?" asked the Bear. "If we could play a duet on something slow and then we could all take a little break?"

"Funny," Haden told him. "After we almost did that rehearsal the other day I wrote a ballad for you in my hotel room. You want to have a look?"

They played it together after three false starts in which the Bear couldn't quite get a grip on the best way to phrase Haden's written line. Once he had it loosened up right, the Bear let Haden's lyric understrumming coax him into deeper seas than he usually travelled. Every time the Bear would play a line, Haden would find something larger to say about it on the bass and the Bear would have to submit to the authority of what he had proposed. Haden surrounded him like an orchestra of basses, lured unknown music out of his lights and vitals, and coerced his consent to a beauty beyond the rim of his circumscriptive troubles of the moment. Did the Bear play well? Possibly. Did he keep to the chord changes? As a matter of fact, the Bear thought he had. When the Bear stopped, Haden took a solo, caressing up from the strings a richness of melody that paid tribute to the beauty of the bass and his own deep human nature. Accordingly, when Haden finished his solo, the Bear played Haden's written theme with unaccustomed literalness and modesty, and it was done.

"Oh, man," Haden said after the necessary pause.

"Really?" said the Bear. "Was it any good?"

Everyone agreed, at least, that it was time for a break. Apparently someone had phoned out for Chinese food and Charlie wanted to make sure there would be enough vegetables. Did the Bear want anything to eat?

"No."

Various people were taking off for the toilet and the coffeemaker. The Bear wanted nothing to do with either. He noted that he had no physical needs: no hunger, despite the fact he'd had nothing since coffee and bagels that morning, no need for the bathroom despite earlier ominous gurglings and the amount of strong black coffee he'd swallowed down for breakfast. He seemed to have no needs at all. No discernible emotion either. No doubt if he didn't have to play the horn he wouldn't be breathing either.

Jones spoke to him but he couldn't make much sense of the words.

"Interview," Jones repeated.

"What?"

"You said you'd do one."

"Oh yeah. Of course."

The Bear sat down with the interviewer on opposing armchairs in the anteroom. There was also a tall thin woman with frizzy black hair and cameras dangling. She circled and snapped pictures, but the Bear shot her a particularly dark look and something went audibly wrong with her motor drive—did I do that?—and she went away for awhile. The interviewer, although evidently Jewish, he looked a lot like Shakespeare—about midway between the Chandos portrait and the Droeshout engraving—had an even more poignant air than Jones of being on the outside looking in. The guy also sort of looked like Anne Frank with a beard. "I'm not really a critic," he explained into the microphone after he had set up the cassette recorder. "—really a critic," the machine repeated back to him, and once the guy had refumbled his papers back into his lap, they were ready to go.

The Bear composed his paws upon his knees, not knowing what to expect. He found the interview process rather odd.

"I was born in a boxcar on a railroad siding on the outskirts of Chicago," the Bear began in answer to the man's first question, and then the interviewer interrupted the Bear to tell him about his own childhood and how he had always wanted to communicate with animals, particularly with birds. He had wanted to convince the birds that he would never do them harm and that they ought to be his friends, but they flew away from him anyway. He had loved all animals really, and although social circumstance had prevented him from meeting up with bears, when he went to summer camp at the age of five in New Hampshire he . . . Had the Bear ever been to New Hampshire?

"Never further north than the Adirondacks," said the Bear, "where basically I was hunting around for lady bears. By the way, it offends me that the human world calls them sows. . . ."

It offended the interviewer too, the guy assured him.

"You see," said the Bear, "due to a whole bunch of unpredictable governmental and bureaucratic wrangles attending the defection of the Great Vichinsky, I wasn't separated from my mother right away. In fact, we were together long enough for me to . . ."

The interviewer commiserated, with reference to the difficulties of his own childhood, while the Bear remembered the Chicago horizon, red lights blinking, while his mother conveyed what she could of the family lore. He remembered the taste of her milk, her warm, anxious, enveloping love. Too soon gone, and a too-cold human world for aftermath.

"My father was American," he said when the interviewer had finished his story, "snuck in one night to diversify the circus' gene pool. My mother found him primitive but affecting. She took to him, I think, mostly out of compassion. There was a certain old-world condescension in her feelings for him. Even though, I was told, he was energetic as a lover he had little appetite for conversation in the aftermath, and however touching he was in his directness, it was felt he lacked perspective and nuance. . . . Anyhow I never really participated in the *snobisme* in which my mother's side of the family indulged itself."

The interviewer spent a lot of time telling the Bear how this story made him feel, particularly in view of how the two sides of his own family had clashed like cymbals, or symbols, and the next time the Bear found a chance to speak, the text was Bird, Ornette and Jackie McLean, but even on these subjects he didn't get a chance to say a lot.

He did get off one thing he wanted to say, though. "I think the only significance of all this activity—the musicians, the industry and all the hysteria that attends it—is that despite all we've done to mar the world with our having been here, and I include myself in that, because I've been here long enough to know that what I leave behind me is less a mark than a stain—is that when you come right down to it we're in love with beauty. You wouldn't think that's what everyone's actually involved with, but I don't know what other significance all this fucking noise could be about, do you? And I think civilization, as currently understood, ought to shut the fuck up and inquire more deeply into what this preoccupation with beauty might mean. If possible before it's too late, you know what I'm saying?"

"You're a Platonist!" the interviewer seemed delighted to discover.

"Of course I am," said the Bear. "And I think an ideal society would be ruled by saxophone-playing bear kings. Besides—"

At this point other voices pressed in upon them. Apparently it was time for him to play some more music, whatever that was.

"Sorry," said the Bear. "There wasn't enough time to really . . ."

"It was fine," the interviewer said, and pressed a sheet of paper into the Bear's paw in place of a handshake. "This is what I really do."

"Thanks," said the Bear, and looked down at what looked like poetry.

"Thank *you*," the guy assured him, and made a little bow.

"Hey hey hey hey *hey*," said someone coming in.

The Bear looked up and couldn't help but grin. It was Lester Bowie, arms spread wide to embrace him, followed by old Doc Friedmann, leaning on a stick, his face reddened by effort. "The two doctors!" said the Bear, and stuffed the interviewer's paper into his trenchcoat pocket. "Glad to see ya."

"Yeah, just blew in on the Tardis," Bowie said, unwinding a length of scarf from his throat. "What's up? What we gonna do here?"

"He inzisted on picking me up," said Friedmann. "Have you experienced this man's driving?"

"No," said the Bear.

Bowie was shaking the interviewer's hand and asking hey, how was he. The interviewer seemed flummoxed, and Bowie, bending over the man's armchair, from which he was ineffectively struggling to rise, began paying him elaborate, somewhat parodic court.

"Sorry you had a rough time getting here," the Bear told Friedmann, who had some trouble getting around the Bowie-and-interviewer tandem. Eventually, however, the Bear had a chance to embrace him. "How're you doing, old man?"

"A couple of chest pains but no luck yet," the doctor told him, wheezing.

"Puh-leeze," said the Bear.

"I have come to feel that the last thing I had to do in this life vas to be of some small help to you."

"You want to sing *Ich habe genug* on my record?"

"I don't feel like singing, Bear," said the doctor. "I feel like taking a good long rest."

"They say it's sweeter to stay on a couple of years after you're done."

"Akh. I don't even vant to know vhich bunch of sadists may have said such a thing. But it's good to see you looking vell."

"I do? I'm feeling a little ragged today."

"Your coat has a nice sheen. And you smell good."

"Hey Bear, so tell me, what're we gonna do?" It was Bowie, appearing over the doctor's shoulder, twiddling one prong of his goatee and doing a little speculative bob-and-weave.

"That depends," said the Bear. "You want to play right away or listen to us do one first?"

"Whatever," Bowie said. "How's the date so far?"

The Bear gestured over his shoulders. "The guys are in the control room. Ask them."

"Yeah, I'd like to see Billy. How do you like the Hat?"

"Hatwell? He's great."

"Yeah, catch him while you can. See you in a minute."

Bowie went past him, a door opened and the sounds of celebration washed against his back. For all his grim existential concentration today, the Bear had to smile. Doctor Bowie was in the house.

They decided to do "Tengri" before they brought Bowie in for his cameo, and the Bear made a mess of it. He had written the tune out of an interest in its Asiatic feel and the laddering thirds and fourths of its melody, and had named it for the Mongolian word for heaven, although he held "Shaman You" in reserve as an alternate title. Out of all the possible chord changes that could be derived from the tune, he had chosen the most complex for the working chart, and as he went into his solo on them he remembered all at once that this was precisely the kind of playing he was most interested in doing these days but also that he had so far been unable to make it work. So for two takes he nattered around within the confines of the harmonic structure, miscounted the twenty-bar A section and the thirteen-bar bridge, and felt, more or less, like a railway stationman out there on the platform with his pocketwatch, hoping for the best but personally unable to make the trains run on time. "Hey, guys," he said, when he had waved the band to a stop for the second time.

"Yeah?"

"I forgot something."

"We noticed."

"I don't want to play these changes," he announced, and a couple of looks passed between the members of his band. "Hey," he challenged them, "you wanna do a couple of choruses of 'Cherokee' or 'Giant Steps' or something? I can run 'em. I'll eat 'em up. I don't feel like playing these particular changes just now for the purposes of making music, okay? It's not in tune with what I want to accomplish at the moment. So. Another way to look at the tune is that the A section is in Dorian with some optional sharps and flats and the B section's Phrygian with a G-minor tag the last five bars. So what do you say let's play it that way for a take and see how it works out."

"Yeah if you can really count to five," Hatwell piped up. "Cause if you can we could all make the end of the bridge together."

"Good point, Bob. Thank you. Shall we try?"

Krieger seemed marginally happier, the Bear noticed, once they did three takes of the reconstructed tune. The first one was still finding its way, the second was acceptable, the third a perceptible falling off, with definite signs of a loss of interest.

"Lester!" called the Bear.

"Come on in here," the trumpeter's voice came over the intercom. "Let's have a discussion."

"You *can't* play 'When a Man Loves a Woman,'" Bowie told him when he had broken the news.

"Why the fuck not," the Bear asked him.

"Because while you were inside, Michael Bolton recorded a version—"

"Who the fuck is Michael Bolton?"

"What used to be called blue-eyed soul," Bowie said. "Anyhow, he recorded it and damn near killed the thing."

"It was everywhere," Billy put in. "It was unavoidable. It was on all the radios. It was on the street. It was like Madonna."

"Not a good idea, the Bear," Krieger said.

"Well I'm a talking bear," said the Bear, "and in the general spirit of the violation of the laws of nature I say let's do it anyway." He grinned and bristled at Krieger and watched the man give way in a series of shivers. It was an illegal use of fur, he knew, and a suspect invocation of nature red in tooth and claw, but what the fuck, it's only a record, only a way of getting by in the world. A way, in short, he had hoped never to think about music, but it was the order of the given day and there he was.

After some fooling with the head, they did it in a take. The Bear and Bowie played the A section in rough unison and Bowie took the bridge alone, giving it his best parodic yowls and whinnies but also rocking nicely back into the cushion of the beat. Billy let his cymbal triplets flex a bit, and played the snaredrum backbeat fat. Haden picked the minimum number of clear, country-true tones, and Hatwell took it to church. It was just what the Bear wanted, and going into his two choruses he did exactly what he had heard himself doing in his head for about a week now. He alternated some rudimentary, comic-Rollinsish linking of the tune's harmonic fundamentals with a repeated rising dotted-eighth-note figure which he let unfold into some fairly Birdlike melodic development on the bridge of his second chorus and then, on the way out, tossed some Cannonball into his last couple of bars: a measured solo: situational improvisation: just this once. Lester Bowie made the best of his choruses—his tone had developed a beautiful sheen and shimmer, a beautiful gleam of brass, and he used it in lovely lyric contrast to his usual divagations from tonal orthodoxy, those yawns and yowls and sidemouth slurs. It also seemed to the Bear that Bowie's phrasing was a bit more developmental than it used to be. The Bear liked that—good as Bowie is, he's been working at construction, and his tone's more gemlike and emotive than ever. Bowie's solo was a moving piece of work that was all the more effective for its relative restraint. For his single chorus Hatwell picked up on Bowie's reticence and suggestions, keeping things mostly chordal and church-solemn. You could hear his youth pushing against this decorum from within, so that there was a feeling of a wave about to raise up and smash some houses on the shoreline, but no actual trace of whitecap showed on the surface. When trumpet and alto returned to repeat the tune's written melody they played it as if with heads bowed. The Bear had the bridge on the out chorus and he elected to rip it with some traditional blues and gospel declamation, then hushed back down for the unison of the last eight bars. Bowie was lovely there, his tone retaining its glow in pianissimo, and the tune ended in a saxophone whisper and the fluttering of Bowie's breath through his horn.

The Bear had wanted this one for Iris and it had come out right.

Back in command central there were quiet congratulations in half-sentences while "When a Man Loves a Woman" was playing back. It was the first take of anything the Bear had listened to, and you know? it wasn't a horrible experience. It even sounded like a record. How strange.

"Yeah when I heard the tune before this one, Bear, I wondered . . ." Bowie was telling him.

"If they removed a critical portion of my brain in stir? Someone play him 'Vehicle' after this."

"You mean you'll sit still for another playback?" Jones asked him.

"I might," said the Bear. He leaned over toward Friedmann. "What do you think?"

"It's not my style of music. I came along in that madman's car to inqvire into your health. Let me look at you." Friedmann leaned toward the Bear across the soft tan leather sofa. "Show me your teeth and gums. A propos, vhat is that good smell? I noticed it before already. Is that your natural smell in good health or is there somesing else?"

"For Christ's sake, Friedmann, it's only cologne."

"Has he been so touchy all month since he left the prison?" Friedmann asked Jones.

"No," said the Bear.

"He's been about like this," Jones informed the doctor.

"Bullshit," said the Bear. "I haven't been like this at all. I'm not like this now."

"So," said Friedmann. "Teeth and gums please."

The Bear obliged him, then let his lip fall closed.

"Your eye please, bend." The Bear leaned in and the doctor pulled his eyelid down. As Friedmann peered in at him the Bear noticed how unwell the old man looked. In the slammer, things looked bad in all directions, but back out here . . . Friedmann looked worn out. There was a new hollowness to his genial ugly features, and the Bear wondered if this was what people meant when they said they could see death in someone's face. Friedmann's examining eye looked dull. "Goot," Friedmann said.

"So I'm okay," said the Bear. "Now tell me what you think of my combo's groovy sounds."

Friedmann might have meant his rough basso to come out in a whisper but it was like a freight train. "Music, shmusic," Friedmann boomed. "Don't lose the girl."

The Bear looked back at the control panel, where most eyes were on the dials and sliders. Bowie was contemplating the ceiling tiles and generally looking innocent.

"Be sure to tune in next week," the Bear told the room. "We're running a special."

"Yes," said Friedmann rather dreamily, "I spoke vith Iris a little on the day of your liberation. Obviously she is marvelous."

"And you're not shocked at the prospect of our . . . ?" the Bear asked him.

Friedmann made a face. "I assume your genetics are incompatible and that you will not between you produce a monster."

"Right."

"She is very intelligent but she tells me she is incapable of thinking. I do not believe this, but clearly you must take specially good care of her."

"She's extremely intelligent but I see her primarily as a sensitive."

"Also essential. I vish I vere her age and in her field professionally. The things I might do."

"She thinks she's old."

"Of course she does," said Friedmann. "If she only knew."

"But about us. What do you think really?"

"I vouldn't vant to vatch. Othervise perfect. And should you two make an arrangement, please do not consult me in any capacity, either as doctor or as elderly friend. There is no ethical problem, but still, I hope you pardon me if I don't vish to know particulars. I'm an old-vorld gentleman of some experience, but there are limits." Friedmann leaned slightly away from the Bear on the sofa. "Of course you realize I am choking vith you."

"I didn't," said the Bear.

"You are an odd character," the old man told him.

The Bear saw Jones swim like a new planet into his ken. On tape, the Bear was into his second chorus on "When a Man Loves a Woman." "You know, Jones," the Bear sidemouthed to him, "what I'd really like to do on this track is lay down a vocal."

Jones looked properly aghast. "Wasn't this man just telling you about limits? Take a look at Krieger."

The Bear took a look at Krieger.

"You've already gotten away with murder today," said Jones. "I'd fold if I were you."

"Yeah, but I wanted to put down a vocal so I could play it for Iris."

"Hey, you big goof." Jones shot the Bear an elbow in his ribs and grinned. "You're in love."

The Bear stifled the beginnings of a growl.

On tape, the Bear finished his solo with a big happy inconsolable blues cry and Lester came in on a sustained and glowing note held long. The Bear looked back at Bowie, who was weaving to the beat back at the control panel. Bowie saluted back and shut his eyes. His head went back.

"This may be as good a time as any," Jones was saying.

"For what?"

Jones squeezed down beside the Bear on the sofa and Friedmann slid back to make room for him. "It seems that I'm, that we're being evicted from the apartment," Jones said.

"You're kidding. Is it about me?"

"Who knows. Maybe you're gravy. The building's being co-opped—"

"That dump?"

"While you were inside, more art galleries crept in from the east and for a couple of mornings in a row the cops sealed off the street and swept the dope dealers off the stoops. You can hear the sound of money getting ready to be made."

"Yeah, but he can't squeeze us," said the Bear. "We've got rent control. We're old tenants. We've got rights. If he wants us out of the building he should have to buy us out."

"Yeah, well, although I'm your average quiet guy, pays his rent regular, in a word the full axe-murderer profile, he did say something about how he knew I'd been keeping an animal in there."

"He said that? He called me an animal?"

"Don't bristle. He's only a landlord."

"Yeah, Jones, but where am I supposed to go? There goes the damn rug from under me again. And just looking at you I know how this plays into your plans about moving in with Sybil Bailey. You're running a game on me."

"What about you and Iris?" Jones asked.

"She wants me to go, and putting your lewd and leering interest aside for the moment, living there is in fact untenable. I've only gone out once or twice around four in the morning and I have to be careful about showing myself in the windows. Usually we draw the shades. What can I tell you? It's a middle-class housing project. I can't live there. It's a holding pattern no matter what goes on between Iris and me."

On tape, Hatwell was rolling through the middle of his chorus. Nice two-handed tremolo there.

"You looking for a crib?" said Lester Bowie, leaning down from control-panel level. "Cause if you are I may know something, long as you're willing to leave town for awhile."

"Am I ever," said the Bear.

"Julius is moving back to the city from up in Woodstock," said Bowie, "and the house is going empty."

"What about Stanlynn?" asked the Bear.

"She's moving back West to raise llamas or some damn thing, but she told me, what the fuck did she tell me? Hey, listen to that." It was Hatwell ending his chorus with a rolling swell that subsided just before the horns came in. "Motherfucker not only has those big hands he's smart. Stanlynn said something about putting the place up for summer rental semifurnished because the resale market's soft."

"It ain't summer yet," said the Bear.

"Yeah, but she's leaving *now*. You ought to speak to her, see if there's anything in it for you. It's a nice place. You could dig getting out of New York awhile, am I right?"

"*Nunc dimittis*," the Bear agreed. "I'll call her. What's up with Julius?"

Bowie adjusted his shirt collar. "We-ell, he was thinking he'd put himself too far outside the scene and wanted to come back into town. But the fact is he's in the hospital just now. They had to amputate one of his legs from the knee down."

"Holy shit," said the Bear.

"Yeah, diabetes and the complications thereof. He still likes to take a drink now and then."

"The leg," said the Bear. "He's losing his leg."

"He's losing his leg." Bowie grimaced at the Bear and the Bear grimaced back. "I'm gonna go see him in the hospital."

"Give him my best. Sheesh."

"Yeah," acknowledged Bowie.

"I love Julius," said the Bear.

"We *all* love Julius," Bowie said.

The Bear faced front again and sat with his paws in his lap. No shoes, and I came upon a man who had no feet. That's some hard blues, Julius. God bless you, wherever you may be. The Bear sat there thinking about Julius and his leg until "When a Man Loves a Woman" ended. They hadn't rehearsed an ending, but they'd pulled off a standard tag smoothly enough, with a little Bowie whisper fluttering off the finish, and it worked.

"Excuse me?" he asked Krieger.

"I said I think we need another one," the producer said.

"Really? I thought we were done," said the Bear.

"In general the session has gone well," Krieger told him, "although nothing since the first tune has risen to the level of 'Vehicle.'"

"Uh huh," said the Bear, who had to admit that the producer was saying what he thought himself.

"'When a Man Loves a Woman' is possibly perfect of its kind," Krieger continued, standing up from his chair and stretching his arms, "but I think even you will admit it is a novelty number still, and we don't have a take of 'Tengri' that is strong all the way through. This leaves us two fast tunes, one of them very long, a duet with you and Charlie, and a well-played novelty item in slow triplets. It's not an album yet."

The Bear wearied himself up from the sofa and scratched the top of his head. "Oh," he said. "Yeah."

"Correct me if I'm wrong. You would like to make this record in first takes all in one day and get out of here," the producer said, getting his licks in. "And I am willing to aid you and abet, but if you want to finish today you will have to work for it some more."

The Bear nodded.

"It is still possible, the Bear. Even so, I would like you to contemplate coming in a second day."

"We could do something tomorrow," the Bear admitted unwillingly.

"Given evidently your frame of mind, I think the day after tomorrow would be better. After you have a chance to clear your mind. Do not understand me too quickly. Extend me that favor, and I may be able to return it you. It may be that I understand you better than you think."

"Could be we have a couple things in common," said the Bear. "I mean, I got a case of perfectionism could kill me if I let it loose, you know what I mean?"

"I do."

"I'd like to close it today if I can," said the Bear. "What do you think we need?"

Krieger seemed gratified to have been consulted. He pinched the bridge of his nose, shut his eyes and thought about it. "A ballad," he said.

"Even with the duet we already have with Charlie?"

"I think," Krieger said.

The Bear stepped up to control-panel level, looked down at the slides, and read the masking-tape labels for the channels: kick, snare, ride, crash, l tom, r tom, f tom, sock—it seemed like almost all the microphones were there to deal with the drums. Where was his channel? There it was. Just one: Bear. Hatwell had three and Haden two. It hardly seemed fair. "You know 'Billy Heart' from the live album?" he said. "I finally got around to writing a B section for it. Which it always needed. Would that be acceptable? I mean, we could always do 'Everything Happens to Me' or 'Chelsea Bridge' or whatever."

"'Chelsea Bridge' would be good," said Krieger. "But I think an original is preferred."

"Long as you don't mind that it's partly a repeat. Me, I'd like to do it."

"All right," said Krieger. "Try."

"Cool," said the Bear. It was a refreshing change to have a conversation with the producer that wasn't an argument or a contest. "Everybody else cool with that?"

"You have parts?" Hatwell asked him. "I haven't seen this tune before."

"Parts I got," said the Bear, bent to his saxophone case and started riffling through his papers.

"These are some damn tough changes," the pianist told him when he had scanned the sheet the Bear gave him.

"Yeah, but they make sense and they come at you slow," said the Bear.

"Kind of a Mingus texture to it," Hatwell noticed.

"There you go."

Charlie Haden was peering at the sheet music over Hatwell's shoulder. He cleared his throat before speaking. "This is really nice, man, but I don't think we should play it cold. Can Bob and I go out there and work it through for a few minutes before we do a take?"

While Haden and Hatwell were out there working on it, Krieger asked the Bear if he had thought about touring when the record came out.

"I suppose," said the Bear, "although there are still security considerations. The last time I played a gig they tried to shoot me. What did you have in mind?"

"It might be safer for you in Europe," Krieger suggested.

"You mean like bears aren't quite so discriminated against over there?" The Bear laughed. "I've always wanted to see Paris. You know, wear a beret and shades and sit around in a café and talk to the world going by, but there are problems. You'd have to fly me over in a private jet and sneak me through customs, cause I'm not willing to fly in a cage as cargo and deal with a quarantine when I get there. And have you ever tried crossing international borders with a bear? Sig, much as I like the idea, I think it'll have to be the good ol' USA, if I can get my security concerns addressed. Billy, can you come out there with me this summer?"

"Actually," Billy said, "I'm kind of committed through early autumn. Doing the European festival circuit, then Japan, get my family expenses covered for the year."

"Huh," said the Bear. "Wonder if I could get McCall."

Bowie and Billy were looking at him funny.

"What," said the Bear.

"You don't know," Lester said.

"Oh shit," said the Bear.

"Steve died," Bowie told him. "Heart attack back in Chicago. Nobody told you?"

"What the fuck is goin' on?" asked the Bear. "A bear goes inside for a few months and when he comes out the avant-garde has been outlawed by Wynton Marsalis, Julius is getting his leg chopped off, and some guy called Michael Dolton—"

"Bolton," Bowie corrected him.

"Some guy named Michael Bolton's fucked up 'When a Man Loves a Woman' for the rest of us and Steve McCall who was forty-what years old?"

"About that," Lester said.

"Drops dead of a heart attack? What is going on?"

"Seems like some more of the famous same-old same-old to me," Bowie said. "And a sort of Rip Van Bear effect."

"Welcome back to the waking world."

Nobody spoke awhile.

"Actually," Billy eased back in, "if you want some people to work with, Bobby Hatwell's got some friends you should get to know."

"They as good as he is?"

"About."

"Huh," the Bear said. "Steve McCall. I'm really gonna miss that guy."

The Bear had to instruct Hatwell on how he wanted "Billy Heart" chorded—not too lush, easy on the pedal, articulate the dissonances enough to bring the bitterness out, think good strong coffee with cognac but don't freeze me out with clusters—then they ran through sections of it twice and were ready for a take. Billy, if you want to go with sticks at some point it's all right with me, and we could belt the out-chorus if it feels right but if it doesn't let's not.

The photographer, still a long slim girl with frizzy hair, was out there with them on the floor. She'd flitted on the fringes of the day all along, but he had excised her from his working consciousness and seemed to have voodooed one of her motor drives. Maybe he should make it up to her now. He walked up to her and watched her try not to retreat.

"Hi," she managed to say.

"Dress me in Chinese colors," the Bear told her, nodding at her dangling Nikons, "for I think the glass is evil."

"You don't like being photographed," she said.

"That's it. But I have a cunning plan."

"Uh-oh."

"You know it's part of my deal with Krieger that there's to be no portrait of me on the album."

The photographer nodded. "I've been taking them for myself."

"Fine, as long as you know that if you distribute them without permission you will be killed and eaten," the Bear told her. "Only kidding," he added when he saw how pale she'd gone.

"What a wonderful sense of humor you have," she said.

"A trifle on the dark side but it's mine," he told her. "I do have an idea for the album cover, though."

"More wonderful news," she said. He was glad to notice some of her color coming back.

"Can we start over? What's your name?"

"Deborah."

"Yeah, I've seen your work in the music magazines and I like it. You do some hand-tinted color, right? How about you take a black-and-white picture of my feet standing on some cables on the floor here, legs in the picture up to the hem of my raincoat or up to the knee, and you tint it realistically but kind of pastel."

"You have a degree in design or something?" Debbie asked, and cocked her hip sideways with ironic self-assertion.

"It came to me in a vision. That's the cover and the name of the album is *Sensible Shoes*. I'm a very graphic bear," he said.

"I bet." Debbie set him up on the floor and shot a quick roll of his feet variously engaged with audio cable, pivoting around him and whirring her motor drive between shots. "I'd like to shoot a second roll," she said, screwing a new lens of choice onto a second camera back.

"I've got to play," the Bear said. "I've got to play right now."

Debbie fired off a quick series of portrait shots as she withdrew. "*Playboy*'s getting these," she said. The Bear whipped his raincoat open wide.

He heard throats being cleared behind him, and a certain restlessness at the drums.

"'Billy Heart.'" Right.

The Bear was glad to get another chance at the bittersweet composition, especially since probably no one would shoot at him this time and the B section had fallen into place. The head went by in an okay mix of passion and clarity. When it was time for his solo, the Bear began it confidently, Haden nudging some extra lyricism out of him with some strums and surges, and the Bear went down into what the bassist suggested. He met Billy there in a rise and fall of cymbals, a troubled hush of drums. Something opened out of him and he let it have its run in the form of multinoted music full of minor sixths and ninths and fourths and polytonal suggestions. This was the second time the tune had worked something complicated out of him, and he was willing to let it happen. Big of me, ain't it, he thought, and blotted a run with a low E-sharp honk before moving on. Two choruses and then Hatwell had it handled. Look at that, thought the Bear. I finally got to play a difficult chord sequence and it worked. Well, it's a tune I already had down.

Hatwell looked at him at the end of one chorus and the Bear nodded him forward for another, or maybe he'd decide to come back in at the bridge. Charlie? The Bear looked over at him, but the bassist shook his head no, he didn't want an outing. Something was happening on the tune and everyone was obedient to it. I'm so great. Shut up and play the head and get out.

At the tune's final cadence, the Bear was surprised to hear the band fall away from him and only then remembered he'd written in a space for a cadenza. Okay, he thought, and went into it feeling nothing much. More or less, he played the current contents of his heart out, summed up the record date for himself, how he'd felt coming into it and what had happened once it started. He discovered significant differences between the bitterness of the Tin Palace version of the tune and the more complex if still soul-puckering bouquet of today's equivocal cup of wine, and he explored for awhile the implications of the gap between them. He took note of the victories and limitations, nodded his thanks to the equivocal riches the moment allowed, tossed some last chromatic skirlings into the day's departing wake, and watched the last waves recede. Justice, thought the Bear. Time spent, imperfectly perforce but all in all not completely bad. As he held up his last high note, inviting the band to set down the final chord, he knew they had played something that reached about the same level as "Vehicle," and that was fine, and also in the oceanic ordered amplitude of the universe no big deal. He said okay to the day's experience and to such world as had brought him to it, acknowledged his still pervasive sense of constricted entrapment, and nodded a last thank-you to whatever grace had supervened to let some not-bad music through. His flawed coin had been accepted and a measure of gold returned him. Good, he thought, and pulled the tune down with a last obeisance of his horn.

"You know," the Bear told Jones in the anteroom while Krieger was there listening to the day's work to see if it made an album, "it's been a little weird."

"What isn't?" asked Jones.

They were slouched in armchairs and the band was wandering around waiting to hear what Krieger thought and would they be coming in tomorrow.

"What I mean," the Bear told Jones, "is that it only occurs to me now that I was probably in a trance for the duration. You know, I still don't need to use the bathroom. That's weird, Jones."

"I see," said Jones. "You don't need to pee equals you're in a trance. How about you levitate and I'll believe you."

"No, listen. I don't feel a thing. I'm anaesthetized. Everything's kind of two-dimensional, flat. Emotionally it's a blank, my body's pretty much not here, and still I was able to negotiate the emotional world while I was playing, because I knew emotion had to be there, but I did it in a very, very detached way. Not to make a big thing about it. It's just kind of interesting to me, as experience."

The control-room door opened and Krieger walked past Jones and the Bear looking somber, but when he reached the loitering band he went into his portfolio and handed out mint-green paychecks that were received with gratitude and thank-you smiles. The band looked at the Bear past Krieger and beamed him grateful smiles.

Then Krieger came back to the Bear. "You did it in one day and it's all right," the producer told him, "but I don't think I will work with you again personally. If you do another record for my company James will produce it."

Krieger may have meant this to sound like a punishment, but "Fine," the Bear said.

"Also I'm leaving the studio open for you the day after tomorrow. I will speak with you on the phone in the morning and we will agree whether or not to come in again."

"*Eh bien, mon prince*. I'll keep an open mind."

Krieger squinted at him but said nothing and left.

There was more human movement around him, the guys in the band coming through, Billy manhandling some black fiber drumcases through the doorway, Haden coming by with a big soft bass case, but the Bear didn't register all these motions in detail. "Right now," he told Jones, "I'm just tired and played out, but I think I was clinically insane for the duration of the date."

"Bear," Jones said, and laid a hand on his forepaw, "I don't think anyone who lived through this one with you would dispute that."

"Really?" said the Bear. "And I thought I was being so cool."

"You were cool like Antarctica is cool," Jones told him "We were up to the neck in penguins here. But you made a pretty good record and that's what counts. How does that make you feel? Just speak into the flower in my lapel here."

The Bear had to think a moment. "Actually," he said, "it makes me feel like quitting music."

What with his dropping jaw and all, Jones seemed unable to form the intended word Wha? "Ww," was what he said.

"I'm serious," said the Bear. "The music came out fine, but if I had to do it like this all the time I'd be destroyed in no time flat. I ain't no burning bush—I'm consumed by what I manifest. I'm clear about this. If getting out of the way stays this hard, I'd have to drink or do drugs to ameliorate the tension. I won't do that. I'd rather not play."

"You talking about stage fright?"

"Oh it's the same old bullshit, fear of judgment, transfer of the inside to the outside and how scary that feels. But the solution that came up today was in certain respects worse than the disease. Too much self-separation. I don't think I can make you see it, but I was so alive and dead at the same time, so full of feeling and at the same time so empty of it, that I was looking around at the guys one time, and nothing mattered so completely that I saw Bobby Hatwell sitting there and it occurred to me how easily I could open the back of his head up with one slap and his brains'd fall out. I could kill him or play the next tune or yawn. It was all pretty much on the same level. It's hard to explain."

"No shit."

"I didn't feel actually murderous, and there was no will to violence as such. It was just that everything seemed about as null and void as everything else. I could swat Hatwell's head open or not. Time was nothing, flesh was grass. I knew I wasn't going to do anything strange, but still it was some kind of controlled psychosis, some fucked-up blend of dissociation and control, and all of it was pretty cold. There were interesting states and waves along the way, but it was not a pleasant way to be. I wouldn't want to live there. It would be intolerable. I'd have to stop or get blotto. If I can't get to some other way of playing music, I'll stop."

"You're serious."

"I'm completely serious. If I had to live like that I'd quit in a minute. It's not the intensity but the degree of self-division. If I can't play like a whole spirit again I'll give it up. I didn't come to music in order to find some new way of being all fucked up. I don't think you should have to cripple yourself into beauty. For one thing it makes any beauty you might arrive at kinda suspect, don't you think? It's too dark, there's a wrong turning in it, and I betcha more than a few cats have gone up that path and disappeared around the bend. Press of circumstance, unskillful means, and hey presto you're a Martian. The next record date, the next night's gig, the apparent demands of so-called art—that's nothing I want to be ruled by. Yeah, absolutely, if it stays like this I'll quit, go live in the woods, eat grass and caterpillars and grubs. Anything's better than this."

It took awhile for Jones to answer him. "You know, Bear, you've got a complicated nature," was what he said.

"You think?"

"With a couple of deepish inner contradictions."

"Me?" the Bear asked, all innocence, but Hatwell had overheard the exchange and was looking on from a discreet distance, staring actually. Had he heard the whole thing? Had he heard the Bear's idea of percussion and slapping his head open? Jeez, he hadn't meant anything personal. The Bear waved at Hatwell with an attempt at easy geniality and got a wary nod back, then returned his attention to Jones. "Who, me?" he asked, with a passing reference to the Coasters.

"Yeah, you."

"But I'm just your simple cuddly basic woodland creature."

"Oh yeah," said Jones. "Right. I forgot."

3

the Bear stayed in the back of the van with the boxes of books and records until they cleared the second tollbooth north on the Thruway. Then he struggled forward to the shotgun seat and sat himself down. "You handle this big ol' van pretty well for such a sweet young thing," he said.

"Give me a break," said Iris, and gave the steering wheel a sideways yank that made the Bear grab the armrest for support. Her voice was ever soft, an excellent thing in woman, but she sure could be tough on a vehicle.

"Look," the Bear said to change the subject, gesturing with an open paw. "Trees. Nature. Green shit."

"I'd like another sip of Evian water," Iris said, "if you can find the bottle for me."

He found it and twisted the plastic cap open. "As Sibelius said," the Bear told her as he passed her the bottle, "while other musicians mix up all kinds of fancy cocktails, I provide clear spring water."

"Thank you," said Iris, and handed the bottle back. Although her tone hadn't varied from its usual melodious politesse, the Bear decided to give up on the charming drollery crap for a few minutes.

"Did you feel the city let go awhile back?" he asked her. "The last ring of its gravitational field. The event horizon."

"Palpably," Iris said. "I have to admit, it is a relief to get out."

"Think about it, global warming has its good side. Anything that puts New York City underwater can't be all bad. In a decade or so there'll be fish swimming through the office buildings and reading old newspapers and personnel files. It'll be a much more meditative place then, and a lot of people will be heading out of town. You and me, we're avoiding the rush."

"I still live there," Iris said. "I'm driving back tonight and returning the van before ten tomorrow morning."

"Well, there's still time. It ain't swimming season there yet."

"I can't swim."

"Oh yeah, I forgot." The Bear remembered the story about some of her cousins repeatedly drowning her in a pond and pulling her out, reviving her, then drowning her again, back in her childhood, when she'd been farmed out to an aunt for a couple of years while her mother had a breakdown. They had bound her arms and legs with rope to keep her from thrashing around and kept an end loose to pull her out of the pond with. Once, they had lost their grip on the end and things had gotten serious. "I could teach you," he offered. "I could teach you to swim."

"I don't think so," Iris said.

"Maybe some other time. It's never too late."

No answer. Maybe it was a mistake to have mentioned it at all.

"Was Jones doing any heavy lifting back in town?" the Bear asked Iris, partly to change the subject.

"He had some people helping him, some hired people and Johnny Coyle. But Jones is fully healed now. You don't need to worry about him."

"He was never very strong."

Jones was moving house back in the city, and so Iris had volunteered to take the Bear up to the Catskills in the rent-a-van. Jones had boxed the stereo for him along with a few cartons of books and records he'd requested, and Iris had picked them up before collecting the Bear just past the tick of noon. For safety's sake—no sense getting your tail caught in the door on your way out of town—he'd been extra careful with his coatcollar, hat and scarf, had taken the back stairs down and exited the building by the laundry-room door.

In general he felt a bit turbulent about the move.

On one paw, it was an obvious good thing. On the other, it cut him off from most of the life he knew. Which might also be a good thing. Still . . . it lacked the homey touch. He'd be on his own up there, although there was supposed to be a sometimes tenant in the basement room to ease his interface with the rest of the world, and both Jones and Iris had promised to drop up frequently to see him. Promises, promises: jabberwocky and air. But then there were the woods. It had been awhile since he'd had a good long ramble in the woods.

Iris was intent on the road ahead. The western sun traced her profile with a single line of white-gold light. He watched a small motion in her throat, and waited for her to speak. He had noticed, only recently, that she was one of those people whose nose moved when they spoke, the dainty tip of it dipping down as her lips and jaw worked. But what was there to say at the moment?

"Nice weather we're having," he said.

"Really."

See that? Even for one semi-sarcastic word, a little dip at the end. The Bear looked off into landscape, out his side an excoriated cliff clawed out of the land by the roadbuilders, past Iris' western window a fringe of trees, then an indeterminate expanse of grass with stray bits of commerce strewn about the middle distance. Soon they'd see the ridge of the Rondout, then there'd be a woodsy stretch through gathering hillocks, and it'd be awhile before the mountains showed, blued by distance. He always enjoyed his first sight of the mountains.

In the meantime there were gossip's flatter vistas. "Did you get the feeling," he asked Iris, "that Sybil was really welcoming Jones into her apartment and life?"

"I think he's a bit nervous about it, and that she's . . . but I hardly know her."

"I think he's sneaking in under cover of crisis," the Bear suggested, "and she's letting him, for whatever her own reasons might be at the moment. But I don't know how secure his position is. My guess is that it's probation at best."

"You think so?"

"Poor bastard," said the Bear, and shifted voluminously in his seat. "I hope he does okay out there without me."

"That's really touching," said Iris, "especially in view of the way you've been treating him lately."

"Yeah, but he's getting so . . . he's getting so . . ."

"You're so used to having him around as a sidekick," Iris told him in her usual tone, "that as soon as he shows a sign of independent life you feel insulted."

"All right, all right," said the Bear.

"You feel deprived of your natural rights. It's egoistic nonsense."

"Maybe I just miss my buddy."

"Maybe," Iris allowed.

The cliff face out the Bear's window slanted off, then vanished, and he had the leisure to observe a stray house-and-barn combo, two piebald horses standing puzzled in a pasture, and just coming up, a large low factory set neatly in a field. Highway coming through. Move your ass or try to like it. Can't stop progress. Bang bang you're dead. "Music?" the Bear suggested.

Iris gave it a shot, but there was nothing on the radio in this region.

The Bear leaned forward and punched the cassette into the slot.

"Do we have to listen to 'When a Man Loves a Woman' again?" Iris asked him.

"But it came out so cool. I wish they'd let me put down a vocal."

Iris said nothing for a moment. Then, "I think 'Vehicle' is the best thing you've done," she told him. "That and the new version of 'Billy Heart.'"

"Well sure. But I have a special fondness . . . and Lester's on it."

"Lester's wonderful, Bear," said Iris. "And I got the message already."

"But wasn't I funky?" asked the Bear.

"You were funky," said Iris, and turned to him, keeping half an eye on the road. "But are you going to start asking me Was I wonderful? Aren't I talented? Wasn't that a great solo? That's not a job I want to take on, Bear. I'd find it exhausting. Is that what you want me to do?"

"Of course not. Keep your eye on the road."

"Thanks for the instruction."

He was not doing all that well today. This move upstate was probably a mistake too. Everything was coming up noses.

The Bear punched the cassette out and fiddled with the radio. Two rock stations staticked their way in, beset by bronchial interference that occasionally parted to reveal full-frequency industrial-strength ear-candy striving to articulate over a range of power chords how, some way or other baby, we were gonna win and make it, were gonna get through the night and take it, gonna climb that mountain, really gonna see the sky. There was nothing out there on this stretch of the American airwaves but striving toward triumph. The big guitar solos were interesting for their first couple of bars, but after the initial liberating blast they had nothing much to say. Iris and the Bear looked at each other briefly and he turned the radio off.

There was the Rondout in the west, a ridge rising out of the land for no apparent reason and with little aesthetic sense of adjacent consequence. After New Paltz—what was wrong with the old Paltz?—a line of power towers strode across the gathering hills, laces of wire strung between them in series. The Bear thought of a TV sitcom husband, hands imprisoned in skeins of wool as his wife wound still more wool around them, the Atropine scissors not yet in view.

The Bear remembered that the mountains would appear, but not quite as soon as he wanted them to.

Then there they were, spreading north and west along the horizon, forested from lap to top, flanks purpled by haze and distance, peaks rounded by modesty or age. The Bear loved the perspective they lent the landscape, the scale they afforded. He had always found mountains a great perceptual aid. Mountains made room for sages. Chinese inkscapes: towering crags, tiny figures. He was glad to see the mountains again.

"That's the turnoff," he said, pointing at the Kingston sign. It was followed by a smaller sign that said Woodstock, a hippy-dippy coda to the main signifier, for those who cared, or just for tourists.

The Bear crawled into the rear of the van as they swung off the Thruway in a long arc to approach the tollbooths. "At the roundabout, follow 28 West to Pine Hill," he told Iris, and pulled a blanket over his head just in case. There were state police around.

When they were established on the straight road west he came front again and sat himself down. When they cleared the car dealerships and the clutter of lesser commerce, the Bear saw the sign welcoming them to the Catskill Forest Park. When a mountainside momentarily darkened the roadway, a grey-white spill of cloud fanning down its front, the Bear assumed the voice of a bored taxi driver. "This is Illyria, lady," he said, but got no response at all.

Oh well, he thought.

"The Woodstock turnoff comes up on the right," he said. "There's a gas station and a light."

When they reached it, Iris steered the van onto the lesser road, and as they entered the lee of Overlook Mountain the Bear felt a familiar sense of welcome from the land coming to embrace him, a female, mothering presence that made for a dramatic change when you were coming up from the city, though you might not notice it once you stayed awhile. Forgetfulness or the fading of illusion? Either way, it felt nurturing and undeceptive to him now.

It was still early spring in the mountains, and the Bear wondered if a few others of his approximate kind were drifting down from the ranges one county north. Woodstock's full summer biped population wouldn't swell the area for another few months, the land was sweet, and there'd be hills to roam and things to munch on. They were black bears, smaller than he was; they'd avoid the lowlands except to hit the creeks for hatchlings. In the Bear's experience, most of them hadn't fallen so far, yet, as to live wholly off the trashpiles, though of course folks tended to raid where they could. It'd be nice to see another bear or so, as long as he didn't have to get into some endless lamebrained fight over turf when all he wanted was to socialize a little, lay back, swap stories. He was a more social being than his country cousins, and wasn't always understood. He was handsomer than they, whatever their color phase, and wondered if they envied him his wider, more dignified head, pronounced, expressive brow, better shoulders, and that distinctive hump of muscle on the upper back—all in all a more pleasing shape, limbs more clearly articulated, his look altogether more detailed, fur more variegated and pleasing in texture, and he moved better than they did, with less bumbling. The males would curse at him and labor their heads through the phantasmal logarithms of their nationalistic conceptions when all he wanted was to express solidarity, admiration, brotherly love. What a way to run a planet. The woods were as mad and racketous with competing delusions as the city he and Iris had left behind. There was so much space and so little room to *move*.

And then there were the lady bears.

They were a different scene altogether. Fun at first, but the mating rituals got boring after awhile—the Bear could splash around in a pond and play clumsy patacake with a lady for an hour or so, but how could he do a *week* of it and still find it interesting? It was touching and atavistic and warm in a dumb sort of way, but the Bear couldn't help but find it kind of rudimentary after awhile, and his sexual interest tended to wane after the fifteenth repetition of Gee you're cute and Gee you're big. And then, if they made it, if they got it going and they were both crooning along, if you tried to turn the beat around and asked if she wanted to try doing it face to face instead of from behind, because, look, it's possible, let me show you—watch out! she'd figure you wanted access to her underbelly and throat only to claw them open, and her face? why, she'd ask you, would you possibly want to look into my face? and to unfreak her out of the horribilitude of your unnatural desire, well, it would be back in the pond and more splashy-splashy for a day or so before she would let you approach again. Afterward it was was all Thanks, that was nice, but who the fuck are you anyway and you only wanted me for one thing and you've had it, so if I see you after the cubs are born I'll kill you before I let you touch them. As if the Bear would eat their babies! How could she think that? How could you talk to anyone like that? The Bear, he had told her, had told a number of versions of her to no purpose, was prepared to be the lovingest dotingest father that universal beardom had ever set forth on this stomping green earth, but the only response that all the warmth of his connubial heart had ever evoked from any she-bear he'd bodied forth a litter of cubs with was blind unthinking fury, bared teeth, unreasoning demented eyes and a bristling back shinnying into place at the door of the cave. Even so, he'd had to marvel at such overwhelming motherbear devotion, and admit in the face of it that in her impersonal singleness of purpose she was better than he could ever be. His trembling sons and daughters didn't want to see him either. Time is short!—he had wanted to tell them—and habitat is shrinking! Men are coming! Wise up! Evolve! The poor dumb darling stumbling things didn't know what he was talking about, and in the instant he understood why his family's wisdom, such as it was, had always been matrilineal. You could only argue with biology's imperatives so far. What kind of place was this? Who ran this benighted planet anyway? There must be some wised-up bears somewhere out there on the continent, but he'd never met up with any. A guardian bear on the higher astral plane, big Kodiak-looking fella about eight feet tall watching him calmly, full of wisdom and compassionate strength, an easy trick to manage, thought the Bear, when you didn't have time and space to contend with; but back here in Mudville he'd never met another soul his soul could peacefully commune with, not a whisper, not a wisp. O for a friend to know the sign!

Well, there'd been Jones.

And now he was in love, he guessed, with Iris, who was driving.

The van braked to a stop and the Bear nearly bumped the windshield with his heavy head. A line of cars coming from the other direction had also stopped. "What is it?" he wondered aloud.

"Look," said Iris, and pointed at the road.

"You're kidding," said the Bear. It was too cartoon-typical: two lines of traffic had ground to a halt so that a slow fat brown caterpillar could cross from one side of the road to the other. "You know what that kind of caterpillar's called?" the Bear asked Iris. He watched its brown fur ripple through quarter-inch after quarter-inch head to tail on the asphalt.

"No," she said.

"It's a Woolly Bear," he told her.

"Omen, anyone?"

"More like one more too blatant signifier, to my way of thinking. Your lane's clear," he said. "You can go ahead."

As she steered around the caterpillar, giving it wide berth, the Bear saw the lead driver in the old Volvo at the head of the opposing line of traffic see him, and they locked in eye contact, the Bear and this older guy with a spreading grey beard, long grey hair, granny glasses, and what might have been love beads around his neck. The Bear watched this man nudge the woman sitting next to him, a refined if odd-looking middle-aged lady with blond hair going grey, tucked into a funny flowerpot hat. They were both looking at him now. The Bear watched the man break into a wide-screen grin and wave hello. The woman looked more startled, but she didn't turn away. The man raised two fingers in a victory V as the van passed the Volvo. The Bear waved, and gave out his mildest, most sociable smile, with a bit of tongue hanging out the side for laughs.

Home, thought the Bear, anyhow for awhile. I can't live around this kind of people forever. It's droll but it'd fuck up my whole sense of outline.

"I think we should detour around town," the Bear told Iris when they had cleared the last of the caterpillar jam.

"How do I do that?"

"I'll tell you when we reach the bridge."

"How far?"

"Not."

There seem to be some new housing installations under the pines, the Bear noted, since the last time I was here. Corporate condo shit of some kind, apotheoses of motels. They look wrong. Betcha people are paying a fortune for them.

The wide brick schoolhouse showed up on the left, the golf course opened out on the right. "Take the sharp left before the bridge," the Bear advised. "We'll avoid Woodstock and come out on the main road just before Shady. The house is in Shady. There, there, no, *before* the bridge, there."

Iris took the turn too quickly and without braking. Once the van regained its balance, they passed alongside the millstream where it widened to the right of the road. The Bear watched it fanning downslope through a series of slaterock shelves, black water swollen with the last of the snowmelt going white at the rips but essentially unperturbed over the shallow falls. The road passed beside a bridge that led off right to town and they began a shallow climb away from the creek past worn wooden houses set amid trees left and right.

"There's a right we take soon," said the Bear, and Iris steered the van smoothly onto it when it came.

It seemed a simple bypass at first, but after awhile the road began curling uphill past houses that showed and others hidden up long drives. Most were basic, foursquare wooden constructions, but one showed antebellum columns astride the white dignity of its door, and farther on, a classic log cabin neighbored some architect's angled glass-and-panel wank. The thickening forest was in early leaf; afternoon sunlight dappled down to warble here and there on the ground. A soft wind sent messages through treetops, and a multitude of leaves flickered punctuation into their body of discourse.

"Is Stanlynn's house like any of these?" Iris asked him.

"Not exactly. The thing about the whole area is that it's zoned into state forest parkland so that roadbuilding is restricted and houses have to be close to the roads. That's the only reason the region has survived more or less intact. We get off this twisty-turny zigzag stuff soon."

"I can handle it," Iris said. Soon they were tipping downhill on straighter two-lane blacktop. They recrossed the stream—wide and slow here, rippling over shallow ranks of small grey stones—on an aluminum bridge with a sturdy wooden surface, and a quarter mile on they rejoined the region's main artery, Route 212, past a playground and the steamed exhaust fans of a woodsy-looking launderette. They turned left on 212 after letting a convoy of Saabs and Cherokees blow past.

"It's not far now," said the Bear, and found his heart beating harder than he would have expected. Well, why not? It'll be home for awhile. Better than being lashed to a wheel of fire which my eyes do scald with tears. Better, most ways, than being back in the infernal city while awaiting the next harsh turn of the wheel of law. But I'll be alone here. Iris seems eager to get away from me and who can blame her. I hope Jones comes up to visit now and then. He said he would, but then he's got his own frail agenda these days, and hopeful fish to fry.

But what was stirring the Bear up for the most part, he understood, was the sense of a page being turned, of a distinct new chapter opening in the book of his life. Who can tell where it's taking me? Especially considering the proven unreliability of its author. The boy would seem to have some problems. Count no bear happy till he's dead. What a terrific gig. So glad I made this deal.

"Take the sharp right uphill here," he said in a bit of a hurry. He'd almost missed the turnoff.

Iris downshifted as the van met the upslope. "Did you see the names of those restaurants back there?" she asked, nodding back toward the road they'd left.

The Bear had noticed a cluster of buildings lapsided in reds and browns, their shingled roofs grey-white. There'd been a parking lot too, and some signs. "The names? Can't say I did."

"One was the Bear Café, the other was the Little Bear."

"You're kidding me."

"And I think the logo for the Little Bear was a bit demeaning."

"Iris. Say it ain't so."

"On the sign, the Little Bear was standing upright, holding a bowl in his paws, and he looked a little drunk to me. Something about the way the tip of his tongue stuck out the front of his mouth."

"No, please."

"That's what I saw."

"Sweet Jesus, where have I come to? Fresh travesty. New farce. One more twist of the plastic knife. Won't it ever stop?"

"I don't know," Iris told him, "but we're coming to a T intersection. What do I do now?"

The Bear was holding his head in his paws, trying on the mask of tragedy and finding out it still didn't fit. He was getting a headache anyway. That counted for something. "The house is just there," he said distractedly, not looking.

"Where?"

The Bear looked up and pointed to the semicircular driveway across the T junction. He indicated the house with a claw. "Yonda is the castle of my fodda," he said.

The Bear saw the house behind its three-deep barrier of evenly spaced, thick-trunked evergreens. Their branches didn't even start till ten or fifteen feet up. From where the van had halted at the T, the Bear could make out new growth tipping the ends of the branches with a luminescent inch or two of brighter green. The earth beneath them was carpeted with yearsworth of fallen needles and broken bits of cone. Stanlynn's house—curiously tall, fronted with dark brown shingles, ornamented with white windowframes, then topped with an off-white circumflex of roof onto which brown needles of pine had strewn themselves—stood behind the guardian trees, a short ell coming out of its left side at the rear. It was an awkward-looking place, but it would have to do. He could see Stanlynn's small gold 4WD Subaru wagon parked on the drive in front of the house, hitched to a midsize white-and-orange U-Haul. She's leaving. This shit's for real. A troubled brow of dark grey cloud, bulging with the threat of rain, was rising to overtop the mountain that rose behind the house, but the rest of the sky was clear, and the sun was still awake in it, even perhaps slightly overeager to show off its post-equinoctial abundance of ideas.

Iris punched the van into first, crossed the two-lane blacktop of the Glasco Turnpike and adjusted right for the leftward branch of the house's gravel drive. The Bear felt the change of traction as the van engaged the gravel, heard the tires crunch and grip, and sensed the sudden hush of pine-tree shade.

"Give it a honk?" the Bear suggested, but Stanlynn had already appeared at the top of the tall wooden stairs, in the doorway of the windowed-in front porch. She was holding the screen door back with one hand and waving hello with the other. Her big dog, Buster, shouldered alongside her and then remained faithfully in place, ears alert and tail upraised. Hi Bus, thought the Bear, and waved back through the windshield, leaning down as the car pulled up the drive and Stanlynn and Buster ascended his limited rectangle of view. Hi Stanny. Stanlynn showed nice white teeth in a smile of welcome. "You've never met her, right?" the Bear asked Iris sideways.

"Never," she said, steered the van alongside the Subaru and its trailer and braked to a stop. She gunned the motor once—a bad habit, in the Bear's opinion—before switching the ignition off.

The Bear listened for a wind in the firs or spruces or whatever—he was a city bear, and knew the names of so few trees—but all he could hear was the absence of the van's own engine and the windrush of the world going past. Then he smelled the living pines, needles lying beneath them, and the rich brown earth. I can live with this, he thought.

They got out of the van and Buster rushed down the steep wooden stairs, upcurved furry tail waving high to meet his big ol' buddy bear. Bus was a roughly arctic-looking fella with blue-grey eyes and long matted fur in shades of grey and streaks of white. The only thing the Bear had against Stanlynn was that she'd had Buster neutered. Of course Buster'd been trouble when young, and that was before she'd had a chance to meet the Bear and talk with him about such things, and actually Buster didn't seem to mind it much, but still . . . the Bear felt a shuddering chill at the thought of it. "Hey Bus hey Bus hey Bus," he said as the dog wagged and tumbled down the stairs at him.

"Hey Bear hey Bear hey Bear," Buster said back, even if Stanny and Iris couldn't explicitly understand his speech. Well, Iris maybe. "Hey Bear hey Bear we're movin' out out out," Buster told him.

"Hey Bus I'm comin' here I'm moving in in in," said the Bear, and thumped himself on the chest to indicate the exact degree of welcome he would like from the joint's previous animal tenant. Buster raised up and plonked his forefeet on the Bear's big pectorals; the Bear bent his face down, touched noses with Buster and let the dog lick his face a couple of times hello.

"Are *we* still on speaking terms?" Stanlynn asked from the top of the stairs. "Or are you only here to see my dog?"

"Hey, Big Strapping Girl," the Bear called up to her, figuring that would have been her American Indian name, if she'd been an American Indian. She knew lots of them, though, had grown up among Indians out West and had always wanted to introduce him to Chief Oren Lyons, who lived somewhere nearby. Maybe someday, he'd told her, and let it go at that. Stanlynn also knew an Indian named Jazzy Wee-Wah, but he was Cheyenne and lived out

West. The Bear thought that Jazzy Wee-Wah was the coolest name he'd ever heard, this side of Vakhtang Gourgastan. He nodded at the car and van in the drive. "I see you're all set."

"Soon's I can get you all set up," she said, and started to step down from porch level. "This is Iris I assume?"

"Hello," Iris said. She was standing beside him.

"Oh yeah, I'm sorry," said the Bear, and took in, by a series of rapid oscillations, this study in female contrasts, Iris all crystalline delicacy and dazzle, Stanlynn a large-sized earthly radiance with curly hair and the apple cheeks of outdoor health. "I should have introduced . . . You mind getting down for a minute, Bus?"

"Course not," said the dog, and dropped back onto all fours with a thump on the boards at the base of the stairs.

Stanlynn was wearing a Western shirt and jeans and the Bear hugged her when she reached him and had nudged Buster aside with a knee. "Well, welcome home, Bear," she said, once she had leisure to pull away.

"You think so?" he asked.

"For awhile anyway. Iris?" Stanlynn said, turning to her. "Where has he been hiding *you*?"

"Not under a blanket," the Bear grumbled, "I can tell you that."

"Tough luck." Stanlynn grinned at him.

"Perhaps I've been hiding myself," Iris said. "I might actually be capable of that on my own."

"Well I'm all ready to go," said Stanlynn, and the Bear noticed her wherever-it-was-from Western accent for the first time that day, "so let me show you what there is."

"Just like that?" asked the Bear. "So fast?"

"Just like that. C'mon upstairs."

"C'mon upstairs," the Bear relayed the message to Iris.

"Oh thanks," Iris said.

It was a strange house, awkwardly divided. The living room, which they entered once they had crossed the windowed porch—"You can take the glass out when it gets warmer and put the screens up," Stanlynn told him—was bifurcated by a bulky greystone chimney rising from the center of the floor, a black iron woodstove set in its mouth. In effect, there was a cutoff living room on one side of the stovepiece and a dining room behind it. Neither was very large. "I left it a little better than semifurnished," Stanlynn said. "I was going to rent it for twice the price to the summer trade, but you're welcome to it now."

"You left the piano," the Bear said in some wonder. A not-bad Mason &

Hamlin upright stood against one of the living room walls. Julius had sanded layers of old paint off it and oiled the original fruitwood, which had a lovely grain.

"For awhile anyhow. You can play it long as you don't claw up the keys. Julius may want it in the city after awhile, and then again I might want it out in Oregon, but you're welcome to it for now."

"Paradise," said the Bear.

"Wait and see," Stanlynn advised him. "There's enough bedding, and there's things to sit on. There's about a quarter cord of firewood left—oak, but sometimes I get ash tailings from a baseball-bat factory a whole lot cheaper. You might need to buy some more before summer sets in and the nights warm up, though there's some deadfall you could cut up out back, and I need to show you about the gas tanks and the plumbing. It's not perfect," she told Iris in sum, "but you could get to like it here."

"I live in the city," Iris said. "I'm going back tonight."

"Oh."

The ensuing pause accommodated the three—make that four of them: Buster was back inside, looking up at the Bear to see if anything fun and interesting was up—and might have made room for a half-dozen more.

"Llamas?" the Bear asked Stanlynn finally.

"Well I bought three breeding pair, the house is in the foothills of a bunch of mountains bigger than these guys here, I can sleep ten between the house and the outbuildings once I finish the barn, and I've worked out some trekking routes for next year."

"So it's not the jazz life anymore."

"Not hardly, Bear. Can I get you something?" she asked Iris, who, looking as delicately radiant as usual, was gazing around in most of the available directions.

"The ladies' room," Iris inquired. "As it were."

"Where'd you find *her*?" Stanlynn asked the Bear once Iris had taken the indicated route.

"Years ago," he said, "and I'm not sure who found whom, much less why."

"How's the house look to you?"

"Fine," he said without looking. "You know, if it weren't for Julius I might not be playing. Not only did he show me a lot of things on the horn, he was . . . an example? Certainly a friend. I know you two broke up, but have you seen him since the leg operation? I spoke with him on the phone and he sounded pretty good, considering."

Stanlynn nodded. "Losing his leg may have gotten his attention. Maybe he'll treat his diabetes with more respect. Maybe he's decided to live."

"Here's hoping," the Bear said.

"But in any case I'm out of here," she said firmly. "So it's a thousand five hundred a month for the joint. D'you have two months' worth up front?"

"Yes," gasped the Bear.

"You're getting it cheap," Stanlynn told him, "especially considering it's mostly furnished. I can get three, even four grand a month for the summer if I want. You've got it for six months clear at this rate, then we can work out whether you want to stay or do I want to put it on the market for sale. It's cheap at a grand five, or don't you believe me?"

"Of course I believe you." He and Jones had been paying two-sixty a month for their dump in the city. He could feel the princely twenty grand he'd been paid for the record date turning pauper in his paws. What am I doing here? What a world this is. How ready it is for you no matter what you've managed to do lately. The acuity of its aim. The bites it takes out of you. The repeated pounds of flesh.

A pattering of rain graced the roof above them, or threatened it. "The weather in the mountains," Stanlynn said, looking up.

"It was a dark and stormy night," the Bear told her.

"Not yet it isn't."

"Listen," said the Bear, "you've got to tell me about the names of those restaurants back down there at the bottom of the hill."

Iris was back among them. "Was that rain I heard?" she asked.

"I never knew," said the Bear, "even though I've been here a dozen times."

"That's not possible," Iris told him.

"You don't get it. They kept it from me. Julius, Stanlynn, Jones."

The facts, as revealed by Stanlynn before she left, were that not only were the two clustered restaurants down the hill named the Bear Café and the Little Bear, but the road junction at whose elbow they were gathered was a town that went by the name of Bearsville.

"I hate it," said the Bear. "They kept it from me and now I live just up the hill. The hell of it is, it's probably not the last straw. No, there'll be more to come. Haystacks, most likely. Farce follows me wherever I go, like shit on a shoe."

"Do you know what a self-fulfilling prophecy is?" Iris asked him.

"Of course I do. Like everything else on earth it's a trick done with mirrors. It's Bearsville."

Rain was sheeting down through the trees and thrumming on the roof, and Iris and the Bear were eating the odd but satisfying Chinese food the Little Bear cooked up downhill. Iris had picked the food up in the van, and the white cartons stood about the table with the tops of their heads unfolded open. Iris performed surgery on her plate with chopsticks while the Bear rummaged around in his vegetables with a fork.

It was getting darker out, and outside the rectangular window set above the long cherrywood dining table a shelf of slaterock gathered gloom beneath it amid leafmeal, ferns bowed to the repeated authority of the rain, and treetrunks ran black. "Bearsville," said the Bear. "I had no idea."

"Maybe it's a good omen," Iris said.

"Phrpphhrrphhr," the Bear remarked.

Stanlynn had pulled her Subaru and its trailer out of the drive—like the sun, heading west—and then the Bear had unloaded the van in the drizzle while Iris wandered through the upstairs of the house, opening closets and drawers and straightening picture frames. Well, I guess I should be going, Iris had said when he was done with the heavy lifting. The Bear rejoined, Hey, I thought we could light up a Kazbeck, lay back and watch a couple of Vladek Sheybal movies. He had pointed hopefully at the black Sony television and VCR that Stanlynn considerately had left behind, but that was not the ticket.

Actually, I could use a bit of food before I drive, was what Iris said.

And although the name bothered him, the Bear said he wondered if the Little Bear delivered.

"What do you think of the food?" he asked her now.

"It's different. Do you think the rain will stop?"

"It always has," said the Bear. "Maybe you should stay the night."

"I don't think so."

"The larger upstairs bedroom looked pretty nice."

"To you perhaps. Sleep in it if you like."

"More brown rice?"

"Please."

The perimeter of a lightning flash reached them as he served her. Then a roll of thunder laid itself down across the floor of heaven. "A definite Elvin Jones influence," the Bear observed. "The sky's been listening to Coltrane records."

"If I opened another beer would you split it with me?" Iris asked.

First it was a hint in the air. Now the smell of rain and the forest took possession of the house.

"Do you think you'll like it here?" Iris asked him.

"At least it's a respite. We'll see. The arrangements are funny."

"But practical."

"You think so? I don't even need a house, me. I could live out there. Why not?"

Iris laughed politely. "Sure," she said.

"I mean, what am I doing here? What do I need this for?"

The rent still shocked him—he had parted with three thousand dollars, cash, in one smooth motion—and there was that photographer using the basement installation downstairs who would do shopping and such, but the Bear hadn't met him yet. It all seemed expensive and overhasty. It felt pretty much as if he were being dumped. By Jones, by Iris, by anyone within range.

"I wish I'd met the photographer," he said.

"But he was called away on—what did Stanlynn call it?—an architectural shoot."

"Money talks and I get to wake up tomorrow morning wondering if there's any coffee in the house."

"Aww."

The rain redoubled.

"It was a dark and stormy night," the Bear said again.

"Please," said Iris, and rose from the table. She walked around the obstreperous chimneypiece and out the living-room door. The Bear heard her footsteps sound as she crossed the porch, then the screen door cranging open on its rusty mortal coil. The Bear remained in place at the dining table and helped himself to another mound of garlicked eggplant. Not entirely bad. More tofu perhaps? Was there not another shrimp in yonder carton?

The return of Iris. He saw three drops of rain arrayed on her brow, and diamonds of it in her hair. "The rain is torrential," she said.

"Biblical," the Bear agreed.

"Perhaps I should stay the night and get an early start in the morning."

"There you go," said the Bear. "Now you're talkin'."

He lay in the under the circumstances preposterous brass bed in the master bedroom offset two steps down off one side of the living room and wondered. He had listened to her preparations for bed upstairs, the workings of her feet on the floorboards, their occasional transfers to carpet, the rustle of cloth, running water, toilet's flush. Iris was heavier on her feet than one would have thought. The rain had stopped, but an enveloping damp had hushed down upon the house. He had heard nothing from her in ten minutes or perhaps half an hour. She had turned over once or twice in bed, if the report of mere springs could be trusted from this distance. His whole life seemed to lie here gathered with him, bunched and waiting in tonight's particular degree of indigo. Should I go up there? Should I go up there? Does it all come down to this?

He liked his bedroom. It was large and amorphous in the dark, although he could make out an edge of Tiffany lamp and a bit of mirror over a dresser in the middle distance.

Maybe she was nothing to him at all in the long run—a would-be shudder in the loins, a misdirected longing that shook the matrix of his genetic code and no more. Maybe it was wisdom to let the figment go, no matter how charmingly it danced through the rooms of his imagination. Could love sum up a life, as it always tried to convince us it could? Could its motions through light and shade really assemble itself into an alphabet to spell out ultimate hopes and meanings, or speak the handful of sentences that might finally make us real? It seemed unlikely to the Bear. On the other paw, wasn't love the last sacred habitat in the portioned-down world, or had that range been shrinking too? And wasn't sex the most rampant, greedy and unregarding of our powers?

How could he go up there with just his immense longing, which might only be a hunger, to justify him? It would take a movement of the Law itself. He had made love to other women, but they had been bought for the night. There had never been any question of penetrating the soul as well as the body, the spirit as well as the soul.

The house, which he was renting for a sum that still shocked him, seemed both larger and smaller than Iris' apartment—it was much larger, of course. In any case it was a wholly different sort of space, not hers, nor yet his either, surrounded by sentinel trees whose language, quiet now in the windless damp and likely fog, spoke words which he neither knew nor understood. What time was it? What could happen in a space like this? What could not? The world had composed itself into unfamiliar music. It was not the city out there. It was forest and clearing, and a mountain grading upslope behind the house. He could smell the sweet and bitter earth of the world as given, dark and loamy after the rain, the scented air amplified by friendly ions. Complex, satisfying, factual, mysterious. I am an ignoramus. Will I lie awake till dawn? Should I go up there now? Wait another half hour? Let the moment pass and do nothing?

He had not heard her come down the stairs, for so much thinking and dreaming, but she seemed to be standing in his bedroom doorway outlined by soft light from the room behind her, wearing what looked to be a sheet wrapped about her down to the ankles, her arms holding it to her body and leaving her squared-off shoulders bare above. "I couldn't sleep," she said from where she stood.

"Oh baby," was what he managed to say, and then she was walking with quick small steps across the room and around the foot of the bed to stand to the left of where he lay, near phantasmal in the relative dark.

"Turn on a little lamp," he said, and she found one somewhere, a little lamp with a leaded jade-green glass five-sided shade and a bit of patterned orange silk laid across it. He saw her clearly in its silksoftened light.

He didn't get up when she stood beside his bed again, modestly composed in her sheet and looking down at him. He didn't move at all. He had never before felt his heart beat so hard for exit from his body or from the world of time entirely.

"Can you make room for me in there?" she asked.

"I'll do my best," he said, slid to the right-hand half of the bed and raised a corner of the comforter for her to enter. She came in smoothly but kept the windings of her sheet still close about her body. "Are you sure?" he asked.

Her eyes looked at him without blinking, and perhaps her bare shoulders, very square for all the delicacy of her build, made the beginnings of a shrug. Then she nodded, or almost nodded, yes.

Your move.

As he came toward her across the sheets he could feel time and categories of being rumple and fold between them like the bedding, or like waves of air anticipating the breakage of the sound or some other barrier: there was a buildup, a ridge of tension being crossed, and when he did cross it the Bear was startled to observe that he had no clear idea what lay on the other side for real.

She lay there looking up at him, oddly immobile until finally she raised her arms to take him in, turning partway onto her side so that the corner of the sheet she was wrapped in fell undone, although this motion still left her covered. Noticing this corner fall, however, she took it in her hand and, after a modest lowering and raising of her eyelids, lifted her body and pulled the sheet off in one motion and there she was.

The Bear paused in his movement and involuntarily gasped at the beauty of her. It seemed to him he had never seen anyone quite so naked, or so finely made, or so revealed. He was shocked to realize how arid his life had been for so long. "There are a few things to say first," he told her with some difficulty.

"How could there be?" Iris asked him, unblinking.

"No, for safety's sake. If you do the wrong things you could injure yourself on me. You're not just dealing with erectile tissue here, there's an actual bone that slides, that is just now sliding into place, and until you know my length and your depth you could rupture your cervix against me. So let me lead you until you know how things are for sure."

"Oh," she said, and that got a long slow blink out of her. Her body seemed to retract slightly, though whether away from him or only into itself he could not say. But just look at her, he thought. How can there be this much treasure all in one place, and the world still here? "Perhaps you should have given me a manual to read," she said.

"There isn't one, I mean I didn't know this was gonna happen."

"Of course you did," she said.

"I didn't," he insisted.

"You weren't born yesterday, Bear."

"Iris, looking at you like this I feel so full of . . . I feel as if I haven't been born yet, but that I might just be about to be."

He had said this awkwardly and spontaneously, but it had an effect on her that no amount of calculation could have done: her physical rigidity, which he realized was fear, seemed to melt, and the Bear saw a blush suffuse first her face and then her upper body. In a moment they were in each other's arms, the Bear was being mindful of his claws and Iris was trying to work out how to give and receive their first real kiss. The Bear had to show her. "You have to cope with my whole mouth," he said, and he opened his jaws and canted his head to one side to show her how it could be done.

"Oh my God," said Iris, not ecstatically, as she looked into his white-and-purple maw. The Bear felt her spine tremble and the effect of it passing into her limbs, but she let his head come down to her.

"Be careful with my tongue," he said, pulling back at the last moment. "It's rough enough to hurt you if you're not careful. You remember the old Turkish story. I told you that one, right?"

She didn't answer, except for arcing her body upward and pulling him down to her and he was on top of her, they were together, he was losing the sense of where he and where she . . . It was happening much more quickly than he had anticipated: she reached between his legs and found his cock emerging ready for her, she was taking it in her hand, she felt it leap in response, and guided it to where her legs were spreading and he could see, could smell, delicious, that she was already thickly wet for him, and before he knew it he was inside her for the first time.

Iris' gasp as he entered was a shuddering intake of breath as if perhaps she had begun to die, and his was one of simpler amazement. Their outbreaths were sighs of release? relief? reception? and then, just as he began to move inside her for the first time, the Bear got the big surprise the night had been holding ready.

What?

He found himself somewhere else entirely, not a trace of as-if about it. Instead of lying in a Shady bed with Iris, he was sitting upright, stage center of a roughly circular cosmological array, in the half-lotus position, which he had never before employed in his life either for sex or meditation, and of which he was no doubt physically incapable. Iris was legspread around his lap, her upper body and breasts pressed against him, her face turned sideways and tongue extended in a ritualized expression of ecstatic reception. He was thrust inside her and they were outside of any time and space he knew about. He noticed, to his increasing surprise, that along with a windmilling multiplicity of arms, he possessed ten or a couple dozen heads stacked and ranked in tiers facing all conceivable directions wearing an implicit infinity of expressions, from lust and rage through compassion and beatitude and every response your average garden-variety deity might turn upon the universes manifesting around him in a ring. As he and Iris made love in this strange configuration—*this isn't my imagery at all*, he told himself, although it sure is easy to see what all those Tibetan tankas are about—their coupling seemed to be engendering the universes—what?—which he saw arrayed around them in ordered spheres.

Is this really happening? Is this what's always happening, only now we're an instance of it? Well it certainly is different, thought the Bear.

Although he experienced this moment with odd objectivity and calm, it would be useless to deny that it also bewildered him extremely. He heard a sharpened intake of breath from Iris, the imagery shook, and when he looked down at her again, it was with one head only and they were making love in Julius and Stanlynn's old house in Shady, New York, and she was more beautiful than he would have believed possible. He was an earthly, idiotically bearshaped being and he loved her with a fire that consumed every possible difference between them.

She had the disconcerting tic, however, of thrusting her face into his armpit, and when he pulled her out of there for the second time, he saw her head go back and her eyes close and he knew that she was going away from him, sailing out from her body much as he had seen her do in sleep. "No no no," he said, "please please please stay here with me." At this her eyes popped open and looked back at him startled from inscrutable distances of swoon. Then they clarified and she was back with him and they more or less devoured each other for the next ten seconds flat. This was well beyond being just in love. Whatever that meant.

All was not joy in the Mudville of this world, however. If the tantric experience, if that's what it was, had demonstrated that their lovemaking was a window opening onto objectively infinite vistas, back here in the Catskill Mountains there still were bodies to negotiate, souls to align, rhythms to coordinate, and, restored to themselves out of the annihilating blur of ecstasy, they experienced a mutual clumsiness that had somehow not obstructed them earlier. It was hard to know how she could accommodate his hips, difficult for him to tell where he should rest his body so as not to crush her, although—and this was some help after all—he hadn't gained back all the weight he'd lost in prison. Why, he probably weighed no more than 350 pounds tops, and that made things safer than they might have been. Beneath him, she was so finely made, so naked, so small.

Following this physically difficult phase, they seemed to lose subtler touch with each other, and where, in the beginning, they had sometimes seemed astonishingly at one, now they tugged and shifted, sought better harbor, firmer purchase, quicker release, or reached ahead for some voluptuous piece of fruit not available on this particular moment's silver tray, but which might lie gleaming on the next, when they might be striving for something else. Huh, what a way to run a world, thought the Bear not for the first time that day, what poor coordination, considering what's already passed between us. Then he thought of a good question: what *has* passed between us exactly?

They made eye contact, lost it momentarily in the near-shame of their momentary disarray. Anxiety and disappointment were on the verge of putting in a definitive appearance when Iris and the Bear rediscovered some portion of their earlier intimacy and began to ride it as far as it would take them home. A certain insecurity travelled with them to vex their journey, but when their climaxes came, about thirty seconds apart—hers first, then his pouring into its aftermath before a sufficient gap could insinuate itself between them—trouble as such was gone from their conjunction, even if it qualified their ending with traces of its having been with them awhile. Still, they broke against each other with cries in whose reaches there might have floated some note of common protest against the limitations of flesh and its perceptions, but the night was annihilated around them anyway and that was it for now.

They wanted to exchange vows of love in the afterpause, but each of them decided separately that it was the wrong moment in which to do so—since, one, it didn't need to be said, and two, were it said now it would be suspect as a possible figment of passionate imagination, the wishful, conceivably corrupt bodying forth of a questionable dream.

"Wait a minute," the Bear said finally, although he did not want to say anything. "That bone I told you about is starting to pull back up into me and I have to get out of you."

"Oh *that's* what it is. I felt this movement and . . ."

"I don't want to leave you, but . . ."

"I understand," Iris said, and the Bear rose out of her before there was any chance of her being injured by the involuntary retraction of his heterotopic baculum.

He was determined that such intimacy as they had achieved should not be interrupted, and he took her back into his arms and looked into her eyes. "Are you all right?" he asked with what upon reflection sounded like perfect stupidity.

"Are you kidding? I'm fantastic," she said.

"You are," he said, meaning several things. "You're . . ." he began, but she placed a finger against the front of his snout and softly went Ssshhh. The Bear subsided like a wave withdrawing from the would-be shores of speech, and watched her in such silence as the night afforded. She had closed her eyes and laid her head on the pillow.

He marvelled again at the beauty of her throat and the lovely thrust of her underjaw—for the moment sufficient emblem of the essential poignant beauty of all manifest existence—watched her eyes moving behind her eyelids and her pulses marking time athwart the channel of her breath. You're a seabird who has fetched up on my shore, he told her silently with a lyricism even he deplored, tired and beating from your long voyage. You're safe, I swear it. When she opened her eyes and looked at him, he understood that she was still awake. No dumbbell he.

"One thing," he said, although she had closed her eyes again. "I didn't wear a condom but you didn't seem worried about catching any kind of disease like the clap or even AIDS from me."

She opened her eyes and blinked once slowly.

"You sly boots you." He grinned as it dawned on him. "That blood sample you took when I got out of jail to look for traces of drugs!"

She said nothing, but did not look away from him either.

"You worked it up in the lab! You checked me out!"

"I did a full blood workup," Iris maintained, "which as a matter of fact included a routine test for AIDS. As a bear you ought to be immune to HIV, even if, with your anomalous genetics, I couldn't be entirely sure: for instance you might have proved a carrier. So yes, I made the test. I enumerated the drugs in your system. I determined that you were dangerously anemic and variously infected. I illegally lifted a number of medications for you and fuzzed the bookkeeping so that I wouldn't be found out. Do you want to lodge a complaint?"

"You sly boots!" the Bear persisted anyway, still laughing. "You had this planned from the beginning!"

"Not so exactly as that," Iris told him, "although certainly I did have it in mind, as a possibility, an option. Don't act so surprised, Bear. I was looking out for your welfare too. And what have *you* been doing these past few weeks? What's been occupying your mind? Have you been comparing metric patterns in Shakespeare and Charlie Parker? Writing a monograph on the timelessness of real identity in Proust? You weren't born yesterday, so stop trying to act as if you were. It doesn't suit you."

It was awkward and unplanned this time too, but he said it anyway: "I feel like I was born just a little while ago tonight, right here in this bed, with you." And it had much the same melting effect his similar remark had had the first time—it occurred to him that Iris could be kind of sappy sometimes; yeah, Bear, and what about you?—and almost before he knew it, they were at it again.

This time Iris took the initiative, and the Bear was amused to watch her place her small hands on his big shoulders and push him onto his back. Okay, he laughed, let himself be pushed and took a fine delight in watching her small pink form climb aboard him and polymorphously explore his relatively more gigantic body: she pushed hands into him, thrust her face into his chestfur where it was softest and pushed against its grain, embraced him now on this side, now on that, grasped with arms, legs, face, mouth, lips, whatever she could use. After a few minutes of this, Iris kissed his throat deeply, as if she could consume it, reared up panting astride his stomach, and looked him in the eye. She looked pretty wild.

"O my America?" he asked her, and laughed.

For some reason this made her laugh too. "My newfound land," she agreed, and stuck her face, still laughing, into his chest.

And fell to exploring him again. The Bear was able, during the course of these explorations, to appreciate, nay, luxuriate in the particular beauties of her form, but what touched him most deeply was the innocent abandon with which she moved on him. The Bear had been lusted over by women before but, it seemed to him, he had never been actively loved. He had not been kissed or caressed with so completely expressed a sexuality before, but there was nothing, even as she took his balls in her mouth—one at a time, of course—and held them there a moment, he would call lascivious in Iris' unguarded hungers, nothing abased by detachment from her entire essential self. There had been women wild for him, but none who had received him so simply.

She relented for a moment and lay on him breathing hard. Poor little lungs, he thought, beating in so delicate a chest. But what had she been in their tanka-moment? She had been nothing less than holiest materia prima, certainly the most beautiful such he'd ever seen. How dare you condescend to her in any regard! In any case, the Bear decided that it must be his turn. He kissed her mouth, he nuzzled the bared delicacy of her throat and shoulders and passed to an appreciation of her breasts, which were not large but were not especially small either: like every part of her they seemed a detailed expression of more deeply organized and beautiful inscriptions and designs. Each detail of her was as finely turned and crafted as the familiar graces of her face, had been the beneficiary of some infallible and affectionate regard. He loved her breasts' pink aureolas and their attentive nipples with their flattened tops, in which his tongue was able to detect further, probably invisible configurations of the script that had written her. Calligraphy? You bet. Iris seemed to delight in the fresh textual discoveries he was making amid her least details. Certainly she was audible on the subject, responding with gasps and *cante jondo* to each fresh subtlety of his reading of her, although once again he had to be careful of the roughness of his tongue for fear of hurting her, a thing he hoped never ever to do. As he kissed and nuzzled and sucked at her nipples, and contemplated her crooning responses with his ears and the intellective entirety of his mouth, his pleasure was not even slightly diminished by the slight striations his eyes detected at the tops of her breasts, traces left behind by her two daughters' passage; neither was he shocked to notice three whorls the size of nickels on the outer curve of her right breast, where a line of cysts must have been surgically excised some time before.

He loved these breasts of hers, these assertive softnesses that seemed the signature of an immeasurate tenderness hidden behind the world but expressing itself here in full. Were they only evolutionary somethings or a pure improvisation on the part of beauty, done for love? Should all animals be adorned with them, or would they present a problem in the wild? The Bear couldn't say for sure, but he knew where his sympathies lay, and lapped, and looned.

After sating himself on these breasts—entirely marvelous things whatever their provenance, he would have wanted the world to understand—the Bear passed lower to nuzzle the twin harps of her ribs, the sweet concavity of her belly flowing downstream from their arch, and then, as he moved lower and opened her legs, he had to tell her again to be careful of the roughness of his tongue and not push against it when he took her. When, nosing his way through a negligible tuft of fur, he tasted her—pink as the incurve of abalone shell, but warmed by her juices that tasted only mildly of the sea—it was the most delicious and accommodating thing imaginable. He used the length of his tongue to taste her entirely, and she cried out above him in what he flattered himself was the full devastation of ultimate shipwreck. She reached down to caress his wide head, pressing his headfur in an appealing syncopation of swirls. The Bear stayed with her through what might have been two or three climaxes, and when she pushed off from the top of his head and pulled away toward the head of the bed, he returned topside to kiss her face, the changed features of which were suffused by a flush he had not seen there or on any face before. Neither had she or anyone else ever kissed him with quite such abandon, sucking her own taste from his tongue so wildly one might have thought it gave her life. Although, as even the Bear had to admit, this interpretation was almost certainly one of the delusions of vanity.

But then Iris was moving down along his body—chest then belly then into the crux of his groin—and when she bent to what his passion ultimately had to say for itself, for all the shocking pink of his presentation the unself-consciousness of her abandon persisted. When her head lowered to his cock, it was as if to sip dew from a leaf at dawn or nectar from a blossom; or she was like Psyche, or whoever the White Rock soda-sprite was on her granite perch, bending to drink from her own reflection in the stream of being. When finally she took his, um, throbbing bearhood in, her mouth felt marvelous, her parted lips caressing him and the slightly beaded roughness of her tongue drawing back and forth along his length conveyed a previously unimagined pleasure to him with great simplicity. Every thing she did was beautiful, everything she did was one more example of the infinite treasure implicit within her finite form. Everything she did, even though he was blown away by the directness of its sexual expression, seemed uncannily, how to put it, pure.

He pulled away when he felt drawn too precipitously near climax, and when, after a short pause, he pulled her small body up to him, turned her with her help onto her back, positioned himself carefully above her and moved to the slightly lesser pleasure but infinitely greater communion of the regular act—her breaking gasp as he entered again, an expression, it seemed to him, of astonished devastation—they were better practiced and coordinated this time, though still a trifle clumsy here and there, and if no separable mystical revelation ensued, the experience of nearly continuous beauty that was their lovemaking was enough. It lasted a long sweet time of which each moment had its particular pleasure. The Bear vacillated, or swung dreamily across an arc, between near-mystical states of self-extinction and greedy pornographic rapture.

He experienced amazement at every detail of her beauty, and if, as the tantric episode had shown him, her physical form, like his own, was a veil concealing greater realities upon which they also, however evanescently, allowed themselves to be projected, for the given moment he was contented with the permissible parameters of the representation. Oh yes, he was thoroughly taken in.

When they were done and the bed hadn't collapsed beneath their last convulsions, the room was quiet again and they lay awhile, rather extravagantly, even ostentatiously draped in the lineaments of gratified desire. After awhile Iris got up and left the room, came back a few moments later with a couple of towels.

"A mess, huh?" said the Bear.

"Quite."

He watched her bend over the bed and wipe it down, then was surprised when, leaning in with a clean towel she had cooled with water, she wiped him dry on his pubic bone, his retracted sex and balls and between his thighs, all very simply and unselfconsciously done. Thoroughly too, he thought. She did a nice job of it, yes.

Iris tossed the towels somewhere onto the floorboards, lay down again, and leaned into him, insinuating one of her legs between his and pressing one of her breasts into one of his, in what seemed a rather practiced gesture.

She knew it, thought the Bear. She wanted it all along. I should have moved on her from the beginning. I've been such a dolt. We didn't need to wait this long.

"Do you know why this happened?" she asked him out of the room's dark blue, at the back of which a lamp still glowed beneath a spill of silk. Was it clairaudience again? The Bear couldn't tell.

"Because we wanted it to," he said, sounding fairly thick but accurate.

"Because you let me have my space," she told him. "Because you didn't try to impose yourself on me and let the right time come around on its own."

"Huh," said the corrected Bear.

"It should take me a week or two in the city to get a leave of absence from the lab and find someone to sublet the apartment."

"Huh?" said the Bear again.

"What's with all these huhs?" Iris asked him, backing off and pushing the heel of her hand against his shoulder. "You mean you don't want me to come up here and live with you?"

"Are you kidding? Of course I do. I'm just a little stunned."

"Stop pretending. It still doesn't suit you."

"You know what an idiot I am. When I say I'm stunned I'm stunned."

"Don't be." And here even she paused semi-awkwardly, the Bear was gratified to observe, and looked away for a moment before looking back. "You were always the one, Bear."

"Huh?"

"Stop *saying* that. It makes you sound so stupid. It makes me feel as if I've made a terrible mistake."

"I'm just a bit slow taking things in, Eye." As he used to call her. "I was always the one? You sure about that?"

"I just didn't know if you'd come around."

"If I'd come around? I was always right there. I was right there waiting."

"That's what you think."

The Bear rubbed a puzzled paw across his eyes, then gave his right eye a thorough rub. "We must be talking about two different things."

"You really don't get it, do you?" Iris reached out to push his paw away and then scratch him familiarly behind his ears. He loved it. "Well, don't worry about it, honey. We wound up where we belong."

"You mean I climbed the glass mountain and did whatever silly shit I was supposed to do to win you?"

"If you have to look at it that way," Iris said a little wearily, "yes."

"If that's what I did, I did it ass-backwards and with my eyes shut, the way I do most things."

"And very endearing it was."

"I sure hope so. Cause, me, I'm happy about this, but when you come right down to it I don't have a clue."

"Men," was all she said, and snorted twin columns of air from her nose.

"I ain't . . ." the Bear began the usual response, but thought better of it. "I know," he told her. "It's as if . . . as if we're two different species, right?"

This raised one of her eyebrows and a hip little smile. "In this case I think possibly yes," Iris said, playing with it but keeping an ironic limit on the smile.

"You mean you noticed?" the Bear said pretty broadly. "I was hoping . . . um . . . uh."

"You were hoping what?"

The Bear scratched at the side of his jaw with partly exposed claws. "I was hoping like maybe you wouldn't notice. I was hoping I could get by."

Iris shook her head. "Sorry," she said. "The fur. A giveaway."

The Bear ran his paw down her side and over the upthrust curve of her hip where it lay under the sheet. "Wow," he said quietly. "All this and comic timing too."

"Good night," Iris told him, kissed him dismissively on the snout and laid her head on the pillow.

They were quiet awhile. The Bear still wanted to talk but he could feel Iris heading in the general direction of sleep. What else had he learned to do lately? Was he a fool for beauty? Of course he was a fool for beauty. Didn't it make him a superficial kind of bear? But she's so beautiful! and beauty's such a shorthand for an incalculable host of other things.

You know, even though her hair's not red anymore still she looks quite Irish. Maybe he should get into Celtic music again, only more seriously. And by the way, he wondered in a sidebar, something that had always bothered him, what did Audrey Hepburn see in Mel Ferrer?

The Bear watched Iris' face relax, its subtle muscles letting go. Iris' body twitched a few times in his arms, first the arms and torso, then the legs, loosening the locks that held her, and then, he guessed, off to sleep.

Iris knew that the Bear thought she was sleeping, and perhaps after all she was, this state she found herself in seemed so strange, flickering in the middle distance between sleep and wake. For awhile she had slipped as gracefully as a seal in and out of the shallows of sleep, cooling herself in its waters, then tasting the freshness of the topside air, newly secure that her simple soul had found harbor on the rocky coast of this world. A sweetness moved with her. What was oddest was that at times her physical form seemed to change. At one point she was unmistakably a pale if not quite luminous sphere, veined and mottled like the, like the, what was the word, like the whatchamacallit of an eye, hovering a foot or two above the bed, and although this too had been pleasant for awhile, the sense of radical dislocation, once her rational mind clocked it, had finally frightened her back into the familiar clash and racket of her insecure and normal body with something like a crash. She slitted her eyes open to see the Bear watching her the way he did, then she shut them again.

Iris had gone down to the Bear's bedroom earlier that night as if to be sacrificed, but also feeling that she was confiding her undefended self to her last true friend in the world. She remembered looking at herself, as if to say goodbye, in an oval mirror set above a small provincial dresser in the upstairs bedroom. Vanity had a last word to say: she fluffed her hair a bit fuller and noted that if she had lost a bit in the face over the years her shoulders were still good, her neck had retained its elegance, and, turning sideways for a last check, the jut of her breasts beneath the sheet was still satisfactory and her nipples poked with sufficient self-assertion against the press of the cloth. Aside from the probable last of her natural modesty, one reason she had wrapped herself in the sheet was that, in order to hold the sheet to her, she would have an excuse to keep her arms in place and prevent any trembling in them from being seen. On the way down the stairs—she had bound her legs too tightly and had to step carefully or risk a fall—she had felt herself confronted with so tremulous a sense of the unknown that her mix of eager and fearful anticipation had been greater, perhaps, than in her first experience of sex way back—that night on which she had allowed herself to feel confused into change on that rough parental sofa from which she could not afterward unwork the awful, undeniable stain about which, in the sequel, her mother, whiskey glass in hand and smiling out one side of her slack mouth, had not cared very much. Iris winced at the dumb and anguished clumsiness of her early adolescence, and the unmerciful world it had left her in once the wraps were off. For most of her adult life, once she had learned the trick of things, Iris had moved pretty smoothly through the sexual world in what now seemed to her a rather superficial way; but at the brink of the Bear's bedroom the sense of taboo about to be broken and of her life being irreversibly changed had been nearly insupportable. She held her winding-sheet closely to her body with the press of her arms and they shook anyway. Going down the stairs she had felt herself descending to other, unprecedented depths.

But she had gone in all the same, hadn't she.

So there. That's what you are really.

And once you got over the fear it was good.

When the Bear had taken her into his arms and then entered her, she had felt a force spreading from her core out to her by now permissibly shaking limbs, and it had been like the return of water to a dry streambed. It had been beyond delightful to feel that newsprung water expanding its influence through her parched impoverished lands, which had so forgotten the touch of deeper life that the response of seed and the promise of blossoms felt almost completely unfamiliar—in any case memory had to work at it. When that final, deepest touch came, it was a stunning something of which she had forgotten the name and therefore no longer knew how to call to. And in the midst of it, there had been something else she couldn't quite place. Time perhaps literally stopping, or looping back on itself? Certainly a fundamental sense of massive reconnection, but to what exactly? What she wanted to believe was that she had heard an audible Click that might have been a sufficient riposte to that other click, the first one, the dismembering one, years back. She was unable to convince herself of it. But there certainly had been an instant in which she almost could have sworn . . . what? She was a millimeter or two short. She had insufficient hands with which to seize it. It was just, it was some intolerable tantalizing increment over the rim of her consciousness. If it was anywhere at all.

What had happened to her really?

She had been taken up by everything in the universe that had always threatened to annihilate her, and it was wearing not only the suspect name but the immense fur coat of love. She had given in and let the pleasure blow her fear away; she had used what was left of her fear as a powerful spice, an additional delectation of this possibly lethal enjoyment. At one point she had rocked her head back, eyes closed, and had seen a spangling millitude of stars, and they had seemed to be her familiars. It had seemed to her that they knew her and knew her name, and that their geometries and lights were obscurely kin to her. When her conventional climax came, larger experiences were blotting her out, and although it was nice enough qua orgasm, in context it had seemed a small event occurring on her peripheries, something between an irrelevance and a sneeze. Well, perhaps not as small as that. But her limbs were shaking without it, and even before it shook her she had felt almost completely gone. She had wished to go completely, to leave any flesh and world she had ever lived in, and for a moment she'd been ready to die if necessary to effect so conclusive a departure, but it turned out not to be possible; although in fact it seemed as if the neural web within her body had been electrified and the major nodal points that stored all her crystallizations of memory and identity and prior self-perception were burning out in dazzles of undoing.

When it was over, she found that she was still herself, however.

In some ways, the Bear had proved a clumsy lover. Perhaps with time he could be trained.

As if that were the point. What had surprised her, leaving aside consideration of his almost insupportable strength, was how sensitive and even gentle he could be.

The second time had been better in most conventional respects, probably the best time she'd had with her clothes on or off in years, but it had also been inexplicably less profound. And how did she feel now? Certainly she had more than just the usual postorgasmic glow on, although by now sufficient time had passed for old demon doubts to rise up and start to tug at her. Could the Bear be trusted? Could anyone? Could she? Could anything as volatile and overmastering as sex be trusted as the basis of any kind of life with anyone? Perhaps part of what nagged at her was the humiliating intuition that her sex was the only, certainly the crucial, coin she had had to offer the Bear. If she let herself, she could feel the beginnings of shame at the thought that her gift should be limited to lying down, opening her legs and being fucked, her body the only card she had to play on the poker table of this world, a wholly brutal place once you took the wraps off and looked at it square. If so, this alleged lovemaking with the Bear was only another hideous transaction, another way of being crushed beneath the wheel and having her soul pressed out of her like juice again. If so, it was only more of the same, only the routine breaking of one more human heart, no big deal in these regions. And if so, what was the point?

She couldn't, she shouldn't, lying here in the stars and blindness of her anchors, give in to this much fear. Didn't she hope for something, didn't she still possess, however deeply it was compromised, some genuine capacity for love? She couldn't be alone in that. There still had to be some correspondence out in the universe somewhere, hadn't there? Some answering call? Otherwise where had her own call come from?

So, of course, she had fucked a talking bear.

She had no doubt that the Bear was in love with her. But he was so romantic about it, and romantic love, she knew, was a stuff that will not endure. The important question was whether or not he knew her from a hole in the wall or the hole between her legs. The question was whether or not he even slightly understood her. The gap between his certain love and his uncertain knowledge was the measure of the risk she was taking with her life. Now that passion had possessed them both, in all its blind imperious power, she could have no clear idea how sturdy or even existent was the rope bridge on which she was walking above that gap? canyon? chasm? pretty little valley one could make a home in? sheer cliffs of fall?

What exactly happens to you after you've fucked a talking bear? You could hardly expect to find a support group, not even in this neck of the woods. Talking Bears and the Women Who Love Them. Right after this commercial break. See? Once your mind and character are destroyed, there'll be a future for you on daytime TV. You might even get a book deal out of it. All eventualities are covered.

She spoke her name to herself: Iris Tremoureux. It was familiar, but what had happened to that faraway person named? What had she been doing to land precisely here, in this bed, listening to a bear's heavy, sated breath as he slept? The urge to run was powerful but led nowhere.

Life had landed her where she had never thought to be. And her vulnerability and special pleading in the face of general circumstance seemed suspect to her anyhow. She had never seriously lacked for food or shelter. No foreign armies, as they did elsewhere in the world on a regular basis, had tramped to her door demanding housing, dinner, daughters, cunt, then her chin pulled back and her throat held naked to the knife. What legitimate right had she, really, to feel so fearful and so desperate? What right to feel that this world was the place in which they caught and killed you if they found out who you really were? She had had it easy. But she was weak and easily deluded, end of story.

And now, she thought, listening to the autonomic repetitions of the Bear's heavy breath, she had engaged, poor fool, with the fundamental monstrousness of the world, and hoped to win something from the encounter. Speaking realistically, where was the hope or possibility in that?

She remembered thrusting her face ecstatically into his fur, its rich scent filling her.

I know an old lady who swallowed a fly, perhaps she'll die.
I know an old lady who swallowed a horse, she's dead of course.
Well, here I am and that's the end of everything I know.

After watching Iris sleep awhile, the Bear eased himself with infinite tact out of bed and headed for the bathroom, but once his feet found the floorboards the call of the wild mingled with the call of nature and he found himself standing on the doorstep of his porch taking in the view like a man of property surveying his eminent domain. All he lacked were pockets into which to thrust proprietary paws.

The wind soughed and woughed in the higher strata of the ranked guardian pines.

The mist had lifted, and behind him, over the mountain, clouds must have parted: past the sentinel bars of the pinetrunks ahead he could see moonlight silvering the meadow on the other side of the road. In the precious-metal shine he could even make out the stand of young birches on the far side of the pasture. A wind was blowing there too: the birches' young leaves were fluttering in an untellable multiplicity of detail, although the essential sum of their language seemed indisputably to be praise. What a night. So quiet, and the vocalist so subtle.

What was happening in him really?

Aside from his entirely satisfactory sense of sexual satisfaction and his preposterous imitation of the landed gentry—certainly he felt better settled in his body, found it, for the first time in ages, a viable, maybe even advantageous object to spend a life in—he was feeling . . . what exactly?

Somewhere in the nave of his ribcage, the transepts of his arms, or the towers of his sight, an unreachable event had taken place, too small or subtle for his grasping, too important for him not to try. But only echoes of it reached him amid the columns, above the altar, beside the font. In this sudden largesse of his inner space it was impossible to trace these echoes to their source. It was an unseizable mustard seed of the beginning of something, but since he could not reach it neither could he be sure if it was there at all.

Better anyway not to soil it with his attempted touch. Right?

The Bear stood at the doorstep of his new house, allowing himself to appreciate the enlargement and deepening of his world by the reappearance of sex in it, or was the right word love.

Is it still possible? Can something out there still respond to one's essential call? Can such fruit ripen through its necessary evolutions and fall to you in its season?

It was a heck of a way to run a world.

For a long time, desire had seemed to exist only in order to be frustrated. Had the rules of engagement really changed?

And for the moment, was it the call of the wild or only the sound of the wind? Or only the urgings of his newfound sense of property.

The Bear thumped down the stairs, stepped across the slithery carpet of pine needles and into the trees. Looking both ways first, he relieved himself against a treetrunk. His urine smelled particularly strong to him, the liquid soaking through the weave of needles into the earth but its steam rising through the open air and the smell of dried sex into his quivering nostrils. That oughta make the local raccoons a little nervous for awhile.

When he was done, he shook his member dry of its last drops, leaned his big head back and looked into the black aproning branches above: a detailed and inscrutable darkness in which the voice of God hummed and hushed.

My trees. Hah.

What had Stanlynn called them?

Blue spruce? Greater hemlocks? Douglas fir?

Well, naming things was pretty much beside the point by now.

part four

Reality being too thorny for my great personality, I found myself nevertheless at my lady's house, as a large blue-grey bird soaring toward the moldings of the ceiling and dragging my wing in evening's shadow.

I became, at the foot of the baldachin supporting her adored jewels and her physical masterpieces, a big bear with violet gums and fur grey with grief, my eyes on the cut glass and silver of the consoles.

All became shadow and glowing aquarium.

—Rimbaud

1

the Bear batted his nose against the bluebells—well there were tiny blue things, delicate white things, some tiny-tongued flower a bit more lyrical in modulating shades of purple, and elsewhere, in greater shadow, magically distributed throughout a chest-high hedge of dusty darkgreen leaves, there were little orange mini-cornucopias hanging from stems attached to their middles, and the Bear ate a few—some kind of wildflowers anyway—and cantered uphill through the meadow. Just before he hit the edge of the forest he bit off a mouthful of young green grass, chewed it thoroughly, and allowed himself to drool its juices out the sides of his mouth like a wild thing before swinging his heavy head upslope and into the shade of the trees. Wugh. It was a delicious experience and he allowed his brain to blur and thicken with it.

After he crashed through twenty feet or so of underbrush, setting loose a racket of birdlife in the treetops, wings clapping off to the hope of peace elsewhere, he allowed himself the luxury of a good long scratch, his back against a rough old wonderful tree and came away from it with bits of bark in his fur and a rich brown fog of wooddust rising around him in the mixed beams of light and shade.

Oh yeah, this was the life all right all right.

Studiously, he licked the fur smooth on his forearms, just for the pleasure of doing something atavistic, and to finish off the gesture smelled the leathery palms of his paws for a long minute as if he might find something really interesting and informative in their mix of tangs and scents. Fuck, he thought, I'm enjoying this. Which just goes to show you, mutation ain't everything. Not by a long shot, no. Roots are cool too.

He stuck his nose into the wind and sniffed deeply. His nostrils quivered volumes of fresh air and sweet decay to his lungs: moss and moldering earth, a continuous undercurrent of insect life, the green difference between the smell of treeleaves and the lolling ferns that found sufficient reason for being in the medallion light that dappled down to the ground through the cover of the oaks and maples. He smelled raccoon and, his mouth suddenly watering, a doe that had come that way and lingered awhile, chewing ferns and pissing there the day before. Oh man, could I? Should I? The Bear doubted he could eat raw meat again, much less tear mouthfuls of it bleeding from a carcass he'd just pulled down . . . but if he did take one he could heft it back home and into the kitchen, cut it up so it'd look civilized, more or less. He doubted Iris would consent to cook it, even if he did the butchering himself, but she wouldn't be back for a week and in the meantime he could feast on venison. *Venison.*

Saliva burgeoned but a shadow crossed his mind: one of the forms in which he had loved Iris—caressing her nakedness and finding implicit in her a host of the world's other beauties, running his paws down her flanks and feeling her muscles tremble beneath his touch—was as a doe, her back mottled by sunlight in woods not unlike those in which he now stood. Probably not a good idea to start killing deer, then. He thought of the blood pulsing thick through arteries in their long lightly furred throats, then suppressed the image in the interest of peace between the species, in which he had acquired a sudden, urgent interest.

He turned to the roughbarked tree which had scratched his back's mortal itch so nicely, bared his claws and experimentally stripped off a piece of bark about the size of a license plate, and there it was on the paler wood beneath: look at all that buglife, see it run: one big black ant, pale white crawly things scurrying for cover, trying to burrow under the nearest edge of bark. Grubs. Now there was something he was not gonna eat anymore. He hadn't entirely wasted his time out there in the human world. *On s'apprend le bon goût* after all. Although Lauren Hutton had made a show of eating termites in Africa, there were limits.

The Bear took off uphill again, enjoying the way his body worked as he loped, the energy of his forepaws' dangle, and when they landed their grasp of earth transmitted smoothly down his spine to where his hindlegs picked up the wave and pushed off full of power. Just for the hell of it he did a short burst of speed and felt like the king of the world, pretty much. I mean, who could compete? Name me someone. Go ahead. Try.

Of course the Bear realized that if he didn't have a woman in tow he wouldn't need a house at all. He wouldn't have to sweat Stanlynn's fifteen hundred a month for one thing not to mention the utility bills on top. And the other morning before she left for the city, Iris had said something about how if they were really going to live there they'd have to buy a car and he said How about if you pay for it and she said Perhaps we ought to share. See, without all that he could den up here in the woods with his saxophone and a handful of books, and his record company advance would last him more or less forever. Now that would be the life.

Wouldn't it?

The Bear paused for a moment in some leafmeal shade and considered Iris under the aspect of "a woman in tow." Touching phrase there. What an advanced brain you have, grandma. All the better to take you for granted with, my dear.

Sounds like a monster movie.

It *is* a monster movie.

If you ever hurt that woman you will never forgive yourself and you know it. Your spirit will haunt you with ghosts of rightful accusation until the dying fall of the last note of the final cadence of the unknown composition that is you really—I wonder what chord you'll resolve on, under what sky—and it won't end there either. Don't harm a hair, don't impede a single one of her breaths or so much as bruise the body of her leastmost, slender wish. Don't, or you will pay for it untellably and forever.

I know it. I may be stupid but I'm not dumb. She is more treasure than you will ever encounter elsewhere and for the moment the world has given her into your care. Try to be equal just for once to so sacred a degree of trust.

The Bear shook his head. It amazed him how, whichsoever way you turned, life kept catching you in its paw. Live solo, den up with Jones, stay clear of showbiz or tangle with it and expose yourself onstage; or finally, take a real live piece of the world's breathing beauty in your arms, and love it so wholly you plunge your dick, your tongue and the breaking flood of your pilgrim soul into it . . . and there you jolly well are, *ahn't* you, signed onto the farce of identity for another full tour of duty and the unknowable pouring in on you from all sides. It never stops, does it?

In any case, it was a long time since he'd had a good long romp in the woods. Come to that, it had been a long time since he'd had a decent run on all fours. It'd be foolish to spoil the simple pleasures of the day by too much thinking on it.

And there it was—omnipresent self-contradiction—the Bear was swept by a wave of love or longing for Iris for the sake of whom he would have traded the rest of life in a twinkling and counted himself lucky in the bargain.

That's the kind of critter you are. Learn to live with it.

The Bear took another good whiff of wind and took off again up the mountain.

He topped it, saw another hill he might like to investigate, peered down into the three available valleys branching below, treetops everywhere and the smell of fresh water at the bottom, and only then did he notice that the specific lay of the land looked unfamiliar. He wondered for a moment if he knew where he was. In the middle of his day's journey, the woods were hardly dark, though evening eventually would come.

Wuf. He was a bear, remember? Did the onset of evening, did the ultimate indigo pitch of this world's darkest night, matter to him a tittle or a jot? How could it possibly?

Going easy but obeying a sense of insecurity he knew he should pay no mind to, the Bear ambled downhill in the direction of the nearest sure thing—a brook beside a road must run somewhere, and he'd follow it downslope to Route 212 and home—and when he got to the bottom of the valley found it wasn't a sure thing at all, just a dry unimproved gully between hills, and no road in it either. Where had the water-smell come from then? Someone's garden sprinkler? From his next ascended eminence he decided that all these mountains looked pretty much alike, and since he couldn't see the fire tower on the top of Overlook from where he was, in effect they *were* alike. Put it simply, he was lost.

But think. He had world enough and time. It didn't matter that much where he was, not for a day or two at least.

Though as he reminded himself when he was better adjusted to the idea, in late afternoon, the sunlight going golden and declining, that he would be spending the night out, you did have to be careful.

There was no bear season in these parts, thank God and the game commission—though who knew what an individual sportsman with a hard-on and a .30-06 might do on the spur of the moment?—but you had to keep clean out of the forest in deer season at least. Anything brown and moving, even a rambling jazz musician, was fair game then. And even at the best of times there could be problems. His rump twanged in memory.

Once, when he was a young bear, just fullgrown, he'd been on a ramble round these woods and had felt a sudden sting in his rear, heard the sound, clocked the scent of man, looked back at himself and seen the dart quivering on his ham, a fan of bright synthetic feathers in its end. He was out cold in two minutes and woke up with a big orange radio collar clamped around his neck and the mother and father of all hangovers driving garbage trucks through his brain and body end on end in a long procession. As for the collar, he couldn't get the thing off even after his head and limbs had cleared of trank. It was bolted together, welded on or something. He took off just in case they were coming back for him with a truck or a copter—there weren't supposed to be any Kodiak-looking brown bears in these woods no matter how relatively small in scale he was for the breed, only American blacks, whatever their color phase. They might decide to put his ass in a sling and, in what later became the time-honored phrase between him and Jones, fly his ass to Manitoba. Where he would be in deep shit, a city bear in rough terrain and no pocket change for a phonecall home. It was also possible the ranger or researcher who had put the collar on him had noticed his anomalous forepaw structure and would want to pull him in for a closer look in electrode city.

So he'd been lucky to wake up before anyone got back. He'd backtracked to where Jones was waiting for him up a dirt road in the Bearmobile smoking a Lucky and reading Raymond Chandler. After Jones finished laughing at how the Bear looked in a radio collar—and it took him an awfully long time to get over it—with the help of a few basic tools from the trunk they got the goddamn misbegotten hellborn contraption off his neck. The Bear had wanted to leave the thing there, but Jones got one of his best ideas ever, and the sequel to the Bear's radio-banding was his little masterpiece.

Instead of leaving the collar in the woods, wouldn't it be a kick, said Jones, if whoever was monitoring it—from a satellite they hoped but a ground-level tracking station would do—found it heading south to the city on the Thruway at a steady sixty miles an hour, stopping once for gas and a couple of times at the tollbooths to pay up? It tolls for thee, motherfucker, they laughed at the presumptive researcher—this bear must have learned to drive! Jones and the Bear motored south, Jones cackling as he punched the push-button tranny, and the Bear got under his blanket when they hit the booths.

When they reached town the Bear wanted to drop the collar in a dumpster, but here Jones exceeded himself, exceeded both of them in his probably finest hour: once the Bear was upstairs in the apartment slugging a beer down and laying the plates out for dinner, Jones flagged down a passing taxi on First Avenue and rode it uptown to Thirty-fourth Street. Veiled by the city's usual loud diversions and a cloud of his own cigarette smoke, he managed to pull up the backseat cushion and stuff the radio collar inside, got it right down there in the springs and jammed the cushion back into place without the driver noticing the move.

Imagine it! They laughed themselves silly in the apartment that night, Monk and Mingus records on in the background, later a little Ornette Coleman. Some nimrod in a radio satellite tracking station is watching a bear cruise midtown Manhattan—down Second and up Third had been Jones' own preferred route in his hacking days, pick 'em up at the movies, take 'em to a restaurant, then tool 'em home to fuck each other silly while he, Jones, wheeled around solo till like four in the morning—this certifiable bear! cruising into the wee small hours and holing up to sleep in a Brooklyn garage—Jones had noted the cab company's address on the door—till about sundown the next day.

What the everloving fuck were they gonna make of *that*?

Howls and cackles. Dreams of youth. Those were the days my friend.

Trout.

It was nearing sunset when he saw them, about a foot and a half deep in a creeklet that fed somewhere downstream into Beaver Creek or the Esopus and hence a sure way home, two young troutlets holding still in running water, biding their time in the lee of a big round stone, their noses pointed into the current. To tell the truth the Bear was getting kind of hungry, but he paused a moment just to watch them. They wavered, coasting, under the eddy of the submerged dinosaur-egg of rock that was going green with algae despite the relative swiftness of the flow and—the Bear tested it downstream of the trout so as not to freak them—the bonechill cold of the water, which argued an underground source not far upstream. Incredibly cold. Look at the fishes. That was what you did if you were a fish, found a spot out of the eternal strugglesome tide pouring down from the peaks or fresh out the granite belly of the earth, and when no more urgent business was pressing you pointed your nose into what remained of its power, flexing your tail left and right in a measured wave to stay in place, keeping yourself upright with countless skilled adjustments of your sidefins, pulsing the water in and out your gills and probably drifting into an alpha state, meditating the Tao according to your capacity and the nature of the particular river you woke up and found yourself in that day.

These two fish were about nine inches each, in any case less than a foot long, not mature, and despite the Bear's insistent hunger, sharpening for the moment into an urgent intestinal pang, it seemed a shame and a trifle unsporting to . . . he tried it anyway.

So that when the Bear plunged his right forepaw in, claws cruelly exposed, that qualm of conscience was probably why he missed, too much contemplation and the compassion for all beings that necessarily followed from it, that and a basic sense of fairness: after all they were hardly grown—and the fish spun away in a quick improvisation of panic, breaking water over a shelf of tilted slate, splashed upstream through some rocks they hadn't expected to encounter, caught up with each other in a deeper pool whose wide round surface was troubled only lightly by a few calm ripples of overthought, where they turned in tight circles to talk about their near-death experience awhile and then began to settle in. Their pool was a fool's paradise but the Bear did not pursue them thither. Thither? Fuck it, he thought. I can spend one night in the woods sleeping bent over the belly of my appetite and not die of it. Hunger was an edge, in other circumstances, he had known how to live with, even profit from.

Then he saw it, farther into the stream than the spot in which the trout had spent their afternoon, a big grey boulder breasting the current and three feet beyond it another of its kind bulging up between white lips of foam that kissed and sucked its body. Between these two stones the water quickened as its passage narrowed, then poured triangulating through the gap, foaming into itself as it met the wave of its own reception, rushing into its own lap, and the Bear settled himself—sharp intake of breath as the full cold hit him—into the spot, hefting his arms over the backs of the two big rocks as if they made a natural armchair, and let the waterflow strike his neck from behind and spill over the breakers of his shoulders. Cold. Holy fuck it was cold. Yes, this stuff definitely came at you from somewhere down under.

He could imagine—or the latent iciness of the flow gradually communicated the image bit by bit to his bonemarrow—he could imagine the water braiding itself onward through primordial rock mile after mile of subterranean dark, brilliantly cold, thrusting for release, full of the hunger for destiny or at least fuller self-expression in daylight.

Water, I'm with you, thought the Bear.

Water, although I'm no longer capable of such singleminded earnestness, I can dig it.

This is the life, he thought. Everything strictly on the natch. Screw the recording studios. Discard the saxophone—well maybe—and later for every assimilationist impulse I ever gave way to. Life, pure and simple. Water, flow.

Damn, but you are cold. What drives you? What powers your engines and replenishments? How do you manage to just keep coming on? How come you are so inexhaustible? Me, I need a rest.

It dazed his brain after awhile, the incredible earth-borne cold of it. It dizzied him and he let it. It was inevitable, he supposed, in this near-mineral submission to the force of purely natural things, that he began to think of Iris—when would she be back?—and doubly inevitable, once he got that far, that he remember their lovemaking, every image he could summon up of the long enduring sweetness of it, each occurrent along the flesh-and-bone continuance of her beauty, the startling glimpses of her cool soul behind the trembling veil of the moment's heat; and although, lying there with the water pouring over him in his granite armchair and his body submerged, he did not get a full erection, after awhile a clear thick gum of pre-ejaculate fluid began to purge itself from him into the water, of which it seemed some essential superconcentration or quintessence, anyhow certainly kin. Good Lord, he thought, he'd never felt anything like this remotely. There must be something abased in it, he felt so voluptuous and strange. He felt himself in some essential sexual congress with not just the stream but the trees leaning perilously over it as the concave earthbank eroded around their roots, and with the forest beyond, and not just the forest beyond but with the blue sky above him and the light cumulus of thought that had begun to gather in the open mind of its expanse.

He was getting really amazingly dizzy in this onflowing unbelievable coldness, and left the water when his head was so dazed by its frigidity he started slipping into dreams in which Iris merged with every possible natural form and shimmered upward into the sun or the other celestial lights . . . actually what got him moving was the stoned, improbable thought that he could drop his head and drown here, not notice it and wake up in another world, his lifework unfinished, his essential impulse unsatisfied. It was not a day for interrupted flow. Once he hauled himself out of the hypnotic weave, the threaded threnum of the water, and shook himself dry on the bank, he had to sit on a big stone streamside for at least ten minutes until his brain began to unwobble, and then there was nothing he could do but lie down on his back in the smaller stones and fall asleep unprotected from all the world, beside the purling stream.

He woke an indeterminable time later feeling . . . what? Not refreshed or renewed, nor any word that came to mind, but something, if too subtle for grasping, akin to every word that came to mind. Jeez, he was still stoned, and on nothing stronger than pure cold water.

He walked upstream minutes later along the pigeon-egg stones of the embankment, then cut inland and uphill into the forest. He was still hungry but it didn't matter.

Night began to fall, if fall is what night did. He found a grove of trees he liked and felt the air going cool after the sun's descent. His sense of smell sharpened.

All he would have to do tomorrow morning was follow the stream down to its last embrace in larger water or look for a well-tended dirt road—a gasoline trace did in fact float upon the air—that would lead him to macadam and inevitably home. But, he thought, why trouble yourself about the morrow? Why not, you rather *embourgeoisé* furball, spend the night out here and enjoy the experience to the full? Tomorrow will see to itself and bury its own dead without you.

As it darkened, the sky turning itself a number of impermissible shades of magenta then purple then blue silk, the Bear loved the way the trees columned around him. He had never managed so constant an upward aspiration as they. He had therefore wandered among the lesser lights, looking here and there for any trace of radiance.

He placed his back against a stout member of this thickbarked community, and decided, as the air precipitously cooled, that this was better than denning up in some cave, not to mention a lot more macho.

Sweet calm feeling as he quieted and night came on in full. He remembered an image from some Sufi poet or other, probably Rumi, since Rumi was the only Sufi poet he had read very thoroughly, and thought that, for all the attractions of the dimming scenery—thank you, it's lovely—to turn your attention on phenomena and their dance is to fix not even on the waves of the ocean but on mere bubble and froth, while beneath them moves depth upon depth through which life sifts itself up and down through varying levels of light and a continuing infinity of configurations, unseizable by either imagination or mind—even desire has better purchase than those. What he wanted was to unconfine the revelation from its specifics. The only way he knew was through immersion in beauty, as sheer as he could stand it. But his mind led him ineluctably back to form, just now to the one form he most loved and had selected, unfairly and according to his hungers, from all others, Iris.

Was such love true expression or only more captivity?

Still, he thought, feeling the rough tree against his back while watching the sky go dark, it's silly to narrow one's eye and finick out distinctions. To squiny up and say this but not that, that but not this. That isn't how the music goes.

As thoughts blurred into image, and wakefulness into the first waves of sleep, he saw a crowd of people lined up shoulder to shoulder in a room, eyes squeezed shut, hats pulled down over their ears.

So silly. What a dumbass way of going about things.

The night had turned surprisingly chilly, but of course he was wearing fur.

His head dipped. He slept.

And woke once, quietly, barely a tremor between the states of sleep and wake, and decided to move his act to another tree at the edge of the clearing over there and walked to it. Looking up when he got there he saw the stars again, long time no sea, glittering in depths of indigo sky.

Decades walking the house of this body, this world, they're enormous.

In the dark I find my hat, high and filled with stars.

I walk into my name as if into open sea.

Well, sorta. Not yet.

He woke and slept several times to see, in stages, his patch of heaven's central piece of drama: the horned moon pulling three bright planets east to west across the sky on a length of string.

With hardly a ripple to mark his descent he slept again.

The next few times he woke he thought—simple, clear, unmuddied by the music of desire—thought of Iris and said, to whoever might be asking or listening, yes.

In the waiting room at Megaton Records, up on the twenty-fourth floor, Jones had a classic view of midtown Manhattan outside the tinted glass window-wall, the office buildings sharply defined in clear sunlight against a blank blue sky. Since Megaton was offset west of center, Manhattan's ranked commercial massiveness was placed at a satisfactory distance and in coherent perspective, so that Jones was able with relative ease to rehearse his old adolescent image of the lined-up slabs, worked through by offices as blue cheese is by mold, collapsing under the weight of their own unreality, toppling into each other like the domino theory, and the whole construct going down in a wonderful upflung cloud of dust—Moloch returning to primal matter in good grace. Jones was not, nor had he ever been, a monster: no one died in this catastrophe; in fact there was a general feeling of release. There were celebrations in the street.

Then Jones remembered that this old image of his had been appropriated recently by a TV ad for an investment company housed in the one computer-generated building that didn't fall; in fact, after a slight wobble on impact, it held the others up.

Well, 'twas better thus. Jones meant no harm. Never had. Not enough to count anyway. And since now he was seeking entry to that world and its stacks of commerce, maybe he should give the imagery a rest.

Stylish, untroubled-looking people walked past him, tall women with square shoulders, high breasts, slim waists, power hair and eyes bright with certainty. The men—everyone seemed so young and tall—had haircuts and wore expensive clothes casually or cheap clean clothes that looked expensive on them. Clothes never seemed to hang very well upon the rack of Jones. In fact, uncomfortable on the sofa, looking up at a lot of hip linen and broadcloth going past, Jones was the only man in view constricted by a jacket and a tie, recent things Sybil had bought him on spec from Paul Stuart—a flash of her plastic and they were his. The guys and gals strolling by had brisk walks, breezy talk, and looked as if they worked out or at least jogged a lot.

In truth Jones preferred the artistic life. It was almost a shame the Bear wasn't dancing in the street for a living anymore.

Feeling more than fashionably thin, Jones sank into the cushions of the sofa, but they were hard and didn't give much. If he had been there on the Bear's behalf he could have handled all these antiquated perceptions of inferiority and alienation smoothly enough, but he was looking for a job for himself this time, and it made him feel weak and guilty and out of place. Just like in the good old days. Maybe big bands would come back too.

The receptionist across from him at her desk, streaked blond hair bound sensibly back into a bun but still luxuriant in tone and volume, looked momentarily up at him from her work. Jones nodded and smiled to indicate that he was doing fine, thanks, and didn't mind waiting a little. When she lowered her eyes again to the things on her desk, Jones saw that she had looked up absently, and only accidentally at him—the point was, she hadn't focussed. He hadn't required focussing upon.

Whenever, as a kid in his twenties, Jones had trudged out for straight jobs—following up those endless ads in the paper, feeling like a dutiful, purblind mule harnessed about the grindstone—he'd almost never gotten as far as the final interview. Usually, once he'd impressed the company with the results of his IQ test, his phony résumé and a little intelligent patter, he'd find himself seized by fierce countercultural emotions—whole armed divisions of feeling massing up in him to rage against business as usual consuming the earth to make billions of shiny objects no one needed, et cetera—and he tended to split the scene before meeting the man or crossing the water. He fetched up, most times, at the Ninth Circle on Tenth Street, over a hamburger with a slice of Bermuda onion on Russian pumpernickel, a mug of dark beer and a basket of peanuts he'd helped himself to from the barrel at the end of the bar, his feet shuffling amid peanut shells to the Horace Silver record on the jukebox: "Filthy McNasty," or sometimes "Señor Blues."

It is human nature to be tormented into a shape which you are then predisposed to glorify, or at least defend. There is almost no way out of it.

In any case, the Ninth Circle had turned into a gay bar before vanishing completely, and corporations didn't give you IQ tests anymore. Everyone had been to college and was smart, the counterculture had become the overculture, sort of, and selling out was buying in. Even he had something of a rep these days, had been semi-responsible for contracts and a couple of records with the Bear. He was a putative someone for all anyone could tell, and not the partly manifested phantasm he still felt himself to be. If it weren't for

Sybil he wouldn't be there, pinned to the sofa and beginning to perspire despite the aggressiveness of the air-conditioning. But Sybil had insisted and he had said okay. She'd made him promise, at the end of a four-course, homemade dinner, that he would go the distance, and then he'd made a joke about the new dessert topping they ought to use on the pecan pie—Pussy Whip, regular or fish-flavored—she was serving him for dessert. He and Sybil had had a good long laugh about it together and then she'd taken him to bed and blown his brains out.

A party of three went past in loose white shirts and smiles, a chic Japanese girl between two broadshouldered American guys, and why were all of them, including the Oriental girl, so fucking *tall*? Jones himself was of average height. Wasn't he? He thought, at five nine, he was still about average for New York, but maybe things had changed while he wasn't looking.

Were these the people, he wondered, who paid two grand a month for a studio apartment or half a million down on a 1BR? then a couple grand a month for the so-called Maintenance Charge—he'd seen Sybil's bill, and despite her explanations it didn't seem a whole lot different from rent. After that, thirty or fifty grand for the right kind of car. Was it therefore possible, considering the degree of tax and other bites, that they were rubes like him even if they got to feel terrific about themselves until Megaton downsized and they found themselves without a rhythm track?

All Jones needed was a shirt, a roof, some Charlie Parker records, a team of horses, a charabanc and a moat around the castle. I mean, fuck all this superfluous American shit.

The horrible thing was, you know? once he got in harness he'd probably make a pretty good corporate shill.

The receptionist called his name. When he looked across she was recradling the telephone on its cantilevered axis. "He's sorry to keep you waiting, but someone will be out to collect you in a few minutes," she said.

Jones put together something made of grin and hands that he hoped would pass for gracious response.

Jones felt that he was being reduced to his leastmost self, to pained, late-adolescent resources that were in fact a set of behavioral recordings he had not sufficiently updated in the decades during which he had lived joined at the hip to a talking bear. These people were as knowing as they looked and he was the one scrambling around on all fours.

Sybil lived in the business world but was more rounded, womanly, warm. What she looked like, in fact, was someone who had borne and raised a child or two, but in fact Sybil had miscarried in her only pregnancy with her former husband. She was still hoping to fulfill her more-than-merely-biological-destiny-thank-you, while her clock still ticked, and it seemed like maybe she'd chosen Jones to be It. Well, it was a long time since anyone had done Jones the favor of thinking of him as It, and Sybil looked so good in the lineaments of gratified desire. On that level, she and Jones got along fine. If he had any self-esteem, her attentions would have done a lot for it.

Though really, he didn't have to think about it much, just sit across the dinner table from her—candles, flowers, wine—to know that she could have the kid with him and if he didn't pan out ditch him and raise Junior on her own. The world had never left him in any doubt about how easily he could be dispensed with. Why did he continue to expect mercy from women when all he'd ever gotten from them was the Law?

Sybil was well enough set up not to have to work outside the house for years if she had a kid and dumped him; and he had to agree, she would probably raise any son or daughter close to ideally well. And the prospect of parenthood had always overwhelmed Jones' sense of responsibility anyway.

The big question was not whether she had Plans A and B on hand, but whether ditching Jones with the afterbirth was A or B. Was keeping him around her preferred option or not? Could she possibly be as cold-blooded as that?

Anyhow, there he was on a corporate sofa, straightening his hip Italian tie. He was individuating, or was trying to.

That self you saw outside of time and space, contented in the garden: did it have anything to do with this?

The distance between here and there made his head spin.

How come I'm still excluded from everything I want to be a part of? Something is happening but you don't know what it is, do—

"Mr. Jones?" a voice asked aloft.

"You came in one bar early," Jones said. He rucked his brand-new crosshatched wheatstraw cotton-linen slacks into some semblance of worldly order as he stood, but the tall young guy with the fashionable flop of hair, square jaw and unshaven look was crowding him still. White shirt, black pants that ballooned at the thigh but tucked back in at the ankle. Jones smoothed his slick new jacket, shot his cuffs, thumbed the knot of his tie: take that. Bears talk to me, not you.

"Mr. Badiyi will see you now."

"Lead on," answered Jones, but called him Osric in his mind. Pathetic.

The guy about-faced and Jones followed him down a corridor, then past a warren of desks fenced off by a flapdoodle of white partitions; there were actual offices for the bigger fish, and a leathery, spartan conference room or two, but when, at the end of a last turning, he was ushered into the expanse of

Badiyi Central, he clocked the simple forthrightness of the power display at once: the narrow door of the private elevator in the rear left corner, the deeper tinting of the window-wall commanding an above-average stretch of urban vista, the unusual species of potted palmetto, the solid teak desk with ebony inlay echoing its contours and, Jones took note, the purposeful absence of a Persian carpet on the expanse of floor Jones had to cross in order to reach the elegant man, about sixty and only slightly reminiscent of the late Shah.

Badiyi rose to meet him, arm extended in an ambiguous gesture Jones had to interpret on the spot as an invitation to a handshake or not. Jones leaned awkwardly across the depth of desk to shake the manicured extremity. His hand was accepted but Jones was still left wondering if he'd made the wrong move.

Jones watched Badiyi's hand withdraw: gold signet ring with an inset diamond, but no watch.

"Please sit."

"Thank you."

"So."

"So-so."

The funny thing was, Jones found himself sort of liking this stylish-looking music-biz potentate, the handsomely modelled face with its savvy eyes and ledge of nose, the assertive hairline from which grey and black swept toward the rear of the head in waves; the suit of light grey fabric that lay upon the man's body like a sort of liquid metal: mercury: communication: of course. Jones liked the expert smile and assessing eyes, and asked himself what he was responding to. A modulation of the power vibe? The parody of a father? The cartoon aspect of the scene?

Badiyi Aga was loaded, sure, but he was a paid employee after all, albeit with a chunk of stock. Badiyi had certainly earned his credentials in the biz over the decades, though he'd never acquired the degree of corporate control the Erteguns had over at Warner—mere Turks: must miff him. Still, the man was a big fish, a real monster of the deep. Jones wasn't sure why Badiyi had wanted to see him.

"Are you a smoking man?" he asked Jones, extending the box, raising the inlaid lid with an index finger. A retro gesture, thought Jones, very 1930s.

"I am."

Jones looked at the cigarette he had taken, thicker than normal, the paper nearly diaphanous and the tobacco curled inside it very blonde. They both lit up, Badiyi extending the lighter; it was a good cigarette, but if you wanted to get technical about it, Jones liked a bit more, um, Turkish tobacco in the mix.

Jones noticed a trim black negative-ionizer ticking discreetly away on the left-hand extremity of the desk. Lots of neat things. A Testostarossa caged up next to the S Mercedes back in Sneden's Landing or wherever?

"Well," said Badiyi, and in order to fill his indicated slot Jones began to speak. This speech, which he was certainly making too soon although it was easy and fluent on his tongue, came increasingly to sound like some kind of incantation, or perhaps he was trying to weave a spell. He began by confessing that he had a couple of good ideas, for example Abdullah Ibrahim, Dollar Brand as was, hadn't put out a record in about six years, wasn't signed with anyone just then and they should get him into the studio with a large ensemble if they could afford it and a small group, anything from four to seven pieces, including Carlos Ward, if they could not. And how about a Carlos Ward record with Geri Allen, Charlie Haden and Elvin Jones? A ballad album by Archie Shepp, if possible with Haden and cameos by Lester Bowie and Tony Bennett. Jackie McLean didn't have a long-term contract with anyone at present, so why not reunite him with Jack DeJohnette and some young fast company? Also, he would personally undertake to talk turkey with Ornette Coleman and try to urge him into the studio with an acoustic group. And oh yeah, did I mention Steve Kuhn has gotten stuck making gorgeous records for minor labels no one hears? Let's call him in from the cold. And there are a lot of younger kids in the post-Marsalis mold that the other majors hadn't picked up on yet, and Jones was out there on the scene spotting them early, and here Jones started to make up names: Ivan Taylor, Anthony Tierney, Jackie Heywood, Wahid McDee, Royal Wheeler, Aaron Chisholme—

"Young musicians are sexier than established ones," Badiyi pronounced, exhaling smoke. "I'm speaking of marketability of course."

Well, sure. By the way, had Badiyi ever heard Florent Schmitt's string quartet, a major twentieth-century composition and still unrecorded, except once uncommercially on a ten-inch disc by the Florent Schmitt Society—you have a classical division, right? and there's also Thomas DeHartmann's classical *oeuvre*—you know, the guy who worked with Gurdjieff?—likewise unrecorded and quite substantial I assure you. But to revert to jazz.

"Please."

Well, there's no end to what's going on, is there? I mean, it ain't like going out in the old days and wondering should I go hear Ornette or Mingus or Sonny or Trane but there are certainly a lot of people around who can play, and it's not all just a holding pattern, keeping the standards up until another genius comes on the line. For example this Hatwell kid, did you hear him on the Bear's record?

"I've listened to it," Badiyi said, and gave out a measured smile.

Well, Jones said, he had heard some of Hatwell's buddies in Brooklyn and thought they were pretty incredible really. They were probably going to tour with the Bear this summer, and Hatwell knew plenty of other young cats who hadn't even come to New York yet, and you could scoop the other majors with these kids and get level on the jazz scene generally. Because if you don't mind my saying so, at the moment you're a bit behind the curve. I mean, I grew up on Art Blakey and the Jazz Messengers and that still seems to be the working model whatever the Miles-and-Coltrane harmonic extensions, but the music is gathering its strength, and even though no one knows when or if it'll get its muscles working for a leap into the next dimension, the time is still propitious for a . . . Jones grew uncomfortably aware that he was beginning to sound impermissibly like an aging hippy in the steely light of a different kind of day.

"All very sound thinking no doubt, but the main point," Badiyi came in on Jones' uneasy pause, examining his cigarette's end . . . But here his speech died on the air.

At length Jones inserted a "Yes?" and this seemed to work.

"The main thing," repeated Badiyi, managing a smile, but fell again to contemplating the castle of ash on the tip of his cigarette.

Jones felt some of his sense of comedy restored. He wanted to slap Badiyi on the back and have a laugh with him about the ornateness of his act. No, seriously, Jones would say, I like you, I get it, give it up, let's relax. Jones had a happy flash of insight: anyone this theatrical couldn't be all that tough. I have to admit it. I keep learning from the Bear on the subject of travesty. This is just one more number from the world's well-worn jokebook. This is more airy nothing on a platter.

Right?

Jones looked out the window-wall at the offering of midtown. If something is going to collapse under the weight of its unreality, it's more likely me than New York. But we can coexist awhile, can't we? It could work out. Imperatives are in play. Demands have been made upon my essential substance. I have to get this job. Afterward, in compensation, the likely meed of sex with Sybil, and then, who can tell and let's not overdo it, a life.

"Usually," Badiyi was telling him, "someone new to the company, like yourself, would not be interviewed by me. In your case I made an exception."

"Thank you," said Jones, and felt his body warming pleasantly. Well, why not?

"I do not ordinarily involve myself in the jazz operation these days. It's not a moneyspinner, nor is it what I was hired for, and my tastes in that area are those of an older generation. The ideas you propose all seem intelligent but I am not the person to discuss them with . . ."

Some modulation in Badiyi's tone, a gathering seriousness, perked Jones' ears up. Is he about to say something real? I think he is. Will I like it? Pigs might fly. Bears might talk, even play alto—as well as anyone since Charlie Parker, don't ever tell him I said that.

". . . and while I'm not sure how much room the young men responsible for our jazz output will make for you, I suggest you get to know them and give it a college try."

Well that sounded good, but Jones began to make out—although it was impossible, at the moment, completely to distinguish anxiety from intuition—the familiar outline of a pie on the event horizon, the pig's bladder full of sawdust being raised into the air . . .

"Of course the most important thing you can do for us, for *me*," and here Badiyi nodded his head with seeming deference, "is to keep your friend the Bear on board. He is a musician of obviously unique potential and it would be a shame for us to lose him. Contrary to the laws of jazz, he might even make the company some money."

Yup, there it was, the familiar cadence, pie encountering face, bladder bashing mazzard. It was all about the Bear, as usual, and nothing in it for me at all. Is this all the world will ever have to say to me?

Jones' heart plummeted, or something did.

Should have seen it coming sooner. Should be smarter than I am.

"Keep the Bear on board and the firm will be grateful to you." Badiyi extinguished his cigarette in an onyx ashtray, and gave the butt a final twist to expunge the last of its smoke. "I am confident that you will otherwise earn your keep. You will easily manage to write press releases and deal with intermediary people of all sorts." Badiyi tossed an invisible object into the air. "Press, management, artists. Whatever."

The rest of the interview got a little blurry for Jones.

"As to the Bear, I should also make clear that once you are employed by *us* you cannot also be working for *him*. . . . I'm sure you understand."

Ah, thought Jones, I'm being offered a morsel of betrayal too. Wouldn't it be simpler just to crush my balls between two stones? Less subtle in its excruciation, perhaps, but fuckin'-A effective, and less ambiguous.

Badiyi mentioned that Megaton had recently opened a film division—who could say what the Bear might make possible in that arena?—and then Jones watched a figure for a starting salary float past him, thirty-seven five plus the usual benefits. Press releases were mentioned again, Jones felt, in order to assure him he had actual duties and to smooth the passage of the blade.

Yes, after all I wrote a couple of columns for the *East Village Other*, he heard himself idiotically assert before leaving.

In the capsule elevator going down, Jones wondered a few things:

Mercy! Pity! Peace! Did they have any place in the world at all? Did he? His demands in the area of human dignity weren't very large. He'd accept simple mousehood as long as someone kept him fed. . . . What about the timeless self in the garden? I must have a place somewhere, here below.

Jones hit the street, too bright, too full of fumes, cars, trucks, buses, people, noise, pain. So much sun, so little light.

Was New York really the condition of civilization these days? New York isn't a city, it's a warehouse for people.

This, he realized, is how powerless people think: it's how I think.

Thirty-seven five. It seemed like a lot to him and might pass muster with Madam.

Jones put his sunglasses on and the street grew easier on his eyes, its lights and shades assuming a marginally less lethal glare. Still, the place was improbably cruel for a prosperous city in peacetime. It's an expensive and ugly mistake.

Yeah yeah yeah, sing the old songs. Join the ghost dance. The buffalo are coming back. The bullets can't hurt you. Write if you find work.

What am I looking for, applause? If so, from whom?

He'd take the train downtown, get to the apartment about half an hour before Sybil, take his jacket off, loosen his tie, have a couple of calming whiskeys over ice—something new, this shift from hops to malt; it went with the change of costume—and talk the Megaton offer over with her when she got home. After awhile, she'd cup his balls lightly in her hand through the cool linen-cotton blend, and stick the smallest pink tip of tongue out between her lips. Then they'd whip their clothes off, fall down someplace soft and froth like lunatics for an hour or so, including intermissions. Human life at last.

And hey, he thought, checking his watch a second time, I'll be hitting the subway ahead of rush hour. He remembered being worse off than this. So it was partly as a gesture of soul-to-soul solidarity but also because he always did it anyway, that when the beggar sitting on the sidewalk one block south of Megaton in his smudge of old clothes put his hand out, Jones emptied his pocket of change for the guy, made eye contact and asked him, "How you doing, man?"

The guy, loose-jawed, mostly toothless, unshaven, swept the buck-fifty and a token into his pants before looking up to speak. "How am I *doing*? How the fuck do you *think* I'm doing?" It was too loud, thought Jones. Mental patient. No proportion. "You must be some kind of *asshole* to ask me how the fuck I'm *doing*. Hey!" he announced to passersby, and some of them turned to hear him. "This asshole wants to know how I'm *doing*!"

"See you, man," said Jones, and started sliding off downtown.

"You're seeing me now!" Oh no, the guy was scrambling, was actually shambling himself to his feet. "You're seeing me now, *maan*." He flung out an arm, five dirty fingers trembling indicatively at Jones. The guy's fly was open too but at least nothing was hanging.

Jones took off at a canter, people staring at him as he ran, the guy screaming obscenities and insults in his wake. And then of course the guy took off after him—it was like being chased by an inkblot he himself had extruded like a panicked squid. Jones feared that the man would cling to him forever, but he got loose after dodging through the crowd for two blocks and turning a corner into the relative emptiness of a sidestreet. He'd cut out of sunlight and away from the subway line he wanted, but he seemed to be free.

Jones got his hankie out of his pocket and swabbed his face down and caught his breath before he could slink off, in clothes that seemed to fit him even less well than before—hitched up here, pulled down there, tangled in his crotch—in what he hoped was the right direction, through falling ash, in a city whose avenues, before and behind, were groaning with the end of day, amid deepening shades.

Iris jumped every time the phone rang and didn't know whether to let her machine screen the calls or pick the thing up and say hello. She already had three prospective sublessees for her apartment, but calls kept coming in. The last caller had hung up when her answering machine came on. No blame. She didn't like the sound of her voice either. Melodious, polite, and utterly false. I'm not in right now. I'd hang up on it too.

She sat in the armchair next to the instrument, rolled herself a cigarette and lit it while the day's declining beam slanted into her living room through the blinds and drew a ladder on the opposite wall. It wasn't a bad apartment. Subletting it is illegal and could cost me my lease. So why not just stay?

She had hoped to be able to sublet without running an ad in the paper, but her application for a leave of absence and a casual word around the lab had only brought Roger to the door of her apartment one evening, taking his last shot at nailing her before she disappeared to wherever. He wore a big untrustworthy smile and his infallible instinct for erotic cliché: a bunch of flowers swirled in green paper, and what looked to be, beneath its festive wrapper, a bottle of jolly champers.

She took the bottle from him and sent him home to his wife with the flowers.

She had handled Roger remarkably well, she told herself while sipping her second flute of purloined Veuve Clicquot. She knew she could be quick-witted when lightly threatened—it was a specialty of hers—but increase the level of threat and she had a tendency to jacklight. The ease with which she'd brushed Roger off owed something to the influence or the . . . what to call it . . . input of the Bear. Input was good. Maybe he was going to be good for her after all. And what she'd said! Roger, if you knew who I'm really fucking you'd die of shock. She hadn't said that, had she? She had. What was happening to her? She was changing. What had passed between herself and the Bear really?

In any case, when it was clear that the lab, and friends, and friends of friends, weren't going to pan out, she'd advertised in the *Observer* and the *Times* but had only gotten a couple of calls. She gave in to the inevitable, placed an ad in the *Voice* and waited for the wave of weirdos to phone. It hadn't been as bad as she feared. There had been a bunch of people she could turn down sight unseen—aggressive voices, voices out of the American wilderness with chaos and dementia blowing through them like wind—men who sounded like they were on the hustle, others who seemed too out of it to be trusted. But there had been other voices too, and she'd let six people come to the apartment for a looksee. She was considering three of them, a poised black woman in her late twenties who worked in an office and was going to night school for an MBA; a probably gay guy from the Midwest who was doing social work in Alphabet City; and a lively young waitress with a lot of contacts on the world music scene—Mauretania, Tannu Tuva, Joujouka—and who, it turned out when Iris let a passing reference fall, also knew about the Bear and liked the Tin Palace record a lot. Of the three, Iris liked the waitress best but thought her the least financially reliable. Either of the other two would do.

So why was she sitting there with her nerves pulled taut as piano wires? It was as if the skin of her world were being stretched thin and was about to tear open, letting in God knew what chaos and destruction.

Could it be because, well, she was preparing to move upstate in order to live in the greatest possible intimacy with, not to put too fine a point on it, a talking bear? Could that have something to do with it, did she think?

Odd, packing a few things up she had found the old issue of *Rolling Stone* she'd made such a big show of reading to the Bear that night before his arrest, the one with the quote from the Gnostic Gospels. If you bring forth what is within you it will save you; and if you don't, tough luck, pfft. . . .

Which was interesting: whatever her professed values, she generally behaved, at least until her recent leap or lapse into sex with the Bear, as if the reverse were true. On the evidence, her working logic had always been that if she hung on to the job and stayed psychically coherent and close to the ground she might get through the whole of her life and die at the end of it without being conclusively torn to pieces; she had already in some measure survived the loss of her daughters, and although the world could always come up with worse just when you thought it had exhausted its ingenuity or its supply, if she hung in there and didn't break the larger laws, maybe she'd make it through—no longer in one piece, too late for that, but without the ultimate atom of her agony being found out, then ripped out of her body and revealed for all the world to see.

RESEARCH BIOLOGIST FOUND IN UPSTATE LOVE NEST WITH TALKING BEAR. Yes, that would do nicely. She knew it: she was going to end up on a supermarket rag rack.

The Bear would bring forth, had already brought forth, some of what was within her, and the experience might have drenched and blessed her but it also scared the shit out of her and screwed her nerves a millimeter short of snapping. They made garrotes out of piano wire, she remembered.

Life with the Bear.

Suck on this and I'll save you. That part of it's usual.

Iris touched her throat with the fingertips of her right hand. There's something predatory in the way he looks at my throat when he thinks I'm sleeping.

Of course, when she wasn't terrified by the prospect of living with the Bear, it felt almost perfect: warm, her only chance of refuge and possibly even transformation into someone braver and more whole and able. And it felt inevitable, fated. One odd thing she remembered: back when she'd been in court with Herb about the kids and hadn't yet understood she was going to lose them, she was going to bed one night in the too-small place she'd been able to afford, Aim and Trace asleep bundled together on their futon, and as she'd put her head down and closed her eyes, instead of darkness trees and mountains had appeared, and in the middle of the apparition stood a bear. At first she'd asked herself, Is that him? but quickly realized that it was not.

She had opened her eyes again and Tracy and Amy were sleeping under their duvet and the nightlight was on. She closed her eyes again.

Looking upslope Iris saw, standing upright on a pinestrewn saddle of land between tall pines, beyond which mountains rose white and craggy above the snowline, the largest bear she had ever seen, built perhaps on the Bear's model but, as she had to admit, incomparably more majestic. His archetype? she wondered briefly, then thought, No, it's not.

Then she opened her eyes again: Tracy and Amy, peaceful and unknowing, breathing softly, as before.

Shut them and there he was. All right, she thought, I'll look at him and let him look at me.

The bear had examined her then. Iris felt his gaze pass like a subtle substance through her from top to toe, and she knew that what this bear was exploring was her fitness to mother Tracy and Amy and to protect them in this world. She could not tell what the bear had decided or seen. As it turned out, she was going to lose them, and it seemed to Iris that he would have known that. So what had he been looking for really? Had he been checking her out for the Bear? For God, justice, the natural order, the forestry commission, what?

When she did lose her daughters in court to Herb's better expertise and more powerful connections, in the aftermath she wondered more seriously if the Bear had sent this big examiner—she wanted to say Protector but no protection had been afforded her—as some kind of immaterial emissary, and she had thought of giving the Bear a call. As perhaps she should have done. Who knows, he might have helped her then, since all the worldly and conventional help of friends and lawyers had been no use to her whatever. The psychedelics weren't helping either. The problem at the time was that she had felt, having in some sense broken the Bear's heart, that she did not have the right to call him up and ask for skyhook service, tea, sympathy and an innocent protective cuddle.

Aim and Trace.

Iris hadn't intended her daughters' nicknames to be a hideous and ironic reproach to her, but it was true: her Aim had been poor, and she'd left almost no Trace on their lives. I released them into the world out of my body and lost them. What greater guilt was there than that? They were on their own and my thoughts were for myself. I deserve to be hurt. Stop this. Stop this now or you know where it will take you.

Iris changed her posture, straightened her spine, which had been bending, clenching. She rearranged her legs and breathed more deeply.

Where was I? What was I thinking?

I am putting out this cigarette, having hardly smoked it.

Would the Bear help her now?

Her cousins had let the rope slip and she had drowned—a surprisingly restful experience with a horrible, choking aftermath. Would it be any different now? There was a voice far back in her head screaming at her with increasing hysterical insistence, Don't go don't go don't go.

The laddershadow on the opposite wall began to slant and fade as degree by degree the day declined. Time was growing short, her nervestrings were winding tighter and tighter, creaking protest under the strain, and of course the devil's instrument on the endtable chose just this moment to ring again, shaking the room and jangling her nerves.

Let's pick it up this time. Maybe it's the perfect tenant. Maybe it's the solution to all my problems. Maybe it's God telling me I should stay in the city.

Iris picked the receiver up and said hello.

"Hey, sweetness," the Bear said in her ear, "when am I ever gonna get to see you again?"

He had the lay of the land down a lot better now. What had happened the first time was that he had gone one mountain north into new country without knowing it, and even when he followed the slope down to a cluster of rooftops he found dirt roads that led him nowhere familiar. It had cost him a second night in the wild, and when he did find his way back to Shady his fur was alive with foraging grubs and other buglife, bits of bark, fragments of needle and leaf.

It was in this condition that he reached the house again and met the photographer. The guy was pretty cool about meeting the Bear on a social basis, didn't mind hosing him down in the yard and scrubbing his fur, all sides, with a stiff-bristled pushbroom and half a bottle of dishwashing liquid. It felt so good! Then the guy drove down to Woodstock with some of the Bear's money and came back with a ton of groceries and beer in Grand Union bags. He was an okay guy, thought the Bear, a tall lean entirely American-looking number with a dirty-blond crewcut and a relaxed, slightly arrogant manner; in any case he was more at ease with talking bears than most folks were. "Though I'm not too comfortable calling you C.J.," the Bear told him as they sat behind the house drinking cold Labatts, the Bear on a treestump and the photographer on a folding beach chair that looked ready to collapse underneath him any moment now. It was a measure of the photographer's cool, thought the Bear, that he did not seem to care about the condition of the chair one way or another.

"The reason," the photographer said, grimaced mildly, and ran the cold bottle around the back of his neck. "My name is Charles Manson. Same as the famous murderer."

"I see," said the Bear.

"Middle initial J, hence C.J."

"We all have our cross to bear."

"What do you know about it?" the guy asked him, then laughed to demonstrate that he'd meant it as a joke. The Bear decided that, yes, the guy did have a sense of humor, but it was a few degrees out of phase with his own. A matter of timing and emphasis, mostly. Nothing crucial.

"What do you say I call you Siege?"

"Siege?"

"Yeah, a contraction of C.J.—Ceej—and also because, well, that's what my life is like up here, a siege, and you're like this messenger who can come in and out."

"Uh huh, I get it. Okay. Fine." Then Siege told the Bear how, generally speaking, he would come and go in his own rhythm, but would also be on call for emergencies and food. "I'll be here now and then to develop some rolls downstairs or do some studio shots. Then sometimes I might stay overnight, if you don't mind, with a lady or two, though nine nights out of ten I'll be back in town with my wife. Barb and I have an understanding," he explained.

"Seems like." Barb. Siege. Parry. Thrust.

When Siege left, the Bear ate cold cuts, bread, potato salad, watched TV, had a few extra beers, and decided being home alone in the country wasn't all that great. He stepped outside, didn't notice the trees or the mountains much, or the fresh, fragrant air, and decided, yes, he was bored. By then it was too late to ring Iris to see how she was getting on. Ah well.

He sat on his front steps and listened to the wind in the pinebranches. After about fifteen minutes he realized that this wasn't an apartment house and he didn't have to worry about the neighbors. He went back inside, unpacked his horn and got in an hour or two of practice. In the absence of anything essential to play, and without much of a sense of connection to the music, he found his technical abilities multiplying as if on their own beneath his paws. He listened to his lines complicate their structures, do rhythmic reversals, end in little filigrees, heard his breath inquire its way into fresh configurations. New details opened their petals, and they were interesting conceptually he supposed, but he sensed little life or beauty in them, and felt no passion in their making. He had always liked a narrative style of playing in which ideas developed in natural, even leisurely fashion before encountering any uprush into greater truth or feeling or thematic transformation, where technique accelerated to match the gathering energies of the moment; but now an overwrought notiness seemed to be encroaching upon him, filling every rift and making such narrative development unlikely if not impossible. It sounded obsessive and anxiety-ridden, on first scan. It seemed like form trying to overcompensate for a lack of animating essence. Where was the beauty in that?

Beauty, he thought, and dropped into a reverie about Iris for awhile, her soul as expressed by her body, her body as expressed by her soul, the arches of her ribcage beneath him, her sweet breasts, the brightness of her eyes.

Baby, come home.

Would she? It hadn't consciously occurred to him that she might not, but now he wondered. The world without a rose. Land without water, space without air. A heart without a heart. A Bear without sufficient reason to do anything at all. I know that to even ask if a love like ours can survive in this world is to invite a gust of comedy into the room. It may not blow out the candle, but it sure does call the flame into question. Even so: Lord please do not deprive me of this mercy.

The Bear went indoors, packed up his horn and began to pace, *kak medved*, like a bear, across his living room, back and forth.

2

"Aw c'mon," said the Bear.

"No," Iris said.

"Ride on my back. I promise I'll watch out for overhanging branches. Come with me for a romp in the forest. You'll love it, I promise."

"I will not."

"It'll be a blast. Can't you see it? Let's go running."

"I decline to be blasted," Iris told him, her face flushing slightly. "Thanks."

"You're missing something terrific."

"I'm not feeling sufficiently in my body to go riding on your back just now."

"Anything I can do to help you with that condition?" he wondered, winking lewdly.

"Not at the moment, thank you. Can't you just let me get settled in?"

Well, thought the Bear, that's the way she is. "Okay, sweetie," he said. "Me Bear, you Iris, it's okay, relax."

The fact was, he was deliriously happy she was back. She'd been home—home!—for four days already, sweeping the floors, cleaning every surface and each tiny item in the kitchen, setting out some of her paintings and bits of ornamental glass, rearranging the furniture and just generally fluffing the place up. He had to admit she had wonderful taste: all these little adjustments altered the house's subtle focus, pointed up its materials and dimensions and even seemed to improve the quality of the daylight coming in through the windows. The only thing he objected to was her insistence on replacing the porch windows with the screens this early in the year.

It's still pretty cool at night, he'd told her.

But it's lovely during the day, she'd objected, and I'd like a place to sit.

We can sit outside, hon.

And be *seen*?

The Bear decided, trying to avoid the more troubling conclusion, that she was looking out for *his* welfare, and was afraid of *him* being seen rather than of *her* being seen with *him*. . . . Can of worms, he'd thought, leave it unopened, hermetic even.

Okay sweets, he'd told her, let's get those dusty ol' screens up then.

We have to clean them first, she said.

Living together, in the full sense of the term, was very different from rooming in her apartment. The space between them, all the space in the house in fact, was charged with new electricity—he almost expected to see flares of minor lightning in the middle of the kitchen or sparks in a corner of the living room—and the territorial issues between them were measurably more complex.

One good thing, touching in its way, was the fact that they hadn't, either immediately upon her return or later that first evening, leapt into the sack slavering and afroth in the throes of mutual lust. The first night they got into bed together, the table lamp dim, neither of them wearing anything, they'd gotten into a quiet conversation, talked about simple, inconsequential things, enjoying the mundane texture of their talk, voices low, and the subtlety or tactfulness of its pacing, and had ended by holding each other until Iris twitched off to sleep and he listened to her breathe awhile before letting go of her, extricating a forepaw and heading off to sleep himself.

Why, it was as if they were, for all the world, two living beings who actually cared about each other in a multitude of ways, some of which did not invariably have to be expressed by means of plunge and shudder. Even better, once they did get going again, her third night back—strange, the Bear couldn't remember what had forestalled them the second night; had she gone to bed without him noticing and fallen asleep before he got there?—it had been amazing all over again. It was no exaggeration to say that the Bear had never before experienced anything like making love with Iris. Her lithe cool beauty, her small body—laughable how once he'd thought her too exquisite a vehicle to accommodate his strength—her subtlety and tenderness opening equivalent worlds in him in response, complex roses of perception unfolding, a series of descents into experience, realm after realm, beauty after beauty accepting him in when so much of his life had been composed of exile and exclusion; pleasure after pleasure, meaning after meaning: a host of new ways to be here, in a body and on earth; although the delicacy of Iris' lovemaking tended to blur the distinction between in- and out-of-body experience. Things tended to refine their colors and waft upward into light.

Days, well, they went by pretty leisurely in these parts—he declined to notice what was happening to his bank balance, and let time pass as the advancing spring suggested, with no more than hasty, sidelong reference to what it might be costing him. Late mornings Iris liked to drive the eight-year-old bright orange Volvo wagon they'd finally agreed to split the price of into town, where she'd stroll through shops, come back with an armful of books and the makings of one more remarkable dinner. (Siege, no longer doing the shopping, had only been by once since they'd bought the car—in the early evening, with two teenage girls who looked like they might fancy being models; photolights had flashed on the windowshades down there awhile, and then there had been a longer stretch with almost no light at all. The Bear found it morally offensive and knew that it could lead to trouble—outraged parents, charges of statutory rape, police. He wasn't about to barge in there, but he made a mental note to have a serious talk with the man the next time he found him alone.)

In any event he had plenty of time for music and an occasional canter through the forest, although he felt he was on a short leash now—when would Iris be back from town? Would she miss him if he wasn't home? Would she go out again if he was out? He enjoyed the woods, of course, but thoughts of Iris fogged his mind, blurred the details of treebark, windscents, the nuances of birdcalls. . . . Wait a minute, wasn't there something wrong with this loss of free perception? . . . Maybe, yeah . . . but isn't it, like, time to be getting back?

"Iris," he asked her one night, in the middle of a heretofore unimaginable domestic scene—if he told her how much pleasure he took in the simplicity of evenings like this, after dinner, Iris with her legs tucked beneath her on the sofa, browsing through three new books to find the one she would read, him in the armchair, the saxophone resting on its case nearby and a Mozart violin concerto on the stereo . . . if he told her what a crazed and muffled ecstasy was born in his heart from these simplicities she'd think he was an idiot for sure, "don't you want to come out with me for a ramble tomorrow?"

Iris looked up from her book and that alone thrilled him, even if she said no it wouldn't matter. "No," she said. It didn't matter. He checked to make sure and it didn't matter.

"Let me tell you what happened while I was out there. It was a very, um, it was a very *jazz* day."

"Yes, dear," she said, put a bookmark in her novel and shut it. "Tell."

He'd been saving it. "I went west over toward Willow," what a country locution; the place was getting to him, "and I was up this one hill and heard some music. I have an ear for music."

"Do you."

"Yup. Heard someone pounding out some complex damn tangled chords on a piano and came downhill following the sound. There was this big modern angled house, slate, pale wood, high triangular windows. I circled it. The music was coming from the basement. Someone was working through a sequence of these really dense ten-fingered chords—one chord, another, then a third, didn't like it, tried it another way, then another, then back, thrash thrash thrash, really beating the shit out of the music. It took me awhile to recognize the style and figure out that it was Carla Bley."

"Did you meet her?" Iris asked him, and the Bear was pleased to hear what might have been a note of jealousy in the music of her voice.

"Not today, but I did meet her one time when I was a cub and Jones took me down to Birdland on a leash. She was the cigarette girl at the time. I don't know if she remembers me from then, but recently I heard through Jones she'd like me in her band. I had to say no, of course."

"Why didn't you go in and introduce yourself?"

"Today? Naw. I just listened to her thrashing these chords out and thought, hey, if it's this much work for her maybe it's okay it's hard for me sometimes. That's intelligent, right?"

"In a touching, rudimentary way," Iris said.

"How I was finally sure it was Carla Bley's house, there were long tufts of frizzy blond hair tied to the chickenwire all around the garden—"

"That's strange."

"I think it's supposed to keep the deer from eating her vegetables. It doesn't work on bears unless they have a sense of honor. I didn't take anything but get this." He was conflating the events of two rambles on two distinct days but what the hell. "I ran into Jack DeJohnette."

"The drummer you're afraid of."

"I was chewing on some flowers alongside a dirt road up a hill and I heard a motorbike coming up from below, so I hunkered down in the shrubbery to let it pass, but when the bike came into view I could see it was DeJohnette. He wasn't wearing a helmet or anything. It was definitely Jack DeJohnette. The guy intimidates me but I thought the best thing to do was stand up and introduce myself. Which was fine, only I didn't calibrate the effect."

"You don't know your own strength, do you?"

"Are you laughing at me or with me?"

"I'm laughing quite impartially. Did he get hurt?"

"I stood up, cleared my throat and sort of extended a forepaw to wave. DeJohnette's feet came off the bike and he opened his mouth about as wide as Joe E. Brown—I didn't know his face could stretch like that. He let out this holler, I ended up hollering too, and so as not to give offense I backed off. He was wheeling the bike around and falling down and there we were, the two of us, hollering like lunatics, waving our arms and trying to get away from each other. Finally I tried to tell him I was sorry but he started yelling louder and waving his arms more. It wasn't a normal encounter between musicians. What could I do? I pretended to be scared off. Come on. It's not *that* funny, Irish."

"Oh yes it is," Iris said.

"Well, see? If you'd come out on a ramble with me you'd enjoy yourself. It's great value for your entertainment dollar."

"Perhaps next week. Did he get hurt, though?"

"Barked a shin, tops."

"So the woods are full of jazz musicians."

"Painters too," said the Bear, but when Iris looked at him he did not elaborate.

Of course the Bear wouldn't tell her about his third significant encounter in the wild. Last week he'd been lolling on his back in the middle of an upland pasture, sniffing violets and looking up at tall grass waving its seed against the sky, when he heard a woman's voice coming his way: a woman's whiskey voice and footsteps coming to him through the high grass, and she was talking, he gathered, to the local poison ivy devas or whatever. Now I know there's poison ivy here, she said, and I acknowledge your presence, but I'm walking barefoot and asking you as a favor not to infect me, okay? The Bear wished her luck, which he thought she might need; the only problem was that she was coming precisely to where he lay concealed in the grass, and he was certainly going to give her a scare. He decided that the right thing was to sit up while she was still about fifteen feet off and try to look placid.

Oh my Gaahd, she said when she saw him, but you had to hand it to her, she held her ground. She happened to be a beauty too, a saucer-eyed black-Irish colleen about five foot seven in a skimpy bandeau top, cutoff jeans and a loose silk overshirt worn open, and once she got her breath back she started talking to him too: Now I know you're a bear but you don't have to attack me, I'm I'm not going to hurt you or anything, I acknowledge your absolute right to be here, and in fact I think you're just beautiful really. Yipe.

I'm the genius of this part of the forest, the Bear told her, and when she looked puzzled he added: in the resident spirit sense of the term. Don't worry, relax.

That got her back to Oh my God and a general announcement to the sky and the surrounding countryside that He *talked* to me! but she calmed down and in about five minutes she sat five feet away from him in the grass, hugging her bare knees. They got to talking and her color started going back to normal.

He learned that she'd recently left her longtime boyfriend, a medium-big-time coke dealer—all her friends thought she was nuts to leave such a great relationship but she had to get away from that scene, and since she'd stopped doing drugs for the first time in about a dozen years it had been hard but amazing things had begun to happen to her, although nothing as amazing as this, as talking to *you*. Are you really a resident spirit? she asked him. You seem so physical to me. And it sounded like you were putting me on.

I was, a little, he told her. You were talking to the poison ivy spirits and it seemed the best thing to say. Actually, I'm new to the neighborhood. And what I am really . . .

And it seemed so easy: they were lying in the long grass in the sun, she had taken off her overshirt and was toying with a blade of grass in her white, even teeth, her big eyes were bright as brand-new days, and it would have been so easy just to reach out and gather her in, and he knew she might be ready to just let this amazing new thing happen to her . . . and the Bear didn't make his move; he felt he would have been taking unfair advantage of the situation, and besides, although life with Iris had turned him on to women and all the forms of nature in general he was still a faithful kind of bear.

And in fact Colleen, for that was her name, looked a bit relieved when she realized they weren't going to do anything. For awhile she grew increasingly flirtatious, batting her eyes and stretching her limbs, but the Bear figured that was because she knew she was safe.

You could come over to my house sometime, she told him. I'd love to paint your portrait.

Maybe sometime, he said.

All in all he'd behaved rather well, considering, but he still wasn't going to tell Iris about it, no, and he'd learned that in a pinch a talking bear could do okay, in this neck of the woods.

As their weeks together progressed, the home fires burned just fine thank you, perhaps even too brightly. Was that possible? The Bear didn't know for sure.

Although they hadn't leapt blazing into the sack at once upon Iris' return, once they did get that look and start moving across the bed toward each other on a regular basis, they learned new and more comfortable ways to couple and discovered some unexpected things to do: one the Bear really loved was doing it upright face to face, the Bear on his knees in the bed and Iris riding him up and down—carefully, because his fur could rub her nipples raw on the upswing. The spice, the kick, the whammy of the posture was that even though he was way up inside her and she was giving her G-spot an ultimate good time, the posture was essentially conversational. Which meant—which made it all the more transgressive and daring—that later, when they were facing each other clothed anytime over a table or whatever, this amazingly intimate image of the two of them going at it like this, her gone face rising and falling before him in the semidark, interposed itself to devastate the quotidian day with something that belonged to another realm entirely. . . .

Another new trick he also did on his knees, he picked her body up in his arms, swung her crotch to him, let her lay her back and shoulders along the length of his arms, cradled her head in his paws and then would lower her onto his mouth, her legs wrapped around his head, then later letting them fall back over his shoulders; using his arm strength to hold her in place, he'd lap her through a series of climaxes, pausing after each so she could just stand the resumption, before lowering her to the mattress, checking his heterotopic baculum for the appropriate angle of insertion, and entering her the regular way. Sometimes she was almost too weak to move. Although most of their lovemaking was a music made between equals, he knew that Iris got off on this demonstration of his strength—so did he—and whenever they did it that way she lay there afterward as if almost lethally extinguished. Him, he tended to croon to himself in a low sweet growl and only after awhile would wonder if there was something faintly creepy and atavistic about the scene.

But the fact that he, and probably they, were growing so centered on sex showed him something he hadn't anticipated at all. Entrance to Iris had been supposed to mean entrance to worlds of unforeseen sensibility and beauty, and their interpenetration had promised all kinds of parallel spiritual fusion. But the way things were working out, as their finesse with each other increased it was getting more and more purely physical between them, wasn't it? and he had to admit that a certain greed was creeping into the proceedings, from both sides of the conjugation he was sure: the way they went at each other, hungrily, progressively more expert, each of them increasingly sure how to procure this particular pleasure or that, whether for oneself or the other or both. It was fine, it was wonderful, it was mindblowing most of the time, but was not a certain selfishness, even cynicism, creeping in?

He was sure she was feeling it too. He could tell by the way she took her pleasures. As for him, even though much of his attention was devoted to her serial gratification, he was taking too: it was less mystically mutual, the borders between them were less blurred than they had been. Meanwhile the frequency of their lovemaking increased. Instead of waiting for the rising of a mutual inner tide or the fall of some subtle cadence and refraining when neither appeared, they had begun to go at it at least once every night, dependably and on schedule. Neither of them mentioned the suspicion that sex was beginning to consume all other intercourse between them, nor did they even allude to it obliquely, but he worried that they were clinging so tightly to their sex life because it was becoming the most important thing they had.

At least—and wasn't this in part a result of their lovemaking too?—he was getting less bored by music, and could sometimes bring to it a less smudged and weary interest than he had been capable of for ages. Yes, whatever the deficits, hadn't life with Iris begun to reanimate his music? It hadn't gotten there yet but it was on the way. Their life was full of subtle ebbs and flows and he could not chart them all. One wave rose, another fell, and it was impossible to sum up their motion or say where it was going. The texture of his life was changing all the time in a way it never had when he'd been on his own or with Jones; then it had been simple enough to confine life to a version, a stableness, a fixity, and factor up a self to live in it. Now it was increasingly sweet to let go, to lapse into the rhythm and the rise and fall, and when some detail wasn't worrying him try to fable out the deepest music of the motion.

The most dissonant chord troubling this music asked a question: how could they be this intimate and he still feel that she was drifting away from him, that he had her less and less and was increasingly inaccurate in his sense of who she was and the life she was living. On the other paw, maybe everything was peachy and in accord with nature and his only trouble was an inability to deal with anything ambiguous. Who knew? He didn't know much of anything at all.

In any case, he enjoyed listening to records more than he had in a long time, and if at first he listened to a wider range of things than usual, before long he had narrowed his focus to the usual gang of idiots in his pantheon:

Bird, Bach, Ornette, Trane, for the sake of *Weltschmerz* the first movement of the Mahler Ninth as conducted by Tennstedt, and lots of Shostakovich. The Bear had loved the Russian long before it was hip to do so—nothing like a posthumous book of anticommunist confessions to reinvigorate your reputation in the West; maybe the Bear should try it sometime; my Russian background, how wild I am about the American consumer ethic generally—and now he listened to his favorite pieces, the Sixth and Tenth symphonies, the Seventh Quartet, the Michelangelo Sonnets in the orchestral arrangement with Fischer-Dieskau singing, and especially the two Violin Concertos: he listened for solace, for the sense of a friend who had travelled through tough times and stayed whole, but also with a certain technical edge to his interest: what caught his ear was the way Shostakovich was able to modulate, often in quirky half-step increments but sometimes unexpectably all over the place, without losing touch with the homing power of a modal root, the soulful unific gravity of a drone. The Bear wanted to take something from that for his own future use, and he listened with special focus to the first crescendo in the Tenth, the passacaglia of the first Violin Concerto—Oistrakh's recording: wonderful how he could pull a viola sonority from his axe when the music asked for that degree of darkness. He listened to the stepwise chord changes in the setting of "Babi Yar" and the colossal orchestral passacaglia from *Lady Macbeth of Mtsensk*, in which the tonal center roamed from key to key but the unifying modal thrust was never dissipated or lost. There was a way to do this, thought the Bear, and it was less about modulating from mode to mode—anyone could do that—than about constructing melodies that yoked such modulations together and disguised their movements in bits of melodic misdirection without losing touch with tonality and mother earth. He might have to crack the books on enharmonic modulation as a way of expanding what he knew about alternative scalar arcs available to a pedal-point ground, but it would be no use unless it became so second nature to him that he could skim it off the top of the passing moment and make it hop three times before going under. There was a way—Ornette had his own inimitable version, and Trane had offered a choice of pedal-point or changes as early on as "Naima" in '59—of developing harmonic variegation, introducing greater chromaticism, even to the point of atonality, without losing touch with the heart.

If only he still had a heart.

It was still lying doggo when he played the horn, whatever its openness and exertions in concert with Iris.

He played the first movement of the Shostakovich violin concerto in unison with Oistrakh on the saxophone, then pieced the violin part out on the piano in order to see the writing set out clearly, left to right on the keys, careful not to scar them with his claws. See? There was a way to do it. If he could improvise melodies that did this kind of work he might escape the harmonic double-bind that even Trane found himself stuck in some nights, when even all the alternate scales he knew couldn't get him off the ground. . . . That's it, Bear. Improve on Trane. Good idea. Ambitions are like assholes, and they smell like flowers to the owner. I must be delusional. Give it up.

When he parted ways with friend Dmitri and started working the horn more purely back into the specific tortures of jazz, the by-now-familiar horror was still in place: for want of a connection to a sufficient sustaining principle, his technique was multiplying as if by itself, notes pullulating like infusoria by the thousand. Which made a kind of sense: if you can't invent anything on the primary level, your energy deploys on secondary and tertiary planes, where invention's easier but a whole lot less significant: the reign of quantity: notes proliferate, metastasize, add up to death or a string of zeroes.

Playing as he was doing now was a largely revolting experience, but the Bear decided that he had better make use of it, let his technique expand, and if he ever came all the way alive again his future fortunate self might make use of the material he was turning up now. Technique was a good servant but a bad master. When a real Idea finally came, if it came, it used all the technique you had developed to make its own way through the stops of your instrument and yourself, but the analytic, enumerative way in which he knew this at the moment was divorced from the ability to put it into practice. He was still living under the aspect of annihilation, in the spaces between the atoms. He wasn't having fun.

But hadn't Trane gotten all analytic too? Yeah, but not by stumbling sideways covered in fur and stupid. Trane got there by consciously impassioned search, all those scalar phrases aspiring upward to the object of his future love supreme. Trane had been progressing. Trane had been making his way. The Bear was losing his way in the maze.

For the sake of getting the *Sensible Shoes* record made, he had managed to dodge the agony of conscience he experienced at playing even one false note. Considering that his performance had been all fake self-impersonation, the album wasn't bad. In fact, since he might never play a true note again in his life, the world being such a fallen place and all, *Shoes* might turn out to be the best he'd ever do.

This was too hard. He turned off his head, put down his horn and went back to records. The Sibelius Sixth, speaking of transmogrified church modes, then on to Bach and Bird. I mean, I love to hear Coltrane bash it out, but Charlie Parker is *the* incarnation of musical genius. Nobody since Bach is even close. Of course when I listen to Trane, he's all there is. Genius by definition incomparable. Sure wish I was a genius too. It would make the music thing go so much easier.

He took a break to drink a quart of coffee in the kitchen.

Iris came up the drive in the Volvo not long after. "You're looking pleased with yourself," she told him once she'd caught her breath and put her new books down and her face had stopped flushing.

"Am I? It's only because I'm seeing you. I've been trying to play music all afternoon and it's been like digging ditches. Feel like taking a romp in the woods?"

Iris shook her head no.

"Baby, you don't know what it's like to ride through a forest on the back of a bear."

"There are a lot of things I don't know," Iris told him.

"Okay, how about a spin in bed?" he asked.

"After I've had a shower, perhaps," she said, flashing a smile and arching an eyebrow as she danced lightly out of the room.

Well, the Bear told himself, in this world you have to take what you can get. He packed up his alto, paused for a minute and went off to join Iris in the shower. Like the gentle rain from heaven. A bear could get used to this kind of life.

One night while washing the dinner dishes—rinsing them preparatory to their ride in the dishwasher, anyway—the Bear heard a fluttery commotion at the oblong window inset above the sink. He looked up. A pale green swallowtailed luna moth with about a four-inch wingspan had entangled itself in a spider's web and was beating itself against the glass: the moth had not so much torn the web to bits as spun it into one thick strand that was fixed to its right wing, but the awful part was that the spider, a large black hinged gothic thing obviously adequate to the task of stinging a luna moth into a trance of death, was advancing arch and sinister along the webstrand to where the moth thrashed and spun like an image, the Bear felt, of all the world's imperilled beauty.

The Bear had always been a Platonist. He took sides instantaneously and banged on the window, a fixed rectangle of glass that could not be opened, until the spider retreated cragshaped back along its strand. The Bear rushed out of the kitchen through the dining room and out the side door praying that the moth would still be alive when he got there. His progress through shrub and branch was slow and tangled, but when he arrived at the outside of the window, the moth was still spinning on the braid of web and the spider was still intimidated into its crux of windowframe.

The Bear bent, grasping the moth as delicately as he could, and two things surprised him: the thick solidity of the moth's wings as they beat against his paws and the panic, greater than anything the spider had inspired, that seized the moth once he had touched it. Still attached to the braid of web, it pulled free of the Bear's overcareful paw and plummeted spinning to the ground, coming down hard, the web stretched but still attached. It lay on the ground, still as death. The Bear caught his breath, afraid that he had hurt it, but when he bent and cupped it in his paws it started flapping again, full of panic and vigor. "No no no," he said, restrained it in his left paw, careful of damaging its wings or its two white headfeathers, and pulled at the thick-wound web still fixed to the right wing just below the false eyemark. The web held for a moment, then, without damaging the wing or its pale green dust of color, it came away.

The Bear cupped the luna moth for a moment in his paws, surprised by the feel of its thick white grublike body, then let it go. It flew like a pair of young leaves rejoining its source in the trees. Night was falling, but there was still some light in the sky behind the knit of leaf and branch. The Bear watched the moth disappear from the last of the windowlight, and felt that his effort on behalf of threatened beauty was a small but touching thing, a confirmation of real substance, however incompletely animated, in his core. This irresistible emotion, he felt, was only partly fatuous.

He looked up to find the spider huddled inside the cage of its legs in the windowframe. "No blame," he told it, but wasn't sure.

Later that night, in bed with Iris as he embraced and entered her, it was hard not to make the comparison and see Iris' small bright form as the luna moth and his prowling mass as something sinister creeping down to consume the beauty that trembled in the lethal geometry he had spun, making sure to inject it so it would hold still in the lens of his desire and he could have all the time in the world to glut himself on it.

I am become death the destroyer of worlds. Stop me before I kiss again.

This self-critique was, however, a flitting thing that passed quickly across the night of his mind and disappeared into the trees. When it was gone, he gave himself over to the extraordinary pleasures of Iris, loving the length of her torso, the arch of her back, the twin choirs of her ribs as they rose and fell beneath the sheet music of her skin. Although Iris still seemed to him a vision of ultimate beauty which the world was inexplicably allowing him to explore in this extraordinary fashion, he could feel their increasingly secular sense of the event. They were still some distance from merely dialling up sensations on each other's bodies and being dialled back in return, but their very expertise was making their nighttime conjunctions an increasingly worldly thing.

The moves were better, the sequences more finely worked, the transitions smoother, the views more gratifying . . . and yet . . . what bothered him? Was there a prude living in some shuttered room in his head? Did this happen to fully human couples? The Bear had no one to compare himself and Iris with, and he wasn't sure it would have helped him if he had.

But he was capable of miracles of pure tenderness!

He bent to suck the raised bud of her breast, then held her throat lightly in his jaws as he thrust into her again. He heard her breath thicken, felt her spine beginning to shake. He loved this. This was purely wonderful. He watched her face contort as it tried to exceed its capacity for self-expression, and her breath came hard as she climbed the invisible ladder. The sight made his own climax begin somewhere below his heels—he held on just long enough for Iris to make it, then finding flesh it climbed his body to the summit and waved a bright flag in the wind.

As for the tantric moment—world-engendering, outside time—if that's what it was, where was it now? He was sure the moment had altered their lives. But what were they making of the opportunity?

The Bear felt an immense melancholy, distinct from his general weariness with being. He had always had a pure belief in love, and he regretted every ambiguity that muddied the view. He was not a realist. He was a talking bear.

"Penny for your thoughts?" Iris had asked him. She was lying on her back and he was canted on his side alongside her, looking down. She had not bothered pulling up the sheet. Her body looked freshly radiant, her skin lightly filmed with perspiration, and there were strands of shed fur around her belly button, a perfect innie into which her flesh poured smoothly from all sides.

The Bear began to brush the fur off with a gentle paw. "My thoughts ain't worth that much," he said.

"I don't believe you."

"You know that line of Rilke's? Beauty is nothing but the beginning of a terror we are just able to bear?"

"You think it might be a reference to you? That's rich."

"No, I think Rilke was wrong. I think Rilke was a beginner. I think terror's the beginning of another, greater beauty we find even more difficult to bear, because it's so beautiful it means our undoing. Because in the face of such beauty, self-extinction is the only honest or appropriate response."

"That's a twenty-dollar thought at least."

"Yeah, but I wasn't really thinking it now. It's an import." The Bear had been looking off into the dimness of the room, but he lowered his head to look at Iris again. "I think I experience the beginnings of this beauty with you, and that because of you I'm beginning to see it everywhere." Was he trying to plead a better moment back into being? Was this some kind of incantation, a prayer, or just another lie? He continued regardless. "You've given me back the trees, the streams, the sky. You've given me back the mountains, the smell of grass. You've given me the sweetness of the world. It makes me want to weep."

But it was Iris who seemed to be crying, and not because she'd been moved by his tender emotion or how he had expressed it. Her face was bright but a tear ran from her right eye and her left was filled with tears not yet fallen. "That's fine for you," she said.

"Iris," he said. "What is it?"

"Look at you, *you're* happy, *you're* winning, *you* get back the sweetness of the world. I'm so tired of being this weak. I want a self."

"But you're perfect."

She shook her head no. "I have no protection."

"I'll protect you."

"I have no *protection*," Iris insisted. "I need a self of my own. I need a self big enough to be in the world in."

"Well," said the Bear, "I'm trying to get rid of a self. If you can figure out how we can make the exchange, you can have mine."

"You mean it?" Iris asked him. It was an odd question if meant seriously, and she was looking at him with what seemed a strange and misplaced ardency.

"Of course I do," he said anyway. "I'd give you my life if I could."

"I don't want your life. You'd give me your *self*?" She grasped his upper arm, and when she couldn't get her hand around it she seized a hank of fur and gripped. "You would?"

"Yep," said the Bear, but he thought the question could not be as literally real as Iris' near-hysterical insistence seemed to say it was. He did not want his girlfriend to be nuts. It worried him. "Of course I would," he said anyway, meaning it, "lock, stock, barrel."

"When we make love," Iris said, "I feel added to for awhile, but it's never quite enough and it doesn't last."

"Funny, after we make love I feel emptied, I feel drained."

"From a little slip of a thing like me?" She was getting her humor back.

"From a little slip of a thing like you."

"I feel filled." She seemed to be reassessing him.

"Well that's what actually happens, isn't it? I empty, you fill." The Bear watched Iris lower her eyes, then raise them again. "I don't mean I feel bad after. I feel terrific, but after awhile I do feel depleted. My bones feel hollowed out and sometimes my brain seems to have emptied."

"Poor brain." She reached up to scratch the top of his head. She was recovering.

"Only in the short term. In the long stretch, in my feelings, my perceptions, in my life, I can't tell you how enriched I feel."

"I give you mountains and trees." She worked her fingers behind his right ear and scratched him there.

"Wuff. That feels good. Absolutely. Mountains, trees, the whole shebang. Wuff. Christ that feels good. Scratch harder. Wuff. And don't laugh at my mammal pleasures."

"You do look funny in dog mode," Iris told him.

"I'd make a bad domestic pet. Wuff. Further down. Wuff, that's good. Won't you come out into those trees and mountains with me? D'you think I meant you to ride on my back naked or something? Wuff. Harder."

"Of course not. You are strange sometimes. You think such odd things of me."

"Because I never meant anything so atavistic. I'd just like to go out there in the wilderness with you and show you around, introduce you to some things I've seen. You wouldn't have to ride me. I mean, we could just go for a walk, hand in hand, I mean paw, if you like."

"We could?"

"Sure," said the Bear, wondering why this should sound so important to her. I mean, what's the difference?

"Then of course I'll come."

"What?"

"I thought you'd never ask."

3

summer should have been icumen in, but spring was slow letting go of the year and the nights were still cool, so for this weekend, when the house would be full of people—his new band, no less—the Bear was out back splitting logs and cutting lengths of lesser firewood from some fallen branches he'd pulled down the slope behind the house. From where he worked at the sawhorse, he could see Iris inside the kitchen through the luna moth window, her face flushed and harried and happy, as she worked at preparing a mess o' vittles for the coming horde. The Bear waved at her, and she smiled in return and wiped perspiration from her forehead. The Bear grinned back and returned to his work. He was cutting two-foot lengths from a long branch of ash with a bowsaw, working the iron band of blade back and forth through the white meat of wood, trying to let the teeth and not his arm do the cutting, as Siege had shown him the week before. He had cut about ten lengths so far, and a not unpleasant sweat, that of honest labor, had broken out beneath his fur. It was a beautiful day and he felt like whistling while he worked. It took him a moment to pick out a tune: "Well, You Needn't."

In a sense, whistling was a greater technical accomplishment than learning to play the horn—not much lip to purse at the front of his mouth—but he had managed it finally, and "Well, You Needn't," which he loved anyway, was one of the handful of things he could whistle in tune. Should the band have the number in its working book? He'd see later.

A section of freshcut log fell to the ground at the right-paw end of the sawhorse, and he advanced the branch from the left and began to cut again, whistling. This would be the first time anyone but Siege would be coming to the house, and the prospect pleased him, even made him improbably happy. It saddened him that she didn't want other people to see her living with him. He knew it was a stretch, he knew some people would see them as unnatural, her as scandalous. He knew, but it hurt all the same. Why was she still so brittle?

"Vice is nourished by secrecy," the Bear had told her.

"Well," said Iris, flashing red and thrusting her hands, what cute little hips, into the front pockets of her jeans, "we're certainly doing that."

What? thought the Bear, just able to keep his jaw from falling open. Is that what she considers it? Vice? He considered their passionate conjugations nothing short of absolute love expressed with staggering, inconceivable beauty, even acknowledging the nagging sense that its most transcendent values were being discounted at the margins. He was sure—he was hoping he was sure—that despite all their due and inevitable settling into a mundane life they still managed to achieve something alchemical and transforming in the conjugation of their absurdly dissimilar bodies and souls. She thinks it's *vice*?

Iris was uninhibited in bed, but she could be such a strange little girl sometimes. At least she comes up the mountain with me these days, though she gets winded pretty quick, hates to break a sweat, and all we do is loll in a clearing awhile before going back home. Won't make love outdoors, which would be really nice, but, face it, you're a pretty strange lovemate and she puts up with you indoors. Good Lord she does.

Another section of log fell to earth, its cut end showing nearly white. His arms felt good, the muscles pumping, blood running warm and strong through his veins. He checked the luna moth window again but her face was gone. Then it was back again. Probably scrubbing vegetables at the sink. He had told her that the easiest thing was roast a leg of lamb or a big bird and boil some potatoes, but she had insisted on a large, labor-intensive pot of chicken and seven-vegetable couscous—bought three organic chickens and a lot of ditto vegetables and spices—and even that was something of a stretch for her: now that she was out of the city and away from the stress of her professional life, she seemed to want to subsist on carrot juice, alfalfa sprouts and, if she was feeling particularly ravenous, a few leaves of salad with olive oil and lemon dressing. She usually consented to eat a bit of dinner with him, just to be nice, and he appreciated it, he did.

He had also tried to get her back into painting, so she would have something to do with herself during the day while he was practicing or roaming hill and dale, and although she'd brought her supplies up from Gotham and had even set up her easel in an upstairs bedroom that got the southern light she did no work of that kind. What she did in the afternoons was dress casually, drive the Volvo into town, buy a few newspapers and sit in some food emporium or other and "have a coffee." She was getting to meet people that way, mostly a bunch of guys running a line of talk on her; she had found out, for instance, which of the local merchants spiced their lives and incomes with a bit of coke dealing and which were making porn films and running a line of hookers out of a bungalow colony near Shandaken. All this information kept her lightly amused, and the Bear could see that she liked the niche she'd found—in town but not of it, a cool mild observer of local life and crime. She had that in her which made men tell all. "What do you think it is?" he had asked her once.

"Perhaps they think I judge nothing and smile on everything equally," Iris said.

"A Garance act. But what are you doing really?"

Iris blew out a line of blue smoke, looked up at him and seemed to shrug. "Who knows. They certainly don't."

Women sat down to talk with her too. Potters, performance artists, wild ladies who'd at last found true love at forty, others in first blush and full fever. Children were drawn to her: two-year-olds toddled across the floor to her table and looked up at her expecting something wondrous or just wanting to babble. The Bear grilled her on the subject of this universal attractiveness she had, but Iris professed not to know that she was so plainly luminous that all kinds of people could see it and were drawn to the light. If the Bear harped on this quality of hers, Iris would roll her eyes and ask him to give it a rest.

What?

Someone uphill was whistling back, the last two *nee*-dn't notes of the Monk tune's A section. There it was again: *nee*-dn't. The Bear spun his head left, right, didn't see a soul. Silence mostly: a slight breeze through the branches: one leaf detached itself, tumbling down in a series of ticks and crashes until it found the earth and settled, rocking on its spine. An odd move for springtime. Omen?

Nee-dn't. There it was again.

Look higher. Son of a bitch: there.

A grey wagtail catbird was observing him from a branch about thirty feet distant uphill. It dabbed its tail twice, raised its head, then sang out again: *nee*-dn't. A compactly formed, glove-grey bird with white markings at the throat and a swatch of brown in its tailfeathers. It sang out again—*nee*-dn't—and looked straight at him with particular intent.

Look at that! He wanted to call for Iris to come check this out, but thought that maybe the bird would split if he raised his voice, and in any case Iris had disappeared from the oblong luna window. The Bear was into the local birdlife—he had adopted a family of swallows nesting under the eaves, sweet birds with charcoal-grey morning-coats, fox-colored weskits and a nest of striving, squeaking openbeaked birdlings whom he protected, when mom & pop were out circling high eating flies and midges, from a local pair of marauding bluejays, the cannibal bastards: the Bear would stand on the steps below the nest and wave his arms at the raiders and occasionally toss a stone at them—"I see you've finally found a family," Iris said of the swallows—and he was courting a pair of sweet but fairly stupid mourning doves who took forever nerving themselves up for a descent to his offering of brown rice and milletseed—but this Monk-attempting bird was something new. He had heard a catbird in the neighborhood, this catbird probably, mewing, imitating other birdcalls and even the electronic warble of the telephone, but this was the first time he had seen it, or heard any winged creature this side the angels attempting a composition by Thelonious Monk.

Which was clearly what the bird was doing: it bobbed its tail twice, gave out with another *nee*-dn't, then pointed its head at the Bear and blew him a confused, catbird equivalent of the two-bar phrase leading up to the two-note tag it already had down. The Bear got the message: the bird wanted the Bear to teach it the tune. Too fucking much!

The Bear laid the saw aside and whistled:

The bird was still poised forward, so he added the two-note *nee*-dn't:

The bird canted its head to one side, then righted it, an obvious request for a repetto. The Bear administered it. This was a trip and a half, he thought.

The catbird muddled its way through the opening bars, mixing a fragmentary cardinal imitation into the middle, but ended on a triumphant fortissimo *Nee*-dn't!

"Not exactly," said the Bear, "but I know you can do this. Trust me." He whistled the tune again.

The catbird got closer to the notes this time and seemed to gain the beginnings of a grasp on the architecture of the piece, but it botched the needn't and got pissed off at itself sufficient to rub its beak, both sides, against the branch on which it stood. Then it directed a series of raspberries left and right.

"You can do it," the Bear told the bird. "I've been there." He whistled the first two bars again, leaving off the *nee*-dn't, trusting that the bird would understand he was getting down to the brass tack of details, and that the part he already knew would still be there when he learned the leadup.

The catbird sang the opening twice, getting it wrong both times, stared furiously at the Bear, rubbed its beak on the branch again, whistled irritated discontent in all directions and flew off through the trees.

"Dilettante," the Bear called after it, and picked up his saw again. Wonderful the smell of freshcut wood. Sorry to burn you in the stove. There must be some prayer I can say to ease the transition but I don't know what it is. The Bear laughed, thinking about the catbird. Iris should have seen it. You know, he told the bird in his mind, it'd be cool if you learned the tune, flapped back out there and taught it to the rest of the tribe: whole flocks of catbirds out there on the branches, working on their Monk charts, forest primeval ringing with minor sixths and getting into the intricacies. Heh. All it takes, bird, is a certain quantum of application. It starts with love, but that's only the beginning. You've got to work against the drift of nature. You've got to breast the current, take a flyer, a chance. *Nee*-dn't. Well. What do you know.

The Bear bent to the labor of the wood and cut more sections that would fit the stove, looked left to the pile of oak and cedar he had split earlier with the axe and felt good about the day's work. Split wood and you will find me there. Well, he thought, that's true. While he mused on this, two familiar notes accosted him from a tree.

"*Nee*-dn't," sang the bird.

Way to go! thought the Bear. You're back! You're willing! Let's work!

It took him about twenty minutes, but he got the catbird through the A section once, even including, well almost, the three slight variations of the principal phrase. The contrasting tag that ended the A section remained beyond the catbird's grasp. The main point was, the bird had hassled its way through. The bird hadn't quit.

"Bra*vo*!" said the Bear, and applauded. "We did it! Let's hear it for all kinds of life-forms. But I hate to tell you this, the tune has a bridge."

The Bear didn't have a chance to observe the bird's reaction to the news, because Iris had pulled open the sliding door at the side of the house to call to him, "I think they're here," and the catbird flapped off through leaf and branch and dappled light.

"You should have seen this, hon," he told Iris. "I called you but you weren't—there was a bird and it wanted to learn—"

"I think they're *here*," she said insistently. "I also think they're lost."

The Bear watched Iris leaning out of the glass doorway on one foot, balancing herself with a light hand on the frame, this small illimitable luminosity of a woman. God, he thought, please preserve this. Don't let us lose it. Is that too much to ask? Probably it is but help us anyway, all right? "Coming," he said, laid the saw aside and asked, "They're lost? If they're really lost they'll phone. What should I do?"

Iris took him by the paw and led him to the front of the house. They stood inside the porch together, looking downslope through the bulging old screens and the treetrunks to the road. The Bear put his arm around her shoulder but she stepped out from under its span.

"I don't see anything," he said.

"I think they might pass by again." Having eluded his embrace, Iris took up his paw again.

Can't we walk into eternity this way? thought the Bear. Can't we get old together and show up at the last roundup hand in paw like this? Isn't this eternity already? I feel that it is.

"There," Iris said, and he saw the car go by left to right, a big gold-brown station wagon with a mound of stuff tied to the roof rack under an army-green tarp. An anxious brown face was looking out the shotgun-seat window as the wagon passed. "That must be them."

"I think you're right," said the Bear, but by then the car had gone again. "What do we do, light a signal fire?"

"They'll come by again," Iris told him. "You could show yourself on the stairs and wave."

“Good idea,” said the Bear, and counted it a victory, since she had been asking him for weeks not to show himself out front. He cranged the screen door open and manifested himself to the world.

“HATWELL!” he bellowed when the station wagon showed itself again, coming past from right to left this time, and the gesture achieved a result: the car juddered to a halt, wobbled front to back on its springs, and gave an answering call on its horn, a D-major third.

Gesturing large—stage acting rather than film—the Bear pointed laboriously to the entrance of the drive, and the car made a series of slow, saurian adjustments before aligning itself to the reality of the situation and beginning its ascent up the gravel.

“The band,” the Bear said semiproudly to Iris and reached out a paw to her, but was dismayed to find her retreating backward through the screen door onto the porch. “Hey,” he said.

Iris waved her hands in front of her face in a gesture of self-erasure and was gone.

“Shit,” said the Bear, and looked back down. There was a lot of blue smoke coming out the back of that station wagon as he watched it crunch its way up the pebbles. It was burning oil. There were three guys in the front seat, just visible through the reflected trees. The brakes sang the car to a stop.

The Bear heard the engine switch off, and he watched the car die: two coughs, three wiggles, one belch and a last blue-grey fart out the rear end before its motion ceased. The driver’s door cranked open on a broken iron tongue and Rahim Bobby Hatwell stepped out of the vehicle and righted himself on the gravel. “Hey,” Hatwell said, and smoothed his jeans down.

“That’s quite a car,” said the Bear from the top of the steps.

“The Lead Sled,” Hatwell named it. “Heaviest thing to come out of Detroit since Motown and Elvin Jones. We can tour the whole country in this car, carry the guys and the instruments, crisscross America ten times over. It is the Car That Will Not Die.”

“The record company’s getting us a bus,” the Bear told him.

“You’re shittin’ me,” Hatwell said, although he was already looking up at the trees and breathing in extravagant lungfuls of country air. “Tour support. I’ve heard about it but I never expected to live to see the day. Lawd Lawd Lawd.”

“Well,” said the Bear, “you should have started playing animal acts years ago.”

“You’re forgetting my glory days with Zippy the Chimp.”

“Why aren’t the other guys coming out?”

“Probly cause they don’t know how to deal with you and still look cool.

Trouble is they don't look cool in the first place so they're in kind of a bind." Hatwell bent at the waist and directed a taunting voice into the front seat of the car, where two forms sat veiled by reflected trees, clouds, sky. "Hey you silly chickenshit musician types, come out the car for a pluck. Meet our horn-player, get face to face with the Boss. Come and meet the Man."

"I am not," the Bear said wearily, "a man."

"That's their problem," Hatwell said, cackling happily, but as he spoke the car's right-hand door opened and two people climbed out of it, first a long-limbed stringy guy about six foot two, very black, with a round elegant head and a loose, graceful way of moving; he wore an oversized red T-shirt, baggy black chinos and white canvas deck-shoes. He was followed, more gradually, by a medium-brown guy with wide square shoulders, a geometrically squared-off fade haircut and a manner that seemed modest and penitent considering the solidity of his build: he composed his hands in front of his navel and deferentially inclined his head; his forehead was high and untroubled, his face wide at the cheekbones and his chin long; he wore a white shirt and a vaguely African vest over faded jeans and Birkenstocks. Like Hatwell, these two were in their middle twenties. The angular guy was an inch or two shorter than the lean guy, but Bobby Hatwell, who was five foot seven at most, did not seem small between them: the strength of his presence. The Bear had taken Hatwell's word on these guys, and whoever else they were, they were his rhythm section for the summer tour and they had better work out. If they didn't, it would be tough luck in a dozen cities and eight thousand miles of road. The Bear trusted Hatwell. Didn't he?

"Hi, guys," the Bear said hopefully.

Got some waves back, and a couple of noncommittal Heys, and the tall black guy broke out the beginnings of a wide bright grin, but shut it down quick.

"Rahim," the Bear said, "what have you been telling them about me?"

"Thatcha eat little children but try to keep it to a minimum in the summer months."

"Thanks," said the Bear. He addressed himself to his rhythm section: "If you come on up, I think Iris bought a case of beer for the weekend, and I could probably let you have a couple cheap."

"Okay."

"Okay."

The Bear heard nothing very rhythmic in their assent. "Names?" asked the Bear. "I mean, won't you introduce us?"

"This is Linton Bostic," Hatwell said, indicating the long tall rangy guy, "on drums, and over here we have the great grey hope of the modern bass, Garrett Church."

"I'm the Bear," said the Bear.

"We figured," said Bostic, and opened that grin again, this time wider.

"And this is the forest primeval," Hatwell explained, pointing at a tree.

"Hm," Garrett Church said, and stuck his hands in his pants pockets.

"That's his bassplayer riff," Hatwell told the Bear. "He's doing this arcane routine about how bassplayers recede into the background and don't talk."

"How long he been doing it?" the Bear wanted to know.

"Since we met him five six years back."

"But we been working on him," said Bostic. "He's gonna crack."

"Hm."

"So," Hatwell cleared his throat for emphasis, "you gonna help us carry these instruments up those stairs or what?"

"Why don't you come up and have a beer first," the Bear suggested. "Cool off after the drive."

Hatwell looked both ways. "Instruments in the car," he said.

"That's right," said the Bear. "We've got some bad raccoons and rabbits around here trying to get their hands on a Fender Rhodes."

"All I brought's a DX-7. Those raccoons like *wash* a keyboard before they eat it?"

"Actually," said Garrett, "I don't like to leave my bass in a hot car. Oh, it's parked in the shade. It's probably okay. Anyone know the temperature today? It's probably all right. Maybe I'll get it. Lin, I'll have to take your trap case out. Well, maybe it's okay. Forget it. Nice place you've got here."

No one paid attention to him.

"Come the fuck upstairs before we die of old age," the Bear finally said.

"Whakinda beer you got?" asked Bostic, showing a sense of enterprise and putting one foot on the bottom step.

"A mixed case. I'm not sure," said the Bear. "Iris did the buying."

"Iris?" asked Bostic. "Who's Iris?"

"The woman hidden in this picture. C'mon upstairs and we'll try to find her."

By the time everyone got upstairs, through the porch and into the cramped if comfy living room, Iris was there too, flushing red and white; the Bear wasn't sure these new guys would spot it, but to him her degree of fluster was obvious. "I think the lads would enjoy a beer," the Bear told her after introducing them, "after the heat and the dust of the road."

"Actually the Sled's airconditioning works fine," said Hatwell, "and they must've paved the Thruway since you saw it, but," he bowed almost imperceptibly, "beer would go down fine, if it's not too much trouble."

"Not at all," said Iris, and began to withdraw kitchenward. The Bear was treated to the extended spectacle of his rhythm section's eyes bonging back and forth between himself and Iris, and the single question almost audible between them in the air: Is he banging her? I always knew, thought the Bear, that this was going to be a complicated weekend.

He indicated the sofa and the armchairs. "At ease. Assume a seated position. Need to use the bathroom? We have two of them. Like anything to eat with those beers? We try to be the perfect hosts, here in the forest of Arden."

The Bear had counted on two long sessions with the band on Saturday and Sunday and thought, well, maybe once everyone gets settled we can set up and do a little playing today, before the Friday couscous dinner special, but the guys were eager to get on with it: with significant ursine assistance Bostic hauled his drums up from the car, Hatwell his DX-7 and what looked like a big guitar amp—"Thanks, but I don't think I'm gonna get enough volume out of your upright," he said, declining the house piano—and only when the other instruments were settled and the chairs and sofa moved aside did Garrett Church walk his nineteenth-century Dutch bass up the stairs and into a neutral corner of the living room.

"Linton," said the Bear, "I think you'll have to keep the cymbal volume down for the room."

Bostic only laughed.

"It's a bright room," the Bear persisted.

Bostic pulled a cymbal stand to full extension and spun a wingnut open. "The Fiend Who Walked the West," he said obscurely.

Hatwell got his keyboard hooked up and the amplifier humming sixty audible cycles a second, and demonstrated some of the DX-7's horrible synthesizer sounds before fine-tuning its most acceptable piano approximation. "I'm getting a good sampling keyboard 'fore we tour but this old thing's what I got for now. We're getting front money, right?"

Garrett Church tuned his bass slowly, meditatively, drawing long pure tones out of it, bending them with large strong fingers, his left hand arched and articulate up the neck, tendons and ligaments and bones defined by the power of his grip. The Bear liked Garrett's sound and was pleased that he was not one of those bassists who lowered their action for speed and glissed their way into every note at the expense of depth and expression and control. He felt right away that Garrett Church would work out fine. And drums? Bostic was still setting up, hefting cymbals into place, checking the height of his toms, brushing some invisible flaw from his ride cymbal with the heel of his hand. His cymbals were on the small side, and had a high bright shine. The Bear preferred darker timbres, but he'd see.

Bobby Hatwell frowned at the ceiling, a window, the floor, shook a cigarette out of his pack and lit it.

The Bear rattled his keys, tuned his horn to the keyboard and looked up. "'Straight No Chaser'?" he said.

"A minute," said Bostic from his drumstool, finicked the tilt of his cymbals a final notch and turned a key on his snare-drum lugs until the sound was right.

The Bear counted off and they began to play.

The rhythm section was going to work out, he thought right away, during the head. They didn't have the weight of Ha Ha Ha, but they possessed a certain hip mobility, and even though it would take a few choruses before all four of them began to find each other, you could see some things early.

Like every good drummer the Bear had ever seen, Bostic played his own physique into a style: looselimbed and eccentric, with great independence of arms and legs. His cymbal beat danced lightly atop the time and he popped odd accents at improbable volume here and there—transmogrified Philly Joe Jones in that—and when he worked some polyrhythms up he'd start his phrasing on a tom-tom or some other peripheral outpost of the instrument, poff, then lay in a cross-comment on the snare, put his boot into time's behind on the bassdrum and only gradually, or in retrospect, did you realize that he was elaborating a line of thought that developed itself into complexities out of seeming random beginnings: hip stuff, thought the Bear, when he peeped it: now if I can only get him to work that level of invention a little deeper . . . well, give him time and he'll probably build.

Garrett Church had a solid, loping way with time, and had found a way of keeping his walking line from turning into a reductive series of quarter notes: he tended to insert the ghost of a shuffle into the walk, hitting before the beat, then after it, not to weaken the onward impulse but to give it a stronger kick, better balance and more dimension. As they played, his note choices kept improving, chorus after chorus he stepped closer to what the Bear was playing on the horn, adding sympathy, nuance, irony, propulsion: the Bear got the impression of a keen ear and fine intelligence. When it was time for a bass solo, the Bear was relieved again to hear him retain command of tone: Garrett could play fast without cheating the strings, and the resultant solidity of sound and intonation made all the difference to the strength of his solo. Another thing the Bear liked, something you didn't hear that often: now and then Garrett played like Mingus—not just the attack but the compositional hornlike sense of line—and the Bear thought this a very good sign in one so young.

Hatwell was Hatwell, God's own *enfant terrible* despite the unnatural sounds issuing from his DX-7. The Bear loved playing with him but he was going to ask him to use the house piano on ballads.

The Bear himself wasn't playing at the top of his game but at the moment it wasn't important that he should. What he had to do just now was listen, and his ears were perked, his mind ticked avidly, and his inward eye screened selected shorts from the possible future. If there was a problem it would be with Bostic, who was plenty talented but might just lack the critical degree of, what to call it, focus? He was a damn good drummer, though, and he didn't try to drown you out. In any case, when they finished "Straight No Chaser"—the Bear coasted through a last solo before the head—the Bear said, "You guys are gonna work out fine. Thank you for bringing them here, Bob."

Bostic laughed behind his drumset and tightened a tom-tom head. "You got to trust the Hat," he said, then did it louder: "YOU GOT TO TRUST THE HAT."

"What's that unbelievable smell coming from the kitchen," the Hat wondered, lifting his sensitive nose into the air.

"Chicken couscous," said the Bear.

"GREAT," said Hatwell, but instead of gravitating to the kitchen door they all got into the music again, played a bunch of tunes one after the other, what would have been a set, including ballads. Skylark have you anything to say to me? You don't know what love is until you know the meaning of the blues. They played "Giant Steps" and "Confirmation" and "Stablemates" and "Impressions" and when they were finished they had pretty much forgotten how to talk.

"We can eat dinner anytime you like," said Iris, coming through the kitchen doorway with four more cold beers on a tray.

"Hah?" the Bear and his band answered in nearly perfect unison. They had nearly forgotten what "eat" meant, who this woman was, and what she meant by "time."

"Dinner is ready whenever you want," she helpfully explained.

It took them awhile. They looked around the room, saw that the light outside the windows was fading from coral to magenta, and after awhile one of them nodded yes, probably it was Garrett, and soon the others joined in, and they agreed, yes, dinner'd be nice, and not long after that they realized that they were all incredibly hungry, in fact must have been hungry for hours already only, playing, hadn't noticed it.

"Oh," the Bear told Iris finally. "Dinner. *Right*."

Half an hour later, once they had splashed themselves with cold water and the food was actually out there on the table and the candles were lit and the wineglasses gleamed with peaked reflections of the candleflames, they ate like true musicians, that is to say like four creatures who had not seen food since early childhood and were determined to make up for lost time.

"This is fabulous," said Bobby Hatwell, holding up a roughcut quadrant of something white and sauced on the end of his fork, "but what is it, some kind of potato?"

"It's a turnip," said Iris from her end of the table. The Bear sat at the other end; the rhythm section was arrayed between them like a string of pearls.

Hatwell stared at the piece of turnip on the end of his fork. "A turnip cannot possibly taste this good."

"It's a very good turnip," Iris told him. "It's organic. It absorbed the other flavors as it cooked."

"It's a *wonderful* turnip," Hatwell announced to the table, his voice booming unnaturally. "This is the greatest turnip in the history of the world." He stood up in place and raised the piece of turnip high. "This is one of the best nights of my life," he said, staring into infinite space, "and I didn't even get laid yet."

"Doctor Jekyll and Captain Schmuck," Bostic explained.

"Damnstraight," Hatwell said. "Fuckin' A."

The Bear had already noted that while they were all drinking good red wine, Hatwell was keeping himself additionally liquid with the aid of a bottle of Cutty Sark, a rocks glass and a blue bowl of ice cubes. Had Iris bought the Scotch in town or had Hatwell brought it from the city? The Bear turned to Bostic and Garrett for a cue but they were looking down at their plates with uniform fixity. Iris was wearing her habitual expression of pleasant interest.

Hatwell sat down heavily and ate his piece of the world's greatest turnip. The Bear noticed Garrett and Linton scanning Hatwell with what seemed practiced eyes. He also had the intuition that Hatwell was not entirely out of control: a whiff of theater: perhaps he himself was being examined: fitted out for a suit: assessed.

Bostic piped up after awhile, the curves of his face so dark they reflected back only muffled bronze from the candleflames; his mouth opened easily into a smile above the finely formed assertive chin. "Yeah this is even better couscous than I had in France," he told Iris.

"She thought of poaching a salmon," said the Bear, "but she doesn't trust me with salmon in company."

"You get down on the rocks with it," Hatwell said, "and growl at the rest of the diners. You attack the young. I saw you on PBS. You were bad."

"I revert," the Bear nodded.

"You're a wild animal." Hatwell poured himself more whiskey and added a single cube of ice to his glass. "You're a hunka hunka burnin' fur. You're—it'll come to me in a minute—a bear. Well, what the fuck, it's just another buffalo show. I should write Zippy. I should write John Carradine. I should write my name on the shithouse wall. I should kick Polly Bergen in the ass. I been cheated. This is not my right life. Nobody move."

"And since I happen to love couscous to death," Linton persisted, leaning toward Iris, "and have eaten it in the best places, I know that this is great."

"Thank you," Iris said.

"You're welcome."

"You've spent some time in France," Iris prompted.

"Better part of a year." Bostic's arms danced briefly into the air to sketch that year's nature, then withdrew. "Went over with a version of the David Murray Octet, you know? Same thing happened there used to happen here, fans trooping in by the thousand, clapping and yelling every time we played two notes right and the guys in the band lookin' at each other and wondering what the fuck? cause the music wudn't nothing much and we all thought that as a soloist David was full of shit a lot of the time."

"It was that bad?" the Bear asked him.

"Nah. Zallright," said Bostic, and took a sip of wine. "Anyhow it was my first time in Europe and I decided I liked the life, so when the tour was over I didn't come back right away. Jammed around Paris with this guy, that guy, musicians who, okay, maybe wouldn't cut it here but could play. Got a little write-up from that guy in the *Trib* and found myself a fine French girl to live with and joined up with this blues band seemed to do most of its gigs for the French Communist Party—a night at the Yuri Gagarin Cultural Center, then the Stalingrad Memorial Blues Shack somewhere the fuck in Normandy. Y'see," he put down his glass the better to explain the point, "Communist mayor gets elected in some town changes all the names while he lasts so you got Rue Lenine, Brezhnev Boulevard . . . Cool with me. The Cocos were a trip, scholarly-looking cats always wanted to talk to you between sets about *lay nwarz*. Then I joined an African band awhile, went over to Germany, Switzerland, Italy, which I loved, the landscape, the renaissance towns, the walls, the towers, the olive trees—"

"Tell him about your career as a terrorist," Hatwell growled, and poured himself another whiskey.

This gave Bostic a moment's pause. "Yeah, okay, it's true." He dropped his head in penitence, but raised it quickly enough. "I took some time off, hitched around Spain a little and got picked up one time by some nice-looking young people in a big white van. We got to talking as we rolled along and it turned out they were Basque terrorists. Must've trusted me, pulled up the floorpanels and there was sticks of dynamite down there, clockworks, automatic weapons, gas masks, grenades, a whole bunch of what-the-fuck. They were cool people, told me they were nonviolent really, only, you know. We stopped in these little red clay towns in the hills and everyone'd come out of the woodwork and feed us bread and wine and olives and fantastic fucking sausages, and these amazing-looking chicks, dusky-looking Spanish chicks only they were Basque, right? would hang around and then want to sleep with us for the cause, or maybe just anyway, and I thought, Heyy, this could be the life."

"Tell them," Hatwell said heavily, gripping his glass of Scotch.

"Yeah," Bostic said. "I was into it. I was into it, I was ready to sign off on America and the rest of my life and join up awhile, all right? So my sign-off was I gave the Hat a call to tell him goodbye."

"He got on the phone with me at five in the morning from Biarritz," Hatwell said, "and told me about these incredible people he'd met, and the cause, and these beautiful Basque women and the little towns in the hills, you had to see them . . ."

"Oh, man," Bostic remembered.

"And what did I tell you," Hatwell insisted.

"He said," Bostic explained to the Bear, "he said, 'Linton, don't be a terrorist.'"

"And what happened," Hatwell said.

"He said, Linton don't be a terrorist, and I woke up. It was weird. I woke up in a phonebooth and wondered what was happening. I said my goodbyes and caught a train back to Paris. I probly owe Rahim Bobby Hatwell my life."

"And one day," Hatwell said, "I'm gonna collect. I'm gonna ask you for it back."

"How about I swear off drum solos for the tour."

"Not enough. See," Hatwell explained to the Bear, "drummers get dangerous if they get too far from their comic books. They can't discriminate. They go where the rhythm is. End of story." He took a sip of whiskey. "Now, as it happens, Linton is a pretty goodnatured guy for someone whose basic instinct is to hit things with sticks and make it impossible for anyone else to hear shit. But you have to watch him, and once in awhile you have to tell him, Linton, behave; or Linton, don't be a terrorist."

Bostic put out sleepwalker hands. "Yes, master," he said.

"And everyone thinks *I'm* trouble," Hatwell said.

The Bear looked across the table at Iris. She was enjoying this pretty much the way she seemed to enjoy the spectacle of life in general when she could find a niche.

Two things happened almost at once. The Bear finally clocked the bottles of wine on the table and Iris rose to say, "I think I should bring out more *semoule*."

The Bear followed her into the kitchen and advanced upon her as she spooned mounds of couscous into the red clay serving bowl. "I just saw the wine on the table," he said.

"Don't you like it?" Iris asked, all innocence.

"Three bottles of Château La Lagune 1990? I love the bouquet, I was admiring the structure and drowning in the taste, but how much did you spend provisioning this little weekend?"

"A couple of hundred," Iris said, smoothing the mound of semolina in the bowl. "Possibly three."

"Gaah," the Bear remarked, thinking about how quickly his advance from BFD was going down the drain. A meal here and there, books for both of them, a used orange Volvo wagon plus maintenance, insurance, gas. The monthly phone bill to her kids in Santa Fe was a disaster on its own. The Tin Palace record was supposed to be selling well but he hadn't seen a check yet. How much was he supposed to clear on the tour? He forgot. "Three bottles of La Lagune in one night? What's that, a hundred?" The Bear ran a paw across the fur atop his head. "Can't you be a little realistic?"

"I see," Iris said. "You expect me to live with *you* and be realistic. Interesting." She bore the bowl of couscous more or less ceremonially in both hands and walked past the Bear back to the dining room, where goblets of La Lagune 1990 were being refreshed and a couple of bottles of Châteauneuf-du-Pape held their spears and wondered if they'd be called into action as reinforcements. The Bear followed his beloved into the dining room and sat down, feeling like an overrun city. Linton Bostic, having completed a tour of the rest of the table, inclined the bottle and refilled the Bear's glass.

"Nice wine," Bostic told him.

"I know," said the Bear. It took him awhile to regain a grasp on the conversation; it was Iris who called him back to attention.

"You know the painting in your bedroom?" she had asked him, in the middle of something or other she'd been saying to the band.

"Whut?" he said, and gathered dimly that recent conversation had turned upon the pivot of Spanish art. "Whaddayou mean my bedroom? Our bedroom, you mean."

"No," Iris said. "*Your* bedroom."

The Bear didn't get it. "*Our* bedroom. I don't have a bedroom. What are you talking about?"

Iris got up from the table.

"What?" asked the Bear. "What did I say?"

"I have to go to the ladies'," Iris said mildly, but turned away in a nearly imperceptible huff that among the initiated would be understood as fury.

Rahim Bobby Hatwell thumped the base of his whiskey glass hard onto the oaken board when she had gone. "Fuck the bitches and make them cry," he announced.

"What?" the Bear asked him.

"I said, *Fuck the bitches and make them cry*!" The Bear saw that Hatwell was sweating and that his eyes were wide.

Bostic got up from his chair, bent to Hatwell and took him gently by the elbow. "Occasionally you have to tell him, Hat, don't be a terrorist," explained the drummer. "Sometimes he gets a little funny when he's had too much of something."

Hatwell rose from his seat and let himself be led onto the porch, then out into the night.

The Bear surveyed the table. Well, everything's just about eaten up anyway.

The Bear and Garrett were alone.

The bassist lifted a chicken leg from his plate and polished it off, then poured himself some dregs of La Lagune. "This is wonderful food," he said, "and I wouldn't worry about Bobby if I were you."

"If you were me. Interesting concept."

The bassist thought about it for a moment.

"Want to swap with me for a month or two?" the Bear asked him.

"I don't think so."

"Well anyway, I like the way you play."

"Thanks," the bassist said. "It's a trip playing with a bear. It's not what I'd anticipated doing this time of my life. Could you pass me that dish of hot sauce, please? I think I'll have another helping of vegetables. This is one of the best meals I've ever had. The other guys'll be back after awhile. Would you mind opening up one of those other bottles over there?"

Half an hour after dinner, to the extended coda of which Iris had only phantasmally returned, flitting here and there in the form of the perfect hostess but then retiring elsewhere, the Bear found himself sitting on the front steps with Bostic and Garrett in the welcome cool of the night.

"The Hat has his episodes of total bughouse but I've never seen him hurt anyone," Bostic said.

"Does he make the gig?" asked the Bear.

"He always shows. Though I'll tell you, get him on one of his total crazy upfucked nights, and he'll play you some surprising piano."

Garrett, sitting two steps higher up, put his oar in: "Bobby Hatwell is the finest man I know."

"I love the guy already, okay?" the Bear told them. "But I've got this band and I'm responsible for what happens on the tour. I'm only asking."

The screen door cranged open and Hatwell, who was supposed to have fallen asleep upstairs, came out and stood unsteadily at the top of the steps. "I love the effect of talk behind my back," he said. "It makes a breeze between the shoulderblades where the wings used to be. Can a man get any pussy around here?"

The Bear turned to look at Hatwell wavering up there behind him. "I believe some of the neighboring cottages have calicoes and tabbies," he said.

"Anyone want to drive to town with me?" Hatwell asked.

"Noo," bass and drums told him, and Bostic patted his pocket and whispered to the Bear that he had the keys to the Sled.

"Are you fucking Iris?" Hatwell asked the Bear.

"I don't believe that's any of your business, Bob," the Bear said evenly.

"I told you he was fucking her," Hatwell informed his rhythm buddies lower down, and kicked Garrett lightly on the shoulder.

"Watch it," said the Bear.

"When?" Hatwell asked him. "Can I take pictures?"

The Bear stood up, fur bristling all over his body and an involuntary growl starting in his belly.

Bostic rose from his step and climbed up to Hatwell. He put his arm around the pianist's shoulders. "The Hat don't know the meaning of fear," he explained to the Bear. "In fact there's a lot of shit he don't know. Come on, Bobby, time for a cold bath and then a few hours in the rubber room. *Come* on," Bostic sang in a descending cadence, and led the brilliant pianist indoors.

The Bear wondered where the catbird was by now. Sleeping in a tree, or wide awake on the implications of Monk's architecture. The Bear sat on the steps with Garrett Church awhile. It was a lovely evening.

"I'm told that in the summer you get the northern lights up here," the Bear said.

"I think it's interesting, your situation being a bear," Garrett Church replied. "You must have had an interesting life."

"Still having it."

"Bobby Hatwell is a genius," Garrett said. "On the musical level definitely. A major cat. If he doesn't fuck up."

"Which he has a tendency to do."

"Sometimes he goes to extremes. But at his level, who can tell what's fucking up and what's pushing the envelope?"

"You think he's a pianist *maudit*? You go for that romantic shit?"

"Not really. I guess a lot of his behavior's worn-out shit he drags around behind him, parts of himself that haven't caught up. He's still young enough to get away with it, but after thirty he may have to pay the bill."

Garrett was showing his youth: thirty wasn't what he thought. "He's half nuts," the Bear said.

"The problem is he thinks that's the good half. He's got the picture wrong but he's a genius and I'm not." Garrett paused. "He's better than I am. Sometimes I think he's my other half."

The Bear looked at Garrett appraisingly.

"I'm impressed by perception," Garrett told him, "and Bobby Hatwell has more of it than anyone I've seen. Intelligence per se isn't as important."

"You think it divides like that?"

"When I was eighteen I joined Mensa for awhile, trying to get up in the world or maybe just show off. I was middle-class IQ over there, a solid one seventy-something. I saw people who were a little smarter than I was and there was nothing much doing there. There were a couple of real brainiacs with two hundred plus and that's what I wanted to have, but they weren't the kind of people I wanted to be. I'm not impressed by intelligence, but I need more of it than I have, another octave, to do the work I want to do. Either that, or the kind of genius Bobby has, which would be better, but it's not possible for me."

"You write," said the Bear, getting it.

The bassist cleared his throat. "I have some tunes with me. Is there any chance we can do a couple?"

"If they work out why not? I planned to run through my originals tomorrow. We can try some of yours. But you have eyes to write longer things, don't you."

"That's it," Garrett nodded. "But I'm not ready yet. One thing I'll say for myself, I know how young I am. I'm not in a rush to be what I can't be yet. Yes I have a decent brain but so what."

"You like Wynton's recent long things?"

"Some of it's very impressive," the bassist said, "though more in the details than in the expression. He's written some amazing moments, though."

"But you're thinking along the lines of Mingus."

The bassist cocked his head sideways at the Bear. "You heard that, huh. You actually listen to the bass. That makes a nice change."

"The most beautiful instrument in the group? You bet I listen to the bass."

"You like bass that much?"

"Absolutely. No contest. I'd play it if I could. It was easy to hear Mingus in you. You ran some Paul Chambers on me too, flatting your notes against the walk on 'Straight No Chaser.' "

"You have ears."

The Bear wiggled them for show.

"I don't think everything Mingus did is adaptable," Garrett said, "and of course it'd be pointless to copy him, but as a composer I'd like to take those tone colors and emotions on, try to get some big stuff down. You listen to *Black Saint and the Sinner Lady* lately?"

"Yup."

"Well, there you go. I listened to one of Wynton's long ones this week, one of those dance company things. It was beautifully worked out but after awhile it sounded like a set of variations on 'Toot Toot Tootsie Goodbye,' all those major chords and cycling fifths, but then he'd write you a slowed-down intermezzo—voicings? implied polyphony? Fantastic things, take your breath away. He's very skilled and he keeps getting better."

"You know," said the Bear, "your name includes the two traditional refuges of the artist. The garret and the church."

"I noticed," Garrett said. "By the same logic you'd be called Forrest Zoo."

"Life," the Bear told him, doing the voice, "is like a box of boxes. We're touring as the Ted Beastly Quartet."

"That's not bad."

"If we were a rock band I'd call it the Return of the Repressed tour."

"That's even better."

"It'd provide some cover. How'd I sound today? I wasn't giving it all I had, you know."

"I heard a cassette of the record you made with Bobby and them. You don't have anything to worry about."

The Bear snorted, then cleared his throat. "I feel like I need some more intellectual voltage too. The things I want to play now, conceptually, I'm kind of stuck. It makes me feel like a bear of little brain."

"We're about the same intelligence, you and me. It's hard to tell. You're not like a guy. You're a bear."

"Oh."

"You're hard to get a read on, but from where I sit, musically, you're okay. The things you want to do? You've got them. They're in you. They're in your hands. Um, paws. You have what you need to work them out."

"That's quite a statement, coming from such a beardless youth."

"I made it up," the bassist said.

Later still, sitting solo on the steps after Garrett had retired, the Bear heard the swish of water indoors and, against the widespread scrim of night—spray of stars beyond the highest reach of pine—the homely chink of dinnerplates. The Bear went into the kitchen to see if Iris wanted any help with the dishes.

"If you like," she said.

He eased the plates and things she had rinsed into the dishwasher racks. "Everyone else in bed?" he asked.

Iris handed him the salad bowl and didn't answer.

The Bear found a place to settle it inside the machine. "Are you mad at me for some reason?" he wondered. "Because you're acting a trifle chilly."

"You know why," Iris told him, and he couldn't remember her sounding this cold.

"I don't."

"You do."

"Pretend I don't and tell me."

Iris got ceremonial about it, put down her scrubbing brush, turned off the hot water, untied her apron, took it off and laid it on the countertop. "You can't be that stupid," she said.

"Of course I can," said the Bear. "Even you underestimate me."

"When I talked about *your* bedroom you said *our* bedroom. You insisted."

"Why the fuck not?" he wondered.

"Do you think I wanted them to know that I'm sleeping with you?"

"They know already."

"Why? I didn't tell them. Did you?"

"Of course not. Don't be ridiculous. They just know."

"They do not just know. How would they know? When you said *our* bedroom it was intentional and ugly. It was one of the ugliest things I've seen anyone do."

"Absolutely not. I couldn't figure out what you were talking about. It didn't make any sense to me at all so I told the truth."

"You're lying. I've never seen you lie before."

"I'm not lying."

"Of course you are."

"Where's everybody sleeping, anyway?"

"Linton and Rahim are downstairs at Siege's. Garrett's in one of the upstairs bedrooms and I'm in the other."

"Oh."

"You finish doing the dishes. I'm leaving. I mean I'm going to bed. You're lucky I'm not going back to the city."

"What? And hey, Jones is coming up tomorrow. Where are he and Sybil supposed to sleep?"

"They're eating here if they want to, and they have a room reservation at the Duchesse Anne in Mount Tremper. Good night."

Wow.

The Bear picked up the scrubbing brush and watched her go. Honestly, he'd had no idea. He scrubbed the remaining dishes reasonably clean, settled them in the dishwasher and set its timer to go off in an hour. He'd had no idea. Had he said something incredibly dumb or was it her problem?

He shut down the lights, listened for snores or signs of other peaceful slumber, sniffed a remaining half-bottle of Châteauneuf-du-Pape and recorked it, then stepped outside for what would have been a smoke, if he smoked. Nice night out. Tomorrow they'd work out some new compositions, not all of them his. "Reincarnation of a Lovebird" especially, maybe something else by Mingus. "Ecclusiastics"? He'd always loved "Ecclusiastics." They'd have to work out a head arrangement, plan the disposition of the tune's three rhythms, figure out what to do with them in the improv. Look at Garrett's tunes before we get started. The couscous had been terrific but Iris was a puzzle to him still. How could she be so uninhibited in bed, then worry so much out of it? Was she two people? Three?

He slouched off to bed, riffled through his bedside novels but selected a hardback history of the Paris Commune that Iris had picked up in town. He had begun to dislike something he found in fiction, that insistent, personal tone, which felt like special pleading, a vain attempt to impose an unreal self upon a larger world. Was that how music struck him too? He wasn't sure, but he was glad he'd only had to play at half strength today. Tomorrow he'd put a bit more effort in, see if it was as distasteful as fiction then. In any case he was committed or condemned to the tour, so what he felt didn't ultimately matter. It was hard to believe that after a life, especially this year, of more or less cosmic adventure, he was being driven by considerations of rent, car parts, Iris' recklessness at the wine shop and the market, and how much was left of the record company cash. It was a more domesticated life than he was used to. He and Iris even had silly arguments, though not about money yet. *Sensible Shoes* wouldn't come out till high summer, when the quartet would hit the road. Would the money hold out till then? And if it didn't, what was he supposed to do? How many records would they have to sell to earn back the advance and bring fresh cash in? The Tin Palace disc was supposed to be whizzing out of the shops like flying saucers and he would have to get some straight talk from Megaton about the royalties he wasn't seeing. He'd start by bracing Jones on the subject tomorrow.

It made his head hurt. It made his ears itch. Was it a law that love always mired you in endless alien consequence? Was that the comedy here? The Bear had no idea.

He read awhile—about the civilian militia of Paris going out to the city walls to keep the Germans away and getting drunk at lunchtime and wandering off with hookers into the byways; later they would murder their fellow Parisians by the thousand and break Rimbaud's heart into the full flood of its genius—in other words, history as usual—then laid the book aside and hoped to fall asleep, but a palpable absence had been carved out of his body with Iris' removal upstairs. He lay on his left side, and his chest and belly ached with hollowness where she would have lain against him. Time passed in this fashion until he heard the dishwasher start up in the kitchen, thrum of machinery, thrash of water, and what sounded like a loose piece of silverware banging against a glass. Iris would let him know about it in the morning if anything broke, he thought, then smiled broadly. The sound of the earnestly laboring kitchen appliance had only partly masked the tread of her small, high-arched foot on the stair. He listened more closely: yes, she was coming down.

He hardly saw her. She slipped into bed beside him. "I miss sleeping with you," she said. "Let's sleep. Just sleep. Hold me."

"I love you, Iris. I—"

"Just hold me. Nothing noisy please. I love it just like this."

"I was lying here," the Bear told her, "with this ache of absence where you would have been."

"I know," Iris said. "First I hugged one pillow, then I put another one between my legs, then I said This is ridiculous and came downstairs."

"But you waited for the dishwasher."

"It helped but I was coming down anyway."

He looked down at this smooth lithe form curled seashell-pink into his embrace, took in her architecture, the chords, the harmonies, the flows. Her nipples, an only very slightly darker tint of rose than the rest of her, were perking erect just then at the tips of the wonderful, fresh-smelling breasts she thought he thought were too small for his liking, a crazy notion of which nothing he said or did could disabuse her. He loved to see her there, like the sweet curve of law, swaddled in his arms. She nestled more deeply, she curved, she curled, she smoothed, she swam. "Venus in furs," he said.

She opened her eyes and rolled them heavenward. "Give me a break."

"You're so incredibly beautiful, Iris."

"Don't overwork it, Bear. It's only skin deep."

"Oh no," he murmured. "Though it is such lovely skin—"

"It's only skin."

"—it runs so much deeper than that." He almost began to say that he had been innocent of all design in saying *our* bedroom in front of the band, but thought better of it just in time. See? Signs of intelligence already. Things are looking up. She eased onto her side to press herself into the treasury of his chest. He held her with the motion of his breath, he enlarged his heart for her, smoothed a paw down the length of her back, playing a fine imaginary melody on the delicate keyboard of her spine, tactfully finishing the motion before reaching her cuppable little ass. A throb ran through him anyway. He suppressed it.

Iris twitched off after a few minutes, the gateways of her nerves letting go, her breath slowing. He watched her face let go of its waking strictures. She slept, it seemed to him, with something like a child's perfect trust in the world's goodness, or perhaps his own. He kept watch over her awhile before lowering his head to the pillow and closing his eyes.

The Bear had never fallen asleep before her. Not once, ever.

4

"it's too tall for itself. It's an odd-looking house," said Sybil Bailey, peering through the windshield of the rented Chevy Lumina as it halted at the T intersection.

"Consider the tenants," Jones advised her.

"There's that," Sybil admitted.

Jones drove the Lumina across the road and up the grey gravel drive beneath the spruces. No one showed at the door to greet them, which maybe was just as well. Jones had a number of reasons for feeling shaky about this little visit.

The first one sat beside him, of course. Sybil had been extra nice to him since he got the job with Megaton, but she was known to have fundamental hots for the Bear. Not that she'd have a chance to do anything about it with Iris around; and the Bear, if phone calls could be trusted on the subject, was sounding awfully happy about his life with the little lady. But Jones found the aggravated sense of possibility a mite destabilizing all the same, and the fact that he was nervous about it only emphasized his general tactical weakness. Which made him more nervous still, so tactically weaker still. . . . Ladies and gentlemen, perpetual motion has been achieved.

Then there was the way the Bear had been treating him lately. Such contempt, when once they'd been so close. Jones had decided two things: that this unfair friction had its origin in Jones' new sense of rough equivalence to the Bear, which in turn had issued from the near-death vision of his eternal individuality in the garden, by definition equal to anyone else's eternal individuality and therefore immutably worthy of respect; his second resolution was that he wasn't gonna take that kind of shit from the Bear anymore. No, things had to be straightened out, put on a new and firmer footing, made fair. I'm not just a sidekick anymore.

If only he weren't compromised by his complicity with Badiyi and the salary he was collecting from Megaton, albeit with massive deductions—Jones had had no idea that such a piratical degree of taxation existed in the world, and he had already shifted his political weight rightward. Taxwise the Bear was not a legal person, so Jones had helped him incorporate as Ursine Enterprise. His publishing company was Improbable Tunes. Badiyi's voice: Remember you're working for *me* now, not him. The posh Iranian had seemed improbably pleased to say so. As if my allegiance could be bought that cheap—Sybil had doublechecked the Bear's contract and it was free of thievery—but in the objective, observable world Jones had nodded yes to Badiyi and muttered a submissive syllable. After that, a tall pretty functionary in a puffy blouse and a tight leather skirt had shown him the way to his new desk and told him how to operate what she called the voice-mail system but what he could have sworn was a telephone.

At least he and Sybil weren't actually sleeping at the Bear's house. They had a room at some inn nearby, and Sybil had already told him that its duck à l'orange and steak au poivre were semi-famous, so they might not even eat dinner with the Bear and Iris and the band. Which was probably just as well.

Jones eased the Lumina to a stop at the Volvo's front bumper and squinted at the huge gold-brown station wagon parked behind it. He switched off the engine and pulled the handbrake tight because he didn't want the car rolling back down the drive. As far as he was concerned, this was wilderness and anything could happen.

Iris appeared behind the screen door at the top of the stairs, waving hello, wearing an apron and a grin. Such an exposed face, thought Jones. So naked a spirit, so visible its hopes of joy. Jones felt a pang for her and hoped the Bear was treating her right.

When Jones and Sybil got to the top of the stairs Iris greeted them with hurried embraces, then retreated, pleading business in the kitchen, and the newcomers had to edge their way into the living room past shunted furniture and Linton Bostic's crash cymbal. "Hey," Jones called to the Bear, who stood in the center of the living room clothed only in his native fur and the saxophone hanging from his neck on a strap. There were no lights on in the room, and little direct sunlight, at that hour.

"Hey," said the Bear, and returned his attention to the band.

From what Jones could tell, the Bear was running them through the chord changes of some tune—it sounded familiar—and it was difficult because the chords were unusual, changed in odd places, and didn't add up to a normal chorus-structure of thirty-two bars or whatever. The Bear kept starting them up, then stopping them. The really stultifying thing, thought Jones, was that although the problems arose during the solo sections, every time something went wrong the Bear dragged the band back to the head and made them play the whole damn tune again. Jones was just on the verge of recognizing it.

"And I'd like it," the Bear said to the bassist, a guy Jones had met and spoken with in the city and liked, Garrett Church, "if you wouldn't play the seventh there, just before the turnaround, because it distracts from the melody line."

Church nodded, and made a pencil notation on his leadsheet.

"Also, Linton," the Bear droned on, "don't feel you have to fill up all the space. In fact, try filling up none of it and see how it sounds."

Bostic nodded from behind his hip little woodgrain drumset, fanning himself with his brushes. "Yeah it's such a beautiful melody," he said. "I didn't know Mingus could be so *tender*."

Hatwell snorted from his place at the piano. "Read all about it," he said. There was a fancy black electric keyboard thingamajig on a table near him, but he had his back to it. The upright piano's lid was open on top and the front panel had been taken off to expose its ribs and veins of gold.

"Excuse me," said Sybil and edged her way toward the dining room and the kitchen. Jones watched the rhythm section and the Bear turn their heads to follow her all the way, until she was gone.

"All right," said the Bear, "let's take it, not from the top but from the half-tempo section in the bridge. Linton, can you find something high and small to hit on two and four until we go back into the main tempo?"

"How 'bout back end of a brush on a cymbal bell? You have the record? What's Dannie Richmond use?"

"Finger cymbals. One," said the Bear slowly, then, "two," and Jones recognized the tune now: "Reincarnation of a Lovebird," a beautiful, sinuous, low-profile line that passed through degrees of light and shade and unexpected chords on its way to resolution, and Bostic was right, for a man best known for the amplitude of his furies Mingus could be almost unbelievably tender. The only thing was, the Bear kept *stopping* the band all the time again.

"Look, you guys," the Bear ground on, "you're just not swinging. Can't you play with this much restraint and still swing?"

No no no, thought Jones. You're taking it too far. This is too much talk, definitely *contra naturum*. You'll shut down the intuitive connection. But, against his expectations, the band nodded seriously, taking it in, still game, still ready to try.

The tune started up again.

See, this was what Jones had never been ever to relate to, all this sweatwork and repetition, these rooms and afternoons in which things had to be worked through atom by tedious atom before anything like beauty could be rendered or achieved. Look at them. I wanted to be like that but I could never relate to the drudgery enough. He remembered the clarinet—more difficult than the saxophone because the octaves didn't finger identically, though he'd worked out on the Bear's alto and eventually it came to much the same thing—and the idea of playing fluently in all twelve keys, well, the fingertangling physical transpositions on their own were enough to boggle your mind halfway to paralysis. Anything you tried to do, there was so much *machinery* to deal with. Was it that he wouldn't do the work, or did he really lack some essential substance?

Maybe now that he was older he'd have the patience to sit still long enough and work something out. Only now he had responsibilities, Sybil, a real job . . . Nothing ever fits.

Jones winced. Look at these guys. It had been the same with acting. There was that point at which things became too difficult to deal with. Something in you acted up and left you sightless. Love wasn't enough. Love had to find its way through the labyrinth of form, and Jones didn't have the muscle or the map. Well, half the musicians in the world didn't either, or lost it on the way. And the Bear had always said that the audience was the music's co-creator and that he, Jones, was an impeccable listener.

Well hey. A plate of cold potatoes.

Oh no. Was the Bear stopping the tune *again*? It seemed to Jones that the band was just starting to get into it.

"Now that we've gotten this far," said the Bear, pivoting to address his rhythm section, "I'd like to try out Mingus' concept of extended form, which means that during the solo sections we can hold any of the chords as long as we want, so we don't only have a forty-four-bar chorus to deal with but something larger and more flexible. The soloist can determine it, but it could also come from one of you when you're not soloing, why not?"

The band was nodding yes and looking serious, and Jones had the dread feeling that they'd been at this tune for hours already and might keep at it for a few hours more. He mainly wanted to hear some *music* and was thinking about extended form and asking himself what does that have to do with anything really? But they were going to keep at it, weren't they. They were.

"Also," said the Bear, "once we've got this stuff down, I want to put the intro together, all those Charlie Parker fragments, maybe not the ones Mingus used, but we're gonna have to play some unisons out of tempo."

The band nodded again. It was incredible. They were still with him.

"After this," said the Bear, "I thought we might do an odd tune. 'Tumblin' Along with the Tumblin' Tumbleweeds.' "

"Something Sonny left off of *Way Out West*?" Bostic asked.

"Sorta," said the Bear.

"Doesn't that have some funny minor changes in the chorus?" Hatwell asked from his place at the piano.

"I thought we'd do it with a two-beat feel and yeah, you have some kind of memory. There are these odd shifts into the minor."

Hatwell pointed to his head. "I've heard everything there is," he said. "Can we get back to the Mingus? Such a great tune. I can't get enough of it. Let's work."

Go figure, thought Jones.

They moved the drums and the keyboard amp out onto the porch when they broke so there would be enough room for everyone to spread out and talk before dinner. There were still no electric lights on in the living room, and outside the windows a bright pastel twilight, diffused as if by mist, an improbably French effect, spread itself through the air and the nodding tiers of the pines and other trees. The house seemed about to levitate, or perhaps deliquesce in light. The Bear opened the side door and a breeze blew through the rooms. Some bird nearby made a two-note call that tugged at the cords of memory, perky, plaintive, reminiscent of, what was it exactly?

The Bear returned to his seat near Hatwell at the dining table.

"Pretty well, pretty well," Hatwell told the Bear, resuming. "Think we need to play some more tomorrow?"

"If we feel like it," the bandleader said. "I think we've done pretty well. I think we've got most of it covered."

"Yeah," said Hatwell, "but you do know the extended-form thing didn't work, don't you."

"Yeah. We'll drop it. You want another beer? Split one with me?"

"Whatever's right."

"You go get it," the Bear suggested, and stretched his arms wide. The heavy wooden chair in which he sat creaked dangerously as he leaned into its semicircular back. "I'm just gonna sit here and lay waste to the furniture."

When Hatwell had gone into the kitchen—the Bear closed his eyes for a moment, then opened them and there he was—Jones took his place in the opposing seat. "Hey old buddy," said the Bear, and laid a heavy paw on the dining table. "So what do you think of the band?"

"Yeah, they're great," said Jones distractedly. "Listen, there're a few things I . . ." For Jones the atmosphere of all that heavy, detailed musical work lingered in the room and bothered him enough so that he left his intended sentence unfinished.

"I forgot to ask," said the Bear. "How's the corporation gig?"

"I'm getting to meet people there, a young, pretty hip bunch. They're okay and there's a lot of goof-off time."

"Around the water cooler, huh. Have you got any input, creatively speaking?"

"Time will tell," said Jones, and tried to look worldly.

"Er uh," said Bobby Hatwell, "I only brought two of these," and raised his sweating bottles of Corona by their necks.

"Keep one and give him the other," said the Bear. "I'll take something later."

Hatwell passed a bottle to Jones and perched on the edge of the dining table. "You know, if we do play tomorrow," he said, "I think you should open up and play your ass off for the guys."

"Otherwise they'll think the record was a fluke?" the Bear asked him.

Hatwell shrugged but obviously meant yes.

"Okay," said the Bear. "I'm easy."

"Did you listen to that cassette I sent you of the final mix of *Sensible Shoes*?" Jones asked the Bear.

"Actually I did."

"No kidding. What you think?"

Sybil Bailey came in from the kitchen and stood behind Jones' chair. After a moment's pause she rested her hands on Jones' shoulders and bent briefly to kiss him on top of his head, where the hair was thinning. When she was done the Bear grinned up at her and she grinned back.

"What a complicated dynamic," Bobby Hatwell muttered, and drifted off to join his rhythm buddies on the other side of the smokestack, where cries of welcome rose to meet him. Ra-*heem.*

"I thought," said the Bear, "it was a pretty good record, considering that my playing was fake. Yeah, as an example of pure self-impersonation it might even be some kind of a classic."

"You're nuts," Jones told him.

"Oh I'm way past nuts," said the Bear. "Tell me something new."

Now Iris came out of the kitchen bearing a stemmed glass of white wine; its sides ran with condensation; she herself was lightly beaded with honest sweat. The Bear watched her clock the grouping, then walk past Jones and Sybil to stand behind the Bear's chair and place her hands on his big shoulders. The Bear watched Sybil remove her hands from Jones' narrower hairless version. This was some exceptionally dumb game of chess, or maybe an alpha-wave contest or something. He had the usual impulse to blow up the set and start over, but in the interest of world peace he suppressed it.

"Well how about a movie," Jones said slyly.

"Love 'em," said the Bear. "We going out or renting?"

"As it happens, Megaton has its own film division, but through recently acquired connections," and here Jones tried looking archconspiratorial, "I got in touch with some of Spielberg's people and they're interested."

"In what," asked the Bear. "The hazards of improvisation without a net?"

"They're interested in a film about you."

The Bear tried not to take this seriously and partway succeeded. "How interesting." Now he wished he had that beer. "Tell me even larger lies."

"I mean even if you didn't want to participate in it yourself—"

"Consider that a given," the Bear suggested. "I'm not gonna play myself. I mean, do I ever?"

"—they can do wonders with animatronics."

"Really."

"Hey," said Bobby Hatwell, who had come around the chimneypiece, flanked by the potentially antic figure of Linton Bostic. "Pardon me—I couldn't help overhearing—who would you want to do your voice?"

"Lee Marvin."

"Hate to break it to you, Bear," said Hatwell. "Mr. Marvin, he dead."

"Okay," said the Bear. "Michelle Pfeiffer." He waited for the laugh and got it. "Lee Morgan, Lee Marvin. All those good Lees gone. It's hard to believe."

"Lee Marvin outswung Brando in *The Wild One*," Hatwell said.

"Yeah, but Brando had all this mystery," Bostic maintained.

"Fuck mystery," Hatwell told him. "Mystery, fuck."

They heard Garrett yawn in the living room.

Bobby Hatwell started to sing "I Was Born Under a Wandrin' Star" in Lee Marvin's voice but he couldn't get low enough.

"I've been sketching out a story proposal," Jones confided to the Bear. "Could be the beginning of a screenplay."

"No kidding? How's it begin?" the Bear asked him.

Sybil put her hands back on Jones' shoulders.

"*Do I know where hell is*," sang Hatwell-Marvin. "*Hell is in hello*."

"I thought maybe getting out of college and looking around for work . . ."

"College?" asked the Bear. "What college?"

"You know what school I went to," Jones told him. "So there I am, not cutting the job market, doing a little acting, and then there was the time I wanted to marry that belly dancer, remember her?"

"I see," said the Bear. "Spielberg's people got in touch with you about doing a Jones movie. First Indiana Jones, now you. They've been working up to it."

"Jeez," said Jones, "I'm getting to you, don't worry."

"*A wandrin', wandrin' star*," Hatwell and Bostic sang in rough unison, then retired to the living room before the shit hit the fan.

"Maybe," Iris suggested, "maybe Jones feels that he could use some of his story as a sort of bridge for the audience."

Jones snapped his fingers and pointed at Iris. "There you go. That's it. A link to common experience. Exactly. A bridge."

"How much bridge you think?" the Bear asked him. "Half an hour?"

"About."

"I can see the card game now," said the Bear. "The cards oversized, shooting across the table like planes of being."

"Too Scorsese," said Jones, frowning.

"Naw," said the Bear. "Steve might do it. He shoots for impact too."

"You think?"

The Bear looked up at Sybil Bailey, who was looking back at him inscrutably but with persistence and intent. "All right," he said, retrieving his intended vocal thunder from the brink, and went on quietly: "Try this. Jones, what the fuck has happened to you? Or were you always like this really?"

"Like what?" Jones asked him.

The Bear found it remarkable how Jones didn't even begin to see it. "You know, a shallow, self-promoting pile of nothing much, just waiting to break loose and rule the world. I mean, what have you done with your essential characteristics, man?"

"I'm trying to improve on them. I'm trying to fit in. I'm trying to help your case."

The Bear looked up at Sybil, then back and up at Iris, who was gripping his shoulders surprisingly hard. "Okay," he said. "I'll try to be kind about this," he began, and by the time he was done Jones had gone upstairs to the bathroom for shelter and Iris was pounding rhythmically on the top of the Bear's head with small hard fists. "What did I say?" he asked her. "What?"

Sybil flopped into the chair across from him, the one Jones had vacated in such a hurry. "I need a drink," she said.

"Did I goof?" the Bear asked her. "Or am I right and does our boy need a little flight correction? Because as far as I can tell he's heading for a crash."

"Fuck knows," Sybil said, and slumped in her chair. "I could swear I saw a bottle of Cutty around here somewhere."

In the upstairs bathroom, Jones found himself unable to pee. His nuts had shrunk into two hard pecans but he still had some beer in his bladder and therefore should have been able to leak something besides the remains of his human dignity. He gave his recently so triumphant member a shake and wondered how he was going to scrape by for the rest of the weekend walled up with the Bear. It was impossible. And, so the knife would not be deprived of its final twist, the Bear had insulted him in front of Sybil. Let's make sure the Jones boy doesn't get a life. Let's make sure he's deprived of everything, and that it is seen. Ah, here it comes. Sometimes, he thought, mere urination can provide as sweet a release as its second cousin the little death. He shut his eyes to savor the moment, such as it was.

And opened them. The male stance at the upstairs toilet overlooked some greenery at the back of the house, and while he was waiting for the last drops to be coaxed up and out he twiddled the stem of the windowblind to provide an optimally downslanted view of the yard—not much of a yard, since the hill began its upslope almost at once—and, wait a minute, a slight refocussing, a slight rejigging of the image and there it was, incredible, too fucking much: the Garden.

He was looking at the garden he had seen before final blackout in Washington Square, the green dappled wood in which he inhabited his real self outside of time in immortal self-contemplation. But this moment, now, was almost as mindblowing: not only did he exist outside of time, this present moment had in some sense preexisted, with himself in it. Ordained.

Intended. All its minutiae included. It was as if a veil had fallen and the real workings of the world had come clear. Teleology. Beneficence. Predestination. Good Lord.

Odd: he had quick flash-memories of certain childhood afternoons, the view from his bedroom window—nothing like the garden—his wars between flying ballpoint pens and his father's nail clipper, the tabletop battles between the foreign coins Dad brought back from business trips abroad—British pennies, French francs, Italian tin, and a heavy brown Mexican twenty-centavo piece that blew all other coins away. He still had the coins in a storage carton somewhere, inside a galvanized iron box he'd made in high school metal shop. Should he go to the warehouse and have a look at them? A thought struck him out of sequence: I wish I'd seen beautiful things from an early age. How can you reconcile your life's transcendent outline and its stupid, negligible contents? Is there a way out of here? He looked down at the garden, identical in eternity and time.

Jones raised his arms, palms offered up, and at least halfway expected to be taken once and for all out of time's illusion into what he really was. He breathed in, then out, raised his eyes and waited a long moment for the drama of his uplift.

Nothing doing, however.

Okay, so it wasn't that simple, but what he had to do, it came to him, was go back downstairs to the Bear and have some conclusive meeting with him, stand up for the real condition of things, tell him I'm not a doormat I'm a man.

Better wash and dry your hands first.

Which he did.

Nice tasseled handtowels. Obviously the Iris touch.

Checked his fly before descending. Jones was ready as he'd ever be.

There was no one downstairs, however. He heard the rhythm section's laughter, three old buddies, outside the front of the house, backglanced into the kitchen as he passed, no one there, and settled on the sliding doors at the far end of the dining room. The Bear was out there waiting for him, and the two women. Iris and Sybil were facing in different directions, looking up into the trees; they were smoking cigarettes, blowing grey smoke into the air, threads of purer blue rising from their cigarettes' ends. The twilight, although diminished, was still doing its magic stuff, and the breeze must have stilled for the moment.

"Let's you and me talk," said Jones, and took the Bear lightly by the arm. There was a path winding away from the house through the maples, or whatever. Behind them they heard anxious undertones pass between the women, a retracted footstep and Iris' voice saying, "Let them." From a branch somewhere up in the leaves a bird gave out with a neat rhythmic figure followed by a sprightly two-note call. Jones doubletaked in its approximate direction. "Wait a minute," he said. "Wasn't that?"

"Monk," the Bear said, nodding.

"What have you been doing up here with your fellow woodland creatures?"

"You wanted to talk."

"Right."

They came upon an oval widening of the prospect, and at the end of the clearing, on the left just before the path resumed, sat a large grey roughly bihemispheric stone about three feet high, lichen climbing it in a slow waveform. Star moss gleamed green about its base.

"Mind if I sit down?" asked Jones.

"Pull up a coffin," the Bear suggested.

Once Jones got his bottom settled on the rock, he told the Bear everything, finishing with how, with a hole punched in his belly, crawling exhausted to the rim of temporal existence while looking for his buddy, he had stumbled into the cool eternity of the garden—which now turned out, ha ha, cosmic sense of humor, to be the view out the Bear's upstairs toilet window. "But was the garden real?"

"It's a pretty well-known establishment," the Bear told him. "And what you experienced yourself to be, what the folklore calls your immortal soul, that's real."

"I don't need you to tell me that. My life down here is some kind of weird malfunctioning dream by comparison. But why was it the same as the view from upstairs?"

"Jones," the Bear said, "if you're gonna try to work out some concordance between that garden and the view from my bathroom window, you're going to get confused. Take it as given, unless you know specifically better. What's real is real."

"Are all gardens the Garden and we don't see it?" asked Jones. He couldn't help it, he expected some kind of ultimate significance to emerge from the moment. He'd say something, or the Bear would, the puzzle would snap into focus and they'd be whisked out of time into truth or at least working friendship. Why wasn't it happening? "We're there now and we don't see it?" he prompted.

"Sure," the Bear said. "But try not to get hung up on the particulars. That's where I think you might be making your mistake."

"Oh yeah?" said Jones, and the Bear could hear him tensing up.

"You saw your real individuation outside time, but even that's only a flickering picture, understand?"

"How could that be?"

The Bear considered using the G-word and decided against it. Even the First Intellect and the Objects of its Self-Knowledge might tense Jones up and start him projecting. "In my experience," said the Bear, qualifying things by his limitations but also feeling that he was bypassing the essential point, "you have to go beyond that selfhood too, or you'll just generate more illusion, get nowhere ultimately real."

"Oh yeah?" Jones said again. The Bear could hear him rising to a purely phantasmal challenge to his right to be.

"Aw Jones, stop trying to *be* someone so hard. Why are you so . . . It doesn't suit you, it's in such bad taste."

"Whereas you're impeccable."

"Obviously not," the Bear admitted.

"So where do you get off still trying to pull some kind of existential rank on me? Look, you may be too big for this world, but I need more of a self than I have so I can be out there and do the do—hold a job down, deal with the dealies, keep the woman happy, have a home."

"But you're pushing in the wrong direction. Listen," I'll try it, he thought, "there's really only one being in existence—"

"Yeah, and he's a talking bear who plays alto."

"That's not what I meant at all."

"That's what *you* think."

It went on awhile longer, but Jones got more and more defensive, and as far as the Bear was concerned the rest of their talk was pointless.

Well after dark and dinner the Bear lay abed, and when he had finished wondering whether Iris would tiptoe down again or not, he thought about how pained his talk with Jones had left him. It would be so nice, he thought, to be free of self-regard. But he hadn't managed it yet, had he? No, he had not.

But you reach a point where it's obvious that the self is nothing. You may still be stuck with the thing, but you can't revive it. You may have your pleasures—they may even, thank God and Iris, increase—but it's beyond your power to revive the self that has them. Jones has his points. The truth is I didn't behave like such a monster of egoism until my ego gave out. I'm probably fooling myself again.

Iris was back in the doorway. "Hello, sailor," she said.

He lifted the topsheet for her and she slid in but kept her cotton nightie on.

"So," Iris asked, "are you happy with the band?"

"They'll do. They're great. I have to impress them with some of my best playing tomorrow, Hatwell says."

"Can I listen?"

"Who could be more welcome?" He gave her a little kiss, and her lips responded lightly. "Actually, I miss Charlie and Billy sometimes. They have such depth. With these kids I have to do a lot of the heavy lifting."

"You're supposed to be the leader," Iris said.

"I'm not used to it. Maybe once we're on the road this summer, after a week or two . . . We'll see."

Iris pulled herself away for a moment to look at him.

"What?"

"That look on your face. Your eyes. This is how you are. All you really care about is the music."

"I care about you."

"Everything is fodder for your art. Me included."

"Aw, you just say that because you've got a fodder fixation."

Iris blinked at him as if he'd said something serious. "Is that what you think I'm doing here? Is that why you think I'm in this bed with you?"

"Wait a minute wait a minute. You're misreading things. That was pure wordplay." But was it? The Bear had thought so, but now, once questioned, he remembered a moment one night the week before, when he and Iris were riding the train of their passion a little more impatiently than usual to the wellknown destination, whereas usually the destination hardly mattered and the ride was all; he was going up and down into her, it was all so quick and easy, then he felt her hands fanning his back, and "Oooh, daddy," she had said. Daddy? the Bear wondered, and paused a moment at the top of his arc. Maybe he lacked a grasp of the vernacular, but it seemed to him, *pace* Freud, that the bed had gotten rather crowded. "It was just a joke, honey. Purest mindspin. Spume and foam. Seadrift. Froth. Fodder fixation. The merest pun." It seemed crucial to pull this off.

Iris seemed to relax. "How did you leave things with Jones?" she asked.

"We had a talk. We're okay."

"What did you talk about?"

"Horticulture. Really, we're cool."

"You do know that you were horrible to him again."

"We aired the subject between us, Eye. Really, it's all freshened up."

"You called him an unrequited narcissist."

"I said that?" The Bear rolled aside laughing, and the bed shook with it. "I said that? It's almost worth being horrible once or twice if you can say shit like that."

"It's still shit," Iris said.

"Aw c'mon, sweets. I had a chat with Sybil and she's worried about him too. He's getting a dangerously swelled head."

"I just had the image of his head expanding like a balloon and his feet leaving the ground."

"That's about the size of it. An airhead making the change to helium and getting into trouble on the transition. He wants to be someone so bad it's painful."

"I want to be someone too, remember? I want a self."

"I told you you can have mine. The main thing is he's offensive on the subject and you're not."

"You mean I sleep with you," Iris said.

"I've never wanted to sleep with Jones since I was a cub and the house was cold and I missed my mother. How can you even make the comparison?"

"You also asked him what he had done with his essential characteristics."

"Yeah, I remember that part."

"What have you done with yours, Bear? When really you're so tender . . ."

"Ssshh." He rolled to her. "Don't tell anyone."

"And, being tender, how can you talk like that to Jones or to anyone?"

"Jones is family. It's allowed."

"Am I family yet? Have I put in enough time yet? Will you be awful to me when I finally make the list?"

"Iris, what are you worried about? I love you so much."

"I know all that. Love love love. It isn't everything, you know."

"It's not?"

"It's what it is." She rose up to kiss him casually, but the moment changed and her mouth opened.

"What about the people in the house hearing us?" the Bear asked, once things started to develop.

Iris reached down, pulled her nightie up from its hem, masked her face in it momentarily, then tossed it out into the room. "Just don't get on top," she said.

"Whyever not?"

"Have you heard this bed when you're going up and down in it?"

"Never noticed."

Iris laughed, an uncharacteristic snort, thought the Bear.

"That I never noticed the noise is a tribute to you," he said. "It's loud?"

"It's catastrophic. This bed is going to fall to pieces one night. You don't know your own . . ."

"Strength?"

"Weight, I was going to say."

"But you know it."

"To my shame, I do," she said. "Tonight let me take the lead."

"Batter my heart, three-personed toots," he said, and rolled back laughing. "I'm yours."

She pushed him back onto the mattress and he let her take the initiative and lay back dropping heavy and easy into bliss.

Afterward he lay on his back watching her sailing off to sleep, and heard her voice even though her lips were as sealed as her eyes, and thought, here we go: their clairaudience act had been one-sided for too long, and she was beginning to come in clear.

He heard her think it, in her own distinct voice: I want them.

What? He almost sat bolt upright in bed.

I must have them, her unmistakable voice pronounced.

He looked at her. Her face was composed for sleep but she seemed to be concentrating on something.

I want *who*? I must have *what*?

The Bear's innards convulsed in what even he knew to be phantasmal jealousy. Who did she mean? The rhythm section? Jones? The entire male population within range? This is idiotic. She's already told me that getting into it with me has turned her on to the world in general, but let's not take it to extremes.

Hallucination of jealousy to one side, it was not so unfamiliar a sensation: he didn't understand her in every subtle aspect, did he. What went on in that cool subtle mind of hers really?

Maybe, big news, he didn't understand her very well at all.

Who was she?

Come right down to it and put his infatuation to one side, did he have a clue?

part five

Many is the caravanserai that must be departed
before the man may come home.

—Rumi

1

the Bear happened to be standing with his arm around Iris at their bedroom window when the powder-blue bus pulled into the drive and ground its way up the greystone gravel to the front of the house. The driver handled the bus neatly—hardly even tore up the gravel; Iris would only have to rake it once to get it flat—which boded well for general safety in the weeks ahead, thought the Bear. He heard the engine noise cease, then the hydraulic doors sigh open.

"I suppose I ought to go out there," he said. At the rear of the bus a last blue figment of exhaust swam up into the summer air.

"You'll have to go eventually." Iris tiptoed up to give him a wifely peck on his jowl, but he could hear the tension of his departure in her voice. As the tour had drawn near, some disquiet or other had risen in her but she wouldn't talk about it. Was she worried he'd get busted again? Shouldn't be. They'd talked that one through—as far as he was willing to share his thoughts on the matter—and had decided between them that the threat was ephemeral and the security setup adequate. What was upsetting her then? He'd tried to broach the subject a few times—over dinner, while taking a stroll uphill behind the house, and intercurled in postcoital warmth abed—but in each instance she had widened her bright eyes and shaken her head no.

"It'll only be a few weeks, kid," he told her now.

"I know."

"And I'll be all right out there." Actually the Bear had determined for himself that in the event of a bust he would not let himself be taken, even if it meant getting killed instead. Even, perhaps, if it meant killing someone else in order to get away. He wasn't going inside again, he was settled on that. If he died, he died, *è finita la commedia*.

"The driver's getting out," Iris said.

So he was. A beefy number with a long dirty-blond ponytail and Mafia shades masking his eyes had stepped off the bus into the hush and dazzle of the global-warming summer beneath the trees. He wore pressed black trousers and a clean white shirt with epaulettes, but he looked like a reformed biker and had a certain lawless vibe. Well, maybe that's good too, thought the Bear. We could use muscle if weirdness turns up.

"Come out there with me?" the Bear asked his favorite girl.

"If you don't mind, I'll wait here," she said politely.

The Bear's things waited for him in orderly formation in the screened-in shade of the porch: his sax case; a briefcase full of sheet music, road money, books, videos, and an anxious profusion of extra mouthpieces and reeds. A small matte-black suitcase and a garment bag completed the family grouping. The Bear hefted the assemblage in one go, stepped out into the country sun and started down the stairs to the bus. Prodigal son seeks readmission, accepts rubber nose and pointy hat.

I know I'm supposed to go out there and knock 'em dead across America, but I still feel more like a question mark than an exclamation point. What kind of statement can I make out of that? Puzzle the fuck out of the country and hustle back home with the cash? Must be what I live for. Iris.

"Hi," he said on his way down the steps.

"You must be the Bear." The driver looked up at him but made no move either to retreat before the approach of monstrosity or to help him with his gear.

"I try to get a break now and then but basically that's it."

"Tommy Talmo."

"Hiya."

Although introduced, the driver was still impassive and unmoving, so the Bear deposited his things at the base of the stepwell and took a little stroll around the veehickle. It had its lines but it was a pretty stubby bus, a light blue two-thirds-of-a-Greyhound with channelled aluminum side panels and a rounded rear end topped by a streamlined airconditioning vent. It was in pretty good nick, and the heavy-treaded tires looked solid enough—he gave one an exploratory kick and hurt his foot on it—and overall the bus possessed a certain retro charm. The speedlined aluminum streaks on its side reminded him of the bus that had deposited Cary Grant at Prairie Crossing so that Hitchcock's cropduster could shoot at him with its machine gun. The air-conditioning unit, unlike Hitchcock's as he remembered it, didn't eliminate the rear window, and no airplanes were in view; even so, his lesser, anxious self had begun to view the bus as the Capsule of Death. I really must learn to deal more gracefully with change. Look: it's a perfectly good bus and I like the band and we're headed west. Where was the trouble in that?

Phantoms of heat rose in waves from the engine box at the rear, making optical waves in the air.

Jones had let the Bear know that it was through his specific influence—he was still beavering away at self-aggrandizement despite the summer heat, it seemed—that the company had agreed to pick him up in faraway upstate New York. "I spoke up for you. Otherwise," Jones had told him on the phone, "you'd have to come down to the city and meet the bus here."

"I don't live in the Arctic," the Bear told him. "It's a two-hour drive."

"And two hours back," said Jones, an ambient recording of office sounds behind him, for all the Bear could tell.

"Oh my God," groaned the Bear. "I've imposed work on another living being. Call off the tour."

Jones' voice had leapt to sudden contralto: "You're not serious, are you?"

The Bear completed his circumambulation of the bus and again came face to face with the driver, insofar as the man's heavy black sunglasses permitted such an encounter.

"Hey," said the Bear.

"Hey."

Not much of a social exchange. The Bear picked most of his things up and carried them on board. The driver gathered the remainder and followed him up the ridged black rubber steps.

On the inside, things were economically disposed about the space, although for the moment some of the lesser fixtures and hideaways were inscrutable to the Bear. There was a smell of disinfectant. Synthetic panels and varnished pine, not too badly worn, achieved a certain balance throughout. Drawing on his experience of the movies, the Bear decided the bus looked like an airliner gone woodsy; he wished the powder blue of the exterior had been continued within. Behind the driver's plush eminence commanding the foreview were highbacked black leather pivot chairs, one either side of the aisle, and past them a pair of booths left and right; it looked as if their woodsy Formica tables could be lifted away and the space between the benches freed up for the meanderings of long-legged bait; a shelf nearby supported a TV/VCR combo; small speakers inset here and there indicated the presence of stereo.

The Bear walked his bags through this first third of the bus into the narrow middle section, where he noted, right, the inset sink, lowboy fridge, coffee machine and microwave oven in passing; he guessed the two flush pine doors, left concealed a toilet and, he hoped and as negotiated for, some bear-adequate form of shower. The sleeping bunks and storage bays were in the rear.

"Does the bus really sleep four?" the Bear asked Tommy Talmo. Turning, he laid a paw on one of the upper bunks. "I see there are four bunks, but they look kind of narrow to me."

"Sleeps four Lhasa apso-lutely," Tommy Talmo told him. "T. Lobsang Rampa," he added.

The Bear could only blink at this. "They still look narrow," he said.

"Yeah but there're only a couple of road nights on the itinerary and we'll be in pretty good motels most of the time."

"*I* won't be," the Bear reminded him. "I sleep here."

"Oh, yeah. Right. We'll work something out."

"Like what?"

Tommy Talmo shrugged. "Something," he said.

The Bear looked Tommy Talmo up and down, sleepy eyes now that the shades were off him, near–Duane Allman moustache, the ponytail, a big frame on him and that gut bellying the shirt over his beltline. The Bear understood that Talmo was part owner of the tour-bus company. In any event he was acting pretty cool about meeting up with his first talking bear; then too he had the half-snoozed, unflappable look of the lightly stoned. Which, if true, was an issue. Because of his own shaky situation vis-à-vis the law, the Bear had stipulated an absolute ban on controlled substances on the bus for the duration.

"Look, I do this all the time—"

"Tour with bears?"

"—and we always work something out," Talmo said. "You ready to go? We have to get in and out of the city before rush hour. Your stuff's on board. We ready?" False toothy grin the Bear didn't especially like.

"I have something to do inside the house." He and Iris had said several goodbyes already but he hadn't heard the cadence he had hoped for in their parting, a solid harmonic resolution that indicated further development ahead, recapitulation, maybe another movement—a set of variations perhaps, or a fugue. He liked fugues.

"Let's do it," Talmo said, and walked back up the aisle.

It was a hot day but even so it was good to be outdoors again, beneath what had become his home trees. He didn't want to leave them, no. As he reached the steps he looked back to find Talmo preparing to piss against a tree. This wouldn't do, but you had to grant the man a sense of atavistic nuance all the same.

The Bear turned on his heel and walked up to the man, bristling, and looked him in the face. Talmo blinked. "You know what a bear does to you when you try that on his territory?" His voice, speaking of atavism, was shaking with suppressed fury, and for a moment he really did want to kill the guy.

"No. What?"

A storm of hormones and power surges was working its way through the Bear. "Usually you die quick," he said simply.

"No shit?" Talmo put it back in his pants and zipped up. "C'n I use the can in the house?"

"No. You can use the facilities on the bus and make sure they work so I can use them later."

"Okay," Talmo said.

The Bear stood there. I know it's petty and I should let it ride, he told his nervous system. On the other paw I could pound him into the ground like a fencepost and see how that affects my position in the industry. That would be one way out of it. He had a moment's discourse with himself: Do I kill him or do the tour?

He knew it all along: he'd do the tour. "See you in a minute," he said, and made sure that Talmo was headed back to the bus before he turned toward the house again.

To save time he took the steps on all fours, but stood up on his hindlegs when he reached the top and walked upright across the porch. "Honey?" he called—although he knew Iris didn't like him calling her honey: she didn't like the analogy—and poised on one foot, he inclined his upper body through the living room doorway. "Hon?"

No response. Then the Bear must go to Iris. He found her sitting on the big bed's edge, her hands composed upon her lap.

"One more big sloppy kiss," he said from the doorway. "Is that too much for a roving bear to ask?"

In view of her recent general attempt at self-composure, he had expected the politesse of a formal farewell at best, but what his lighthearted question from the doorway provoked from Iris was a terribly ardent look in which sex was not very prominent, from which she launched herself to fling her arms about his chest as powerfully as she could manage. She thrust her face into the depths.

"Hey," said the Bear, returning the hug but finding her gesture surprisingly operatic, "it's only a few weeks, and I'll come back to you rich as a merchant prince and his two kid brothers." Iris pulled back far enough for him to see her face: so intense: what was going on in there? "You worried about a bust? It's not gonna happen."

"It's not that." Her crystalline features seemed rounded and transformed by depths of feeling the Bear hadn't expected to rise to the surface of the waves today.

"Wow, you love me," he said, amazed.

"Of course I do," she said, and shook her small head clear. "Have a great tour, Bear. Goodbye." The words, spoken in her usual lilting tone, didn't seem to go with the convulsiveness of her hug, but that kind of fragmentation was typical of her sometimes.

"What is it really?" he asked.

She shook her head rapidly no, seemed to suppress the big emotion and change the subject to something factual that enabled her to recompose: "I have to ask you: are you planning to have other women out there?"

"Is that what's bothering you? The idea has no appeal to me. I am completely satisfied in you—satisfied? I'm in bliss—besides which I am the most faithful furcovered soul in the God-wide, breathing world. What can you possibly be thinking?"

Iris hugged him with that strange intensity again, then they kissed, and Iris hauled herself up onto him and embraced him around his hips with her legs. The Bear thought: a quick trembly one standing up? but felt no, that's not what's called for. It'd seem sordid. The moment was about emotion even if he didn't understand what the referent was.

"You should go," she said, and relaxed her legs around him but did not descend to the solidity of the floorboards.

"I know," he said. "Okay. I'll miss you terribly, but I'm gone."

She let go of him, dropped and stood back.

"Walk to the bus with me?"

"I'll stay here."

"That's it, then." She nodded yes. He paused at the bedroom door. "Do you have enough house money?"

Iris nodded again.

"Remember to feed the doves," he reminded her. The timid pair he'd started feeding in late spring were showing up with their offspring—incompletely fledged, white stalks sticking out of their partly completed heads and backs—so there were five regulars now, and a second pair had begun scouting the area, occasionally coming down on shrieking wings for a peck.

"I said I would," Iris said. "I'll feed them. Don't you trust me?"

"Another pair has started showing up sometimes. Probably they'll become regulars," he said. "I love the doves."

"I know you do. I'll look after them."

"And the swallows."

"My eye is on the swallow," she said.

The Bear nodded. "I have to leave sometime. This is it."

And he managed it.

The stairs, a last inhalation of home woods, his patch of earth and sky.

Inside the bus the airconditioning was kicking in, the doors whirred hydraulically shut, the muted engine wound higher. Tommy Talmo punched the machinery into gear and let out the clutch. The Bear saw Iris in the bedroom window as the bus began to move, her hand raised in farewell from the only house in the world that had ever been his own. Is this really my life? Is it possible I can come back to this?

The bus pulled onto the asphalt, took a hard right downhill, and before the Bear knew it the house was out of sight.

The Bear waited until Tommy Talmo was finished swaying through the curves of the countryside, then used the stability of the Thruway to dispose his things about the bus, his few clothes and such in the back and his briefcase handy where he sat. As to that, he tried the banquettes, then settled on one of the highback swivel chairs. It accommodated him pretty well. He had also noted that the toilet was wide enough to do the same and that yes, gratias Deo, the shower would do.

Now he felt the wrench of leaving her. They'd been together almost continuously for the past months, apart for perhaps three hours the longest stretch. It was completely different from anything he'd known, and he'd begun to get used to it.

Iris. It was still incredible.

The bus whooshed its way down the Thruway to the city, almost as smooth as life had been over the past months, from the gathering muscles of spring and the long slow lope of summer: smooth as the practiced motion of their bodies had become, smooth as the ease of talk between them and their mixed lives, only . . . only it was hard not to feel that the deepest resonances had been stripped from the harmony of their discourse, and as if from the poem of their sexual motion the subtlest sinews of their coordination had been taken out of action so that, so that what exactly? It was as if, perhaps, their most precious treasure had been taken from them atom by atom without their notice and only the mere effect of its glows and glitters had immaterially remained . . . well, something like that. It had been as if they hadn't been paying sufficient attention to the value of what passed between them, or had settled for something less without knowing how.

Their quality of life, as long as you weren't paying strict, or perhaps overscrupulous attention—who knew?—had seemed extraordinarily fine: the ease of conversation in the morning, at table, in passing, whatever, and the practiced wonders of the bed. What had ever been as good as this? Probably he was some overfinicky fuckhead to trouble himself over the imperfections of such sumptuous congress. Did he have a problem with continuous sweetness? If so, then whythefuck? That's what he wanted to know.

Whatever the judgment, his sexual life with Iris left him in a different relation with life in general, more deeply implicated in its workings, more in touch with its flow and, who knows, its teleology too. He was deeper in. He was in it. It was living him. So?

Maybe all that bothered him was that they weren't talking. Or, they were talking, but not about anything of consequence. They talked about the daily round—an exotic subject to the Bear, whose relationship with everyday life had always been tenuous at best, and so he delighted in it—about their food, the wine, their books or the weather; and since what the Bear had most deeply to say to Iris generally summed itself up as some variant of I love you I love you I love you, the cheerful trivia of their daily prose possessed a strange elegance for him: how graceful to only allude to the overwhelming fact of what had them in its paws. Only gradually did he notice that they weren't saying very much, and that the territory of their real intimacy had been ceded almost exclusively to a coalition of silence and the pleasures of the bed, which sometimes they transferred to tables or the living-room floor for the sake of a variety they had not needed earlier.

But maybe this was the normal what-the-fuck motion of life. What did he know about the normal motion of anything? This was life, wasn't it? Hadn't he always wanted one?

Tommy Talmo got into an argument with the tollbooth guy at Harriman about the length of the bus, the number of wheels and how much money was owed, but they got it settled short of fisticuffs and the bus plummeted south toward the grey-brown fug of exhalations that overhung the beating, panting city.

The rhythm section had foregathered at Linton Bostic's place on the Upper West Side, which they had judged most convenient to the highway system, besides which Linton said he wasn't gonna haul his drumset halfway 'cross town when they could pick him up at home and Garrett could get his bass there by car service down from the edge of Harlem so there.

It was only an hour later than it was supposed to be when the band muscled itself onboard in a bluster of black luggage. Bostic was first on deck. He did a quick survey. "Old bus. Did the last refit 'bout two years back," he said. "Starting to run down but I seen worse. Whassup, B?"

"I don't know yet," said the Bear, seated in the black leather swingchair just inside the door. "I was hoping you guys could tell me."

"Road virgin," Bostic laughed.

"Not entirely."

"Got to check the rest of this water hazard out," Bostic said. He dumped one of his bags under a wingtable and took strides toward the back of the bus. The Bear heard Bostic's drumcases sliding into the luggage bay beneath him, and he looked out the window to see Tommy Talmo's bent back beneath the upturned edge of aluminum door, the bottom of his shirt bulging. Garrett stood behind Talmo holding his bass in a large white molded hard case; he was saying something to Talmo's back.

Rahim Bobby Hatwell climbed on board and looked around.

"What do you think," the Bear asked him.

"Free chicken and beer," Hatwell said. "Though I'll tell you, we still have time to rent a trailer and hitch the Sled on behind so we'll have a ride when this piece of shit breaks down. Where'd you find the driver, ape house at the zoo? You seen the list of towns we're going to? You ever see a tour booked like this? You sure you wanta do this thing? How long did it take you to develop an embouchure? How'd you get that much articulation in your paws? What's your favorite Monk tune? Did Trane or Sonny win on 'Tenor Madness' or was it a draw? You doped out the unified field theory? What is this thing called love?" Hatwell coughed into his right hand. "How you doin'? You look kind of tense."

The Bear shrugged.

Hatwell rocked on his heels and came briefly up onto his toes. "Don't go batshit on us, Bear. That's my job and I'll fight you for it if I have to. Oo-bop sh-bam da *Fledermaus*." Hatwell raised his voice to a shout: "Hear ye, motherfuckers. I'm filling the fridge with frozen Jamaican meat patties. Anybody takes one he dies."

"Yeah, eventually," Bostic said as he came out of the rear of the bus. "I guessed right and you guessed wrong," he told Hatwell, smiling happily. "Storage space upstairs is for shit and you're stuck with your bulky soft-sided they-came-to-Cordura crap and I'm slick with Samsonite."

The pianist and the drummer got into a highly technical luggage discussion, much of it turning on the advantage of being able to pack your shit in halves that folded flat. The Bear didn't track all the detail. He did know that the band was to wear suits, however loosely defined, onstage; initially he was supposed to wear a suit himself. Iris had had a tailor she had met in town come up to the house to fit him out with a set of double-breasted items in grey pinstripe and summerweight blue serge, but once she'd seen the cloth laid out on him and the paperwork patterns set forth she'd looked aghast. You'll look like a medieval fortress, she said. Actually, more like a brick . . . you know. That had been the end of it, and the tailor went home with a hundred for his trouble. Then Iris had gone to a Big & Tall shop in one of the malls across the river and come back with the best raincoat he'd ever owned—a hip modified charcoal trench that actually looked sleek on him despite the usual ornate flap-and-belt aspect of the thing—and two jumpsuits—one dull gold, the other black, both showing a lot of zippers. He was big, though not tall for his breadth, and she'd had to do some alterations. The Bear learned a new word when she was working on the seams around his crotch.

Which side do you dress on? she'd asked him.

Which side do I what?

After a few repetitions of this exchange she'd rolled her eyes and finally asked him, Where do you put it?

Oh, left, he told her, laughing and feeling pretty cool, not making the obvious lewd joke about where he really liked to put it, and he let her move it and pin the seam.

The clothes looked fine, and the week before departure Iris had gone back to the Big & Tall store and bought him the same trenchcoat in tan and two new hats, wide-brim things, one black one brown, with countrypolitan silver-studded hatbands, that looked better on him than any hats he had ever owned. Iris knew him, and had infallibly fine taste.

It was true he'd gained some weight in the past months—a consequence, he was sure, more of life with Iris than the amount of food he was scarfing down: a sign that his space in the world had expanded since spring. More room had been made for him to live in it. It was her.

He looked out the window. Garrett was shaking his head no to Tommy Talmo and keeping a grip on his bass case, and back by the storefronts a youngish couple were staring up at the Bear. The Bear made a toothy grin and nodded hello. The couple nodded back on a reflex basis, then looked at each other for a reality check. I'm not your problem, thought the Bear. I'm my problem. What also occurred to the Bear: it's a grey stone world out there, different from upstate. How did I ever live here for so many years? Such a limitation of scents: so few of them, and those few without much interest. For another there's no shading in the colors, jumble in place of detail and almost no nuance.

The couple weren't going away. He waved again.

"I know the unit," Hatwell was saying, and the Bear returned his attention onboard. "Screen's small but the rez is good." He had switched the television on and was waiting, more or less in the pose of Aristotle contemplating the bust of Homer in the Rembrandt painting, for the picture to appear. "I brought some videos," he said.

"Good."

The picture beamed on beneath Hatwell's hand: one of those sick afternoon talk shows full of dysfunctional families, sexually rampant or omnidirectionally abused, UFO-abducted, women who live with talking bears, that kind of thing. "Cool, it's Rolonda," Hatwell said.

The Bear looked at the screen, where a bunch of people were yelling at each other and the network was beeping much of it out; Hatwell was laughing at it in a good-natured way.

"Could you turn that off?" the Bear asked him.

"What for? We ain't going nowhere for a few minutes."

"It's too much of a learning experience."

"We're just starting out," Hatwell told him. "This is nothing. Wait a hundred miles and we'll be ready to kill each other."

"I see."

Hatwell turned the TV off with a minor ironic flourish. "What the fuck is keeping Church?"

"I think it's about where to store his bass," said the Bear.

"Why did I even ask?" said Hatwell. "I'll handle this." He adjusted his invisible gunbelt and stomped down outside.

Bostic dropped his long form into the pivot chair across from the Bear. "Instead of doing the tour," he said, "let's hide out."

"Makes sense," the Bear told him.

"When drummers rule the world," Bostic began to say, but fell into a silence with his mouth partly open, and after awhile the Bear stopped waiting for him to finish.

A flash of light caught his eye: the couple outside had pulled an instant camera from a pocket or a purse; the guy had it now, and raised it to his eye. You won't get much of a picture through the windowglass, he could have told them. You'll mostly get the glare of your own regard, and is there not a lesson for us all in this?

The flashbulb went off notwithstanding.

Bobby Hatwell had involved himself in a highly gestural threeway with Tommy Talmo and Garrett Church.

Another flash, and when the Bear's eyes cleared Garrett was bending to pull a bundled softcase from the belly of the bus. While Hatwell unfolded it and held it up to receive the instrument, Garrett cranked his hardcase open and uncovered his bass. Look at the beauty of the wood, thought the Bear, the craft, the patience, the love that went into its making.

"We gonna be here forever," Bostic told the air.

But in fact they were not. The hardcase was slid empty into the luggage bay, the padded, softcased bass went to bed in one of the bunks at the rear of the bus, everyone climbed aboard, and the engine ground back to life.

When the bus lurched into motion, the Bear had a sense of being launched, but into what? The world streamed past in a clutter of commerce and stacked residential prospect. The bus swung toward the river, its air and light.

"Yo, Rondo!"

The rhythm section had taken to calling the driver Rondo Hatton because, they told him, he was taking them Round Manhattan, but actually, as Hatwell whispered to the Bear, because they thought his jaw sufficiently prognathous and his nose enough of a slab for him to resemble the grotesque actor who had once played the Creeper, among other roles, in movies of the thirties and forties. The Bear didn't see the resemblance, but what the hell.

"Rondo, pass us the itinerary. You got it, right?"

A folder was duly handed back as the bus, declining a plunge into the Hudson, orange flame under afternoon sun, hooked right onto the highway and pointed its nose north.

"Looka this." Linton Bostic had commandeered the itinerary folder and was flipping through its sheets. "Amazing. We get to miss every major town out there. What idiot put this tour together?"

"This one," said the Bear. Although Jones had done the actual bookings.

"Monongahela stead of Pittsburgh? Waukesha stead of Milwaukee and we don't even touch Chicago? I understand the coupla college towns, but the rest of it don't make sense."

"How about the last time I played a gig they shot at me and I spent a winter in the slammer? I'm being cautious. This is the only way I can do it. We've worked it out in detail," he said as the bus brought the arches and girders of the George Washington Bridge nearer through granulations of haze. He had his band's attention, everyone angling toward him in varying acuities of interest, Linton the most eager, Garrett the most laid-back.

"Speech," Bobby Hatwell suggested.

"*Sensible Shoes* is coming out more or less as we speak," the Bear began.

"Yeah I saw some ads in the paper," Bostic said.

"And Megaton's supposed to do a bunch of publicity nationwide," the Bear continued.

"I always said," Hatwell put in, "that if more furbearing higher mammals played jazz we'd see some respect around here."

"So," the Bear persisted, beginning to get a fix on what this tour was going to be like day-to-day, "every area we're playing they put out specific publicity for the album—"

"But we're billed as the Ted Beastly Quartet," Garrett said.

"—and the day before each gig," the Bear pressed on, "Jones calls the local jazz radio station and tips them that the Ted Beastly Quartet is us and we are them. There's also supposed to be some kind of clue in the ads but I don't know what it is. So the idea is—"

"We get what the idea is," Hatwell said, "but these places we're playing, I don't think they're on the big huge side, so I don't see how we're gonna earn our keep. This fabulous bus," he said dryly, "all those Comfort Inns, those nice checks we got in the mail last week, the per diems you're supposed to give us along the way . . ."

"Yeah, those were nice checks," said Bostic. "We don't make that kind of money in New York much."

"I've got some cash for per diems with me," said the Bear, "and the rest of it's supposed to come out of the nightclub money—"

"You don't get it, Bear," Hatwell said.

"No, see," the Bear tried to tell him, "what isn't completely covered by the nightclub fees—and in each case, on top of a flat rate we're getting a percentage of the bar—"

"As counted by who exactly?" Bostic wanted to know.

"Yo," came a voice from the driver's seat, "I can do that."

"Rondo!"

"Ron-*do*!"

"Cause if I don't do it," Rondo-Talmo's voice said wearily, "I can see where this whole thing's goin'."

"Into the shitcan," Bostic said.

"T. Lobsang Rampa," Rondo said.

"Tee what?"

The Bear got the orchestra to pause with a broad gesture of paw. "What is it I'm not getting," he asked.

Hatwell leaned toward him. "Where does the rest of the money come from," he asked the Bear with the air of one speaking to a dim, resistant child, "if the nightclub receipts don't cover it?"

"From the revenues of the record," the Bear said, extending both paws, claws held inoffensive, leathery palms up.

The three members of the rhythm section looked at each other, then back at him. Tommy Talmo Rondo Hatton began to whistle "Dixie."

"What," said the Bear.

"The money comes from the revenues of the record," Hatwell ground on, "which there aren't any yet because it hasn't come out, and before there are any they get to deduct your advance and what they paid Billy, Charlie and me, also various other operational costs they'll make up as they go along, also the salaries and per diems the three of us are pulling down on the tour, also the nickel-down-for-every-sparrow-the-bus-hits-during-the-tour charge . . ."

"The fried-chicken charge," Bostic said.

"The chord-change tax," this from Hatwell.

"The thirty-two-bar-chorus toll."

"We don't play too many of those," the Bear said hopefully.

"Speeding tickets."

"Uptempo fines."

"Modulation fees."

"Blues deductions."

"Lyricism surcharges."

"Mode loads."

"Clinker penalties."

"Uhh . . . wait a minute," said Bostic. "I'm working on one . . . shit."

"You getting a flat salary on the tour?" Something Garrett wanted to know.

"Not exactly," said the Bear. "See, what I get—"

"You been turned over to Creative Accounting," Bostic told him. "What you get is fucked."

"We gotta protect this guy," Rahim Bobby Hatwell announced. "We got to take this boy in hand."

"We coming in kind of late," Bostic said. "How we supposa do it?"

"STEAL!" Talmo Hatton shouted aloft. "They left us an opening wit' this percentage-of-the-bar bullshit. Put me on the bar and give me room to operate, this could be the winningest tour you ever seen. A little move on the register when no one's lookin' and hey fuckin presto. Put me on the door and the club only gets to see the littlest bitty piece of the action." The bus began weaving from lane to lane, cutting off innocent commuters in sedans. Rondo seemed to be unbuttoning the front of his shirt. "Theft! I knew I was gonna come in handy."

"But Jones told me everything was cool," the Bear told Hatwell as the bus swung onto the approach ramp to the G.W. Bridge.

"And who does Jones work for?" Bostic asked him.

"Maybe," Hatwell said, "we should change the subject."

"Yeah," said Bostic, pivoting toward the Bear. "Read any good books lately?"

"Lookit this little asshole," Talmo Rondo shouted amid a sigh of airbrakes.

"I oughta crush his fuckin' car for him. Somebody get me a beer outa the fridge."

The bus swayed its way along a high stone wall and an overhang of trees, then ascended a seasick curve leading to the bridge.

The Bear washed his face with a dry right paw. "Is this what's really happening? Is this the straight shit on the deal?"

"We changed the subject," Bostic reminded him. "And we gonna look out for you. We gonna cover your ass."

"Garrett?" the Bear asked the bassist, looking for a lifeline, a straight line, a hint of objective hope.

"So far this is exactly like every tour I've ever been on," Garrett said. "It's a mess and you're in trouble. Tradition supports you. Don't fight it." He got up from his seat. "Rondo, where's the stereo?"

"Right-hand cabinet over the microwave. Who's gonna get me that beer? There some people I know in Detroit could set us up to do a bank. We got a day off after Ann Arbor. We could do us a bank, get our money squared away and set our minds at rest."

"A bank?" the Bear asked weakly.

"How the fuck you think I bought into the music business, got me a piece of the bus comp'ny, production outfit and the little jingle studio which let me tell you may look like shit but is one fucking moneymaker? See, Tony 'n' Don are my old good buddies but I still had to come up with a share legitimate if I wanted into the partnership. Only fair."

"Banks?" Garrett asked him from the stereo cabinet. "Isn't a little discreet drug dealing more conventional?"

"I go for the direct approach," Rondo said. The bus swung up into daylight and soared out over the river. "Stick 'em up. Hand over the cash. Nice tits. Nobody move."

"You think we could get away with a bank?" Hatwell asked the driver.

"You kidding?" Rondo asked him. "Easy."

I'm just a simple musician, the Bear wanted to say. I want to carry a tune in this complicated world, but even he couldn't buy the poignancy of the statement. Not in the middle of this racket.

"How much you clear your typical bank job?" Hatwell asked.

"Depends," the driver said.

"This is gonna be a great tour," Bostic told the Bear, leaning confidentially toward him across the aisle. "I was worried at first, but now it's shaping up pretty good. I was afraid it was gonna be boring but we're doing fine. Yoo hoo. Bear. You with us? Call your office."

"Yeah. Sure. Definitely. What?"

Garrett got the FM on and diddled the dial down to KCR, everyone's favorite station. "Now, as it happens," a man's pleasant voice was saying on the radio, "Monk's band had lunch between takes two and three of 'Bye-Ya.' That's right, on this particular record date, between takes two and three of 'Bye-Ya' Thelonious Monk's band sat down to lunch, and I invite you listeners out there to discern such difference as you can between takes two and three, because Thelonious Monk's great band sent out for sandwiches and had lunch right there in the studio, between takes two and three. Of 'Bye-Ya.' That's right, we're listening to the music of Thelonious Monk today. Today we're listening to the music of Thelonious Monk. It's our little tribute. To Thelonious Monk, to whose music we are listening today. And now we'll listen to takes two and three of Monk's tune 'Bye-Ya,' take two being what we might call the 'hungry' take, and we'll go on to the next take without a break, but we'll try to remember that the band took their own break, for lunch, between takes two and three of that particular tune, 'Bye-Ya,' on that particular day. Now I don't know what deli they ordered their sandwiches from, although they were within range of both the Carnegie Deli and Max Asnas' Stage Delicatessen, or what kind of sandwiches they had, though I've heard from several sources that Monk himself was partial to corned beef—"

"I love this guy," Hatwell said.

"We all love this guy but we need some music," Bostic insisted, "and he got at least another five minutes to go before we hear any. See what's on BGO."

"And bring me my beer," the driver said.

"—whereas Charlie Rouse, well actually I don't know what Charlie Rouse went for in the way of sandwiches, but he probably had something substantial to eat, with maybe some potato salad on the side, so when we listen to take three of the tune we might try to imagine what—"

Garrett twirled the knob and found the Jersey jazz station and within a bar and a half everyone's head came up. "That sounds good," Hatwell said. "That a tenor or an alto?"

"Alto," said the Bear. "I should know who that is but I don't."

"'But Not for Me' in Coltrane's reharmonization," Garrett said of the tune, correctly.

"He's good," said the Bear. "I hope he's not some kid the same age as you guys 'cause if he knows that much at twentysomething he scares the shit out of me."

"I know who it is," said Bostic, smiling smugly, "because I got the record."

"Who?" asked the Bear.

"*Uh*-uh." Bostic shook his elegant African head. "Sweat it out. Blindfold test."

The Bear lowered his head and listened. Plays better than I do, he thought. Listen to him work his way through the changes. A relaxed way with alternate chords and scales. Swings. Nice rhythm section sounds like some old hands. Who the fuck is it? Not Frank Morgan. Plays almost as well as Jackie, though not as distinctive a presence. . . . Damn, but he can play. I shouldn't be out here. I shouldn't be on a bus heading into America. What business do I have blowing on a horn in public again?

"It's not Kenny Garrett," Hatwell said.

"It's not Kenny Garrett," Bostic confirmed.

That's a relief, thought the Bear, and raised his head in time to catch a spectacular aerial view of the Hudson River, the Palisades, a downpour of light upon what once must have been a spectacular piece of wilderness, and then the bus was negotiating its way through a maze of lanes branching in all conceivable directions—Route 4, Route 17, Fort Lee, Palisades Pkwy, NJ Tpk, Springsteen Expwy, whatever. The Bear surrendered control to Rondo Talmo, who seemed to know the way to whatever unexpected doom the world was cooking up.

"Hold the beer till we're past this shit," Rondo said—and this was encouraging—as he slipped his mafia sunglasses on and primped himself erect on the elevation of his seat, then relapsed back into kidney-fat and cushions.

The Bear watched the bottom of Rondo's shirt rebulge and thought, Damn, that altoist can play. "Rhythm section's good too," he said aloud.

"You don't get off that easy," Bostic told him.

"He doesn't have that Ornettish burr in his tone anymore," said the Bear, "but . . . is it Gary Bartz?"

"Bingo," the drummer told him. "You win the dinette set and the lifetime supply of dog food. Gary Bartz. Read it and weep."

"I always liked Gary Bartz," said the Bear, "but he didn't play like this before. Where's he been the last few years?"

"I'd say he's been putting in some serious time in the shed," said Bostic.

"Where's my horn?" the Bear wondered.

"Where you put it," Bostic said. "Yeah you better start worrying about the real shit. See, the money's always fucked, the business always got you by the balls. That's the law. Don't waste your energy on it. Get to work on your horn. Where you're sure to lose too but the time passes better."

"Bostic the Gnostic," Hatwell nodded.

"Let me hear the rest of the tune," said the Bear.

Fuckin' hell, he thought as he listened. Gary Bartz. I could have gotten by without hearing alto playing this good just now. Fluent. In command. Comprehensive. Relaxed. Well, he'd always liked Gary Bartz but at the moment he kind of wished Gary Bartz had stayed out there in the commercial wasteland making repeated attempts at some pseudofunk radio hit except Wynton hit and jazz was hip again and Bartz was back for real and better. I'm trying to get a tour going and I can't deal with this information at the moment.

Deeper down, the Bear envisioned himself spending a lot of his coming roadtime in the back of the bus, huddled over the bright curve of his horn, working everything he knew to death trying to squeeze some music out. He'd better. And he'd better have luck.

The tune ended after about five more minutes. "That was Gary Bartz," the radio said in a deep cool radio voice, "and now a word from the absolute masters of the budget oil change, the folks at Blink-a-Lube, that's right just shut your eyes and the next thing you know your vehicle is running smooth and sweet as the day it was born because at Blink-a-Lube we understand—" Garrett was waiting, and the dial whirled back to KCR to tell them, "So when you hear take three, see if you can detect any change from the second take, after which Thelonious Monk's quartet paused for lunch in the studio, ordering sandwiches from the local deli, before proceeding to the third take of 'Bye-Ya,' even though the very first take they did that day turned out to be the keeper. But what we'll hear now are the second and third takes, respectively, between which, that's right, the band paused for a taste of lunch, and since we're listening to Thelonious Monk's music today, exclusively, I thought we might take a closer look at . . ."

The bus ran on an even keel now, having completed its choice of road on the multifarious earth, and settled into a steady groove west. "I think I could deal with that beer now," said the voice behind the wheel.

"Rondo!" came Garrett's voice from the rear.

"Scherzo!"

"Allegro!"

"Harpo!"

"You drive like God on acid," Garrett's voice resumed, "but your taste in beer is, can I say this? Your taste in beer is for shit."

"Bring me the fuckin' can."

"Bring Rondo the fuckin' can."

"Bring Rondo the fuckin' can," two knocks on a wingtable, "and two hard-boiled eggs."

"Okay, here they are then, takes two and three of 'Bye-Ya,' as played by the Thelonious Monk quartet, separated by a lunch break—the takes, that is, and not the band, which I presume ate their lunch together, although knowing Monk it's possible he might've taken his sandwich and enjoyed it in a corner . . ."

Garrett came past, bringing Rondo the fuckin' can—"Green death," he told the Bear, who wondered what he meant—then resumed his seat.

Linton was thumbing back the pages of the itinerary printout: "Holiday, Holiday, Quality—I like Quality cause the rooms are new and the bathtubs are fiberglass and kinda soft so if you happen to meet a mermaid at the gig and take her home it's easy on her hips—McIntosh, Scottish Inn—meaning cheap, you dig?—Red Roof, Holiday, Shylock's, Ramada . . . I've seen worse. Heyy," he said, looking up at the Bear and a slow smile spreading across his face. "Hey Bear, you can't stay at the same ho-tels as us, can you? Guys, hey guys, the Bear can't stay at the same ho-tels as us. He got to stay at some hotel for bears exclusively. You think that's fair?"

"Maybe," Hatwell piped up, "we could put together some kind of a protest. At the ho-tel."

"Or stop off, pick up a case of Nair, wipe him down and maybe he can pass." Linton folded up his long body in the seat, cackling.

"Or electrolysis," Hatwell suggested. "Less greasy mess. Just stick a wire up his ass and plug him into a wall socket. All you need's a broom after. You know how to use a broom, doncha Garrett?"

"Hey," said Linton, "what color is he under all that fur anyway? Peel a dawg back he *white*."

Garrett looked up from his book of crossword puzzles. "What does the chief of the Nez Perce Indians wear?"

"A perce-nez," said Hatwell. "Next."

"Peel a dawg back," Linton was persisting, "he this funny sickly kind of *white*. We Nair the Bear or fry him with a wire we got to finish him up with Man-Tan or somethin'."

"Now back in the o-old days," Hatwell reminded the bus, doing a movie cracker sheriff, "we-uh didn't use no Nair, we always used *tar*. Cause you can set *tar* on *fire*. See what I'm sayin', with tar you got *options*."

"So what you're trying to say," Linton asked him, "we set the Bear on fire and walk him into the Holiday Inn?"

"*Got* to set him on fire," Hatwell said. "He too big for the microwave, though maybe we cut him up he'll nuke okay in pieces—hard to tell if we don't try."

"We could practice on Rondo," Linton suggested.

"Not enough fur."

"Fur ain't everything."

"True, and with Rondo you could cut his head off for practice and he wouldn't notice it. No one would."

Garrett raised a pen above his crossword. "Instructions for Tabriz, fifteen letters, Turkish."

"*Git ve bashsiz gel,*" Hatwell told him.

"Hat," Linton said. "Help me with this. I'm still stuck on walking in the Holiday Inn with the Bear on fire."

"It's something we coulda done for the Fourth of July," Hatwell said, "if we started this tour a couple weeks earlier. But as things stand it's pure head-theater is all. I'm kind of stuck on the imagery too but that's it."

"Uh huh," Bostic said, "but what I was wondering, you think Nair *burns*?"

The Bear yawned and Garrett muttered into his crossword, but this line of talk was good for another ten miles before Linton and Bobby got bored with it and wound it down.

"Bear," Rondo asked when there was silence, or something like it. "There anything special I c'n do for you?"

"Yeah. If you see Sheryl Crow's bus, run into it a little. I'd like to meet her."

"Bear meets Crow," said Hatwell, pleased. "Another shaggy dog story."

Later, a leafy landscape going past, green but soiled with the soot of commerce. "See," Bostic was telling the Bear, who was getting used to the motion of the bus, "one of the drags when you road, first you got all this New Jersey Pennsylvania shit to deal with. You movin' but nothin's changed, still looks like New York out there."

"Whereas when you get to Ohio," Bobby Hatwell said, his voice flat, "there're all those palm trees and tropical birds and volcanoes and the occasional passing dinosaur. Linton, what the fuck you trying to tell the Bear? You're more than six years old, right? So unless there's something wrong with your rock country head you already know all we're ever gonna see is another steaming heap of the same old shit all the way to the end of the line."

"The Mississippi River? The Kansas flats when you see a thunderstorm fifty miles off?"

"Linton, just to be a bro I'll try not to be bored out of my skull but I can't promise."

"Colorado," Bostic proposed. "The Rockies."

"That's just mountains. I want something different."

"What kind of different you want, Ra-heem?" Linton asked him.

The pianist thought for a moment. "Vanadium-based life-forms. Thoughts made of colored light. Emotions with visible nine-sided crystal structures. Solar-powered vegetables writing comic books. You know what I'm saying? *Different.*"

"Talking bears not good enough for you?"

Hatwell glanced at the Bear. "I got used to it," he said. "Rondo!"

"What?"

"Tell us about the bank job."

Rondo began to tell them about the thrill of bank robbery—"when you go in there, man, I tell you, it's a bigger charge than sex," he said, and all three rhythm section guys looked at each other, made faces and did jerkoff motions in their laps.

The Bear watched Garrett unpacking some things from his blue canvas briefcase: a pocket chess set, a heavy hardback—what was it? The new translation of *The Man Without Qualities*; Garrett was into the second volume; the Bear had read the old translation ages back. See, the Bear told himself, that was the idea, bring along a big doorstopper of a book. He was aware of the anxious profusion of paperbacks in his own bag: his three favorite Shakespeare plays, *Lear*, *Hamlet*, *The Tempest*—why hadn't he packed unfamiliar ones, *Troilus and Cressida*, *Cymbeline*, *A Winter's Tale*?—a couple of Elmore Leonards he'd already read twice, a biography of Talleyrand he knew he wasn't going to read, a beat-up Penguin *Charterhouse of Parma*—the only great book, in the Bear's opinion, with a sufficient sense of the preposterous, but maybe he was prejudiced in this regard—from which he might skim a favorite passage or two . . . dumb, *dumb*: he was doing everything wrong. He was born under a bad sign. If he didn't have good books he wouldn't have no books at all. "Garrett? You don't happen to have the first volume of the Musil with you, do you?"

"Sorry."

Linton leaned in to read the title off the fat spine of the book on Garrett's table. "*The Man Without* . . . Whoa, Hat. Garrett's reading a book about *himself*."

Hatwell stretched his arms aloft, yawned extravagantly and spun his pivot chair through a few degrees of arc. "Gametime," he said, and without much enthusiasm pulled a laptop computer from his chairside bag, started punching keys to wake it up.

"Another thing," Rondo said, still pursuing the happiness of a well-run bank job, "we'd be interracial plus a talking bear extra, and that'd fuck 'em up enough on the IDs so if they remembered anything at all they'd only remember one of us, see . . ."

"Excuse me," said the Bear, "but if one of the bank robbers was a talking bear, wouldn't they tend to remember *him*? And wouldn't that kind of point the finger at *me*?"

"Yeah but you'd be fuckin'-A effective," Rondo said. "Their brains'd go into paralysis. They'd get all fucked up. They'd hand it over, we'd split, and they wouldn't remember shit and the cops wouldn't believe 'em anyway."

"Who has the power to cloud men's minds?" Hatwell asked Bostic.

"The Shadow do," came the reply.

"The cops'd know they were running some shit on 'em must be an inside job and we're clear," Rondo resumed. He cleared his throat heavily. "So whaddayou guys think? I could call my friends in Detroit 'n' they'll set us up for twenty percent, twenny five with the local cops paid off to be on lunch break. You interested, Bear?"

"I think I'll pass," the Bear told him.

"Typical musician," the driver said. "Long on dream and short on action. No offense."

"None taken," said the Bear.

"And if the tour money's short?"

"I'll think about it," the Bear told him.

"Well, *I'm* up for it," Hatwell announced. "Banks, Fort Knox, the Mormon Tabernacle Choir. Long as you can promise me I won't be bored."

"Bored? *Bored*? Fuck no," Rondo said, turning heavily to look over his shoulder at the pianist. The bus stayed true in its lane. "Not a chance. On a bank job? Never."

"You don't know me," Bobby Hatwell said.

The Bear leaned over to watch him working the joystick on a baseball game, a layout of flat primary colors on the screen: here's the windup, the pitch—the ball seemed a little slow and it moved in visible increments—a swing and a miss, strike two, one and two the count.

"Want to play?" Hatwell asked him.

"I'm not into these things," the Bear said.

"After this tour I'll get me a new computer, faster chip, more RAM, get into some of the newer software. This one's not too hip."

"Wait a minute," said the Bear, leaning in farther. "That's weird. Are all the players white?"

"What'd you expect, realism? Wake up and smell the bullshit."

"They're all white? I don't believe it."

"Ah," Hatwell said, drawing in a lungful, "the smell of day-old bear. You oughta bottle it. Born yesterday and still going strong. Rondo, can I have one of your beers?"

"Yo-ho," Rondo said. "Take anything you want, man."

"You can have one of my meat patties on a three-beer exchange rate if you want."

"Naw, that's okay. Too spicy for me. Just take the beer."

"Peckerwood motherfucker must think I'm for real about the bank job," Hatwell told the Bear sotto voce as he rose. "Probly thinks *he's* for real about the bank job. Meanwhile it's payday." He went back to the fridge for his tallboy can of beer. "Rondo," he called from there.

"What."

"This is Rainier Ale. Green Death."

"Yeah I got a trucker friend brings me loads black market from the Northwest special."

"Rondo. It's Green Death."

"Fuckin' A."

"Why would anyone want to bring this shit in?"

"Man," said Rondo, "if you got to ask, you'll never know."

The Bear looked down at his feet for a minute, wiggled his toeclaws on the indoor-outdoor carpeting. The band had only been on the road an hour or so and already there were all these competing subjectivities thickening the air. You were supposed to do this for weeks and get inspired on schedule every night. Piece of cake. Tea for two. Milk run. Love Theme from *Terminator 2.*

On the other paw, some piece of him envied his rhythm section their youth—less their sense that there was plenty of time to fool around in than their living in a world without real consequences—but maybe that wasn't youth. Maybe, because all time does is heap illusion on you till you stumble and go under, maybe that's the way it really is. If so, he had been that young once, and hoped to be that young again.

"Hey you guys," called Hatwell from the fridge, "I'm turning off the radio. We're getting out of range of New York and the static is getting to me."

"Kill it," Bostic said, and the sound was gone. "Uh," Bostic said aloft, "maybe we could watch the box a little? Now?" The Bear detected something uncharacteristic in his tone.

"Yeah," said Hatwell a bit overemphatically, coming back with the tallboy can of Death, Green. "Let's watch a video."

"I brought a two-cassette version of *The Children of Paradise,*" the Bear offered.

"Naw, got something here," Bostic said, rummaging around in a bag at his feet.

"I smell a setup," said the Bear, sniffing the air.

"Setup? Setup? What's a setup?" Hatwell asked him.

"We don't need no steenking setups," Linton said. "Whynchoo come over here and sit with us?" He patted the benchseat beside him while Hatwell fiddled with the video player.

"Okay," said the Bear, got up, went over there, sat down. "What is it."

Garrett put a bookmark in Musil but didn't shut it. Hatwell addressed himself to the buttons on the video set. Bostic laid his hands demurely in his lap.

"It's three against one," the Bear told them, "but I can take you. One at a time or all together."

"Here we go," Hatwell said. "An art film. A bit of esoterica."

The fifteen-inch screen flared into life, first as a field of video snow accompanied by white noise, then as bluescreen with the number three on it, and finally as an oldish black-and-white movie image from the fifties, the middle of a movie, Donald O'Connor wearing an army uniform in a barn, leaning on the side of a stall and having a conversation with Francis the Talking Mule.

"This must've been hard to find," the Bear told Hatwell.

"Not really, with my connections."

"But Francis," Donald O'Connor was saying in evident panic, "you can't expect me to tell the general *that*!"

"See," Hatwell said professorially, left hand cupping right elbow, index finger accenting points in the air, "I always thought that Mr. Ed was the commercial bullshit version and Francis the Talking Mule was the real deal. But," he told the Bear, "I wanted to check it with you. Because, although I don't want to imply that you necessarily feel a solidarity with other talking animals—that would be insulting, that would be animalist of me—still, I thought you might have a means of knowing something pertinent and not widely known. . . ." Hatwell almost blew his professor act but covered the laugh with a cough cycle and a quick hand to his mouth. Once he recovered himself, the hand, now holding a conjectural pipe, indicated his readiness to hear the Bear's reply.

The Bear was trying to make up his mind whether to tell them this was a bunch of juvenile bullshit or if he should come up with something that would pass the Humor Test and join up.

Bostic, seated at the Bear's immediate left, also trying to look serious, said, "If you can't think of anything to say just stamp on the floor. We'll keep count."

Garrett shut his book on his bookmark. "Linton and Rahim," he explained to the Bear, "are relentless practitioners of Musicians' Humor. Sometimes, the operative word is relentless."

"Hey *hey*."

"And sometimes," Garrett allowed, "it's the other way around."

Hatwell was waiting, Bostic fingertapping paradiddles on the stonewashed denim of his knees and humming the four-note bassline of "Hambone, Hambone, Have You Heard."

On the screen, behind Donald O'Connor's back, a sergeant had walked into the barn without Donald O'Connor noticing his entrance. The Bear watched Donald O'Connor complaining to Francis the Talking Mule some more. Then he watched Donald O'Connor waiting for Francis the Talking Mule to talk back. "Come on, Francis," Donald O'Connor said. "Tell me." The movie paused a long beat for the theater audience to laugh. Then the sergeant laid a heavy hand on Donald O'Connor's shoulder, and Donald O'Connor did a large-sized double take with a last flip at the end, making it a triple.

"I always felt," said Hatwell, "that Francis was, like, Duke Ellington to Mr. Ed's Stan Kenton. But what do I know? Donald O'Connor is an obvious Jones figure but he can also dance, and this is confusing. So I came to you. With this dilemma."

"Well actually," said the Bear, "despite your lack of inside information you've hit the nail more or less on the head, Bob. Because, as it happens, when I was a lot younger, when I was about your age, I knew both Mr. Ed and Francis the Talking Mule, although Francis was advanced in years by then. I think I can call them both dear personal friends and wonderful talking animals both of whom influenced me deeply. And in fact, although I was a mere cub at the time, they were kind and generous enough to let me jam with them."

"Uh huh."

"And fundamentally you're right. Ed would frequently pull up lame at the critical juncture. Sometimes count off a tune with his forehoof, One, Two, Three, and not infrequently Francis the Talking Mule or even I would have to tell him, 'One more, Ed. Come on, Ed, you can do it.'"

"A time problem," ventured Bostic.

"A labored conception generally," said the Bear. "An inability to cut loose, although Francis wouldn't let anyone say a bad word about him. Another thing about Ed. When he ate too much fermented oats you'd see the real horse start to come out."

"An asshole?" Hatwell wondered.

"Anger, and despite all his success insatiable envy. In a word, your typical mean chewer. Whereas Francis, oh man, what can I say? He was a Charlie Parker among mules, a Diz among pack animals, a Prez among beasts of burden. And his girlfriend, Clare? You want to talk about singers? You want to talk about Make Me an Instrument of Your Peace? You want a vow-of-poverty I-talk-to-the-birdies two-step with the Renaissance as a follow-through? Words fail me. Francis lives."

The Bear had scored: the laughter and applause that obliterated the end of the Bear's riff included even Garrett, although Rondo seemed unaffected: the bus cruised in a straight line through the world. Maybe the Bear should have worked crime into the speech so everyone would have felt equally involved in the categories he had proposed. But that was the way of improvised solos: they were provisional, in the best sense of the term. It was true, he loved jazz and the stuff it was made of. Besides, working Rondo in might have risked a crash.

Meanwhile, Bostic was climbing out of his benchseat and clambering atop the wingtable. Once up, he shifted his right foot to the other table so that he bestrode the aisle, the Colossus of Roads. "AAAHHHHH!" Bostic said, and banged his head into the ceiling panels. "AAAHHHHH!"

"Are you guys always like this?" the Bear asked Hatwell across the aisle. The pianist was folding his laptop computer away so that if everything collapsed under Bostic he would still be able to play in the Digital Ofay League.

"Touring with you kind of stimulates us a little," Hatwell said. "Things get Out There a little quicker than usual. But basically, yeah, this is us."

Bostic banged his head into the ceiling harder. "AAAHHHHH!" he said again. "I can't stand it! We finished all the humor and we're still in Pennsylvania!"

"Actually, " Garrett told him, tilting his head up to catch his eye, "we haven't crossed the river yet. I hate to tell you this but we're still in New Jersey."

"AAAHHHHH!" the drummer cried, and resumed smashing his head on the roof.

The Bear wondered if Bostic would beat the roof of the bus apart and let the air in, but everyone settled down after awhile, and quieter miles resumed. The Bear and Linton traded fours, Garrett reopened his book, Rahim Bobby his laptop. Bostic had opened an issue of *Modern Drummer*. "Looks like Ludwig got a good new hi-hat pedal here," he told the Bear.

"Great," the Bear replied, and twiddled his thumbclaws.

"I wish I had it now, on this tour."

"Uh huh."

"They didn't price it high the way the foreign companies do, and it looks pretty good."

"Oh."

"Here's the picture of it. Pretty slick, huh."

"Yep."

"Got two parallel springs but they didn't overbuild it just for show."

"I see."

"The way it is," Hatwell told the Bear, leaning across the aisle, "after a week or two of this, none of us is gonna be able to stand each other. The way to road, you have to find a distraction, something that passes the time for you, otherwise you'll die or go out of your mind with boredom. Pussy's good, but there's also drugs and alcohol. I'm a pussy man myself, but between engagements I do computer games and sometimes take a stimulant to close the gap. We need our pastimes and compensations. What's yours?"

"I don't know yet." The Bear felt the road rising, and outside the bus the trees were thinning out. "Is this the river?"

"It's Dodge City out there, Bear, a whole country full of haw-haw cowboys and their gals, and you're gonna have to figure something out. I'm gonna intentionally walk this batter. When you figure out what it is, let me know."

2

bypassing Pittsburgh—probably a mistake, the Bear realized as the bus hit the bypass and swung away from the city amid its rivers under gathering clouds near the end of day—the bus travelled in one side and out the other of a brief fierce squall of rain in hill country and at length descended into a car-culture strip of gas stations, convenience stores, Blink-a-Lubes and the usual round of Macs and Kings until they reached a central, tilted town of clapboard houses under sulphurous lamplight. Behind the houses rose the onion tops of Slavic basilicas and a looming herd of extinct industrial immensities lit here and there by a few last productive fires.

"Interesting," said Hatwell, looking out the window. "Let's fly Jones down and buy him a ride in a blast furnace for booking this shit."

"It's not his fault," said the Bear.

The bus blundered twice down narrow streets past clapboard tenement and warehouse sets, then found a long straight street with a tall green neon sign angling out from a building about three blocks distant. When they reached it they saw a tattering JAZZ NIGHT sign in one window and a hastier placard in the other for the Ted BEASTLY Quartett.

"What I want to know," said Bostic, looking out—no one had made a move to leave the bus although the engine had been off for a long minute—"is what the fuck kind of name for a club is Nancy's Cabbage."

"Betcha dey got beer," Rondo said, sighed the doors open and struggled off the driver's seat and down the steps. They watched him push his way through the bar's double doors. Then they looked up and down the street. There was no one out there. There was really no one out there.

"Are we insured?" Garrett asked.

"In case of death," said Linton, "we get to go to hebbin."

"I'm the bandleader," said the Bear, "so I'll go in first."

"See, honor among bears," Hatwell said.

"I read the rulebook once," the Bear told him. He put his rust-colored countrypolitan hat on and stepped down to the street, then across the sidewalk and through the doors into the barroom darkness of Nancy's Cabbage.

Not a promising prospect, thought the Bear once inside, but then Rondo, arrayed backwards across a stretch of bar, raised a mug of beer into the air. "Hey join me, Bear," he called. "Cause I'm comin' apart."

Nancy's Cabbage was a long dark bar with a bandstand in the dimness at the rear. Forms in workshirts and baseball caps huddled over dregs of beer along the bar and in one or two sunken booths toward the back of the room. A bass-heavy blur was playing at uneven speed on a jukebox whose lights were dying. The Bear heard the band come in behind him.

"I've seen this somewhere before," he heard Linton say.

"The ad campaign for Snafu, the new men's fragrance," Hatwell said, too loud. "Situation Normal, All Fucked Up."

The Bear watched pale faces turn their way along the bar but nothing happened so after awhile he and the band came the rest of the way in.

"Line 'em up," Rondo told the bartender, and in short order a row of foaming mugs began to appear atop the oak, or whatever. "The beer's pretty bad so let's have a lot of 'em."

Rondo was right. The beer tasted of iron pipe and the Bear had three of them while Rondo walked around the room looking for a conversation and Bobby Hatwell tested out the upright piano at the bandstand in the back. The bartender was back there with him, watching as Hatwell plinked around, just in case he did something to the piano like put a spear through it or try to cook it up in a pot. The Bear tried not to hear what the piano sounded like, nor to count the notes that sounded like bedsprings or did not sound at all. He kept his hat on snug and his raincoat collar up, but nothing had budged the dead energy in the room.

Hatwell was back. "John," he indicated the bartender thumbwise, "says they get a lot of organ trios."

"I don't see no Hammond B-3 back there," said the Bear.

"No. *Organ* trios: stomach, liver, spleen and all you can drink. They use *sampling* keyboards," he explained to the Bear. "Welcome to modern times."

"Doesn't look it. You play Hammond, work the pedals and all?"

"Oh, man."

"We oughta try it sometime."

"Well, tonight all you get's the sample and for bass you're stuck with Garrett here."

"So kind of you to mention me," Garrett said. "Another beer please."

"Thanks for letting me get a word in edgewise, Church," Hatwell said, then turned to the Bear. "Though I'll tell you, playing the house piano would be great mental exercise." He paused to swallow down half a beer and make a face. "I'd have to remember which keys don't work and how to get around them in all the different keys we play tunes in. Four-dimensional chess with earlaps. The piano didn't sound like shit I might even try it. This is beer? Jesus. Rondo, how much Green Death you got on board?"

"Four cases down the bay."

"Rondo, remind me to thank your mother for fucking you up right. So Bear, I'm playing electric and Garrett's got his amp, but if you were expecting a usable PA for the horn forget it. You'll have to play to the room."

"Linton'll have to play soft," said the Bear.

"Ha," said Linton. "Ha ha ha. Ha. Ha ha. Ha ha ha haah."

Hatwell leaned across the bar and wagged John closer with his index finger. "The Klan got a branch office in town?" he inquired. "Or you just use a website."

While the band set up, the Bear decided not to watch Hatwell kick his amplifier one more time. He recovered Rondo from two iron men and a longneck Bud in a booth, went back to the bus and tried to raise Jones on the cellphone. "Don't you know how to use that thing?" Rondo asked him finally.

"The on switch. Where is."

"Jesus H." Rondo hit the switch for him and left.

The Bear was grateful Rondo gave him credit for knowing how to dial, but it took him awhile to figure out he had to hit the send button after.

Sybil gave him a nice, surprised hello and said she'd get him.

When Jones came on, the Bear heard ice cubes in a glass but Jones sounded fairly straight. "We figured you could use Nancy's Cabbage as a nice safe easy way to get up to speed," Jones told him. "You should pull some people down through the NPR station in Pittsburgh, where they're giving you extensive mention after sundown—I checked, they promised—and the other venues are all gonna be much more to your liking I swear. Remember, you're the one putting the constraints on where we book you—nothing too big, nothing too wide open, the usual shall we call it your guarded attitude."

"Shall we call it my rational disinclination to get busted again?"

"We're accommodating you the best we can, but you have to deal with the accommodations."

"Sure," said the Bear, "but why at Nancy's Cabbage?"

"Mostly because the conjunction of Nancy's Cabbage and Monongahela was pretty much irresistible on a nomenclatural basis, is that a word? Besides which there wasn't anything lower-pressure out there within a one-day drive for a startup."

"Monongahela? Is that where we are?"

"You didn't look?"

"In a general way." The Bear meant he had looked at the tour itinerary several times and his eyes had gone out of focus. He was looking more seriously now, flipping through the pages on the clipboard. "Jones, did you really do this? We're playing Rockford, as in Jim, Illinois, and Parma, as in Charterhouse, Ohio?"

"I couldn't resist. We've got upfront guarantees at every venue and you'll exceed all of them. Think college towns. Ann Arbor and Madison are gonna be good financially four nights each, and very safe. You know how much you're gonna make five days in Boulder Colorado alone?"

"That's the end of the tour."

"The club there's brand-new, a real palace they tell me, and the front money alone will be enough to get you clear. That's where you record if you feel ready, and there's an option on a second week if the nice folks keep coming out to see you."

"It's weeks away, if I live that long, and what I'm looking at here is not inspiring."

"You'll live that long and the inspiration's up to you. You still do irritation great."

"Thanks."

"And you miss me, don't you. Fess up."

It was true. The Bear felt an illogical, out-of-sequence rush of his old affection for Jones. Was it because he was locked up with four lunatics for six weeks—well, three lunatics and a bassplayer, which came to pretty much the same thing—or was something more fundamental working? The Bear pawed his way through the fog of his current irritation re Nancy's Cabbage and would have sworn that some of the old unqualified camaraderie was coming back into play. It didn't make a lot of sense but it was welcome anyway. Why do things happen when they do? "Jones," he said, "I'm pissed off about the nightclub but it's good to hear your voice."

"*Vesti la giubba*, B."

"What?" The Bear repositioned the awkward headset at his ear. They should design these things more considerately for ursine use.

"I said, I wish I could be out there with you."

"You do?"

"Course I do. You kidding? Listen, they'll send me out if you're ready to record in Colorado. Keep in mind Boulder'd be a low-pressure recording situation. Not up to snuff for full release, it goes out to radio stations and other promotional purposes, keep the pot boiling for *Shoes*, for which there's a good buzz in the industry."

"You've been looking out for me," said the Bear. "Doing toil and trouble."

"Front and back, like always. How you feeling really?"

"Strange," the Bear confessed. "It's a wrench leaving Iris, and I'm out here with Groucho, Chico, Harpo and the ghost of Jesse James."

"Talmo's a trip, ain't he? He tell you how he got into the music biz?"

"The world is a foreign country."

"What else is new. Wish I could be there with you, B."

"Wish you could too."

"Sounds like old times, don't it?"

"Ain't it strange? How're things at home?"

"Actually," said Jones, lowering his voice confidentially, "life at home has begun to improve. It's like maybe I'm not on trial anymore. She's beginning to appreciate me for the find I am."

"She knocked up?"

"That's the good part. Far as I know she's not. It might be true love at last."

"I always loved that old sweet song," said the Bear. "No, really: best wishes."

"Want to call me after the gig? I'll stay up."

"Get some sleep, or something even better," said the Bear. "I'll call you tomorrow." After a ceremonial exchange of goodbyes and best wishes he switched the headset off—Rondo would applaud him—and stuck it in the holster hanging from the backrest of the driver's seat.

Was it too late to call Iris? It might be. She'd begun going to bed nine, nine-thirty. Country life. He'd give her a honk tomorrow.

Time to shuffle into place, stand there and see what happens.

He banged back into the club and found Hatwell standing just inside the door. "Let's go up there," the Bear suggested, "and smite the sledded Polacks on the ice."

"Just what I was thinking," Hatwell said, and thrust his hand quickly into his jacket pocket, but not before the Bear noticed the small white pill the pianist was trying to hide. Hatwell knew he had seen it, he knew Hatwell knew, Hatwell knew he knew . . . and the Bear decided to let it ride. Hatwell cleared his throat. "All the same, I'd watch what you say about Polacks in here. Me and the guys already feel a distinct chill in the air, you know what I'm saying?" He worked a finger between his shirtcollar and his neck.

"I'm good in a barfight," said the Bear.

"I'm sure, but it's not the way to start a tour unless you're Mingus. Funny you should bring it up though. See that guy at the bar with the bandage on the side of his head? Don't look right at him, dummy."

"I see him." A hulking young guy in working clothes draining a beerglass: a white crosspatch bandage covered the rear-right quadrant of his head: his lank black hair had been shaved around the perimeter of the wound: he didn't look terrifically bright.

"Well," Hatwell told the Bear, "he gave me a Hey good buddy and asked me to have a beer with him. After a sip or two I asked him about the bandage and he told me about how he was shooting pool the other side of town last night and got into a fight with like a dozen black guys and one of them hit him on the head with a poolcue and then they threw him out into the street and he had to crawl home. So tonight he's getting together with about twenty colleagues and they're goin' over there and beat the shit out of the black guys. One of his old buddies is bringing a blowtorch and the rest are packing chains. He asked me if I wanted to go along."

"No shit."

"I wondered if he was being ecumenical or if it might be a sneaky way of getting me beat up, like maybe they could warm up on me in an alley on the way over."

"What'd you tell him?"

"I said there was a chance his buddies might get me confused with the bad guys when the shit hit the fan. He said I could wear a hat so they could tell me apart. Did I want a John Deere or a Pittsburgh Steelers. I told him Chicago Bears and it was an interesting proposition and it'd make a change but if he didn't mind I'd pass."

"I think you made the right decision," said the Bear.

"You think?"

"I can't spare you."

"Bear, this is the weirdest club I've seen since I did the tour with Mr. Tim, John Carradine and the monkey. Not," said Hatwell hastily, "that I'm making any comparisons between you and Zip."

"I could wear a hat," said the Bear, "so you could tell me apart."

"Please don't make me laugh. The guy's looking over and I think he can smell we're talking about him."

"Rahim," said the Bear, "just tell me about the pill."

"Okay. I owe it to you." Hatwell dropped into a vaguely penitent slouch for a moment but didn't like it and straightened up. "It's a Percocet."

"I don't know anything about drugs."

"A painkiller."

"Are you in pain?"

"I'm alive, ain't I. Look, I had a small, manageable habit going and I tried to get clean before we started out but my timing came up a week short. I'm tapering off with Percocet. I'm not carrying anything heavier, I'm not high, I'm not fucked up, and in a week I won't even need Percocet—for which, by the way, I have a completely legal prescription. You won't see any shakes or diarrhea or any sweaty Hollywood bullshit, although I do have a small involuntary tremor in my legs, and on the way out of town I won't tell you I have to stop off at that jewelry store a minute where they were fixing my watch, I'll just be a minute and don't come with me. That won't happen. I'm fine for the music, and beyond that, if you don't mind, it's not your business. A small habit, you understand? I've slipped once or twice, but it's under control."

"I've heard that song before," said the Bear. "It's such sad old shit."

"Yeah well I have a feeling for tradition."

"It's a mistake, Rahim."

"Well it's mine to make, isn't it." For a moment a curtain rose and the Bear could see Rahim Bobby Hatwell as someone fundamentally stymied by the terms of life as he himself was. Then the curtain dropped. "Anyhow I'm using Percocets to taper and Lomotil for my bowels, otherwise I might have to get up in the middle of a piano solo and go to the can. Is that enough information? Are we cool? Is it okay?"

The Bear gave Hatwell an assessing look. Hatwell looked as if he might be about to blow smoke out his ears and fire from his nose, so nothing seemed unusual or out of order. "If it has to be," the Bear said.

"It has to be."

"I worry about you sometimes."

"Thanks, Ma."

"Right. So let's go up there and, um . . ." The Bear checked the house and his voice trailed off.

"Sled the fucking Polacks on their ass."

But the house had been augmented, the Bear realized when he came onstage and looked out at it for real. The radio strategy, or word of mouth, or some other song, had done its work, and there were new people who looked as if they'd come from somewhere else. Only one couple had been brave enough to occupy one of the four front-row tables: students, he supposed. The male half looked like a twelve-year-old with intense eyes, a dark goatee and a cigarette he was smoking to death; his blond girlfriend was so pale and her features as yet so unaccented by character that she seemed incompletely formed. The Bear would have taken them for sixteen, tops, but either they were old enough to drink those beers or they had fake ID. The beard wasn't fake, though. The Bear would have to recalibrate his human-age scale for the tour. They looked like children.

He heard the band settle into place behind him, complaining softly about this and that, and he felt the usual flutter of anxiety, then thought: No, we're good, we know how to do this; and he stamped off the tempo for "Straight No Chaser" medium up.

He felt it going wrong from the beginning but was sure the band would get it together on the repetition of the head. After that he thought they'd pull together after a few choruses of improvisation. After that he told himself he had to get used to playing with his back to the band, when circularity in his living room had been so easy, and accustom himself to facing a not particularly impressive house on a quotidian night in the known world. The band—they'd have to get used to it too. Bobby would stop laying in the wrong chord at the right moment, Linton would get his cymbal sound integrated with the drums and more nearly on the dime, and as for himself, he'd remember how to play before long. Garrett was the only one among them displaying anything like his usual competence, but although his steady walking quarter notes were all in a row and in tune, they were essentially indistinguishable from each other—One could be Three or even Two or Four—senseless, robotic, indiscriminate. Soon, though, one of them would pull it together and the rest would fall in line.

But once the Bear finished eight undistinguished unswinging choruses and Bobby Hatwell began his own solo by stumbling over his own fingers, the night's real aspect rose definite and clear from these clouds of supposition. Unless they could do something about it soon, the night at Nancy's Cabbage was going to be an avatar of Every Musician's Nightmare.

After Hatwell's embarrassment Garrett wisely declined a solo, and when the Bear initiated an exchange of fours with his drummer, Linton dropped his left stick first time out and dropped a beat finding another one, so that no one came in together on the way back in. The Bear sustained the fours through three choruses, listening to both of them lose count, went back to the head and got the tune done the best he could.

Then he made the mistake of calling "Reincarnation of a Lovebird," a beautiful, difficult tune that cried out for long, reflective solos, and just wanting to get out of there they finished it in five minutes flat. The Ted Beastly Quartet had full leisure in which to contemplate the mystery of four entirely competent, frequently inspired musicians passing what seemed like hour after interminable hour unable to play anything but notes. Their senses of time never meshed, not on the subtle, breathing level necessary to living music, and everything they played was reduced to mechanical gestures of tone production of no inherent meaning. The sounds went separate ways into the air or lay there on the floor like disused and misbegotten objects. None of them understood, given their known degree of talent, how this dispiriting thing could be, but evidently it was. It had not happened to any of them for a long long time.

"Someone chop my fingers off," Hatwell said behind him.

"Too much work," Bostic said.

"It can't go on forever," said the Bear over his shoulder.

"Oh yes it can."

The Bear called "Skylark," one of his favorite ballads, and some cold-hearted and murderous hunter shot it on the wing, but only wounded it so that it lay there flapping on the ground for the duration. Each time he came to the tune's bridge, the Bear played it as written, with only the lightest embellishment, so as not to spoil such a lovely thing completely.

The house was pretty much silent when it was over. At least they respected the dead.

Maybe, thought the Bear, a little uptempo energy will cure us. He called "Oleo" and heard the rhythm section lose itself in the stalls and disjunctions of the head, and when that was done he tore into the "I Got Rhythm" changes as if volume and attempted passion might be enough; but the insistence of the rapid tempo seemed like a whip lashing them to no purpose, time a maniacal insistence to produce energy and heat and light no matter what. Who decreed this? The rhythm at the heart of jazz had always seemed to instance the inexhaustibility of life itself, a ground for hope, a reason to go on living, an emblem on the prow of grace, but at the moment the whole of American music seemed to him, and perhaps to the rest of the band, a ship on which a blind god beat the drum and men worked themselves to death at the oars on a doombound, pointless journey. Others were under orders to listen and find pleasure in the spectacle. The world turned, laden with pain and weariness, and even in peacetime the population ate shit, which it was musicians' job to dish out in steaming heaps. Is this a great country or what?

Such, at least, were the Bear's impressions of this version of "Oleo."

The Bear tried another ballad, but its wings were broken too. After that he managed a limping, semisentient blues, and watched it die on a dirt road a hot mile short of home. Vultures descended like slow applause, necks bent, beaks hooked beneath unblinking eyes, and wings clapped the night to a pause with at least another set to play.

On this first set, of all the tunes in the band's provisional book, only "M Squad," Count Basie's shuffle blues written back in 1960 for a TV cop show starring Lee Marvin, used now as an out-theme, worked at all. The Bear took three solos to stretch it out and close the set. If you can't play a Count Basie shuffle blues you were dead, most likely.

"Thank you thank you thank you," he announced into the microphone, hearing his voice split and shriek on the Martian PA. "That's Rahim Bobby Hatwell on piano, Garrett Church bass, Linton Bostic at the drums, and on alto Lieutenant Frank Ballinger, yours truly." When no one laughed he added, "That's okay, I'm used to telling jokes no one gets."

"We don't get it either," Bostic said from behind his drumset.

"We'll take a short break," the Bear announced, "for suicide and surgery and we'll be back to torment you in twenty minutes."

While the band beelined for the bar he strolled into the audience compulsively apologizing to the folks at the tables. "Just our first set," he told them. "We oughta do better in a little while."

"That's okay," the college-looking kid with the goatee trying to look adult and world-worn—if he only knew—said, looking up, one hand tangled in his beard and the other in his vague though lovely girlfriend's froth of hair. "That's about what we expected to hear from a talking bear and his band. Who really played on the record?"

"Perfect," said the Bear—the kid was polite, and seemed to mean no harm—and he walked to the bar feeling shot neatly through the middle.

The rhythm section was sucking down draft beers and not looking at each other.

"Don't say a thing," Hatwell told him.

"We'll be fine the next set," said the Bear.

"Didn't he ask you not to say a thing?" asked Bostic.

"Garrett, let's hear from you."

"Well," Garrett said, but declined to elaborate.

"They keep the money," Rondo reminded them, "in banks."

"Listen, guys," the Bear began.

"Don't say. A fucking. Thing," Hatwell warned him.

The Bear deferred, and they drank some so-called beers.

"We'll straighten out," the Bear insisted on the way to the stage for the second set, but halfway through he felt obliged to call "M Squad" again.

If you couldn't play a Count Basie shuffle blues what could you do?

You bussed back to the motel, where Rondo had confirmed the reservations. The band went inside and you got to sleep in the parking lot up against some decorative shrubbery and two willows that screened a view of the highway and a mall that had died in midconstruction. You popped open the roof hatches for ventilation but you didn't sleep. You looked down at the horn in your paws, tried it out—you could play, almost—and thought about it all. You told yourself, in a rational tone of inner voice, that if it went on like this you would either . . .

Couldn't sleep, didn't want to play horn, so figured out how to turn on the video and push in the first cassette of *Les Enfants du Paradis*, watched truth in the form of Arletty regard itself in a mirror, turning in the fake depths of her well, then thought Nah, and punched up Buster Keaton, watched him run down that hill pursued by a world of bouncing boulders. The Bear had long thought it the funniest thing ever put on film and he watched it a few times through, getting more technical-headed with each viewing, until he heard a knock on the door of the bus.

"Who the fuck is that?" the Bear bellowed, scared himself and hoping he'd scared whoever it was. Then, "*Who?*" when he couldn't make out the voice.

"Garrett," Garrett said louder this time, and "How you doing?" once he'd come inside. "I couldn't sleep either. What're you up to?"

"Sitting here watching TV and wondering what it would cost to cancel the tour and pay you guys off."

"Aw, don't do that."

"I keep vacillating."

"Then you need vacilline," said Garrett. "Who's that, Keaton?"

"Yeah, end of *Seven Chances*. Ever seen it? No? You're kidding."

The Bear summarized the plot for Garrett and wound the tape back to Keaton waking up in church with a few hundred women who want to marry him for his money. Then they watched the chase through to the end of the picture, laughing and stomping.

"What else you got there?"

The Bear held up the two cassettes of *Les Enfants*. "Ever seen it? Really? You've got a treat coming, if you have the time. It's a long movie."

"Let's see."

While the Bear set up the tape, Garrett had a few things to say. "You might think of treating tonight as a hallucination. You know you can play. I know you can play. I know I can play. And so on. This happens sometimes. Because it was so distasteful it will cling to us awhile. All we have to do is work it away bit by bit. The music will come back."

"It will?"

"It always has. Don't let the tension flip you. I'm not saying we'll be cured tomorrow, but you know how it is: one of us will start playing and someone else will catch it and pretty soon, you know. We might start having a good time."

"We lost money tonight," the Bear said. "I can't go on doing that. I'll have to pay you off and cancel."

"Didn't Jones tell you the other clubs are for real? Chances are if Nancy's hadn't been like that we would have played okay."

"I don't believe that," said the Bear.

"It *could* be true."

"And it was all Jones' fault for booking us there? Jeez, just when I was starting to lighten up on the guy."

"It was an honest mistake," Garrett told him, "but the point is, you're the one who'll have to deal with it, not him. If you can get it out of your mind completely, that's the best, it never happened. But chances are you won't be able to blow it off so you'll have to use it."

"How would I do that?"

"You'll figure it out."

"You sure?"

"Absolutely."

Garrett spoke without any special emphasis, not pushing the beat, his note choices discreet and subtle, and the Bear didn't think it was a particularly rousing old-school pep talk or anything, but by the end of it he knew in what he could contact of his better self that Garrett was right. Right enough to take a chance on anyway. And, oh yes, do remember to thank him for dropping by. "Okay," said the Bear. "We'll try it for a few more nights. Now, as to this picture . . ."

As to the picture, they watched it medium-impressed until—and for the Bear it always happened at the same moment, when the apoplectic owner of the Théâtre de Funambules raised his hands in the air and cried that his theater was torn by rivalry and hatred—it turned into the greatest movie ever made. "Wow," Garrett said, in all the usual places, and then "Really? You sure?" when the Bear said he was going to lie down in the back but Garrett could keep watching the movie if he wanted.

After Garrett left, around first light, the Bear woke from an hour's nap lying on his back and with his eyes still closed saw, as if it were proposed to normal sight but without final clarity or focus—saw by analogous light as it were—the limit of the world as a series of worn grey wooden slats with gaps between. Through the gaps stretched a bluegrey slate of sky against which white birds passed, their tapering, hooked-back wings spread wide.

Which was interesting.

But it was a little while later, after he'd washed, had some coffee and run the engine to get the airconditioning going and blow off the night-damp, that the tour began to assume what would be its real aspect for the Bear. He unpacked his horn, examined it for traces of last night's insult, worked the keys and fixed a new reed to the mouthpiece. At first walking up and down the aisle and later perched on the edge of a bunkbed in the back, he played, alternating scraps of tunes, scalar explorations and technical workouts for embouchure and paws. He played for an hour, spelled by a few mugs of coffee and the occasional pause for thought; and while he didn't want to make too much of it, didn't want, in his usual graceful fashion, to pounce on the poor thing with all four paws and worry it to death before it had a chance to live and breathe a little, he had a feeling, a certain intuition . . .

Despite having pulled off a largely successful record with *Sensible Shoes*—a triumph of self-impersonation, done under unsustainable stress—and having coasted his way through an agreeable weekend of rehearsals with the band at home that spring, the Bear felt that his relation to the music had been inauthentic at least since the night of his bust at the Tin Palace. Oh, his technique had multiplied and his harmonic knowhow had deepened and taken on detail, but had done so in a sort of vacuum. He had practiced a lot, but it had been busywork, bereft of essential savor. Now, oddly enough and who knew for what reason, he was starting to get something: the float was dipping on the surface of the water and he was pretty sure he felt the beginnings of a tug on the line. Who'd believe it? Something living down there yet. He played for a second hour and most of a third and didn't feel tired. What he felt was . . . interested. Quietly interested.

Yesterday Hatwell had asked him what his pastime on the tour would be.

Well, you never know, it might turn out to be music.

The daily rhythm of bus and road, the nightly rhythm of club and crowd, assumed their place in some external orbit of his consciousness, almost as peripheral as the billboards ticking past in the summer haze of highway America. It may have helped that Monongahela had provided him with such a deep pit to climb out of—on their second night at Nancy's they occasionally achieved the competence of a student band—since shame was such a long-familiar motivation; but the Bear's new descent into the music, whether alone in the back of the bus late at night or rolling between towns on long afternoons and sometimes even in a nightclub, quickly acquired a contemplative aspect, his large form bent above the fall and rise of his horn, making what he hoped was the beginning of a fresh adventure into the intricacies, the matrix, the logic of the given forms. Eventually he might find his way out of the maze and back to beauty—who knows?—but for the moment there was work to do.

"It's a Coltrane thing," was Bobby Hatwell's opinion.

"Am I starting to sound like Trane?" the Bear wanted to know. "Because it's true I'm getting pretty scalar."

"Naw, I just meant I never heard of anyone else practicing that much. You must be playing ten twelve hours a day by now? Oral fixation I figure. Maybe we could all chip in and buy you a lollipop. Or some animal tranquilizer so the rest of us could live in peace."

The Bear stumbled forward guarding his alto as Rondo jammed the brakes on and screamed at some fucking fool in a Japanese bug-car ought to get crushed by a bus only I got a tour to do don't I? The bus rocked front to back to front before changing lanes and passing.

"Join us awhile," Linton invited him, "before you hit the windshield."

The Bear dropped into a seat by a wingtable. "Really, am I bothering you guys playing this much?"

"Let's hear it for the higher mammals," Hatwell said. "You ever see a human musician this considerate?"

"Not me," Linton said. "Want an Earth Chip?" offering the bag.

"Actually," Garrett began, and Linton and Bob groaned in rough unison. A carhorn blared past.

"Fuck the fuck you too," Rondo remarked.

"Actually the Coltrane question is pretty interesting I think," said Garrett.

"Who cares."

"Yeah who cares."

"Because although you're getting pretty scalar I hear a more muscular grip on the beat than Trane had—"

"Puh-leeze."

"—because Trane had this soaring thing going and you, well, you—"

"Garrett please shut the fuck up."

"Okay."

"Looka that," Rondo announced. "Three clear lanes of interstate in fronta me. I can drive."

"So you say," Linton said.

"News to us," Hatwell agreed.

Whenever the Bear phoned Iris to tell her that the imminent rebirth of his musical sense was thanks to her, really, because beauty is truth and truth beauty, she said Thank you very much, and when he asked how she was doing she answered Fine, and sidestepped further inquiry, repeating that she, and things, were fine.

What? the Bear wondered, and: Luminous being on the end of my life's line what's up with you? but once he got off the phone the music quickly reabsorbed him, and with stabs then flickers then mere wisps of misgiving he consented.

In Youngstown they played a club that would have been in the middle of the tracks, had there been a train coming through: a neighborhood bar on the line between the white and black parts of another dying American industrial town. The stage was an alcove across an open wooden floor from the bar—did people dance here?—with mismatched tables and chairs set around the edges. The street entrance was on the left, the room deep toward the rear of the club on the right, and this place did have a Hammond B-3 organ: Hatwell licked his chops and rubbed his hands together at the sight of keys and pedals and especially the big old Leslie unit. "Ventilation," he said happily. "Garrett, you can take off and read up on chemistry tonight, and Bear you can go visit your folks in the zoo, cause Linton's all I need and I'm not sure about him."

"Plug in your sampling devil just in case," the Bear advised.

They started the first set playing to a scattering of neighborhood drinkers, and sounded pretty good, opening with a version of "Giant Steps" on which the Bear had to growl at Hatwell to lay off the footpedals and let Garrett play bass. The band achieved a certain amplitude of swing, and toward the end of his solo the Bear got where he wanted to on the tune, vaulting over those steeplechase changes with a fine gathering and ungathering of muscle, notes fluently cascading, making Coltrane's obstacle course sound inevitable and easy. Hatwell had some trouble with the organ—all of it mechanical, he swore later, stuck keys, bad action, electrical fluctuations—and switched to piano-sample midway through.

The Bear got through the first set without embarrassing himself. In the middle of the second, the bar revealed its true nature as a place for all the musicians in town to jam in after the gig or instead of one: a bunch of young guys with instrument cases began strolling in, assembling at the tables to the left of the stage, nursed their beers and looked up at the bandstand with the usual contradictory mix of cockiness, skepticism and diffidence: the Three Fates of jamming. I wish, thought the Bear as he called "Skylark"—love that bridge—I wish these guys'd show up a week from now, when I could handle them fine, instead of now, when I'm not so sure; and in a flash and with some surprise realized that he knew exactly how he would be playing in a week's time. This was a faculty he'd possessed in the old days: pick out a musical target, see it clear, intuit the trajectory between here and there, know how long it would take, and fill the space between with the necessary but secondary details of work and hit the mark cleanly at the appointed time.

This recognition of what might prove to be the old acuity threw him off for two beats, and he saw the faces at the musicians' tables all come up, a clutch of predators. He made sure to play especially well through the remainder of "Skylark," employing viciously complicated reversals of accent out of Bird and Sonny Rollins, and, having at the moment no shame, he took care to employ every trick of inflection and tone that his ursine embouchure made easy: those slurs and grace notes, that thickening of timbre, the sardonic growl amid lyrical blossoms: no shame at all. He watched the faces recalibrate the parameters of night as he drawled his solo's end into Hatwell's opening.

Finished the set with "Take the Coltrane," played well although he knew he was still pretty much faking it, irritated that the stuff he was playing in the bus had yet to swing into full function, and stepped to the floor when he was done to gladpaw the young lions, already unpacking their axes, and rough out a solo order.

A quick six beers at the bar, a little light humor with the band, and the Bear was as ready as he would ever be. He attained the stage all huffed up for combat, called "Oleo" at a less than prohibitively fast tempo, played three professional choruses of "Rhythm" changes with lots of chord substitutions on the last sixteen bars just to show the kids where Bobby, Linton and Garrett would go if beckoned thither; then he waved the first kid up, a tenorist, and stepped to one side of the stage next to Hatwell. Linton tucked his ride cymbal time back in, chicked the hi-hat tighter on two and four than usual and cracked out the occasional Philly Joe Jones accent on the snare. The Bear nodded at Bostic to acknowledge this kindness to the kids coming up.

It turned out that most of the youngsters would need it: a tenorist who made his way through the changes with some esprit until the rhythm section responded to him, opened things up so that he responded to them and got lost; three trombonists, no surprise, who couldn't work the slide sufficient to bebop at this tempo, although one of the three was an interesting colorist; a guitarist who plugged in and did a credible impression of Kenny Burrell until he got ambitious and ended in a tangle of fingers; two altoists with a certain amount of talent still working their way through the fundamentals who were not ready to play with this rhythm section, which was beginning to lose its patience and make trouble—the Bear stepped in for a couple of choruses to restore due process; a guy on flugelhorn who would almost certainly lash himself to tatters in the next few days over the shame of it all, although the Bear was careful to give him a friendly nod and wave at his departure from the stage and then hurriedly out the door into the night, where the weather obliged his sense of personal drama by starting in to rain; a tenorist who had some Sonny Rollins together but probably had downed a beer or two too many while mustering up his courage; another tenorist who swaggered his way through five ill-fitting choruses in which it was painfully obvious he would have been happier playing in another key: he came offstage with his swagger not just intact but inexplicably magnified. And then there was Jerome Parris.

A shy brown bony kid maybe nineteen with big eyes, a long jaw, cheekbones the rest of his face hadn't made friends with yet, a head shaven just short of clean, and rumpled slacks too long for him that wreathed to a gradual halt on reaching at last his worn-out shoes. He was so shamefaced in his climb to the stage that the Bear prepared himself to hear the night's most uncertain music so far. And in fact the trumpeter did start off a tad uncertainly, hesitating at the top of the chorus for two bars, head down, watchful, licking his lips, then pursing them and lowering himself to the mouthpiece to meet his rising horn halfway, rather than raising the horn all the way to his chops. By the time he finished the first A section he had shown a fluttery, cumulative sense of line out of Clifford Brown's lyrical side—Dupree Bolton and Carmell Jones instead of Lee Morgan—and the Bear exchanged a round of small nods with his rhythm section to acknowledge the young man's gift; but by his second chorus the kid began to unwrap a gleaming, forthright, brass-proud sound that straightened the Bear's spinal column and won his complete attention.

Bobby Hatwell looked up and raised impressed eyebrows. Garrett deepened his traction. Linton broke out something wide and shining from his storehouse of grins and came up with a big pressroll out of Blakey to cheer the kid on.

The complete second chorus was an impressive construction with only one clinker that came in his transition to the bridge, when the kid let loose a lick he had too much practiced or too long treasured—his sincerity betrayed him—but he recovered quickly and the chorus ended on the upsweep to a climax in the third: an array of lines arcing upward to a set of clarion calls at the top of his range at chorus' end. Then he delighted them all by coming down from this peak in his fourth and last chorus—Brownie liked to put Mount

Everest in the middle of his solos too—in a series of fallaways, back-references and interstitial spurts of fresh invention before ending just short of fluttertones at the bottom of the horn.

The house applauded, and Hatwell's solo and the Bear's pro-forma wrap-up had the aura of an aftermath.

When it was over, the kid tried to escape the club alive but the band encircled him at his table before he could shake his spit-valve clear and get the mouthpiece back in its pouch.

"Jerome," he said. "Jerome Parris. Excuse me? Yes, nineteen. Oh thanks. Thanks very much." He was unable to retract his head beneath his collarbones. Linton came back with ten longneck bottles of beer on a tray and, although there was some momentary doubt on this score and a quick helping hand from Garrett, got it onto the table without tipping them over.

"Definitely," Hatwell was telling the young trumpeter. "You definitely ought to come to New York and fuck your life up with the rest of us. I mean, I don't care what you think is wrong with Youngstown, but if you want to see brutality and ugliness, if you want to be shit on enough to make you sing, you got to come visit. We'll show you the town, Jerome."

"Well, actually," said Parris, "I was thinking of going to the Berklee School of Music. If and when my folks can spare me."

"Been there done that," Hatwell told him, "and . . ."

Well actually the Bear was thinking what it might be like to have a quintet, another horn to spell him and a bright young talent to introduce to the greater world, and were it not for the fact that he was still basically hiding out, not really on the scene, only emerging for the occasional peep and payday . . .

"Actually . . ."

"No shit?" said Linton. "Trane's father was a tailor too."

"Really?" And it seemed that Jerome's father's tailor shop had closed down lately, all the jobs leaving town and not a lot of work in the neighborhood, so that Jerome felt he had to stay on just now, help as best he could and continue his trumpet studies with Mr. Middleton—any of you hear of Mr. Middleton?—for the next foreseeable while . . .

"Aw c'mon, man," Hatwell told him. "You old enough to disappoint your parents by now. Get with the program. Come to New York and get fucked up."

Parris' eyes grew even larger, and looked as if they were welling up with tears. "I love this music so much," he said, and even Hatwell had to put a hand on the kid's shoulder and stop talking.

They were a quintet for the last set, but it seemed to the Bear that Parris had retreated back into the shell of a Clifford Brown impersonation and that those peaks and gleams of his real, illumined self were less readily seen. "What do you think of him," the Bear asked Hatwell privately after the set.

"I'll be twenty-six in October. He makes me feel like a dead old fuck."

"No. Really."

"Really?" Hatwell asked. "If he doesn't blow it one way or another he could be immense."

"Hope for the future, Pappy?"

"Up yours, Ma," Hatwell said.

Gedunk, gedunking over seams of road north to Parma—he would not let Jones pull these gags on him again—the Bear fuddled himself in a forest of notes and was able to recall how easy it is to lose track of yourself in even the simplest search. Music ought to be simple enough—right?—it was just a bunch of notes and not a terribly resistant medium compared to life in general, so how could you lose the essential thread in anything as simple as that? Yet one did it all the time. Like money, the essential thread was only important when you didn't have it.

He phoned Iris in the afternoon and she came close to getting normally conversational with him but eventually reverted to being fine, fine, and telling him she hadn't been doing much really. Tension in her voice? Tension? What tension?

The Bear made another call.

The club in Parma, Jones told him, was supposed to be the hottest venue on the tour outside a college town, and as usual there were college towns and larger cities within National Public Radio range.

"A rock joint," Bostic said when the manager let them inside before sunset.

"I guess," said the Bear. There was a bar on one side of the club, a stage way over there on the other, but no tables between, and everything—floor, walls, pillars and heating ducts—was painted black. There were blue and red neon signs high up the walls saying PARTY ON, and neon martini glasses blinking GO GO GO in the corners. Daylight slashed into the space when some secondary attendant banged the loading doors open.

"Typical American music installation," Hatwell said.

"Really?" said the Bear. "Looks pretty strange to me."

"I didn't say it wasn't strange," Hatwell told him. "You're gonna learn something about the country tonight."

"What?"

"That Americans are the most miserable bunch of motherfuckers on the planet but they have to keep pretending on pain of death they're having a great time. The country fucked up its last chance in the Sixties and been dying ever since but that don't stop it from getting bigger and louder, does it."

The sound check went well, however, and the Bear had his first experience of decent stage monitors: it was interesting to hear the band clearly, even if the instruments' true acoustic was lost in the crudeness of the circuitry and cones. What would it sound like in the room?

The Bear would never know.

When they attained the stage that night the club was packed pretty much wall to wall with white kids whose main problem turned out to be that they had to shout at each other in order to be heard above the band. This was a new experience for the Bear, and he stepped back from the microphone after two choruses of "Now's the Time" that the band heard okay but probably no one else did.

"Take a long one," he said, bending over Hatwell.

"Welcome to America," Hatwell said, chording. "Let me show you how it works."

"At least the place has a piano," the Bear said hopefully.

"Is that what this is," Hatwell said. "Watch."

Hatwell played two impeccable bop choruses, then began his third by quoting "Amazing Grace" fortissimo in block chords with both hands, forearm muscles bulging below his pushed-up jacket sleeves. This elicited a round of applause, some stomping feet and a scattering of wolf-howls.

"Get it?" Hatwell asked the Bear. "Q. E. fucking D."

A brief allusion to "Ain't No Mountain High Enough" yielded a somewhat smaller roar. The Bear walked to a rear corner of the stage to contemplate the situation. It made him feel like a hamburger joint. It made him feel like he was working the drive-thru window. And it wasn't just a rock joint, he noted. There were posters in the room celebrating past gigs by Son Seals, the Meters, Luther Allison, Bela Fleck.

When he stepped to the microphone for his solo he got a roar just for being who he was, but the noise subsided only slightly as he began to play. Conversation was widespread and energetic. He played the house some Dave Sanborn, and when this proved insufficient to inspire a response he hit them with a medley of the world's hoariest blues clichés high up the horn at top volume—held them up and fairly shook them at the audience—and this yielded an ovation that did not diminish as he performed a cheap trick and held one note through a full chorus without recourse to circular breathing. He finished off by biting the reed into a high squeal and got a wicked grin and a nod from Bobby Hatwell on his return to the rear of the stage at solo's end.

This is the way it's supposed to be, he figured, and decided to go with it for the rest of the night.

By set's end he had realized how soul-destroying the setup was and saw how the vulturine cynicism of the tactic would pick his liver clean. He remembered seeing older musicians back in his clubgoing days, when he still looked credible on the end of a leash—Max Roach, Art Blakey, Coleman Hawkins, Sonny Rollins—and now was able retrospectively to recognize a certain presence in them—a granitic solidity, a massif of stoicism at the center of themselves—and the Bear understood that it was only by this kind of inner substance that you could endure decades of unbelievable bullshit and still have something left to play. You had to be some kind of colossus to keep anything going out here down the years.

Jesus, he remembered Sonny Stitt, who never had a band, always played with the house rhythm section and usually found someone to insult in it, and who delighted in tearing to pieces anyone unwise enough to bring a horn onstage and match wits with him. The bitterness in that man's face. Sixty years old, play better than anyone alive, and they still call you Sonny.

I'm not him.

The Bear finished the set without superficial flourish and decided to play the second show as if he were in the back of the bus meditating the puzzle of his being through the maze of chordal structure and the volutions of pure sound. In any case there was a big ovation at the end. It even rose above the roar of talk for a good ten seconds.

"Jesus," he remarked to Hatwell in the greenroom, which was blue.

"He don't come here," Hatwell said.

Garrett told them the story about how one night Mingus stopped in the middle of a bass solo at the Village Gate and told the audience that he hated to interrupt their dinner conversation, and had the waiter bring a table onstage and set it for two, and sat down with Dannie Richmond and ate three full courses, occasionally chatting about this and that with the audience over the microphone.

"They don't serve food here," said the Bear.

"We could play cards."

They began the second set with "Well, You Needn't," and the Bear tried to keep his concentration despite the ubiquitous bellow from the pit. He almost managed. Toward the end of his solo he was pleased to see Jerome Parris climb up from the audience horn in hand: true, it would have been better if he'd said hello first and waited to be invited, but think of it: he must have driven a hundred miles to be here.

The Bear ended his solo that chorus and leaned down to the microphone to introduce him—"Let's hear it for Jerome Parris, for the young, the astounding Jerome Parris, everyone!"—and as Parris began to play, the Bear pulled the mikestand higher for him and screwed it tight before stepping back.

The kid began his solo with a bit more confidence and brass than he had in Youngstown, and built his way nicely through Monk's chordal motion in the first chorus, developing some phrases in the last eight bars that he had set forth in simpler form in the first two A-sections, and in general beginning to pile things up. Sure enough, came the bridge of the second chorus Parris climbed his first peak, effectively moving stepwise up the range of his horn as Monk's harmonies moved stepwise down: nice contrary motion opening up massive archiectures in conceptual air. Bobby and Garrett responded happily and emphatically to the tactic, and Linton accorded it something like applause on the snare. As for the audience, forget it, except for a few souls near the lip of the stage, who had raised their faces from the start and were still listening.

Parris brought his solo to a second exclamation point and then began the expected decline—at nineteen it was probably too soon to tell him that this Brownian motion sounded increasingly mechanical with use, and that he shouldn't tongue absolutely every phrase with that little upflick into clarity the way Brownie did—but then, at the end of his fifth chorus, which everything in his solo had foreproclaimed the last, Parris went on into a sixth chorus, and a seventh. The ninth confirmed it: he was turning into the Soloist Who Wouldn't Stop. By the tenth his chops were failing and when he wasn't recycling ideas he'd already played twice he was fingering complicated new ones that maybe he could execute at home but had no idea how to fit in or swing with now.

The Bear knew the kid was in the middle of his worst nightmare and didn't know how to end it. At the end of Parris' eleventh chorus, just as he was inhaling the air of a twelfth, the Bear stepped to the microphone, signalled to the house and began to applaud. "Let's hear it for the wonderful Jerome Parris, everyone!" he said, obtained the ovation, and when Parris, looking shamed and panicked, made an attempt to bolt from the stage, the Bear, wearing a big showbiz grin, seized him by the arm and walked him off, stage left, and into the greenroom.

"Listen," he told the poor kid, who looked like nothing so much as an engorged and palpitating ego caught in the cruel light of day, unable to either expand or contract or get it over with and blow up. The Bear himself had no ego problems of course, but he was sufficiently learned in the ways of empathy to offer effective commiseration of a kind. "Listen. You're a terrific young player and the whole band loves you but you really shouldn't've . . . Aw forget it, sit down and have a beer. Have several, and don't try to leave. Because I want you onstand next set."

The Bear didn't really, but, you know . . .

Between sets the whole band went to work on Parris, telling him how good he was and what he'd done on the Monk tune was not some terrible debt he owed to suicide, only something less than à propos. It took awhile to calm him down, but the invitation to join the band for their third set and the insistence on giving him gas money practically collapsed him with relief.

We're all the same, thought the Bear. We're idiots together, behind the mask and beneath the fur, aren't we.

So it was a busy night, but what amazed the Bear at the end of it was that Bob and Garrett and Linton had managed to abstract a woman each from the general blur below and it looked, at spotlight's last gleaming and despite all the gosh-golly tremors of maidenly embarrassment at the musicians' unmodulated directness, as if at least two out of three were going to get laid.

A number of women gave the Bear himself a still more nervous eye, and one or two came up to him gushing fantasy on the protective arms of edgy boyfriends, but the Bear contented himself with parkland outside town. After Rondo headed back to the hotel in the taxi that had followed the bus out, he enjoyed the late-night cool amid trees under stars and wished it weren't too late to phone Iris. Although, if their only fitfully communicative telephone conversations were to be believed, she was doing fine, relentlessly, unambiguously fine.

After fifteen minutes back on the bus and some desultory diddling with the television, practice claimed him, and he submitted to its complexities until even a bear had to get his rest.

"I'm out here in America," he said that morning.

But Iris seemed a flickering presence out there on the line, and their conversation that day could have been any of the others they'd had since the Bear had hit the road.

Fine.

And the doves?

They're fine.

The swallows?

Also fine.

Any trouble from Siege?

She had hardly seen him. Everything was fine.

I miss you.

She missed him too. How was the tour going?

Well, he allowed, things were beginning to look up.

Okay then, bye.

What? Iris . . . Iris . . . are you there?

Of course I am. Is there something else you wanted to say?

How about, thought the Bear after he had replaced the receiver in its sling, how about Duh, what's happening, sweetie?

The Bear retired to the back of the bus, sat down on the edge of the bed, hooked his saxophone back on the neckstrap and thought about what to work on next.

What he was beginning to find was that all the work he had done piecemeal and in the dark over the past year was beginning to cohere: it was precisely as if the essential work had been done without his consent—in fact he had fought it all the way, hating to be imposed upon by these false, misleading complications of quantitative harmony, these million-odd notes all over the place—his necessary music assembling itself as best it could without him, knowing he'd come around and join it sooner or later. The Bear would have resented this intrusion into the workings of his will were he not beginning, if not to see the light, then at least to take some pleasure in the sweetness of the first fruits of this odd and self-divided labor. He also began to have the old feeling that he and not the saxophone was the instrument, and that all the work he put in was no more than making sure the keys worked smoothly, the pads didn't stick and the reed wasn't thick with slobber. After that, if and when the right moment came, it was time to step aside and be played upon. Listen to this reed reborn. He wished.

The first of the tour's college towns gave him the leisure for a prolonged taste of these new pleasures. Ann Arbor: meaning nice woodsy club with a decent Baldwin baby grand and an attentive if sometimes overstudious young audience: impossible for him to get through a set without noticing all the elements he'd been struggling with starting to line up and dance. He felt like a supersaturated solution into which the crucial crystal had been dropped, and now all this music was precipitating out. Even so, he had to admit that he was being outplayed by his rhythm section; the good part was that it didn't especially bother him: he knew his place on the tour's evolutionary curve and did not try very hard to exceed its limits or run ahead, look back and see how he was doing. It was almost like being intelligent again, and besides, he could rationalize the situation a bit: most of the interesting playing going on these days was happening in rhythm sections anyway: he could abide a week or two of looking secondary. More than that, of course, he'd be thinking bloody murder.

His dreamlife was popping, though, parked out there in the campground outside town. One dawn, just as he was starting to nod off, a typical pale Mid-western type in neat hair, madras shirt and chinos appeared, leading a small boy by the hand. "Hi, I'm Tom," the man said, extending a friendly hand, "and this is my son Kevlar."

This jerked the Bear's head up, and he woke up laughing rather stupidly. After that he went back to sleep and about half an hour later had the most charming dream of his life. He was standing in a grassy field, feeling large and awkward, surrounded by a three-deep ring of children, five or six years old, dressed in bright colors. When they began to sing their voices were exactly like those of real children, reedy and only approximately in tune with each other—nice touch, thought the Bear—but the song, in the simplicity of C major, was even better.

—such a nice reversal, thought the Bear,
I don't mind them calling me a man.

—I get it, he thought, but then the kids
skulled him by adding, by calling him:

He woke in a state of addled bliss, feeling graced, as if he had been promised something much better than he could consciously imagine—not just a restoration of lost innocence but something finer and more fully formed. One question: in the fourth line had some of the children sung "You will see what I *am*"? It was possible. It worked either way. Kids had always loved him.

He wrote the tune down even though he knew he would not forget it—the dream had been so clear, and he had awakened from it in a wonderful brightness of mind—and before going back to sleep he parted the window-curtain with a claw and looked out: a few bodies in sleeping bags beside their cars, no one stirring in the early light. Perhaps some child had run past and that had . . . No, the dream had come from some other place entirely.

In a soft doze on another morning, he had had an erotic dream about doves: twenty or so descending on him, and he died in the rose underblush of their breasts as they pressed upon him, beating their wings. He understood that it was a dream while he was having it and knew that he would wake up with a lapful of seed, but even as the beating of their wings—ribbed, delicate—took him deeper and as he began to come he thought that there was nothing in this much beauty that was not implicit and surpassed in the embraces of Iris. Or maybe, he thought in his slow persistent way when he woke, that while he might be taking the world on one species at a time, Iris was their sum.

He liked the club in Madison Wisconsin too, though for some reason he experienced a shiver of fear on entering. He had Rondo double-check the security arrangements and back-door access, and made him promise to keep a particularly sharp lookout for anything that looked even remotely like the Law. All that happened was that he caught up with his rhythm section and had a few nights of feeling inhabited by an increasingly large body of music.

On the way out of Madison to St. Paul a few salient points were confirmed by phone: the guy from *Down Beat* would meet up with them in Minnesota and yes, they were getting the cover of the September issue. The Bear spoke with the interviewer on the phone, and after the ritual prelude of childhood reminiscence about animals, the man had wondered if the Bear was basically pro-Wynton or anti-Wynton, and this seemed a dire omen. Don't fence me in, he'd told the guy, I love everything Wynton does and he keeps getting better at all of it, and if an art form that throughout its history seemed to invent whole new forms of consciousness every ten years now seems to be pausing for thought and codification that's not Wynton's problem though occasionally it's mine. Yes, the parameters of a classical art form chafe some, but as it happens I'm working my way more deeply into them myself at the moment.

Now, rolling between cities, he was working up a speech that would compare the explosion of genius in jazz this century with the Italian Renaissance—good sense of scale there, he thought—but would point out, however, that there hadn't been a major innovator in the music for thirty years. . . .

The more he thought about it the more he lost himself in a thicket of qualifications: the early moderns possibly equal to the *cinquecento*—nah—or the unimportance of innovation to traditional art forms outside the insatiable maw of Western Sieve, etc. . . . There was no end to it. I'm not talkin', it just don't pay. The interviewer is gonna have to spin the usual line of crap about his childhood and Baloo and Smokey and make the rest of it up.

With time to spare between Madison and St. Paul, Rondo had taken a byroad along which farmland swept radially past the window, crops of corn fanning past in ordered rows, white farmhouses in the medium distance beneath aluminum phalloi full of grain.

"Buncha people fucking farm animals when they can't get ahold of their daughters," grumbled Hatwell. He was off Percocets, had begun to tipple and hadn't gotten laid last night.

The Bear reholstered the cellphone and told the band the news.

"You mean *you're* getting the cover of *Down Beat*," Linton laughed. "Don't you."

"All they're getting of me," the Bear told the band, since they were watching, "is the back of my hat, a few inches of neckfur and the general shape of my shoulders in a raincoat. You guys get to face the camera and smile for the people."

"What human musician would treat us this well?" Hatwell asked aloft. "From now on I'm working with paranoid higher mammals exclusively."

"Also," said the Bear, "the guy just told me if you hook your laptop up to the cellphone in five minutes he'll modem us an advance review of *Sensible Shoes*. He says they liked it."

"Modern times," said Hatwell, rummaging in his gigbag for the wiring. "News from the mothership. He said five minutes?"

But they had to wait ten.

"C'mon Rahim," the Bear asked Hatwell, who was hogging the screen and slapping Linton away, "what's it say?"

Hatwell pivoted away from the Bear on the chair. "The album got four and a half stars, I'm a precociously gifted young pianist—we all knew that—and Krieger's meticulous production style, get this, 'failed to capture the Bear's real furriness.'"

Laughter generally.

"Would there be anything in there about how I played?" the Bear wondered.

"Yeah," Bostic interjected, "what's it say about *me*?"

"I seem to remember you're not on the record, Lin," the Bear told him.

"So the fuck what? I'm on the bus."

"Wonder what you lost the half-star for," said Hatwell, scrolling up and down. "I know it wasn't me."

"Actually," said the Bear, "don't tell me anything else, it'll only fuck my head up."

Bostic started laughing again. "Bear, you're a show," he said.

"Maybe I'll go in the back and practice."

"And I *love* the way you do dedication," Bostic said.

"'Not so much an excellent new jazz record,'" Hatwell read aloud, "'as an unprecedented act of God.'"

"It says *that*?" said the Bear, dropping back into his seat and putting a paw to his brow.

Hatwell snickered at him: "Gotcha."

"River coming up," Rondo announced from the driver's seat. "The mighty Mississipp in just another mile or two. Real nice crossing on this road. You want to take a look."

"Yeah, you should check the river out," Hatwell told him. "Where I come from it's all industrial sludge—not to mention the floods this year, though thank God my folks' place is cool. East St. Louis Toodle-oo."

"We could visit them when we . . ." he began. Oh but look at the river. The bus soared out, and the Bear looked through the aluminum girderwork at the expanse.

The light that day was golden: long grassy islands lay here and there shouldering the blue immensity, and the declining sun spilled gold on tall grasses and bluffs back on the eastern bank.

"Is there any way," the Bear asked Rondo, "we can pull up somewhere on the other side, stretch our legs and have a look?"

"Sure thing."

"The Bear discovers America," Hatwell said.

"T. Lobsang Rampa," the Bear agreed.

Rondo cackled happily. After landfall the bus turned north along the river and followed two-lane blacktop until they came to a place where the shoulder widened sufficient for scenic overlook. Rondo checked the prospect and said it looked cool for wary mammals.

The Bear was first out of the bus. "See you guys later," he said, waving a vague paw in the air, and dropping to all fours he began to shoulder through the tall dun grass down the bluff toward the blue.

"Half hour tops," the Bear heard Rondo call, but didn't bother to acknowledge him. It was hot and humid but still sweet rumbling down the bank, a hint of cooler scents coming up to him on a gust from the river. The Bear broke into a trot and let the hillside take him, faster, stumbling, then letting the slope spill him into a somersault—cries and whoops from up there on the roadway as he went over—dry grass breaking under his weight, sweet friction, and an explosion of dust flurrying up into the sunlight and working into his fur. Righting himself, he accelerated to his fastest pace, his head full of pleasure atop this power and pull of muscle, free, then one more tumble over a stray redoubt and a last gallop to the blue running edge of the river. He hit the water fast and hard, stumbled a moment in the unexpected mud underfoot in the shallows, but finally reached sufficient depth and pushed out from shore, volumes of water bellying out from him in waves. Not as cold as he would have wished but it would do.

During his swim he was unable to rid himself of anxiety over the chance of being observed by cops or other strangers, although he knew that once in the water and from sufficient distance he could be mistaken for a log. He dove, couldn't see very far down there, and came up wuffing his mouth and nose clear. Give me a decent stretch of natural landscape and I'm at the top of the enjoyment chain, I swear. No creature alive takes greater pleasure from the premise of the world as given than I do. So what's my problem really?

The Bear dove again, deeper this time, testing the capacity of his breath and bumping nose-first into riverbottom—whut?—long before he'd expected it to be there. Having a great time anyway. Wish you were here. Why was she so uncommunicative on the phone?

He came out of the river in what he figured was ten minutes, shook himself dry and climbed the bank to where the grass was tallest, chomped down some sweet-tasting green shoots and reclined on his back and elbows to admire the prospect, glad to be delivered from the labyrinth of music back into the apparent simplicity of the world—look at that river; put your nose into that breeze out of the north and wuff down the insinuating texture of its woven scents: there is no end to this except the one we make, sheer tedium. All the same, within a very few minutes his mind wiped an eraser across the view.

Something in his playing oppressed him, something, it might be, unpleasant about him generally. It had to do with the heaviness of obsession.

Look at the wind combing waves through the grass on that island. That's music for you. That's the way to play. He felt the same wind ruffle the fur on his head. You've always been ambitious. It's fouling your music. There's a heaviness, an obsessiveness, to your work. You're not having enough fun with it. Why can't you play more like the guys?

What?

He heard it again, a voice calling from up the bluff, and understanding it was time to go he took in the blue of the river and the gold of the banks and islands one last time, turned his head uphill, and caught Bobby Hatwell skylighted by the reddening sun. "What?" he called.

"Come back to the raft, Huck honey," came Hatwell's voice, brought nearer by a change in the wind.

The Bear shuffled to his hindfeet, waved acknowledgment, and shook himself dry one last time.

Back on the bus again, rolling away from the river, music was declared necessary, but there was some discussion as to what to put on the box.

"*Black Saint and the Sinner Lady*," was Garrett's vote.

"Again?"

"There is no end to Mingus," Garrett said.

In the end Hatwell insinuated a Keith Jarrett trio disc into the machine, but after awhile he began imitating Jarrett's vocal impression of a goat being horribly tormented with a sharp stick in its privates—"I think I'll start doing this onstand," he said, "but I'll do it during the bass solos"—and since he wouldn't stop bleating Garrett got up and switched the music off.

"You're no fun," Hatwell told him.

"I know," Garrett said.

"You know what?" Bostic asked, settled low in the benchseat, legs draped over the table—it had taken him weeks to find this posture but once he had achieved it he could stay in it for hours at a time. His right foot nodded in its hi-top canvas sneaker. "We oughta work on our shit for the *Down Beat* interview."

"Good point," Hatwell said. "Bear, you spoke to the cat, dinchoo. He white?"

"The interviewer? Think so."

"See," Hatwell explained, "Linton's right. We should work our shit up. We should keep it dignified—Garrett, I'm talking to you—and we should be extra extra careful not to bring up any unfortunate cultural stereotypes." He leaned across the aisle toward Bostic with an empty beercan in his hand and extended it like a microphone. "*Down Beat* here. First question. How do you like to beat yo' ho'?"

Bostic laughed. "I likes to give de ho' the back of mah hand," he said into the beercan, "when de ho' ain't lookin. Trick is, look left, hit right, 'cause if de ho' see it comin' she move her head and I could hurt mah hand and den I has to cut her."

"And how do you like to *cut* yo' ho'?"

Garrett got up, walked back to the CD player and rummaged amid the plastic boxes. Bostic watched him.

"Appalled?" Hatwell asked the Bear.

"Yes thanks."

Garrett had selected a disc, and they could hear the anticipatory whirr of the player above the roadnoise and the air conditioner. Coltrane came on.

"Oh shit. God is in the house," Bostic said. "We have to cut this shit out."

"Our bassist has shamed us," Hatwell said, and hung his head.

It was "Crescent," and they sat listening to Trane's evolving solo, the gathering crests of his phrasing, the periodic releases as thematic waves broke smooth and ordered on the shore.

"Well," said the Bear, "there it is."

"Yeah let's all play like that," Hatwell agreed.

"You ever see Trane play live?" Bostic asked the Bear.

"I was just a cub."

"We hate you anyway. Tell us about it."

"Jones took me down to Birdland on a leash. Don't laugh. We used to play with the imagery. Once or twice Jones wore shades and acted blind and I'd lead him. Our surrealist phase. You should've seen the double-takes."

"Coltrane," Hatwell reminded him.

"He was pretty hard to hear over the drums once Elvin Jones got going."

"C'mon, what was it *like*?"

"Something like being burned alive," said the Bear, back there, seeing it. "I was still a cub but I thought I'd experienced everything there was in the world and Trane was this enormous dose of Oh no you haven't, either. It was too much for me but it left a deeper mark on me than anything else I've ever heard."

"Uh huh."

"Part of my problem was that I had to keep acting like your typical animule and instead I kept moving to the music and watching Trane. Jones kept yanking on the leash and telling me to keep the act up. You guys really interested in this?"

"Yeah."

"What can I say? I remember thinking once or twice that there was nothing left for Trane to do but levitate or burst into flames. Because the resources of music as such were over, exhausted."

"Look at his eyes," Hatwell said.

"Nice glaze," was Bostic's comment.

"Elvin used to come over, hunker down and play with me between sets. You have any idea how strong his hands are?"

"I shook hands with him a couple times," Linton said. "It hurt."

"Then you know. He practically tore my head off. Trane came over once or twice and just stood there looking at me."

"You talk to him?"

"Are you kidding? I couldn't have talked to him if I tried, I was in such awe of him. I loved looking at his face, though. Those eyes. That smile. He smoked cigars."

"Thank you for that important fact," Hatwell said.

"Carla Bley used to stop by the table and scratch me behind the ears too. She thought I was cute. You know she was the cigarette girl at Birdland, right? her way of getting in to hear the music for nothing, but she did the whole thing, pink costume, fishnet stockings, big tray of cigarettes and teddy bears. Jones was hung up on her but she just wanted to play with me."

"You was coppin' feels off her," Bostic said laughing. "I know it."

"I really don't remember," the Bear sniffed. "Jimmy Garrison wanted to bring me some food from the kitchen but Pee Wee Marquette told him no . . . You know who Pee Wee Marquette was?"

"The midget emceed the place," Bostic said.

"The guy Lester Young called 'half a motherfucker,'" Garrett remembered.

"Right," said the Bear, "and Jimmy got in an argument with Pee Wee about feeding me and once the band went back up Pee Wee told us we had to leave. His cologne smelled worse than anything. God, he stank."

"We're so privileged just to be on this bus with you," Hatwell said piously.

"He saw Trane."

"He copped feels off Carla Bley in her prime."

"He has experienced more than we will ever know."

"He weighs more than all of us put together."

"He smells like shit from the river."

Onstand in a suburb of St. Paul that night the Bear felt something in himself let go. He uncovered a creamy lyricism on ballads, a greater amplitude of swing on the mid-tempo tunes and didn't feel rushed on the quick ones. Toward the end of the evening he experienced the first flutters of something like the old bliss at the entrance to his heart, and visions beckoned him from beyond the edge of things. He wasn't ready for that yet—too much work to do down here—but he began to experience, for the first time in ages, the music actually beginning to lift him, to invite him level upon level through higher, ampler, more satisfying worlds. Not yet, he said firmly. I've botched this stuff before, but I hope if the time is right again I'll be ready.

If you stand where I stand you will see what I am.

Little one.

When he went to sleep after the gig that night, the Bear had no idea he was dreaming when he walked into a theater that might well have been set up in a tent. The stage, brightly but not harshly lit—in fact the light was exceptionally pleasant—had a square of white canvas for backdrop, and when the jugglers were introduced, a number of red, orange and yellow geometrical objects—circles, triangles, squares—appeared onstage and began tossing themselves to each other across the stage, sometimes changing into each other—red triangle into orange square—as they were caught.

The Bear thought it was the most wonderful thing he had ever seen.

"And now," a voice announced from offstage, "ladies and gentlemen, the Circle."

The brightly colored objects now began to whirl in a circle against the white canvas backdrop, going faster and faster, wider and wider, and beginning to blur slightly with the speed of their motion. The Bear was so completely taken with the charm of the show that it did not even occur to him to laugh or applaud: he felt like doing both, but did neither because it would distract him, and besides it wasn't needed. As the circle widened, the whirling shapes began turning green, blue and purple at the edges of their orbit and the light onstage brightened still more pleasantly. It was wonderful to watch. That was when the Bear woke up.

He lay there in the bunk awhile, enjoying the memory of the show and wishing he could see it again. He knew he would never be able to explain to anyone, or even to himself, how enchanting a dream it was: the bright colors, the cheerful light, the sense of play. It took him about five minutes to realize that these "jugglers" were in some sense the guys in the band, and that what he had been enjoying was their essential freedom, unmediated by the conditions of world and place and time: what he had called their youth.

The funny thing was, every time he went outside the changes on them, which he'd done once or twice on an experimental basis and for a whiff of the old days, for all their hoo-ha freedom the guys didn't know how to come up with a group response. Bobby, who had done so well when they were taking it outside on the *Shoes* session—but he'd had Charlie Haden to steer by—now either laid out or played meandering empty octaves, looking for home and a glass of tonic. Garrett tried to follow the Bear's tonal drift but unlike Haden had to think four beats and by the time he'd made his choice the Bear had moved the action elsewhere. When Linton heard the Bear going out, he played more eccentric polyrhythms and left some of his phrases unfinished—you know, *weird*—which didn't really cut it. The Bear gave up on it after two tunes and wouldn't try it again. It must be a generational thing, he supposed.

The other funny thing: driven by his own imperatives and without reference to the music's current neoclassical moment, the Bear had drifted more than a few degrees from his roughly free jazz habits to reinvestigate the details of the harmonic tradition. It shocked him how much he was a bear of his time.

But you know? We might play some interesting music by the time we finish the tour in Colorado. God, I wish Iris could be here to see it.

3

the Blue Note in Boulder Colorado was the coolest-looking, not to mention the most luxuriously outfitted, club they played that tour by a long shot. The Bear sat at the bar, wearing his full nightclub rig of jumpsuit and raincoat, his hat on the bartop, sipping a Myers' rum and orange juice and enjoying the prospect in advance. It was a barn of a place: from his end seat on the bar's rounded wooden corner—American oak—he could look through a big square archway into the club's main room: high walls of nearly midnight blue, around which ran a fine line of royal-blue neon about ten feet up, enclosing rows of clean tables, with dark violet tablecloths believe it or not and orderly chairs; and although from his seat he couldn't see all the way front to the stage, the Bear knew that the band's instruments stood under modulated spotlights, preparatory to a final sound check, and the band was chatting up a bunch of pretty waitresses—the Bear had felt his own presence spook the lasses, so he had retired to the bar until the crew was ready for a last runthrough. The place had everything: good acoustics, onstage monitors that gave you an honest image back, and not just one acute weird pothead techie soundguy but an actual crew that adjusted microphones, stands, dials, slides and whirlies as if it mattered. Good Lord, this gig might be more than the usual struggle against the force of circumstance.

Which was especially welcome, in view of the record or quasi-record they would make their last two nights here.

The Bear sipped his drink. He had never been treated this well in a club, and the band had clocked in to tell him that Boulder had the finest-looking women they had seen since Paris, Milan, Stockholm, Urbino, Rome, yeah maybe anywhere. . . . Anyhow it was the right cap to a tour that had gone pretty well after its unforgettably bad beginning. Even the *Down Beat* interview had gone well, although the issue wasn't out yet. The Bear got in a few words edgewise, the band had had their fun with the guy, and the Polaroids from the photo shoot promised an interesting cover: the Bear's back and shoulders massive under the raincoat and the guys looking pleased with themselves into the camera in front of a textured grey backdrop. Yeah, it had gone well, and Hatwell and Bostic hadn't given the interviewer too hard a time, considering.

Although, thought the Bear, the genuinely odd and interesting thing was how quickly and without fanfare the band's social act had changed once the

Bear loosened up and from St. Paul onward joined the general sense of fun. Everything got quieter—Hatwell less cutting and acidulous, Linton accordingly more laid back, and even Garrett began to enjoy something like free speech and equal time—and the Bear had blinked at it, amazed, because it seemed a subtle and instantaneous response to his own inward unconfessed change of state, a balancing act gracefully, perhaps perfectly achieved, as if the guys in the band were enlightened representatives of some higher agency, and had clowned around and made a lot of noise until he got the message and rolled away the stone.

It was pretty unlikely, but that's how it looked. Elevated unspoken stuff going on behind the scenery. When people talked about the subtle interaction between musicians they didn't know the half of it.

If only he could get a little interaction out of Iris. She was still relentlessly fine on the phone, and if the Bear could have afforded to worry about it he would have worried a lot. Finally he decided, since he couldn't do anything about it, that the best he could manage was pretend it wasn't happening, and if it was not just a quirk of hers but bad news, he would deal with it when he got home. Which was pretty soon. Of course it worried him.

At least he was having all those good, seems-like-the-old-days conversations with Jones. Speaking of whom . . .

The Bear watched Jones, must be fresh from the airport because he was carrying a suitcase and a garment bag, walk right past him and thrust his face through the archway as if he might just find the Bear in the next room. The Bear grinned as Jones halted with a characteristic wobble beneath the arch.

"Hello, sailor," the Bear called, laughing.

"Bear!" said Jones.

It really was great to see the old boy.

Jones dropped his bags, the Bear got off his barstool, and they managed a series of big imbalanced hugs and backslaps.

"Together again after all these years," said the Bear. "Back from the dead."

"We're friends again?" Jones asked him.

"Seems that way, doesn't it. You look terrific. You look all different."

"Yeah," said Jones. "It's possible I do."

"Come to the bar and have a drink with me."

"Come with me if you wanna go to Kan-sas City."

"Been there, done that," said the Bear.

They hunkered onto adjacent barstools.

"Yeah," said Jones, "Kansas City. What was so important about Kansas City that you wouldn't tell me about it on the phone last week?"

"I wouldn't? Funny, it doesn't seem important now. I went out to visit Charlie Parker's grave, and even though the guys in the band were ragging me all the way through the cemetery—ooh, spooky, ooh look, a UFO shaped like an alto—I was hit by all these powerful emotions, and I felt sure, sure that I was, um, you know."

"You were gonna encounter his spirit."

"Like that," the Bear admitted. "But when I found the actual grave, all those big emotions vanished, all that sense of being greeted—zip."

"And this is what you wouldn't tell me on the phone?" Jones asked him.

"That night," said the Bear, "I had a dream in which I had a long talk with John Coltrane. We sat in two armchairs and I think I asked him all my deepest questions about, um, being out here and trying to do something real with the music."

"What did he tell you?"

"I can't remember. By the time I was aware of the dream the talk was almost over."

"Tough luck."

"The only specific thing I do remember," the Bear went on, lowering his voice, "is that he looked at his watch and said, 'Oh, I have to go. Why don't you come over to the house and have dinner with us, and then we're going to this little club in Brooklyn'—I knew he meant the old Club la Marchal—'nobody knows we'll be there and you could sit in with us, you could play.' And I blurted out that I was just this little cub from the sixties and I used to come see you on a leash and there's no way I could ever . . . et cetera. And he said—I remember the sound of his voice and it was his—he laughed and said, 'Aw, never mind all that stuff. Just come along with us, have some dinner, and play.' And I woke up."

"So whaddayou think?" Jones asked the Bear. "You think it was a real encounter?"

"No idea," the Bear told him.

"Oh?" Jones remarked suspiciously.

"Maybe it has to do with me making some kind of a shift. I don't know." The Bear shrugged. "It's a mystery to me. I've had a very active dreamlife out here, but I don't know what it signifies, if anything. Could just be subjective stuff. Dreams is tricky, Jones."

"What's that you're drinking?" Jones nodded at the Bear's glass.

"Rum and orange. Have one. Sally?" A tall dazzle of redhead appeared before them and answered yes. Sally was not wearing very much and the Bear still couldn't figure how anyone could get a body to grow into all those shapes and fit them together so well. "One for my buddy and one more for the road."

"Okay, Frank," Sally said, and turned to the ranks of bottles.

"Where did *she* come from?"

"Take a stroll around town. Must be the mountain air. Place is loaded with Tibetan monks too."

Sally set two drinks in front of them, smiled and said Hi to Jones in such a way that he nearly fell backward off his barstool.

"Jesus," said Jones. "What're the monks like?"

"Orange robes, nice smiles," said the Bear, and took a sip of his drink. "You know? Now that you're here we oughta rent a van and get up into the mountains in the afternoons. The bus isn't built for it, and it's too conspicuous."

"I think I can put a car on the company and tool the two of us around."

"Yeah, what's up with the music biz? How's *Shoes* doing? We making a record here or what?"

"*Shoes* is doing fine and we can record two nights here and it's either another record or a radio show. How good's the band?"

"You can hear them in a minute." The Bear leaned to look past Jones into the main room but didn't see signs of anything happening yet. "Only place I've ever seen that wants to do a second sound check because the first one didn't come out perfect."

"Your wide experience," said Jones. "How you like touring?"

"I haven't been arrested yet and we're sounding better. Jones, I don't think I've ever seen you this relaxed and cool. You don't mind my asking, is this the result of Sybil loosening up on you or did you get a stock option?"

"It's the result of realizing that a tense, crummy, frightened life shot through with occasional visions and lately some pretty amazing sex wasn't . . . um, probably I shouldn't be talking about the sex."

"Nah, I like it."

"I don't know, Bear. Things started working out. Sybil did reconcile herself to the idea that being with me wasn't the worst thing that had ever happened to her, but I think I changed first. I saw that I was in something like a state of grace and always had been. So I learned to stop worrying and love the bomb."

"Ah ha," said the Bear. He squinied up his eye at his old buddy, looking for signs of the Higher Fatuity as Jones had practiced it, but didn't find any. The old boy seemed surprisingly well settled in himself. The Bear raised his glass of rum and juice in salute and hoped it would last.

"Why're you looking at me like that?" Jones asked him. "A flower just pop out of the top of my head or something?"

"I'm just enjoying you."

"That makes a change. We were drilling on opposite sides of the mountain for awhile. How you doing otherwise?"

"I'm music stupid. The music's working out but I don't know nothing about nothing else. Occupational hazard. I took a swim in the Mississippi River and thought about chords. I sat on the grassbank and forgot that the Mississippi was being taken over by zebra mussels flushed from European tankers and that they were using up all the oxygen in the river and everything else was dying."

"What would you have done, eat 'em all with pasta?"

"I forgot the river was flooding people out of their homes further south—"

"You were gonna drink it?"

"—and forests were going up like matchsticks in the drought, habitat was still shrinking, the sun was burning hotter—"

"Think you could blow it out?"

"—and the sky'd gone bad."

"That's a lot to remember."

"I know," said the Bear, and sighed. He wanted to ask Jones if he knew what was going on with Iris, but he hesitated, then disgressed. "Some nights now when the music opens up I go into visionary states, little ecstasies and flutters, and I'm happy to forget everything else. When I'm in those states everything isn't so much forgotten as subsumed. But how real is that? I wish I knew."

"Having a second cubhood?"

"It's been awhile," the Bear agreed. "It's nice, but it doesn't mean what it used to. I mean, life is more . . . um."

"Life is definitely more um," said Jones. "Is there something you want to ask me?"

"Actually . . ." the Bear began, but then he heard the rhythm section starting up in the other room, an arpeggio on the piano, a rap on the snare drum, then Hatwell and Bostic starting to make animal noises into their microphones. The call of the wild.

"How've they been?" Jones asked the Bear as they dismounted from their barstools. "You get along? How're they playing?"

"They're geniuses," said the Bear. "And a pleasure to live with."

"Don't you find Bobby Hatwell just a little intense?"

"The man's a pussycat. Wait'll you hear us play."

"Um," said Jones, holding the Bear back a moment with a pull on the sleeve of his raincoat.

"Um?"

"See if you can guess who might be coming out for the recording nights."

"The Great Dane?"

"No, Krieger said he'd never work with you again and he's keeping to it. James'll be out day after tomorrow to hook up with a local studio and a mobile unit and get everything set."

"We ought to be able to give them something worth taping," said the Bear. "The band's great, and I don't want to sound pretentious but I think I might finally be coming into my . . . my real, maybe . . . but, you know, I could choke when I know the tape recorder's on. We'll see."

"You're still funny," Jones told him.

"Thanks. So who's coming out?"

Jones looked at him oddly. "Bear, you're shitting me. You really can't guess?"

4

iris sat in the bus, her hands composed upon her lap, and waited for the Bear to get the news of her arrival and come out of the club to see her. Since the Blue Note fronted on some kind of pedestrian mall or walking-street, Tommy Talmo had pulled the tour bus into a service alley behind the building: dark night, utility ports blowing exhaust above hulking dumpsters. The Bear wasn't supposed to know she was here, but she was sure that Jones had told him. The Colorado night was cool even though it was summer in the mountains. Tommy Talmo had switched the motor off and, clumsily, elaborately polite, opened two small square hatches in the roof before he left. Iris had asked him to please lock the door. She didn't know how long she would have to wait. A powerful force knotted her small bony graceless hands together atop her thighs, and she had the familiar sensation of being about to break apart and fly off in bits and pieces. She had grown stronger and more peaceful in her domestic months with the Bear, but now that she was daring to make this journey . . .

Iris heard a heavy key turn and the door sigh open. The bus dipped to take his weight, and then the Bear burst upward into visibility, his head turning every whichway in search of her: he was, thought Iris, like an irruption of primal chaos, and she was both happy to see him and scared half to death.

How odd that he hadn't seen her. She was right there in front of him, in the chair, although it was true she had switched off the overhead light, as soon as she had found the button.

"Bear?" she said, and the degree of emotion in her voice sounded inappropriate even to her. After all this was supposed to be a meeting of old friends.

The Bear made a noise of discovery and welcome, and even though he halted for a moment before advancing upon her arms outstretched, Iris could feel the swarming shape of his affection and all his heart's warmth coming at her like a huge wave. It threatened to overtop her, and she had to keep intact every scrap of courage that had brought her this far. She must keep her will intact regardless, and her consciousness organized. She had vows to carry out, commandments to bear witness to and obey. "Here I am," she said, and stood.

"Ba-by," the Bear bellowed all too predictably and took her in his arms. He enveloped her for a moment, then tilted back to have a look. "It's beyond belief incredible to see you here. Let me take you up into the mountains tomorrow. You gonna ride back East on the bus with us after we're done? You know we're recording tonight? It's our last night and we got so much great stuff on tape already we don't know what to do with it. You've got to hear us play. We're unbelievable. We've had incredible luck. You look more beautiful than ever, you're straight off a nonstop out of heaven. How was the flight? I love you so much my heart's about to burst. The music is getting incredible. How do you expect me to be able to hug you if you get back down in that chair? Iris for Christ's sweet sake say something already."

It was pretty much what Iris had expected. "Take a seat," she said, and indicated the matching chair across the aisle.

The Bear lapsed backward into black leather—Iris had a brief preposterous sensation of seeing herself in a mirror as the Bear—which sighed its protest and widened a split in its left side but settled beneath him at last. "Jones told me you were coming out but he wouldn't say a word about why."

"I don't believe you," she said.

"Pardon?"

"I don't believe that Jones is capable of keeping his mouth that completely shut."

"We're going down to Santa Fe to get your daughters," the Bear admitted.

"Did he say why?"

"I don't need a why. You want to get your daughters and you want my help is enough. I'd do anything for you, you know that."

"Are you sure?"

"Santa Fe," the Bear ruminated. "That's in Arizona, right? The saint of faith in the arid zone. Perfect."

"Santa Fe is in New Mexico," Iris said.

"That's like a couple of hours' drive from here. Half a day? I know. Rondo told me. When do we go? Tomorrow? Want to go tonight? I'm supposed to make a record but fuck it, who cares, baby I'm so proud of you. Let's get you your daughters back. We'll all go back home together on the bus. What are you looking so worried about? Something wrong down there? If that son of a bitch Herb is treating them wrong I'll pound him to a pulp. I'll grind him up like coffee beans and scatter the grounds all over Arizona. I'm with you, I'm here."

"I would be awfully glad of your help and support, Bear," Iris told him.

"Look at this face," said the Bear, indicating his own. "Is this an expression of positivity and good will or what? You want to leave now or come into the club and hear us finish up our fifteen-CD set?"

"I'd like to hear you play and then if everything can be arranged we can spend the night together and start out tomorrow morning," Iris said.

"It's beyond perfect," the Bear told her. "I'm so glad to see you. Come on inside and I'll play a beautiful set for you, special."

Later, she would remember very little of the Blue Note: a large place with high walls of midnight blue, and the guys in the band coming up to her all smiles. "Hi," she said, and involuntarily laughed. Months back, at the rehearsals in Shady, all their affection had been for each other, with some left over for the Bear and no essential mind paid to her at all—she might have been a piece of talking furniture. Now she felt an unmistakable warmth of affection swarming down on her from these three young men as they surrounded her at the table. Was this because of the time and the miles and the music, so that she was a sideline beneficiary of their affection for him—or was her link with the Bear such an amusing sexual idea? Finally their obvious sincerity relieved her of this distress. ". . . delayed two hours at Kennedy," she said, "but a very nice flight after that, thank you."

"Rondo hold up a 7-Eleven on the way back from the airport?" Linton asked her.

"Who?" But Iris didn't find out who Rondo was. The Bear stretched out his arms and hugged his band all in one. Bostic affected to collapse beneath the weight of the embrace.

"Ain't they terrific?" the Bear asked her from between Garrett's head and Linton Bostic's.

There was a momentary blur, and then the Bear noticed four Tibetan monks in orange robes seated at a table behind him. "I'm sorry were we crowding you?" the Bear asked them. "No?" and then the Bear looking down at them while they grinned up at him.

"Whea you ah *from*," a roundheaded monk with short black hair, golden skin, and a wonderfully open smile asked the Bear finally.

"New York City, trailing clouds of glory," the Bear told him. "You?"

"Tibet," the monk answered.

"Oh yeah? What part?"

Iris was surprised to see the tableful of monks get the joke right away and break up laughing. They must have been around awhile.

Speaking of which, it seemed to her that just before the Bear departed for the stage—he had his arm around her and was being obnoxiously expansive—the monks registered her conjunction with the Bear and exchanged rapid parenthetical words in Tibetan between themselves on the subject: offensive, and once the Bear left they smiled and nodded hello and best regards at her too much.

At the time, Iris was intent on getting ahold of Jones, who seemed to be fussing at details between the lip of the stage and a booth along the right-hand wall at the rear of the club, to which a skein of shielded black cables led.

When the band began their set with a shuffle blues that sounded half-familiar, Iris was able to wave Jones over. "I hope you're coming down to Santa Fe with us," she said, pulling him nearer by his wrist so that he would not run off.

"Of course," he said.

"Good," she nodded. "It's such a comfort to me."

Jones put a theatrically sincere look on his face and bent to hug her awkwardly around the shoulders. "You're getting your daughters back," he said.

"I hope I am."

"Hey, the Bear's great in a rescue. Don't worry. We'll do it. It'll be a blast."

"This isn't going to be a picnic," she said. "It might not work out. You don't know Herb."

"Don't worry, kid. We got him covered."

They just didn't get it, did they?

Later, after a three-set night that had been well received by the audience, the moon was heading down and the mountains were a jagged line of script rising against the stars as Rondo drove Iris and the Bear north out of Boulder on two-lane blacktop to the campground. Garrett and that pretty redheaded barmaid followed them in an old Volvo. Iris only half listened to the Bear telling her that Rondo would take them to Santa Fe and back for two hundred dollars. And should he take the extra week at the club or not?

"Why not decide when we get back?" she advised.

Perhaps five miles north out of town they turned left on a dirt road that led them into the lap of the mountains, the bus jouncing over the irregularities of the way. Iris went forward to look through the windshield: peaks swam up the sky swallowing ranked stars and the declining quarter moon as the bus drew into their shade. Iris shuddered. No. It will work, she thought. It has to.

"Almost there," Rondo said.

She felt the Bear's paw lightly on her shoulder and she moved from under it. "It's beautiful here," Iris said.

"This is where I've been staying since we got to Boulder," the Bear told her. "The best layup I've had the whole tour. Usually I sleep outside. There's the gate."

Iris saw something indistinct to left and right as the bus passed through.

"It's a campsite supposed to be closed right now while they do some kind of work on it, but Rondo here picked a lock or two and found the right people to pay off—"

"Heh heh heh," said Rondo thickly, and Iris heard gravel under the tires as the bus swung left and eased ever so gracefully—he really did have a touch at the pedals, Iris thought—to a stop, and Iris saw the Volvo pull up alongside the bus on the right.

"Home sweet home," said the Bear.

Rondo explained that he was leaving them the keys in case they wanted heat or cold or whatever the fuck, excuse me ma'am, and he'd see them, was eleven in the morning too early? cause let's figure six hours down to Santa Fe and what time did they want to get there? Okay, see you at ten. You know what time it is now? Okay, bye.

The Volvo tooted twice in farewell, arm of Rondo waving from a rear window as the taillights swung away.

Iris and the Bear stood outside the bus, letting the silence resume. Something yipped way off, and when Iris heard leaves rustling she looked left and was just able to discern a spaced planting of young aspens, silver leaves aflutter in starlight and the aura of a last-quarter moon down behind the jag of mountains.

"What do you think?" asked the Bear.

"It's a lovely spot. This is a campsite. We're in a parking lot. Why isn't anyone else here?"

"Rondo didn't say. Are you complaining?"

"No."

They made love in a bunk in the back of the bus so quickly and in such a fever the intensity startled them all the way through. Afterwards the Bear started laughing.

"What?" Iris asked.

"It was like being electrocuted, only in the nicest possible way," he said, and she laughed with him. After awhile they went outside again, Iris lightly wrapped in a topsheet.

"Looky thar," said the Bear, and they stood awhile watching frequent streaks of starfall race down the outspread wings of night: it was the meteor-shower time of year, and this was an ideal sky to see it in: a fine dust of light, seminal wash of materia prima behind billions of bright particularities. Down here among the aspens, other constellations flickered, reconfigured, reappeared: fireflies out courting. "There goes another one," said the Bear, pointing up at a meteor streak quickly followed by another a few degrees down the sky.

"I stood outside the house and watched them in Shady before I flew out," Iris said. "But what a sky you have here, Bear. Clearer. So many stars."

"You think it's mine?"

"Have I been mistaken in you? Don't you own all this?"

"Huh? What? Excu—" said the Bear, then by unaided starlight saw Iris' smile. "Why d'you always tease me?"

"Because you're easy," Iris said.

They went back inside the bus because in fact it was getting a little cool, wasn't it, and when they made love a second time it was with a gentleness and a delicacy of consideration neither of them could remember having felt before. Almost like a farewell. The Bear switched off the little light.

"I never knew it could be like that," Iris' voice said in the dark, then she laughed. "I don't believe I said that."

The Bear laughed with her but added, "I didn't either."

They were quiet awhile, each remembering favorite details. "I've never understood," the Bear finally told her, "why anyone would experience tristesse after."

"We don't. I don't. Do you?"

"Why would I? Listen, tell me about what's happening with your daughters. Do you want them back on general principles or is something bad happening down there?"

"Both. They don't say much, but I was always afraid that Herb would crack up, even in his strong days, and now I hear it in my daughters' voices and I'm sure I hear it in his. I'm afraid for my daughters, Bear."

"Don't worry, kid. We're gonna rescue your kids from the Ogre."

"This is not a fairy tale."

"Oh yeah? Look at the company you keep."

Iris' was voice serious, level: "I know I'm taking them back. I've seen it."

"Are we talking precognitive flash here?" the Bear wanted to know.

"I wouldn't have the strength to do it if it weren't for you. I don't mean your coming with me now, although that's important, believe me. I mean that without your influence . . . Without the strength you've given me I wouldn't have dared to try. I want you to know that, whatever happens."

"What could happen? We'll get your kids back and we'll live happy ever after. You're doing a good thing. But would you mind if I ask a simple question? Why didn't you tell me? Why nothing for months at home and then all this fine fine fine on the phone? Why such total secrecy?"

"I wasn't sure I'd have the strength until the plane actually lifted off for Denver. And I didn't want to get into a, what should I call it, thing with you about it in advance."

"What thing? I'm with you all the way on this."

"I didn't want you pushing me into it either, if I wasn't sure it was right. I had to be sure, myself. Do you remember telling me that you'd give me your self if you could? I think that's what you've done, and I'm grateful."

"I don't think that's possible," he told her. "It's all you and it's great."

"You're so undiscriminating. And you can't take a compliment."

"That's true. Can I turn on the light?"

"Do we have enough blankets to keep us warm if we sleep outside?" Iris asked him. "If we stay here the bed's too narrow and we'll have to hold hands across the aisle. I would rather sleep in your arms."

"We can take two of these mats outside and some blankets, besides which we have our love to keep us warm. Not to mention the usual bearskin rug."

"This is still so strange," she said. "Let's go."

In the early morning the Bear watched her walk pink and naked—such a nice little tush—on the grass, then among the aspens. Neither of them had managed much sleep that night. They'd done a lot of stargazing and listening to the wind. Before first light they dozed off, but the Bear, moved by his usual worries of being discovered in inappropriate relation to the known world, woke with a start not long after, and this pulled her awake before he had a chance to watch the sweetness of her sleep.

They'd washed up a bit in the bus's small facility, and he had given her a clean toothbrush from his bundle since she had forgotten to pack one. Now she was walking tiptoe through the morning dew as the Bear watched her from the stepwell. The sight of her like this—a sprite whose walk was so like a dance there was no difference—conformed to some essential notion he had always had of her: he almost expected to see her bend to sip a breakfast of dew from a grassblade or a leaf extended her by some solicitous aspen. Her refinement was so extreme that despite all the dinnertable evidence day to day he half-thought she really did sustain herself on something as barely material as stray condensation or the rain. Ridiculous thought. The Bear watched her walk lightly on the tidy grass between the aspens, behind her the mountains soaring up in dark green drama to greystone crags, and the Bear knew that this image of her, at this moment, was inscribing itself on his memory and would remain as long as he did. Look at the grace of her step. Wings might sprout from her back at any moment.

But she was strong enough to come out here and get her daughters. He was proud of her.

The Bear heard an approaching engine and looked back along the dirt approach road east. "Come back to the raff—" he called before remembering that he'd heard the phrase somewhere lately—where? "Iris!" he called. "Visitors! Guests!"

The Bear squinted up the road. Two cars coming, a minivan he hadn't seen before . . . and last night's Volvo. Had the whole band come out to see them off?

Iris dressed in the bus and watched the group of them in the parking area through the tinted windows as she smoothed her white blouse and checked the zipper on her jeans: the band, the Bear, Jones, two sleepy waitresses beside the idling cars, and Rondo peering over toward the bus. Iris didn't think anyone had seen her naked.

The Bear and his band were exchanging a series of embraces so hearty and intense that the implied degree of male bonding almost frightened her: she had to remember that the fear issued from her thoughts of Herb and what might happen when she confronted him. The Bear and the band were innocent.

She slipped her shoes on, checked herself a last time in the narrow insufficient mirror, and when she came carefully down the stepwell she was surprised to see that it was Linton Bostic who trotted over and turned up toward her—she was still on the last black rubber step, hadn't quite come down to earth yet—his handsome young face and brilliant smile. "We all want to wish you luck on this one," he said. "Me, I'd like to come along and help you out, but everyone tells me no, the Bear and Jones and Rondo got it covered. How you doing?"

"I'm touched," was all Iris could find to say.

Linton extended his long, loose-jointed right arm and steadied her way to the ground. By then everyone was surrounding her with good wishes, and Iris didn't clear her head of the general clamor of farewell until the bus had regained the blacktop south and Jones was rustling two large white paper bags open. Iris smelled something good.

"We decided to come out early," Jones was saying. "Maybe we shoulda called—why didn't we call? I forget—but Rondo did a time-and-motion study and threw the Ching, and maybe you should make a pot of coffee. I know I'd like some, and look what I brought."

Jones had brought, complexly wrapped in paper, bagels loaded with cream cheese and onions and tomatoes and especially lox from the New York Deli back in downtown Boulder, one each for himself and her and four for the Bear plus a couple extra with cream cheese only just in case. She and the Bear competed awkwardly at the coffee machine and dropped the brewing papers twice, but they got it settled and the bus was steady south.

"Fantastic breakfast," said the Bear, before popping another bagel in.

"We got a long day ahead of us," Rondo said from the wheel. "Can we hear some music?"

The Bear was wise enough to give the man a dose of country.

When it came to country music, Iris divided it simply: there was Willie Nelson and there was everyone else. This wasn't Willie Nelson but she could live with it. The coffee was good and she poured herself another cup, and it was almost home life with the Bear again: she watched the Bear ingest half a bagel in one mouthful and remembered that this was his personal favor to her, his version of being dainty: usually he liked to eat them whole. The cream cheese frothing out the sides of his jaws made him look rabid anyway.

"There it is," said Rondo, pointing left when they were ten minutes south of Boulder, and they bent to look at an expanse of low dun buildings about a quarter mile distant on the plain behind a series of protective fences. "Rocky Flats."

"Where they made plutonium triggers for H-bombs," Jones explained. "Now they're cleaning the place up. As if, heh heh heh, they could."

"Yeah, that's the place," Rondo brayed from his seat, and turned toward them while still driving. "Radioactivity all over the place out here. That's why that campground you stayed in was all closed up. All this country's lousy with waste." Rondo laughed while hauling the bus back into lane. "Lousy with the shit all over."

The Bear and Iris stared at each other for a long moment, then decided that one night's dalliance there in her case and a week in his could not possibly have been sufficient to . . . especially since neither of them had sipped the local water—a lucky thing, since if not for everyone's early arrival a mutual, possibly impassioned dip in the stream at the edge of the parkland would have constituted an irresistible temptation.

"Bear?" Iris asked him, staring at his fur. "You haven't been bathing in that stream, have you?"

The Bear shook his head no. "Someone must be looking out for me," he said.

They hugged the line of mountains as it veered off south and west, although here and there the prospect seemed to crumble into less dramatic statement, and once or twice the road was drawn away from them by some lesser territorial imperative.

Iris declined most conversation and watched the landscape pass. The more that did pass, the less she watched it, her mind trying to get a fix on what lay ahead. Suppose it proves impossible to get Aim and Trace out of there without Herb calling the police? There she'd be in a bus with a talking bear and two young girls over whom she had no legal right of custody. On the other hand, who but the Bear could help her? She had gone about this in what had seemed the only way available. Suppose it was precisely the wrong way—what then? Perhaps the Bear had not helped her to be brave but only foolish. It can't be. It can't be that way. She had to get her daughters out of there. The rest was irrelevant. She didn't want revenge on Herb, did she? But what if she had gotten it wrong?

In her conscious mind Iris did not believe in paybacks, still less in revenge. She believed in moments, their authenticity or more often their lack of it. But what kind of moment was this? Iris didn't, in her conscious mind, believe in wellmade lifelong dramas with a coherent skein of consequences and redemptions, but deeper down she felt intensely, and wanted to feel convinced, that if she could safely retrieve her daughters from what she knew was a dangerous situation with Herb, it might just save Tracy and Amy from a chaos they had done nothing to deserve, and begin to redeem the defining failure of her life.

They stopped once for burgers and Iris declined to join in, obeying an obscure but potent urge to purify herself for the ordeal ahead, although she did step outside to take the air. What surprised her was how completely she had failed to notice the landscape's transition from green and granite to a red land she had never seen. The air was hot and dry and clear and the sense of place dramatic, and, she felt compelled to say, sacred.

"Ma'am," came Rondo's voice behind her. "We're ready to go again."

Fifty or a hundred of these red, lightswept miles passed, slants of sandstone tilting out of the earth beneath crumbling hills, and then, after what she was told was a series of wrong turns that Rondo had undertaken in an attempt to approach Santa Fe from the most propitious angle, the bus pulled crunching onto a roadside curve of scenic overlook. They were just outside of town, and as they all descended from the bus Iris felt her tense little heart punching at her breastbone. All the forces that had ever attended her life were drawn up like armies and the outcome was uncertain—all that Krishna and Arjuna crap that frightened her and she didn't like to believe in.

She was the last to join the grouping at the outlook's edge, and almost had to elbow her way between Jones and the Bear to get a peek at the prospect. So this was where Herb had taken her daughters. It was new land to her entirely: the corrugated earth so red and the sky above it bereft of lighter harmonics rendered a flat cyanic blue in which long clouds lay, their undersides tinted brick-red by light reflected from the earth beneath. The hot dry air helped to clear her mind. What an unambiguous place this is, she thought. And how susceptible I am to the sense of place. Suspect it.

"Holy ground for sure for sure," Rondo said of it.

Past a stretch of flat country Iris saw a complex rectilinear grid of steel fences where sodium lamps an evil grade of yellow gleamed over low buildings even though the sun would still be up another couple of hours.

"See that's the prison there," Rondo continued. "Bear, shame you and me can't go down there and bust some good ol' boys loose. I prolly got a couple friends in there. We can't, huh? Ma'am, you sure we don't need no more help?"

Iris shook her head.

"How much time you do?" the Bear asked Rondo.

"Oh," Rondo said, "me and time we go way back."

Iris tried to focus on the business in hand. Past the prison, to the left south and east, Iris could see the car-culture sprawl and ingathering verticals of a city that must be Santa Fe. There. It was there.

Jones had the map outspread in his hands and rustled it importantly before him.

The Bear put an arm about her shoulders and she accepted it, then took a half-step forward to the map.

"Now we have a decision to make," Jones was saying. He pointed below them to a dusty-looking stretch of land into which some houses had been spilled like dice. "Jim Wilson's house is down there—you remember Jim, don't you Iris? I made a few calls and found him—amazing what you can do with a phone billed to the company—and we're invited to rest up, spend the night at his place and go get your daughters tomorrow, great dinner and good wine if we come. Either that or we go right into Santa Fe and do it now. If we do it now we should get out of town right away, no stops."

"We're doing it now," Iris said.

The two men and the Bear looked at each other and nodded. Oh thanks for permission, Iris thought.

"Okay," said Jones. "If the information Rondo got in Boulder is correct—"

"It is," Rondo said.

"—then your ex-husband's house is in a rich folks' canyonland just outside town on the northeast." Jones pointed off to the left of the city, then down at the map, but Iris couldn't quite make the connection between the two planes of reference. "You sure you don't want to reconnoiter, lay up a night and make our move tomorrow?"

"I'd like to go and get my children now," she said, "and drive back to Colorado right away."

"Then it's done," said the Bear. "Let's take another breath of this good air and get on with it."

Jones tapped the map and pointed beyond Santa Fe to where mountains rose jagged out of the earth, their underslopes shading blue to purple in the day's declining beam. "See those lights at the bottom of the mountains there?" Jones said. "Los Alamos. U-235. The Bomb. Radiation City."

Rondo gave a low whistle. "The serpent's glowing eggs," he said. "Very dangerous if you steal them."

The Bear did a classic double-take, then said, "Right on, Rondo. Right on."

"What?" Iris was momentarily confused by the appearance of this inappropriate subtext, then realized: of course: this whole spectacular landscape is poisoned and my daughters are caught in it.

Jones began folding the map, getting the conformations wrong. "Santa Fe's all right—fucking thing—but I understand the cancer rate in Los Alamos is—fucking thing."

Rondo took the map from him and folded it so the city street map came out on top.

"I've never even seen a picture of Herb," said the Bear, aside.

"I prefer not to keep them around," Iris told him.

"What's he like?"

"Sephardic."

"That doesn't make a picture for me."

"He's a very handsome man," Iris said.

An abashed-looking Bear blinked at her. "Better-looking than me?"

Iris was grateful for Jones' bony shoulders to collapse on shaking with laughter.

"What's so funny?" the Bear wanted to know.

Iris looked up at him and laughed more convulsively—but wasn't this beginning to border on hysteria?

"You're . . . different," she managed to say.

"Different how?"

"Bless you, Bear," she said, getting control. "I needed that."

"Yeah, so what's the cancer rate in Santa Fe?" Rondo was asking Jones.

"Boys," Iris said finally. "Do you see that?"

Off west toward Albuquerque a fanshaped cloak of dark grey cloud was spreading swiftly toward them across the sky, shadowing the land beneath and raising its horns toward the sun, which ran down shafts of fire that pierced the fabric here and there.

"Jesus," said Jones.

"Man I love the fucking West," was Rondo's impression.

"Storm," the Bear said intelligently.

"Whatever," Iris, surrounded by loonies, said. "I'd like to be on my way out of here before it hits."

But the weather system had scattered, mere scraps of grey in the sky, by the time they found their way out of central Santa Fe and an unobstructed sun was going down behind them. After halting on an upslope while Rondo consulted his notes, the daylight darkening down from gold to orange, the bus hauled a hairpin left into a road forking its way out of a sage and mesquite canyon up onto one of its ridges. The low white adobe houses that emerged as they neared the top offered the road a modest prospect but seemed to stretch to the rear over large areas, dark antiqued beams poking out from under pueblo roofs: what ethnicity would look like if the ethnics had cash. Cactus, more mesquite, dark green silver leaves on twisty trees, impeccable gravel walks and exposed rough rock fell away from the houses in landscaped gradients to afford the folks who lived there ordered and gratifying views of the world, such as they had earned it, on all sides.

"Big money," said the Bear, bending to peer ahead through the windshield. "Probably worth a few hundred thousand each."

"Nearer a million," said Iris. "This is just where I'd expect to find Herb. Do you see any numbers on the gateposts, Ron?"

"I'm lookin', sweetie-pie. That it over there?"

"Let's look."

Rondo pulled the bus up on the right in front of a house still being built across from what might be Herb's hacienda, a wider spread to it than most other places on the road.

Iris saw the stubby black Porsche sniffing the Range Rover's rear end in the driveway and knew that this was it. He's still rich and powerful. Get on with it. God help me.

Rondo confirmed the number.

"Want me to come with you?" the Bear asked her.

"No," she said, "let me try it first," and in a sort of dreamstate Iris descended, crossed the road, stepped along the white sand curving walkway through low dry greenery, turned the facetted knob, pushed open the heavy wooden door and walked inside. Left, past a barrier of entrance shelves, two steps forward, turn right and there Herb was in the middle of his living room, spinning to the sound of the opening door and seeing her, a rocks glass in his hand, arms spread wide and his face wondering what the fuck? and once the gears engaged and he recognized her he still didn't get it.

Iris did a quick scan, detected no sign of her daughters and looked at her ex-husband again.

Herb looked shockingly bad. His frizzwired hair had gone half grey but that was only the normal work of time. His staring eyes looked fried—evidence his brain must be—and his features were still in place but looked shot to hell. The air around him was full of alcohol and drugs, of which last shrinks have their pick of course, as she'd had once. His skin, although sunbrowned, wasn't doing well, and in his burst face Iris could read the trails and creases he had ridden from the intellectual and chemical bravado of his youth to this degree of wealth and collapse and what might be near-psychosis. Or was she reading too much into a few burst blood vessels and the luggage beneath his eyes.

"What the fuck?" he managed to say finally.

His voice: he was rotted out inside. Was it possible that, even without the Bear's revivifying input, she had done better with her life than he? It seemed obvious that she had, but old habit and accustomed shame made it hard for her to assimilate the idea all at once. He had been such a powerful figure looming over her past, just like the other men to whose usually inexistent mercy the circumstances of life and her own helplessness had confided her. You're better off with talking bears, though of course they have their problems too. For a moment Iris watched this former superpower staggering before her, and she felt an involuntary smile tug at her lips. Revenge.

But she must keep her attention fixed on the present moment and all the things there were to do in it.

"What the fuck are you doing here?" Herb asked her, his first complete sentence.

"I've come to get my daughters," she said, and was pleased to hear her voice sound entirely normal. "You're fried," she added. "You're a wreck."

"I'm at home on Sunday evening," he said, slurring some of it. "Tomorrow in the office I'll look like an apoth, a poth. I'll look unassailable."

Iris looked him up and down. "That's no longer possible," she said.

"Excuse me?" said a female voice, but it wasn't one of her daughters. A form stood itself into view from a sofa set at the windows at the far end of the long white room, and the girl walked toward her. Where were Tracy and Amy? This little piece, a fringe benefit no doubt of the New Age end of Herb's practice, couldn't have been more than a few years their senior. Certainly her physique—no waist, flaring hips, large self-lofting breasts—would not survive its teens. Even by her twenties she would succumb to gravity or fill out or deflate. In the meantime she was just the sort of troubled, hypersexual young thing a rich deteriorating shrink might still be able to get ahold of in a place like Santa Fe. The girl walked steadily but too slowly—grass or tranks at least, Iris thought, noting the dreamy eyes—high-breasted beneath a cutoff T-shirt that lifted as she stepped, a curtain threatening to rise on what Iris had no doubt was Herb's favorite show. The girl looked at Iris with still innocent youthful insolence. Iris was surprised Herb could satisfy her, but maybe expertise could pass for vigor with one so young. But—Iris warned herself—wasn't this speciously, transparently self-defensive? not to mention some idiotic form of outworn jealousy. Reject it.

"Mom?"

Tracy—thank God she was home: Iris had asked them not to go out all weekend, but they had whined about it, and you never knew—appeared in an archway to Iris' left and stared at her with only seeming calm in her dark eyes. Tracy's face was longer and more serious than when Iris had last seen it at Herb's mother's apartment in Chicago. A corridor behind her led to a bedroom in which some rock record or other was playing. Amy wandered out of this room up the corridor and stood partly behind Tracy, her blond head down but her eyes looking toward her mother, and Iris knew what she had to do.

"You really came," Tracy said, and Iris could hear that her elder daughter had had no faith in her arrival. Perhaps no faith in her at all. It hurt but perhaps over the years she had earned no better. My two daughters, dark and light. Tracy was beginning to become beautiful. That Mediterranean coloring, the Moorish modelling of her eyes beneath their arches. Aim was still cute, with a pale saddle of freckles across her *nez retroussé*; Iris smiled just to see her. My heart might burst. Can I get away with this?

"Are you packed?" Iris asked, but Herb was on the move and she had to keep an eye on him.

"What the fuck are you talking about?" he said, and blundered toward a rank of shelves on the living room's right-hand wall. There was a fireplace and a mantelpiece, left. His hand found a squat round piece of Indian pottery, earth-brown triangulated with gridded slants of black, then rejected it for something larger but less well made—even in near-delirium he retained his sense of property. Once he had grasped this second pot by its lip he stepped forward and swung it at her head, missing widely, and then, either by a continuance of his motion or deliberately, flung it into the opposite wall, where it shattered over the mantel and knocked over two kachinas and some photographs. Tracy ducked away from the flying pieces and Herb came toward Iris.

"That's it," said the Bear at the first sound of breakage, out of the bus and covering the ground to the house on all fours at speed. He was upright once through the open door and inside the house, however. It looked bad, he thought, but he thought he could manage this.

They must have exchanged positions, thought the Bear, because Iris was farther inside the house than the man was, and the man, in a black short-sleeved polo shirt and loose khaki slacks, was advancing upon her with his arms outstretched, a whiskey glass raised in one hand. Off left under an archway stood two adolescent girls presumably Iris' daughters, one dark the other lighter, and there was another girl, probably a friend of theirs, who had fallen backward onto a sofa beneath a sweep of windows at the far end of the room. Amazing tits, he thought.

There had better be enough space between the man and Iris to forestall any violence until he got there, because if the man hit Iris the Bear would likely kill him and that would lead to complications. The Bear knew it was fatuous and cheesy, but as he made his approach he couldn't help thinking of it as a Jim Rockford moment. The man was raising the whiskey glass higher to threaten Iris.

The Bear hit the guy—Herb—between the shoulderblades with the flat of his forepaw, not hard enough to knock him down—didn't want him falling into Iris—but sufficient to stagger him and command his attention, and when the handsome ravaged face spun toward him and its eyes went wide and jaw fell open—the Bear was bristling atop the jumpsuit collar and baring most of his teeth—the Bear spoke: "You'd probably deal with this better if you were a Jungian. But it's already too late now to make the change."

Herb didn't deal with it well. His face reddened abruptly enough for the Bear to worry about the possibility of a heart attack.

"Sit down," the Bear advised Herb, and prodded him down onto the loveseat. "We'll be out of here in fifteen minutes. You want another drink?

cause I think you spilled that one. In fact, show me where you keep the liquor and I'll join you."

"Fffffff," Herb said.

"You don't want to say that," the Bear confided. "Iris? Jones and Rondo can help you carry that stuff. I'll just sit here with your ex." He patted Herb on the knee. "Nice to meetcha. What? In fact yes I am," he assured the man. "Real as real can be. That girl's underage. Amazing body. She much fun? Don't you fucking move."

Of course the girls had not packed everything their mother had asked them to, and it took twenty minutes, Jones and Rondo shuttling in and out of the house with their arms loaded, Iris in the girls' bedroom most of the time, pulling things out from under the bed, insisting to Tracy that if she couldn't find it she would buy her a new one in New York. When everything had been loaded into the underbays of the bus—Rondo made a last appearance, grinning, with all the house's telephones in his arms—Iris came out looking admirably calm and addressed herself to the girl in the cutoff T-shirt.

"I don't think you want to stay here now," Iris told the girl in her normal conversational tone.

"He can be a lot of fun sometimes," the girl maintained.

"Not for the next day or two, I think," Iris said. "Has he ever beaten you?"

"I'll get my things," the girl said hurriedly.

"Can we drop you somewhere? Home, I mean your parents' place?"

"Sweet Jesus not there it's worse," she said. "I have friends. Could you drop me downtown?" The Bear watched the girl as she jammed things into a backpack, put on a torn denim jacket and told Iris that she was ready. She didn't seem to remark the Bear's existence at all.

"It's been a blast," the Bear told Herb in parting. They'd had a couple of whiskeys together, straight. "But don't try to find us. Nobody'll believe you about me and you'll hate the countercharge of statutory. You're not in shape for this. You're fucked."

"By the way," Iris said. "Your mother's on my side."

They dropped the girlfriend—Annie—in the day's last light at a square in old Santa Fe, and the Bear saw her skipping away under mission arches in deepening twilight—he felt a mixed pang of natural concupiscence and conscious worry—as the bus pulled out. He rode standing up in the middle, kitchen section of the bus with Jones, holding onto the walls for balance. They didn't speak much, and both felt constrained to keep a distance from the wingtables farther front, where Iris was consoling and reassembling her daughters. One of them might have been hysterical: the Bear heard one voice alternate weeping and laughter in unnatural succession. The one with dark blond hair, he thought. Amy? The other one seemed almost unnaturally self-contained.

By the time the bus found the highway north it was dark out. The windows gave back reflections of the bus's occupants through which the red taillights of cars ran front to back along the tinted glass—Rondo was driving fast, passing them all.

Twice the Bear went forward to visit Iris and her daughters. Tracy, the older one, was a beautiful child of at most fourteen with silky dark hair parted in the middle, a long serious face, and deep eyes that did not blink or look away from him as he approached. Amy, with light eyes and those freckles across her cheekbones, seemed to have inherited some of Iris' Irishness and what looked very like a sense of humor: in any case something irrepressible gleamed from her eyes and tugged at her wide mouth as she looked at the Bear not as if he were a joke but as if perhaps they shared some joke between them. Then she began to cry again.

He tried to place a helpful paw on Iris' shoulder but she squirmed away from his touch. The second time he came forward, holding onto the booths for balance, she came to meet him halfway and barred the path. "Don't even think of coming up here now. They've had enough to assimilate for one night."

The Bear was irresistibly reminded of a she-bear at the cavemouth, ready to kill him if he took so much as a glance at her cubs. He retreated back to the kitchen area and Jones. "Kids always love me. Remember how it was in the street act? What's Iris' problem?"

Jones wouldn't say anything.

The funny thing, the Bear had always recognized the suprapersonal justice of a she-bear's motherly ferocity even if her judgment of his intentions was way way off the mark, and he knew that despite his attempts at protest now and possibly in the future, he would submit to Iris' biological imperatives whatever they cost him, although he expected more consciousness from her than he did from the usual run of mother bear. He shook his head regardless, expecting to hear the rattle of two dried peas, wondering at the way of the world and the clumsy laws of his own construction.

After a few minutes Iris came back to where he and Jones stood. Iris looked remarkably self-contained and despite the obvious intensity of her emotion—he saw her suppress the trembling of her hands—she spoke calmly. "I think it would be best," she told the Bear in a voice that retained much of its habitual music, "if you stayed in the back of the bus until we get to Boulder. The girls and I are flying to New York tonight if we catch the last plane in time, and I think it would be best if you and the band would take the extra week of work so that the three of us have this time together before you come home."

Iris walked back to her daughters down the aisle, her step light, her balance good.

She had spoken with explicit correctness, and although any motherly fury in her was well hidden, the Bear was not so dim that he could not read handwriting when it appeared as if by magic on the nearest wall. He had the nearly literal experience of scales falling from his eyes, and he believed that he could see the future as the bus rocked northward through the dark. There was also the chance, of course, that he was getting it wrong, as usual. The Bear wobbled slightly where he stood and placed an ineffectual paw to his brow. "Wow," he said softly, and shook his head.

"You mean you didn't see this coming?" Jones asked him.

"Not even slightly," said the Bear.

"I sort of tried to tell you."

"You did? I don't remember."

"You weren't listening."

"What was I, starry-eyed and wanting to see her win the big one?"

"A little in love with yourself too," Jones said, "and the prospects of the role."

"Yeah," the Bear nodded. "The Rockfish Files."

"You really didn't see it coming?"

"Nope. Not a jottle. Not a tit. I mean . . ."

They had a mirthless laugh together at that one.

"It'll work out though, won't it?" the Bear asked his buddy.

Jones shrugged.

The bus continued north.

5

after Iris' departure east with her daughters, the Bear took her suggestion and picked up the option on a second week at the Blue Note. Though it was the rhythm section's week really. His own playing had lost its glory and his mind was elsewhere. The fact that he played with an unfailing competence he might have wished for in vain two months before didn't cheer him much. Oh all right, he came alive once or twice even so. In the afternoons he ran his worries off through high-altitude woods while Jones ate lunch at the Gold Hill Inn (elevation 9,500 feet) and kept a New York eye on the rent-a-van parked on the one dirt road that ran through town.

The Bear roamed the forest higher up, giving his legs and lungs a workout. Even though it was high summer there were caps of snow on the peaks and the sky behind them was a brilliant unbroken blue to which warmth seemed alien. The Bear was stirred by the majesty of the view—even remembered it was the material emblem of the higher ranges of consciousness—but it had no power to intercede for him. He had the sickening suspicion that had he run into any hikers he would have tried to tell them all about Iris.

For the ride back east Rondo cranked himself up with some crystal meth he'd scored outside the Jack Kerouac School of Disembodied Poetics, man, right there in downtown Boulder. The band, down with the road cold that had spared them until a day or two before departure, spent most of the ride in the bunkbeds all adenoidal honks and misery and where the fuck's the paper towels.

Rondo sang at the wheel much of the way and kept Waylon Jennings on the box, with occasional remissions of Willie Nelson. When anyone tried to interfere with the program Rondo warned them not to fuck with him when he was crankin'.

I'm gonna kill him, said Garrett.

He's gonna kill us first, Linton told him.

We're already dead, Hatwell said. We died in a crash forty miles back and this is a bad dream.

The Bear's immune system permitted him to recover first. By the time Pennsylvania came around again he was up at the windshield watching the whiteline miles come at him and Rondo, paste-faced and driving with unblinking white-eyed concentration, had stopped singing.

She loves me, thought the Bear. Too much has passed between us for everything to. Burger King. Price of gas going up.

She's a good-hearted woman in love with a good-timin' man, Rondo remarked.

Is that my story? the Bear wondered, and watched the city slowly assemble itself out of busted warehouses and industrial scrapyard as the bus passed through Jersey, the air thickening with humidity and smog, buildings raising up out of the earth, radio waves multiplying in air racketous with commerce and banality and dream.

Hello walls, Rondo piped up.

You keep surprising me, the Bear told him.

Hello windows, Rondo added.

There's that, the Bear allowed. The air's filthying up. You think it's smog, or tons of mental waste and the stupidification of the idiosphere?

Hard to tell ain't it, Rondo said. Look there's the city.

The band was slow debarking in Manhattan, making the most of how sick they were and how heavy everything was to lift, Rondo getting lost after dropping Garrett and his bass up in Harlem and starting to worry would he ever get out of here and Jeez, look at all the niggers. Rondo's face started going grey on the ride up to Shady and his eyes looked fried.

You want to come in and have some coffee, use the can? the Bear asked him. Take a nap?

Naw, think I'm gonna get the bus back, take the engine apart and either grease it or piss on it.

Well, bye.

It's been a pisser. Don't forget your alto.

Iris was cooking dinner when the Bear came indoors. She hadn't come to the front door to meet him. The girls were upstairs. We have to talk, Iris told him. I know, he said. But they didn't talk.

Dinner was a strained affair, the four of them sitting mostly speechless over roast chicken and wild rice, Iris looking radiant and only mildly electrified, Tracy keeping her long beautiful disapproving face turned away, and Amy suppressing a giggle.

"I see, now that you're back," Iris managed to say, "I'll have to start shopping for eight."

"Naw, that's all right."

"If you had phoned a bit earlier . . ."

"Sallright."

The Bear filled up on bread and had a bottle of Côtes du Rhône almost completely to himself, with Iris sitting not precisely beside him in the wilderness, and he could see it coming.

But in bed that night Iris surprised him. She curled herself into him with a slightly suspect ease of movement—sure of her effects, knowing where to press her breast, where to lay the leg—and only adjured him to keep it quiet. Lying there afterward with Iris sleeping under a single sheet—easeful cool of summer night—the Bear thought for the first time that things might just go back to normal.

Still, he could not but be aware that there was a new experiential alphabet for him to learn.

The next morning he woke to the sounds of Iris and the kids at breakfast.

Feeling uncomfortably like a stranger in his own home he stayed in bed until Aim and Tracy headed into town to hang—well, after all those miles he probably would've stayed in bed anyhow—drifted back to sleep, and when he woke Iris had gone out too. There was a note saying she'd be back by evening, so the Bear spent the day blundering upslope through the shrubbery and, telling himself the long evening twilight was too good to miss but also calculating uncomfortably that the kids might have dinner early, he came back down to the house around nine. Iris had saved him some dinner, and her daughters were already upstairs. Of course he knew he was acting like an idiot, but if there was catastrophe in the offing, he was forestalling it, wasn't he?

The house had filled with an unfamiliar geometry by which the Bear felt himself intimately constricted. He tried to abide by its parameters and succeeded for days, trying to make friends with Tracy—impossible—or get inside Amy's sharp little smile—a more difficult operation than he'd thought—and show Iris that he was doing everything not to rock the boat or strike the keel or whatever the fuck, but one sit-around evening he heard Amy tell Tracy something had been "so fun" and he criticized the locution, explained his critique in detail, then defended himself from an all-round accusation of pedantry by saying that language was particularly precious to him because of his, well, unique situation, and usage therefore important. Then, before he was aware of it, he found himself mentioning the dirt the girls had tracked into the house, and they could listen to his CDs but not his LPs until they learned to treat them right, or at least put them away, and he knew they'd taken his saxophone out and fiddled with it and put things back wrong and would it be better if he locked the case, and by the way your rooms upstairs are a mess and I think you should have more consideration for your mother and keep the place shipshape . . . This speech seemed to pour out of his mouth unbidden, and somewhere in the middle of it he looked across at Iris for confirmation or approval and saw her startled, jacklighted eyes, and swore he could hear the gears and wheels of decision turning—no, it couldn't be, could it? he thought, then heard a clairaudible snap and saw something change in his beloved's eyes.

But after the girls had gone up to bed, the rate of vibration went back to nearly normal and everything seemed okay.

Iris was placidly unavailable in front of the television with a glass of chilled white wine. A few minutes after he sat beside her on the sofa, she confessed that she was tired, and before heading off to the bedroom she handed him the remote. The Bear listened as she showered with what he knew to be cool water, wanted to taste that water on her body, and stared blindly at a sitcom for two commercial breaks before his own hesitant approach to bed.

She was awake, reading by the bedside lamp. He slid beneath the sheet and lay beside her.

"Iris," he said, with a sigh behind it, wanting to talk, moved toward her, and even though he did so with no explicit hardcore sexual intent she rose onto one elbow to hold him at arm's length—her thin arm's length, held not very rigid, sufficient.

"You know," she told him, "the situation has changed and what's needed here is not a lover."

"Huh?" he was able to remark.

"Please don't say Huh. I know you're not stupid. Sex is just not that important right now."

"That's not what I would have thought," the Bear said, "from the way we go at it. Not to mention the meaning sex takes on between us. Okay, *most* of the time," he said, qualifying this hopeful statement when she gave him an Oh really look. Even so, he did not detect in her any listening ear.

"Sex is not that important," Iris resumed. "Context is everything, and everything has changed. What's wanted here is not a lover anymore. I am not primarily a lover. I'm the mother."

"Well I guess I know what that makes *me*," the Bear said, always quick to pounce upon a straight-line, and whoops, saw it was the wrong thing.

Iris gave him the darkest look that could issue from so luminous a creature, and a disappointed curl of mouth. "Nothing doing," she said.

Before turning over and going to sleep, "Make an effort to understand," she advised him.

Well, wasn't that what he did all the time, in all situations?

The next morning he woke before she did, an unusual occurrence.

There was sunlight in the room, the beginnings of day spilling through the bedroom windows, beams of it all fair promise and illimitable light. Iris and the Bear lay facing each other, he on his left side and she sleeping on her right, their heads cushioned on opposing pillows. She slept as beautifully as she ever had. The Bear blinked himself more nearly awake without moving so that she would not wake. After a few minutes he couldn't help it: telling himself, falsely, that he only wanted further warmth against the last of the morning cool, he withdrew his head beneath the white double sheet that lay upon them both, and for good measure pulled her edge of it up so that he'd see her face under there too.

He knew at once that he would never forget this sight, perhaps his last? of his fondest paradise. Lost? In the unconsciousness of sleep Iris had crossed her arms across her breasts against him, their incurves visible but the nipples covered by her forearms, although it could hardly be comfortable to sleep placing so much weight atop that angularity of arm and elbow. In any case he had never seen her sleep in that position before.

He raised the edge of sheet on her side so that he could see her face better. Sunlight shaped the view and softened it through white cotton, her body blushed with warmth in its shelter. He admired it, the lovely face, graceful throat, square delicate shoulders and the momentarily concealed tenderness of her chest, but was compelled to recognize that below, all the interflowing concavity of divided belly, from arch of ribs to folded triangular groin, which received the descent of the body's converging lines in the merest curls of hair, had been designed in the interests of procreation, and that it was precisely this beautiful irrefutable logic, to which the whole of his soul succumbed, that excluded him now—what legitimate issue could there ever be from a monstrous talking bear? Her daughters slept upstairs, had been sleeping there for weeks already, and everything he might want to say was contradicted past any possibility of argument by her eloquent sleeping flesh and the blunt fact of his own mass of breathing fur. His brute unsubtlety compared to her delicacy and finesse: a not very good or useful joke. Of course it had to end. The surprising thing was that their love had happened at all. It had happened. Hadn't it?

Iris sighed, not very dramatically, in her sleep.

A fat bear in prison lies.

It was clear to him that had he ever actually made love to her he would have corrupted this beauty with his own freakishness and nullity. So all that lovemaking, he concluded, had been fiction, written by the unnatural author who wore his form. He was a talking bear, he was illegitimacy and collapse. He wished to be without blame but there was no way he could manage it.

Did he love her or did she just make his dick sing? Impossible to tell at the moment. He would have sworn his heart had precedence, but to judge by the visible evidence, there it goes . . . Iris, let's not lose this.

My God we fucked each other beautifully.

Didn't we?

Maybe he should face it: all his attempted romantic poignancy was frustrated appetite and nothing more. But was that so bad? That kind of love, especially the way he and Iris made it, had long seemed innocent enough. And now it wasn't anymore? He lay there, stunned by her beauty, now unreachable, all his life summed intolerably up. It was hard to know how his body could contain this much erotic sorrow.

"Really, Bear. How can I deal with that much emotion?"

"What?"

"I can't," she said, awake, and when he had gaped at her long enough she added, "Oh come here you idiot." She smiled, took his tongue into her mouth and raised a limb to wrap him.

Title of his next album: *Angel Takes Amazing Mercy on Melodramatic Fool.*

But the next night Iris placed her pillow at the foot of the bed and, giving him a measured look and saying something about just for tonight, laid her head upon it, and they slept head to toe for the better part of a week. No intercurlings intervened.

That done, and despite occasional passionate intermissions, further removes were easily accomplished.

See, this was the demeaning thing, that their story could be spelled out so simply, and without, it seemed to the Bear, much nuance or honor. As he saw it, the decline of his romantic fortunes took place in one smooth swift motion, even if it took a month or two. What he liked least, aside from the fact of it happening at all, was how blatant and legible the process was: you could write the story with Iris' body and his own, each new word spelling out some greater gap between them. At first, the orthography could be accommodated by the white page of their double bed between its brass margins, but then the words began to get too long and the spaces between them too wide for the binding, and the text expanded to the oval bedside carpet—I'm more comfortable on the floor, she said, because the air is cooler—and later to other rooms.

It was clear to the Bear that sex had been too central to their relationship all along—his increasing clashes with her daughters were irrelevant to the process, secondary at best, whatever she said. They should have learned to talk more; all those exquisite intimate nuances should have found some other arena to spell themselves out in than bed, though their lovemaking had seemed to say everything at the time. Had they learned to talk better, thought the Bear with no great certainty, they'd be able to manage things more intelligently now. They would be able to work things out.

Well, maybe.

What amazed him was how, just when you thought you had safely reached home, the world assumed its alien aspect again. Was this something *he* was doing? If so, he didn't see it.

The Bear's head hurt and he was beginning to feel abnormally tired.

The Bear saw nothing, Iris thought, heard nothing, noticed less and less. Certainly he should know better than to keep crossing Tracy as if he had something to teach her or could put her in her place. Didn't he know, when

Tracy punched the refrigerator and stomped out of the kitchen after he had won some minor argument, that this rage was nothing compared to what Tracy self-contained, stored up and wielded afterward in all directions but especially at her mother—and Tracy has longtime legitimate claims. I know the Bear's a big dumb horny one-eyed romantic but can't he see what fighting with Tracy is doing to my loyalties?

And when you try to tell him he says . . .

Tracy's mad at me even when I'm extra nice to her, so I figure as long as she's mad anyway I might as well tell her how things really are.

Bear, that's the worst thing you can try to do.

Why? I've been walking on tiptoe since I got back and I can't keep it up forever.

Who said forever. Just bear with us for a little while, and—

You're *leaving*? he says, all gapmouthed and sorry-eyed.

Who said anything about leaving?

You're l*eaving*?

. . . impossible! Why, whenever she tried to tell the Bear that she and her daughters needed time to themselves so she could get them settled and perhaps eventually adjusted to the idea of him, why did he take it so personally and read it as rejection and abandonment? Iris knew that he had been early, perhaps traumatically separated from his mother, but . . . do I look like his mother? Can't he see straight?

He no longer hears anything you say. Then you have to trudge to the other end of the house, where Tracy is steaming, find the valve and try to ease that pressure off . . .

He thinks I'm this *kid*, Trace would tell her. He thinks I'm this chump kid who has nothing better to worry about than him. And if that's his attitude it's not going to change, is it, because once you bring that energy in, it stays there.

I agree with you about the energy, Iris would tell her—although it seemed to her that Tracy was repeating something she had heard somewhere—but if you'd just give the Bear a chance . . .

Does he give me one? No, he pulls one of those tirades on me—whammo—because he thinks I breathed wrong on his stereo. Who does he think he is? What does he think *you* are, Mom?

You don't know him, Iris said, watching her daughter smirk at her.

I may not know him but I've *seen* him. I'm sure I haven't seen as much of him as *you* have, but—

Tra-cy . . .

Well it's true isn't it so you don't have to take offense, because it *is* true so how can you then?

. . . and she stamps her foot and walks away from you, happy in her triumph of spite.

It was exhausting. Even these internal playbacks were exhausting. Iris had hoped to be able to deal with her daughters and the Bear at the same time, but the logistics were too complicated, and she would have to reconfigure. Everyone thought she was so fluid, but she knew that she went at things in fixed ways, and she would have to reset herself. This was just too hard.

Iris had to stop and pause for thought. Real thought. A long time since she'd had the luxury of any. Life had turned into event event event. She had hoped to have a triumphant feeling after her daughters' rescue, but it had turned out to be a million tiny things, endless complications, just more life as usual. It was like working for a living again. It was worse.

She put her fingertips to her forehead and stood by the window and tried to slow things down.

Iris was no longer guarding her own fragile light but her daughters' bright-dark souls. They had seen too much, too young. Herb's decline into a drugged amoral world, and now their mother with the Bear.

Tracy had grown judgmental and severe, perhaps above all with her mother, whether for abandoning her initially or rescuing her now it was hard to tell. Iris remembered adolescence: you were out there on your own, no one around understood what you were going through, and the quickest cheap relief lay in finding someone to blame.

Amy, doing the standard younger-daughter two-step, had learned to be charming. Iris herself remembered becoming so charming that she could hardly breathe—it was still a problem—and behind Amy's levity there was a scary disarray in which Iris could recognize something akin to her own fractured counterfeit of grace and ease—so young, so soon!

If only the Bear could be a little more intelligent about it, but he refused to see what her daughters had been through—technically short of sexual abuse perhaps, but depravity enough. But what could you expect? The Bear was more deeply human than any of the men she'd known, but he was also several times more male. Why should he be able to see farther than his cock? Why should she be surprised if he couldn't?

A period of graceful abstinence might have given her daughters time to get used to the idea of this . . . um . . . talking . . . *bear* . . . um . . . living with their mother—*fucking* their mother: they knew the word. Well, perhaps not. But she had done everything on hope for so long. It was all she knew, and hoping for the best she had brought her daughters safely home.

It wasn't only that he expected to be loved or that he had no notion of how he looked in her daughters' eyes. He seemed to have no idea what sort of life they needed.

Had she misplaced her faith in him?

She had tried to tell him some of this—and this might have been her first mistake—in bed, and when talk all too predictably ran out she had tried to communicate the facts to him with her body—with the finest demonstrations she could manage of tenderness, sensitivity, compassion, tact—and he had seemed to understand her. But when she talked with him afterward she saw that no fresh cognition had taken root. She must have been addlebrained to imagine that the necessary viewpoint could be communicated by means of sex. In any case that attempt was over.

She was trying hard not to snap into automatism—what the Bear called her tendency to jacklight—and cut him out, but it wasn't easy. She was being pressured from all sides. He knows how I am. Couldn't he ease off awhile? Couldn't he stop pushing me down when I'm trying to get up and walk?

Iris sipped from her goblet of chilled Australian chardonnay.

She didn't want to remember what Tracy had suggested at breakfast that day, but she couldn't help hearing it again. "Maybe after the Bear leaves," Tracy had said, her face lowered but her dark eyes brightening, "do you think you could like buy us a dog?"

Sometimes Iris wondered if the Bear was plotting something intricate and obscure. For instance, when all was pretty much lost between the Bear and her daughters, after weeks of petty argument and social frost, then, *then* he began making pathetic attempts to win them over and be charming.

He actually—it was hard to believe it—told them the Turkish story.

The Bear descended upon the girls in the living room after their early dinner one evening. Aim and Trace were dawdling over their homework on the floor and Iris was on the sofa idling through a magazine. The old and under the circumstances obscenely hideous Turkish story had rattled through the branches of the Bear's family tree for generations, and Iris knew it all too well; it had been part of his tentative lovesong to her in the old days.

Didn't he know, the idiot, that it was precisely the wrong tale to tell Tracy and Amy? This degree of impercipience had to be some kind of put-on. What was he plotting? What was he up to really?

Iris listened acutely, ready to intervene if the Bear crossed the line when he came to the crux of the story.

"You see," said the Bear, "in the old country, the bear who may have been my great-great-great-great-great-great—"

"We get it," Aim told him, not all that unsympathetically, Iris thought.

"—grandfather," the Bear said.

Iris heard Tracy sigh heavily. Don't tell the story, Iris urged the Bear in her mind. Although she knew that he could hear her sometime, he wasn't listening now.

"In the old country, there was a family that lived at the edge of a forest, and they had a beautiful young daughter who was betrothed to the eldest son of a family of hunters who lived nearby. Now, as it happened, the bear who was my great-great-great, um, you remember, used to watch this young woman from the edge of the forest, and the morning before her wedding day, when she went out to fetch water from the well . . ."

Iris let him get through the bear's abduction of the young woman betrothed to the hunter's son, and allowed him to describe how, once he had carried her to his cave, he licked the bottoms of her feet with his rough tongue to make them so tender she couldn't get away—the Bear was beyond oblivion in his failure to note the tension rising in the room, the incredulous looks on her daughters' faces, and the speed with which their minds had solved the equation that ended X = Mom—although the Bear did bring a certain, if overemoted, poignancy to the story-bear's primitive attempt to build, with branches he pulled from nearby trees, something that never quite resembled the house he intended as a wedding gift. When this gesture began to win the young girl over, Iris prepared herself to stop him before the story achieved full sexuality, but here the Bear surprised her with a certain reticence and delicacy of detail, and she was ready to let the story run to its bloody conclusion—the hunter family's final revenge, led to the cave by a path of branchless trees—but before he could get there Tracy said, "I can't *believe* you're telling us this horrible story," took her younger sister by the hand and swept out of the room with a look of infinite loathing.

Iris watched the Bear blunder up to her looking utterly clueless. He raised the palms of his paws like Job and intoned the story's punchline in an approximation of the peasant girl's voice: "It was only a pile of sticks but it was my house; he was only a bear but he was my husband."

"Tracy's a bit hard on you but I agree with her," Iris told him. "How could you have told them that story?"

"I wanted them to see, I wanted them to appreciate . . ."

"All they see is a bear with an erect penis violating a woman in a cave."

"The longing . . . the poignancy . . ."

"What poignancy?" Iris asked him, but she did have to reconsider: the Bear wasn't plotting anything: he was in fact at sea. She felt for him, tried not to, felt for him again.

What had happened to him? Couldn't he see anything at all?

Iris would have wanted to include the Bear in her current world, but it wasn't working. She could configure her inner geometry only once in a moment of crisis or decision, and the resultant crystallization included what it could and lost what it could not. Initially, she had set herself to save Tracy and Amy and include the Bear, but it was becoming increasingly apparent that she would have to make a change. Circumstances were compelling her to put the Bear on a back burner.

She knew, she knew: it was unskilled of her, but what was she supposed to do? There were so many competing individualities in her she felt more like an orchestra than a person. Poor Iris. Poor Bear. My daughters! The Bear was purely, typically intent on living as he had before, and wouldn't see how impossible that had become.

It all seemed logical enough, but it left her with a familiar feeling of panic-stricken weakness, of impotence before the brute facts of life, and therefore . . . maybe she was only repeating a familiar error. What was she supposed to do? What?

And Iris also detected a certain vengeful glee in herself at the Bear's failures of perception—a horrid involuntary grin tugged at her mouth sometimes. This smirk rendered her whole line of thought suspect and odious.

Also, what she couldn't say to her daughters and, these days, hardly even to herself: God help me I love the Bear, and the conflict between life with him and life with my daughters is tearing me apart. Aim and Trace must have precedence of course, but what can I do?

Iris melodramatically wrung her hands, saw it, couldn't stop.

What was she supposed to do? What?

She would have to separate her daughters from the Bear. But how was she to do it, and for how long?

Would three months be enough? It would be simplest to move back to New York, but the last thing she wanted to expose Aim and Trace to, after what they'd been through with Herb, was the brutality of the city, not to mention the horrors of its public schools. They were enrolled here, and even though they couldn't invite anyone home they were making friends.

How was she to get ahold of some time apart? Could the Bear move down to the city for a few months? But Jones was living with Sybil, and they would make an uneasy threesome.

And besides—this was the incredible part—she didn't want him to go. She was an idiot. She still loved him.

These small waverings in her decisiveness had their material result. One stray afternoon, when she and the Bear were wandering around the otherwise empty house at the mercy of the nonintersecting geometric lines of force that dominated the space, they exchanged a series of involuntary looks and within a minute the Bear had her up against the wall and she had raised her skirts and wrapped her legs around him as he entered her: a quick, shuddering, full-body trembler that possessed them completely while it lasted but must have shamed them both in the aftermath: neither of them looked at the other or spoke as the day turned suddenly sordid. They saw themselves in its harsh light, stooped guiltily to pick up every scrap of torn clothing, and bumped into each other going for the bucket so they could wash the floor and the wall clean. This wasn't Eden anymore.

"I can see the dreams you're having about me," Iris told him after another night she'd spent on the living room sofa. They hadn't touched each other for a week.

"I'm not surprised," said the Bear. "They're pretty vivid."

The Bear volunteered that he would sleep on the sofa instead, maybe even try a night or two outdoors, and they both pretended that would fix it.

He made his bed in the outer darkness of the living room, dutifully tended the fire in the woodstove and hefted in big armfuls of logs: autumn was coming in and heat was necessary at night, especially upstairs, where her daughters slept. Caliban has a new master.

And habitat is shrinking all the time.

Some nights he couldn't sleep, sat up and watched TV with the volume down. One night he saw a nature documentary about a valley in Africa, desert most of the time, which burst into bloom for two weeks a year when the runoff from the neighboring region's rainy season reached it—a brief explosion of color, then back to desolation—and the Bear felt like that valley.

Once earnest autumn set in, a number of uses were found for him. Gathering deadfall from uphill and sawing it into useful portions, and then—they took instruction from an article in the *Woodstock Times*—he learned to snuffle morels out of the underbrush so that Iris could cook up fine new things in the kitchen.

The Bear went out on early-autumn expeditions with Iris and her daughters, on the end of an improvised leash in the interest of decorum and against the possibility of unwonted discovery with the girls present. But the plain fact was that he got into it, and along a side road up Mount Tremper way he uncovered a positive wealth of small black wrinkly things whose tang attacked his nostrils with fierce, irresistible insistence. He wuffed them out from under fallen leaves clodded with moist earth and passed them back to Iris and the burlap sack she carried, Aim and Trace dawdling behind, tangle-footed, bored, conversing inaudibly with each other. Amy had a tendency to trip and bark her knee and whine about going home; Tracy would tell her not to be so *wet* and they'd keep on awhile longer.

What had happened to the trace of humor he'd seen in Amy? Tracy had her under orders and under thumb. Tracy's detestation of him was plain, though God knows he'd tried to get her to like him. She was unapproachable, even sometimes by her mother, toward whom she seemed almost to condescend. Was it conscious, the way she wielded the whip of guilt over Iris? Or just a survivor's instinctive strategy. It occurred to him once or twice that even if he were not around, Tracy might be taking it out on Iris, avenging herself for being abandoned, perhaps even for being rescued—whatever she imagined the central wounding drama of her life to be. This insight seemed intelligent, but there was nothing he could do with it.

"Here's some more," he said, snouting a bunch of fallen maple leaves aside and uncovering a fat black scrotum of morel.

"Can we go back now?" Amy asked the grey upward air, and in fact it did look as if it might begin to rain.

On the end of his leash, the Bear looked up and back at Iris, who wore a long Scottish cloak and was peering uphill into the trees. She couldn't have looked more beautiful and he still admired the fineness of her jaw, but he wasn't happy about the leash he was wearing.

This was not what he had envisioned doing, this time of year.

They made other attempts to behave like a family.

Later in autumn, when the woods were in the most spectacular flame of their seasonal decline, they packed themselves into the orange Volvo wagon and tooled east along the curving blacktop to Lake Hill, where they took the side road that ran around the placid man-made lake: a reservoir for the locality when the rest of the area's watershed—fifteen towns and valleys flooded by edict and charter—ran away by conduit back to the insatiable city south. It was one of their better days. Conversation in the car remained civil, almost sociable, and the drive was picturesque, especially when they reached Cooper Lake's farther shore, where Iris pulled the wagon to a halt on the roadside and the four of them ambled through evenly planted spruces to the calm water of what appeared to be an eye of wide blue contemplation beneath blue unfathomable sky.

An inverted forest braved the ripples at the edges and pointed down to the reflected immensity above, inexactly rendered clouds passing west to east—another slash of rain approaching?—although to see real mountains you had to forsake reflection and raise your eyes: attentive, calm, gone bare where deciduous trees predominated, dark green swathes where pine held sway.

The Bear tried to talk to the girls again—hope against experience—telling them what he knew about the woods, trying to get them to appreciate the scene set forth—see how different it is from the Southwest you've come from but just as beautiful in its way, don't you think?—before all that was left was winter's bare branches.

Tracy turned her back on him to look at the Volvo, if at anything, and after a short perhaps confused pause Amy looked down at her feet and scuffed one shoe against the other.

The Bear looked at Iris and she looked back at him. What can I do? he thought. What? I try my best but do you really think it's fun to have your heart so systematically rejected?

"Can we go now?" Tracy asked her mother.

"Not before I go in for a swim," the Bear said in what he thought might prove a clever gambit—it might prolong the trip at least—speaking to the girls even if the way they looked at him was not exactly encouraging. "This is a reservoir, see, and people can't swim in it by law, but me," he thumped his chest, "I'm wildlife, me."

Tracy rolled her eyes to heaven, but Amy could not quite stifle a laugh.

Iris' unblinking look, as she stood there in the brown and dun squares of her soft Scottish cloak when gladly he would have kept her warm himself, was enough to make his rolling, four-legged passage to the water feel like ignominious retreat.

Under the circumstances he had to go in, didn't he, even though the lake was colder than he had expected, and no birds sang. He breasted the water anyhow, breathed out hard, shook, pushed on into colder flow.

"He looks like a log," he heard Tracy say back onshore once he was well into the lake and paddling away, but he grinned back over his shoulderhump anyway and said he'd be back in about five minutes. Pathetic.

A third of the way into the lake and really beginning to enjoy the swim, warming to the cold, he heard Iris calling from the shore, and looked back to see her waving her arm above her head.

"What?" he yelled back, turning, but got a mouthful of water, and as he watched, expecting further discourse, he saw the three of them walk back through the spruces to the station wagon, Tracy fictitiously clutching her behind—heard the thunk of three shutting doors after space and time interposed their delay—and before the parping of the old engine's idle came to him across the water, he saw exhaust puff out of the tailpipe in a fade from blue to grey as the car cranked into motion. He watched the orange Volvo wagon that he had paid for, mostly, roll along the shore of the lake until it disappeared among pines.

His swim had lost its savor but he persisted in it anyway. The chill wasn't bad and water, at least, was still water: he wished he could melt into it and fade away.

On the trot home he avoided the openness of the road and followed the course of Beaver Creek downgrade beside it, going deeper into the forest halfway home to squat and have a large-size satisfying dump into leafmeal. Does the Bear shit in the woods? Yes, and it's one of his last remaining pleasures. He wiped himself with a swatch of leaves and a patch of moss that grew at the base of the greying stump of some forgotten tree.

En route he reminded himself that Sonny Rollins probably had days like this, perhaps not in detail but on the essential plane. If not Sonny then Ornette, Monk. Shostakovich had Stalin. Bird had junk. All I have is busted love, which is par for the course, an unavoidable thing.

But nothing eased the ache.

When he got back to the house, Tracy was helping Iris make dinner and Amy was dancing alone to a rock record in the living room—conventional progressions, beat all insistence, no nuance: not a world she should really want to live in. If he couldn't help the girl, who would?

The Bear waved to her and retired to the front steps and sat down.

Two minutes later the rain. It began thoughtfully, not unlike the quality of mercy, but before long an angry wind piled up behind it and the air went sharply cold, about ten degrees in half as many minutes. The Bear stood up and put his face into it. Crack your cheeks, he thought, and then realized, not likely. The rain and wind blew harshly in his face but it didn't help him feel Shakespearean or even Byronic.

Winter was not far off.

The wind intensified and his senses went keener. The land was lit by bruised, inverted stormlight, sun dropping beneath the cloudline and peering under the heavy weather.

Across the road on the other side of the pasture a gust of wind hit the trees and seemed to lift the whole grove of birches, but in fact it only took their last, most persistent leaves with it up into the air, and he wanted to call back into the house so that Iris and the kids could appreciate the moment's vehemence and beauty, but it was over before he could raise his voice and they wouldn't listen anyway.

The moment was happening to him alone.

When he came indoors again after shaking himself dry on the porch, Iris greeted him alone to apologize for their departure from the lake—the girls' insistence on the need for a toilet—and he sensed an opportunity for some real communication between himself and Iris hidden in the moment but could not make out its face and it passed by unspoken.

Iris adjusted a bright silk scarf about her throat and said that dinner would be ready soon and he could join them if he liked.

Alone in the afternoons he went downstairs to Siege's basement room and practiced bebop in all twelve keys. He put on early Ornette Coleman records and thought, all things considered, he'd be wise to give up music entirely. I mean, how could he, how could anyone ever play anything as beautiful and unexpectable as what Ornette had done? Not to mention Charlie Parker.

In a bout of weakness he thought of calling up Charlie Haden so Charlie could tell him how great he played. He had just enough character left to resist the impulse.

Afternoon declined, daylight modified its expectations, and at length a sequence of footsteps would give laggard testimony to the girls' return from school. They'd make dish-noises in the kitchen, then go upstairs to listen to Prince's *Black Album* and giggle over a video.

Iris would come home. When she and the Bear took their mostly silent dinners together late, Amy and Tracy would pretend to go to bed but actually, as the Bear's directional ears told him, would hunch in the halflight at the top of the stairs listening, so that if he had wanted to say anything significant to Iris he was prevented from doing so.

He might mention that he needed reeds.

Iris favored the weather, car repairs, what to eat tomorrow.

He had begun loving Iris knowing that in loving her he was loving all the beauty and spirit allowable in this world or any other: through her he had all of it compact, and in scenes of staggering intimacy had actually embraced it. Now he was beset by minute, purely personal considerations, each one a door closed upon the greater world and the beauty of which she had been the sign. . . . He knew he was being stupid, but he couldn't get the halves of the picture to coincide, nor could he reconcile the experienced breadth of the universe and this undeniable constriction. It was probably too late to plead that he was only a joke of a talking bear and could Iris clue him in please.

Dinner would end without a significant word being said by either of them.

Sometimes the simplest communications would . . . how was it possible? He could offer to make a pot of coffee and she would ask him, Do you intend the whole pot of coffee for yourself or can I have some, and if I *can* have some does it mean that I *must* have some because you're making some and you want me to join in, or do I have a choice?

His own answer would turn unintelligible in his mouth, his attempts to untangle it only further confuse the issue.

His eye was perturbed by something he had never seen, or thought to see: she's become afraid of me. Why?

Do you mind if I turn off the light in the room? he might ask.

Does this mean, she might answer, that control of the lightswitches in the house now belongs to you and I have to ask your permission if I want to turn one off myself? And by turning off the light do you really mean something else much more serious?

Clearly, the woman was getting hysterical. What could he have done to provoke this? True, lately he couldn't help walking around the house, sometimes, with an unconsolable erection that even his raincoat was unable to disguise. He knew it made the rest of him look like a walking rationalization for the pole in his pants, but Iris was supposed to know him better than that and that his love for her was deep and true.

Was it absurd to protest the depth and sincerity of his love when what he most wanted at the moment was to sup upon the impeccable curvature of her breasts as they lifted to his delectation the perishable imperishable buds at their tips?

Probably it was.

No: what amazed him was that they were both caught in some unknowable geometry, some overmastering rectilinear design. Neither of them knew how to bend anymore, all the sweet curving subtlety of their loving world gone.

All he had to do was open his mouth for the wrong words to leap from it into the air. All he had to do was attempt a physical gesture to feel himself constrained by some behavioral straitjacket: his body rigid with it, hers rigid in its own bonds. They couldn't move or talk, and her daughters, who ought to have responded to a warm and sympathetic talking bear with a sense of liberation from the narrowness of the quotidian . . . with laughter and a sense of high adventure . . . well, let's not even talk about it.

His brain felt mazed and inextricable. He wandered room to room, blundered through bare trees in the bereft, forsaken forest, and only when he found himself for the third time in the crawlspace underneath the house, scumbling around on all fours with no clear aim in the damp spidery semidark, did it occur to him that he was looking for a place to go to sleep for awhile and he noticed that it was the beginning of winter.

No, he thought. It's not possible. It's undignified and atavistic, not to mention overreactive and silly. But how come I feel this tired?

He slept outdoors a few nights, or tried to, but it was not sufficient. He found himself underneath the house again with no clear memory of having gone there, the scent of earth heavy as a drug in his nostrils.

No no no, he thought. I won't.

"What about I went to sleep in Siege's room downstairs," he wondered aloud to Iris finally. His grammar was slipping. "Yeah and how come I never see him anymore."

"He seems to know when you're here," Iris told him. "He turns up sometimes when you've gone up into the hills on one of your romps."

"He knows when I've left?" the Bear asked her.

"I don't think he *knows* when you've gone out. He just seems to . . ." Iris laughed. "You know? He's started trying to talk me into a mother-daughter scene. He brought it up once or twice."

It took the Bear a number of questions and answers for him to understand that what Iris meant was that Siege wanted to go to bed with Iris and one and if possible both of her daughters at the same time. "I'll kill him," the Bear said seriously. "I'll claw the son of a bitch open and feed his liver to the crows."

"Don't be ridiculous," Iris said. "I know how to handle the Sieges of this world. Do you know how he pronounces my name? In front of the girls and even alone now that I've rebuffed him, he's taken to calling me something like Mrs. Termaroo. I wouldn't worry about Siege if I were you."

"Let me get this straight," the Bear asked her incredulously, and began pacing the living room. "Siege wanting to get into bed with you and your daughters rates a polite little laugh, but I'm too shocking and obscene for anyone to live with?"

The Bear repeated this question in a number of forms and in diminishing volume until he gave it up. Or actually, until Iris began harping on a single point.

"Bear," she said, her face brightening as he had not seen it brighten in months: a big smile at the prospect of his disappearance. "Do you mean you want to go to sleep down there for a long time? As in months? Bear! That would be perfect! I feel like I'm about to break apart, as if my head's about to fly off! A few months would be perfect!"

The Bear was aghast. "You mean you're that eager to get rid of me?" he asked her, tears welling up his eyes.

"Bear, don't you understand anything? Three months would be perfect! Four better still." She seized his arm. "At last, a use for bears!"

"My God. You really want to get rid of me."

"Oh stop being so melodramatic."

"You want to get rid of me."

"What's the use of talking to you? You're deaf as a post. Trust me. Oh do stop looking miserable. You know, you can sleep down there for as long as you want," Iris said thoughtfully. "Siege can take his photo things out. I don't think Stanlynn would mind if I asked him to leave. Do you think she would raise our rent? How much money do we have in the bank, do you remember?"

But the Bear was still trying to grope his way along the contours of the old point: "Siege wanting to fuck you and your daughters is okay and I'm this shocking illegal banished entity when all I want is for us to love each other in a healthy, loving, fundamentally nonperverted way? Allowing, of course," he admitted, "for the slight unconventionality of the interspecies aspect of the thing. And now you're thrilled that the one piece missing from my full suit of mockery has arrived and I'm going to hibernate? Iris, it's total loss! It'll be like dying! It'll be worse!"

"Oh lighten up and stop being such a drama queen. You know, if you're going to sleep for a few months," she said, in what sounded like her capacity as a biologist, "you might think about putting on some weight. Can I bring you anything special from town? I could work up a list of supplements."

"Iris," he said, feeling that he was about to go drastically wrong but unable to stop himself. "Is this all I get of heaven? There has been nothing like me in the whole history of the world! I'm unprecedented, I love you in a way few bears have ever loved a woman, and I wouldn't harm one hair of your daughters' heads. Is this my reward?" Yes, he was going wrong but there was no stopping it.

"I was under the impression," Iris told him in her usual tone, with a bit of laughter in it—now that he was vanishing from her life she was blithe and untroubled again—"that there were at least twenty generations of talking bear before you came along, and the lore and skills were passed down in each generation—at least so you've told me—and that—"

"There has never been anything like me!" He tromped up and down the living room, waving his arms in the air in what even he knew was uncivilized fashion. He had the useless intuition that he was about to make the ugliest speech of his career. "My forebears were primitives! They spoke with accents! Their taste in music ran to circus marches or at best some tawdry tearjerking Gypsy violin! Their view of the world was simple! They were innocent of literature! Some of them were rudimentary animal Marxists! Their mysticism was rudimentary! They never developed a sense of irony adequate to the nuances of their situation! None of them was remotely capable of either the music I play on my horn or the greater music of my love for you, which is now, I grant you, only a stunted little tune!" Yes, all things considered it was one of the ugliest speeches he had ever made. "Twenty, forty, fifty generations of talking bear striving across the genes and generations have produced nothing even remotely approaching me!"

"Oh Bear, what are you going on about?" Iris asked him, with not the least audible strain in her voice. "Whether twenty generations or fifteen thousand: you didn't produce yourself. You *were produced*. What's your problem?"

The Bear's mouth clacked open and shut. Iris was not only unanswerable, she was just.

"That being so," she said, driving the nail farther in with no apparent effort, "I don't see how you can claim credit for being who you are, or, more to the point, demand a reward."

The Bear let his jaw fall open and didn't clack it shut again. When you're unmade, you're unmade. Give up.

"In that respect," Iris pressed on, "you're exactly like the rest of us. The most that can be said of you is that you're here. Beyond that, you have no special edge or any special right to blow your horn. I'm speaking figuratively of course. Play the saxophone all you like."

The Bear dropped to the sofa and smelled the dust rise around him. "Wuf," he said.

"So if you'd like to move downstairs," Iris told him, "it's perfect. I'll call C.J. and give him a week to get his equipment moved. Our problems are solved."

The Bear's last comment was a heavy wondering sigh.

About the time of the first light snow, he found himself more or less unconsciously adapting Siege's room to his purpose. Siege had taken his tubs and his enlarger out. It was cool, Siege said, but looked pissed off. Iris had fixed it on the phone with Stanlynn. You want to speak with her? The Bear said Hi Stanny. Yes I know I should go see Chief Oren Lyons and I'm sure he would be good to talk to and it would help. But. But. You know me. Yeah I think the money is together for the foreseeable future. How's the llama-trekking biz? Great. If there's a problem here we'll handle it. Fine. Bye. Yeah, here's Iris. Bye.

Down in the basement the Bear switched off the thermostat, then thought better of it and turned it up to the minimum so the pipes wouldn't freeze and burst while he slept. He hauled armfuls of fallen leaves in for the scent, pulled the foam mattress down from the built-in bed, jammed it into the room's rearmost corner and fell into it to test its suitability for a long stay and because he felt like falling down.

One thing he wondered: if he hibernated would he lose the capacity for speech and wake up in springtime a garden-variety bear? It seemed possible. He felt too tired to care. Besides, it might prove a relief. Naw naw naw: this was some *regressus* he should avoid. This was happening on some deeply stupid perhaps he meant unconscious perhaps he meant deeply stupid level. Getting too sleepy to think.

Still trying not to give in to the tide of granular dark seizing him body and brain, he trundled somnambulist-insomniac upstairs for a few last items one day when the house was empty.

Just himself and the fading echo of the life he'd tried for.

Pulled some cartons down through the attic hatch and fumbled through old stuff of his with blundering paws. Rummaging through his trunk he found what he was looking for, and clutched his old worn raincoat to him, felt a tide of absurd self-pity rising but was powerless to stem it. My old raincoat, he thought helplessly, and convulsively gathered it to his chest, once thought inexhaustible, and took in the old scent of himself from the fabric. What he was getting was nostalgia, but what he wanted was Lethe, Nepenthe, Oblivion, Death.

There were baggy corduroy pants too, which although they'd been washed retained some essential tang of the past; and, good Lord, that bathrobe, its looped and windowed raggedness, could it still be said to exist?

The Bear pulled these tangled things to his chest—impermissible self-pity at work but I can't stop myself—and, rheumy-eyed and stupid with want of sleep, he stumbled heavily into the doorframe on his way out of the room but succeeded in getting down the stairs without an arse-over-teakettle whoop-de-do.

In the master bathroom he did the worst, and added a bedsheet rich with the scent of Iris to his hoard.

In the basement he added these new treasures to the pile, pulled apart issues of the Sunday *Times*, wound the Iris-smelling sheet around his neck, lay down in his nest, stuffing the bathrobe under him, the raincoat on top, then thought, No, sat up and pulled the raincoat on. Tore some lining as he pushed his right paw through the sleeve but that was okay. He pulled the pocket inside out: toothpicks, a paperclip, clumps of grey-brown pocketfluff spilling from the seams, and a worn-out Rico reed.

The Bear felt unbelievably sleepy. He laid his head. Really coming down, such a weight of sleep never before. Fine dark dust. Tons. And tons.

He felt his blood thicken, the big muscle of his heart gear down, brain descending into dark, lights dimming down, blinking out . . .

You're getting more skillful with these descents, he told himself in a last waking blink of clear mind, smoother with these small deaths and late declines. You argue less, consent quicker. But is that wisdom or fatigue? Who knows, it might work out. Perhaps after all you're being shriven of the uses of this world. No telling what you'll be left with when you wake up from this one. Let fall. Hope still talk.

Rear corner of basement room under blankets dried leaves newspaper sheet with scent of her fading and old raincoat, other odds and ends, sometimes it seemed to him in the early stages of his sleep that he drifted upstairs through the floorboards and joined Iris in her life up there in the light. Her daughters doing okay. But all so vague. Drawn there. Wasn't sure he really went. Once saw birds like that but where. Brain thicken. Heart slow. Whelmed in big slow wave. What he wanted, sleep so deep, deep so sleep, world gone only thing down there barely audible last link far dark center long low humm.

Pilot light. Need one while off sailing. Where?

Went deeper. Knew that Friedmann had just died.

After while—how long?—phone rang up there. Wun't anawon home? Anaboda pick it? Up? They all move back city leave me? House around him dark. Walls all run down rain. Soak rain earth smell. Try raise head heavy wugh. Put head down longer wider wugh. Thick slow brain tongue. Long slow heavy head. Sleep. He slep. t.

part six

Thou art the unanswered question,
Couldst see thy proper eye;
Alway it asketh, asketh;
And each answer is a lie.
So take thy way through nature,
It through thousand natures ply;
Ask on, thou clothed eternity;
Time is the false reply.

—Emerson

I practice all the time, to be there when the spirit comes.

—Rollins

1

"It's an incredible idea," said Jones. He had never been inside the body of the Brooklyn Bridge before—who had?—and he stared up with undisguised amazement into the vaults and archways, where workmen in coveralls negotiated the scaffolding to smooth down ocher plaster, reinforce brickwork with fresh mortar or lay in large rough-cut light brown ornamental squares of facing-stone. Some lateral daylight pillared through the floating workdust from a couple of remade windows off to the right, but most of the illumination came from hanging bulbs in safety cages and, where men were plastering, brighter banks of floods. The matte-green steel balconies, a vaguely maritime curve to their fronts, supported below by thin steel columns of an identical green, had already been built into place, but virtually everything else was somewhere between shadow and act. "Though really," Jones told Bob Levine, "you should get Sonny Rollins to open the place. He's so identified with playing music on bridges and all."

"Uh, yes and no," Levine said. "Yes we should, no he won't do it. The Bear's like an automatic second choice."

"Is he?"

"As far as I'm concerned. The mythic note. This place wants the mythic note. Don't you think?"

"What about Ornette?"

"Hard to deal with and he'd want to bring in his electric band."

"The Bear would say Jackie McLean."

"If the Bear says no I'll try to get Jackie to say yes." Levine laughed. "I can actually do this stuff. I haven't had this much fun since kindergarten."

"That a Romanesque arch up there?"

"A Renaissance adaptation. You see those men up there? A family of Tuscan stoneworkers. *La famiglia Fusi. Mia famiglia. Io trovato, lei fatti.* I brought them over from La Fattoressa and I leave it to them. They can even overrule the architect if they want, who basically is me anyway. Well I had a little help at first but after awhile I kind of took over. How do you like the hi-tech sound insulation? You hear any traffic? I don't hear any traffic, but right above our heads at this time of day there are five lanes of cars fighting their way down to three so they can all get across the river to Brooklyn. God knows why."

"Mrs. Stahl's knishes?" Jones wondered.

"You think? Myself, I go for Yonah Schimmel. Kugel that lays in your stomach like a rock for a week."

"I can hear horns." Jones, posing with a hand at his ear, thought that it was no more than fair to point out this simple fact. "It'll put a crimp in your ability to record live."

"We won't be recording at rush hour and they can shield the mikes. And the city's putting up a sign."

"Cool," Jones said, beginning to wonder about Levine. "Put it next to the one that says Okay Please Don't Murder Nobody Today."

"Ha ha, that's funny," Levine said. "They said they'll back it up. And even in Carnegie Hall you hear the IRT."

"Not since they renovated," Jones broke the news. "The sound's not what it used to be but you don't hear the subway anymore." He had read about it in the *Times*.

"I couldn't have put this place together without the support I've had from the city," Levine said seriously. "They could've had a dozen hot name boutiques. But I've had a lot of good support."

"Uh huh," said Jones. That was one of the first things Sybil had been able to find out about Levine's finances in her first few sweeps of the datasphere: most of his money was inherited, although he had made some on his own in residential real estate at the right time for the market; there was some import-export action without the usual hint of drugs, but then the story beaming back from dataland grew harder to substantiate. It seemed that Levine, true to his name, had invested in some promising vineyards in Chiantishire but had fallen, one heard, beneath the wheels of hard practice, local corruption and the generic fate of even partly absentee landlords—word was the manager in question had retired to Sardinia cooled by a purloined million and an unassailable team of lawyers hooked up with the Camorra. Levine's family had thumped the escritoire, reeled him back from Tuscany to New York and ordered him to retrench. But was this retrenching? The only thing more quixotic than opening a jazz club was aspiring to play in one. Levine's clothes looked pretty hip and his Mercedes was sufficiently blunted with use not to look vulgar, but the man had unsteadiness in him, Jones was sure, even if the stories were unverifiable.

But he was tight for sure, he was hand in glove with some of the movers and shakers of the city. Which meant that the Bridge—the first nightclub since Birdland to pay tribute to a living musician with its name, since it pretty much translated as Sonny Rollins—would probably pass inspections and open on schedule after all.

Jones half-recognized Levine's face from around the circuit over the years, someone he'd seen at this table or that, or leaning in a doorway with some musician at the back of the room, sharing a laugh with Elvin Jones in the Vanguard's so-called kitchen, Elvin dripping sweat and showing his teeth in the usual crazed grin beneath black Mongolian cheekbones.

Jones fixed a closer look on the man in the hope of some conclusive insight, but didn't learn anything new. An intelligent-looking guy with good features but an uncertain chin, in silver-rim glasses, fortysomething with a headful of wavy hair receding at the front and going harmoniously grey along the sides; hip expensive-looking casual clothes—something indefinably privileged about the simple crewneck sweater and the drape of those cream-colored corduroy slacks—and the stippled black leather bomber jacket was probably some upper-class kind of goatskin; and Levine had a certain set look about his face that made him look as if he knew something about money and its ways. But what about the Italian rumors and why was he investing in a jazz club? not to mention one as visionary as this place was fixing to be. He had weirdness in him. Which might be why someone as outside as Jones felt so comfy jawing with the guy. A brother spirit, perhaps, beneath the skin of money and above the feet of clay.

"The sheer weight of stone up there takes care of most of the traffic noise," Levine was telling him, "but you get potholes in winter and God knows what kind of never-ending repairs, three years of steel plate, whatever. So, make a long story short I was able to wangle a research grant that covered some of the cost." Levine smiled fondly, as if he amazed himself sometimes.

"And you'll open in six weeks?"

"Why not?" With a gesture, Levine ushered Jones deeper into the wonders of the construction. Jones stepped over the ends of some stacked two-by-fours and wondered if he should be wearing a hard hat just in case.

"Watch out for that hole in the floor," Levine advised him. "We're still running wire and pipe."

"I have to know about the six weeks part of it."

"The Bear has such a busy schedule? I heard he wasn't working just now."

"Sometimes he's kind of touchy." Jones was pleased that he was still capable of understatement. Things had been going so improbably well in his life he tended to tell all, in the full confidence that you could show your hand and it wouldn't affect the basic onflowing Tao of things. And if people looked at you like you were an idiot when you told your all? That was their problem. "The Bear may have to think about it awhile. The last time he played New York he got busted and spent the winter in jail."

"The Tin Palace," Levine said. "You should see the security I'll have in place by the time we open. What do you think of the back of the room?"

"Great," Jones said even before looking. Most of the interior walls between the big grey stone supports had been bashed away; the scaffolding and joists seemed strong enough. Jones saw an occasional leg of stoneworker up there in the vaults and arches, and missed stepping into another hole in the floorboards mostly by luck. "Whatever the city's doing for you, this must cost a fortune."

Then Jones had an unnaturally clear attenuated moment in which to open his mouth, begin a pointless gesture with his hands and watch a chunk of masonry about the size of a television drop out of the vaulting toward the floor about fifteen feet behind Levine. The crash, when it finally hit the floor, was enormous, and Levine leapt forward almost into Jones' arms. Jones was able to steady Levine on his feet just short of a full embrace.

"*Va bene?*" a voice came from somewhere up there in the heights.

"We're alive, Amedeo, *grazie*," Levine called back. Then to Jones: "Maybe we'd better go back outside."

"Sure," said Jones. "I can relate to that."

Levine gave a last anxious look back over his shoulder, where fresh dust was rising around the fallen masonry chunk, took Jones' elbow and steered him past all obstacles toward the club's proposed front door. "Most of the work's not structural. By now it's mostly decoration. We're together."

"I'm sure," said Jones, thinking about traffic vibrations and falling rock. It won't collapse and kill the band the first week. A couple of months later, who knows? The opening is safe. That's what I'll tell the Bear. And what'll he tell me? Find me two pillars and place my paws on them.

They had made it to the greater safety of the entrance area, and peered out the small square of plexiglas set in one of the steel utility doors. After a dumbshow of head-gestures that ended in reasonably unison nods of yes let's go, Levine pushed the left-hand door open and they walked outside into Tuesday afternoon and what was left of the uncertain midwinter lull—storms had come and gone, and presumably would come again, but meanwhile there was a kind of peace. A damp gust of wind had a go at them, but there was no ice or hatred in it, and after this first gesture it let them be.

"Wow," was what Jones managed to say.

They stood on the large square landing atop the roughed-out stairway and looked riverward across to Brooklyn. It was an indecisive afternoon: the small rain down had rained and now, south on their right to the Battery, a white winter sun alternately masked and unmasked itself behind migrating cloud. The grey underside of the bridge soared out over the river and diminished toward its farther landing, the water beneath the bridge dull as lead except where sun found it and tipped the surface. They could hear the sound of traffic above them on the bridge, and pretended they were too cool to notice, about at eye level on the right, cars driving past them on the elevated bridge approach road slowing down to rubberneck, the occasional window rolling down, one guy trying to get their attention, calling, "Hey. Hey!" By now, of course, it was too late for them to respond and they were dealt the regulation New York epithet: "You stoopid fuckin' assholes, *hey!*"

The car passed on and was eaten by other cars where the lanes narrowed before the hairpin bend that would swing them up onto the bridge.

"He probably just wanted to know what was going on here," Levine explained of his fellow New Yorker. "The staircase, the couple of opened-up windows, all that."

Jones nodded. "It would have been hard to establish an adequate dialogue," he said.

For years, or perhaps decades, Jones himself had wondered, passing by in cars, about the brick walls and bricked-up windows that filled the arched space between the hulking grey stone supports at the Manhattan landing of the Brooklyn Bridge. He had wondered what had filled those bricked-in spaces once, a customs house? some composite Abe Lincoln Walt Whitman Hart Crane enclosure of abstract historical space? the dusty, preserved aether of another epoch? what?

"If the club succeeds, the city'll let boutiques move into the other arches. It could turn into a neat little bazaar here and I could keep the place open in the afternoon for lunch, maybe hire a piano player."

"Actually," said Jones, "there's a neat little bazaar in the neighborhood already. Best smack south of 110th Street, though most people don't make the trip and settle for bags of Laundromat or Bag-in-a-Bag on Avenue D."

"Down here? I didn't know."

"Sure. Right here on Pitt Street." Jones didn't know where Pitt Street was, so he waved in some direction or other.

Levine reset his head atop his neck the better to direct an assessing look at Jones. "You have a habit?" Levine asked him.

"Naw," said Jones. "Just trying to sound street. I have an informant who tells me these things."

"Who's your informant?"

Jones decided to look cool and say nothing. The lunchtime piano gig might be worth something, and why should he queer it for Bobby, who said he was kicking again anyway. "I used to wonder about these bricked-up arches," Jones said, looking back up at the body of the bridge.

"I did too," said Levine.

"But you did something about it," Jones prompted.

"Yeah," Levine grinned, then did an assortment of aw-shucks gestures before getting into it. "I decided to make a couple of maneuvers. I decided to get down with the city and see if I could *hondle*. . . ."

Jones let Levine tell him all about it.

After shaking hands on a definite maybe, Jones made a credit-card call on a payphone just the other side of the bridge in the lee of Police Plaza—he wouldn't mention the nearness of the police to the Bear if Iris could wake him up and get him on the line—but no one picked up. He tried the number again and let it ring about a dozen times—Jeez, people go outdoors and actually do things in the country. Jones decided to try again that night after dinner. He thought he might have a dram before going back up to Houston Street and waiting for his honey. Or, better yet, go over, browse J&R Jazz World and see how *Sensible Shoes* was doing, tell the manager the Bear would be opening the Bridge in six weeks and wouldn't it be good to put up a display for the album now?

He doesn't hibernate does he, ha ha ha? Levine had asked him in parting, and Jones had answered Of course not, ha ha ha.

The sun had gone down behind the buildings when Jones made it from Police Plaza to City Hall.

When Iris woke him—as gently as she ever had when they were lovers, so gently for a moment he thought they might be lovers still—several clouds of thought assailed him. He had been aware for some time that her voice was calling his name softly, an excellent thing in woman, and then that a gentle familiar hand had laid itself upon his shoulder; but he was deep down, he was all the way asleep, and that voice and hand reached him only through veils of dream and interpretation, not to mention the memory of desire, and something like his love for her was groping upward out of sleepdust toward her but it was a long long way to go . . . it had been so long since he . . . there was so much he wanted to say . . . did he still know how to say it?

When Iris' familiar hand took hold of his right foot things started not to fit into the pattern of his loves and wishes, and that was when he began to wake into the familiar world of mixed light and dark, time resuming its steady motion, and he remembered loss.

When he opened his eyes he couldn't see her clearly. She seemed to shimmer there as if only partly manifested out of aether. He wanted to speak to her but couldn't find a word anywhere, and for a moment was afraid that he had lost his grip on language. "Ssss?" he said finally. Maybe he had lost it. "Ssspingyed?"

"Is it spring yet?" Iris asked him. "Not quite."

"You do me wrong to take me out of the grave," he told her. Looked like he still had language. Was that a good thing? Maybe he could have done with a change. Where had it gotten him? "Thart so bliss." Tongue still thick in his mouth though.

"Jones wants to talk to you." Her voice still had that melodic lilt, and was still pretty much inscrutable. "He says it's important. Can you wake up? Do you want to wake up? If you're having trouble waking up, I could make some coffee."

A yawn pulled his jaws wide. "Thart a soul in bliss," he finally managed. He tried to look up at Iris but the daylight was unfamiliar and dazzled him.

"I could leave you alone and let you decide. I could come down again tomorrow."

It seemed he had managed to nod yes. But he didn't want her to go away. He raised a vague paw but she was leaving, the door swung shut, and she had left. And now he had some sort of decision to make. Even though he was for the most part unconscious, he nosed his way forward through the veils and made a selection among the levels of mind available to him; he found a band of unassuming sleep in which he could put off immediate decisions and coast with the currents until he could meditate the situation through, maybe wake up for real tomorrow. Three notes chiming down there in the bass. How strange to deal with all this multilevelled vagueness when the only issue really was a love supreme. Three, make that four notes chiming, an old favorite long-familiar tune, he thought, wiping from his mind a momentary confusion with Bostic's humming version of "Hambone, Hambone, Have You Heard." Once the Bear got Trane back in focus he sailed off to sleep on the notes—low sleek planar sleep, not the insensible depth dive of the last few months—a boat gliding out from shore on smooth dark water. He smiled at the simplicity of the notes. Admired their economy and efficacy. Dreamed.

"Iris and I hardly talked," he told Jones, climbing forward as the van swung away from the ticketbooth along the curving ramp and found the straight vein of the Thruway south to the city. "Though she said we had a lot to talk about when I come back after the gig next week. The kids and I kept out of each other's way. It was some kind of a truce, I guess."

"Did you practice?" Jones asked him pointedly.

"Yes, I practiced. And I can still play. Thanks for the empathy."

This exchange yielded a few miles of silent highway, bare trees flicking past. The Bear fiddled with the heater and unbuttoned his raincoat, the snazzy charcoal-grey one, and adjusted his hat.

"I think we might be getting married," Jones said finally.

"That's sweet, man," the Bear told him, thinking that sometimes Jones had an unerring instinct for the wrong thing to say, almost good enough to match his own. "I'm touched of course, but you know I don't really need the ceremony. And seriously, Jones, what church would have us? You know I love you anyway, right?" The Bear batted his eyes and placed a paw atop Jones' right hand where it held the wheel.

Jones turned his head as if it were mounted on gimbals and gave the Bear a Look. "I was thinking of marrying someone else. You remember Sybil." His head returned its attention to the road.

"Oh yeah, *her*. I think you'll make a lovely couple. If you need a band for the reception you should call my guy and have him book me. He works at Megaton, he'll set it up. Yeah, give yourself a phonecall and negotiate a deal."

"On the other hand," said Jones, "for our wedding entertainment you could just go fuck yourself." He pulled the van left to pass a long black tarp-shrouded truck laboring on an upgrade, ends of rope flapping here and there at its edges. Once past that, he joined a line of cars doing seventy-five in convoy against the legal limit, tucking into the slipstream at the rear.

"I was trying for humor," said the Bear, "but it came out kind of testy, huh."

"You? Testy? Never happens. Well, hardly ever."

"Jones, let's clear the air. Of course I'm happy for you. I'm bitter about my own losses. Which is an explanation, not an excuse. Are you and Sybil really doing well? That's terrific."

"Everything is lox, clam and velouté. It seems we've worked our issues out."

"Jones no shit that's great to hear." The Bear looked his buddy over head to toe. He seemed better settled in his flesh than ever, yes. Marrying Sybil was probably the best thing that could happen to him. "She coming down to the club tonight?"

"Of course she is." Jones cleared his throat and fiddled in a stage-business way with the knobs and levers of the heater. "She'll whip up a gala post-gig supper and be down for a late set at the club."

The Bear reset the heater the way he liked it once Jones was finished fiddling. Of course she's coming down. And of course Iris is staying home with the girls. He was still sure that Tracy and Amy were supposed to love him, but some unaccountable error had interposed itself on fate's necessary pattern so that all of them—he, Iris, Trace and Aim—were missing the moment's intended boat. If he could somehow manage to reposition this presumptive boat at the dock they could all climb aboard and eventually learn to enjoy the ride. It should be the simplest thing in the world to clear the entire misunderstanding up, but trivial, idiot, unimportant things kept barring the way. Passing Tracy on the stairs last night for instance . . . the look she'd given him . . . how it had made him stumble into her and she had made *that* look as if he had tried to grope her . . . Could she really be that malevolent? It wasn't possible. She was a smart, nice kid. If she'd only understand that he was no threat to her possession of her mother. If Iris would only be less brittle and afraid she'd see there was room in her world for all of them. But they were riding on rails like locomotives powerless to alter course. How was it possible that none of them could summon up the necessary quantum of clear-eyed, liberating perception? What was wrong with them? Who had cast the spell? It was such a waste.

"You want to talk about things?" Jones asked finally, his voice wavering up out of its usual range. "You want to talk about Iris?"

"Do I want to talk about Iris?"

"I think that's what I said."

"Do I want to talk about Iris."

"This is getting repetitious. Maybe we should forget it and turn on the radio."

"You can't pick up anything on this stretch of road. Why would I want to talk about Iris?"

"Because it's happening to you. Because it's happening to you and it's important and you might want to talk it over."

"I never talk about anything important," said the Bear. "You know that."

"You could experiment. You could consider the possibility that not talking about it might be part of the problem."

"Humans," the Bear said, "and their human ways."

"Let me see if I can make this clear to you," Jones suggested. "Iris . . . is a human. You, who are a bear, are involved with Iris, who, you remember, is a human. Her daughters, also human. That means there is a four-person situation here, in which three of the four persons are human. To talk about it with a friend is also human. So is the friend. He's human too."

"What's your point?"

"You don't see a connection here?"

"Where?"

"Iris human. Kids human. Situation therefore mostly human."

"Yeah that's pretty much what's wrong with it," said the Bear, "as far as I can see."

Jones persisted. "Talk like human to human friend about human situation."

"Mud upon mud. Only make it worse."

"Maybe good. Maybe help. Don't you see? Human-human-human-human."

"Jones, you're talking like an idiot. What's up with you?"

"You're giving me a headache."

"Funny," said the Bear, "I didn't know you could give someone a headache by pulling their leg."

"You're pulling my leg?"

"Jesus, I *hope* it's your leg. . . ."

They watched the miles go by awhile. Jones futzed with the radio and found that what the Bear had said about this stretch of road was true. The Bear checked his gig-bag for the umpteenth time to make sure he had packed enough reeds, then waved hello to some astonished, happy kids in the back of a slick new Volvo wagon. They were jumping up and down, baring their teeth and fingernails, and the Bear was smiling back and showing them nature red in tooth and claw, revised version. See, he told himself, they like me. "See," he told Jones, "they like me, and they don't even know how wonderful I really am once you get to know me."

"It might help that you're not fucking their mother."

"I'm not fucking anybody's mother," the Bear grumbled.

Jones decided to pass the Volvo before the kids' parents scoped the Bear and things got out of hand. He gunned the engine but it was awhile before the van was able to gather sufficient speed to creep ahead, the kids jumping up and down all the way and the Bear waving back and making faces.

"You know," said the Bear, "if Iris and I had known how to talk a little better . . ." He lapsed into silence. "Maybe . . ."

"Uh huh," said Jones.

"But the way it turned out . . . We just . . . you know."

"Yeah?" said Jones.

"We just . . . yeah," he sighed.

"You still know how to tell a story, Bear."

"Yeah," the Bear nodded, then looked down at the backs of his paws, something he had done in cubhood to assure himself that he was there and at the same time wonder why. "Like that."

"Thank you for sharing that with me," Jones said.

"It was nothing," said the Bear.

"Pretty close."

Bare woods still flicking past, stripped branches reaching up to white winter sky as Jones eased off the gas and let the van fall back. As the van dropped into the right-hand lane, the truck they'd passed before whooshed ahead of them looking like death with flapping cloaks and ropes, and left them rocking in the afterdraft.

It's preposterous, he told Iris in his mind, gnawing at the subject like a paw caught in a trap. You'd think we would be able to walk and chew gum at the same time. I could have my music, you could have your kids, and we could meet between sets and work it out. It ought to be simple but there we are without a clue between us. Who would have believed it?

He kept turning their failure over in what passed for his mind, trying to rejig the picture, see it clear, get it right. They'd both been given an unconditioned opportunity—for him best typified by the astounding instant he had first entered Iris and woke up wearing a cosmic multiplicity of heads and limbs—and they'd each made of it what they'd known how to want or ask for. I got sex and bliss and music, she got her kids. Not enough. What a loss.

But if their tantric moment, if that's what it had been, represented unconditioned opportunity, and the botch they'd made of it was a result of selfhood, how was that different from life in general?

Jones cleared his throat. "What I was wondering, if you don't mind telling me, what was hibernation like?"

The Bear looked out at the woods whipping past. "Deep," he said. What am I doing going down to New York City to play some gig? What he wanted was more sleep. What he wanted was to hold Iris in his arms and to believe that love still meant something. "It was deep," he told Jones, nodding his big head.

"Restful?"

"Not the word I'd use."

"Restorative?"

"I couldn't say. At the moment I feel not so much restored as emptied out.

Annulled. Most emotions neatly excised." Why was he saying this? It wasn't literally true. But it felt true. Something had been taken out of him. What?

"A liberation?"

"I'm not sure but I keep looking." He wanted neither self-acceptance nor self-rejection but a state in which self was off the map, but he hadn't reached that point yet. What he had reached felt suspiciously like the Lesser Void, not a plenum but a blank. Empty world, and cold.

"Tell me about the club," he prompted Jones, just to get out of the rut.

"It's pretty trippy, being in the bridge and all. It's like a metaphor, a symbol of something."

"I meant how are the acoustics."

"It's like the bridge between two orders of perception, two worlds."

"I hate to be pedantic," the Bear began.

"You *love* to be pedantic."

"But if the club is set in the piles at one end of the Brooklyn Bridge, then it can't possibly suggest a transcendent crossing to the farther shore. The imagery doesn't play. I understand we have a cash guarantee up front and otherwise we don't play note one?"

"That's the way I set it up."

"When'd you become such a hardass?"

"I'm in the business. I've been observing. It's how these things are done. Trust me." Jones reached out and patted the front of the Bear's raincoat. "Hey, you really lost some weight there, all that sleeping."

"If music gets too tough I could do an infomercial. Sleep It Off: The Ancient Ancestral Wisdom of the Bears."

"Tollbooth coming up soon."

"Should I get in back?"

"Just pull your hat down and drool and they'll know you're a musician."

The Bear shunted his body into the rear and sat down on the edge of a wheel-hump. Smell of oil, trace of other industrial substance. It seemed strange that the sweet immaterial motion of music should require such heavy instrumentality: vans, buses, heavy flesh. It ought to be subtler. He sighed. Iris. How was it possible to lose that much beauty and wind up riding in a van that smelled of oil to play some music?

Maybe the music would rise to meet him when he got there. Or maybe someone'll do me a favor and shoot me. I can't do another few decades of this shit. If Iris and I can't work it out, maybe I'll just bag it, go off into the woods and do the rest of my life on the natch. Why would I want to play a bunch of notes?

The van approached the tollgate in a series of lurches, then stopped. The

Bear watched Jones pass the ticket and a couple of greenbacks out the window, and the gesture reminded him he had to talk to Jones about money. Jones rolled the window up as the van accelerated back to normal. The Bear gave it another thirty seconds, then climbed forward. "Another thing," he said. "If *Sensible Shoes* is selling so well and the single of 'When a Man Loves a Woman' is a minor radio hit, how come I'm not getting any royalty checks? Iris says our money's getting short."

"Sybil and I looked through the papers, and it's all straight."

"Iris looked through the papers too and there's all this money the album has earned that I don't get yet. Why?"

"A lot of the money's coming in from foreign sales, and Megaton uses that to pay themselves back for the twenty grand they gave you in front. As soon as that's earned back the money starts to come to you. But not before."

"The way it looks to Iris," said the Bear, "the album has already earned the advance back but because this money hasn't *officially* come in, I don't get any yet. Which sounds like a bunch of shit to me."

"That's because there are scheduled royalty periods twice a year, so when the money comes in at the European end there's a lag before the payout, and when the money's shunted to the company's American end, the six-month period in America doesn't coincide exactly with the European six-month period, so—"

"Oh I think they've got their six-month periods coinciding just the way they want," said the Bear. "They get to keep money I've earned for up to a year before I see a nickel. In the meantime I'm running short of cash, though it's hard to believe it given the way the album's doing."

"They also have to deduct bus and hotel money and per diems from the tour from your record sales account—"

"Wait a minute. I thought that was covered by income from the tour."

"I could lend you a few bucks if you need it," said Jones, "though tell you the truth I'm barely clearing forty grand a year and there are *secretaries*—do you believe it?—secretaries with seniority who are getting—"

"They're paying a flack like you forty grand," the Bear exploded, "and running all this doubletalk on me? Without me there wouldn't be any music for them to make their money on!"

"It's not all you. There are actually some other musicians on the label."

"I was speaking globally."

"Big of you."

"I'm getting screwed."

"Welcome to the real world."

"You want to see reality? I'll show you reality."

"Look, Badiyi's supposed to be coming down to the club tonight," said Jones, immediately wishing he hadn't. "Maybe you could talk with him about it."

"Ain't no fucking maybe. I'll crucify the executive son of a bitch. I'll punch his lights out. I'll eat his liver. He's not a drinking man, is he? Persian, right? I love foreign food."

Jones let the Bear grouse the frustrations out of his system as the van hauled south to the city, its signature fug of toxins visible up there in the sky ahead, hovering like whatever the night would bring.

2

"**okay** I admit it," said the Bear, his eyes beginning to adjust to the light after coming into the club through the heavy green doors. "It really is a hell of a place."

"Thanks," said Bob Levine, but he looked uncomfortable, kept smoothing his hair back and looking off to one side. Well, reasoned the Bear, by now I ought to be used to people acting nervous when they meet me first crack out of the box. So why was a warning-bell dinging softly in a small room in the rear left quadrant of his brain?

Rahim Bobby Hatwell rose unsteadily from the dimness at the rear of the club and, lurching sideways, grappled with a momentarily treacherous chair-back before emerging from behind a table. The Bear squinted: a tilted Hatwell was leaning much of his weight on a wooden cane on which his right hand and arm were pressing down. "Brooklyn Bridge?" Hatwell said, grimacing with the effort to suppress pain. "You'd think it's the Bronx Zoo the way they let the animals in. Ouch. How you doing, you fat furry fuckhead? Christ it's good to see you. Ouch. Shit. Fuck!" Tottering, Hatwell lapsed backward, and one of the club's woven rattan café chairs caught him as he fell, juddering backward on the floor. "Fuck! Shit. Ouch. Ahh."

"A cane?" asked the Bear. "What the hell is up?"

"It's temporary," Hatwell said, and settled himself more deeply in his safe harbor. He managed an old-man pose with his hands folded atop the cane-handle in front of him. "A purely temporary thing."

By the time the Bear got over to him, Linton Bostic had come away from behind the bar, where he'd been making an informal census of the bottles. "Bob here was trying to paint a moustache on the Statue of Liberty and he slid off her nose and fell down," Bostic said.

From a dim table off left came Garrett's voice: "Bobby fucked up. It comes as a big surprise to us all."

"But I can play," Hatwell said, looking at the bright side of things and up at the Bear with an uncharacteristically hideous grin. "The perfect jazz musician: half dead but still able to play. There are noble precedents. Plug me in. Bury me later. Send the check to my mother. He had so much promise. Boo hoo. Who can we eat now that's he's gone?"

The Bear reversed a nearby rattan chair—these things take up more room than the usual sardine jazz economics allow; did Levine know what he was doing?—and sat down across from his piano-playing outlaw genius buddy. "Are you all right?"

"Fuck no, I'm still alive."

"You don't have to tell me anything you don't want to."

"Which means I do have to tell you. I expected a higher grade of hypocrisy from you, but why? Fur? Fur's not enough." Hatwell came out with a stage sigh. "I went up to 120th and Adam Clayton Powell one night on my motorcycle to cop—don't interrupt, okay?—and I have a reputation, they know I'm carrying a lot of cash—my metabolism, whatever; it takes ten bags a pop to get me high instead of one or two. So I was cruising down the block and a coupla guys jumped out from between two parked cars and tried to take me off."

"Ah shit," said the Bear, and placed horrified, belated and inefficacious paws atop his head.

"One of them tried to get my neck from behind and the other one came at me with a tire iron from the right. I got my leg up and kicked him and he went down, but the one behind me got my shoulders and I pulled him down the block till the bike came down with both of us attached. That's how I got this," he said, and raised the cuff of his pants up his right leg. A deep scabbed-over gash, cruel and serpentine ran dark red down to his ankle.

"No wonder you're on a cane."

"That's not what put me on the cane. My helmet was still on and the guy couldn't do shit to me, so I worked him over pretty good while lying in the gutter on my side with half the bike on top of me." Hatwell snorted proud air from flared nostrils. "That's when an unmarked car pulled up. The other guy tore ass out of there and the cops decided why not bust me. They went through my pockets and found no drugs but did find three hundred dollars.

Pissed them off they didn't have enough dope to plant on me for a felony bust and three hundred wasn't gonna make their night and I called them on it. See, time passes but they still don't like an uppity Nigra. The mistake I made wasn't doing dope but talking back."

The Bear put a paw over his eyes.

"They got me in the car, drove me to the river by the sanitation plant, pulled me out and beat the shit out of me with their nightsticks. Kicked me too, thanks for asking. Fucked up my ribs, my kidneys and both knees. I crawled awhile and found a gypsy cab that would take me. Believe it or not, when I got back to where it happened my bike wasn't torn up too bad and there was some kid I gave twenty who told me he watched it for me. I should've died from the beating the cops gave me, but all I did was piss blood for three days and live. It wasn't one of my better weeks but I can still play piano."

"Bob Bob Bob," said the Bear.

"Bear Bear Bear," Hatwell said. "I take a lickin' but I keep on tickin'. You want to do a sound check or you think you're such hot shit you don't have to anymore?"

"Where'd Garrett go?"

"Standing right behind you," the familiar voice said.

"Bassists," Hatwell grumbled. "That's what they all say. But where are they when you really need them?"

"Someone needs them?" Linton wondered.

"We'd better do that sound check," said the Bear, "before war breaks out."

In the event they didn't do a sound check. They played what amounted to a set, all of them laying back a little to save their energy but nudging the music hard enough to be sure that it was there. It felt good to be able to do that, bring the music up to the brink and leave it for later. Everything they'd accomplished on the summer tour was still in place. All the ease they'd earned. They looked at each other in the middle of a laid-back, humorous "Doxy" when the Bear quoted "The Battle Hymn of the Republic" in a related minor, and exchanged small knowing smiles, savvy laughs, nods of the head. What arrogance, what cool. It still felt pretty hip to be a musician. The Bear figured if he could make it through the night without getting shot he'd feel cool in the morning.

Hatwell was in obvious pain, though, and the Bear wondered if he could carry a trio, like Sonny or Ornette. If he had to he would. You had to be such a melodist. He didn't want to say it out loud, but the Bear felt that he had again become such a melodist. Which was an interesting way for life to turn out. Come back to where you started and wonder if you've gone a few turns up the spiral or only made a circle, flat, for all the experience you've been through. No: he still had nothing, but he wasn't who he'd been.

The place had interesting acoustics. The club's main floorspace was roughly cruciform—or maybe say a plus sign or a crossroads for safety's sake—and the low square riser of the bandstand was set slightly to the rear of the center point so that, playing, they faced a broad inverted T-shape of tables with green metal graded balconies above in all four limbs so that there were box seats not only out in front of the band but behind them as well: the Bear didn't like playing to people who could see him but whom he couldn't see, but it couldn't be helped. Behind the bandstand on ground level was an oval service bar—the Bear could see a sound-problem coming up, cocktail shakers during the bass solos, blenders whirring up daiquiris, all the usual nightclub bullshit—but he had to admit that the acoustics were interesting. He made the mistake of mentioning it to Bob Levine and had to listen to a speech about the acoustic engineer Levine had brought in at great expense. Whatever. The sound went up into the arches and came back sweetened without losing much definition or detail; the PA had been intelligently integrated into the space; everyone in the band could hear everyone else without special effort; and the Bear, walking out front during a Hatwell solo—he sounded only slightly handicapped so far—found the house sound satisfactory, only a trifle bright without the hush of seated bodies. All in all, it was the best-sounding place they had ever played in. Even the guys in the band said so.

"Just don't tell Levine," Hatwell warned them. "He's insufferable already. You believe the guy?"

"No," Garrett said. "I don't think I do."

The Bear took them through tunes they'd played on the tour, and a few stray standards they hadn't. He also passed out sheets and worked up a head arrangement for a little waltz he had lifted from the soundtrack of *Gigi*: "Say a Prayer for Me Tonight." He thought he might use it for a light touch, a bit of comedy, something like the way Sonny had done "Shadow Waltz." As the light in the windows declined from twilight to early dark and the kitchen and the bartending and table staff came in—a lot of aspiring fashion models, tall girls of all colors defying gravity in a number of ways, their architecture closely followed by the band—the Bear found that Sonny Rollins was much on his mind. How could he not be? This was, after all, the Bridge; and even though Sonny had spent his famous nights practicing on the walkway of the Williamsburg, this place was close enough for a brush with the legend. Even the Bear would have preferred that Sonny Rollins was opening the joint.

They finished the rehearsal set with a rambling but together version of "Oleo" in which Bobby Hatwell, picking it up from the Bear on "Doxy," kept quoting "The Battle Hymn of the Republic" even though it didn't fit the changes. The Bear cocked an appraising ear toward the pianist; he was playing fine, although given his leg problem he wasn't using much pedal. Fair enough. We'll get through tonight, do three sets tomorrow, take Sunday and Monday off, and ought be in shape to play five days next week, assuming they don't shoot me.

But . . .

What was it? Something important was missing or had been left undone.

Yes—he'd forgotten it completely, and where was Jones?—they weren't supposed to even set up their instruments before the cash guarantee was in hand, in full. They'd acted like musicians and played a warmup set. "Jones?" the Bear called into the obscurity of the house. "Where the fuck is he?" he asked the band when no answer came. "If he doesn't have our front money we've already played more than we were supposed to according to the deal."

"Hey guys," Bostic asked, "isn't this just like playing with the Bear? This is exactly like playing with the Bear."

They stepped away from their instruments and scoured the house—no Jones—but finally heard voices coming from the greenroom offside the kitchen doors.

"Why not let's go in there," the Bear suggested.

"Kill," said Bobby Hatwell, hobbling across the floor on his walking stick. He poked at the greenroom door with the rubber end. "Pillage. Maim. Cheese dip."

The Bear stepped around Hatwell and pulled the door open, then led the way inside and surprised Jones and Bob Levine in the act of vigorous conversation. Jones had been reading Levine a version of the Riot Act, but he barred the Bear's way across the room and said, "Let me explain."

"The front money's not here," said the Bear. "Am I right?"

Hatwell bypassed the cheese dip, found the tub of free beer and fell into the sofa beside it.

"I hate it," said the Bear once the situation had been explained to him twice. The band was eating antipasto from the trays and pulling bottles of Feathered Serpent from the big iron tub of cold water and ice. "The money was supposed to be here in front. We weren't even supposed to set up our instruments."

"The money will *be here*," Levine began explaining for a third time, "only I don't have it right now because basically the whole house is comped for the first set—the whole world of press and the music business is coming down to hear you—but they'll pay for their drinks and once the bar receipts start coming in . . ."

"I have to wait for a bunch of critics and music-biz vampires to order Perrier with a water chaser before I can pay my band?" the Bear asked Levine.

"White man speak with forked tongue," Bostic explained.

Levine didn't look so good: the Bear knew flop-sweat when he saw it. The man was leaking gesture: he ran his hand through his hair front to back, took his silver-rim glasses off, put them back on, picked imaginary lint from his Italian sweater of many colors, pulled a handkerchief from the back pocket of his cords, seemed to forget what he wanted to do with it and put it back; all this as he paced back and forth across the room. "Jones," said the Bear. "You were supposed to take care of this."

"He's good for it," Jones told him, but Jones looked tired. "I mean look at all the money he's put into the place."

"How much he got left?" Bostic asked the ceiling. "I think that's the question. We're sposed to have two thousand dollars in our pocket before we play note one. He got that much do you think?"

Levine fretted the hair that protected his temples. Maybe, thought the Bear, it will go an increment greyer as we watch. "I'll tell you something I'm not supposed to," Levine told the room. "It's a fucking event, the opening of this club. Salman Rushdie's supposed to be here tonight."

"He comped too?" Bobby Hatwell wanted to know.

"British Secret Service," Levine told him.

"Then I hope he's got lots of guards and they drink," said the Bear. "I find his books unreadable but it'd be a welcome change to see someone in greater danger than I am." He began to visualize the worst of all possible worlds: Iranian fundamentalists busting the door in and heading for Rushdie, the Bear getting in front of them with quotes from 'Arabi or Rumi to convince them they'd misconstrued the dispensation, cops rising up to turn their guns on him and the final battle commencing—a typical Friday-night gig in New York. The fruitiness of the imagery helped relax him somewhat.

Bostic was playing foghorn sounds into the mouth of a beerbottle, Bobby Hatwell was paring his fingernails with the end of the corkscrew on his Swiss Army knife, and Garrett seemed interested in Bob Levine.

"I can't tell you how much I wanted you guys to open this place," Levine said.

"Tell us anyway," Garrett said.

"You think we fucking care?" was Hatwell's question.

"You were supposed to come up with two grand," the Bear said again, feeling calmer now. "A lot of money went into putting this place together. It shows. But it's not fair if there's nothing left over to pay the musicians. You know what I mean?"

"Look," Levine said, "once people start coming in . . ."

"But the house is comped," the Bear persisted.

"Your own record company has got like six tables down."

"My own record company has like six tables down? Jones, is there something you haven't told me? Do I own a record company?"

"I'll get you money from the door," pleaded Bob Levine. "From the bar as soon as they start drinking."

Silence, untrusting looks.

"Okay," said Levine in final desperation. "I'll give you my car. Actually, my girlfriend's car."

"What's wrong with *your* car?" Bostic wanted to know.

"For Christ's sake it's a Mercedes."

"And he's a bear."

"Yeah but Georgia's Accord's got a book value of fifty-five hundred and you can have it clean against the guarantee if the cash doesn't come in, which it will. I'll sign the title over to you right here."

"You asked her?"

"I don't have to ask her."

"Aw man," said Bobby Hatwell, "we can't take your girlfriend's car . . ."

"I'd give you my wife's car but we're separated."

"They throw a bucket of water over you?"

"Look, we can't take the car . . ."

"Naw, we can't take the car . . ."

Levine paced the room in a tightening ambit. "I'll talk to her in a minute. She won't mind. The club's gonna work. It's a great place. My father's gonna kill me. It's gonna do business. Help me out, guys. I swear I'm doing this with the best will in the world. You think it's easy to have money? It's not easy to have money. I don't have money. I mean I have money but I don't have money. Maybe people have been coming in by now. Let me go out and check receipts at the bar. There's like a three, four hundred percent markup. Couple bottles of champagne and I can pay you for the week." With a sweep of his hand through his hair, he left.

"I trust the guy because he's so together," Hatwell said, and tossed an empty bottle into the trash. "If there's anything I'm a judge of, it's character. I trust him because he acts so cool. Who's gonna drive me home?"

"We can't take his car," Linton said.

"Of course we can't take his car," said Garrett.

"What would we do with his car?" asked the Bear.

"No point taking his car," said Jones.

"Then it's settled," Hatwell said. "We're not taking his car."

Long pause, a furtive exchange of looks, then all five burst out laughing. The Bear was the first to say it: "Let's take his fucking car."

Hatwell lapsed laughing onto Linton Bostic on the sofa. Garrett hooted.

Bostic summed it up. "Okay let's take his girlfriend's fucking car."

"You seen his girlfriend?" Hatwell asked. "Cause maybe we could take her, instead."

"Actually," said Jones, "we could raise two grand on his sweater."

The Bear stomped wheezing laughing around the room. "Car," he said. "Car. Car. Car."

"Hey," said Bostic, "Bear learned a word."

Who could tell, the Bear thought while gasping, maybe this would be a good night after all.

They took his girlfriend's car. Jones had signed the paper, in lieu of a pawprint from the Bear. The girlfriend, a nice one, alternated anger and anxiety but let it happen. Levine told her she could have the Mercedes if the deal didn't play. The house had filled, and down in the parking lot at the base of that long stairway a white-hot pivoting searchlight lanced and circled at the sky. "He can hire a fucking searchlight but he don't have dime one for us?" was Hatwell's reasonable remark. Hatwell bit a fingernail. It was almost time to play.

The Bear wandered out in front of the stage for a moment to glad-hand a portion of the house, partly to say obligatory hellos but also because he had security concerns in mind. He didn't see Salman Rushdie. There was a back door accessible from the stage and it had been left unlocked for him, but that had not been enough at the Tin Palace, and this particular escape hatch gave onto an exposed metal stair slanting to street level down a bare brick wall with no cover and no future to the gambit if the law was waiting at the bottom. The Bear expressed some of his misgivings at the first stageside table he approached.

"You see these good old boys here?" Rondo grinned up at him.

"I see them," said the Bear, looking down at five other big strange white guys—swollen T-shirts, black leather, guts, bad skin, tattoos, sloppy distracted grins, straggly beards, long ponytails and lawless almost certainly demented eyes. "Hi. Hah. Yall. A fragmentary greeting I'm afraid but the fact is I'm glad to see you. Yall."

"Anything happens," Rondo told him, "they run loose like you wouldn't believe and the world better duck and cover."

"Rondo," the Bear said, "I thank you from the available bottom of my heart but don't start anything just for the fun of it, okay?"

"Do my best to keep the guys in line," Rondo said. "This's Dooky, that's Pap, this here's Clancy, Case, and Bugle-Ass. Y'oughta take the time to get to know them individjly."

"Maybe after the first set you could all come back to the greenroom," the Bear suggested.

"The fuck's this 'Rondo'?" one of the faces at the table asked as the Bear headed over to say hello to Tim. Rondo was answering; if they were old movie buffs there could be trouble. The Bear could feel the house watching him, faces pivoting his way as he moved from table to table, nodding and sociable as he could manage.

"Hey Bear," Tim's familiar voice asked him when he was still looking out at the house and raising his saxophone aloft—pure social weakness—to wave some species of generalized hello: lot of tables out there in the relative dark, and a smattering of applause even though he hadn't played a note yet. "I don't see any cops in here, Bear, in case you were wondering. And I oughta know," Tim said.

"Hey thanks man," said the Bear, and nodded to acknowledge the information. "Is this Mrs. Tim here? Hi." Still somewhat distracted and looking around, definitely impolite; the Bear attempted a correction, and labored to focus his eyes on the woman.

"Miranda," she offered up, and took his paw with less than the usual trepidation, a wide grin beneath lofted red-dyed hair.

"O brave new world," the Bear felt obliged to say, still turning a wary eye upon the house. "Nice to meetcha. Creatures in it."

"Really, Bear," Tim told him, "the law ain't here."

"The law is always here," said the Bear, "even when it can't be seen."

"Tim has told me so much about you," Mrs. Tim said, perhaps conventionally, and tugged lightly on his paw.

The Bear finally looked down at her and liked what he saw: behind the woman's face widening and flattening into middle age he detected an indiscriminate light, more pleasing than the attempts at makeup or the aura of hair that framed the display suggested. "Look after him," he told Miranda, feeling a sudden tenderness for both of them, making their efforts at identity in the midst of such immensity. "He needs looking after." As did all sentient beings, he thought, his heart swelling with unthought love for every creature his eye might propose to consideration that night. What's happening? he wondered. I know it's true but what's working in me? What is going on?

"I will look after him," Miranda said.

"I know," said the Bear, and it seemed for a moment that he could see Tim and Miranda as God might have thought them up; how precious and impossible not to love, how undiminished and untravestied while deployed in time. What could he do for them? The Bear was unable to think of anything adequate.

What is up with me tonight? he wondered. If I get too floaty I won't have enough concentration to play.

Levine came up behind the Bear and placed a hand on his shoulder. "Stanley Crouch just bought a magnum of our best champagne for his table. God bless the MacArthur Foundation and the markup on booze in general. We're making money."

"You mean you want the car back?"

"Only if I pull in the two grand clean above what I have to pay the kitchen staff. I'm ready to introduce the band. You ready to play?"

"One never knows, do one." The Bear looked at the brick and ocher masonry walls, the stonework trim, and reminded himself: material world: you play music in it: your role here: you signed on again, remember: but why?

"I'll just say a few words to welcome the audience." One more shoulder-pat and Levine made for the stage, where he tapped the chrome and webwork microphone, cleared his throat and bestowed upon the house his best attempt at a relaxed, hospitable grin. "If I could have your attention for a minute . . . just a minute please . . . hello ello . . . thank you . . . ladies and gentlemen, welcome to the Bridge."

A dutiful round of applause, quick fade, the sound of drinks, provisional hush of patience.

"And welcome to the Bear too. Didn't mean to leave anyone out."

The Bear dropped into a chair next to Tim and listened as Levine began a surprisingly long speech about how he had always dreamed about opening a jazz club in New York, if at all possible in just this particular, quite extraordinary location, and as the Bear heard a certain tearfulness beginning to crest in the man's voice he cast his eyes around the room to scan his almost fully comped public. That might be Stanley Crouch over there pouring out champagne—nice suit for a man his size, wonder if his tailor could make me one like that; orange label on his champagne bottle; the Bear felt a sudden purely phantom thirst—for his large round table of eight; but the man the Bear wanted to find was that creep Badiyi so he could brace him between sets all bristling fur and flashing teeth to ask him about the small matter, the rather too small matter of those royalty checks, hm? Instead his eyes encountered, at a small table set against a masonry wall, the Shakespeare-looking guy who had interviewed him at the Power Station—he was sitting with an attractive Middle Eastern–looking woman, who seemed, to the Bear's lipreading eyes and directional ears, repeatedly to be calling him Winkies. Note to Iris: people are funny.

Levine, poised at the microphone in the spotlight at the edge of the stage, had begun talking about how important animals had always been to him, especially in childhood, when . . . the horse he'd always wanted . . . the birds he had wanted to befriend . . . White Fang . . . The Jungle Book . . . Akela . . . Baloo . . .

What was it with people? the Bear wondered. I get so tired of being everybody's sentimental inkblot.

Bagheera . . . Kaa . . . Levine said he had always seen himself as, well, how should he put it, a sort of Mowgli-figure . . . empathy with his childhood dog . . . the raccoons that used to raid the trashcans at his parents' country place those long summer nights . . . and don't we know New York's a jungle? So . . . in a certain sense . . . the bridge above our heads . . . and the appearance of the Bear in it . . . as cars rush over us . . . signifies . . .

The Bear had had enough of this—Jones had taken a run at this near-metaphor on the ride down from the mountains, but as far as the Bear was concerned it was twice-idiotic hooey, signifying a double dose of nothing. It was time to cut the talk, time to strut your hour upon the stage and hope it swings despite the odds.

The Bear rumbled up from his seat, rehooked the alto to his neckstrap, nodded farewell to Tim and Mrs. Tim, and walked up to the stage playing a bit of intro to what was supposed to be "Doxy" but might actually prove to be a blues: he'd think about it. Turning heads, startled looks, one glass breaking, and a smattering of applause as Levine stepped back looking confused from the mike and indicated with a flawed sweep of arm the advancing Bear. After a momentary dissociative blur, he found himself fully onstage, nodding into the lights as he played, acknowledging the applause with inclinations of his trunk and hearing the band attain its instruments behind him—tink of piano, ting of cymbal, thrum of bass—as he played a couple of blues licks in F up into the arches and thought it might work out.

It only then occurred to him that walking onstage playing was another Sonny Rollins reference, something Sonny sometimes liked to do—considering the venue, it was no more than good form, due tribute—but he thought that opening with Rollins' "Doxy," as he had planned to do, might overegg the custard, and he cued the band with a couple of passing references to "M Squad," the Count Basie shuffle blues they'd had fun with on the tour, but noodled and divagated his way through some further asides before settling on a tempo and pulling the band in with a downward sweep of his horn. Four bars into the head the house unloosed a round of applause—they know "M Squad?" it'd surprise me—and he looked up past the spotlights' mix of white and blue and red into the balconies, which seemed well freighted with listening humans. The house might be comped, but at least it was full. He finished the repeat of the head and heard the guys prepare the way for his solo: a climbing Tynerish cadence, a cymbal flurry with a press roll behind it, and a friendly nod to the subdominant from Garrett. Okay, thought the Bear. What should I play for these nice people?

In any event, he thought after a couple of choruses, this is an interesting way to stumble into the music. What he had done, pretty much, was keep Sonny Rollins in mind: gradually, teasingly, he'd been evolving the beginnings of a new melody from the fundamentals of the tune, underlining the process with a blatant, half-comic tracing of each cadence and chord change—first, um, this chord, then that, and at the end of every twelve bars it all comes down like *this*—in a way the audience might find familiar if they'd heard his recording of "When a Man Loves a Woman." What he usually liked, when his head was working along these lines, was to build up, by means of overstated basics and interstitial runs, a long and ruminative architecture which he could later tear to pieces for catharsis; but as he put the solo through these somewhat accustomed paces, he had occasion to wonder how much this really had to do with Sonny Rollins, because maybe it really came down from Monk.

Rahim Bobby Hatwell seemed to think it did; in any case, he salted the way ahead with an exploratory alternation of major and minor sixths, and when the Bear acknowledged them the band dropped into a meditation on "Misterioso," the almost unrecognizable abstract Monk had built out of the barest fundamentals of a blues, and they might even have taken it out of tempo to explore the implications—Garrett and Hatwell climbing those laddering sixths, the Bear continuing to augment the nearly contrapuntal bass component of the line to draw out its aspects one at a time, so that the four of them were slowly being led by the tune's abstraction into a kind of stalled, Cubist consideration of its workings, Monk's corners all so brilliant—had not the Bear pressed onward into the next chorus, and the next, with a willful plurality of new ideas in order to jettison the already known, or at least the sufficiently obvious. The band fought him at first—kids, he thought, and we can work this stuff out some other time—but after awhile they seemed to accept his terms and give way before his insistent push ahead. They set up a little modified shuffle groove to see if he might enjoy the ride, and after two more choruses it seemed as if he did. Garrett's time broadened to accommodate the larger melodic ambit the Bear kept proposing and reproposing; Linton widened the shuffle into a lope and set cymbal ornamentations shimmering in the gaps; and Bobby Hatwell began to leave uncharacteristically long spaces between his chords—the Bear looked over his right shoulder to check and yes, to spare himself Hatwell was holding his hands down on the keys rather than using the pedal to sustain their resonance: a partly practical consideration given the state of his legs, but it also invited the Bear to occupy the lengthening gaps with whatever the freedom of the moment might suggest.

These were three very smart musicians. The band was sounding good. And how much room they give me. As a matter of fact I do feel a bit expansive.

He felt his body find its ease, his lungs expanding on the inbreath, tone enriching itself on the out. He doubletimed the next four bars, did a little accent-switching turnaround, thank you Bird, into the release, and felt cell after cell in the large dark shape of himself begin to come alight. Oxygen. Inspiration. I like it. He took the saxophone from his snout for a two-bar lag and laughed aloud as his heart began to open—lots of room in there, and something more knowing than emotion. Yes, he thought, as he had sometimes on the tour but never at the beginning of the first set, this is what the music's for. What I feel right now is worth a life, even one as preposterous as my own. Certainly worth all the sweat and study. In the city of himself, lights went on in the apartments, people settled down to dinner or got up to dance, block parties started up in the sidestreets, and the simplest facts of life were celebrated: memory was accorded a specific rhythmic nod and the basic functions of the brain inspired spontaneous group gyrations here and there. The basic stuff of night and day embraced and the undecided sky filled with a rich blend of color. The Bear took a stroll along the boulevards and liked the look of everything he saw, the way people were, the things they loved and the way they loved them. One more significant step onward and he saw the labyrinth of streets begin to assemble itself into that ideal geometry of light in which identity was spelled out whole beyond the passing chords of space and time—a radical shift in the angle of view but not yet, he noticed, an essential change of substance. The process so far was only implication not ascent, and what he felt now was deep pleasure in being who he was, where he was, and if that necessarily included all the gain and loss that had brought him to this point, he had a few objections but was ready to say yes. The Bear felt an anticipatory flutter in his heart, the familiar trembling of the veil at its entrance, but suppressed the urge toward ecstasy, or laid it aside for the moment in the interest of the continuing particulars of this satisfactory little solo on a Count

Basie shuffle blues as played on a worn Martin alto in a club called the Bridge.

So that, standing on recognizable earth, the Bear played a long arching trill in alternating seconds and thirds through the better part of a chorus—lungs still good, he thought—leaned back into the rhythm section to play one more long-breathed chorus that casually summarized the preceding architecture and stepped aside to let the guys have a go. What surprised him was that Hatwell kept his outing short, Garrett declined a solo, and the Bear traded three choruses of fairly elegant fours with Linton before taking "M Squad" out. But you know—he told himself, still riding on the warmth and illuminations of the performance—these are familiar, well-worn pleasures: they only add up to just more Me. However cozy the sensation, it's within known limits, and less than ultimate. It's still within the prison walls. Looking down into the mostly bungled immensity of himself he felt the coarseness of the puppet on him, the cheap fur, the glassy inexpressive eyes, the corruption of its known coordinates, its unsuitability as essential statement, and he decided that any amplification of the mostly comical dingus could not satisfy him or anyone finally. But did you really expect to bust out of here completely? It would be nice, and I'll put in the obligatory essential request, in triplicate if need be, but it's not the kind of thing you can expect to happen really, is it, in the persistent narrowness of the given world.

"Thank you thank you thank you," he said into the ovation anyway. "I'm Lieutenant Frank Ballinger and I wish Sonny Rollins was here tonight too. We all know he should be opening this club, but he turns down more gigs than the rest of us get offered and his price was high for the house, so welcome to the real world and we will do the best we can. Rahim Bobby Hatwell only slightly crippled at the piano, Garrett Church wisdom itself on bass, Linton Bostic hitting things with sticks until he thinks up something more sophisticated, and I am exactly what I appear to be. My friend Tim assures me there's no danger of arrest tonight and Rondo looks particularly ready to resume his dialogue with the law should occasion arise. Jones is watching the receipts, I've already won a car and you could be next. Keep your coat-check tickets and thank you thank you thank you. We hope you're not sitting up too close or back too far and we'd like to play you a tune from the score of *Gigi* Sonny should have played back then but somehow missed out on: 'Say a Prayer for Me Tonight.'"

He had almost said Iris instead of Gigi.

The Bear nodded the band into the pirouetting little waltz before the applause had quite died away. Such a pretty tune. The way he'd found it, Iris had a video of *Gigi* up at the house and the Bear used to watch it some nights.

Like most talking bears, he had sentimental notions of Paris, and he used to sit there with *Gigi* on the box and in the middle of some random scene of no particular emotional import tears would pour down his face and he'd watch the rest of the movie dripping and not knowing why. He liked the score, but none of the standout tunes would work for the quartet—and could you imagine practicing "Thank Heaven for Little Girls" in a house full of Iris, Amy and Trace? But this slender little waltz charmed his pants off and he was happy to play it now, lightly, graciously . . . though now it occurred to him that Frederick Loewe had fudged the resolution of the B section and that if Sonny had wanted to stroll these boulevards he wouldn't have been embarrassed to play "Thank Heaven"—the luxury of being a primary creator—and if the tune was going so dancingly well why was he getting those jabbing discontented chords in his back from Rahim Bobby Hatwell?

The Bear looked over his shoulder to find the pianist glaring at him from his station at the Steinway. Really? thought the Bear. Hey Bob, if I'm playing such utter bullshit how come Garrett and Linton are enjoying themselves on the tune?

Hatwell looked over at the bassist and the drummer, then back to the Bear as if to say So What and hit him with a minor ninth.

Surly motherfucker, thought the Bear, but when he returned his attention to his solo he found that much of the charm had gone out of it and he let it end.

Much to his surprise Hatwell took a long, rather lyrical solo on the tune, probably exacting some convoluted form of revenge, although there was no way to tell: the man's facial expression was triumphantly unreadable. The little wars of bear and man. He played some needless background figures for the pianist and grinned around his embouchure. But felt, whatever the moment's small ironic pleasures, that the set was at risk all of a sudden, and he wondered, since it must continue, what they might play next. He didn't feel like doing one of his own tunes. More Sonny? Wouldn't that be overdoing it? He riffled through the band's working repertoire, discarded it and finally thought, yes, maybe that, although we've done one blues already.

After Garrett's two delicate choruses—substantial melodies teased out at their edges by lithe, guitaristic, single-finger strummings along the E-string, all wings and flutters, reference Mingus on Duke's "Fleurette Africaine"—the Bear played the out-chorus of "Say a Prayer" as if the alto were feathery and breathy as a flute—a departure from his usual muscular presentation. He bowed to the polite, proportional applause and stomped off a dangerously fast tempo without telling the band what the tune was going to be, but they peeped it in two bars of course, and got behind him on the downbeat of the third: "Pursuance," the B-flat-minor blues that formed the third part of John Coltrane's *A Love Supreme*. But, thought the Bear as he lit into the tune's scalar ascents, Trane's ladders to a possible heaven, it ain't no simple minor blues either. Anyone who thinks Trane got harmonically simpleminded once he went into his modal phase should listen closer to the way he put this thing together—Bostic I love you, he thought as the drummer put his boot behind the tune's written rhythm; thank you for knowing that there is no such thing as too much propulsion this tune this night. In tribute to the tune's generative impulses and the band's acknowledgment of them the Bear repeated the head an unconventional third and fourth time to build up a sufficient head of steam and think about it because hey lookit:

It's a B-flat-minor blues all right but Trane built it on the F-minor pentatonic scale, which through the flat seventh opens onto A-major pentatonic and anyhow resolves in the logical though unexpected daylight of B-flat major, so you can play it as a straight blues if you want but even without pushing the tune's composed parameters you're already out there in a wealth of alternate scales . . . so that if you want to take it out the tune will hold you—obviously Trane wanted to indicate a plurality of possible ascents to a single illumination, and you had to admire the economy of means with which he had expressed the idea. By the end of the head's fourth repetition the rhythm section was playing with greater interior velocity than he had heard from them ever, and the Bear lit into his solo loving what contemporary piano bass and drums could do—Linton springing loose a multilimbed complexity of polyrhythm that acknowledged all manner of detail within the larger motion of ruling onrushing time; Garrett moving his attack just slightly ahead of the beat and cutting it back in uneven groupings of three and four while his note choices worked their way along an axis arrayed between B-flat and F natural, nodding hello to the implied tonalities along the way but pursuing a forthright central course nonetheless, good man; and Hatwell shunted some powerful Tynerish stacked fourths into place while audibly waiting to see where the Bear was going to take his line before committing himself to personal response. It was just this side of inconceivable, thought the Bear, that mortal musicians could converse on this level at this speed—flash remembrance of the juggling triangles of his dream: who are we really? The Bear wished he could play nearer Trane's level of inspiration, less for reasons of insane ambition than because life seemed to require it of him just now and anything less would seem like failure. In admission of this unpayable debt he quoted early some lines from Trane's recorded solo on the tune, that architectonic upsurge through detailed obscurity until the soul, having exhausted its own and music's known resources, could legitimately tear itself open before the hoped-for illumined face of God—something, the Bear remembered, that Trane had achieved in a studio on a solo lasting four minutes tops.

Ambition, take note.

It would be nice to be able to play that well, but what are you gonna do really?

After a chorus and a half of mixed invention and quotation, he thought to settle into a simple pentatonic scanning of the tune's written parameters, and hoped he might eventually begin to build something out of its rhythms. He played fluently and at speed, paws working well, lungs and embouchure dispensing power smoothly into the music's rush.

I may be a long way down from Trane, but it feels cool to play even this well. Parenthetically it occurred to him to wonder why he was adapting the dynamic of Trane's calamitous argument with the nature of things when Ornette's subtler elision of dispute had always seemed the wiser course; but then the Bear had always had a difficult nature and it was too late to change now.

Besides which, listen to how well it's working at the moment.

The Bear took so much pleasure in how he was handling things he hardly noticed it when his attention began to wander; in fact it seemed to him that his straying thoughts detailed both the tune's legitimate business and his own: he saw himself heading upstate in a car—odd, when the plan was for him to stay at Jones and Sybil's through the weekend and the Monday off, and only van it back to what no longer felt like home at the end of the following week, an intelligent conception of a break from the family scene—but there he was, in foresight or imagination, heading north with Jones behind the wheel of what might be the new Accord they had farcically lifted off of Bob Levine. We're sure to give it back to him once the till is full and he can pay us the agreed amount, so the image didn't make sense as precognition, but it was vivid all the same. As the car headed up the Thruway, shadows of bare trees along the road fell across his eyes through the windshield, sun low in the eastern sky: is it morning? The mixed pattern of light and shade through which they sped seemed very like the pentatonic glide of chords—Trane so smart and subtle in his constructions—through which he urged the fluency of his evolving alto line. Well of course he dreamed of the way upstate. Wasn't he in love? Wasn't he doing what he knew best, banging his head into the world's brick wall in the name of the truest thing he knew? He knew nothing truer or better than his love of Iris. It was worth a life, wasn't it? And it seemed to him that the tune's goal, like the road on which he dreamed his way to an imagined Woodstock, was Iris, or was subtly encoded in her bones and lights and motions. Listen to how the music goes, Iris, up there into B-flat major: we can work things out. Look at the scales, observe their ideal tendency. See what the whole wide swarming composition is searching for. Get with me on this. Having wonderful time. Wish you were here.

Even he could hear the fatuous pleading note in that.

And if all the inclinations of his enraptured artifice were aimed true, why was Bobby Hatwell—exactly what the fuck was Hatwell hitting him with now? You could hardly call it accompaniment: that bare repeated minor seventh, C to B-flat without the ameliorative F between, and for emphasis Hat was doubling the bare, forked thing in octaves. What, the Bear would have liked to know, was the source of this violence, this assault?

He looked over his shoulder to see Hatwell glaring at him from the keyboard. The Bear gave him a what's-up look and Hatwell laid a minor ninth and eleventh on top of the seventh, already sufficiently tart, thank you.

Look, the Bear thought at Hatwell furiously, just because you're more heavily invested in an ethos of struggle than I am, that doesn't mean . . .

Just because you've confused death with daylight, that doesn't signify . . .

Just because you've been beaten up more recently than I have, that doesn't indicate . . .

Besides which, I know my way around this complicated chromatic labyrinth as well as you do, so what's your problem, Bob?

But gradually the Bear's busy protesting mind ground to a halt and shut up, because whatever Hatwell's motivation might be, his aggressive chording had in fact begun to give the Bear's easy pentatonic fluency the lie; and, um, it did finally occur to him that he had played the last five choruses while thinking about riding upstate in a car.

The Bear decided not to shoot the piano player, and thought, All right, I'll take you on, I'll dig in, I'll hit the tune's particulars as if they mattered and I were really capable of all their implications. Will that make you happy? Probably not.

The Bear strengthened his stance at the microphone, lowered his center of gravity, filled his lungs, thickened his tone by choking up on the reed a bit and headed for the bottom of the next chord—digging in, he wished he had himself a tenor now, closer to the range of his speaking voice and not the alto's more specialized song. But songfulness was what had drawn him to the smaller instrument in the first place, that and how it felt in his paws, so probly he'd better get off the Thruway and deal with it.

Vee vill do vhat vee can, he thought in the late Doctor Friedmann's voice. As a bonus I'll try not to get blood on the stage.

Place does have nice acoustics.

Love the sound up there in the arches.

Still don't see Salman Rushdie.

The Bear took still firmer hold of the reed in his snout, directed its vibration with fiercer intent and sent his breath down the length and curve of horn with such power as he could muster up from his feet and legs and let branch breathwise in his ribs and assemble toward final form in the wide house of beating dark . . . anything to get this shit together . . .

. . . and played some angry chromatic enumerative bullshit . . .

. . . and heard the rhythm section let him know it.

He shut his eyes to the room and wondered, as he had several times before in his life: if I could really play my ass off, what would it sound like? and he almost laughed into the mouthpiece because, as had happened several times before in his life, some part of him—convinced, no doubt, it had outfoxed the vanity trap—responded to the gambit, got up on its hindlegs and proposed the beginnings of an answer.

As he dug in he heard the rhythm section respond—Jesus this tune is fast; faster, once you try to work some substantial phrasing into it—with such telepathy and invention what could a poor dumb bear hope to do? But hope had nothing to do with it, nor Trane nor Bird nor Ornette nor Sonny: he would have to shake this ragdoll bear and work sufficient sense or stuffing from it on his own.

He dug the alto deeper into the tenor saxophone's timbral range than he would have believed possible—Jackie McLean call your office—and was doing this whirring arpeggiated thing in F minor that got up under the architecture of the changes and began to breach them: not outright demolition so much as the bending of structural oak, a creaking protest from the fundamentals. The rhythm section responded quickly to this information, which of course only increased the level of demand on him. Before I find my way out of here I might have to play some serious music: and what a shock that would be. Although imagery was a distraction at this level of play, behind his shut eyes he saw himself hibernating in the basement these past months as some phantasmal marrow of his being struggled up to inhabit the rooms and join Iris' life in the light; he remembered the rich dark earth outside, beneath; some fugitive and unseizable seed struggling to germinate deep in the mothering dark. Maybe you should try to remember you're trying to play music here; no, I want to gather these scents and memories, make them part of what I'm trying to evolve for these nice people, who for some reason have let loose a ripple of applause.

He felt the beginnings of cramp in his right paw—the repeated reach, on the run, down to low E-flat—and changed its angle of address to the keys at the bottom of the horn; obtained some momentary relief by moving the action higher up, where his left paw was working fine; and stayed obstinately in F minor against the recurring pull of the tonic B-flat. Go further, he told himself, and shook his right paw loose. Pull the sucker apart.

Garrett was with him on this and Bostic, in the probable interest of countervailing centripetal force, was altering his attack to generate a less disparate sense of his drumset, pulling together its timbres, relating cymbal more closely to snare, deepening his relation to the beat, thickening its pulse—which, face it, was the way the Bear loved to hear the drums really—and what was more gratifying still, Rahim Bobby Hatwell was giving him room and support again. Sensing it, the Bear looked over his shoulder at the pianist and saw that he was using the pedal on those sustained chords, taking the pain and looking through it at the Bear.

That's probly overdoing it, Bob, but you're great anyway. Thing about the great players is how events never seem to impinge on them. How, unlike me, they always have so much time.

The Bear faced front, raised his alto up into a high cry before redescending into dark, and if his eyes were open he didn't see the room. What he did see, and didn't at the moment particularly want to see, was the edge of the world beginning to rise up.

The vision thing.

Not now, he told it, and fixed his attention on the workings of the music, bringing his line back up into the instrument's middle range—seemed he'd snuck around that threat of cramp, he noted—obtaining the chords' permission to blur the edges between their transitions and getting a firmer grip on the floorboards with his feet, careful not to scar the new wood with his claws but hunkering in, finding a place in which to stand, given the flimsiness of the world, stable enough to launch what had begun to ache in him already, if only things would stay put long enough for him to play it. He saw the edge of the world start to raise up again and slapped it down, repeated: Not yet. More development wanted here, more motivic working through, a more comprehensive gathering of the tune's particulars and my own.

Toward the end of the summer tour, when the music got going particularly well, the Bear would begin to leave this world: things would start to drift loose from their moorings, and as his heart opened he'd begin to vanish into ecstasy or vision, the immaterial air of higher worlds making its way through the intervening veil at the entrance of his heart: something he loved but from which he had turned aside because of a necessary focus on the music and because such ecstatic departures seemed a suspect, too-sweet indulgence. He had also turned aside for love of Iris, since if he lost touch with the world of form he would in some sense lose her too. Now, having lost her, he felt the same. She was more meaningful to him than any solo on the horn or visionary flight he might take on the moment's provisional wings. So he repeated his refusal to fly out of here. He would hold to these notes, he would hold to particulars still.

He brought the next chorus up from the bottom of the horn in a dazzle of cross-accented sixteenths—paws working fast and brilliant, tongue turning out complexities of accent, wind unending—and reprised Trane's written near-triadic melody, butting against its limitations the way Trane himself used to those fettered nights he couldn't quite break through. That's what there is to play, he told himself. Stick to that. Hold to the known. See what it yields.

On the other paw, it occurred to him, why does it take so much work to keep infinity out? And why should I bother? When have I ever lost anything by dying?

The Bear stumbled over this dilemma for an instant and, hearing a certain hesitation in mid-chorus, an alert Bobby Hatwell scattered an inquisitive handful of notes across the keyboard. The Bear nodded yes: good question. Who am I really?

He reviewed the chromatic possibilities he'd enumerated—a flying analysis of an audible rainbow, a detailing of intelligible lights—as if they might yield a clue, and it seemed to him that for all its apparent variety his solo was a smallbrained semihysterical run up and down the keyboard of known ideas in the hope that some unknown chrismal coupling of its numbers might somehow free him. This seemed neither essential nor very likely. The Bear wanted what he had always wanted: music that ate life and death for breakfast and drank down time and space like morning coffee. It had seemed easy enough to him in cubhood, but he'd never really been good enough and by now he was older and had seen too much empirical detail. He had passed the point of believing that his life's transcendent meaning—assuming it still had one, which since the loss of Iris he frankly doubted—would ever be revealed to him or very easily fulfilled; and in the absence of that fulfillment, compensatory visions and ecstasies were nice enough entertainments in their way, but were bereft of final meaning or importance, a string of zeroes without a signifier. After so much life and change, vision was just more exile. What could be hoped for from music, in these conditions?

The Bear listened.

The past, present and possible future shape of his solo was powerfully present to him—as dramatic structure, as pure form expressing itself in the air of time, as a shape assumed by his own inmost urging, for which even music was clumsy flesh: perhaps one day, if not tonight, he might play such a solo for real.

Was that still possible?

He felt his harmonic center of gravity shifting gradually, almost imperceptibly upward to the composition's last four bars, the promised land of B-flat major—but Trane had the resources to reach that journey's end, to satisfy the musical demands and live through all the meanings along the way—an eye of a needle too slender to admit a talking bear. But think, if you put everything you have into this music, whatever the terms of your personal farce and the limitations of the given night, who knows what might come into it and join the ride? Tonight could be the night, and if not, so what? The first step is as good as the last, and the end will come sometime. So what the hey, let's try.

Gusts of notes took off from him and whirled into the air, achieving a certain lyricism despite the tempo's unceasing rush. These fluttery, fanning arpeggiations—when had he played so fast with such articulation? It was like watching a bird extend its wing to stretch it, detailing its feathers along the arc of its embodiment, and he thought in some surprise and perhaps impersonally: how beautiful you are. He sensed fresh air begin to reach him—scent of garden, waft of home—as if there might actually be an opportunity latent in the moment for him to come out of the endless maze of worry that was his solo, his life, his place in the world, his shot at love, and all the rest of the wellknown weary round, into free expanse, clear mind, fresh radiance.

Really?

He would find a way up or out if he could.

Raise me up into that music by which all things are changed.

And look there: exactly as if they'd read his mind, Garrett pushed his attack into the front of the beat, Linton stepped up the intensity to match him and Rahim, hearing the moment take form, started laying those powerful two-handed block chords in no matter how much it hurt him.

Almost at once the Bear felt something larger descend to seize the reins. Here we go, he thought, but as he rose through notes as if through worlds, worlds as if through notes, and laid aside successive versions of himself as the air grew finer and the light more uncompromised, he neither saw offered, nor knew how to accomplish on his own, a fundamental annihilation from flesh and time entirely. Even though B-flat major was taking on the transcendent meanings Trane had assigned it, the Bear was still stuck inside the puppet, the cheap fur and glassy eyes, the essential incapacity.

He played a chorus of upward arpeggiating major and minor triads, closely bunched, and to his surprise a version of the world appeared almost cinematically before him in the air: a geometric knit of fields, alternately green and dun, set between encirclements of forest beneath a sky of mixed sun and cloud, and it occurred to him that it was a place it was his responsibility to protect, but you know? he'd never really done much in that line, hadn't loved it as he should, or seen it as it was. Looking through it at the people at their nightclub tables, seated as if at their stations of being in the grand scheme of things, points of candleflame marking out each position, he knew he hadn't given them their due either, and the Bear was surprised at the sudden intensity of love he felt for them, and for each mundane thread of which their threadbare mortal coils were spun. He would have liked to play better notes than these, or stand there a more amazing instance of the inexplicable, not for anyone in particular but just, you know, for love.

The Bear found himself playing a classically structured blues chorus and heard the band fall gratefully in behind him: cool. He played another: even cooler. And could have played a third it was such a music of celebration and regret. Come on, Bear, cop to it: whatever the intervening veils and thickness of disguise, whenever we do it real we do it for love, though, true, once you say the word you tend to lose it. Things go bust so easy in these parts.

Say this much: Iris.

Say too: gone.

That was the important thing in your life and you blew it.

He looked back over his shoulder at Hatwell but the pianist wasn't looking back. His face, grey with probable pain and dripping sweat, was bent to the keys, and what issued thence were empty fifths, so bare, so spare, in octaves: he's fading: he's blown it too, so young. Why are we so stupid to ourselves?

The Bear wished he could play an answer, but he was a specialist in error and regret. He was a mote in the world's eye. Nothing could be seen through him. He would just not get out of the way.

He started working his next chorus further away from the changes, confusing the issue with chord substitutions and the occasional frank anomaly, but ended it with a well-turned resonant shining G: really put it up there as if he meant it: sounded pretty good: tone holding up, the rhythm section behind it like the heroes of perception they were, and there was even some applause, but the Bear knew in himself that the moment wasn't real.

Which made it all the more surprising that this was when things began to change. He couldn't have said whether it was the music's complex joy, his life's simple sorrows, or the tension between them, but his heart finally broke and something greater than he was began pouring through the gap.

The Bear was unable, as he played, to prevent himself from seeing:

In both the nightclub and the represented patch of pastoral world superimposed upon it, he saw everything in the manifest order, all material things and beings, begin to rise free from imprisonment in condition; saw materiality's prayer outwear its given vehicles, watched notes give out, words give out, vision, ear and paw give out. Saw all he had ever seen or touched or thought or loved or tasted, expiring before him, streaming upward into the music from which their notes had first spun themselves into form, arpeggiating their way back to their light of origin until lost in the shimmer through which they had entered the theater of being. He saw the tremulous rainbow, the iris tremoureux, whose delicacy eased their passage between worlds. He tried to play this music of which all things were made and unmade but the notes weren't on the horn.

Briefly he saw Trane's well-remembered face: my friend.

Well of course: who else would be here with me?

Though truth was, it was hard to play in these conditions, since what he saw happening to the world was also happening to him. The things you had to put up with, when all you wanted was to play some jazz on the familiar curve of light in E-flat thank you. It wasn't fair. Look: all the world's conceivable notes trying to burst in upon him and be played: all keys, all rhythms, all sounds clamoring for impossible simultaneity and the death of all condition. Look, he had to tell them, I'm in the middle of a chorus in front of a New York audience, backed by a handful of kids I have to keep an eye on all the time: they think I'm taking it too far already, and look what you're asking me to do. What do you want me to say? Yes yes yes yes, Holy holy holy? It's not very New York. It's such bad form.

It was the Bear's last attempt at irony, and the music blew it away, its tempo gathering and the rush of his own ideas blasting him into regions unforeseen. He saw the treasured geometry of his lights and vitals, the wellscanned signature of his timeless self erased by waves of greater light, the vessel bursting. As the Bear sped to the limits of his own transcendent outline, he could discern details—gardens, geometries, geometric gardens, fine dust and starry singularities, all the declensions of Life into lives—rushing toward annihilation and embrace, their mayfly constructions swept away, since under these circumstances even metaphysical flesh was grass.

He felt the the wellknown fluttering veil at the entrance of his heart give way as a greater paw lifted it like a piece of pop-up tissue paper.

I don't believe this is ha—

The whole world vanished. In fact all worlds vanished.

The Bear was plucked out of existence like a cheap suit. He had once thought the cloth so finely woven.

Not just outside time and space, but blown clean out of individuation too.

Complete break.

Despite all his stoopid efforts to the contrary, he was gone.

Am I dying? Have I died? Did someone shoot me? Just look at this.

That sun. Those seas of light—ocean upon ocean of unconditioned being, seen as fire. These receding scrims of sky—at the center, a single, inconceivable sun. Life without limit. Sheer being, set free from all constriction. If you stand where you stand you will see what I am. Little One.

The light and warmth feel so *good*. What a relief.

That sun. The Bear had never seen, nor even nearly conceived, anything approaching such generosity. You could not say that the sun was the source of this vista, since everything was so beyond duality there was no possibility of particularized attribution, or that a distribution of that sun's light had placed these seas rank upon rank like a series of theatrical scrims in the sky; but that was how it seemed to be. Just as worlds by the million were perpetually born and annihilated in those seas, rising and falling away like foam, so did these serial unscalable shores of light seem implicit in that central sun. Good grief, he realized, this was a conventionalization, a display. He was being given a show.

This was what he had been looking for all those years, room after room in the wide house of himself while hoping for a window or an exit, and had sought through the intervening veil of every passing form. But he had never himself existed and there had never been anything but this. Where was that cartoon bear? Vanished in the neverwas, drowned in what hand has not touched nor eye seen, ear heard, tongue spoken, mind conceived, heart encompassed nor love nor hope framed its image: the Bear had come home.

Who could have imagined how large joy is once you're cut loose from the farce of having to be someone? or dreamed life freed from the stricture of things and all conceptual limit? Rolling upon rolling sea of light without end, space not even the memory of being cramped, time less than a fidget. If it had been possible to laugh, he would have laughed—he laughed—and the laugh went generous into the oceans, those fugues of recirculation and embrace.

Notes were nothing. Each note was infinite. It made perfect sense.

Had the Bear still existed he would have laughed beyond being drunk on beauty and drowned in light. Had the Bear ever existed he would have plunged into these seas and tried out his stroke in them. Were he not himself these seas, and these seas him. It was so simple it was inconceivable not to have seen it all those blinkered bearshaped years. It was the basic fact of life and he'd walked right past it. How? How had he got his paw so painfully caught in so illusory a trap?

A press-roll broke behind him and a crash cymbal seared the sky.

What?

When the world reappeared and he found himself onstage in a New York nightclub, finishing up a four-bar phrase over pedal-point that he remembered starting an eternity, that is to say an eyeblink ago, he was unable to feel that things were substantially different from what they had been in that unbelievable serried sky. It's all here. Was and will be. What a hoot.

Since it was not his business to laugh, he continued to play: a series of choruses that didn't have a lot to do with the changes but weren't willfully outside them either: they pursued their proper business according to laws they brought into being as they went along, for the pure pleasure of invention—and wasn't it interesting to hear how the guys in the rhythm section responded, how they adapted each according to his character and the moment's possibility of sight? Ain't that just like life?

How much more should I play? he wondered.

As much as I like, was the answer.

Which was funny, because when you dropped back into the world and into yourself with it, full of indiscriminate love and good vibrations, everything was exactly as it had been and utterly transformed. It was to laugh. He was so blown out by radiance that all he could find to play was one high repeating torn and happy cry not quite at the top of the horn: as if to say YOU! YOU! YOU! or HA! HA! HA! or perhaps indicate that compared to infinite Being one note was about as good as a million of 'em so let's play one good one and call it fair enough. Musician: always an imperfect profession.

After two recapitulatory choruses of pretty swinging B-flat-minor blues he played a third that glossed the melody, then stepped back from the microphone and lowered his horn.

Whew, that was a long one. I feel good. Is everybody happy?

Nice big ovation there, a few kind folks leaping to their feet, a bunch of people yelling and carrying on. Wonder what they heard. I have no idea, but maybe it was good.

He pivoted and turned his bright, refreshed regard upon the band: each of the three bent to his instrument. Bostic was just coming off the drum-and-cymbal flourish that had capped the Bear's solo, the cymbals still loud enough so you couldn't hear anything else. It looked like Bobby Hatwell had begun a solo but it was hard to tell. Everyone was dripping sweat, and Garrett was bent in so intent an embrace with his instrument that the Bear couldn't see whatever expression might be on his face. In any case Bostic finally consented to subside, the drummer peeping at the Bear as he went back into time over the top of his Istanbuls—he was using larger cymbals, darker in timbre than the high bright things he'd played on the tour, and they gave the Bear more of that dusk-bronze tone he wanted. How sharp-eared Linton was, to have known it: must remember to thank him. He seems to be working pretty hard and he looks kind of tired but he's still quite watchful and alert. Tight around the mouth, though, and dripping sweat.

What's Bobby Hatwell up to now that I can hear him?

The Bear listened to the beginnings of his solo, heard the pull of rhythm against rhythm within the phrasing—the music sleeking down into something leaner, more efficient and economical than it had been during the Bear's outing, and for a moment he felt an odd, hallucinatory shame for the disorder he'd unloosed upon an after all wiser world during his solo—Garrett's flex and bend of the beat running alongside the piano line from idea to idea beneath the fleetness of Linton's cymbal-time and, the Bear's odd flash of shame to one side, the music moved him. That is to say, he moved. A little Monkish cross-accented stumble to his left, an apparent flail of his arm into an interesting little gap between the beats, a pivot of his body on the floorboards for pleasure and, you know, things in general . . .

It took him longer than the audience to recognize what he was doing, took a long minute for him to realize, as one of Hatwell's choruses rose to a hint of climax in its middle but then fell back into its long smooth stride, that he was doing something he would have sworn he would never do in front of an audience again on this side of the sky or any other: a shuttle of hips, a dip of shoulder, the feel of boards beneath his feet, the happiness of the wood. It was hard to believe it but he liked the way it went down. He was compelled to admit how pleasant and inevitable and unconflicted it seemed. There were an odd few hundred reasons for him to object, but he submitted his essential substance to none of them. The rules were blown.

The Bear did what he felt like doing.

He danced.

In the greenroom afterward the Bear encountered a small social problem: he couldn't stop laughing, and his tongue kept lolling uncouth out the side of his mouth as the laughter seized him but aw what the hell how can I help it? My manners were never much anyway. Always stood out in a crowd. Maybe what I need is another beer. Amazing how dehydrated I am, and all it was was a B-flat-minor blues.

Laughing, even though I know if I'd gone all the way through there wouldn't have been any sky imagery only light beyond form. Laughing, even though if I'd entered that world completely I wouldn't see even this vestigial distinction between that world and this one here. Laughing, because it had to count as a good night anyway, all things tallied. There comes a time when even a Bear has to quit grumbling and give up the funk.

He rummaged among bottles and icewater in the galvanized tin tub beside the sofa he was overstressing with his weight. The Bridge seemed to specialize in the world's most obscure microbreweries: he paddled his paw through the jetsam until he came upon a bottle of Buzzard Breath, and he popped it open for a taste. And you know? It was good.

The Bear had a certain tendency, at the moment, to confuse himself with other people walking by, this world still so suffused with the nondifferentiation of the other that sometimes he couldn't make routine distinctions. Didn't we have a good time though? Hey guys—he either thought or said as Bostic, or himself, walked past to stir the contents of the beertub in a sort of cosmic ruminative gesture that for the moment he felt too lazy to decode in detail—didn't we? He squinied up his eyes for a clearer look around.

Rahim Bobby Hatwell sat in a straightbacked wooden chair, hands perched atop his walkingstick, face grey and glaring as he purged in large clear drops of perspiration his evident physical and perhaps after all moral pain. Garrett Church, plunged in the depths of a winged green armchair, held a bottle of beer between his knees while he taped up the tips and sides of the fingers of his right hand with strips of surgical white adhesive: you could see fresh blood red on the windings. Linton had transferred his bottle of Brooklyn Brown Ale from his right hand to his left, and bent to show the Bear the tremor convulsing his cymbal hand, the fingers twitching inward toward the palm as his thumb spasmed in less regular rhythm side to side. "You played that solo for twenty motherfucking minutes," he told the Bear.

"I timed it half an hour," growled Hatwell, shaking a band of silver on his wrist above the crook of cane, "and then my watch died. Next time you want to kill us use a gun, all right?" He breathed out heavily, then slumped. "I'm gonna come up to Woodstock, kick your door down, insult your woman's cooking and break all your Coltrane records."

Garrett dropped his spool of tape and it rolled across the concrete floor to the feet of the furred and guilty party and tipped over. What have I done? the Bear asked himself, looking at the fallen spool. Violence to everyone around me, the usual price of my obtaining any kind of pleasure at all. Does making an artistic statement sufficient to the fundamental questions my existence has proposed really require this much breakage? For others probably not. For me, always. I am a blot, a smirch, a . . .

"Maybe you could play the next set *a cappella*," Hatwell suggested.

The Bear was in too good a mood to sustain the hysterical note of inquisition, and Bostic had started laughing too: "Or buy us health insurance," Bostic said, and Garrett looked up from his bloody fingers to ask if he could have his adhesive tape back please.

"Speaking of tape," said the Bear, leaning with what seemed a strange elongation of his body across the room to hand the spool to Garrett, "I wish someone had recorded that one."

And along came Jones. "Actually Levine made a DAT off the board mix," he said, and peered into the beer tub as if he might find his reflection there.

"Kill the bootlegging bastard," Hatwell said.

"I'll settle for the tape," said the Bear.

"Will do," Jones promised, holding up a bottle of Encantada.

"Because I'd like to listen to it someday." The Bear leaned back into the sofa and allowed himself to lose track of any specificity of event. It was enough to know that things were cool between now and the time they'd have to go out there and summon up another set. Ballads, he decided. Nothing but ballads, and perhaps one businessman's bounce. He wondered what the "Pursuance" solo would sound like on tape, what trace the experience of playing it had left behind. Maybe nothing at all.

People were coming back to shake his paw and say Nice set. He grinned at all of them and said whatever he said back. Tongue lolling out the side of his mouth again most likely but he couldn't be bothered to check. In this manner the Bear received some emissaries from the press, miscellaneous well-wishers, a few musicians—it was all pretty much a blur—and a shy tall blond gorgeous giggly patrician girl from Connecticut quickly appropriated by Linton Bostic. Garrett rose to welcome his tall elegant Ethiopean-looking friend Sistine: briefly, with an intimacy that would have been shocking had it not been informed by love—marriage was imminent, and the Bear invited—she folded her undulant form into the bassist's more angular sense of line. Momentarily, the Bear confused Garrett and Sistine with himself and Iris, until a dull interior thud reminded him of the facts upstate. Oh why wasn't she here?

Then he remembered: Garrett had asked him to have a word with Bobby, who wouldn't listen to any of his human friends about how his deathwish might be getting out of hand. "You know," he confided to the pianist, who appeared to be searching for a better pose with the cane, "if you could see the real object of your quest you'd know how unskillful your current means are, Bob."

Hatwell just looked at him, and even the Bear was aware that his statement lacked sufficient context. Given those skies, those oceans upon oceans of being, the ruling blur of the current room was excusable, but still . . . "Next time it might be your hands," he added, nodding at the cane.

"It might," Rahim allowed.

"Don't do it. It's beneath you. It's antique. It's reflexive, atavistic. I can see you in your spiritual aspect. You're free of it on the essential plane."

"Cats and dogs play the same game," Hatwell said, "but only rats can dance."

"That's bullshit, Bob. C'mon, Rahim. The universe loves you. There's no end to you. Give up."

"This is so touching I think I'll puke," Hatwell said.

"Forgive me for intruding. I mean no condescension. You should see my problems."

"I do."

"Well then," said the Bear, feeling that the conversation wasn't working, "let's all get together and lose the whole fucking load."

Jones came in holding up the tiny box of DAT cassette and jerked his head back toward the emissary from the music biz and peacock throne. The Bear looked at Badiyi and laughed at the smoothness of imposture. He knew he should slice the man into sandwich meat, but he was in too good a mood, and on too generous and elevated a plane to stoop that low just now. In short, he acted like a musician, which is to say a fool for beauty. No wonder they keep eating us for lunch. "Hi nice to meetcha," was what the Bear managed to say before letting Badiyi escape in good grace.

He watched Jones off to one side, doing the ritual steps of the Old Gettinpaid Waltz with Levine, who had returned from his nervous supervision of the house for a looksee behind the scrim. Jones looked at the Bear and made a steering-wheel gesture, so he guessed there wasn't enough money in the till. So what? The world had been overwhelmed, conclusively, by a far greater Accord.

The Bear may have intended a second set of ballads, but when the band regained the stage to a ripple of applause that swelled into an unexpected wave midway through as the nonpaying house remembered what it had heard last set and perked up for more, the Bear called "Reincarnation of a Lovebird" and they played it for more than half an hour—the Bear took three different solos, Hatwell two, Garrett one long very lyrical one, and the house quieted down to hear it while Linton shaded his way through on brushes, the solos moving in and out of each other smooth as scenes in a dream; and the Bear thought through all of it, We are rich in this music, and this is the best ever, the everbest, best. The band exchanged looks, nonlooks, private grins, tacit nods. Even some of the people in the house knew it.

He was still grinning in the greenroom after the set when Jones came in with Sybil Bailey. The Bear thought they looked great together, the air between them bridged and harmonious with what after all might pass for love: in any case he could see a nice exchange of ions. The Bear smiled back at them. “Hello, young lovers,” he said, “wherever you are.”

“You playing a third set?” asked Jones. “A short one? Whatever. We were thinking you could invite the band back to the apartment after, Sybil bought a few bottles of good champagne, there’s some caviar that fell off the back of a truck, and then the three of us can have a late supper that needs to be warmed up in the oven and you can sleep through to tomorrow night. You must be bushed, huh.” Jones put his arm around Sybil’s shoulder and grinned as, only a slight move but spontaneous, she snuggled closer into him.

“Actually,” said the Bear, grinning wider too. “Actually . . .”

3

the Bear rubbed the top of his head with the flat of his paw again.

“It’s out,” Jones told him. “You’re clean. Stop it already.”

When they’d come out of the nightclub a seagull wheeling on an updraft in the lights above the bridge had crapped smack dab in the center of the Bear’s head, and although he’d washed himself clean at Jones and Sybil’s place the sensation of being fundamentally stained persisted. This feeling was for some reason associated in his mind with the short royalty money from Badiyi and with not having been paid for the gig and ending up with this car instead. “How’s it go?” the Bear wondered.

“Nice smooth ride.”

“You get enough road feel?”

“Just.” Jones gave the steering wheel an approving pat.

The light passed rapidly across them laddered with bars of treeshade, their eyes slow to adjust to the rapid changes of illumination since neither of them had slept that night. Early-morning light coming from low in the east as they hauled north on the Thruway. A rough red rockface rose up on their right to grant them a respite of unbroken shade.

“I really appreciate this, Jones.”

"Think nothing."

"You doing okay?"

"Only taking short naps behind the wheel. Sing me a song or something. Keep me awake."

"I really need to see her."

"Don't just recite the lyrics. Hum a few bars."

The Bear turned on the radio and twiddled the dial until love began struggling toward electric triumph in D major.

The Bear may have needed to see her, but his eyes were a little tired this morning. He should have taken a nap after late supper at Sybil's, but he'd found the energies of the night still working in him—had he really played all that music? Jones had sat up with him, swapping jokes and stories, and before they knew it first light was grey then blue then blazing sunup over the city slabs, and they hit the road. Had he really played all that music? That was the funny thing: he had no problem assimilating the experience of eternity but found it hard to believe he'd played that solo on the Coltrane tune—he'd listen to the DAT one day, see if it was any good. "Reincarnation of a Lovebird" hadn't been bad either. He'd never been able to frame a musical hope large or wide enough for that kind of play. Was it possible he was actually doing it? Maybe he was still blissed out, not seeing it clear. As for infinity, eternity, seas of unconditioned being: well, sure, of course. What else is there to see around here anyway? The glow was still with him, and he wanted to take it upstate while it was fresh and perhaps even communicable. Was he really feeling love without limit for everything that breathed and even for what didn't? Yes, it seemed he was.

"You know, it would have been easier to take the van," said Jones.

"Yeah but I wanted to show her my new car." The Bear knew even this much sounded fatuous, and he was ashamed to confess his still more fond and foolish ulterior motive, dared not confess that the name Accord seemed significant and hopeful, an omen, a portent—good Lord was he really thinking this?—a kind of automotive prayer. Accord! he sang absurdly to himself, and over the distance to Iris. Harmonic Resolution! Major Cadence! It was such a long chord progression. Certainly he was acting like an idiot. But there was such hope in the world, in the word, in this merciful, look at it, light. Iris! Accord! Idiot! What is a Bear that Iris should be mindful of him?

Yes, he decided, maybe a little blissed out, a little stupid. It's a brand name, not an omen. But it seems so generous a morning, so promising a day.

Still, how different the ride up from the ride down. Coming down to the city with his mind fogged in, worried about playing and the possibility of arrest. Going back flush with the afterglow of vision, his heart expanded another couple of octaves: room enough for Iris and any number of difficult daughters. Room enough for anything to go rolling through it in a great wheel. Like that sky he'd seen. That sky he'd been.

"*May you be an old man,*" the Bear began to sing, "*May you be as tall as I am . . .*"

"What's that?" Jones asked him.

"Something I dreamed up."

"It's pretty cute," said Jones. "Not your usual thing."

"Well actually . . ." said the Bear, and told Jones about the dream in which he'd heard it.

"What a beautiful dream," said Jones, and the Bear looked across the seats to his fellow struggling creature.

"Jones Jones Jones," he said.

"Bear Bear Bear," Jones replied.

"Nice to see you again."

"Likewise, baby."

So they were cool. This life stuff remained complicated, didn't it, however friendly the supervening skies.

You know, he said to the moment's partial patch of blue, leaning into the windshield to get a better look up at it, the sun some degrees higher in the east brightening the expanse with colors that were no longer winter light but not quite yet the light of spring, you know, you ought to show yourself for real more often. Would it hurt the overarching order of things if you'd show your true nature to us dumb motherfuckers down here on a more regular basis? It would do a power of good here in Mudville, cut the war and slaughter bullshit down and vitiate the power of delusion generally. Would it hurt to see the peasantry blundering around wondering who to love first? I know you've got the conclusive argument and all, but do give some thought to what I'm saying, won't you. Because it hurts down here even in peacetime.

"How'd you like the guys last night?" the Bear thought to ask.

"They were cool, but you kind of left them bleeding."

"Sometimes you got to show the young whippersnappers a thing or two. How'd you like the solo on the Coltrane tune?"

"Pretty energetic. Maybe a little over the top."

"Over the top," the Bear laughed. "That's perfect. That's what it was, all right. Way way over the top. And the kids're gonna have to get used to it."

In a few more miles the mountains put in their first appearance, and the light above increased.

When they were approaching Woodstock the Bear told Jones never mind the cutoff by the creek, drive straight through town.

"Feeling cocky?" Jones asked him.

"Nah. It's early morning, not too many people out."

They passed through the supermarket-and-gas-station gauntlet without significant incident, but when they took the curve through boutiqueville and the Village Green there were some early strollers out, newspaper underarm or takeout coffee in hand, and a few of them clocked the Bear through the windshield. Some did slight double takes and one or two waved hello.

The Bear waved back: he hadn't been in town much, and he certainly hadn't been so brazen as to play a gig there, but one way or another folks knew he lived in the area—many knew in which particular house, Iris said, and with whom—but it seemed that Woodstock offered freaks of nature the same discreet lack of fuss they afforded rock stars and movie people, and on this particular morning those who saw him took his apparition literally in stride: the merest hesitation, that's all.

There was the guy opening up the Turkish carpet shop, where Iris had bought a couple of kilims surprisingly cheap. There was the bookshop. There was Taco Juan's—Iris had brought some first-rate burritos home for dinner once or twice.

It was an artificial little place and at the same time a nice town the Bear felt a momentary longing to be able to hang out in like everybody else.

On the way out of town, some character with streaming white-guy dreadlocks finally got fazed by the Bear going by and ran his bicycle face-first into the bushes.

"My first drive-by," said the Bear, pivoting in his seat to see if the guy was picking himself up okay. "Maybe I'll get a write-up in the *Woodstock Times*."

After about a mile of straight-line two-lane they arrived—the Bear still had some trouble with this—in Bearsville.

"You want to pull up over here on the left?" said the Bear, flinging a paw in the direction of the forecourt of the restaurant complex: the Bear Café, the Little Bear with the tip of his tongue still stuck out on the sign. The turnoff up the hill toward home was opposite on the right.

"You want to collect yourself before you make your presentation?" Jones asked him as the Honda ground to a halt on the roadside gravel.

The Bear peered forward through the windshield and nodded. "I see some activity in there. They're open."

"Whoopie," Jones said.

"They do a nice Saturday breakfast, Iris tells me."

"So?"

"What I'd like you to do, Jones, is go in there and enjoy a big one, on me, and I'll take the car up to the house. I'd like to see her alone first. Stroll up later when you have breakfast inside you. I'd like some time with her, kids permitting and if you don't mind."

"I could drive you up and drop you."

"I'd like to show her the car myself," the Bear said, trying not to let the absurdity of his sentiments show. Accord.

"You remember how to drive?"

"I used to handle the Bearmobile."

"An experience I have yet to forget." Jones sucked his teeth. "I could do with some coffee. How good's the breakfast here?"

"Had I your tongue and eggs I'd use them so that heaven's vault should crack."

Jones made a face and popped his door open. "You need to get out and come around, or can you slide across without destroying the gearshift?"

"Slide."

Jones unhooked his shoulder belt and watched the Bear slide across without destroying the gearshift. "Next," he said, "don't crack it up and die cause I'll owe Levine money."

"Bye, Jones. Why'd they make the clutch so small?"

"Because they're thoughtless brutes. Because they're unable to foresee so simple a contingency as you. They deserve to have their livers eaten. Shove back over and I'll drive."

"I can hardly . . . there."

The Bear lurched the car across the road and got it smoothly into second on the way uphill. He scraped some branches on the right, pulled away from them and looked into the rearview mirror to see Jones holding his ears onto his head with both hands. The Bear honked the horn twice and steered the car up the middle of the road. What a lovely morning, he thought as he gained the crest and open sky emerged. He tried to set a hope stage center in the arena of his heart and give it a song to sing. It managed a few lines in a too wavery tenor. I'll see her, she'll see me and she'll feel the change. She's so sensitive she'll pick it up right away. She'll know there's more room for us than there was before. I'll walk her outside—it's not too cold a morning, is it?—show her the Accord and we'll have our talk without the kids listening in. They'll love me eventually too. How could they not? The tenor in which he sang his hopes sounded increasingly equivocal, however, as he drew nearer the house.

What if the kids are up but she's not yet? What if they're sitting down to breakfast together? What—this is not gonna happen—if she's in bed with some guy? How am I gonna play this?

I want love to win out, not just for my sake but so that the picture of this world will line up right with the picture of the other. The dissonance is a figment, it's unreal.

The Bear tried this sentiment in his normal baritone but couldn't find the right key for his range.

The car crested the rise, made its gradual descent, and as he reached the T junction, life, doing what it did best, presented him with a picture he had not anticipated: the house standing there okay, looking as usual a trifle dark and tall, but the Volvo nowhere to be seen in the semicircular drive beneath the guardian trees. No one home. Or the kids were home and Iris had run into town to pick up some delicacy or other. Had he passed her on the road without seeing?

The Bear braked the Accord—Accord?—to a halt and looked both ways before driving across.

Worst of all, it occurred to him as his heart hit bottom, she's taken the occasion of my New York gig to split, pack up her stuff and daughters and take off, just the way she did with Herb years back.

As he urged the car across the turnpike and then up the grinding-stones of the drive—exceeding small—he felt with heavy certainty that this worst-case scenario was the one in play. She's flown the coop. She's gone. The vocalist stepped out of his heart's spotlight and stumbled backstage, perhaps to drink himself insensate.

The Bear stopped the car at the foot of the steps and fumbled twice at the key before switching the ignition off. Is she gone forever?

When he got out of the car he saw what he should have noticed from the T junction: a homely blunder of woodsmoke wooling its way out of the chimneytop into the trees. Although he did not entirely recover his uphill hopefulness, he felt a palpable lightening of his burden as the worst-case scenario fell away, its pages crumbling back to native dust.

There was hope yet, or something like it.

He turned to survey his old domain, amazed for the first time in his life he had really slept away the winter—how quaint—and his eye encountered, timid and lovely on a patch of stray grass and bare ground, the doves. Six mourning doves in fact, the rose underglow brightening the dun swell of their breasts, their delicate heads held aloft and watchful, a ring of bright aqua circling each round black eye. Of the two males he saw, one's neckside iridescent patch was magenta, the other's a luminous chartreuse. Two of the females pecked watchfully at the bare earth—a clever supplication to him, or a means of conjuring food from heaven? It came to the Bear in a rush. Iris hadn't fed them! She hadn't fed the lovey-doves, the doves of love, and it really pissed him off. In fact, so blinding was the disproportionate, preposterous rush of rage that he wasn't aware of himself galloping up the steps and bursting into the house through the door left open—standing open! Fucking kids!—although he came to himself once inside and rose to his hindlegs, nostrils quivering for some niff of what might actually be going on. Faint smells: no one home, but they hadn't been gone long. No smell of Siege or some strange man. He took a few steps forward and peered around the rustic grey massif of the chimney: breakfast still on the table: two half-finished bowls of some breakfast flakes or other, cold toast and a mug of abandoned coffee. The wreck of the *Marie Celeste*. The Bear had come home.

The Bear walked closer. At Iris' place, at the head, beside the mug of black coffee, on the blue plate that held the slice of wheat toast, he could see the crescent shape of his beloved's bite; in the children's places—how he hated the ungrateful look of uneaten food—blue bowls of flakes decomposing in milk amid the eyeless gazes of stranded raisins. He did some rapid calculations, emptied one bowl of cereal into the other, crumbled the toast into the mix and carried it outdoors all altruistic for the tenderhearted timid-souled doves, to feed their beauty.

"Here you go, kids," he announced on the approach, and they took off for the trees in a panic of shrieking wings. The Bear stood there with his begging bowl, revealed again as walking wrath and a terror of the earth. He scattered the sodden flakes and toast on the ground and poured the milk into a hollow in the top of a low grey rock before retiring houseward with the bowl in his paw, trying to feel virtuous but not quite making it. "I know you'll come down when you're ready," he said over his shoulder, and had the strength not to look back to see if the birds were fluttering down.

He was lousing up. He was losing his temper. How dumb could you be? Keep cool.

But back in the living room his mind acknowledged what his eye had already seen: the half-open black iron woodstove door. Even before things had gone sour between him and Iris this had been a bone of contention: she liked to load the woodstove up with oak and then, as if she had not the least knowledge of the principles of convection or any sense of the price of firewood she would—it was hard to believe it—*she would leave both doors of the woodstove open*. Often she would pull up a chair and sit in front of it in the morning with her mug of coffee, dragging herself back to consciousness while split oak went up like matchsticks. Okay, he understood that she woke to a difficult, fragmentary state of mind, but allow nature more than nature needs and even beast's life don't run so cheap. Two hundred dollars a cord! and that cord dubious: a local tendency to give short weight.

Prithee, do not make me mad.

He shut the door of the woodstove, reuniting the halves of its bas-relief mountainscape—and turned the handle snug. Will she never understand? Good oak burning up by the ton in there. Do not make me mad.

Then the Bear had an odd experience: he saw a chill malignant fog emerge from within his body and begin to fill the house to its last beam and leastmost corner. He recognized it as a monstrous instrumentality of control. This was what had screwed everything up between him and Iris and the kids. From his side, this.

Free me from this delusive nonsense, he asked. Help me now. There must be some grace left over from last night. And to the monster inside himself said, Leave me, fall away, begone, fuck off, die . . . and hey presto, these things happen, it fell, shucks, husks, fell from him like the heavy inert qlipothic carapace it was.

So that, when he went upstairs to niff around the rooms, it was without the slightest trace of wrath that he unmade Trace's and Amy's beds when he found pistachio shells, candywrap and shards of tortilla chips in the bedclothes—bugs, chipmunks, mice!—and it was in a nicely balanced, reasonable frame of mind that he returned downstairs and stood meditatively in the living room, ready for Iris and the kids to come home from wherever they were. He would greet them expansively and with love. Then he would have a private talk with Iris and explain that he understood how difficult, make that impossible, he had been, and how he felt for the situation of her daughters, understood the peril in which she felt them to be, and acknowledged the unusual, some would say unnatural, picture he made in conjunction with her; and would end with the certainty that love could find a way. No matter how long it took. He would talk about love. Not just their love, but love in itself. As it shaped and made the forms of nature and refrained from overspilling the conventional skies, exquisite consideration, only in order to preserve intact the individuated forms of its making, of which, Iris, you and I are two who have recognized the trace of that original love in each other, and . . .

No one came home from wherever they were, however—Jones'd be up soon, he knew—and a light dusting of drowsiness fell upon the Bear. He really ought to have a nap. Had to play again that night and all.

Without thinking about it overmuch he wandered into the master bedroom and the big brass double bed that had seen such pleasure once. If things broke right with Iris, the Bear thought sleepily, and with the royalty statements, maybe we could buy the house from Stanlynn, hire an architect to cut a hole in the bedroom floor and plant a tree down in the crawlspace, let it grow up into the bedroom and flourish there like the one Mr. & Mrs. O'Dysseus had. Yeah, if things break right and we put aside enough college money for Aim and Trace maybe, Iris, you and I could get ma—

I must be idiotic with lack of sleep.

He tumbled into the bed but came alert when he encountered that much-unmitigated scent of her—Iris!—and it was several minutes before sleep began perceptibly to descend again and he started edging into dream, images of Iris blending with thoughts of music, thoughts turning into images, images turning into sound so that, when it came, the familiar rumble of the Volvo rattling up the drive blended with the mumble of his mind rolling down the slope to sleep, and the shock of waking recognition only came as the engine switched off, the handbrake ratcheted tight, and one door cranked open on its busted iron tongue.

"No," he heard Iris' voice say, "I don't know whose car it is either."

The Accord, she meant. He didn't know what to do, and decided in default that he was much too sleepy to arise. He heard them hesitate on the boards of the landing at the bottom of the steps.

"I'm sure there's nothing to worry about," Iris told her daughters in a voice disguising its worries, and then, after a very slight pause they began their way up the steps, Iris in the lead if his ears did not deceive him.

They were at the door. He heard Iris come in alone.

"There's no one here," she said, and then her daughters' footsteps followed her hesitantly in.

The Bear's heart beating.

More footsteps, one set of them lazy, dragging their way across the floorboards: Amy. Amy would come to like him first, then eventually she'd bring Trace along.

"Hey," he heard Amy say from the dining room, "someone's been eating my breakfast."

Once upon a time, way back, way way back, shortly after he'd broken with the family secrecy and made himself known to Jones—he'd been a little harsh about the old boy's clarinet playing, but he'd been tense—Jones, in a rather touching, unconscious parody of protective fatherhood, thinking that the Bear still needed to be taught to read, had brought home an armful of threadbare grade-school textbooks, generic tales of Dick and Jane and Spot—you could see them run, first severally, then together—when in fact the Bear had already made his way through most of Hemingway. There had been a story, in one of these books, about a little bearcub who had lost track of his mother and gotten stranded in the woods as night came on. That Mom would find him eventually was a sentimental given of the genre, but before she did, the little cub would have to spend a night on his stony lonesome. The passage the Bear particularly objected to came when, as dusk fell, the abandoned cub curled into his own warmth at the base of a tree. First he closed one eye, the text said, then he closed the other. The Bear had found these sentences odious and objectionable. That's not how bears go to sleep! he had announced with disproportionate outrage to Jones. That's not how anyone goes to sleep! How could anyone write this crap! It took Jones awhile to joke him out of it, and after awhile they managed to defuse the moment and have a laugh at the silly shit someone thought kids were supposed to learn from. More of the same dumb hustle. Human civilization a laugh, et cetera.

But now, as he heard Tracy join her sister at the dining table and could hear the whole freight train coming around the bend as Tracy said, "Someone's been eating my breakfast too," the Bear closed one eye.

Whosoever diggeth a pit, he thought, shall fall in it.

"My toast is gone but my coffee's still here," came Iris' voice, and although he was grateful for the minor variation the Bear closed the other eye.

It took only a very basic talent for endurance to wait while the other shoes dropped, Amy and Trace running upstairs to announce something only partly audible about the state of their beds, but when Iris appeared at the bedroom door, her eyes wide, her hair as if on end and not one visible trace of irony or recognition of what she was enacting, to say, "Someone's been sleeping in my bed, *and he's still in it*," the Bear was wide and appallingly awake. In a life, in a long life of tired, in a long life of tired and weary, this was the tiredest, this was the tiredest, weariest, worst. This was one to break the back, the heart, the hope, the sense of humor about this long, tired, flat, stale, weary, profitless, entirely.

"What are you doing here?" Iris asked him in an outraged stage whisper, her face blotching red and white, and when he tilted upright and humbled himself to his hindfeet saying something about how he had played a minor blues by Trane and had to show her the car, she didn't seem to calm down much.

"Listen," he tried to tell her, but she wasn't doing it. Trace and Aim were clumping back down the stairs. Iris was blocking the doorway with her body, and despite her petite personal radiance he could recognize without difficulty the mother bear in the cavemouth, protecting her young even though he would never do them the least harm, and keep them from the unnatural, obscene sight of him even though he had made no move toward the doorway or the room beyond. In short, the known world, with all the tedious weight of its serial limitations, came crashing down again, and it was so unbearably dull, its recognitions rehearsed a thousand times, its roles played a thousand thousand times and now played out. "Aw please listen," he said, which did no visible good. "Why do you hate me?" he was finally able to ask.

"I don't hate you," Iris said. "How could I ever hate you?" A plaintive look took possession of her face for a moment, and for a moment a major cadence popped its head above the clashing chords that after all might be his own hallucination to say, If you reach me we can make peace right here. But something happened, and the resolution sank beneath the waves of working dissonance as the composition advanced barline after barline piecing one moment from another, and he and Iris remained similarly apart, across what might as well have been an infinity of wooden floorboards, Iris in the doorframe and the Bear on the edge of the bed, springs and mattress sagging catastrophically beneath his weight, while he was saying, or trying to say, "Wait a minute, can't we slow this down?" But once again, despite the overwhelming waves of unconditioned being he'd seen last night, he and Iris had reached the shore on which ignorant bozos clash by night.

"Go upstairs for a minute," Iris told her daughters over her shoulder, and as they audibly obeyed her it occurred to the Bear that this provided at least the possibility of another opening.

"Can't we just be ourselves awhile?" he asked her. "If it doesn't work we can go back on automatic after."

"I don't know what you mean," Iris said, but she seemed to go slightly softer.

"Look," he tried to say. "Look," but got no farther. He was tired. And had no words. All these years, he should have learned to speak.

"At what?" Iris wanted to know.

At me. At the monstrous face love wears in this world. At what might work out yet. At the unacceptable face that life perhaps for good reason is intent on showing. At the inconvenience and insult of it all. At who we really are. "At me," was all he managed to say, the room already heavy with failure.

"*You* get all the breaks," Iris told him. "Everyone has to make allowances for *you*. What about me?"

"I'm sorry," the Bear admitted. "I love you. I feel like I'm dying here. I died last night. I'm tired."

"Well, you shouldn't sleep it off here." Iris thrust her chin indicatively at the bed, then flicked her eyes upstairs to her daughters. "I wasn't expecting you."

"Iris, my heart is breaking."

"Oh that," she said. "You still notice things like that?"

"Iris."

"Bear."

"If there's something new I'm supposed to put on the plate, I don't know what it is," he said. "Tell me what you want from me. Give me a hint. Offer a clue."

"You don't have children. You wouldn't understand."

"No," he told her, "I wouldn't understand. How would I understand a single thing you're going through?" He waved his arms in exasperated semaphore. "I'm just a puppet you can find lovable when occasion suits and toss out after."

"That's not how I think of you. Is that how you think I think of you?"

"I don't know what else to think." Whenever he got in an argument with anyone he was automatically unjust, and with Iris invariably also wrong. "You know, I might have a cub or two out there," he told Iris anyway, "but their mommies treated me about the way you're treating me now. Hands off, fuck your clumsy impersonation of love, you're here to eat my kids. Iris, I'd love your daughters if they'd let me. That I love you, albeit in my dumb fatal way, hardly needs repeating. I understand the imperatives of your motherhood. I would help you if I could or if you'd let me. I think I've been good for you. I could be good for them. Let me in. Give me a cognitive kiss. Here I am. Tell me what you want. You think this isn't love?"

"You're impossible," was all Iris found to say, but she fretted her hands and looked desperate. "I wasn't expecting you today."

"Of course I'm impossible. But from you I'd hoped for recognition." He saw a moment's helplessness in her face, a hint that she felt caught in the web of her own reactions and might welcome release, if only he could find the lever and pry back the jaws of the trap. "Iris," he said. "Get real with me. Remember who we are."

"Give me a minute." Her hands flustered into the air. "Why couldn't you have spent the week in the city as we agreed? I'd counted on that week. I know I've had my months with the girls but I needed that week."

"For what? You were going to leave?"

"Why do you keep saying that? We have a lot to talk about, if you'd only listen."

"Really?" He stepped closer to her and he felt himself enter a palpable aura of confusion and pain extending at least three feet from her body, poor kid, a sort of whirring blurring of the air.

"But not this minute. I wasn't ready. Not just now."

"When?"

"I don't know," Iris said. Did she look helpless or just exhausted?

"Do I . . . Iris, do you mean there's actually some hope?"

And then the strangest thing happened. Iris' face went bright red, her hand flew to her mouth, and her body began to hoop, to jacknife over, and the Bear's first impression was that she was about to projectile-vomit at his mention of hope, but what happened instead was nearly as bad: she began to laugh.

"That's it," he told her, "laugh at me. Thank you very much."

She shook her head furiously but continued laughing, bent into her hand, her body convulsing and her right foot stamping on the floor. "Oh my God," she managed to say before fresh gusts convulsed her.

"Yes," said the Bear. "That's what I get for expressing something as unrealistic as hope when I should have learned from your treatment of me that there was none. Well, I'll be out of your hair in a few minutes. Jones should be coming up the hill soon and we'll get in the car and . . ."

Iris, her hand still cupped to catch her laughter, shook her head from side to side. "I just realized," she managed to say between gasps, "just realized what I said . . ."

"Well yes perhaps we've both said too much. Don't worry. I'll be out of your hair in a minute, and your life after that."

This statement only served to render Iris more helplessly hysterical. ". . . what I said when I came in and saw you there. *Someone's been sleeping in my bed* . . ." And off she went into fresh convulsions at the thought of it.

"Yes, and much as I like to be insulted and laughed at," the Bear told her, "it seems to me . . ."

"Oh you poor dope," she called him between spasms of laughter. "Don't you—"

"Thank you very much. I need a breath of air. Can I get by?"

Iris, still seized by laughter, pulled herself aside, and he went through the bedroom doorway.

Past her probably for the last time.

Leave 'em laughing when you go. My policy always.

Went through the living room, slid the glass door open and stepped out into the air of the world, which had sweetened since earlier that morning; hint of new wine in the breeze, spring around the bend. So why do I feel like pulling a blanket of earth over my head and sleeping like the dead for another season? The Bear stretched his arms aloft for greater inbreath, reconnoitered a moment and started up the path that led away from the house along the base of the slope, kicking idly through twigs and leafmeal.

Feeling the touch of someone's regard, he looked back over his shoulder to see fair-haired Amy framed in the sliding glass doors, dressed in white, posed like an emanation of hope: she might almost have raised her hand to wave to him but it was hard to see her through the reflections on the glass. The Bear walked on.

Shortly he came to the clearing in which he remembered having a particularly fruitless talk about gardens with Jones. He began to pace its perimeter in the rough circle it allowed, head down, *kak medved.*

He and Iris had almost achieved conversation, he thought, before shearing off into nullity and hysteria. Wonder how soon Jones'll be here so I can go. What a sight the sky was last night, superabundant being without the least possibility of loss, the most ultimate, convincing vista he had ever been witness to. And what a sight I am pacing the limits of my old circle now.

How can I possibly buy this smallbrained dichotomizing razzmatazz? It should be possible for a bear of any brain to hammer out a better working relationship between the poles of spirit and the manifest order than this.

Then of course there was always the possibility that he was misunderstanding everything.

Naah.

He thought of all the changes he had lived through since he'd stumbled lit by vision down Second Avenue to the Tin Palace to play. Certainly he had grown in experience and understanding since then. He might even be a shade or two wiser—but with so little material result! and the stone so incompletely rolled from the mouth of the cave. Why should ignorance and coarseness always drag us down and render our efforts null?

Despite the dimness and confusion of the moment's current blink of sight, he felt a parallel consciousness working in him: gratitude to the past, gratitude to the present as an instance of available grace, and as to the future, how could it be less blessed than what had come before? How could he waste his time on regret?

He regretted everything.

The way was clear: ahead, behind, and where he stood.

The way was muddied: he saw nothing in all directions, he was walking in a circle. Rumors of an upward spiral were just that: rumors.

A fluttering in a nearby tree did not distract him from his brooding.

One thing, this side of the sky or that, he told himself, I won't give up on love, however imperfectly I may have felt the thing. I refuse this crimp, this crink. I deny this cheap constriction any final say on the sight of things, this sky-above-mud-below dichotomizing dumbhead fracture of the realms of experience, this lucky-in-music-unlucky-in-love routine: I won't have it. I do not accept. I won't give up on love no matter what mess the two of us have made of it.

"*Nee*-dn't," came a two-note call from a branch a short distance up the hill.

"Damn right I needn't," said the Bear, although, although . . . he hated to admit it, but he knew . . . that when things had begun their still delicious decline between himself and Iris, his choice to make love to her every night—to fuck her, call it that—instead of only when the spirit spoke, had been an attempt to bliss her into complicity and submission. Had been a selfish attempt to hold on to what was already being lost. He had employed unskillful means. And here's the payback.

"*Nee*-dn't," sang a silver voice from a tree.

"Needn't *what?*" the Bear roared in anguish. "Needn't love? Needn't strive? Needn't worry how it works out? Needn't bleed? Needn't sweat the details because loss is illusion and love is universal and unlimited? I know *that*, but meanwhile I have time to pass down here and it's not working."

"*Nee*-dn't."

The Bear looked up, saw the grey bird fluttering to a higher perch affrighted by the violence of his roar, and for the first time realized who'd been tweeting at him. "Oh it's you," he said. "Back from Florida already? Is it really spring? How come I still feel like sleeping the world away?"

"*Nee*-dn't." The catbird worked its beak against the branch and seemed to nod at the Bear. "*Nee*-dn't," it sang again, and bobbed its tail up and down, quite perky.

"Easy for you to say. And where's the rest of the tune? That all you remember?"

The catbird regarded him with fresh attention, tailfeathers ticking the air with what might have been time, head canted, dark round eyes expectant, alert.

"All right already," the Bear conceded. He wetted his leathery lips, pursed his snout and whistled the first bars of the tune.

He waited, but the bird was waiting too. The Bear performed the phrase again. "Your turn," he said, adamantine, all teacher, and folded his heavy arms across his chest.

His student showed the usual stage tremor and reflex reluctance, twitching a wing out of place and back into tuck for diversion, but then opened its beak a crack, worked its throat and sang forth—the Bear loved to see the movement of its throat. The song began well with four of Monk's true notes but got lost in the middle: the bird inserted a scribble of redwing song and dropped a beat before finishing with a clarion *nee*-dn't it obviously hoped might pass.

"Faker," said the Bear.

"*Nee*-dn't," the bird insisted, with all the overmelodious fruitiness of a bluff. The Bear had used similar dodges himself. He had even tried it once or twice last night.

"Let me get this straight," said the Bear. "You've been down there the whole damn winter in Miami Beach or wherever without working even once on your Monk charts. If you think you *nee*-dn't practice you're wrong. You *need* to practice a lot. You didn't do a lick of work, did you. I can hear it. Nowhere to run, nowhere to hide. The Bear sees all."

"*Nee*-dn't," the bird insisted, and attempted to eye the Bear down.

"Bullshit," said the Bear. "Everybody's got to practice. You can't get away from it."

"*Nee*," sang the catbird, but the Bear didn't let it finish.

"Look," he said philosophically, "if you work the tune out, learn a couple others and mate, you might pass it on to your descendants, and a few generations down the pike where the fuck will they be? I'm speaking to you from my own blind alley here, okay?"

"*Nee*-dn't," sang the bird.

"You're right. It's a mistake to be that determinist about the prospects. No doubt your offspring will have better luck. I had an amazing night but it's been a difficult day." The Bear resumed walking in a tight argumentative circle, and readdressed his central fury to himself. "Maybe the whole enterprise of loving Iris was assimilationist weakness and a fallacy from the start. Maybe I should have been happier with my original lot. Maybe trying to enlarge my world was a mistake."

"*Nee*-dn't," the bird affirmed.

"Oh what the fuck do you know about it?" he asked the catbird. "Could you enumerate her beauties? Grasp the sum that overtops all addition of her parts? The dreams of angels outside time would be confounded into song by her, birdbrain, much less anything fools like you or I could come up with."

"*Nee*-dn't," sang the bird.

"Needn't pile metaphysics atop what is after all a pretty simple appetite? What a bunch of crap that is. You sound pretty sure of yourself, but how much of the world have you experienced really?"

"*Nee*-dn't," sang the bird again.

"The more you travel the less you know? The old Taoist party line? I only ever bought that in an abstract sense. Practically speaking it doesn't play."

"*Nee*-dn't," sang the bird again.

"It's boring but at least it beats the shit out of Nevermore," the Bear allowed. "How is it possible," he asked in a calmer voice, "that I've seen so much and trust so little? Can you tell me that?"

"*Nee*-dn't."

"Needn't tell me? Needn't trust? Needn't ask? Needn't for fuck's sake *what?*" The Bear looked around him, woke briefly to the encircling scene: the earth beneath him, patient pines, bare deciduous trees praying their way nearer leafdom as the sun inclined, and just look at *my* bare branches. Why am I having this idiotic conversation with a bird that is only repeating a couple of notes it less than learned from me? What a pathetic fallacy. For the first time he noticed the massive grey nearly bihemispheric boulder at the clearing's edge that had once reminded him so vividly of a brain.

And maybe it was a sort of brain.

He attuned himself as best he could to the infinitesimal pace of its cold deliberate mineral cognition. Lichen climbed its sides, and star moss, already refreshed into edges of brilliance by the changing weather and the inclining sun, gathered at its base greedy with what it no doubt took for an unprecedented radiance of green, something the world had never seen before. Egoism identically stupid on all levels everywhere. Phantasmal all my scalar attainments.

Had Jones come uphill yet, his mortal body warmed by one more breakfast?

Tick tock clock. Another day.

The fatuity of individuation generally.

Its incomparable beauty.

How reconcile? How make sense?

"*Nee*-dn't."

"Oh fuck off. Stop impersonating the voice of wisdom." On the other paw, who was to say what was speaking through the catbird's limited voice? God had all the voices, except one's own. Unless you're obliterated and indistinguishable, as he'd been last night. Look at the dumb dualism he was mired in now. So quick. Pure stupidity, utter mindblock. It was a simple problem really, and the real solution perfectly obvious.

Whatever. The Bear was tired. Whatever's right.

He would go back to the house after awhile. He would manage, if not now then eventually, to talk with Iris outside the dominion of their blind opposed compulsions. If he had to wait for Aim and Trace to go off to college, that would be okay. That was the kind of Bear he was. Dumb but willing. Earnest to the end. Life has found me out. This is who I am.

"*Nee*-dn't," sang the bird, then made a new attempt at the whole two-bar statement.

"Better," said the Bear, "though you're still trying to fake your way through the middle."

And so was he. For all last night's glory, he was not an example of spiritual victory. He had bifurcated and botched it. What good were big visions if you spoiled everything that came your way by what you made of it? if you had the big Hollywood moments but breath by breath lived your life like a dog?

The Bear had not arrived where he had hoped to arrive.

"*Nee*-dn't," sang the bird, returning to its known, too simple certainty.

"I suppose you're right but I'm tired anyway," said the Bear.

To that large grey rock, thought the Bear, and the longdrawn processes of its mineral cogitation, the interchange of day and night was no more than the flickering of a film. Even less. To the rock, day and night were imperceptible in themselves, for all their vital gestures and chambered drama. Probably Bach knew this better than anyone else doing music: the law, excluding no beauty or intellection along the way, proceeding in ordered fashion without stopping or special cry. But the rock didn't know much about beauty. To the rock, the eyeblink rise and fall of walking lives, the barely more persistent flickering into leaf then back down to dust of trees, were all hysterical illusory gestures of self-assertion quickly gone.

Under eternity's eye, as he'd seen through it last night, the stone itself was only another blip, its persistence illusory, its substance insubstantial.

Down here in the passing world of the Bear's life, the rock of fact was still obdurate and immovable, however, and circumstances solid. There were conditions to deal with, this side of the sky. Down here the Bear was still the Bear, Iris still Iris, and any essential movement between them difficult in the extreme. Spiritual vision offered to ameliorate the difficulties but only served to confuse the issue.

For instance, at the moment his attempt to think clearly was clouded by a wish made visible posing as psychic second sight: in his mind's eye he saw Iris leave the house by the glass doors and start up the path toward him. If the Bear believed that his psychic faculties 1) still worked, and 2) signified anything, then he might put some faith in the sight of Iris coming his way, her finelined features rounded by excess of merriment, but he knew it for the wishful hallucination it was.

If we could see things with the eye appropriate to each world in which they had their being and know false invariably from true, we might get somewhere. We might even begin to swing. But as things stand . . . pphhht, it's a wash.

His mind's eye continued watching Iris come up the path but he didn't give it any credit, because to think that Iris was really on her way to him would be to believe that grace had significant consequence not just in the spirit but down here on the ground, and from long habit and frequent rehearsal he doubted it.

He saw her brush a dark green branch of pine with her shoulder as she came: more psychic flimflam, another hustle.

In another few minutes he'd go back to the house and see what the true day would put on show. But in the meantime he'd have what passed for a think, beneath these passing trees, provisional skies.

"*Nee*-dn't." Another catcall from the catbird seat.

What do you know about it? he asked the bird, in what passed for his mind. Budge that brute rock with your bit of misremembered, half-accomplished song. That's what I've tried to do all my life, and look where it's gotten me. The familiar weary round. Budge that.

The Bear walked up to the rock and sat himself down.

Iris swept into the clearing still laughing, her arms open wide, and fairly skipped across the intervening distance to embrace him.

acknowledgments

I am indebted to the generosity of the musicians who have allowed themselves to be represented in this book: Lester Bowie, the late Steve McCall, Arthur Blythe, Roscoe Mitchell, Joseph Jarman, Malachi Favors, Don Moye, Ornette Coleman, Billy Hart, Armen Donelian, and Charlie Haden. Similar thanks to non-musicians Bob Cummins and Stanlyn Daugherty. Julius Hemphill hovers but never appears; neither does he die: were it so.

The book owes a large debt of gratitude to Peter Giron (bass, Paris and Bordeaux) for his road stories and buffalo shows; for providing/confirming the book's harmonic content; and for the use of his tune "Billy's Heart," slightly retitled. Wayne Reiss (piano, Brooklyn) worked out the changes of "Book the Hook." Bruce Jackson (drums, New Jersey) confirmed Giron's road stories, lent the Lead Sled and only one one-liner; but Jackson is one of the funniest jazz people alive, and I have learned extensively from his example. I must also thank Branford Marsalis & Co. for showing me road-humor at its most scabrous; and Peter Himmelman & Co., especially Jeff Victor, for all those road-miles across the Caucasus and Central Asia. Ronald Shannon Jackson, for the loan of his Accord. Robert Rahim Harwell, in England, for the use of his name. David Breskin, for an early review of *Sensible Shoes*.

The author owes a special debt of gratitude to Jack DeJohnette for a world of education at the drums, all those sessions at the Power Station, and much insight into the music and its musicians, to which Lydia DeJohnette contributed much. I owe all kinds of musicians all kinds of debts, and hope the book begins to thank them.

Other bills due:

A nomadic author benefits from many hospitalities: In Konya, Turkey, that of Ali Bey at the Olgun Palas, where the book began; Asim and Muzaffer Kaplan, Jemal Palamutçu, Ahmet Kavut and Yashar Kemal. To Atesh Baz Wali and the town's other elders the author owes an unrepayable debt.

In Sherborne, Gloucestershire, Siddiqa Cass, in whose house I drafted most of Part One, performed feats of hospitality above and beyond the call of duty; her back garden also provided the songbird with an interest in Monk.

Sam Holdsworth and Gordon Baird offered me the amazing hospitality of their magazine when I sent them the first chapter from Turkey for safekeeping; they printed it and serialized the creature for a year.

Many people read the manuscript and offered help and support. First among them was Brian Cullman, than whom few authors ever can have had so expert and sympathetic a reader. I incorporated most of his suggestions immediately; the rest I incorporated after awhile. Others who contributed time and wisdom were Daniel Furman, Salik Chalom, Sara Sterman, Eleanor Butler, Aaron Cass, Bulent Rauf, Mahmut Rauf, Kathryn Dunn, Jane Winsor, Jacob Lampart, Barbara Pecarich, Maura Ellyn, Bibi Wein, Karen Burdick, Abdullah Gündogdu, Vic Garbarini and Jerome Reese.

The author is grateful for the generous, nay, crucial support of the New York Foundation of the Arts. And to Bruce and Susan Kovner, near the end, for shoveling me out of my Brooklyn bunker and flying me to the straits of Vancouver; as to Kate Wilson for prolonging this paradisal intermission: between them they saved the end of the book and made its central pair of lovers happy.

To Mary Cunnane for bringing me to Norton even before I had a bear in tow, and for persisting in her interest when he wandered off to brood for fourteen years; regret that she left as he reached home; gratitude that Gerald Howard was on hand to smooth the book's fur (and ruffle mine) at the finish.

Two brief memoria to close:

To the gifted young altoist Alain Tabar-Nouval, whom I heard and played with in Paris in 1966, and who died in a freak train accident en route to a festival in Oslo in 1969. His tone and, alas, embryonic style, I realized as I went along, had evolved post mortem into a basis of the Bear's.

To Jim Schjeldahl, who was beaten by police and died, in New York, in 1995, in circumstances more innocent than those of Bobby Hatwell's beating—indeed, in circumstances that were entirely innocent. R.I.P. if you can manage it, and leave your enemies, as your friends, to God.